# The Four Streets Saga

NADINE DORRIES grew up in a working-class family in Liverpool. As a child, she spent a great deal of time in Mayo with her Irish grandmother, Nellie Deane, and for a time she attended school in a rural village close to the Atlantic coast. She trained as a nurse, then followed with a successful career in which she established and then sold her own business. She has been the MP for Mid-Bedfordshire since 2005 and has three daughters.

## Also by Nadine Dorries

***Standalone Novels***

Ruby Flynn

***Short Stories***

Run to Him

A Girl Called Eilinora

***The Lovely Lane Series***

The Angels of Lovely Lane

The Children of Lovely Lane

**Coming soon**

The Mothers of Lovely Lane

# NADINE DORRIES

# The Four Streets Saga

*The Four Streets* first published in the UK in 2014 by Head of Zeus, Ltd
*Hide Her Name* first published in the UK in 2014 by Head of Zeus, Ltd
*The Ballymara Road* first published in the UK in 2015 by Head of Zeus, Ltd

This omnibus edition first published in the UK in 2017 by Head of Zeus, Ltd



9 7 5 3 1 2 4 6 8

A catalogue record for this book is available from the British Library.

ISBN (HB): 9781786692375
ISBN (E): 9781781857571

Typeset by Adrian McLaughlin

Printed and bound in Great Britain by
CPI Group (UK) Ltd, Croydon CR0 4YY

Head of Zeus Ltd
First Floor East
5–8 Hardwick Street
London EC1R 4RG

WWW.HEADOFZEUS.COM

# Contents

# The Four Streets

*For my beloved and much-missed brother, John*
*1960–1986*

# Chapter One

Let me take you by the hand and lead you up from the Mersey River – to the four streets, and the houses stained black from soot and a pea-soup smog, which, when winter beckons, rubs itself up against the doors and windows, slips in through the cracks and into the lungs of gurgling babies and toothless grannies.

In May 1941, Hitler bombed Liverpool for seven consecutive nights.

All four streets survived, which was nothing short of a miracle.

Home to an Irish-Catholic immigrant community, they lay in close proximity to where the homes of families far less fortunate had once stood. Life on the streets around the docks was about hard work and survival.

Children ran free, unchecked from dawn until dusk, whilst mothers, wearing long, wraparound aprons and hair curlers, nattered on front steps and cast a distracted eye on little ones charging up and around, swallowing down the Mersey mist.

They galloped with wooden floor mops between legs, transformed into imaginary warhorses. Dustbin lids became shields and metal colanders, helmets, as they clattered and charged along back alleyways in full knowledge that, at the end of the day, they would be beaten with the smelly mop end.

The women gossiped over backyard walls, especially on wash day, whilst they fed wet clothes through a mangle and then hung them on the line to dry.

In winter, the clothes would be brought in, frozen and as stiff as boards, to defrost and dry overnight on a wooden clothes maiden placed in front of the dying embers of the fire.

Such was the order of life on the four streets. All day long housewives complained about their lot but they got on with it. Through a depression, war, illness and poverty they had never missed a beat. No one ever thought it would alter. Their way of life was constant and familiar, as it had been as long as anyone could remember. When little boys grew up, they replaced their warhorses for cranes and, just like their da, became dockers. Little girls grew up and married them, replacing toy dolls with real babies. Neighbours in Liverpool had taken the place of family in Ireland and the community was emotionally self-supporting.

But this was the fifties. The country had picked itself up from the ravages of war and had completed the process of dusting itself down. Every single day something new and never before seen arrived in the shops, from Mars bars to Hoovers. No one knew what exciting product would appear next. Liverpool was steaming towards the sixties and the Mersey beat. Times were about to change and the future hung heavy in the air.

It smelt of concrete new towns and Giro cheques.

The economic ebb and flow of daily life on the streets was dominated by the sound of cargo ships blowing their horns as they came into the docks angrily demanding to be unloaded. A call for the tugs meant money in the bread bin, which was where every family kept their money. An empty bread bin meant a hungry home.

The main source of income for each household came from the labour of the men who lived on the four streets. Liverpool stevedores were hard men, but the bosses who ran the Mersey Dock Company were harder. Wages were suppressed at a level that kept families hungry and men keen for work. It was a tough life for all. Childhood was short as everyone pulled their weight to live hand to mouth, day to day.

Each house in the four streets was identical to the next: two up, two down, with an outhouse toilet in the small square backyard. Upstairs at the top of the landing, a new enamel bath, courtesy of the Liverpool Corporation, stood exposed under the eaves. The water to the bath was supplied via rudimentary plumbing in the form of two pipes that passed through the landing roof into the loft and attached straight to the water tanks.

Although some homes had discarded kitchen ranges for electric cookers, and back boilers for the new immersion heaters, those on the four streets enjoyed no such new-fangled innovations. The open range remained, doubling as a back boiler and a cooker.

Running past the back gate to each house was a cobbled alleyway known as 'the entry', which was odd as it was in fact 'the exit'. People only very occasionally entered by the front door, and they always left by the back, although nobody remembered how the habit had begun. No one ever locked their doors; they didn't need to.

The entry was a playground to the street children as well as the large brown river rats that grew fat on the spewing contents of the metal bins overturned by hungry dogs and cats.

At the top of the four streets lay a grassed-over square of common land known as the green, which in school holidays hosted the longest ever football matches, sometimes lasting for days on end. Rival teams were formed from each of the four streets and were in perpetual competition. Matches would begin with a nominated goal counter, who at the end of each day would collapse in his bed, exhausted and mucky, with the score scrawled on a precious scrap of paper tucked under his pillow, ready to resume playing the following day.

St Mary's church, which stood at the end of Nelson Street, was visited at least once a day by every woman on the four streets. No one missed mass. The priests were hugely influential amongst the community and combined the role of law keepers, teachers and saviours of souls.

No two front doors in close proximity were painted the same colour. Black followed blue, followed brown followed green. On almost every window in every house hung a set of net curtains, each with a lace pattern different from any other window in the street. Even in homes that could boast nothing in terms of material wealth, individuality fought to be expressed and admired.

Aside from the practical function of the nets, their existence played a significant role within the community. The degree of their whiteness and cleanliness invited verbal judgment to be passed upon the woman responsible. They had to. Women needed a yardstick by which to measure one another's competence as wives and mothers. Men didn't wash nets. That was women's work. Men were judged only on the number of sons they spawned. For women, it was the nets. A barometer and a source of gossip, which was essential. Gossip was the light relief between household chores. Football for men. Gossip for women. Religion for all.

Maura and Tommy Doherty lived in Nelson Street. Although they had a brood of children, they continued to breed, and were passionate, loving and caring neighbours to everyone in the streets. Tommy was short and muscular. If he hadn't been a docker, putting in ten hours a day of hard manual labour, he would have been short and fat. He was bald on top and sported a Friar Tuck band of hair around the back and over his ears. As a result, he was very attached to his cap, which he wore indoors and out, rain or shine. Not one of his children had ever seen him without it, except when he slept. If Maura hadn't insisted he remove his cap before he got into bed, often flicking it off herself, he would have worn it there too. Tommy had vivid, twinkling blue eyes, the kind that can only come from Irish roots, and his eyes reflected his personality, mischievous and kind. He was a proud and devoted husband and father, and was possibly one of the few da's on the streets never to lay a finger on any of his children, a fact that bore testament to his temperament. All he desired in life was peace and quiet.

Tommy had grown up in Cork and had travelled to England to work on the roads. On his first night in Liverpool, he was waylaid by a prostitute at the Pier Head. On his second, he met Maura. Penniless by the third, he got taken on at the docks and, to his great sadness, had never been home since.

Maura was thin, taller than Tommy by a good two inches and, as Tommy often joked, her almost-black hair and eyes were proof that her granny had lain with a tinker: a joke that often resulted in Tommy being chased around the kitchen with a wet dishcloth.

Maura liked to travel, sometimes managing the whole mile and a half into Liverpool city centre, known to everyone as 'town'. She had been born and raised in Killhooney Bay on the west coast of Ireland and, until the day she left home to work as a housemaid in Liverpool, had never ventured any further than Bellingar, on the back of a mule and cart.

'Sure, why would ye need to go into town?' Tommy could often be heard exclaiming in surprise when Maura told him she would be spending extra on shopping that week and would be taking the tram. 'Everything a man could want can be got on his feet around here.'

Without fail, an almighty row would ensue and Tommy could often be spotted running out of the backyard gate as though the devil himself were after him, when it was in fact Maura, brandishing a rolled-up copy of the *Liverpool Echo* to beat him around the head with, the children scattering before them like cockroaches in daylight, in case they got in the way and copped it instead. He regularly sought refuge in the outhouse, one of the few places where no one troubled him, and took his newspaper for company. Tommy may have craved peace but, with seven kids and a wife as opinionated and as popular as Maura, it was just a dream.

He didn't much care for the news, although he read what he could understand. His relief from hard labour was to check out the horses running at Aintree and to study their form. Tommy had spent his entire childhood helping his father, a groom for a breeding stud. He knew something about horses, did Tommy. Or so he thought. It was his link with home, his specialist subject, which made him feel valued when others sought him out for his opinion or a tip. He was right more often than he was wrong. In his heart, he knew it was the luck of the Irish, combined with Maura's devotion to regular prayer to the Holy Father, far more than his dubious unique knowledge, which sustained his reputation. He still lost as much money at the bookies as every other man on the streets.

If there was anyone in the backyard as Tommy left the outhouse, whether anyone looked at his *Liverpool Echo* or not, or was even paying him a second's attention, as he walked to the back kitchen door he would nod to the newspaper in his hand and loudly pronounce, 'Shite in, shite out.' Social skills were strangers.

Life was lived close to the cobbles.

Maura was, without doubt, the holiest mother in the street. She attended mass twice a day when everything was going well, and more often when the ships were slow to come in and work was scarce.

She was the person everyone went to for help and advice, and her home was where the women often gathered to discuss the latest gossip. On the day one of the O'Prey boys from number twenty-four was sent to prison, the mothers ran to gather around Maura's door, each carrying a cup of tea and a chair out onto the street to sit and gossip, watching the children play.

'I'm not surprised he's gone down,' Maura pronounced to the women sitting around, whilst standing on her doorstep, arms folded across her chest, supporting an ample bosom. Hair curlers bobbed with indignation inside a pink hairnet whilst, in order to dramatize her point, two straight and rigid fingers waved a Woodbine cigarette in the general direction of the O'Prey house. 'Look at her nets, they're filthy, so they are.' In Maura's eyes, there was a direct connection between the whiteness of the net curtains and the moral values within. No one ever challenged her assertion.

The women turned their heads and looked at the windows as though they had never noticed them before.

'Aye, they are that too,' came a murmur of acknowledgment, led by Peggy, Maura's next-door neighbour. They all nodded as they flicked their cigarette ash onto the pavement and took another long self-righteous puff.

The mother of the son who had provided a poor household with stolen food was damned by dust. But Maura's condemnation wouldn't stop her sending over a warm batch of floury potato bread, known as Boxty, as an act of commiseration when she made her own the following morning, using flour that was itself stolen from a bag that had fallen off the back of a ship in the dock. Maura was as kind and good as she was opinionated and hypocritical.

# Chapter Two

Jerry and Bernadette Deane lived across the road from Maura and Tommy in number forty-two. Like many of the men on the four streets, Jerry had arrived in Liverpool from Mayo, hungry for prosperity and advancement that weren't to be found in rural Ireland, where levels of relative poverty remained almost unchanged since the sixteen hundreds, and where, right into the winters of the nineteen-sixties, children still walked to school barefoot through icy fields. It was as though the land of his birth were caught in a time warp. The outside privies on the four streets were a luxury compared to the low stone-and-sod houses of Mayo, where an indoor toilet of any description was mostly unheard of in many of the villages.

Jerry and Bernadette had met on the ferry across from Dublin to Liverpool on a gloriously sunny but cold and very windy day. Jerry spotted Bernadette almost as soon as he boarded the ferry, her long, untameable red hair catching his attention. Jerry was mesmerized as, from a slight distance, he watched Bernadette do battle with her hair, which the wind had mischievously taken hold of and, lock by lock, teased out from under her black knitted beret. She struggled hard to force it back under the hat.

Jerry had been on his way to the ship's bar when he caught sight of her, her beauty stopping him in his tracks.

'Jaysus,' he would often say to anyone who was listening, 'she took the eyes right out of me head, so she did.'

Instead of moving into the bar for a pint of Guinness to settle his stomach, he sat down on a painted wooden bench, bolted to the wooden deck, to watch the young woman standing at the ship's rail and wondered to himself why she didn't step indoors and into the warm. Surely, it would be much easier than taking on the sea wind and trying to tame a wild mane of hair outdoors?

Her already pale complexion turned a ghostly ashen as she gave up on her hair, staggered forward a few steps and grabbed the rail with both hands, looking more than a little queasy.

Aha, Jerry thought, seeing an opportunity in the girl's problem, thank ye Lord, a hundred thousand times, for here's me chance. He embodied everything everyone knows to be true of an Irishman. He was as bold as brass, full of the blarney and didn't know the meaning of the word shy. That was until he met Bernadette.

Taking the initiative, Jerry nipped into the café, bought an earthenware mug of steaming-hot sweet tea and took it over to the strange but beautiful girl. In his grinning, cheeky Irish way, he tried to introduce himself, but he was so struck by the size and the blueness of her eyes that, for the first time in his life, he could say nothing.

Bernadette didn't notice Jerry as he approached her, so focused was she on holding onto the rail of the ship and on keeping in her stomach the fried eggs and bacon she had enjoyed that morning. She was sure she might faint, and was wondering how she would cope all alone if she did, when she saw Jerry's tall, broad form standing next to her. It was hard to look up as it meant breaking her concentration, but she managed for a few seconds even though she felt like throwing herself overboard. A slow watery death was surely more pleasurable than feeling as she did right now.

She was distracted by his large black eyes that made her forget her sickness for all of thirty seconds. 'I felt as though they were burning into me very soul,' was how Bernadette described her first meeting with Jerry, wistfully and often, her eyes welling up at the mere memory of the day.

It was obvious to everyone who knew their story that Jerry and Bernadette had benefited from that all too rare but wonderful thing, love at first sight.

He realized as he walked over to her that there was no reason on God's earth why he, a complete and total stranger, should be taking a mug of sweet tea to a woman he had never met in his life before and might never meet again. Jerry introduced himself, as best he could, but it came out as a prolonged and indistinguishable jabbering.

Holy Mary, he thought to himself, where the feck has me sensibility gone and why is me hand shaking like a virgin on her wedding night, spillin' the bleedin' tea everywhere?

Although Jerry was talking gibberish, Bernadette could tell he was offering her the tea. So desperate was she to feel better that she accepted it, assuming that he could see how ill she felt.

'Thank ye,' she whispered, as she took the mug out of his hand, managing a very thin and feeble smile that she didn't for one second feel herself. 'I'm so glad there is someone who knows the cure for how bad I feel.' She tried to improve the smile and look grateful, whilst her stomach did an Irish jig in her belly.

Jerry's stomach also began a jig, but it had nothing to do with feeling seasick. He smiled to himself at how it seemed to have gone into free fall, something he had never experienced before.

Bernadette was doubly grateful for the tea as she had only half a crown in her purse and hadn't wanted to waste a penny. She wasn't sure if drinking tea with milk was the right thing to do in the circumstances, but she trusted him. He looked trustworthy – and gorgeous; even through her sickness she could see that. And why shouldn't she drink the tea in any case? In Ireland, strong, sweet tea was the cure for everything from scurvy to colic.

As she drank slowly and tentatively, Jerry studied every detail of her profile, her neck and her hair, which kept blowing across her face, covering it like a lace veil. Finding his sea legs at the same time as his courage, Jerry played the fool with his best show-off jokes and Bernadette tried her best to laugh at his audacity. After all, he was outrageously flirting with a sick woman. Suddenly, without warning, they both saw the tea again, all over the deck and Jerry's shoes.

Jerry sprang into action. The wind had met its match. He gathered Bernadette's flyaway hair together and spun it into a knot, before tucking it back under her cap as tightly as he could, for fear she would vomit straight onto it. Bernadette was beyond caring that a stranger was stroking the back of her neck and whispering soothing, comforting noises into her ear. Her eyes had filled with tears of shame and she looked as though her knees were about to buckle at any moment.

Jerry kept hold of Bernadette, and her hat, keeping her hair away from her face for almost the entire crossing. The seasickness claimed her as she vomited over the rail all the way to Liverpool during the notoriously choppy journey across the Irish Sea.

As deathly as the seasickness made her feel, Bernadette had noticed Jerry's black wavy hair and, for an Irishman, his unusually broad shoulders. He wore a typically oversized cap, which, although pulled down low over his forehead against the wind, blew off to the other side of the deck so that Jerry, thrown from side to side by the rocking of the boat, had to run like a madman to rescue it. Despite how ill she felt, she laughed. It was impossible not to laugh at this cheeky Irishman.

They didn't leave each other's side for the entire crossing. If they had, Bernadette might have fallen over. By the time they docked at Liverpool, she felt she had known him all her life. To be fair, she had: not necessarily Jerry, but many young men from home just like him. However, it was the fact that there was something very chippy and confident about Jerry that made him different and extremely attractive, despite her self-imposed intention to meet a rich American traveller who would sweep her off her feet and carry her off, away across the Atlantic, to the country where so many of her Irish ancestors had emigrated to live.

'Never worry, Mammy,' she had said to her mother, who was upset at the thought that soon all her children would have left her to work abroad. 'I'll send ye me pay and when I'm in America, oh sure, won't ye be the grandest woman in all of Killhooney Bay, I'll be able to send ye so much.'

Bernadette was confident that she would be massively successful in the land of milk and honey, and her generosity was such that she was determined everyone she knew would benefit too.

She already had a job waiting for her as a chambermaid in Liverpool's Grand hotel, with staff accommodation provided in the maids' dorm under the roof, boiling in summer and freezing in winter. Bernadette did not care. This lowly position did not deter her from her grand ambitions. She would have work. That was something many in rural Ireland did not. It hadn't stopped raining in Mayo for weeks before she left, and although she loved her home, she was looking for adventure and a way to earn a living, not to grow a set of gills.

But she hadn't reckoned on meeting Jerry and she also hadn't expected to fall in love within minutes of her feet leaving the Irish shore. It wasn't the most romantic or conventional beginning to what became the deepest and truest love affair, but it forged an immediate deep bond.

Jerry told Bernadette he was off to stay with a widowed aunt who lived on the four streets. Although he didn't have a job already lined up, he knew there was plenty of work in Liverpool for strong Irish navvies. Work on the docks, the roads or building the new houses was not too difficult to come by and a slice of a pay packet earned in England could transform the life of a family back home.

As soon as they docked and Bernadette set foot on dry land, she started to feel better. On board the ship, she had felt as close to death as it was possible to be, having vomited what felt like the entire lining of her stomach. Never had she experienced anything as unbearable. She knew if it hadn't been for Jerry's company and the fact that he had looked after her, it would have been a million times worse.

Jerry turned to look at her and laughed. In the five minutes since they had docked, the colour had risen in her cheeks. Her eyes had begun to take on a sparkle and her smile was less forced. Jerry didn't want to part from her. He needed to know the Bernadette who wasn't distracted whilst vomiting over the deck.

'Let's go in here,' said Jerry, pointing to a rough-and-ready port-side café. 'Ye need to get a lining on your stomach before ye set off to your hotel, and I sure need to eat before I set off to look for work. Let's grab a bite together, eh? It'll set us both up for what lies ahead for the rest of the day.'

Bernadette willingly agreed. She had no idea when she would get the chance to eat again, and she also wanted to spend some time with this handsome young man when she wasn't embarrassing herself and could act in a more dignified and ladylike manner.

The café smelt of damp wool, stale bodies, fried steam and blue cigarette smoke. They walked across its floorboards to a newly vacated table with a red gingham tablecloth, next to the open fire. The waitress came and removed the overflowing ashtray, replacing it with a clean one as she took their order. Jerry offered Bernadette a cigarette, a Capstan Full Strength, which made her choke, and both of them laughed a great deal as they began to talk.

Very shortly a large brown earthenware pot of tea was placed on the table with a plate of thickly sliced white bread and butter, followed by two plates piled up with chips and two fried eggs on top. Bernadette hadn't realized how hungry she was until they both devoured the food.

Finally, Jerry plucked up the courage and, cheekily, reached out and took one of Bernadette's hands in his own. She didn't pull away.

'Does ye not know any modesty at all?' she chided playfully, hitting the top of his hand with her free one as though to knock it away, something she had no intention of doing.

Bernadette might have been play-objecting to Jerry's romantic advances but really she was giggly and delighted. They talked about their homes and family, the places they both knew and the people they had in common.

'Do ye know the O'Shaughnessys from Mayo?' asked Jerry.

'Ah, sure I do, from Bellingar, I know the mammy and daddy and their daughter Theresa,' replied Bernadette. This was Ireland. In the rest of the world they say you are only ever six people away from someone you know, but in Ireland it has to be two.

Jerry was nervous, turning his teaspoon over and over between his fingers, making a constant tinkling sound as it tapped the cup. On a normal day, he found it hard to remain serious for more than a few minutes and here he was, for the last hour, pouring out his life plan to a woman who had thrown up over his feet. He had never before had a conversation in which he talked out loud about the things that made him hungry for the future. Jerry was stupidly happy. They both were. Emotions were gripping them both so fast they had no idea what was happening but neither resisted.

By the time Jerry delivered Bernadette to the tram stop for the hotel, he had decided she was very definitely the woman he was going to marry. There was no doubt. She was the one. It was just a matter of time until she realized it too.

As they said their goodbyes, neither could believe what had happened. A few hours ago they had boarded a boat to take them to

Liverpool and a new life, and here they were, both without a shred of doubt that, just those few hours later, they were in love; their new life had arrived. It had jumped up and whacked them both in the face with no notice whatsoever. Things were about to change, forever.

Jerry promised to call at the staff entrance of the hotel and find her at the weekend. They walked away from each other, waved, then both looked back and laughed. Jerry ran back.

'This is ridiculous,' laughed Bernadette. 'I don't even know ye.'

Parting was physically painful. Both were secretly worried they might never see the other again, that the magic bubble might burst. As Bernadette turned to walk away for the second time, Jerry reached out and grabbed her by the wrist, and that was when Jerry, in broad daylight, with people walking past and with the Mersey River watching and a thousand seagulls soaring, kissed his Bernadette for the first time.

It was a kiss that was so daring, Bernadette often recounted it to her friends.

'Sure, he was so bold I had no idea what was coming and when he kissed me, I lost me breath and almost fainted, so I did.'

It was very different from what Jerry told his friends. 'She was so keen, she couldn't keep her hands off me and begged me for another, in front of everyone and in broad daylight too. I thought we was going to be arrested right there.'

If Bernadette heard him, it would be followed by squeals and play fighting. No one ever knew which version was true and no one cared. Their storytelling infused everyone with warmth and laughter.

When they finally parted, Jerry went straight to his aunt's house, deposited his bag and, after a quick greeting, took himself straight down the steps at the end of the street to the docks. Dock work was casual. He would walk the entire length of the waterfront and visit every dock if he needed to in order to be taken on. He now had a new imperative, a spring in his step. A reason to find work and good, well-paid work.

As he ran down the steps whistling, he couldn't get Bernadette out of his mind. For what felt like every moment until the weekend, he relived each second of their conversation. In bed, in the minutes before sleep, he relived their kiss as his stomach churned at the excitement and expectation of another. Might there be more? Could this be possible? Could life really be that good? Could Jerry, a farmer's son from Mayo, really be this lucky?

He was. They met almost every night until the day they married, even if it meant Jerry had to walk to the hotel when Bernadette had only her break time free. He would stand at the staff entrance until she could slip out, just for a snatched kiss, to reassure himself she was happy. On her day off she would run down to the docks and spend it at his auntie's house on the street, enjoying the comfort of having a place where she could spend her time and wait for Jerry to finish work. On Sundays they would attend mass at St Mary's church together and walk along the shore as far as Waterloo.

They were blissfully in love and, after nearly a year of steady work, Jerry asked Bernadette to marry him. He popped the question in the café at the Pier Head where they had their first proper date. Bernadette could not have been happier. He even got down on one knee as the customers and staff cheered and clapped. They both cried a little as an elderly man from Eire came up to them on his way out of the café and pressed a brown ten-shilling note into Jerry's palm as he left.

'For the babby when it comes,' he said, and winked as he left.

They both thought they would burst with joy. But this did not distract them from the plans they had. Jerry and Bernadette spent a great deal of time mapping out their future. When Jerry's aunt suddenly died, it was a shock to everyone, but luckily, shortly after Jerry had moved in with his aunt, she had put his name on the rent book, which meant that he could remain in the house without question. The houses on the streets had transferred from one generation to the next in this manner ever since the first wave of immigrants had flooded through the gates of Clarence dock during the potato famine.

However, the pressure was too great for Jerry and Bernadette to put off the wedding until after the full twelve-month mourning period. Bernadette was helping Jerry to cook and clean and look after the house, and not being able to run up the stairs was driving them both mad with desire. But Bernadette was a good Catholic girl and she was taking no chances with sex before marriage.

No shotgun wedding for her. Suddenly, being alone in each other's company in the close proximity of a bedroom was becoming an almost unbearable temptation. Bernadette would never stay overnight and the pressure built to an almost unbearable pitch.

'Just stay tonight,' Jerry begged, one Sunday night as Bernadette was leaving. 'Please,' he murmured into her ear in the midst of a very passionate kiss. 'I promise I will be good and ye will still be a virgin in the morning.'

'Not at all!' replied Bernadette forcefully. 'Are ye crazy? Can ye imagine what they will be saying here in the streets tomorrow when they see me leaving in the morning?'

Her resolve did indeed drive Jerry crazy. He wanted to put his fist through the wall, but he also knew she was right. They were married within three months.

During those three months Bernadette got to know everyone on the four streets as well as she did her neighbours back home. Bernadette and Maura came from the same village, Killhooney, and had known each other since Bernadette was a baby. You didn't need to travel far in Liverpool before you met someone from back home. The two women became special friends, which extended to Tommy and Maura's children, especially their eldest daughter, Kitty, who spent as much time with Jerry and Bernadette as she did in her own house.

Although Maura was older, she and Bernadette had attended the same school, knew the same families and had a shared history. Their deep yearning for home had drawn them together from the first day Bernadette had arrived in the street. Maura was daily homesick. Both their families came from the sod houses, close to the coast. Every day they talked about how there was no better view of the Atlantic than that from the cliffs overlooking Blacksod Bay. No better dancing at a ceilidh than that to be had at the inn. No better fish to be tasted than salmon poached from the Morhaun River or fish from the Carrowbay Loch. They had so much to talk about and their conversations about home acted as a salve to Maura's always aching heart.

Neither mentioned the poverty, the lack of shoes, the rain, the hunger or the wet ceilings. The sun always shone on Mayo when it came to the reminiscing.

Bernadette spent hours talking about her work to Maura, who loved to hear the chambermaids' tales about the guests staying in the hotel. Stuck in a life that would never alter, Maura found every detail fascinating, from what the ladies wore to the staff-room gossip, especially about the head housekeeper, Alice Tanner, who had worked at the hotel since she was fifteen and who was legendary for never having taken a day off or having had a visitor since Bernadette arrived.

'Sure, that Alice is a mean one altogether!' Bernadette would exclaim, at least once a week, as she flounced into Maura's kitchen. 'I cannot wait until Jerry and I are married and I can give in me notice. She would drive a saint to drink. I have never given out like some of the others, Maura, but God help me, I will one day soon.'

Maura was all ears.

'She knew Jerry was coming to the staff entrance for me last night and she deliberately sent me off on a wild-goose chase across the hotel to make me late for him. Out of my half-hour break I got ten minutes with him. Jeez, that Alice Tanner is a spiteful bitch. She never sets foot outside of the hotel, and no one ever comes to see her. She's just wicked jealous, so she is, and here's me, always protecting her from the others. So help me God, I cannot any more, the witch.'

Maura loved these days. She would make Bernadette a cup of tea, sit at the kitchen table and listen to her talk for hours on end. The most interesting conversation Maura ever had with the other women on the four streets was how to keep your milk from drying up when you had half a dozen kids to run after, with not enough food to go round for everyone, and how many black eyes there were in English potatoes. Bernadette's chatter was a ray of sunshine.

Just talking to Maura would calm Bernadette down and they would move onto the more interesting gossip, such as the wedding that took place at the hotel on the Saturday. Maura could not believe the things they did with a salmon at the Grand and who knew people ate lobsters?

Everyone on the four streets looked forward to Jerry and Bernadette's wedding with huge excitement. There was something special about them both. They were always laughing and making everyone else laugh either with them or at them.

There was no salmon or lobster to be had at the Irish centre, but the Guinness flowed as fast as the laughter was loud.

The wedding reception had been in full swing for just a few hours when Jerry dragged Bernadette away to carry her over the threshold. The gentle ribbing from their family and friends carried them down the street as they ran giggling to number forty-two.

'What in God's name will they all think?' protested Bernadette, tripping on her new heels. 'Running away to me marriage bed and not staying until the end.'

Jerry's response was to scoop her up and sprint with her across his arms the rest of the way. A Lord Lochinvar stealing away his princess.

The river was black and still. Watching and listening. Holding onto what it knew ... and their shrieks and squeals of laughter echoed out across the water and were surely absorbed into eternity. They were, after all, the happiest couple to have ever run along the river's bank.

The wedding reception carried on way into the early hours, long after their marriage had been consummated a number of times.

In the early hours of the morning, spent and exhausted, Jerry and Bernadette made plans for the future yet again. They knew they were special. They knew they were different. They knew that the brightest future awaited them.

They also knew they were lucky to have a house of their own, even one owned by the Liverpool Corporation. It was the norm for young couples to begin their married life by moving in with their parents. Bernadette and Jerry were a novelty. Jerry's aunt had been barren, and had lavished her attention on her immaculate home, on the rugs she had been able to buy at the docks and the nice chest of drawers from Blackler's department store. Although slightly fancy and dated for Bernadette, with far too many fringes around cushions, lampshades and curtains, it was still the best-furnished and decorated house on the street.

Bernadette strove to be different. From the day they married, she learnt how to sew and cook, acquiring any little skill she could master to keep them one step ahead. Life had yet to wear Bernadette down, to disillusion her, to possess her womb. She embodied the arrogance of youth, combined with a hungry, impatient aspiration for a better life away from the four streets, although she and Jerry were yet to work out how it would be achieved. Even when there were only two of them, a docker's wage merely covered the bills and provided food, with just a little left over. Most couples in the streets had at least six children, which made life much harder than it should have been.

The neighbours nicknamed her 'Silver Heels', so grand were her dreams. Bernadette was aware that she had almost set herself apart from the community by talking about the future she wanted. If she hadn't been so popular, she might easily have succeeded in this. But how could anyone dislike Bernadette and Jerry? They were so in love, so idealistic, so happy.

A natural good neighbour, she always helped her friends. Whether it was to take a crying baby into her house to give a mother in the street some time off, or buying a few sweets for the children on the green. She attended mass every day and never gossiped – her heart was pure.

'Bernadette, ye are too good for this world, so ye is, sure ye must be an angel come to spy on us,' said Maura, who said she sinned so often she needed to go to mass twice a day. 'Feck knows, if ye are, I'll never get through them pearly gates now, no matter how many times I go to confession. I don't confess everything, ye know!' Maura would exclaim in mock indignation every time Bernadette refused to join in the gossip or say anything unkind about another woman in the streets.

Bernadette was godmother to the Doherty twins, which made her broody for her own, but with an iron will she maintained her plan to have everything in her house perfect and some money saved before a baby arrived. And besides, she and Jerry loved their Saturday nights out, and their short trips back to Ireland to visit their families and to take home presents. The young married couple with no babies and a bit of money were accorded a similar status as the film stars of the day. They knew that once babies arrived, all that would stop.

Jerry was so content that he could find nothing to complain about, no matter how hard he tried. Whereas many men feared going home on a Friday night after they had drunk half of their pay packet, Jerry ran home to his wife. He took a great deal of ribbing from the other dockers, but they all wanted to be him. Why wouldn't they?

He never stopped grinning. He and Bernadette were the only couple on the streets never to be heard having a row.

The fact that they didn't have a baby straight away was the subject of daily gossip amongst the women.

'He must be jumping off at Edge Hill,' was a theory thrown over garden walls by women with a dozen children each.

Edge Hill was a train station just a few minutes outside Lime Street station in Liverpool city centre, and 'jumping off at Edge Hill' was the colloquialism used for the withdrawal method of contraception favoured by the Pope. Not that the Pope ever had to use it, despite being such an expert. It was highly unreliable; even more so when practised by dockers who selfishly, after a few rum toddies, forgot to jump off and went all the way to Lime Street.

Jerry never forgot. Life to him and Bernadette was about careful planning and being responsible. They were going to get on in life and nothing, but nothing, was going to be left to chance.

When Bernadette finally became pregnant, there was no one on the four streets who was not caught up in the joy of the news. Babies were not an uncommon occurrence on the streets, but the arrival of Bernadette and Jerry's first baby had everyone excited.

'That child will be surely blessed when it comes,' said Maura. 'Was there ever a child more wanted or which could bring more joy?' No one could answer that question. It was as though Bernadette was the only woman ever to have been pregnant.

Bernadette had broken the news to Jerry whilst they were in Ireland visiting her family. They were standing on the cliff at Killhooney, overlooking the inky depths of Blacksod Bay. Jerry had almost fainted and had to sit down.

'Oh my God, Bernadette, are we to be a mammy and a daddy?' He took off his cap and rubbed his hair before putting it back on. Bernadette tucked her calf-length skirt in behind her knees as she sank to the ground to sit next to him.

'We are that,' she replied, looking shocked, and then they both began to laugh and cry at the same time. They kissed and hugged each other as the sea roared with laughter all around them. That night, the villagers attended the ceilidh in the pub arranged with an hour's notice and, pregnant or not, Bernadette danced into the small hours.

When the time came for the baby to be born, news had spread fast that Bernadette was in labour and that she and Jerry were at the hospital. Already the women were falling over themselves to help. They let themselves into the house by the back door, cleaned it from top to bottom despite the fact that it was unnecessary, stocked up the fire ready for a match to be thrown on and left a stew on the side of the range. Bernadette was one of their own, a young woman from the bogs in search of a better life. Disappointment would certainly be just round the corner but, until it came, she had friends and the four streets to count on. Whilst the women were being good neighbours and dusting down her new cot, Nellie Deane made her entrance into the world.

Jerry had been absolutely convinced that Bernadette had been carrying a boy, and the fact that it turned out to be a girl threw him, but only for the few seconds it took him to fall madly in love with his new baby daughter.

For hours, he had nervously paced up and down, waiting. There were no mobile phones then and although there was a public payphone in the hospital entrance, no one they knew could afford a telephone. All communication was by word of mouth or letter. Everyone knew it would be over a week before their relatives in Ireland received the news announcing that Nellie had arrived.

Jerry was beside himself with excitement. Their new baby's birth was the manifestation of his and Bernadette's life plan. He had the perfect wife in Bernadette, and at last he would have the perfect baby. For months he had told everyone he was going to have a boy. That was all forgotten now.

'Jeez, I knew from the day she told me she was pregnant it would be a baby girl,' said Jerry in a very matter-of-fact way to the midwife. 'I have always wanted a beautiful daughter.'

'Oh my,' laughed Bernadette, 'have ye indeed, is that why ye have been saying for seven months ye can't wait to get him to the football, was that our little girl ye was talking about then?'

Moments after she had given birth, they were both laughing together. He and his Bernadette, with her long red hair and bright blue Irish eyes, had spoken in detail about this day ever since they had first known she was pregnant. Not a drink had passed Jerry's lips from that time, as they had saved every penny to buy a cot and turn the second bedroom into a nursery fit for their child. They had managed to completely refurnish and decorate their home. Each time a room was finished, almost forty couples traipsed through the rooms to ooh and aah. Bernadette was meticulous. She fought the dock dust and smog hand to hand; the windows shone, the nets gleamed and pride reflected from her white windowsills.

Once Bernadette had been cleaned up, Jerry was allowed into the labour ward. He had paced the corridors the entire length of the hospital during the birth, desperate for it to be over so that he could be allowed back at Bernadette's side. No father was allowed in a delivery room in the nineteen- fifties. The baby business was women's work. He held his precious bundle in his huge muscular arms, more used to lifting cargo than babies, and could barely see her little face through his tears. Being careful to protect their tiny, fragile scrap, he turned towards his wife and their eyes met.

'She looks like ye,' whispered Jerry. His voice was thick with emotion as the tears trickled down his cheeks. 'She is the most beautiful baby in the whole world.'

Before Bernadette could protest, she gave in and didn't argue. Was there ever a man who could love his new daughter more? Let him think what he wants, she thought.

'Ye will have your lad next,' she said with a smile and such confidence, he believed her without question.

She smiled up at him tenderly, her love for this man who was different from all others pouring out despite her exhaustion. He leant over and kissed her dry lips, thinking that he had never seen his wife as lovely as she looked right now, after twenty-four hours of hard labour and no sleep. His tears wet her face and as she laid a hand on the side of his cheek, she kissed them away and tasted the salt on her lips. Between kisses, they were quietly sobbing and laughing at the same time, flooded with the love their new baby had brought to them as her gift. Jerry hitched the newborn up so that she was wedged between them both and they each gave a nervous laugh as they leant down and kissed her too. The three of them, wrapped in one warm embrace, filled with the smell of the newborn. They were both high on the miracle of life.

'I feel so scared,' confided Bernadette to Jerry, looking up at him. 'We have this little life to look after, she needs us for everything, Jer, we can't fail her.' Bernadette spoke with a degree of urgency, referring to the conversation they had had many times into the small hours of the night.

'Shh, I know, my love, and we won't,' said Jerry. 'She will be a princess, she will have everything she needs. I will never be out of work or let her down.'

Bernadette smiled up at him again. She felt safe and secure. She had no idea how happy one could possibly be, but she couldn't help worrying about money.

Worry was in her Irish DNA. Famines had left an invisible footprint. Jerry and Bernadette had plans for their baby daughter. For months they had talked and plotted about how their children would be schooled. Regardless of what the priest said, they would have just the two, so they weren't reduced to total poverty. They wanted their children to live a better life than their own had been and that of others on the streets. Bernadette was surely right: a son would be next. Jerry did not want his son to have aching bones every day from a lifetime of hard toil, or to be injured in one of the accidents that happened all too often on the docks, or to develop premature arthritis due to the excessive wear and tear on his joints from manual labour. He wanted his daughter to be more than a shop assistant or a cleaner. He wanted her to be a lady, a beautiful, kind lady who possessed all her mother's gentleness, but who could grasp life's opportunities and make something of herself.

Leaving them to have a few private minutes alone, the midwife went to fetch them both a cup of tea and some hot buttered toast. This baby had been a tricksy delivery and at one point she thought she was going to have to call for the doctor to assist. But just at the last minute, with the help of a pair of forceps, the baby shifted position and made its entrance into the world. The midwife had been touched by the obvious love and affection Nellie's parents had for each other; knowing that the special first hour with a first-born came only once in a lifetime, she made herself scarce as quickly as she could.

Even though he had been up all night, Jerry would save the bus fare and walk back home. He could not remember ever having been as hungry as he was right now. After he had eaten breakfast he would change into his work clothes and be in time to clock on at the docks for the first shift. This was no time to miss a day's pay.

Exhausted from her long ordeal, Bernadette lay back on the hospital pillows, feeling drowsy. She turned her head to one side and smiled at her husband, the man she loved more than life itself. Jerry had moved and was sitting on a chair next to the hospital bed, cuddling their baby, still unable to stop looking at her tiny face. Bernadette's eyes were still full of tears as she gazed upon the manifestation of all their hopes and aspirations for the future, the baby, who was falling asleep on his chest, flooding his thoughts, absorbing every ounce of his new love and devotion. Watching them together increased her happiness, if that was at all possible.

As sleep fought to claim her, she tried to say his name and to reach out and gently stroke his hand. She looked down at her arm in confusion. Her hand was like a lead weight and, no matter how hard she tried, it wouldn't respond. Unnoticed by Jerry, who at that very moment had eyes only for his new baby, panic slipped past him into the room and settled itself down upon Bernadette.

She tried to open her mouth, but it wouldn't work, and despite her best efforts, her arm would not move.

Jerry's name urgently beat against the sides of her brain but could get no further, as she managed to part her lips and move her tongue, which felt twice its normal size. But no sound escaped. A black haze had begun to blur the edges of her vision. She struggled to maintain her focus on the adoring father and their baby lying in the cradle of his arms, trapped in their bubble of wonderment. She lay, silently imploring, desperately willing Jerry to move his gaze away from their baby girl and to turn round. Her mind screamed: Look. Look. Look. At. Me. He didn't hear it as he kissed the downy hair on his baby's crown.

Bernadette's head became lighter and the sounds around her more acute. She could hear people outside in the corridor, giggling and talking as though they were standing right next to her bed, laughing at her.

And then, suddenly, she sank. The screaming in her head ceased. She felt as though life itself were draining out of her very soul as a chill sped upwards from her toes and fanned across her body like an icy glaze. She could no longer move her tongue and her eyelids felt leaden; there was no energy left to fight, no will to prise them open as she wearily succumbed to the dark cloak that enveloped her which was so heavy, so oppressive, that, try as she might, she just couldn't lift it off.

'She hasn't even murmured a sound yet, she just has these great big eyes lookin' at me now, just like her mammy,' said Jerry, as he turned himself and the baby towards Bernadette.

The last thing Bernadette saw, as her eyes slowly closed, was the smile evaporate from Jerry's face and transform into a look of horror as he suddenly looked down at the floor and saw a steady stream of blood, dripping from the corner of the bed sheet onto the floor, as though it were running from an open tap on a slow flow, creating a puddle of blood that had reached his own boots.

## Chapter Three

It was bitterly cold in the early morning half-light as heavy rain washed over the streets on the crest of gales swept up from the

Mersey River. A fresh squall every minute relentlessly pounded any unfortunate soul who had reason to be outdoors.

'It's as though an angel is chucking a bucket of water down the street, so strong it is,' said Peggy to her husband Paddy, as in her half-sleep she opened the bedroom curtains.

Peggy was a plain woman, with a face that had never experienced even a touch of the cold cream currently flying off the shelves in Woolworths in town. Peggy had no beauty routine. Peggy had no beauty. What she lacked in looks she complemented with a mental denseness that made much of what she said hard to comprehend and frequently funny. Peggy was also a stranger to housework and, unlike the other women on the streets, made no effort to dispel the English urban myth: that the Irish were a dirty breed.

Peggy hurriedly drew the curtains again when she remembered that they had been closed all week as a mark of respect and needed to remain that way for another day. She peeped through the side of the curtain and stared at the fast-flowing rivulets of water gushing down the gutters on either side of the entry.

Paddy turned over. He wasn't going into work this morning. He and Peggy were a good match. Paddy wasn't a pretty sight at any time of the day. With red hair and cheeks to match, from his high blood pressure brought on by overeating, over-drinking and over-smoking, he had aimed high with Peggy and got lucky.

'The ships will wait,' he had announced as he turned out the light the night before, which of course they wouldn't, because their time in dock was dependent on the tide, not Paddy. This morning the men and boys who normally struggled to be taken on by the gaffer would fill the places of those from the four streets.

Peggy lifted the net and raised her hand in a half-hearted greeting as she saw Maura run down the entry and in through her own back gate from early-morning mass. Maura's head was bent against the wind and rain and she was holding onto her hat, but as she put her hand on the gate latch, she looked up towards Peggy, as though she knew she were watching.

If Peggy pressed her face full against the net and onto the glass she could just see halfway up Maura's backyard to the outhouse.

An acute nosiness, born from an idle existence, forced her to strain to see if that was where Maura went next. Peggy knew Maura was returning from six o'clock mass and felt guilt stir itself somewhere in the depth of her belly. Maybe she should have made the effort for first mass today. Sure, didn't she have enough to feel bad about, without having seen Maura playing the Mary goodwife? She made a mental note to attend mass in the evening, after the funeral. A note she would have lost by the end of the day.

For every other street in Liverpool, it was a day of heavy rain. But those who lived by the river had to contend with the squalls that battered the docks on a regular basis. The four streets took the brunt of every storm that had gathered pace and momentum across the Irish Sea, only to be broken up and dispersed when buffered by the houses. They stood out against the tempest like a policeman's upturned outstretched hand, yelling 'stop' to the wind and rain as they whipped round the houses and then subsided into a flimsy breeze, on their way across the city.

Peggy and Paddy were right to be surprised by the weather. It was one of the worst days anyone on the four streets had seen for many a long year. But the residents weren't fazed. Those from the west coast of Ireland had seen as bad, if not worse.

Just as Peggy was putting the kettle on and beginning to make the watery porridge that passed as breakfast in her house, Maura was on her knees in front of her kitchen range, sobbing again, struggling to light the fire, which had gone out overnight.

Her children were yet to leave their dreams behind and the baby, just into its third month, slept in a small cardboard box, wrapped up in a multicoloured, hand-crocheted blanket, made from scraps left over from knitted baby cardigans and school jumpers, with odd ends of yarn salvaged from the wool stall in the market. The box was pushed securely to the back of the armchair, one of only two comfy chairs in the house. It was upholstered in a bottle-green knobbly wool, flecked with the occasional splash of dark orange. The legs were chipped, the wooden armrests worn and two of the springs, covered in brown rubber, which ran underneath the cushion, had snapped. This meant that anyone who sat on the chair sank down into the middle and, having been grabbed on all sides by the cushion and springs, found it difficult to get up again. The baby was just a scrap and the weight of the box was evenly spread across the chair, so the infant was safe enough.

Maura had only a cardboard box in which to put her baby girl, her seventh child, Niamh. For the first, Kitty, there had been a Moses basket, which had fallen apart after both sets of twins and had never been replaced. Maura had thought the twins were to be her last. She had assumed that every baby after the twins was to be her last and then came Angela. However, her Tommy's virility showed no sign of waning and they had coped up to now. Maura's baby might have been in a box, but she was warm, clean, dry and well fed.

Even indoors Maura was still battling the elements, as the wind blew the thick white smoke back down the chimney, refusing to allow the fire to draw and forcing the smoke to billow back into the living room, making Maura cough and splutter. She was shivering, cold and drenched to the skin, having just run the hundred yards or so from the church to the house, far enough for the rain to have found its way through her coat. She thought about the expression she had just glimpsed on Peggy's face at the window. She had raised her hand in greeting. But for both women there had not been a hint of a smile.

A less devout person than Maura would have skipped mass in this foul weather and, indeed, there were only half the usual numbers for the early-morning mass. Shame on them, Maura thought, as she took communion. Today was not a day to skip mass. By the time it was over, Maura would have entered and left the church four times, regardless of the weather.

'There's already more water running down these gutters than they can cope with, without you adding any more,' said Tommy, as he passed behind her on his way to the outhouse, carrying the *Daily Post*.

Maura sat back on her heels and covered her face with her hands. 'I just can't stop meself,' she whispered back to him through the gaps in her fingers, catching a sob at the end of her breath.

Tommy knew that if he put his arms round her, she would disintegrate. Better to keep her mind busy on the important daily routine. The things that mattered.

'Two rashers, two eggs and fried bread in ten, thanks, Queen, once you get that fire going, mind,' he threw over his shoulder as he bustled past her to the back door.

Tommy was the only person in the house to eat meat and eggs for breakfast. For the rest of the family it was bread in watered-down warm milk. Tommy had to unload a cargo ship each day. Without decent food of some kind he would slack and be laid off. As he was about to make his way into the yard, he was hit by a wall of water as though it had been waiting for him to open the door at just that second. Maybe Maura's trip to mass hadn't been in vain after all. Retribution.

'Fecking holy fecking Mother of God!' she heard in decreasing decibels as his blaspheming words were snatched away from him by the wind and rain and flung into the air. The back door slammed shut with such force that the sleeping baby startled and jumped in her box. Her eyes opened wide and her little arms were rigid as they shot upwards with tiny fists clenched. Her lips puckered up and for a second Maura thought she was about to wake and cry.

'Please, God, no,' she whispered, 'not today, I need another hour to get everything done.'

She stroked the back of the baby's hand, making gentle shush, shush sounds to try to prevent her from waking fully. It worked; as she leant across and looked into the box, the baby's eyes slowly closed, her arms softened and dropped gently back down to her side, her face relaxing into a dreamy smile as sleep and innocence won the battle with the slamming door.

Today, as Tommy used the outhouse for his morning ablutions, he was more preoccupied with the state of Maura's mind than on the running order of the horses.

His reverie was suddenly broken by an urgent call from his oldest child.

'Da, will yer hurry now, I'm desperate!' shouted Kitty, her voice cutting through the wind and rain from the back door. On a finer day, she would have been knocking on the outhouse door itself, giving him no peace.

Kitty was his eldest; she was five going on fifteen and, now that she was in the infant school, had refused to use the pot that was kept under the children's bed. Kitty might have been only five but, as the eldest of seven, she could change a nappy and soothe a crying baby as well as her mammy. With her auburn hair and her mother's eyes, she was one of the prettiest and sweetest little girls on the four streets and definitely took after her father in temperament.

The sleeping arrangements were cramped, with the girls in one bed and two sets of twin boys sleeping behind a curtain in another. The new baby would join the girls' bed soon enough and be trusted into Kitty's care.

'I'll be out in a minute, Queen,' shouted Tommy loudly.

He would do anything for their Kitty, his first-born and the apple of his eye. He would even abandon his normal morning routine of studying the horses' form whilst sat in the outhouse with a pencil behind his ear, ready to mark out a promising filly. As he prepared to vacate his throne for Kitty, Tommy wondered, yet again, what they were going to do to prevent Maura getting pregnant again. It wouldn't be long before all the children were refusing to use the pot and demanding the outhouse, his morning sanctuary. Seven little ones in their two up, two down, was as much as the place could take.

Tommy had a great deal to concern him today. He was also worried about the tears that had poured continuously down Maura's face during the six days since Bernadette had died. It was too much. She had cried for too long. One of the neighbours had told him that she felt Maura was making herself sick. What could he do to stop her?

Last night, when they were in bed, Tommy had clutched at straws. He was lying on his back and Maura on her side, her arm propped up with her hand behind her head.

'If ye keep on crying like this, the upset will get through to the babby and make her ill,' he told her.

He was no master of the art of child rearing, despite the fact that they had so many of their own, but he had heard enough women in the four streets say exactly the same thing to Maura over the last few days to know it was a comment that carried some collective weight. And anyway, imparting such wisdom made him feel authoritative and useful, rather than just criticizing Maura for crying all the time, and, other than Tommy, God alone knew how much she had cried.

His stress management technique was rewarded as Maura responded, 'I know. I feel so sick and I can't eat for crying. I know ye are right.'

Her breast had fallen free from her nightdress, which was still open from the baby's last feed, and lay bare against Tommy's chest. That was enough. His hand moved from stroking her arm to stroking her breast for just a minute, which was all it took.

As she quietly sobbed into his chest he pulled his arm from underneath and rolled her over onto her back. He kissed her lips gently as he lifted up her nightdress and parted her legs with his knee.

Somewhere in his Guinness-addled brain, Tommy thought sex would help Maura. It was life affirming, it was comforting, it was a relief in the midst of despair. For Tommy, that was. For Maura, it just made her feel more isolated and bereft.

As soon as he had finished and heaved his last sigh, Maura left the bed for the bathroom. As she stood to go, with her back to him, Tommy slapped her backside playfully.

'That's a good girl, now isn't that more like it, eh? Bet you fecking loved that. Now if you're still feeling bad tomorrow I'll give you another.'

She heard him chuckling to himself in the thirty seconds he took to fall asleep. She looked back over her shoulder. He had no idea. She watched him beginning to snore as he fell into the first folds of sleep, pleased with himself, a self-satisfied grin on his face.

She would always be with Tommy, she knew that. She loved him. He wasn't perfect, but he wasn't bad either. He was a man with simple needs, who had no idea how to emotionally support his wife, but tried his best, even though sometimes he got it horribly wrong. She knew she would never have emotional support, unless she asked for it to be expressed physically. Tommy thought that making love to Maura was the best and only way to show his love and, in doing so, in the years they had been married had knocked her up five times and impregnated her with two sets of twin boys. A double feather in his manly cap.

Before she went to the bathroom, she wondered how he would react if she were to die tomorrow. Would he be a shadow of himself in the way Jerry was?

When Maura returned to the bed she moved against Tommy to be wrapped in his arms, the only place she felt any comfort or relief. The only place where her tears stopped flowing, even if only for a few minutes. He would hold her tight across her back and she would inhale the smell of him deeply as each breath brought with it a wave of calm and sweet relief to her anguished heart. Maura knew she wouldn't sleep tonight. How is anyone going to sleep, she wondered, as she thought of Jerry and his mammy and daddy in the house with baby Nellie. She felt their heartache as raw as her own and began to cry again.

Tommy knew Maura had hardly slept at all since they heard that Bernadette was dead. Later that same night, somewhere between sex and dawn, he had been woken by her sobbing as he had been every night since Bernadette's death.

Tommy was confused. At a loss to know how to comfort her, he had tried everything he knew. He had felt irritated and impatient with her one minute and overwhelmed by love and compassion the next. He desperately wanted normality to return as soon as possible. Life was hard enough, working on the docks every hour God sent, without the unexpected calamities that were thrown in their path every now and then. Sure, Tommy was upset too. Who wouldn't have been? Kitty and the other kids were also distraught. There wasn't anyone on the four streets that hadn't cried and wailed upon hearing the news. Bernadette was a legend.

The women all liked her, the children loved her and the men lusted after her. There wasn't a man who hadn't envied Jerry, the man who had it all. No kids until he wanted them, a bit of money in his pocket for the extras, a trip home to Ireland every now and then, and as much Guinness as he could drink. Aye, Jerry had had everything, the lucky bastard, until now.

'Come here, Queen,' he had whispered to Maura in the dark of the night as she woke him with her muffled sobs.

There was the slightest hint of exasperation in his voice. He knew she was trying to do everything she could not to wake him and yet he wasn't sleeping as well himself. She shuffled over from her side of the bed to his and laid her head on his chest as he put his arm under her back and round her shoulders. With his free hand he stroked the cold out of her other arm, which lay on top of the blankets. And there he had lain, holding onto his Maura until the sobbing had passed and she had fallen into a fitful sleep, until the baby, who was in her box on the floor down at the side of the bed, had woken them both for her feed at five.

As he did every morning, Tommy lay on his side watching Maura feed the baby. Maura lay on hers. They were facing each other with the baby resting on the mattress between them. The room smelt of warm milk, wet nappies and lanoline. Tommy stroked the baby's head but she didn't break her stride to look at him as she sucked furiously at Maura's breast. Even at three months, she knew the rough scaly hand stroking her downy dark hair was only that of her da; it was something he often did when she was lying in her box. Maura and Tommy smiled at each other and that was the last Tommy knew until Maura woke him again just before six.

'The baby is in her box, she's all fed and changed and will sleep now. Look after her, I'm off to mass.'

It wasn't yet six o'clock. Tommy smiled. If anyone got to heaven it would be Maura. There was no better Catholic than his wife. She set the standards in the street for the other women to follow and she was definitely Father James's favourite.

When Maura returned from mass, she quietly checked on the other children, who were all sleeping soundly. It was still early and what she couldn't get done in the hour after mass and before they woke wasn't worth doing. Whilst Tommy was in the outhouse and she waited for the fire to catch, she leant over to check on the baby in the box. The child was full and sleeping, but that didn't stop Maura from picking her up and holding her against her whilst she rocked. Although the baby needed no comfort – not a sound did she make – Maura did and the only solace she could take right now was to hold her sleeping baby close.

The fire suddenly caught as flames raced up the chimney. The bricks on the inside heated quickly, chasing the smoke back up the stack and out of the top to mingle grey smoke with grey mist. Maura was now shivering violently. Putting the baby back, she jumped up quickly and pulled off her coat, which smelt of wet wool and stale chip-pan fat.

Both she and the other women had agreed the previous day to send the children off to school early and to keep the little ones indoors. Today was no day for footie games or laughter on the green, regardless of the weather.

She looked up at the clock on the mantelpiece above the fire, next to a pair of Staffordshire pot dogs. They were the only things of value in the house, although they spent more time in the pawnbroker's than on the mantelpiece.

The morning routine of feeding and dressing seven children began in a hurry. Kitty took Angela, and Maura the twins. Tommy helped today as he was at home, and took over from Maura as baby Niamh had her next feed. Kitty took the twins to school and then returned to help look after the little ones until Mrs Keating, a neighbour, came in. The teachers wouldn't bat an eyelid. They were all from back home and knew of the terrible tragedy that had struck the four streets.

Tommy had brought chocolate back from the newsagent's, something they had only ever had at Christmas before.

'Don't let them have any until ye see us turn the corner at the end of the street, now, Kitty, do ye hear me?' Maura said as soon as Kitty came back in through the door. 'What did Miss Devlin say to ye? Was she all right now about ye coming back home?'

'Aye,' said Kitty, 'she was grand, Mammy, and she asked me to tell ye she would be putting in a prayer card in St Mary's for Bernadette.'

Kitty was smart and older than her years. Her childhood was doomed to be short as she shouldered the responsibilities of an elder sister. She didn't need to be asked or told anything twice.

The church bell began to ring out the death knell. A Liverpool funeral wasn't worth having without the solemn, dramatic accompaniment of the slow, steady call to a requiem mass. They told everyone on the four streets it was time to leave. Put on your coat. Check your lipstick. Put on your hat. Leave the house.

Maura looked out of the window to see if anyone else had begun to drag their hard-backed kitchen chairs outside into the street. The rain had petered out into a drizzle. How did anyone cope in this life without prayers to be answered, she thought. She put on her funeral black coat and mantilla, shouting to Tommy to come and help her put their own chairs out onto the pavement.

As she stepped outside she looked towards the top of the street and noticed that the dogs had ceased to bark, the tugs had stopped blowing and every curtain in the street was drawn in respect. Most houses had been in darkness with their curtains drawn for the last six days and no curtains would be opened until after the interment.

The cranes, visible on even the murkiest day, stood motionless like dormant lighthouses in relief against the flat landscape of the harbour. Even the dockers who didn't live on the four streets, and who hadn't known Bernadette, knew Jerry. They wanted to pay their respects and show solidarity in his worst hour. The Mersey Dock Company, the stevedore bosses and even the gaffers knew this wasn't a time to pull rank or to lay down the law. The faces of the men were too grim, too set to challenge. The docks were as silent as the four streets.

A hush had fallen over the cobbles and the only noise was that of wooden chair legs being scraped across the pavement as they were dragged outside to be lined up in a row along the pavement edge. Along with softly falling tears and the occasional sob, this was the only sound to be heard. No one spoke, but everyone crossed themselves each time they looked towards Jerry's house.

There were no words to be said. The feeling of loss was so acute, the shock so profound, that normal chatter had ceased.

People were used to grief. Everyone knew at least one person who had suffered as a result of the war even if they hadn't lost someone of their own. Infant mortality rates were high and maternal death from childbirth the biggest single killer of young women, particularly those from impoverished backgrounds like their own. Death was no stranger to the families on the four streets but, still, they hadn't expected it to snuff out the very brightest light that burnt in their midst. They were grappling in the dark. She was too vibrant, too noisy, too vital to be lost.

It was nine-thirty as everyone took their seat and lined the pavement in a guard of honour. At just that moment, the clouds parted and a ray of sunshine broke though. The older neighbours, who weren't going to the church or the graveyard, came out, the women with their headscarves fastened over hair curlers and heavy dark woollen coats flapping open on top of faded nightdresses or, for the men, stained pyjamas. They wore outdoor shoes with bare legs and no stockings, or work boots unlaced with no socks. The laces flapped around bare ankles and soaked up the rain from the pavement. No one batted an eyelid at the coats worn over nightwear. Everyone had wanted to say a last goodbye to the young, exuberant girl with the flaming red hair and the infectious laugh.

The women took their places on the chairs lined up in the street as their men stood behind, holding onto the backs. Some were shaking, some were tearful, and all were in shock. Today was a day they all wanted to be over as soon as possible. Even Maura. Despite her inner torment, her unstoppable tears and the acute pain in her diaphragm, the survivor in her knew that once a line could be drawn under today, she could take a fairy footstep towards normality. Life had to move on. She had her own children and family to hold on to, and if there was one thing she had learnt from death, it was to love and appreciate those around you because you never knew what tomorrow would bring.

None of the women were strangers to death from childbirth; Bernadette wasn't the first woman on the four streets to meet her maker that way. But Bernadette had done something different: she had chosen the hospital over a home delivery.

'I'm taking no chances,' she had told her neighbours. 'It's all the rage with the fancy women,' she had declared, laughing her decision off when the others asked why a home birth wasn't good enough.

'Ooh, get you, Silver Heels,' they had all teased her.

But Bernadette hadn't cared; she thought no ill of anyone for laughing at her. She had just wanted the best for her baby. None of the other women had a clue what plans they had in store for their child's future, and for Bernadette a hospital birth would lay down the first marker of change. It would be the first of many steps she wanted to put in place to break with the past. Their child would not be living its life on the four streets, but she couldn't share that desire with anyone. Never mind the fact that she knew, Bernadette just knew, that life for her baby would be very different from that of any of her neighbours' children.

They heard the horses' hooves before the gleaming black and glass hearse reached the top of the road. The first thing they saw were the white bouncing feather plumes attached to the horses' brow bands as they came into sight and turned the corner. Bernadette was coming home, back to the door of her proud, pristine house for one last time. She was coming to say one last goodbye to them all.

The men removed their caps and, casting their eyes downwards, clutched them to their chests. The women held each other's hands along the row, like children in a playground, and sobbed. Squeezing each other's hands tightly, they were holding one another up. The sudden emotion that had flooded the silence of the street as Bernadette had turned the corner was in danger of knocking them over, of taking one of them down. The shock of knowing that she was only feet away from them, that they could reach out and touch her coffin if they so tried, had brought up sharp the reality of her loss. There but for the grace of God could go any one of them. Most of them had at least half a dozen children each. At the rate they turned out babies, on any week Bernadette's fate could be theirs.

At the top of the dock steps, they heard the slow, steady ascent of footsteps as, one after another, dockers appeared and removed their cloth caps as they gathered along the top, stood in silence and watched.

As the carriage horses slowed to a standstill, everyone's eyes were on the house as Jerry's front door opened. For a few moments there was nothing. Not a sound. It looked as though the door was going to close again without Jerry coming out; then suddenly he stepped out with his baby cradled in his arms. For a second, he held onto the door frame, then looked down as his foot came off the front step and he stood in the street.

Hardly anyone other than Maura and Tommy had seen Jerry since Bernadette's death. The neighbours had been in and out of the house but it was Jerry's parents, who had got straight onto the ferry as soon as they heard the news, who had sat and talked with neighbours for hours, entertaining in true Irish tradition. No one had paid their last respects at the house and left without a glass of Irish whiskey and a sandwich in their insides.

Jerry had lost a great deal of weight and seemed ten years older than his age. His face looked grey and lined, and his red eyes were sunken and surrounded by dark circles from lack of sleep and continuous crying.

'Have ye ever seen a man so heartbroken?' Peggy could be heard to whisper.

She said that at every funeral of every widow, and it could have been the case; however, on this day, it was a fact. The truth. A statement exaggerated in a way only the passionate Irish could manage. Truly, had anyone ever seen a man more bereft or heartbroken?

Jerry's mother and father stood one each side of him and, without touching, were providing the invisible support to keep him upright. They were coping and giving no sign of being under stress themselves. Jerry's mother, Kathleen, the true matriarch of the family, was doing what all mothers do, being strong for her boy. No one could have mistaken Kathleen for anything other than an Irish mother. Fair, fat and looking like fifty. Her once light strawberry-blonde hair was partly grey and fresh out of rollers. Her eyes were also heavy but shone with a determination to get her son through this awful day in one piece.

Behind them came Bernadette's brothers. As soon as they had heard the news, they had packed up and made their way straight to Liverpool, just as they knew their mammy and daddy, who had both passed away, would have wanted them to do. The landlord at the Anchor pub on the Dock Road had rung the owner of the pub in Bangornevin, who had sent out a cellar boy on a donkey to the pub in Killhooney Bay, where there was no phone, who had sent out Celia, their cleaner, who was related to Bernadette's brother's wife, to break the news. The Irish mule telegraph. Both families had all arrived by coincidence in Liverpool on the same boat three days later.

In the meantime, whilst Jerry had waited for family help to arrive, Maura had kept him fed, watered and sane, but only just.

Each morning when he woke he felt a huge shock as the realization washed over him that Bernadette was dead. In the first few seconds as sleep half left him, he would reach out to scoop her into his arms; sometimes he would smile to himself, believing her still to be there. Every day since their wedding, he had woken as the happiest of men. But now, leaden dismay slowly descended upon him as it filtered through the haziness of sleep until suddenly, as though he had been slapped on the face, his eyes opened and the adrenaline kicked in, ready to help his body handle the shock, as fresh every day as it had been on the first.

It began with a hint. A small clue. A question. An odd pain between his ribs. A feeling that all might not be quite right and then, with a rush, the thought, *she's gone,* would flood in so quickly that even the adrenaline had no ability to protect him from the sudden pain and outpouring of tears.

If it weren't for Maura and Tommy, he would never have got out of bed in the morning. One or the other was always there, shouting up the stairs, telling him the kettle was on and the fire was lit or there was a stew or a pie on the table. How did they manage to smile and laugh as they did, as though nothing had happened? Had they cared nothing for Bernadette? Did they not understand his agony?

The hospital had insisted on Nellie remaining there until Kathleen arrived. 'Ye cannot be dealing with managing a first newborn now, in the midst of all ye grief,' the Irish ward sister had told him kindly. 'I do know what I'm talking about. Now, get yer mammy and daddy over and come back to the hospital, and by then baby Nellie will be settled on a bottle and ye can take her home.'

Jerry felt as though the hospital were kidnapping his baby. No. No. No. The words screamed in his mind. This is not what Bernadette wanted. This is not what she had planned.

'Now come along,' the sister said kindly but firmly. 'If Bernadette were here, both of them would have been with us for a week. Nothing is different for the baby.'

And so he had returned home alone. He had walked the full length of the city back to the four streets, unaware of where he was going. Unable to see through his tears. Unable to comprehend what was happening. She had been dead for only an hour and here he was, out on the street alone.

When he had spotted the blood pouring onto the floor, he had slowly stood up and, disbelieving, taken the three steps from the chair to his wife.

'Bernadette,' he whispered. 'Bernadette, what's wrong with ye?'

Only minutes before they had been kissing, crying and laughing, and now she lay deathly silent with a complexion of sallow wax beaded with clammy cold perspiration. He reached down and took her hand to shake her awake but dropped it just as quickly as the wet, unnatural iciness seeped from her fingers into his.

He ran into the corridor screaming for the midwife. In what seemed like seconds, it was as though all of hell had broken free. They no longer cared whether or not he could hold a baby's head properly as they had done only minutes earlier, as he was yelled at to take Nellie and to get out of the labour room.

Doctors in white coats stampeded down the corridor, with nurses running after them, pushing metal trolleys, their shoes on the floor sounding like waves of angry thunder coming towards him. He saw his beautiful wife thrust out of the room on a gurney and he wanted to shout at the doctors to be careful as it smashed against the side of the narrow corridor, leaving black rubber skid marks on the pastel wall as hospital staff became clumsy in their haste. Bernadette was as white as the sheet upon which she lay, with her long red hair splayed over the pillow, as the nurses, with panic running alongside, yelled at people to get out of the way.

It was too late. Within six minutes, she had haemorrhaged to death.

And at that very moment, as the last breath left her body, Bernadette heard their baby cry for the very first time … as though Nellie knew and were calling her back.

As Jerry left the hospital, the only lucid thought he had was to get to Maura's house. When he got to the back gate, he staggered and almost fell through into the safety net of their yard. Maura ran out of the back door, wiping her hands on her apron, imploring him to tell her what was wrong as, not knowing why, she began to cry herself, fearing the very worst, which transpired to be worse than even she, in those few seconds, had imagined.

On the second day, Maura and Tommy left yet another meal on Jerry's kitchen table. He didn't want to go back to their house. He couldn't face leaving his own or having to speak to anyone – he felt an inner resentment at their ability to carry on as though the most tragic, world-stopping event had not occurred. He wanted to scream and shout at them: 'Don't you both know she is dead? How can you both be so heartless? How can you just carry on with your lives as if nothing has happened?'

But he couldn't shout that, because they were there, at the beginning and the end of every day, acting normally, giving him quiet and unobtrusive support as though nothing had really altered, as though life must go on just as it had before. Except he knew that could never be the case.

He fell into step behind the funeral cortège, with Nellie in his arms. 'Here's yer mammy,' he whispered into the side of her face as he lifted her up onto his shoulder. With one hand on the back of her head and the other across her back, he cradled her to him. He was the only person who felt Nellie should be at the funeral. Every other woman on the four streets thought it was wrong and that a funeral was no place for a week-old baby. She shouldn't even breathe fresh air until she was a fortnight old, or so the mantra went.

He wouldn't give in. Nellie was Bernadette's daughter. She had been the most important person in their lives whilst she had been growing in Bernadette's womb. To Jerry, for Nellie not to be there was as odd as it was to the other women that she was. Nellie was going, in his arms, and that was all there was to it.

Bernadette was now only two feet away from them both. He wanted to rip open the wicker casket in which she lay and touch her. He wanted to stroke her hair, to look at her. He wanted to join her, to lie down next to her. He wanted to die and to be with her. He knew that in less than an hour she would be underground. Somewhere he and Nellie could never reach her, buried beneath the dirt, in the eternal darkness.

Tommy was at his side, and behind him four other men from the street who were acting as pall-bearers. He was about to carry his wife for the last time. The moment was coming when she wouldn't be there any longer, when his mind would have to let go and accept there was nothing else he could do for her. He had chosen flowers for her grave, picked a dress from her wardrobe for her to be buried in, combed her hair when she lay in her casket.

Every little thing he had done since the moment she had died was for her. He had given their baby her bottle, for her. He had cleaned the house, for her. 'She would want me to keep the place clean, Jaysus, she would go mad if I didn't,' he said to Kathleen who was making a good job of cleaning up whilst he insisted on feeding the baby.

He was about to take Bernadette in his arms for one last time and then she would be gone and there would be nothing left for him to do for her. He wouldn't be carrying her as his bride, shrieking and laughing down the street. Not as the girl he sometimes playfully carried upstairs and threw on the bed with her squealing, 'Put me down, put me down, you animal,' as she pounded on his back, unable to squeal for long, laughing so hard she had no breath left for words. None of that would ever happen again. It was gone forever.

He also knew, without any doubt whatsoever, that distraught with grief and desperation as he was, Bernadette would never forgive him if he didn't look after their precious daughter with every bone in his body. Bernadette would never rest if Nellie wasn't well loved and cared for by him and him alone. His life was to be a living nightmare as there was no escape for him. He could not die. He couldn't follow Bernadette. He could not stay with her. He had no option. Here, looking after their child, was where he had to be. There would never be a way out.

He knew this because he had dreamt it, as though Bernadette had lain next to him and whispered it with imperative urgency into his ear when he slept last night. The dream was so real, it had given him some comfort. It hadn't taken away the pain, but he felt as though she were, somehow, somewhere near. When he woke, he thought he could smell her. The room felt as though she had just walked out and was standing at the top of the stairs. He was sure that if he shouted her name, she would shout back, 'Yes, I'm here, Jer,' with her tinkling laugh.

Only in the dream, she hadn't been laughing. She had been urgent, imploring, instructing him to take care of Nellie. He had felt her fingers intertwining with the hair on his chest. He had felt her leg cross over his as she kissed his ear and her free hand stroked his hair, just as she always had. She was loving him in his sleep and giving him a list of instructions. These instructions were about Nellie and, when he woke, he could remember every single one.

The dream had given him purpose. He had been starving with grief and, in his sleep, Bernadette had fed him. That was his job now, to look after Nellie in the way Bernadette would have wanted. She was their legacy. This was his purpose. When he felt sorry for himself and trapped in a living nightmare, he would remember that dream.

Nellie began to whimper against his chest.

'It's yer beautiful mammy, don't cry,' he croaked. His throat had closed; it was on fire, thick with distress. He could say no more. His legs felt like jelly and his arms began to shake. 'Oh God, make me strong, let me cope,' he quietly prayed. He looked up and could just make out all the familiar faces around him, down the street, at the top of the steps and on the green. Neighbours who had spent hours talking to Bernadette. She had been in every house and had dispensed her own kind words to almost everyone in front of him.

For every woman who had cried tears of exhaustion, Bernadette had lent a hand.

She had hugged away the fears of some of the wives and laughed with the men as easily as he did.

His own eyes swam with tears to see so many people lining the street to say goodbye. As he looked towards the steps he saw the men from the dockyard lining the top together and, on the edge of the green, the shopkeepers and the ladies from Sunday school where Bernadette had helped with the classes. They all swam before him, blurred.

He felt Kathleen's hand in the small of his back, pressing gently as she stood behind him.

'C'mon, lad,' she whispered, 'one foot in front of the other, steady now, you have the babe.'

And as she nodded to Mr Clegg, the funeral director, who signalled to the horsemen, the wooden carriage wheels slowly inched forward, lurching to the left slightly, lifting from a groove in the cobbles and settling into the next, then lifting again, until the horses increased their speed to allow the wheels to glide over the top.

As they moved down the street, the sobbing of the women could be heard, following them in waves, the slow repetitive peal of the death bells ushering them along.

Jerry had used the money saved for their future to buy his love a wicker casket and to use Clegg's best horses and carriage.

Bernadette had exchanged her silver heels for silver wheels.

As the procession slowly moved towards the end of the street, those who were attending the requiem mass got up from the chairs and fell into a regimental order behind Jerry and his family. The sound of their footsteps took on the rhythm of an army of mourning soldiers, as they marched in time, as methodically as the horses' funeral walk.

Those still in their headscarves and nightdresses, battling to keep out the cold with their overcoats, watched as the last black mantilla turned the corner. And then silently, they watched some more, before, with heavy hearts, they took the chairs back inside.

Jerry handed Nellie to Kathleen as he and Tommy moved towards the carriage. And now their friends would support him. The men he lived alongside and worked with every day of his life were about to help him to carry Bernadette in love and duty, and he needed them, as the tears poured down his face so hard he could barely see where he was going.

'Hold up, mate,' said Tommy, as he steered Jerry to the foot of the hearse. 'We need to unload her.'

Tommy used the language of the docks, as though the hearse were a ship. He was worried about Jerry's ability to walk straight, having never seen a man cry like this before. None of them had. Jerry seemed to have lost all composure.

'Me and Jerry will lift from the front, Seamus and Tommy Mac, get the end, Paddy and Kevin, move into the middle and bear the weight even. Now, steady, after three.' Tommy was taking charge, his way of coping.

Jerry began to shake. At first it was just his hands but as soon as he had handed Nellie over to his mother the shaking seized his whole body. When the men slipped the coffin along the waxed wooden runners, the shaking became violent, as he and Tommy lifted Bernadette up onto their shoulders, in unison and with the same control that they lifted heavy weights every day of their lives.

He felt Tommy's arm slap across his back, grab him firmly and rest on his shoulder, hugging him as close as possible. The men were carrying Jerry, a human wreck, as much as they were Bernadette. Their footsteps shuffled, haltingly at first, and then fell into time as they slowly marched up the path and in through the church doors.

At the moment the large wooden doors of St Mary's church closed, the bell above the door of the bakery tinkled as Mr Shaw returned from the green and let in a customer who had stood outside, patiently waiting. Life on the streets had already begun to move on.

The men who were returning to their work on the dockyard slowly replaced their caps and turned to walk back down towards the river in groups of two and three. Within minutes they began to discuss the Everton away match on Saturday.

The children began to filter into the entry one at a time. Everyone began helping the older residents to put away their chairs before they made haste to check the babies and little ones they had been allocated for the morning so that the younger neighbours closest to Bernadette could attend the mass together.

They had all been too solemn, preoccupied and tearful to notice the thin young woman who had arrived at the top of the street and now stood at a distance.

She hugged the wall of the corner house, more to remain discreet than to shelter from the wind. She was dressed in a sage-green coat, fastened with a belt, and a matching green Napoleon hat with the front flap held up by three fashionable brass buttons.

She had a thin face, pale and pinched except for her nose, which appeared unusually large for her narrow face. Wisps of shoulder-length fine dark hair escaped from her hat to blow around her face.

Unemotionally, with small, dry, hazel eyes, she observed every second of the scene before her. She scanned the houses, all with curtains drawn both upstairs and down, and noticed, as the carriage had arrived in the street, a flurry of small faces dip under the upstairs curtains as, in one house after another, little noses pressed against the glass to view the horses.

She gave an involuntary shudder. She had the same distaste for children as she did for vermin.

She observed, with interest, that one of the women mourners appeared to be more distraught than the others. As she raised her hand, kept warm in her brown leather gloves, to tuck back an errant wisp of hair, she made a mental note of which house the woman had come out of.

As the mourners dispersed and went about their business, she moved away to catch the bus back into town. She was the only person that day who entered the four streets and smiled.

Most of the inhabitants, especially Jerry, felt as though they would never smile again.

# Chapter Four

When the last of the mourners had left the house, Jerry's daddy, Joe, managed to get the best part of a bottle of whiskey into Jerry with the sole intention of knocking him out. It worked.

Once Kathleen and Joe had him undressed and tucked safely into his bed, they tiptoed down the stairs and closed the door at the bottom behind them, just as they had done when he was a young and vulnerable boy. They looked at each other and breathed a sigh of deep relief.

'We haven't put him to bed in years,' said Kathleen, tears quietly trickling down her cheeks for the very first time.

Joe put his arm round her shoulder for comfort, struggling to contain his own worry and grief. The way Jerry had cried over the last week had torn at his father's heart.

'He's hardly put the baby down and he's going mad with no sleep,' she said, as she pulled her hankie out of her apron pocket to wipe her eyes. Kathleen was a strong woman and unused to crying. Joe had known the whiskey would push Jerry off the cliff. He knew how strong his son was, but he also knew no man could last a week with hardly any sleep.

'A night's sleep and all will be different in the morning, you wait and see. He will be stronger and we can all move on a bit,' he said reassuringly.

They had to return to the farm and their younger boys soon. Kathleen hoped Joe was right.

At five-thirty the following morning, Kathleen placed Nellie in the pram Bernadette had chosen, covered the hood with netting, to keep out the flies, and placed her in the backyard to sleep after her morning feed. It was the only day she had been able to get her hands on the baby for more than a couple of minutes, since she had carried her out of the hospital, five days ago.

Kathleen looked through the kitchen window, at the pram stood against the brick wall in the grey morning light, and whispered to no one other than herself, 'Thank God for Maura.'

Maura had offered to have Nellie when Jerry went back to work, which would have to be within the next few days. Kathleen knew, with such good friends and neighbours, Jerry and Nellie would survive.

Jerry slept for fourteen hours and, for the first time in a week, woke with dry cheeks. Alarmed, he fell down the stairs and into the kitchen, frantically looking around him.

'Where's the babby, where's Nellie?' he almost yelled at Kathleen, who calmly nodded towards the window and the pram outside.

'She's been fed and changed twice and is doing what all babbies should do, sleeping in the fresh air,' she said gently. 'Now, sit down, lad. We've buried Bernadette, it's time for you to eat a proper breakfast and for us to talk about the future.'

For the next few days, Jerry learnt from Kathleen most of what he needed to know about running a house, and what he didn't know once she went back home, he was assured Maura would fill in.

Over the following weeks, absorbing himself in the challenge of being a single father, running a house and keeping down a manual job brought him back onto the path of sanity and exhausted him to such an extent that he was able to keep all thoughts of Bernadette at bay. He pushed her deep down into a room in his heart and locked the door, whilst he focused on rearing their daughter in the way they had both planned. Bernadette's memory constantly banged at the door to be set free, but it remained firmly locked. He knew this was the only way he could survive. But there were days when she burst out and took him by surprise. When she overwhelmed him and flooded his mind with her image he found it painful to get out of bed. To shave, to eat, to walk, to work, to pick up Nellie. These were the days when the pain in his chest made him bend over double. With all the will in the world and all his strength, on those days, he couldn't stop her.

Exactly a week after the funeral, when Kathleen and Joe were at mass, there came a knock on Jerry's door. Haggard and exhausted, dressed only in his vest and trousers, he almost left it unanswered. He had been worried about possibly getting a visit from the council, telling him he couldn't bring up a child on his own and that they would be coming to take Nellie away. That fear kept him awake and was the basis of all the discussions with his parents. He was terrified that his visitor was from the council and he might be about to lose his baby. His tiny Bernadette.

He opened the door, holding Nellie protectively in his arms, and stared at the woman standing on his doorstep. She was smartly dressed and holding a parcel wrapped in a muslin cloth.

He looked across the road and saw that every net curtain was twitching. Some of the women were standing on their steps, arms folded, watching the house. A visitor knocking on any front door was an event in a street that was a stranger to surprises.

'Good afternoon,' said the visitor confidently. 'My name is Alice. I used to work with your late wife, Bernadette, and I have come on behalf of the hotel to pay my respects.'

When it dawned on Jerry that his visitor had been someone who knew Bernadette, he was so relieved that he immediately invited her in for a cup of tea. Today was one of those days when he wanted to talk about Bernadette to anyone who would listen. This woman looked as if she wanted to talk about her too.

'Forgive the mess,' said Jerry. 'I have me own mammy and daddy here and I'm sleeping down here for the while whilst they have me bed.'

Jerry didn't follow through with the information that he was relieved by this arrangement. Getting into his own bed was something he hadn't done willingly since the day Bernadette had died, preferring to sleep on the sofa when Kathleen let him. This way he never truly gave in to sleep, using the excuse that he could keep the baby warm in the kitchen. Having to sleep alone in his bed, without his angel to pull into his arms, was more than he could face right now. Physically walking up the stairs and getting into bed was normality. He wasn't ready to cross that line and accept that life without her was now the new normal.

'Did ye know Bernadette well?' he asked.

He was completely ignorant as to who Alice might be and was racking his brains to try and remember whether she was one of the girls from the hotel who had come to their wedding. But they had all been Irish lasses and this lady was definitely English. She had an air of stuck-up-ness about her which no one from Ireland ever had.

Nellie stirred and, suddenly, it was as if Alice wasn't even there, while he turned his full attention to the babe in his arms.

'Shush, now, Nellie, don't fret ye little self, shush,' he whispered tenderly, as he rocked her up and down.

Alice looked at them both with a curiously expressionless face, clearly untouched by the scene in front of her and regarding it with, at best, mild curiosity.

'Here, let me make you some tea, you look worn out,' she said, and walked over to the kettle, making herself slightly too much at home, although Jerry seemed not to notice as he laid Nellie down in her basket.

Stiffly, almost reluctantly, Alice walked over to the basket and leant over. 'Goodness me, she is a beautiful little thing, isn't she, and with such a look of Bernadette about her,' she said with a false brightness.

'Aye, she has that,' said Jerry, whose eyes didn't leave Nellie as he straightened up. 'I'm overrun with cake, so would ye like a slice with ye tea?' he asked politely. He didn't really know what to say to this very proper and posh stranger, but the Irish gift of welcoming friendliness automatically kicked in.

'Oh, yes please,' said Alice as she handed him her muslin-wrapped gift. She seemed embarrassed as he opened it to reveal a cake and for the first time he looked at her and smiled.

'Oh, I am sorry, I didn't realize, I am such an eejit, thank you so much,' he said. 'I will be the size of a tram by the time I have eaten all this cake but it is all very welcome, I can tell ye.'

They sat down and Jerry sliced the cake. The conversation was slightly awkward, but she managed to keep it going while they drank their tea. Although he couldn't have said why, Alice made Jerry feel slightly uneasy. She spoke in a clipped, accentless tone and her smart clothes made him feel inferior. He found himself gabbling.

Fear of ruthless British dominance runs deep into Irish roots and Jerry had no idea that, from this inbuilt default position, he was already losing.

When it came time for Alice to leave, Jerry politely showed her to the door. He hardly took in her promise to return soon to see if he was getting on all right. As he turned back to Nellie in her basket, he was already dismissing from his mind the whole strange episode and the unexpected visitor.

From behind her nets, Maura watched Alice leave. She had been standing at the bedroom window since the moment Alice arrived and she saw Alice smile, rather smugly, as she walked away. This disturbed Maura so much that she crossed herself.

'That one's up to no good, you can be sure about that, it's written all over her face. Holy Mary, Mother of God, I've a bad feeling about this, so,' she wailed to Kitty, who had brought them both a cup of tea sent up by Tommy and was hiding behind the curtains with her. As Kitty was growing older, she was becoming her mammy's best friend as well as her little helper. Maura gave a dramatic shudder.

'Jaysus, Kitty, someone has just walked over me grave, so they have.'

Maura went in search of Tommy to give him the news. As she passed through the kitchen door, she picked up her rosary, hanging off the big toe of the plaster cast of Jesus mounted on the wall, and thrust it into her front apron pocket where she stuffed both of her hands. A stranger on the street at any time was big news. A stranger arriving a week after Bernadette's death, who had been hovering around on the day of the funeral with a smirk on her face, was worrying news.

'Tommy, a strange woman has turned up twice this week, looking as though she has a stick up her arse, when Bernadette's still warm in her grave. She's giving me the creeps. You find out from Jerry who she is, now, or I'll be givin' out to you.'

'Calm down, Queen, it'll just be a mate of theirs,' said Tommy, trying to return to his newspaper.

'Are ye mad?' she yelled at him. 'You stupid man. What mate? I knew Bernadette better than anyone, I've known her all me blessed life, longer than Jerry even, and this woman is no mate, or I'd have known for sure. There's something bad about her, so there is, I can feel it in me water.'

'You and your feckin water,' snapped Tommy. 'Can ye water tell me what's going to win at Aintree today, am I right on the two-thirty with Danny Boy, eh?'

Tommy didn't see what hit him smack on the side of his head. It was Maura's knitting bag, the first thing to come to her hand, as she went to chase him out of the kitchen. Maura had a dreadful feeling. She had felt it before on the day of the funeral, when looking up the street she had seen that sly-looking woman, and she knew all was not right.

Distracted by her thoughts, Maura went into the yard to take in her washing before the damp air set in. The other women were still in groups of twos and threes standing outside their front doors. This was like an afternoon matinee at the cinema. No one was going inside until Alice had left and they'd all had a good look at her. Now silence settled over the chattering groups, while each woman stared at Alice and took in every detail from the shoes on her feet to her smug smile and purposeful stride as her shoes clicked and her hat bobbed down the street.

'So, she's up to no good, that one,' said Peggy.

'I've never seen a woman smiling, coming out of a house of death before,' said Mrs Keating.

'Aye, looks like she has her eye set on being the new Bernadette if you ask me, that high and mighty one,' said Mrs O'Prey, as she dropped her ciggie on the pavement and stubbed it out with the toe of her slipper, scorching the sole with a reek of burning rubber.

Nothing would get past the women on the street. They might not have been endowed with academic brilliance or good looks, standing there in their housewife's uniform of curlers, headscarves, wraparound aprons and baggy cardigans, but their emotional intelligence was as sharp as a new razor.

'Aye, so it does,' said Peggy, as Mrs O'Prey's words sank in. Peggy was always the last to catch on. 'My God, the brass neck of the woman. She's as brazen as yer like and, mark my words, I bet we will see her back here soon enough, Jaysus, would yer so believe it not?'

It was often hard to understand what Peggy was on about, even for her neighbours, but they all got the gist and never questioned her.

They carried on watching Alice, walking with a pert step back up the street towards the bus stop, and gave each other a knowing nod and a smile. Peggy put her hands on her hips and began to wiggle, imitating Alice's walk behind her back. They all began to laugh. Peggy always made them laugh.

On the bus back to the hotel, Alice knew she was going to have to play a long game. A thrill of excitement shot through her stomach as she thought about what she had set out to do. The first step had been easier than she had imagined it would be, although her nerve had almost failed her as she walked down the street towards Jerry's house, carrying the fruit cake she had paid the chef in the hotel to make. All of her brave thoughts over the last few days had deserted her. The plans she had made in her head did not seem so attractive in the cold light of day as she attempted to put them into action. It was the children on the street staring at her that finally drove her the last few steps to Jerry's door.

She noticed that front doors on the street were beginning to open and women were gathering in twos and threes, folding their arms and staring at her, as bold as brass. They intimidated her and left her in no doubt that it was her they were talking about. Her heart was pounding in her chest and her throat was so dry it had all but closed up. It had taken all her courage to knock on the door.

'The nerve of me,' she said quietly to herself, as she took her seat on the bus. She almost laughed out loud and looked around to see if anyone had overheard.

There was no doubt in her mind what she wanted, but it wouldn't be fitting for anyone to guess that yet. She wanted Jerry. It wasn't that crazy. The feelings she had nurtured for him over the years were so intense, he would surely feel and share them once he got to know her.

For years, Alice had been obsessed with Jerry. The man who had raised his cap to her. Who had looked into her eyes as he greeted her. The man who had once smiled at her in a way that made her stomach churn like it never had before or since. It was only Jerry who had entered Alice's thoughts over the last few years. Bernadette had been barred. Jerry was important; he mattered, Bernadette did not.

Alice had first met Bernadette when, as a new chambermaid fresh from the bogs, Bernadette had reported for her first day at the hotel. She had immediately caught Alice's attention. Not only was she not scared stiff and whimpering, she was positively bursting with energy, had bright shining eyes and was eager to start work.

Alice managed to remain hostile and distant with the impetuous, bubbly new arrival, who settled into hotel life very quickly.

Bernadette spoke and interrupted Alice so often, she felt her face burning with anger. However, it was impossible to shut up this girl who, even when chastised for talking, appeared never to take offence. Nothing, not even the worst telling-off Alice had ever given to anyone, using the harshest words, seemed to penetrate her happiness.

Alice was fascinated by Bernadette. By her hair, her accent, the way she smiled, the blueness of her eyes. She stared at the freckles on Bernadette's arms, the shape of her teeth, and she was transfixed by every word that came out of her mouth. She felt that if she was an oddity, so was Bernadette, just in a different way. But Alice didn't bond with Bernadette. She didn't like her.

The same couldn't be said of the young man who met Bernadette at the end of each shift every day. That young man did stir feelings in Alice and she was as obsessed with him as she was by Bernadette, but for very different reasons.

Alice had never before seen a man kiss a woman the way she saw

Bernadette being kissed. It happened by accident, late one night, just as Alice was closing the blind in her attic room at the back of the hotel. She heard Bernadette's incessant laugh as she turned in to the back gate and watched as, bold as you please, she put her hands on either side of the man's face and kissed him. And then he kissed her back. Alice held her breath, stunned. She felt a thrill of intense excitement run through her entire body, something she had never experienced before. Rooted to the spot, she stared, open-mouthed, and watched them.

And this she did from the very same place, on every night Bernadette went out. Alice lived her life through a pane of glass and in secrecy.

One evening, just as she knew Bernadette was about to leave work to meet her mystery man at the gates, Alice sent her off on an errand whilst she herself slipped outside, under the pretence of dropping a note to the gatekeeper. She wanted to see his face, to look at Bernadette's man close up. She wanted to hear his voice and get close enough to smell him.

As she crossed the yard, with her keys jangling against her long black skirt, she tried not to stare, but it was impossible. She suddenly felt stupid in her housekeeper's long apron. Bernadette's beau was the most beautiful man she had ever seen.

He obviously felt her eyes on his face because he turned, delighted, and chuckled, raising his cap in polite, almost extravagant acknowledgment, and shouted, 'Top of the evening to you!' as she walked past. It was the nicest, warmest smile she had ever received from anyone.

She noticed his hair was almost jet black, curly and slightly too long. Alice felt as though she had had an electric shock.

'Good evening,' she managed to reply primly, but she felt as though she was trying to talk with a mouth stuffed full of knitting.

He was wearing a long dark overcoat and a sombre checked scarf, but she could see that this made his eyes shine even brighter and show off his face, which was tanned, not pale like her own and that of most of the men who worked at the hotel.

Alice felt her cheeks burn red and her heart beat fast. The blood rushed to her ears and she couldn't tell what she was saying to the gatekeeper, who was looking at her oddly. Her heart was pounding and her breath came short from rushing. Her eyes were gleaming at her own audacity. She had done it. She now knew his face. That was all she had wanted. For now.

Every day that Bernadette worked at the hotel, Alice watched her being met and dropped off by her man. She waited, like a voyeur, to see every goodnight kiss at the back gate. She closed her eyes and imagined it was she, not Bernadette, being kissed by the tall handsome Irishman with the gentle smile and laughing eyes who let his hands roam over her buttocks. It was she, not Bernadette, who lifted those hands off and playfully chastised him.

One Saturday morning, there was a knock on Alice's office door, and Bernadette burst in.

'Oh, Alice, I have the most fantastic news!' she announced, bouncing up and down. Bernadette was totally unaware that Alice didn't like her. It was not something she had ever experienced before and she didn't recognize hostility.

'I'm to be married and I would like to give you my week's notice. I'm to become a lady of leisure,' she trilled, as she turned round and round on the spot, her arms open wide to include the entire office in her exuberant embrace. 'Or more likely,' she enthused, not giving Alice time to answer, 'a hard-working housewife.'

Her laughter escaped through the open door and bolted off down the staff corridor, where the chambermaids looked up and smiled at each other, already knowing Bernadette's news.

Alice felt the blood drain from her face. Jerry was about to exit her life. She would no longer be able to see his face every day and imagine he was meeting and courting her, not Bernadette. She nodded in acknowledgment and told Bernadette she would leave a letter in her pigeon hole with her stamp card and a reference for the following Friday. She didn't wish her well, because she felt no such goodwill. She couldn't get her out of the office fast enough. Bernadette was so high on her own happiness, she didn't even notice.

From that Friday onwards, Alice never saw Bernadette again, but she never forgot Jerry. She thought of him every single day. When she slept at night, she dreamt of him. Vivid, detailed, dreams. Once she had seen his face and known his voice, he dominated her waking thoughts and, somewhere in her head, she lived in an imaginary world. One where he was collecting her, waiting for her, kissing her. One in which he was hers and whisking her away to a life in a comfortable house, where she could make a world of her own. A life void of Bernadette.

When years had passed and Alice read the announcement of Bernadette's death in the *Liverpool Echo*, she was breathless with excitement. All those dreams seemed suddenly within her reach. Jerry was alone.

The bus driver approached Alice for the money for her ticket. 'Lime Street station,' she said, as she handed over the money without removing her long gloves, of brown kid leather with six buttons. Alice hadn't bought them; she might have been the housekeeper, but her wages took into account that she was provided with board and food. She certainly couldn't afford gloves as fancy as this herself. They had been left behind by a guest, placed in Alice's lost property box and never claimed.

The bus driver raised his eyebrows. Fingerless knitted mittens were the best he ever saw on a cold day on his bus. Alice saw his look and loved it. Her plan had been developing in her mind by the minute. She wanted Jerry, but not his circumstances. She was not going to live a docker's life. She wanted better than that. That was what happened to the Irish girls at the hotel. She would have to work on Jerry to leave the four streets and use what little money she had to get them away. Alice had worked amongst guests who were travelling on from the Grand to America. She had overheard their conversations and read the letters and leaflets they had left behind in their hotel bedrooms. Alice was taken with the idea of America. New York sounded like the most amazing place in the world.

In a few short minutes she had transformed an idea into a certainty.

The only dent in her pleasure was the unwelcome news that Jerry had been left with a daughter. The wording in the newspaper announcement had repelled her: 'A beloved baby daughter left with a broken heart.' Alice loathed children and in Jerry's kitchen it had taken every ounce of resolve and determination she had to walk over to the basket and make the ridiculous sounds she had heard other women make when they saw a baby. Seeing Jerry's obvious love for Nellie roused no answering tenderness in Alice; she was more curious as to why a man would want to hold a baby and not look displeased. She knew this was something that made her different from other people, and she must disguise it.

It was not entirely Alice's fault that she felt this way. As a child herself, she had been so unloved and neglected that normal emotions were now almost impossible for her. From the age of three, she had known that her parents neither loved nor wanted her. Sitting in the doctor's surgery, suffering miserably with a nasty case of chickenpox, Alice had looked around at the other children, cuddled on their mothers' laps, while she shivered on a hard chair by herself. Her mother sat in the chair next to her, staring straight ahead with a rigid back, managing to look at no one, ignoring the reproachful stares of the other women. Alice leant back against the chair, wondering what it would be like to be touched and kissed like the other children. Alice was never touched at all.

Neither of Alice's parents had wanted children. From the day she was born neither of them took to her. Her conception had been an 'accident'. One they had learnt from, because they never had sex again. The consequence of sex, Alice, scarred them for the rest of their married life.

Alice's father was a clerk at a solicitor's in town. The couple were just about comfortable, one and a little bit above poor. Alice's mother was a hypochondriac who invented a new illness each week, and her father worked hard to pay the doctor's bills. He was a suppressed, quiet man who accepted his lot in life, did everything he was instructed to do and never complained. Alice sometimes thought he would like to talk to her, that he wanted to be kind, but that he knew it wouldn't be approved of. Only one female in the house was allowed any attention from her father and it wasn't Alice.

As the years passed, Alice became almost invisible. You could walk past her in the street and be totally unaware you had done so, so slight was her presence. Her parents didn't talk to the neighbours and she had no friends to speak of, because she wasn't allowed to play with the other kids in the neighbourhood. She spent a great deal of time at her bedroom window, watching as other children wheeled push-bikes in and out of the houses up and down the street, sometimes pointing up to the window and laughing at her if she didn't move away in time.

'Oi, Miss Havisham,' shouted the boy from across the street to her, one afternoon when she had spent a particularly long time at the window, 'come out and play.' She ducked and hid behind her curtains and didn't go back to the window for days.

When she was about seven years old, she saw a small child and her father walking hand in hand past her window. No one had ever held Alice's hand. She watched intently, unable to look away as the little girl and her father passed by. She stared at their hands, clasped together, at the father striding on ahead laughing, his head bent forward against the wind to prevent his grey trilby hat from blowing away, and the flaps of his long dark grey overcoat kicking out in front as he strode purposefully forwards. Her eyes fixed upon the little girl, giggling, tripping along behind like a balloon bobbing around in the wind, about to break free and take off. She had to resist the urge to run out into the street to follow them and see what they did next.

What is he doing holding onto her hand? she asked herself. She sat for hours, replaying the image over and over in her mind. No matter how long she pondered, it made no sense to her and added to the confusing questions that were growing in her mind about her life.

It wasn't as though she was entirely short of physical contact. The impaired hearing in her left ear was surely due to the fact that whenever she did something wrong, apparently often, her mother hit her with such force across the side of her head that her ear blew up like a cauliflower for well over a week. During this time she couldn't eat properly or close her jaw fully until the swelling had subsided.

And that was about it. There was never any talk other than what was essential. No affection. No interest. She could never remember a meal with her parents, although every night it was her job to lay the table and then to clear the dirty dishes away, when her parents signalled to her that they had finished. She ate her bread and dripping each morning in the scullery, alone, whilst her parents sat at the kitchen table. She was never allowed to join them.

'Don't make any noise when washing up, Alice,' her mother would bark, as they left the room. When Alice made a noise, she reminded them she was there. Noise pricked their collective guilty conscience.

One evening when she was fifteen, while she was washing the supper dishes at the kitchen sink, her mother made a rare appearance and picked up a cloth to wipe down the table. Alice knew straight away that something must be wrong and nervously took her hands out of the dishwater.

'Your father has found you a job,' her mother said to her, without any preamble or niceties. 'On Monday you will start work as a chambermaid at the Grand hotel in town. You will live in at the hotel and earn your own keep. You can pack your bag over the weekend.'

With that, she put down the cloth and left the kitchen. Alice stared at her back as her mother walked out of the door.

The following Monday, Alice stood at the staff entrance to the Grand with her small suitcase at her feet, watching her father walk away without a backward glance. In her pocket was a bag of barley sugars – the first, and last, sweets her father had ever bought her, perhaps in response to the unspoken distress in her eyes.

She never saw either of her parents again. Within a year, they were both killed in a tram accident, having never written to her or visited her since the day she left. Alice inherited just enough money to bury them, and their furniture, which the hotel manager kindly allowed her to store in the hotel basement. Alice received the news of their death with composure and dry eyes. She was swamped by a feeling of relief. No one would hit her, ever again. There may have been no money, but she suddenly had possessions and had lost the people who inflicted so much pain upon her. Alice felt rich and, for the first time in her life, moderately content.

However, this contentment was destined not to last.

The bus pulled up outside the gates of St Mary's and through the window, in the graveyard, Alice saw the freshly dug mound of earth laid over Bernadette's grave like a quilt. It was covered in home-made wreaths and bunches of pink and white flowers. Alice smiled to herself. My turn now, Bernadette, she thought to herself. My turn.

What happened next was a mystery. There was a wire running along the roof of the bus for people to pull to ring the bell in the driver's cab, should they want to alight. As the bus pulled away from the church the bell rang, seemingly of its own accord, and the driver slammed his foot on the brake. He thought something must have been very wrong for the bell to ring as he was pulling away. The conductor, standing in the aisle, suddenly lurched forward and his ticket machine slammed into the side of Alice's head.

'Bloody hell!' he shouted as he grabbed the chrome rails on the back of the seat to steady himself. 'What the flamin' hell are you doin'?' he roared at the driver in his cab behind a screen of glass. Turning his attention to Alice, concerned, he enquired, 'Are you all right, luv?'

Alice was pale and still. She hadn't even flinched. Turning towards the conductor, she smiled as a trickle of blood ran down the side of her face.

'I'm very well, thank you,' she replied as she held her handkerchief to her cheek. 'Very well indeed.'

'As long as you are sure,' said the conductor as he walked away. When he reached the platform at the front of the bus, he turned and noticed Alice look out of the window, talking to herself.

'Nice try, Bernadette,' Alice had whispered.

*

As the bus approached Lime Street, Alice pulled the cord and stood up. She stepped off the bus and swept in through the staff entrance of the Grand. She made her way up to her own room, acknowledging the curtseys and bows of the other staff with a stiff little nod. Entering her bedroom, she shut the door behind her and looked around her at the room she had occupied ever since she had become housekeeper. Although vastly better than the rest of the staff accommodation at the hotel, it still was not much to show for her years of service. A single sterile room at the top of a hotel with an iron bedstead and a sink. She had a little money put by, but not enough to give her any degree of comfort, come the day she had to leave the hotel. Not enough to buy her a house or to pay for a lifetime of rent somewhere respectable. And Alice knew that, once she reached a certain age, the end would come for her at the Grand.

She had seen it happen to the previous housekeeper, Miss Griffiths, who had been forced out by rheumatoid arthritis at the age of forty-two. Not long after Miss Griffiths left and Alice was promoted to take her place, the hotel manager asked Alice to take a letter and some personal belongings around to Miss Griffiths' forwarding address. What she found there shocked Alice into a fear that was never to leave her. This fear had occupied her thoughts after she turned off her light at night, keeping her awake into the small hours, and was now propelling her into action.

According to the address on the envelope given to her by the hotel manager, Miss Griffiths lived in a large terraced house on Upper Parliament Street, in the not-so-salubrious part of Liverpool. When Alice knocked at the door, she could smell the stench wafting from within.

A young woman, no more than eighteen years old and only half dressed, had answered after the fourth knock.

'What d'ya fuckin' want at this time?' she screeched as she yanked open the door. It was two in the afternoon. She had the grace to say, 'Oh sorry, luv, thought it was one of me customers who couldn't fuckin' wait.'

'I am looking for Miss Griffiths. I believe she lives in flat number two,' said Alice once she had got over her shock.

'The spinster? Is that her name? Yer, luv, she's down the 'all. Close the door after youse, will yer, it's fuckin' freezing,' said the girl, leaving Alice standing on the doorstep. She almost fell back up the stairs, where Alice could hear a baby screaming its lungs out.

Alice stepped inside, reluctant to close the door, as there was no window. A dark brown wire hung from the ceiling but with no bulb attached. The floorboards were bare and filthier than any Alice had ever seen in her life. Rubbish was piled up against the wall in an open wooden box that obviously contained the remains of stale food, even though there was a metal bin outside. The smell of rotting food competed for dominance with that of cat pee, which was definitely winning. Next to the box was the shabbiest pram, with barely any rubber on the wheels, and two skinny, flea-bitten cats asleep inside. She could hear the noise of a man and a woman arguing, and the baby's crying hadn't stopped. It was relentless.

As Alice tentatively clicked the door shut behind her, she was suddenly plunged into darkness and stood still for a few moments to let her eyes adjust. Within seconds, she heard the sound of rustling coming from the box on the floor and realized she was probably sharing her air with rats or goodness knows what other vermin or wildlife.

'Don't panic, just breathe,' she told herself, as she placed her scarf over her mouth to reduce the stench of cat pee and whatever else was making her gag. She heard muffled music coming from down the hall and then saw a faint light struggle to penetrate the darkness from under a door. Alice gingerly made her way towards the thin strip of light, step by step, one hand holding her scarf against her mouth and the other flat on the wall to feel her way along the hall corridor. Suddenly she stood on something that moved so swiftly from under her feet, it made her lose her balance. She put both her hands out to save herself, but to no avail, ending up face down in a new musky smell she recognized. Shaken and shocked, she picked herself up as the door tentatively opened and, to Alice's huge relief, flooded the narrow hallway with light.

'Hello, Alice,' said Miss Griffiths, 'My poor girl, I am so sorry, are you all right? Can I help you up? How lovely to see you, please come in.'

Alice looked down at herself. She was covered in black dust, having fallen over a pile of coal outside the door. She took a handkerchief out of her handbag and began to furiously brush herself down.

'It is my fault,' she said, seeing how much worse the rheumatics had made Miss Griffiths and how gnarled her hands were. 'I will just put this back.' She bent down and retrieved the coal scattered around the hallway.

'I am relieved to see it's you,' said Miss Griffiths. 'Some of my coal is stolen every day and I don't ever get to the door in time to see who it is.'

Alice wanted to ask why it was kept on the floor outside the door but the answer awaited her as she stepped inside.

The room was hardly big enough for one person and Alice noticed that it was not as clean as Mrs Griffiths had kept her room at the hotel. Her housekeeper's eye took in the dirt on the floor around her fireplace and the smoky grime on the mirror hung on the wall. Alice wondered how Miss Griffiths managed to cope as she noticed her hands were so bad that her fingers appeared to have closed over on themselves. A badly made bed occupied one corner; at its foot was a table with a pot, bowl and a matching jug. Another small table stood against a wall with wooden chairs on either side, the seat pads covered in green leather. On this table stood a radio playing classical music, a bowl of sugar, a brown teapot, a milk jug and a cup and saucer. Two red velvet armchairs flanked the small range in which a pathetic fire with the remains from a handful of coal smouldered. Against the opposite wall was a cupboard that obviously contained food. A chest of drawers stood to the side of the door and above it hung a picture that Alice thought she had once seen in one of the hotel bedrooms before it had been redecorated. The cold from outside had seeped into the room and the dwindling fire had allowed the damp to take hold. On a diminutive rug in front of the fire slept a ginger tomcat with a battle-chewed and bloody ear.

Alice didn't like being here. Miss Griffiths had been her superior. Never a personal word had passed between them. Their past conversations had been about bathrooms, sheets and chambermaids. Alice knew nothing about Miss Griffiths but, over a short period of time, she had watched the older woman's hands turn out sideways to resemble a pair of fans and her back hunched, until she was so debilitated that she could no longer work.

'Would you like a cup of tea for your trouble?' asked Miss Griffiths, as she struggled to take the envelope and the bag from Alice.

If Alice felt awkward, Miss Griffiths felt diminished and embarrassed by Alice seeing her in this condition. Her job had been her world and she had been very professional, running a tight ship and managing the chambermaids as though she were a strict hospital matron. If only she had known, she was friendliness itself compared with Alice.

'Er, no, thank you,' said Alice. 'I had better be getting the bus back now. We have a new girl arriving off the boat from the bogs this afternoon and, as you know, I need to be there to sort her out.'

She had no idea what to say and took her leave within minutes, not noticing the look of acute disappointment in Miss Griffiths' eyes. It would never have occurred to Alice that she was the only visitor Miss Griffiths had received in many months. It never crossed her mind to offer to carry in some coal, or ask if there was anything she could help with. It was now almost impossible for Miss Griffiths to pick up a cup and saucer, but she would never let anyone know that.

Those thoughts still didn't cross Alice's mind when she heard three months later that Miss Griffiths had been found dead in her armchair, having died of dehydration and hypothermia. It was the constant wailing of the cat and the lack of coal to steal that had attracted the neighbour's attention.

Alice knew that if she didn't act quickly, this could be her fate. She would become the next Miss Griffiths. She was prepared to do whatever it took to make sure that never happened to her. Come hell or high water, her future would be secure.

Later that afternoon, at the end of their shift, the crew from the bus enjoyed their mug of tea in the Crosville hut down at the Pier Head.

The conductor filled in his accident book and noted what had happened for his supervisor.

'She was a fucking loony,' said the conductor to the driver. 'Posh gloves, but away with the fucking fairies, if you ask me, talking to herself out of the window. Not even so much as a flinch when the ticket machine caught her in the face.'

'You're the nutter,' said the driver, 'pulling the bleeding cord and then saying you didn't.'

They finished their break in an acrimonious silence, the conductor not wanting to mention the woman with long red hair that he thought he had seen jump onto the bus just before the bell rang, but was nowhere to be found afterwards.

# Chapter Five

Over the next year and a half, Alice put her plan into action with great skill and single-minded determination. She was living a lie but she was excited and fired up by the fact that it was no effort whatsoever, and she could very easily see the results of her scheming slowly and steadily becoming her reward.

She had hoped that the baby would travel back to Ireland with her grandparents or maybe even be popped into a convent. To her huge disappointment, she discovered on one of her first visits that the baby was going nowhere. It was a blow, but Alice even had a plan as to how to cope with Nellie. Week by week, she eased herself a little more into Jerry's life and each week made it a little harder for him to manage without her help. Without his even realizing it, Jerry was slowly becoming dependent upon Alice.

Alice was as cunning as she was cold. She paid her second visit almost a month after the first and then the next three weeks later. Each time she came with something delicious to leave behind and, by the third visit, she had begun to help with little things, like the ironing, or making a pie, with food she had taken from the hotel kitchen. This food was divided out amongst staff who worked at the hotel. For the lower grades, it was the leftovers from the table service; but for the more senior staff, it was a cut from the butcher's and a share from the fresh fruit and veg delivery.

Alice had never previously taken any, but now she pulled rank. She brought fresh beef and chicken to Jerry's house and, having taken lessons from the hotel chef, could cook a decent stew. The chef made her the odd pie with buttery hand-rolled puff pastry and steaming gravy, which, delivered in a wicker basket wrapped up in a tea towel, lasted Jerry a few days. In return, Alice supplied the kitchen staff with bedding, blankets and pillows. The hotel trade was doing well in Liverpool and everyone had their cut.

After the first six months, Jerry would arrive home some nights to find Alice in the kitchen cooking a meal. She always left straight away, insisting she didn't want to encroach upon his time. This made him feel bad and he implored her to stay and eat with him. He had never invited her to the house, but she quickly worked out that the back door was never locked and took the daring step one day to let herself in.

For Jerry, the pleasure of coming home to a clean house, with the range lit and a meal cooked, quickly surpassed his shock at finding a near stranger in his kitchen.

One day, when Jerry and Tommy were sitting on the dock wall having a ciggie break after unloading a hull, they began to talk about Alice.

'She is a strange thing, this Alice,' Jerry said to Tommy. 'She seems to like helping out and I can't work out what she wants in return because she won't let me pay her nowt.'

Eejit, thought Tommy, but kept his thoughts to himself. He wasn't going to start a row with his best mate. He also wasn't going to repeat to Maura what Jerry had just said, because she would kick off. Instead, Tommy made a few enquiries of his own.

'Was she a friend of Bernadette, then?' he asked, as subtly as a brick. 'It's just that I was wondering, like, why I never saw her before Bernadette passed away and, the thing is, I don't remember her from the wedding, either.'

'She was nursing her sick aunt in Macclesfield,' said Jerry, who had already asked this question of Alice during one of their first meetings. He had tried to place her in his mind and tried to remember meeting her. He couldn't. It was a mystery. He knew the name, he had heard Bernadette mention an Alice, but in what context he had no recollection. But he didn't have time to dwell on it and, anyway, she was obviously just kind and trying to help.

'I do feel a bit uncomfortable, so I do, just sometimes,' said Jerry. 'I mean, what would Bernadette say? But, Tommy, I swear to God, it's nothing like that, I never so much as touched her or had a thought like that cross me mind. Anyway, as soon as I gets in, she leaves.'

'Aye,' said Tommy, nodding. Maura had mentioned that. 'You know what I think, Jerry? I think she's broody and it's all about the babby. She has none of her own and I reckon she's hanging around 'cause she has a nature for Nellie. Not having had a baby of their own by the time they are twenty-one does strange things to a woman's brain, so it does, and the more time goes on the worse it gets. I don't know how Bernadette stayed so normal, I don't. Best thing to do is bang 'em up as much as ye can and as soon as possible and then ye can't go wrong. It's natural.'

Having both spoken enough for working men, they sat on the wall in silence, looking down at their boots while they finished their ciggies. Jerry was lost in thought as to how things would have been different if he had led his life according to Tommy's simple rules.

One day, Jerry invited Alice to stop, spend the evening and eat with him and Nellie. He felt bad that she had arrived with a meal and wouldn't take a penny off him.

His mornings were always rushed. On his way to work he took

Nellie down to Maura's, with a basket full of nappies, and collected her on his way home. He often left the kitchen in a mess and felt horribly guilty at how much this nice, kind woman, who wouldn't stay longer than five minutes once he and Nellie got in, did to help them. He felt he should do something in return. Initially, she refused every single time but then slowly she began to accept the occasional invitation, always manufacturing reasons as to why she couldn't accept most times he asked.

Over time, although he had never so much as touched her, Jerry realized that Alice was becoming a fixture in his life and that others would regard her as more than a friend. Alice was odd, he recognized that.

Maura remembered the stories Bernadette had told her about Alice. Maura hated Alice, which made things difficult. Every time Jerry dropped Nellie off at Maura's, he was assailed by a storm of questions. He assumed that Alice didn't relate very well to Nellie because she didn't want to step on Maura's toes. Even he was aware that when Maura came into his house and Alice was there, the hostility between them froze the air within seconds. However, he knew that when Alice wasn't around, life was just that bit harder.

After about a year, he began to invite Alice to go with him to the Irish centre on a Saturday night, and on Sunday afternoons she would occasionally meet up with him, as he pushed Nellie around in her pram for a change of scenery. Jerry would do anything to keep moving and to blot Bernadette out of his mind. Thinking about her wasn't the source of comfort he once thought it would be; it was torturous and painful.

As Alice became a regular feature at the house, Maura grew spitting mad. If she could have poisoned Alice and got away with it, she would have. One day, when Jerry wasn't around, Maura decided to meet Alice on her own terms. When she saw Alice enter Jerry's house via the entry, she followed her into the house and pretended to be shocked when she found Alice in the kitchen. Alice was so much at home that there wasn't much acting involved in Maura's being stunned.

'Can I help ye?' she said. 'Are ye here for anything special? Only Jerry didn't mention youse was comin'.'

Alice knew she would have to deal with this one carefully. Maura might be bog Irish, but she could tell she was sharp.

'He doesn't know,' she responded, without a hint of friendliness in her voice. 'I finished early at the hotel and thought I would pop down to help him out.'

'Did you now,' said Maura, instantly affronted and her temper rising. 'Well, let me tell ye, miss, there are plenty of us here on this street to help out. Jerry doesn't need a stranger to do it for him.'

'Oh, I'm no stranger, Maura,' said Alice tartly. 'In fact, Jerry is taking me to the Irish centre on Saturday night. So I am sure we can chat there, but for now, if you don't mind, I have a meal to make.'

Maura stared with envy at the meat Alice had unpacked from her basket. A dark piece of brisket sat on the table covered in a dark-veined, deep-yellow fat. Maura could never afford meat like that in her house. The two women looked each other in the eye. Maura had met her match. As she retreated from the kitchen, Maura spotted the statue of the Virgin Mary on the mantelpiece, facing the wall, as if in disgust. She immediately thought Alice had done it.

In an act of defiance and with a determination somehow to leave her mark on the kitchen before she exited, Maura stormed over to the range and reached up to the mantelpiece.

'The Virgin Mother doesn't put her back on us,' said Maura, as she turned the statue round. 'She keeps an eye on what we're up to.' Then she flounced out of the kitchen.

Confused, Alice looked up at the statue and at the door Maura had just slammed behind her. It is true, she thought somewhat ironically, the Irish are mad.

It was after a particularly bad second winter alone, with Nellie now toddling around the house, that Jerry asked Alice to marry him. He hadn't planned to and for days afterwards he regretted what he had done, but there was no way out of it. He had committed a mortal sin. He had made his bed and now he had to lie in it.

Two weeks earlier, measles had swept the streets and Nellie had been ill for the entire time. Jerry had barely coped. Maura was at her wits' end, with her own seven children all down with the same illness, including Kitty, who was usually like a second mother and a second pair of hands for Maura.

It was the first time Nellie had been ill and despite Maura's protestations that she could handle one more sick child, Jerry wanted his Nellie to have all of his attention. He took the whole week off work and didn't go down to the docks once. It was Tommy who kept both houses fed that week.

Jerry hadn't seen much of Alice while Nellie was ill, although it was the one time he could really have done with her help. He wondered where she was and why she hadn't called in, but he was too busy nursing Nellie to think too much about anything, other than keeping her temperature and her food down.

It had never once occurred to him to ask Alice to marry him. He didn't think about it even for a second, not even when he hit his lowest point, boiling Nellie's vomit-soaked sheets in the copper boiler in the yard, with the cold rain pouring down the back of his neck and the steam from the boiler scalding his face. Not even when he cried again and his tears ran into the trickles of steam on his cheeks.

Definitely not then, because that was when he thought he heard Bernadette say his name. As he looked up, he saw her through the steam at the kitchen window, like he used to. She was standing at the sink, smiling out at him. Definitely not then, because that was one of the few moments he felt Bernadette was somewhere near, when he needed her, when he knew he wasn't alone. One of the very few moments he allowed himself to think about who and what he had lost and lived without, when he let her memory roam free. And he was filled with shame at how angry those moments made him feel, the fury rising like acid in his throat.

It happened on a Saturday night. Jerry had invited Alice to the Irish centre, something he now did on a regular basis as a way of saying thank you. He didn't really know what else to do. Even though he'd worked out she didn't have much of a social life, he told himself that she appeared to enjoy herself and the odd glass of Guinness, so it usually turned out well enough.

The dockers worked hard, their wives struggled to manage every day, but it was all made bearable by the fun they had down the club on a Saturday night. They spent the first half of their week talking about the previous Saturday and the second looking forward to the next. So special were Saturday nights that it was the only night of the week the headscarves came off, the curlers came out and the Coty cherry-red lipstick was taken off the top of the mantelpiece, where it stood all week like an ornament, and was applied carefully in front of the mirror that hung above. Lipstick cost money. Nothing that cost money was hidden away. A lipstick was a possession to be admired and it remained on parade, ready to hand, to apply at a moment's notice. Maura dusted her lipstick, along with the pot dogs. The family lived hard during the week but there was no better fun to be had than in the Irish centre, or in the Grafton rooms on a Saturday night.

There was a comedian over from Dublin that night to do a turn and a band from Sligo playing afterwards, which everyone on the docks had been talking about for weeks. Jerry knew the craic would be good and he would be able to have a few drinks himself and relax, not something he did often. It didn't really worry him that Alice was intense and slow to laugh, that she never spoke to Nellie, that she avoided any intimate contact with him and was the coldest fish he had ever met. He didn't care. He just liked to have the company. Another human being to relate to. Someone to keep him talking about little things and stop him thinking and remembering.

The women in the street reminded him every day. They knocked on his window as they walked past and shouted to him, 'On me way to mass, Jerry, and I'll light a candle for the angel Bernadette when I'm there, so I will.'

He would stand and look through the nets as the women's shadows passed by, and feel nothing. He hadn't been to mass since the day of the funeral. He never opened the door to the priest and he hadn't prayed a word since the day Bernadette died.

The women on the street mentioned Bernadette every single time they saw him. They spoke to him with manufactured expressions of acute pain etched on their faces.

'Oh God, ye look like a man broken with tears,' said Molly Barrett, as he bumped into her in the entry. He had no words to reply with, as she dragged on her ciggie and went on her way. He knew she meant well.

Mrs McGinty would touch his forearm and look at the floor as though suffering an attack of acute colic before squeezing out a tear and saying, 'God, I imagine the pain, Jerry, is more than ye can bear, Jer, ye must weep ye'self to sleep every night, ye poor, poor man, and how is the poor wee motherless babby?'

The past two weeks had been tough. He was haunted by the fact that people kept telling him he couldn't manage, that he needed help, that he shouldn't have to cope. He knew people frowned at the thought of him bringing up Nellie on his own. As he walked out of a shop one day with Nellie in his arms, struggling to carry his bag, he heard the greengrocer whisper to the next customer, who nodded in agreement, 'It's unnatural, so it is, he won't keep that up for long.'

He realized he needed Alice's help. Alice never mentioned his pain. She never spoke of Bernadette, ever. He had heard her mention Bernadette's name only on her first visit. With Alice, he hid. She was a life after death.

He drank too much that night. Alice didn't like to socialize and, although she hadn't ever said so to him, she made it known. It wasn't that she was rude to people, she was just quiet. She never asked a question and never fully answered one, either. And she was asked a lot of questions. No one on the four streets knew where Alice had sprung from. Some of the women, especially Maura, knew what her game was, but there was nothing they could do. Alice gave them no ammunition to use against her. She didn't engage or converse. She knew their game, too.

Jerry had to sit on a table for two with Alice, not on a big circular table for twenty as he had with his Bernadette. The nights at the Irish centre with Bernadette had been some of the best in his life, full of dancing and laughter. Bernadette would often run down to the centre first when he was getting changed after work, or watching the footie, and he often tried to stop her.

'Jerry,' she would protest, 'we have no babbies, we aren't as busy as the others. I like to keep a seat for everyone at the big table.' And that is what she did and everyone knew she would.

'Keep me seat on Sat'dy night, our Bernadette,' neighbours would shout to her, during the week. 'We'll be counting on ye, Bernadette, me corns won't take the pressure stood.'

It was just one of the little things she used to do that made her, a new wife, one of the community, from the day she arrived on the four streets.

Alice had no intention of saving seats for anyone. God, how she hated the Irish centre and everyone in it. She hid it well, but not enough to join in.

'Are ye not good enough to sit with us then, ye two?' the odd person would say, as they passed by their table.

People were trying to be welcoming and willing to have Alice on their table for Jerry's sake. Jerry hadn't told them that Alice was a Proddie, but they had all guessed. Everyone had wondered whether she was part of an Orange Lodge and would be out on the march in July. But, as it was, they saw her going into Jerry's house just as the big march was taking two hours to pass through the city and so they knew Jerry was safe on that score. It was the nineteen-fifties, but in Liverpool it was as if the battle of the Boyne was only last week.

Some of Jerry's friends would be more insistent, trying to get them to bring their drinks over and join them on their table. Jerry wanted nothing more. But always, the answer was no. Alice would shake her head, look down into her Guinness, smile sweetly and appear shy.

She wanted to reply, 'No, you aren't good enough to sit with us, never mind us with you.'

God, how she hated Guinness too. Alice looked around the club on this particular Saturday and tried to hide her discomfort at the cigarette smoke stinging her eyes. When would he realize he needed her? When could she stop pretending to like this foul drink?

Alice had reached a wall. She had no experience of romance and no idea of what to do to take her plan to another level. For the first time since she had left home, she was lost for ideas.

Alice was the only person in the club who didn't laugh at the comedian. The only woman not to dance to the band. Jerry, a fun-lover, who had spent most of his life laughing, recognized that he wasn't enjoying himself. In fact, he didn't even feel comfortable. He and Alice had run out of things to say half an hour ago. He had managed through the measles without help and, sure, hadn't he come out of the other side all right? The house might be a mess today, but Nellie was better and had wanted for nothing. Measles killed toddlers, but not his Nellie. He had passed the biggest test of a single father, one many women struggled with.

Time to stop this, he thought to himself. I will not ask Alice to come any more and in future will come here on my own and sit with the others.

Jerry was feeling stronger. It was almost two years since Bernadette had died. He could do this alone now. He took a deep sigh. He had just taken the first decision of his own in two years and he felt good. Empowered. He was going to get a grip, take control of his own life and look forwards for him and Nellie. It was time to make a visit home and take Nellie to see her family and the farm he grew up on. His mammy had written to say Joe had been ill, and Jerry was keen to visit him. He would arrange that tomorrow.

He looked at Alice, knowing she was about to become a thing of the past, and he felt lighter at that thought. No sense of loss, just relief.

A minute later, Alice took a very huge risk and slipped her hand on top of Jerry's while he sat and laughed at the comedian. As she lifted her own to put it on top of his, it shook. Her mouth was dry, and she was breathless. This was the most daring thing she had ever done in her life. The comedian sounded louder than he actually was and as she looked around, no one was looking at them. Everyone was laughing loudly and hysterically. It was a good moment.

She had no idea what he would do in response. She was terrified, but knew that, as he had already drunk a fair quantity of Guinness, now was as good a time as any. She had seen the look on his face, the expression in his eye when he had looked at her a moment ago.

It was as though he had stepped back. She saw in his eyes the slight flicker of a decision and his body language spoke volumes, as he leant back in his chair and sighed. For the first time, she felt as though she was losing control. She had slipped backwards in the flash of a second and she knew that she had nothing to offer that couldn't easily be supplied by any other woman. A woman he could easily pay a few bob a week to and who would look after Nellie in her own home. Her capital was shrinking. His gratitude diminishing. She had to think fast.

She didn't look at him, as she felt the dark hair on the back of his hand bristle against her palm. Her heart was beating too fast; she couldn't catch her breath and she didn't dare look up.

She heard him say, 'Alice,' but she still couldn't look.

He said her name again. 'Alice, Queen.' This time she made herself look him straight in the eye with a bold stare.

'Would ye like another drink?' he asked, not knowing what else to say. He thought initially her hand on the back of his was to catch his attention above the noise. It was only when he saw the look in her eye that he realized he was wrong. Something else was going on with Alice.

She felt a small self-satisfied warmth with the sense that she had just taken a gigantic step. Emboldened, she radiated a new self-confidence.

The Guinness and Alice's hand on his were confusing Jerry. He was a sucker for human contact and had missed that a great deal over the last two years. When he looked at Alice, she smiled sweetly. That was hard for Jerry. He was still vulnerable and loved a woman's company. It was so long since he had had sex, he couldn't remember what it would be like to have a woman in bed next to him.

Hand on hand … skin on skin … limb on limb.

The thought of moving on from Alice to a future on his own flitted away, as quickly as it had arrived.

He turned over Alice's hand and laid his strong, brown docker's palm on top of hers. Her pale white fingers and delicate nails were almost half the size of his. He gently lifted both their hands to face upwards, still joined, palm to palm, as if in prayer, as he stared at them both. Jerry was lost in the moment of fusion. It had been so long.

There was no real beauty in Alice, no vibrancy, no passion. He couldn't compare her to Bernadette. Chalk and cheese. It was futile to compare any woman to Bernadette; she would fail miserably. After Bernadette, one woman was as good or as bad as another but only one woman was cooking his meals, cleaning his house from time to time and had her hand on his.

The band would play until two in the morning but it was now midnight and, much to Alice's relief, Jerry stood to leave.

'Come on, Queen,' he said, 'let's go.'

He had no thought other than that this was a new and strange situation, and he didn't for one moment want Maura or anyone else for that matter to see him and Alice holding hands. They would want to know what was going on and he had no idea himself. Five minutes ago he had decided it was time to move on from Alice, now here he was holding her hand. How had that happened?

Halfway to the bus stop, Alice slipped her hand into his again and held it.

'Jerry, can we go back to the house tonight for a drink?' she whispered. She did her very best to appear seductive although this was so new to her that she had never even been kissed.

Jerry was thrown. They had not done this before. Through the fog of Guinness he tried to recall what time the last bus was and whether she would make it home if they went to his house first. Nellie was sleeping at Maura and Tommy's where all the children were being looked after by Mrs Keating's daughter, so he had no reason not to leave the house later and walk her to the bus stop.

'Sure, but the last bus goes in an hour,' said Jerry.

She kept her hand in his and turned to walk back towards the house, pulling him round to follow her. There had been no conversation as to what was to happen – there never was much conversation between them – but Jerry didn't argue with the fact that they were deviating from their normal routine. He was too far gone. It was the Guinness holding Alice's hand, not Jerry.

She thought she knew what was coming. They would sit down and have a cup of tea and chat about how difficult Jerry was finding things. He would tell her that she had become the centre of his universe and that he couldn't manage without her, he needed her. That he was beginning to love the times she came round, their walks and occasional evenings out. He would tell her he loved her more than anything in the world. That he admired her cultured ways and wanted to move away from the docks, to make a fresh start together in America or somewhere better than the four streets. Maybe he thought about New York where Alice had always dreamt of living, amongst more ambitious people.

Alice had talked to Jerry about going into insurance and she was sure he was clever enough to get a job at the Royal Liverpool. They had been advertising this week and Jerry had a nice hand for writing. He would tell her he was going to take her advice and apply for jobs, and he would finish his little speech by getting down on one knee and asking her, would she marry him? This was in the world according to Alice. This was her plan.

Alice knew she might have to try to seduce Jerry. This was something she had only ever imagined, but it didn't matter, she would manage. She had overheard enough conversations amongst chambermaids to know what they got up to and wasn't she better than any of them? There were ways to avoid getting pregnant and she would use them. She might have to do this thing with Jerry to get him to propose. She had worked hard to get to this point and she wasn't going to let the time pass any longer. He was an honourable man. Once he had laid with her, he would propose. It couldn't go wrong and if an Irish slut from the bogs like Bernadette could manage it, then so could she.

Jerry's ideas were different. He had two bottles of Guinness in his free hand. He thought they would have a drink, and then he would take her for the bus or if they had missed the last one, he would walk with her down towards town to hail a cab. Then he would be up, bright and early, to play the ritual Sunday game of footie with Tommy and the other men and lads on the green, whilst Kitty looked after Nellie. He would then go to Maura's house for the usual big Sunday roast. Nellie loved nothing more than sitting in Maura's kitchen, eating her dinner in the company of seven other children. It was the one meal of the week when they pushed the boat out. Jerry always gave Maura money to contribute. He and Tommy earned the same wage. Jerry's had to keep two people. Tommy's had to stretch to nine, and it wasn't easy.

As they went in through the back door, Alice took off her coat. She was wearing a dress that evening that she had bought in town that day. It was cut lower than she would have ever dared wear before and she was self-conscious about the fact that she was displaying too much cleavage. All evening she had wished there was spare material she could pull over her breasts and she regretted not wearing a cardigan. She had spent the entire night trying to draw the neck of the dress closed. She had bought the dress only because she remembered Bernadette's beautiful figure and how the hotel porters used to comment about it when they thought she was out of earshot.

Whilst Jerry hung up her coat, she took another huge leap. She put her hand inside her dress and lifted each breast up and out to make it more prominent, pushing the material aside to display more cleavage. She took a deep breath. She had no idea what came next but hoped something would give her a clue. She wanted him to look at her breasts, which she had boldly presented, and then kiss her. That must be how it went.

Alice hadn't been round to the house for a couple of weeks, because she knew Nellie had been sick. Any child was bad enough, but a sick child was intolerable. She realized that while Jerry was trapped in the house with Nellie, Alice was safe and no other papist whore would be getting her nose in. She calculated that to stay away would be a good thing. It would make him see how useful she had been over the last two years and how much her involvement in Jerry's life made sense.

She was wrong.

She had almost overplayed her hand.

As Jerry switched the lights on, she looked around at the kitchen. The floor was disgustingly dirty. She shuddered. Filthy dishes met her eye, and mouldy remains of dried egg and fat clung to the greasy oilcloth on the table. It looked as if it hadn't been wiped once in the two weeks since she was last there. Jerry's and Nellie's dirty clothes were piled up on the corner of the kitchen floor, not even in a basket or a box. Jerry had spent all day washing the sheets and hadn't got round to the clothes.

A white enamel bucket of cold, pungent, dark-brown water sat under the sink, full of Nellie's soaking dirty nappies. In the dim light from the overhead bulb, the indoor washing line had been pulled out across the top of the range, on which were pegged the few nappies Jerry had managed to wash out that day, now filling the room with steam. Its smell, and that of the enamel nappy bucket, mingled with that of Jerry's sweat-soaked work clothes and made Alice's stomach heave. She just about hid her revulsion.

Pull yourself together, you are nearly there, she told herself, as she forced another smile and looked Jerry straight in the eye. She wanted to leave the service of the hotel and begin planning a new life with the man she hadn't stopped thinking about since the day she first saw him. Having seen him treat another woman and even his repulsive child with so much kindness, she was determined to have him for herself.

Jerry opened the bottles and drank deeply from one. He looked at Alice as, without a word, he handed her hers. Alice took it from him before picking up his free hand and placing it on her breast. Jerry was stunned. Repelled. No. He didn't want this at all.

He could feel that Alice was shaking, as abruptly she moved his hand down and onto her abdomen and then slid it between her legs. This is what she had seen the girls do at the back gate with the men who walked them home to the back of the hotel. They didn't know Alice watched them every night. She had seen them put their hands down men's trousers and undo the buttons as they got down onto their knees, or sometimes if the men were in a hurry they raised the girls' skirts and almost lifted them off the floor as they pinned them against the wall and took them quickly.

They always reminded Alice of animals. Of the roaming dogs she had watched in the street when she was a girl. She had seen neighbours run out with buckets of cold water to throw over those that were locked together, howling and snapping, stuck in mid-copulation. She had only to step away from the window to remove herself but she never did. She had watched every chambermaid who had been taken at the back gate since Bernadette had left. Voyeurism had been Alice's life.

In those few seconds, whilst she moved Jerry's hand between her legs, a switch flicked on in Jerry that had been shut down for a long time. Suddenly, in the passing of a single second, he knew what he was about to do. He pulled away from her abruptly and staggered from the door with his back to the range. He stood looking at this plain, skinny woman, whom he didn't really know. Was this really about to happen?

He realized he had no idea how this situation had come about. He was deviating from his path of strict emotional control, a path he had walked in a steady line for two years. Now that he had stepped off he was beyond help. At that moment, his love for Bernadette turned to hatred. His anger at her leaving him bubbled to the surface for the first time since she had died.

He had drunk too much to control his fury. He felt hatred for God, the world, the priests, his neighbours who pitied him, for his parents for being elderly, for the life he had inherited and for the impossible job of being a father. He felt hatred for this scheming devil woman who was not the shy and proper Alice he knew. He hated himself. He hated everyone and everything and he was about to explode with anger.

'Come here,' he said roughly as he moved away from the range and towards her.

Alice stood frozen to the spot. If she did move towards him, she didn't know what to do.

'Come here,' he said again, only louder, with impatience and irritation.

For a second this shocked Alice, terrifying her into silence. This was the opposite of kindness, this was not what she had planned. This was not the fumbling she had seen at the back gate of the hotel. She was rooted to the spot, as he took the few remaining steps to stand in front of her. Without even kissing or touching her, he roughly pulled her dress up to her waist and her panties down over her suspenders and stockings. He took the bottle out of her hand, and placed it on the draining board. Jerry was an Irishman. He might have been about to have sex for the first time in almost two years, he might have been angry and have lost all reason, but he wasn't going to spill the Guinness.

Afterwards there were very few things Jerry remembered about that night. It would take too much time to go through the niceties and get Alice to bed, so he took her over the kitchen table.

He couldn't make love to her and look at her face at the same time, and so he turned her over. He could do this only if he couldn't see her eyes. He couldn't kiss her. Kissing her was the last thing he wanted to do. He wanted only sex, not affection. He wanted to punish her, badly. He remembered holding the back of her hair and accidentally pressing her face into the table without meaning to. His instincts were basic and animalistic, and if Alice hadn't deliberately engineered this, his lovemaking would have bordered on rape.

Making love to Bernadette had been nothing like this but that was what he wanted right now. No affection, no loving conversation, no kissing, no laughter. He wanted nothing to be like it was with him and Bernadette. Nothing. His anger with Bernadette for leaving him with a child and his intense hatred for life spilt out of him and into Alice as he pounded and punished her. And she didn't make a sound.

So angry was he and so consumed with loathing, he didn't notice the tears he cried all the way through. He didn't hear his own sobs.

She was relieved when he finished, staggered backwards against the range and picked up his bottle again.

'Oh God, for feck's sake,' he said, as he wiped his mouth with his hand.

Was that a good thing for him to say, she wondered? Did that mean he enjoyed it? She had never imagined she would lose her virginity, ever. But when she had, she had not imagined it would be like this. She was horrified and in shock, but she was tough. She was repelled by the surroundings and the smell, by the fact that nothing tonight seemed to be going to her plan. She knew what she was aiming for and if this was how to get there, so be it. She saw the tears pouring down his face, but pretended she hadn't.

Alice felt physically sick. She felt worthless and abused. She had thought that Jerry would at least kiss her the way she had seen him kiss Bernadette, night after night, from her bedroom window. That her first time would be less brutal than this. Tears pricked at the back of her own eyes and she willed them to stay where they were. If this was what she had to do to get his ring on her finger, she would go through it in silence. If it took her one step away from her single room in a hotel attic, if she had to endure this night, she would do it.

Pushing down on the table with her hands, she levered herself up from where he had left her. Her dress was around her waist and she frantically pushed it back down.

She turned round and looked at him. So acute was her embarrassment that it was one of the hardest things she had ever done in her life. He wouldn't meet her gaze, as he wiped his tears away with the back of his hand. Not looking at her was, in a way, a relief as he drank from the bottle.

'Get undressed, Alice,' he said as he undid his belt. 'Get all your clothes off now.'

For a second, with horror, she thought he was going to beat her with the belt but realized it was to further loosen his trousers. She had walked into enough hotel bedrooms and seen enough men naked not to be shocked, but she knew he would never have spoken to Bernadette in that way. Alice was jealous of a ghost.

'Get on your hands and knees on the floor,' Jerry said and Alice didn't recognize his voice. It was guttural and thick from the tears choking his throat.

She shook like a leaf and felt humiliated as, naked and cold, she obeyed awkwardly. Her face was feet away from the stinking pile of washing. Stale remnants of breadcrumbs and food dug into her palms and knees, stabbing into her skin like sharp tiny pins. As he pounded her repeatedly, this time for much longer, it took all her strength to keep her arms rigid to support herself. The buckle from his belt pierced the skin on the back of her thigh almost causing her to scream out in pain. She could not withstand his weight and when he finally came, her arms collapsed and her entire body crashed forward onto the floor with Jerry laid fully across her back. A virgin no more. She was at one with cold, dirty concrete. Her face was pressed downwards and she smelt urine where, earlier in the day, Nellie had had an accident while she toddled around.

'Oh God, I'm sorry.' Jerry sobbed and sobbed and, for the second time that night, Alice did not know what to do.

She lay perfectly still and waited for the sobbing to subside. What had she done wrong?

When Jerry finally stood up, he staggered up the stairs to his bed, saying nothing to Alice. She heard him crying, so loudly and painfully that she knew the emotion locked her out of the room. She gathered herself together, snatched up her clothes, holding them tightly in front of her, and collapsed onto the small sofa against the wall. She was scared he would come back down the stairs and demand more, but after half an hour or so, she heard the sobbing subside and knew he had fallen asleep.

Even though she hated the stuff, Alice went over to the Guinness and gulped the rest to calm her nerves and, even though she didn't smoke, she lit one of Jerry's cigarettes. She was in shock. But that was all. It was done now. She was no longer a virgin.

There was now something she knew she had to do. She took out of her bag the potion she had bought at the chemist's and put the kettle on the kitchen range. She might have got what she wanted, but she wasn't going to get more than she had asked for.

Of the two of them, only Jerry knew that there were sailors taking whores up against the dock walls with more feeling than he had felt before or after sex, with Alice in his own home. Alice had no idea that what had just taken place had nothing to do with her. That she could have been anyone.

Now she was occupying the bed he had shared with Bernadette. He had woken up in the middle of the night and become aware Alice was there, lying next to him but as far away as she could be. He felt worse with Alice in his bed than if he had been alone.

When he had been on his own, he would place his hand flat onto the mattress and slowly pass it over the bed. It didn't always happen, but sometimes it would stop as it came up against her form. He would close his eyes and, as he breathed deeply, he would move his arm up and onto the milky-soft skin of her abdomen, which he knew as well as his own. He would run his hand up and across her breasts, over her face and into her wild hair. In the moonlight streaming in through the window he would see her eyes twinkle at him. And, just like that, he would lie and talk to her about Nellie and work, Maura and Tommy, and would fall asleep with her breath on his hand.

He knew now that would never happen again. He had never talked to Bernadette about Alice and here Alice was, lying in her place.

At first light, Alice slipped out to the outhouse to clean herself up. The sticky mess, which had spread across her thighs, had made her legs itch all night. She couldn't get it off her skin quickly enough as she scrubbed and scrubbed until her legs were red raw.

Whilst Jerry still slept, she cleaned the kitchen and put the nappies into the boiler. When he came down the stairs, smelt the frying bacon and potatoes and saw the clean kitchen, he was grateful. He knew what had happened the night before and he knew his duty.

He was ashamed. He knew he had behaved like an animal. Catholic guilt swamped him. His emotions had been primeval. It hadn't mattered that it was Alice, who had been good to him. He felt as though he had been possessed by something bad and vowed to himself that, as long as he lived, he would never behave like that again.

The previous night had been a passage back into the real world. He had vented his anger, which had bordered on loathing, at his Bernadette. His anger and venom extended to the hospital, the midwife and everyone else he had blamed for her death and for leaving him with the life he now had. He had been consumed by an evil rage that had been locked deep down inside him since the moment Bernadette had died and last night it had erupted with a Vesuvian ferocity.

He had taken it out on Alice. He had abused her. He had punished Alice for things that had nothing to do with her. Jerry had heard men talking at the docks who had treated a whore better than he had treated Alice last night. As he woke his first thought had been, Oh God, what have I done?

He was worried about facing Alice, but that was secondary to the realization that he knew what he had to do and what his responsibility now was.

'Morning, Queen,' he said nervously, as he came downstairs.

As he looked at the clean kitchen, it occurred to him that it really didn't matter who took the role of a wife and a mother in his house. He didn't love Alice but he needed routine and order back in his life, and this woman could give him that. He needed someone to share rearing Nellie with him. The women were right. It was near impossible for a man to bring up a daughter on his own. It wasn't the proper thing to do. He owed it to Nellie to find her a mother.

Before he sat at the table she had scrubbed, the table on which she had lost her virginity, he walked over to the range where she was leaning over the pan, frying his breakfast.

'Alice, will ye marry me?'

He said it too quickly. It was too complete a statement; he left no room for ambiguity. The hangover from the Guinness blended with Catholic guilt and a misplaced sense of duty. Prompted by loneliness and despair, he had proposed to a woman who was as far from Bernadette as it was possible to be.

Alice smiled. She had got there. Not in the way she had thought, but she had achieved her goal. Neither of them had wanted emotional contact; only one had wanted sex, as a means to an end; and she had got there. Just as she had surmised, he felt duty bound, out of decency and honour, to propose once he had slept with her.

Now she had to leave the house quickly, before any of the neighbours realized she had spent the night. If they saw her leave, they would also know the truth: that Alice had won.

*

She sat on the bus back to the Grand, looking out of the window. The seats were made of green leather and the windows were so dirty she could barely see outside. She rubbed the condensation from the inside window with her gloved hand and stared through the circle she had made at the passing houses, at smoke billowing out of chimneys, at the warehouses, pump rooms and workshops.

She was sore. Walking to the bus stop had been painful. She felt as though the back and inside of her thighs were bruised. When she had gone to the outhouse, her urine had stung, and her scalp hurt, where Jerry had pulled her hair. She felt as though every breath she had taken since last night had been a shallow one.

She was tense and confused but, as always, acting and hiding it well. When she closed her eyes, she could see and smell the hard dried egg and grease on the kitchen table into which Jerry had pushed her face, as he had forced his way into her. But it was over now. She was betrothed. It had all been worth it. And here she was, thirty- two, smelling of sex and had still never been kissed.

## Chapter Six

Jerry and Alice married less than a month later. Alice wore a very expensive outfit that had fortuitously been left hanging in one of the hotel rooms by a guest travelling on to America. It fitted Alice's short and skinny frame well. The label said Moda Paris, London and New York. Alice had read the label over and over again, when she realized the outfit was going to remain unclaimed. This was now hers. Her wedding outfit.

'How many women from the docks have married in anything as grand as this,' she said to the head porter, who was disappointed that Alice was keeping the outfit. As Alice was head housekeeper, all unclaimed property was hers to do with as she wished. As head porter, he would have become the beneficiary of anything Alice didn't want for herself.

The wedding was to be held in the register office and Alice had decided that Jerry needed a suit, something there wasn't much call for on the docks. Jerry was puzzled by this and his first inclination was to pay a visit to Eric Berry, the pawnbroker's. Not only had he never owned a suit, he didn't know anyone else who had one either. On the day he had married Bernadette, he had worn one of his uncle's, which his auntie had kept in the wardrobe since the day her husband had died. It had originally been bought in from Berry's shop for his uncle's own wedding, which Jerry remembered attending as a child. Since the day Jerry had married Bernadette, it had hung in the same wardrobe as always, with a calico cloth draped over it to protect it from the moths and dust.

When he brought the suit downstairs to show her, Jerry found Alice's indignation hard to understand. Was it because he had worn it when he had married Bernadette? He couldn't have been less bothered about that; for all he cared, a suit was a suit. He hadn't enjoyed wearing it on the day he had married Bernadette and he was sure it would be equally uncomfortable this time around. Jerry had no emotional attachment whatsoever to a suit, which rubbed his neck and made him feel as though he had a wooden coat-hanger stuck down his back. One reason for dragging Bernadette away from their wedding so quickly hadn't just been about ripping her clothes off as fast as possible; it had been about getting out of his own too. His suit hadn't made it as far as the bedroom and he remembered it had been strewn on the stairs along with Bernadette's dress.

'That suit can go on the rag and bone man's cart in the morning,' said Alice, her nose and lips visibly turned upwards, 'and we will go into town, when you finish work, to have you measured for a new one.'

Jerry was in shock; this took some digesting.

'I know exactly where to go,' continued Alice. 'Some of the guests who stayed at the hotel often needed to have a suit run up quickly. The concierge knows a Jewish tailor on Bold Street who would run one up in forty-eight hours. I will get a good price for it too.'

She didn't even look at him for his approval. As far as Alice was concerned, she had spoken. It was done. Jerry's expression was the same as if he had been told the following afternoon's football match had been cancelled.

'I don't have the money for new suits, Alice,' he replied very quietly and firmly.

An extravagance like that was not in his scheme of things. Jerry liked to live within his means. He saved half a crown every week and always had, but that money wasn't for him, or to be thrown away on suits. Even in the weeks he never quite made half a crown, he always managed to put something by.

Alice had found a new confidence since losing her virginity and receiving a marriage proposal, a confidence that was not to be challenged. 'I have some money saved, Jerry, and we will use it to buy the suit,' she said with an air of finality. 'I won't be embarrassed by either of us not dressing for the occasion.'

Was Alice, a woman, proposing to buy him a suit? Jerry was bombarded by a new set of uncomfortable emotions that he had never before experienced. He felt torn between wanting to keep Alice happy and being affronted at her telling him what to do. He and Bernadette had never operated like that. Throughout their daily lives, every decision had been taken by mutual agreement. Or so Jerry had thought. For the last couple of years, he had made every decision alone. Some had been challenging and far more difficult than others but he had grown used to that.

He looked at Alice and silently, almost submissively, nodded. This was all very new and for now, he decided to avoid a scene. Alice smiled briefly as she folded up the old suit and laid the bundle by the back door, ready to be thrown to the rag and bone man when he came down the entry the following morning. As she flung the suit down, she shuddered and walked over to the sink to wash her hands.

Jerry looked at the garment he had never before much liked. He now wanted to grab it off the floor and smell it. He wanted to hold it to his face and breathe in deeply the happiness of weddings past. Instead he lit a cigarette. Five minutes ago he hadn't given a fig for the suit; now he was fighting to overcome an almost overwhelming desire to rescue it from the rag and bone man and tell Alice it was this suit or none. Deceitful notions were dancing in his brain: of pretending he had thrown it out and hiding it in Tommy's house. Jerry dragged deeply on his cigarette. These new feelings were confusing and he had no idea what to do with them.

'Jeez, I'm just a bloke, what do I know,' he said as he shrugged his shoulders. He had given in. Alice had shifted herself into position.

He wore the new suit for the first time on the morning he and Alice were married. He had never felt more uncomfortable in his life.

'I'm trussed up like a bleedin' turkey,' he confided in Tommy with a hint of anger. 'Why would she be wanting to spend so much money on a suit for a register office?'

'Aye, yer look like one too,' responded Tommy, which made Jerry feel no better. Jerry and Nellie had arrived at Tommy and Maura's house for breakfast, before they left to go into town for the not-so-big day.

Alice was taking a cab from the hotel, an extravagance Jerry failed to understand. The register office was a ten-minute walk down Church Street. It would never enter his mind to take a cab if the destination was within walking distance, or if you could jump on the bus.

Tommy had more to say about the suit, without being asked. Maura had taught him well.

'Look on the bright side, ye will never be stuck for money again. Ye could always get a few bob for that suit, when it runs in and out of the pawnshop, and ye could always sell it, if times were tough. After all, ye can't eat a suit now, can ye? Alice is buying an investment, as well as summat to wear, though I'd never let no woman buy me a suit and that's for sure.'

Jerry looked at himself in the long dressing mirror in Tommy's bedroom. He didn't look or feel right and Tommy's comment, brutally honest as it was, niggled him. There was nothing he could say or do now. The die was cast.

Tommy and Jerry left the house to carry Nellie down the road to the green to play with Kitty. She was already looking after the twins and Angela and would be taking care of Nellie for the day. Jerry and Tommy were quieter and more subdued than they would have been on a cold morning heading off to work.

'Good luck, Uncle Jerry!' shouted Kitty as she ran to greet him and threw her arms round his waist.

Jerry loved Kitty and even he knew it was because she had been Bernadette's favourite. Quite often, right up until she died, when Kitty was still a little tot Bernadette would bring Kitty home from Tommy and Maura's house to stay with them for the night and play mothers and daughters. Each year since Kitty had been born, Maura had delivered a new set of twins and two new sisters, making a grand total of seven children in five years. It was a huge treat for Kitty to be in a house that was quiet and tidy and not full of smaller children expecting her to do things for them. Bernadette would fuss over her, paint her tiny nails in bright-red nail varnish and buy her special treats for the night. Kitty had cried a lot when her Auntie Bernadette had died. She was only little and had no idea what death meant, but she sensed it was a tragedy.

'You're getting married today,' Kitty sang, and all the little ones followed her lead and began laughing and singing. 'You're going to get married today, you're going to get married today,' they chanted, as they jumped up and down on the spot around Jerry and Tommy.

Tommy laughed at the kids, as Jerry watched his Nellie grab hold of Kitty's hand and try to copy the other children, by taking her thumb out of her mouth to jump up and down and sing. She did so with both feet on the ground, bobbing around, trying to jump, although all she achieved was to bend and straighten her knees. Nellie had no idea what she was singing about, but she grinned from ear to ear, looking from her da to her heroine, Kitty. It was the first time Jerry had smiled all morning, seeing his Nellie infected by the excitement.

'Thanks, Kitty, ye are a grand lass,' shouted Jerry, as he and Tommy walked away to collect Maura. 'Thanks, kids,' he shouted and waved his hand above his head. They all crowded round to wave goodbye.

'Who's he marrying?' asked Kitty's brother, Harry.

'Mammy says it's a witch,' replied Kitty, watching her da and Jerry walking away.

All the children stopped laughing and running about. This was big news. Jerry was marrying a witch? A witch was coming to live on their street? In unison, they all looked first towards Jerry's house and then at Nellie, who followed their lead, looking at the house and then seeing their reactions. She put her thumb back in her mouth. Something was up.

'Poor Nellie,' said Harry. 'What will happen to her?'

'I dunno, but it's strange, so it is,' replied Kitty.

'Never mind, Nellie,' said Harry, as he took hold of Nellie's hand. 'I will look after ye and save ye from the witch.'

Harry was only two years older than Nellie. Nellie took her thumb back out of her mouth and grinned up at him appreciatively. Nellie already truly loved Harry, who always looked out for her. As Harry took Nellie's hand, his hair gently ruffled and blew in the breeze, a soft kiss landed tenderly on his head and a warm cloak of protectiveness wrapped itself around his shoulders. Harry didn't feel a thing, but Nellie did and smiled.

Jerry and Alice had struggled to find witnesses for the day. Alice had no friends. Jerry didn't know a single person in Liverpool who wasn't an Irish Catholic and for a while they thought they might have to ask two strangers on the street to come in and stand for them. No God-fearing Irish man or woman would attend a wedding that wasn't a nuptial mass, held in a church and witnessed in the eyes of God and every saint that a day had been named after.

When Father James from St Mary's got wind of what was happening, he had called round to the house and given Jerry hell, without him having had to live a life and die for it. The women on the street could hear the priest's voice booming out of the front-room window and bouncing off the cobbles, and slowly they began to gather round. Within an hour, everyone in every house on all four streets knew every word of the conversation.

'The windows rattled and shook with such a force they almost broke with the sound of his voice,' said Peggy, which of course wasn't true, but this was Liverpool; no story was worth telling without a good dollop of exaggeration.

In the end, Maura and Tommy had agreed to stand witness, Maura for no other reason than she wanted to know exactly what was occurring and wanted, self-importantly, to relay back to the other women every detail of the event. Knowledge was king and, with it, she would be queen of the streets, if only for a day. Tommy agreed, because he was a decent man who would do anything for his mate and, once Maura had decided, he would also do anything for a quiet life.

Jerry, Maura and Tommy took the overhead railway, known as the Dockers' Umbrella, into town to meet Alice. It ran along the full length of the docks, looking down on a panorama of containers, crates and cranes, with stack upon stack of timber strapped together, waiting to be collected and dispersed to timber yards across the country. The murky horizon was sharply broken by the sight of billowing red ensigns, the merchant navy flags on the docked ships that were having their loads lightened and on the ships sat out at the bar, patiently waiting for the pilots to guide them in.

For the first time since setting foot on Liverpool's soil, Jerry longed deep down inside to return home to Ireland. It was a longing that had crept into his chest earlier that morning and had now settled in for the day.

His view from the window of the overhead railway made him feel low and depressed. A mist was rolling up the Mersey like a bolt of grey chiffon being randomly unfurled above the surface of the water and there was not a blade of grass in sight. As they passed by large areas of wasteland and rubble, interspersed by rows of blackened brick-terraced houses, much of the area looked as though the bombs had dropped only yesterday. The bleakness was made vaguely opaque and eerie by the combination of the grey mist and yellow smoke spewing from the chimneys of the factories, workshops and pump rooms, as well as those homes that could afford to keep a fire lit all day.

Since Jerry had vented his anger that fateful night, he had thought about Bernadette daily. He could remember everything as though it were yesterday. He knew now that he could let her in and dwell on his memories, and that afterwards he would still be whole in body and mind. He could think about her and not go insane. He wouldn't fall apart.

As the train moved slowly on past each dock, Maura and Tommy chattered away. Jerry imagined what the small farm his parents owned would look like this morning. He leant his head against the window and closed his eyes for a minute. The jolting of the train made his head loll backwards and forwards against the glass, but he went with it and didn't move or open his eyes. Within his own dark world, he could replace the smell of dirt and damp and cold steel with the rich, wet grass and peat of Ballymara.

The contrast between the view from the railway carriage and the image of home was intoxicating and dragging him in. He could see his father returning from the milking shed, with his faithful cows on their way back to the field. The cap on his head that he had worn for the last thirty years, a stick in his hand, the crazy dogs barking at his heels and the sun rising behind him, making the same journey he had every single morning of Jerry's life. The gentle rain was falling in the sunshine but, as always, it fell soft and pure as only Irish rain did.

He could hear the Moorhaun River tripping over the pebbles as it skirted Bangornevin and passed round the back of the farmhouse, which stood only two hundred yards from the banks. He heard the plopping of the salmon, jumping as they made their way upstream. And his heart clenched, as the sadness in the pit of his belly deepened.

In his longing thoughts of home, Bernadette drifted in. How different would their life have been if he had met and married his Bernadette back in Ireland, instead of in Liverpool? The farm wasn't big enough to feed two families and, for sure, there were plenty of siblings, as well as Jerry, to feed. But he liked to imagine that he could have found a way to have reared his Nellie in Mayo. To have lived with his Bernadette on the farm. To be living a very different life from the one he was today. For the last four weeks, each time Jerry felt low or down, he had escaped to an imaginary other past, full of Bernadette and Nellie. He knew such thoughts were crazy just when he was about to wed another.

Tommy suddenly nudged him in the ribs. 'Ready, Jerry, we're here.'

Jerry dragged himself back from the farm and Ballymara. He left his da locking the gate to the field and his mother walking up the path, carrying a pail of unpasteurized milk, straight from the milking shed into the house, battling the midges and wafting them away from her face with her free hand. He left his brothers in the kitchen, making plans for the day and finishing their bacon and tatties; the youngest carrying a large bucket full of brown bricks of roughly cut peat into the kitchen to stack by the fire for the day's baking.

He left Jacko, the donkey he had ridden when he was a lad, who was still alive today and up to his usual tricks. Jerry took himself up the hill directly opposite the front of the farmhouse and looked down across the fields to find Jacko as he had so many times before, and there he was, two ears stuck up in the field of oats, the rest of his body hidden.

And there was his Bernadette, in her red dress. He had been looking for her and there she was, sitting on the long five-bar gate to the farmyard, the gate she had sat and swung on every time they went back home. It disturbed him that she looked so sad. Sadder than she ever had when she was alive. He closed his eyes and attempted to draw her smiling image back into his mind, to look into her eyes – as he often did now. Today, she refused to be drawn.

Tommy nudged him again. 'Come on, off, now!' he said with a sense of urgency.

Tommy was worried. Never before had he seen a man less enthusiastic to attend his own wedding. Maura linked Tommy's arm in hers as they walked up into town and tried to make happy chatter. They were meeting Alice at the register office doors in fifteen minutes.

'Have we time for a quick one?' whispered Tommy to Maura. 'We need to put a smile on yer man's face afore she sees him or we'll be taking the blame for making him look like he's going to a feckin' funeral.'

'Don't talk about funerals, or ye'll set me off, and sure if I start, I won't stop,' replied Maura, as they both turned sharp left and up the steps of the Grapes pub. Jerry silently tripped along in their wake, deep in thought and looking for all the world like a man heading to the gallows.

Alice had tucked herself away at the bottom corner of the square, with the doors of the register office in sight, giving herself good warning of when the others entered the square from Water Street. She did not want to be standing alone outside. She knew she looked conspicuous in her wedding attire and couldn't help wondering how many women had stood in this same spot, dressed for the biggest day in their life, only to be humiliated in public as office workers looked out of their windows and saw them walk away, alone. She was far from sure that Jerry would turn up. This was her final concern. She was quite convinced that Maura and Tommy would do anything in their power to persuade him that he was making a mistake.

Alice had spent her life as a bystander, observing the lives of others, and today was no exception. She felt a familiar sense of continuity as she watched shoppers, office staff, sailors and businessmen bustle across the square. Here she was, ironically, on the day her life was to change, doing something that was second nature, watching others. The knowledge didn't make her feel as good as it could. Narrowing her eyes, she peered into the distance as she pulled herself back from the edge of her reverie, aware that time was ticking by. Her heart was beating so fast, she could feel it thumping against her ribs and her mouth was abnormally dry. Had Jerry stood her up? They were due to be married in six minutes and she still couldn't pick him out across the square.

Suddenly, she felt her anger rise inside her like vomit, as they came into sight and she saw the three of them together, Maura in the middle and Tommy and Jerry each holding one of her hands, running up the ginnel that fed onto the square. The ginnel was dark, deprived of light by the tall buildings on each side. At first Alice couldn't believe it was them but there they were, suddenly bathed in light, as they broke cover and ran into the open square. If she hadn't seen them with her own eyes, she wouldn't have believed it. All three were running as if the wind were chasing them, with Maura squealing and laughing loudly as she tried to shake Jerry and Tommy's hands out of her own so that she could slow down to a walk and catch her breath.

'How dare they run up here at the last minute and forget about me,' muttered Alice to herself. As she took a step forward, she realized they were about to run through the doors of the register office. They had obviously assumed she was inside, waiting for them.

'Well, there's a mistake and make no mistake,' said Alice, as she began to walk purposefully across the square towards the building. She was attracting the attention of office staff leaving for their lunch hour. For a few moments, Alice had forgotten she wasn't looking in on the lives of others from behind a pane of glass; this was for real. This was her life.

The others first spotted her just as she reached the oak and glass revolving door to the lobby. They had been looking for her inside. Jerry immediately noticed something different about her face. It was cold and hostile, shrouded in anger.

Has she changed her mind? he wondered. Is that what she's coming through that door to tell me? Is that why she isn't already in here? Am I to be let off? Relief hovered expectantly.

The revolving door ejected Alice into the lobby. The hostility fell from Alice's face as she gave Maura a tight and brittle smile in response to her overly effusive greeting.

'Good morning, Alice, that's a beautiful outfit ye are wearing and would ye look at them gloves, go on now, let me take a closer look.'

The three of them smelt of the two hot rum toddies they had each just downed in the Grapes. Maura was nervous, talking too much and too fast. Alice knew that she could possibly risk everything if she remonstrated with Jerry for smelling of alcohol. He looked less than happy.

As Alice turned to show Maura the gloves, which Maura was by now just about peeling off her arm, Jerry realized that it was over. All done. The wedding would be going ahead. He was still in his twenties and the best of his life was already behind him.

They called into the Lyons Corner Tea Rooms for lunch afterwards, where they had shepherd's pie followed by apple crumble and custard with two large pots of tea. Most of it was eaten in silence although Maura did her best to keep the conversation alive, in order to find out as much as she could about Alice, the Protestant cuckoo who had forced herself into their Catholic nest. Tommy smoked more cigarettes than usual. A man unused to social niceties, he found the whole day extremely uncomfortable. If he had a Cappie in his mouth, no one would ask him a question, or expect him to talk.

As the waitresses bustled around them in their black uniforms, they would never have guessed that the very quiet party on the table in the corner had just been to a wedding.

When lunch was over, they took the Dockers' Umbrella back to the four streets. As they entered their own houses, Jerry, Tommy and Maura closed their doors on each other and their shared past. No longer would Jerry be able to raise in conversation some of the fun nights they had shared together. Maura wouldn't call round with her letters from Killhooney Bay and news of her own and Bernadette's family. That was the past; a new future was about to begin.

'You would have thought she'd have been grateful to have me standing for her and not be so snooty with it,' said Maura to Tommy, in indignation, as they walked into their house.

'Ah, let it go now,' said Tommy. 'We've done our duty, so we have, we can sleep easy tonight. Not that yer man will be doing much sleeping, I shouldn't think!'

Maura grinned and slapped him on the leg. She was thankful she had her Tommy. They might not have had the most exciting life, but they were secure, emotionally stable and, for what little they had, always grateful.

Within thirty minutes of arriving home, Maura had curlers back in her hair, her floral overdress apron on, and was away next door to Peggy, to recount the activities of the day.

'Quick as yer like, I'll put the kettle on,' shouted Peggy, out of the open kitchen window, as she heard the latch rise on the back gate and saw Maura walk up the path.

She picked up her mop, which was leaning against the wall, and ran with urgency back into the kitchen, where she used the end to bang hard three times on her kitchen wall adjoining the house next door. This was to alert Annie to hurry away in; it was the code that Maura was back with news.

'Get ye away here now, quick, missus, O!' shouted Peggy at the wall, when she finished banging, and was reassured to hear her neighbour's back door slam shut in acknowledgment, as Annie rushed down her path to join them. But not before she had used her own mop to bang on the kitchen wall to alert Sheila, who in turn used hers.

In the absence of telephones, it was an efficient system. Within five minutes, six women were sitting round Peggy's wooden kitchen table, in front of the range where a tiny fire burnt, just enough to boil the kettle slowly.

Peggy had nine children. Every penny and every lump of coal was counted. She was as sharp as a box of knives and God help the coalman if he tried to short-change her weekly hundredweight of coal. If she caught him in time, she made him wait whilst she inspected the sack to see if it was full to the top. A short-weight sack was a day's warmth and, in winter, that mattered. Between her nine children there were five pairs of shoes. Whoever's turn it was for the shoes would play outside, or go to school that day.

Peggy and Paddy lived an entirely different life from that of

Bernadette and Jerry. Bernadette, who bought the occasional new dress, but never without giving away to someone else something she already had, had been the glamour in their lives. No one had ever seen Bernadette outdoors with her curlers in. Today wasn't just a day to gossip about Alice, it was a day to talk about their Bernadette too.

Sheila, who was only twenty and as yet had just two children, walked through the door with a shovel of coal in one hand, a baby in the other arm resting on her hip, and a two-year-old holding onto the end of her long apron trotting along behind her. Before she sat at the table, she threw the heaped shovel of coal on Peggy's fire and no one questioned it or batted an eyelid. She wanted to stay and hear every word of the gossip rather than be driven out by the cold and, besides, they would need the range.

'A lot of tea will be drunk this afternoon, so it will,' Sheila announced, as she closed the range doors to let her shovelful of coal catch.

This morning was one of those days when something had happened to lift the daily monotony and the relentless grind to pay the rent and feed a family. It required a sense of occasion and urgency. The air in the kitchen as they all settled down was tight with expectancy. Everyone needed to concentrate on Maura's every word, each being too important to miss.

Whilst Maura had been at the register office, Annie had made oat biscuits, with syrup that had found its way from a ship into Annie's kitchen en route to the Lyons factory. Peggy and Annie had given all the children a delicious, chewy biscuit and sent them into the front room, or out to play. This morning wasn't about changing nappies, scrubbing floors, washing nets or making bread. The tea and biscuits around the table powwow were as important to the women on the streets as a meeting of world leaders was to global security.

Maura sat and waited for everyone to settle down, for the tea to be poured and babies calmed, before she commenced. This was her moment. She was queen of the news – and what news she had to impart! She began with the gloves and ploughed on straight through the oohs and aahs to the ceremony itself.

'It will all end in tears, such as every ungodly marriage does, so it will,' said Peggy with absolute authority.

This seemed to be the general opinion when discussing Jerry and Alice on any day, not just their wedding day, and no one present had talked about much else since Alice had arrived on the street. It was true that no one could find anyone who had taken to Alice, or had a word to say in her defence. She gave people good reason to distrust and dislike her.

'That Alice, she's no better than she thinks she is,' said Peggy.

Everyone looked at her for a moment trying to fathom what it was she meant and then, giving up, moved on.

'Alice is a Protestant; she has probably been in the Orange Lodge. What in God's name was Jerry thinking of, marrying such a woman and bringing her amongst us?' said Sheila, if for no other reason than to make her own contribution.

As different from every one of her neighbours as it was possible to be on a practical level, Alice just wasn't the same as any other woman; she was slightly unusual, odd even. Alice would never belong. That much had been decided from almost the first time the women on the street had been aware of her existence. Each one round the table knew exactly what Alice was up to. They had all seen right through the game of the plain spinster preying on a grieving man.

'God help me, it was so hard,' said Maura, putting one hand onto her left breast and the other to her brow for effect. 'I had to get meself half piddled in the Grapes with a couple of rum toddies, which went straight into me blood, so it did.'

All the women gasped. Not one of them had ever before drunk a rum toddy during the day, let alone in the morning.

'It hasn't even been two years since our own Bernadette was sitting round this very table with us, before she was taken,' said Maura.

They all looked to the floor and crossed themselves simultaneously, muttering a chorus of, 'God rest her soul,' and then for a moment lost themselves in their own thoughts of remembrance. Bernadette, who had made them all laugh within seconds of walking in the room. Who never arrived without a plate of food she had made, for them and any little ones around. Bernadette, who had amazed them all with her ability to control her own reproductive organs, whilst unable to control her wild red hair. She had become pregnant only when she decided it was time to, thereby keeping her richer and more beautiful, and, sure, who would have denied her that?

Her soul had been as beautiful as she was. Bernadette, who if the women in the streets had their way would by now be canonized. Even if Bernadette had been a demon, she would have seemed a saint compared with Alice.

The gossip continued for well over two hours and the women savoured every minute. Grand events like this didn't happen every day and this one would be relished for a long time to come.

When Jerry and Alice walked into their kitchen for the first time as a married couple, Alice announced that she would like her own furniture to be moved out of storage at the hotel and into the house.

'It's the very best quality and I've cared for it well. It will improve the place no end,' she said to Jerry, walking over to the range to put the kettle on.

Jerry was taken aback. The house was how Bernadette had wanted it to be. She had lovingly invested herself in every little detail. He wanted to keep it that way. The realization swept over him afresh: marrying Alice was going to be about more than he had bargained for.

'That's fine,' he replied, with a smile he didn't feel. 'I'll borrow the coal wagon from Declan, after he's finished his drop-offs on Wednesday, and get yer man Tommy to help me.'

Alice looked at Jerry without a hint of softness. 'I want better than a coal wagon for my belongings, Jerry. I want a proper van.'

Jerry decided it was time to tell Alice a few home truths about how much he earned and how much life cost. She had been protected by having full board in her hotel accommodation and free food, and probably felt more secure than she should do with the small nest egg she had saved. She had left the Grand only yesterday and now wouldn't be returning except for her belongings, so it was time to talk facts.

The row about the housekeeping budget began when they had been married for less than four hours, and the row about Jerry having no intention of ever leaving the four streets or the docks to emigrate to America began after five.

In his effort to put right a night of shame, haste had taken over from common sense and he had never considered the practical issues of their living together. He had just assumed that life would become easier, with a housewife at home. Alice had been very keen to leave the hotel as soon as possible. And here they were, on their wedding day, arguing. The contrast between Jerry's two weddings could not have been greater.

The row about Nellie was the third and last on their wedding day. Nellie had blossomed over the last two years, her days spent in the midst of the hullabaloo at the Doherty house, her evenings and weekends basking in the one-to-one devotion of her father. Her hair was short, strawberry blonde and curly, but was already showing signs of darkening and taking on her mother's wild untameable redness. She was described by everyone as a little cherub, because that was just how she looked, like a tiny angel, and she brought out the protective instinct in everyone who met her. Nellie had never carried her father's sadness. She had never known a mother's love, other than the next best thing, which had come from Maura. But Jerry had done more than his utmost to compensate. It was the next to best life for an only child, but all that was about to change.

As Alice was preparing their supper, she announced that she would like to eat at separate times from Nellie.

'I also think it would be a good idea, Jerry, if just the two of us eat at my table. You could get something for Nellie to sit at. Maybe turn one of the tea chests in the backyard upside down and put an oilcloth on it?'

Alice had completely misjudged Jerry. Like a lion, he roared, 'We will not, she eats with us, so she does, she's not a dog being sent to eat in a kennel!'

Nellie, who at two years old joined in the rough and tumble at the Doherty house and had been brought home by a very grown-up, seven-year-old Kitty, knew full well that this argument was about her. Putting her thumb straight in her mouth, she began to cry. All was not good. Everything was different and she had no idea why. Alice was here again but this wasn't the normal routine; she was usually gone by now, much to Nellie's relief. Nellie knew Alice didn't like her, but she didn't have the words she needed to communicate this to Jerry.

The row about her raged over Nellie's head. She had never seen her da angry before, but she wasn't frightened when he scooped her up into his arms and held her tight, as he gave out to Alice. Nellie didn't know why, but she understood enough to know that her da was fighting her corner. She put her arm around his neck and placed her head on his shoulder. Her fingers twiddled the hair at the nape of his neck round and round between her fingers, as the shouting continued.

She looked at the statue of the Virgin Mary on the mantelshelf above the fire, which, now that she was in her da's arms, was directly at her eye level. Nellie had often stared at the statue. When she was laid in her crib in the kitchen as a baby. As a toddler sitting in her wooden playpen, and often when she was in her da's arms, as he sang her to sleep. Now Nellie stared intently at the statue and was rewarded as, through the tears swimming in her eyes, it smiled. Nellie grinned back and hugged her da tighter. It had happened so many times before.

That night, Jerry and Alice lay next to each other in a hostile silence. Alice lay, waiting to be assaulted, but hoping the row had been enough to deter Jerry from lovemaking. They hadn't had sex since the night she had lost her virginity and although doing the deed had got her here, where she wanted to be, it was not something she relished doing again.

Jerry, lying on his back looking at the ceiling, decided that they couldn't go on like this. He had to do something. It was time to perform his wedding-night duty and get it over with. They had to put behind them an awful day. This time he kissed Alice. He had kissed her a number of times since the night they had crossed the line and it had never been unpleasant. Kissing Alice didn't stir him in the way kissing Bernadette had, but, as the sailors said, any port in a storm. Maybe having regular sex would make him feel happier in himself.

This time he tried to be as gentle as he had once been rough, he really tried. He tried to make it responsive and special. Alice didn't. It was over in five minutes. When he said goodnight, Alice didn't respond. She hadn't made a sound or moved a muscle from beginning to end. Five minutes later, as he began to drift into sleep, he heard the latch of the bedroom door lift as Alice left the room.

Jerry lifted himself up onto one elbow and lit a cigarette. He looked out through the bedroom window at the stars illuminating the inky-black sky. There was a full moon and he could hear a tug out on the river and a tomcat fighting in the street, screeching like a baby. As he blew out smoke, he lay back on his pillow and felt lonelier than he had ever done in his life. His eyes filled with tears brought on by the familiar pain of loss, enhanced tonight by guilt and shame, as he gazed up at the sky and whispered, 'I'm sorry, angel, I'm so sorry.'

# Chapter Seven

Maura knew it would be just a matter of time before Father James called round to the house to ascertain for himself the details of the wedding. He wouldn't want to hear it in bite-sized chunks, from women who he knew were exaggerating their own sense of importance in the situation and embellishing their second-hand knowledge. At the six o'clock mass, some of the women had tried to engage him in gossip and ask him what he thought.

'I have no opinion now,' he replied sternly, brusquely dismissing the invitation to gossip, 'until I hear it from the horse's mouth meself.'

'Well, they are legally married in the law, so they are, Father, and that's a fact,' said Peggy indignantly, affronted at being put down so abruptly in front of the other women. Peggy was never quite as deferential to the priests as the other inhabitants on the streets.

Father James shook his head in disbelief and boomed, 'The only marriage that matters, Peggy, is a marriage made before the eyes of God.'

He was as keen as the women to know what had happened. He also knew the best place to find out was to get himself to number nineteen as quickly as possible and inveigle Maura into giving him the unfiltered version.

Maura had missed the six o'clock mass and was in the process of wiping the dust from her windowsills for the second time that day. Cleanliness was next to godliness. She felt guilty at having attended a Protestant wedding and missing mass. She knew that Father James wouldn't be able to keep away and that she would see him walking through her back door at any minute, now that evening prayers were over.

The Father often liked to visit Maura's house, which annoyed Tommy.

'Jaysus, Maura, we get more visits from the Father than the whorehouse gets from a sailor,' he liked to complain. 'Everyone will be thinking we are the biggest sinners in Liverpool.'

'Go wash yer mouth, ye heathen, ye,' she would shout, as she flicked him with a rolled-up tea towel.

Tommy had learnt from bitter experience not to say a word against Father James. The tea towel hurt. As he walked out of the house, sulking, he shouted over his shoulder, 'I'm away to the outhouse for a shite. Maybe ye can leave me be in peace in there, eh?'

Tommy didn't get it. He didn't understand the prestige or the feeling of self-worth and status that being popular with the priest gave Maura. She liked the fact that the others saw him tripping in and out of her back door; it made them jealous, so she thought. Maura wouldn't have a word said against Father James. It was her dream that one day Harry would become a priest or Kitty enter the convent.

Father James was a disciplinarian who brooked no dissent from his flock. Jerry's marriage in a register office to a Protestant had been undertaken in defiance of the Church and God. The Father had a sinner in the midst of his flock and he wasn't happy. It was the first step on a road that could lead a community into ruin and it had to be stopped in its tracks.

Sure enough, an hour later, as Maura was washing the dishes, after what felt like the feeding of the five thousand in her kitchen, she heard the click of the gate latch and through the window saw Father James's hat, darker than the night sky, loom towards her up the back path.

'Come along in, Father,' said Maura, 'and have some tea. Tommy,' she shouted upstairs, 'Father James is here.'

As he took off his cape and placed it over the back of the kitchen chair, Maura noted that, yet again, the Father's cassock was dirty with what looked like soup stains down his front and he never looked as though he had managed to shave as well as he should have, with clumps of whiskers around his mouth clinging onto the remnants of food he had eaten that day. He always left on his ostentatious hat. Father James thought it gave him an air of authority, especially with the children.

Tommy was tucking in Harry, who hadn't been sleeping so well. His asthma had been worse than usual that evening, as it always was when there was an unloading of stone on the Herculaneum dock.

'Night, night, little fella,' said Tommy, as Harry finally closed his eyes and Tommy could creep down the stairs.

'Jaysus, Maura, it took me half an hour to get him off, what are ye doing shouting like the foghorn up the stairs?' said Tommy, as he entered the kitchen, closing the door behind him. Maura gave him a look that told Tommy to shut up quickly, just as he saw Father James out of the corner of his eye, standing by the back door.

'Oh hello, Father, how are ye, 'tis a pleasure as always, are ye staying for a cuppa tea?' Despite the resentment Tommy felt at once again finding the priest in his kitchen, no one observing would have guessed that Father James wasn't Tommy's favourite person.

Everyone had to be courteous and grateful to the Fathers. They were the community pillars of truth, morality and discipline. When times were desperate, they provided food from the sisters, or sometimes clothes from a big house in town. Almost every family in the street had, at one time or another, found itself knocking on the Priory door on a dark and cold winter's night, looking for help in the form of food or coal. The Fathers and their housekeeper were the last port in a sea of poverty. Their authority came from God, not the City Corporation offices or the government. They were the mortal representatives of God's voice on earth and no other office could match that.

'I am indeed, Tommy; I have come by, though, to hear about how the sinful service that calls itself a wedding went today and which you yourself and Maura took part in.'

Maura wasn't expecting that and looked quite crestfallen.

Tommy left Maura and Father James to it as they took a tray of tea and fruit loaf into the front room. He made his excuses and sat at the kitchen table to do his pools and read the *Liverpool Echo*. He lit his Capstan Full Strength ciggie, put on the radio, stoked the fire and poured his own tea. He grinned as he cut himself a slice of fruit loaf; Maura had made it that morning by soaking overnight in cold sweet tea a large pocketful of sultanas that had been Tommy's share from a chest that had split the day before. Tommy often joked that he could fit a small baby into one of his jacket pockets, but promised he never would.

Just the one tall lamp, with a large red lampshade, was lit in the corner by the table. It had seen better days but despite its shabbiness, along with the glow from the fire, it bathed the kitchen in a warm light. Tommy inhaled deeply on his cigarette. Everything was all right in his world. Wasn't this just the best bit of the day? His family were well and asleep on full bellies, a blessing in itself and not something that could be said for every child on the four streets. Each one tucked up in their beds, dreaming their own dreams.

He looked down at his paper and heard the murmur of Maura's and the priest's voices.

Father James was the only person who was ever taken into the front room. In Maura's eyes, the kitchen wasn't good enough for someone of Father James's standing and importance. Father James was the 'other man' in Maura's life, the only person towards whom Tommy felt any resentment. It was a sin he couldn't take to confession and so it festered and rotted in his gut.

He knew that the Father and Maura talked about the oldest twins becoming altar boys and entering the priesthood, and that they did it behind his back. As God was Tommy's judge, that would never happen. Maura would witness the wrong side of Tommy's temper if she ever tried to overstep her matriarchal mark to pull that one off. Being the mother of a priest brought with it a sense of pride and an elevated standing in the community. Tommy knew this was something Maura craved and would seek through the advancement of at least one of their sons to the priesthood.

'Even a worm can turn,' whispered Tommy to himself. He had rehearsed the words in his head ready for the argument that would come one day soon. He knew everyone thought he was a push-over but he also knew the boundaries he would allow himself to be pushed to. Even a worm can turn.

He sighed and leant back in the kitchen chair as Maura walked into the kitchen. Tommy looked up with an element of surprise and, thinking he might have left via the front door, asked, 'Has the Father gone?'

'Not yet,' said Maura. 'He's gone up the stairs to bless the kids whilst they are sleeping. He's a bit mad that none of them were at mass this weekend. I asked you not to stop them going, Tommy,' she half hissed.

'Aye, well, did ye tell him that football's a religion too, so it is?' said Tommy, through his chuckles. He had beaten the priest. One up to Tommy.

'Hush yer mouth,' she hissed. 'He may hear ye.'

Tommy leant over and turned up the volume on the radio and, as he did so, winked at Maura and they both giggled. She moved over to the sink where the bowl of cold greasy water awaited her with a knitted dishcloth floating on the top. It would have never entered Tommy's mind to wash the dishes. That was women's work and the dividing line was strong and well understood. Maura plunged her red, weather-chapped hands into the bowl and carried on where she had left off with the dishes. Whilst she waited for Father James to come back down the stairs and into the kitchen, she and Tommy chatted in the same relaxed way about the travails of their family life, as they had every night since the day they had married.

Kitty was exhausted and had fallen asleep as soon as her head had hit the pillow. She shared a large bed with her sister, Angela. The boys were behind the curtain and also shared a bed. She had heard her da comforting Harry and sitting with him, having put a towel over Harry's head and made him breathe over a bowl of steaming, medicinal-smelling water, and then that was it; she went out like a light. She sometimes thought that being the eldest, and a girl, was a curse. She had spent the day looking after her four younger brothers and her younger sister, and she had looked after Nellie too. But she hadn't minded looking after Nellie.

'Sure, Mammy, Nellie was a dream altogether,' she had told Maura when her parents returned from their exciting excursion into town.

Nellie was a good kid who did everything she was asked as soon as Kitty asked it. She never cried or whined, unlike Kitty's younger sister. Kitty would rather have a dozen Nellies than one crying, whinging Angela, any day. Since she had been able, Kitty had helped her mother with childcare as soon as she was big enough to carry a child on her own small hip. She accepted that she was the working, practical appendage to her mother's ever-productive womb and that was her lot in life. At such a young age, she not only knew what her future would hold, she was already an expert at it.

When she looked back, she couldn't remember how it had begun. She didn't know what had woken her. Was it a noise or simply a sense that there was an alien presence in the room? She turned over onto her side to make herself more comfortable and to move their Angela's feet out of her back. Even when she was asleep, Angela could be difficult. Kitty had to put Angela next to the wall to sleep. She cried if she was on the outside because she was scared, and would lie next to Kitty and spend her nights kicking, or crying out and waking up the others.

Kitty opened her eyes slowly, taking in the familiar shadows in the room but aware something wasn't quite right. She froze as she saw black skirts swish across in front of her face and then let out a startled gasp. He very swiftly clamped his hand firmly over her mouth.

'Hush now, Kitty, 'tis only I. Don't make a noise and wake the others.'

As he moved his hand away from her mouth, Kitty realized she couldn't make a sound. She had been about to say sorry after she had gasped, but there was something unnatural about how hard his hand had pressed on her mouth. She could smell the stale tobacco on his stained fingers and an acrid aroma of unwashedness that had rubbed off his hand onto the skin under her nose. She could taste blood on her inner lip where his hand had so suddenly slammed on her mouth. Her heart was banging against her chest wall so loud she could hear it. Could Angela hear it?

She had known Father James all her life. He had christened her and taken her first Holy Communion, but he had never before touched her, other than to lay his hand on top of her head. She was confused and afraid. Waking up to find him standing by her bed was not a normal occurrence. She could hear music from the radio and her parents laughing downstairs. If Father James was in her bedroom, her parents must surely know. Why weren't they in here too? Why was Father James alone? Why had he banged her on her mouth and nearly stopped her breathing? What was she supposed to say or do?

Questions chased each other and, trapped, ran wild in her head. But she didn't speak or move. He had told her not to make a noise. Kitty did as she was told. Father James was an authority that even her parents obeyed; she wouldn't dare make a noise.

She lay with her eyes wide open, looking at his face and wondering what on earth she should say. She had no idea how old he was. Much older, she guessed, than her parents. His hair was grey all around the sides, and she knew, from the increasingly rare occasions he took his hat off, that he was bald on top. She hated his scary hat, which made him look like the pictures she had seen in school of Guy Fawkes. She could see the dark hairs erupting out of the end of his nose and protruding in huge bushes from both of his ears as though they were trying to escape, screaming in terror, from the unnatural thoughts inside his brain. His skin was pale, with a dark shadow where he had shaved, and the wide brim of his hat meant that when his head was bent down, as it was now, his face was in total darkness. She couldn't see anything of his expression, except the gleaming whites of his eyes.

There was silence while he stood leaning slightly over her, staring intently at the outline of her thin body under the pink cotton candlewick bedspread. She noticed that he seemed agitated, pressing his knees into the side of the mattress, pushing his weight onto the bed and grabbing hold of the headboard with one hand to steady himself. He thrust his hand through a fold in his black skirt and Kitty immediately screwed her eyes shut. This was very out of the ordinary. The black material of his skirt was brushing against her arm and she wanted to lash out and knock it away. His knees, pressing into her mattress, were less than a finger's width from pinning down her arm. He hadn't told her not to look, but she knew she didn't want to see what he was doing right now.

What was wrong? Why was he here? Why had her parents sent him upstairs to her? Did they think something was wrong? What were her parents doing laughing whilst he was here scaring the life half out of her? She wanted to shout loudly, 'Mammy, Daddy!'

She had never wanted to be close to them as much as she did right now, not even on the odd occasion when she had awoken in the night with a high temperature, shivering and shaking, feeling so ill that she couldn't stay in her bed and needed to be with her mammy. On those nights she would wander into the kitchen half crying and flushed with sickness. Within seconds Tommy would scoop her onto his knee and hug her, making soothing sounds, whilst Maura fetched a bowl of tepid water and a flannel, and sponged down her limbs with long strokes. Both of her parents concerned, both flapping, emitting soothing noises until the temperature finally subsided. She would spend the rest of the night fitfully sleeping, watched over by one or the other, no more than a hand's reach away. She wanted her mammy desperately now, in the same needy way, even though she wasn't sick.

But she knew that if she woke the kids for nothing, she would probably be in trouble. She lay with her eyes squeezed tight shut as she heard his breathing become rasping and rapid.

'Hush now, Kitty, you good child,' he said breathlessly and gratefully.

She hadn't spoken or made a sound, she had nothing to say. Why was he hushing her? She lay deathly still and didn't move a muscle. She heard the muffled friction of his vestments rhythmically moving and she could feel the mattress slightly shifting under her. What in God's name was he doing? He would wake Angela and the boys. Why was he making that noise?

She opened her eyes, to tell him in a whisper that he would disturb the others because the mattress was shaking, and to ask him to stop doing whatever it was he was doing. She was ready to call her mammy right now. In her role of junior carer of the little ones, she had the confidence to call for help. Not because she was frightened, or because she felt as though the precious space of their bedroom was invaded and no longer safe. Not because the inside of her lip was bleeding, or because she felt scared and violated, but because this was now breaking their carefully managed routine of domesticity. The little ones were her responsibility and were about to have their sleep disturbed, and that now gave her the confidence to shout for her mammy in the presence of the priest. They wouldn't tell her off, because she was just doing her job in looking out for the others. Father James didn't have children, he didn't understand. Her parents would know she wasn't being disrespectful to the priest.

As she opened her eyes and turned her head to shout for her mammy and daddy, his ejaculation left him, like an opaque milky fountain, and hit her full in the face.

And then again. And again. Again.

He was still holding onto the headboard as he slumped forward and let out a low groan. She gasped in horror. The bitter smell of his close proximity robbed her of her ability to inhale. He was leaning so far over the bed that he was less than six inches away from her face. She stared in transfixed terror, her mind screaming a rejection of what she was seeing, as the final flow of his exudate slowly oozed out onto the end of his langer and formed into a threatening drop. Her fingers clenched the bedsheets tightly. She was too terrified to raise her hand to her face.

He gave a last irregular gasp and spat out the word, 'Feck,' as, spent, he leant more heavily on his knees into the mattress. Less than an inch from her face, the last milky drop dribbled slowly and clumsily, still attached by a thread of slime, onto her chin and slithered down onto her neck. She screwed her eyes tightly shut and swallowed her breath in gulps, as she fought off the instinct to scream repeatedly and loudly, and to prevent the contents of her stomach from discharging themselves onto the bed.

She couldn't scream. She had to protect the others from the badness in the room. They were safe whilst they were asleep.

She could feel his sperm, now cold, slowly crawling down her nose and cheek. She felt her fringe, wet and sticky, clinging to her forehead. Her stomach leapt in revulsion as a puddle halted its downward journey and settled in the dipped valley of her cushioned, clenched lips. She could faintly taste salt, seeping through her teeth and onto her tongue.

Helpless, trapped, terrified, she felt as though she was about to choke. She could not breathe and although she would rather die than open her lips, a low cry, beyond her control, escaped her. Shocked, at first she wondered whether the sound had come from him, then recognized it was coming from somewhere within herself. She fought to stop, but was driven by fear. Surely she was ensnared in a nightmare; this couldn't be happening. She was terrified he would now ask her a question and she would have to open her mouth to speak. All she could think, as she cried, was, Oh God, please let this end and take him away.

She longed for Angela to let out one of the noisy, tortured cries she sometimes did in the night, as though she had been poked unexpectedly with a sharp stick. This quite often brought her mammy running up the stairs to check she was all right. The boys were so used to Angela's noises that they slept through, but Angela always woke Kitty or her mother, and either one or the other went to her side, checking her to make sure she hadn't woken herself. Please scream now, Angela, Kitty silently begged.

She kept her eyes firmly shut and played dead. Every muscle in her body was rigid and tightly sprung, ready to do battle if he touched her again. He didn't say a word. She almost lashed out in terror at the pressure of his leg and let her breath out suddenly with shock as his hand came down to wipe her face and rub and rub at her skin, with what she assumed was his skirt, or maybe a handkerchief he kept somewhere in there, just for this occasion. She was pathetically grateful to him. Removing the slime was a huge relief.

'Stay quiet now, Kitty, there's a good girl,' he whispered in a thick voice, as his breathing returned to normal. 'Mammy and Daddy will be very angry with ye if ye say anything about this to anyone, even to them. They don't want to hear a word of this, do ye understand what I'm sayin', child?'

He knew she was a child.

'God will be very angry, and throw you into the fire and flames of hell and eternal damnation if ye so much as let the words pass ye lips and upset ye mammy and daddy. Do ye understand, Kitty?'

She nodded. She still hadn't opened her eyes.

'What ye have just done, Kitty, was very bad, a bad sin, ye have been a very bad girl.'

She thought she had always been good. She strove to be a good girl. Why had she been bad? What had she done wrong?

He had stopped talking. He was quiet, but he was still there, and although she could now hardly hear his breathing, she could sense him. She still didn't open her eyes. And then she heard him whisper, asking God to forgive her for her sins and save her from the fire, and then, with a flourish of his vestments, he was gone.

*

'I will be away now,' shouted Father James, as he strode through the kitchen purposefully, on his way to the back door, his black cape billowing out behind him.

'Ah, thank ye, Father, for blessing the kids,' said Maura. 'It is so kind of ye. I know they don't always go to mass, but they are all good kids.'

'Aye, they are that,' he replied. 'Don't fret, Maura; if they miss a week I will always pop in. It's no trouble, but they must make confession and communion now.'

'Yes, Father, they will that,' promised Maura to his departing back, as the door closed. She turned to Tommy. 'Sure he was in a hurry tonight.'

Tommy wasn't listening, he was somewhere else. He put his hand out to Maura to hold hers and pulled her down onto his knee.

'Ye know, Maura, as you and the Father were talking tonight, I was sat here, counting me blessings and thinking how lucky we are, ye know. Maybe seeing Jerry's fall in fortune has made me think, but there was once a time, I am ashamed to say it, when I envied him, as he always had much more than we did. We are always struggling, but look at us now, eh? We are warm, I've good work, the kids are fed and all safe and asleep in their beds, and they've even been blessed tonight. Life can't get much better than that, now, can it?'

Maura cupped her man's face and they kissed tenderly. They were united in their love for each other and for their children, whom they adored and who were their pride and joy. They had little else, but it was enough.

The room smelt funny. Kitty thought to herself that this wasn't the first time the room had smelt like this. She had woken up on a number of occasions, feeling something sticky and itchy on her skin and smelling this smell. She had thought it was snot. She remembered waking with the itchiness and wiping it away with the back of her hand and the corner of the pillowcase.

Kitty began to cry, quietly. She didn't know why. She didn't know what had happened. She just knew it was something bad.

With brothers to look after, she knew exactly what a langer looked like, but she had never seen a grown man's before. Tommy was very careful to maintain dignity within the family and none of his children had ever seen him undressed. Something she had never before seen or encountered had been violently thrust upon her and rent her childhood apart.

Father James, God's voice on earth, had told her she would be thrown into the eternal flames if she told anyone what had just happened, but she wanted her mammy so badly. She could hear her parents laughing downstairs, all the familiar sounds of family. Security and safety in love. She wanted to run down the few stairs that separated them, the few yards of distance between her bed and the kitchen table. To be in the same warm, brightly lit, protected space they were. She wanted to wash the lingering smell from her cheek at the kitchen sink with the distinctive clean and antiseptic smell of the Wright's Coal Tar soap, which lived in a broken grey saucer on the windowsill. She sobbed quietly until, once again, exhaustion claimed her.

She didn't open her eyes again until the next morning, when an unexplained feeling of badness and shame was quickly drowned by the calls of siblings asking for her help. She could tell no one. No one knew about the evil that had crept uninvited into her room. When she washed at the sink, she plunged her face into the bowl of water with a force that made Maura shout out at her for splashing the floor. Finally, Kitty got to hug her mother. She flung her arms round her waist and buried her head in her chest. Maura kissed the top of her head and rubbed her shoulders, too busy with the morning routines and the chores of daily existence for procrastination.

What Kitty had suffered that night was the by-product of being poor. It wasn't the outward signs of poverty or the lack of shoes and clothes that defined a poorer child and brought the deepest lasting misery. It wasn't even the hidden hunger pains, pale skin and pinched cheeks, an unheated house or broken furniture. It wasn't having to share a bed with springs protruding from a stained mattress or having to walk on cold, bare, splintered floorboards. What often defined a poor child was shame. Shame not just from being without, but from having encountered something dark that roamed the streets and homes of the vulnerable. An evil that did a greater damage and left a deeper mark than an empty belly. Hunger could be fed, a numbed body could be clothed, but a damaged soul could not be seen or healed. Poverty, gratitude, a sense of inferiority and insecurity made children prey to the things that were invisible and were never spoken of.

## Chapter Eight

Time rolled by and life on the four streets altered very little. People still existed rather than lived, and Alice, wallowing in the residual memory of a dream, withdrew into her familiar pattern of isolation.

She had given up any pretence of enjoying Saturday nights at the Irish centre and had no interest in the new band, the Beatles, that Jerry and the others had been raving about since they had played at the pub.

Through her window, Alice watched life on the four streets. She was the first to see Peggy, an unsuspecting follower of fashion, walking down the street with no curlers in and her hair piled up on top of her head like a beehive. Alice thought she looked ridiculous, but she didn't say that to anyone other than Jerry, because she didn't communicate with anyone on the street. Instead, she preferred to stand at her window and watch as the world around her went on with its business through a pane of glass, just as she always had.

Alice had been unable to make the leap from her past into her future. She had worked hard and put everything in place for the life she wanted, but she never once accounted for her own social inadequacy or her history to date. Observing life was very different from living it.

She struggled most with Nellie and for much of the time made sure the child was out of the way. She couldn't touch her and never spoke to her. Throughout her upbringing no one had ever spoken to Alice. She didn't know how a normal family worked.

When deep in thoughts of regret, Jerry often pondered on how he had ended up where he was. He now recognized that he hadn't been given much of a chance. How was he supposed to have known what was going on when Alice had arrived at his house only a week after the funeral? But now he knew he ought to have done. He had at last realized that, even at the time, her knock on the front door had created a stir on the street.

The only person who had ever knocked on his front door before that day was the man from the Pru, who collected the sixpence club money every Friday night. The man from the Pru knocked on everyone's front door. It was an act of significance that highlighted his status and degree of importance in their lives. Most of the people in the street handed over the sixpence without question. The money would pay for a burial when it was needed. This was a big deal. For Catholics there was a stigma attached to being buried in a pauper's grave, an end met by many in years gone by.

But no matter how much thought Jerry gave to his predicament, the fact was he couldn't get out of it. And in truth, he and Nellie were finding their level; they were managing, with the help of people he would be grateful to all his life, especially Maura, who constantly gave out to him about Alice.

Nellie never got the chance to talk at home, when her da was out at work. That was why, whenever she found herself in the company of others, she never stopped talking. It was as if all the words she hadn't spoken in her own house and all the thoughts in her head, unvoiced and unheard, came pouring out. It was impossible to stem her enthusiasm, or to stop her asking questions and laughing. Nellie saved up everything she had to say. She was irrepressible. She was beside herself with happiness in the company of Maura's noisy family from up the street, and if she didn't have her da at home, she would have happily lived at number nineteen. Over time, she ended up spending more hours at the Dohertys' than in her own home.

But now, at five years of age, even Nellie was beginning to sense that Alice was different. Nellie desperately wanted Alice to like her. She wanted to make Alice smile or get out of bed in the mornings. Or to stop Alice snarling and being grumpy to her da. She wanted not to be scared of Alice and for her to be nice, like Maura.

Maura and Tommy often discussed the 'Alice' situation. Sometimes it felt as though they discussed nothing else. Maura was concerned by Alice's behaviour. Even though there were net curtains on the upstairs window, Maura could often make Alice out, a ghost behind the nets, staring down at the street. Neither of them knew what to make of such very odd behaviour.

Over the last few years Alice had retreated into a place Jerry couldn't recognize. She often didn't get up in the mornings and, more often than not, he had to see to himself and Nellie before he left for work. Alice did the basics, the washing and cleaning, and there was a meal ready each night when he got home. But she wouldn't go outdoors any more, so all the shopping fell on Jerry. The last time he suggested that they go into town, to buy Nellie a new coat at C&A, his request had been met with recriminations and tears.

'Why are you asking me to do that, Jerry, why? You know I don't like to go out.'

'For feck's sake, Alice, why won't ye go outside the front door?' shouted Jerry, more in exasperation than anger.

'Because no one round here likes me and I don't want to be seen. I never wanted to live here, I wanted us to be better than this and for you to get a better job, so we could travel to America or somewhere more civilized than these dirty streets.'

Alice wasn't budging but she also wasn't being truthful. Stepping outside the front door was something she had found difficult since the day she moved in.

'I never said I was going to leave either my house or my job when we married, Alice. There was no discussion along those lines and there never will be. If I don't end my life here, I will do it back home in Ireland, but I am not moving away from the people who have looked after me and Nellie so well!' By this point Jerry was roaring in anger, hurt by what he saw as an attack on the home he and Bernadette had made. 'They are like me family and if I live to be a hundred years old I will never find enough ways to thank them.'

'Thank them, thank them?' screamed Alice. 'What about me, what about the sacrifices I have made? I gave up my job to look after you and your snotty kid.'

Jerry stormed out of the door before he did something he regretted.

The women on the street had now, by and large, forgiven Jerry for marrying Alice. Things had moved on. Everyone had accepted that Jerry had to remarry, and quickly, and he was an attractive option for any woman. There was no man in Liverpool as good-looking or as good-natured as Jerry. What had upset them had been the shock of a woman getting her feet under his table and the eejit not being able to see what was going on. Their worst fears had been realized. He would never have sought out a wife and a mother for Nellie, and so one found him.

It was not so easy for Maura. Although she struggled hard to keep on an even keel with Alice, Maura would never accept her. From the moment she had first witnessed Alice's arrival in Jerry and Nellie's life, Maura had known it was bad news.

One early morning, she said to Tommy, as she had a hundred times before, 'That Alice is a Protestant whore, coming to Jerry's house with her brass neck, Bernadette not yet cold in her grave, and her banging on the door, trying to get into her bed, and him so torn with grief he couldn't see through her.'

Tommy could not for a second see what the problem was now. They were years into the marriage already, so surely it was time for

Maura to move on and change the tune? But always aware of the need to dodge the wrong side of Maura's tongue, he didn't dare say it. Anything for an easy life.

Alice had pulled the rug right out from under them and usurped the places of both Maura and everyone back home in Ireland, and to her dying day Maura would never forgive her.

'Between us, Tommy, after a decent passage of time, we would have found a good Irish Catholic girl for Jerry,' she insisted. 'God knows, there's enough of them to pick from.'

Tommy, as usual, wasn't listening. Instead he was worrying about Kitty, who was becoming more and more withdrawn with every day that passed.

'What's up with our Kitty?' he asked Maura, as Kitty passed through the kitchen, without a word or a glance in his direction.

'I think she's about to start, but she's too young really she is,' Maura replied in hushed tones. Tommy understood, without her having to spell it out, that Kitty's period was about to begin. 'She's so sour and miserable, so she is, I can't get a word out of her.'

'No, nor can I,' replied Tommy, who was more worried than he was letting on.

He and his Kitty had a special bond. Sure, he loved his twins. Not many men could boast two sets of twin boys, surely a testament to his virility. There was no better joy than playing footie with his lads on a Sunday morning on the green, or going up to Everton on a Saturday afternoon to watch a home game. He always walked the distance to the match with one of them perched on his shoulders on the way, singing footie songs and hooking up with other match-goers. But it was different with him and Kitty. She was his first-born and they had a great rapport with each other.

Kitty was clever and liked to talk about everything she had heard on the radio, or read in a book. Her mind was inquisitive and probing, though Tommy had no answers for any of her questions.

'Da!' Kitty would squeal in exasperation. 'Why don't ye know about Africa? I want to know who lives there. I heard the man say on the radio that there was summat called apartheid in South Africa, tell me, da.'

Kitty would playfully shake her da's shoulders, as though she could shake the knowledge out of him. But instead of feeling inadequate, Tommy burst out laughing.

'Kitty!' he would splutter out through his laughter. 'I can't even say it, Queen, never mind know what it is, for God's sake.'

Kitty would laugh too and stamp her feet in exasperation, often pulling a face, which told Tommy she thought he was useless, but she loved him anyway.

Tommy was relieved to take on board Maura's explanation that the way Kitty was changing was to do with her monthlies. There was none of that with the lads, thank goodness, and he reflected on the fact that with Maura, Kitty, Angela, and now Niamh, one day he would be living in a house where at least one woman, out of his wife and daughters, would be out to murder him as soon as look at him.

Telling this to Jerry one day, he told him how lucky he was. 'Can ye imagine anything worse, four of them all out to kill me? You should think yeself lucky, mate, you only have Alice and little Nellie.'

Jerry smiled. He had confided in Tommy many a time that he would now like another child. He thought it might be what Alice needed, to bring herself out of her shell.

Tommy, in turn, confided in Jerry about Kitty.

'Ye expect Angela to be miserable, she's been fucking miserable since the day she was born. If Angela had been the first, we would have dreaded the second, but our Kitty is different and I'd hate to see her good nature disappear.' His face creased into a worried frown. 'When I came down this morning to light the fire, she was already sitting at the kitchen table, crying. She wouldn't tell me what was the matter and I must have asked her ten times. All she made me do was promise that I wouldn't tell Maura. Why would she ask me that, eh, Jerry? Why wouldn't she want her mammy to know she was upset?'

'Women,' replied Jerry. And that was it. Neither knew what to say. Women were as unfathomable as the ocean itself. They hadn't got a clue.

Tommy had no idea how to deal with the problem of Kitty, or how to make it better. He had promised he wouldn't tell Maura.

Kitty was the one child he wouldn't betray in that promise. He put to the back of his mind the sight of her crying quietly to herself at the kitchen table and got on with the routine of his life. Almost.

Kitty felt as if she was dying inside. As though each day a part of her crumbled away. Father James had taken to coming upstairs to 'bless the children whilst they be in innocent sleep' about once a month. Whereas once she was the first to fall asleep, now Kitty lay awake every night, until she heard her parents switch off the kitchen light and rake down the fire. That blessed sound, that familiar click, the sound of her mother washing their cups in the sink and her father closing the outhouse door, before he came up the stairs to bed: all those familiar bedtime noises told her that now she was safe for the night and she could sleep.

Kitty was reaching adolescence and the first sprouting of tiny breasts had begun to appear. Embarrassed and bemused, she had been shocked when they appeared almost overnight. Maura noticed them too and assumed the physical signs of womanhood were the source of her moodiness.

Maura wasn't the only person to have noticed the changes in Kitty's body.

She always pretended to be asleep when he came into the room. He had begun fumbling around under the bedclothes to feel her breasts. When his hand found one, it didn't move, just rested there for a while, deadly still, before he removed it and began his fumbling. His jerking and panting and gasping.

As the years moved on, she had learnt to roll over, pretending to be asleep with her head buried in the pillow, and thankfully she had never again had to endure him wiping her face. Even if she were lying on her front when he came into the room, he would still push his hand under her slight frame to find her breast. He couldn't risk being heard trying to wake her up.

Kitty screamed, not only in her head, but in every nerve of her body. But she lay there rigid, not moving a muscle until she heard him rush down the stairs. Then she could cry her silent sobs into the dark and to no one else.

What could she say? What could she tell anyone? No one would believe her. They would think she was away with the fairies. They would call her mad Kitty and send her to the mission, where the old people who had lost their minds and who had no family went to be looked after by the nuns. Father James was the most important man in the whole of Liverpool, wasn't he? Even the head nun in her school, Sister Evangelista, had him come in every week to take prayers at the assembly.

Only last week, Kitty had been putting out books for the geography lesson to help the teacher when Sister came into her classroom.

'Kitty, Father James has asked especially that you make his cuppa tea and take it to him in my office,' said Sister Evangelista.

Kitty froze to the spot.

Sister Evangelista began talking to Kitty's teacher. 'The Father's a saint, he's so many families to look after he must work all the hours God sends,' she said.

Sister Evangelista thought Father James was a saint? Kitty felt as though she lived on a different planet from everyone else in the world. She was remote from everyone and everything that made any sense.

'Father James is going to stay after prayers and help with teaching the Bible to the little ones in the infant section. I'm sure they could have no better teacher. He's so devoted to the Word.'

'Aye, that he is,' said Kitty's teacher. 'He lives and breathes "suffer the little children"; he sits each child on his lap when he is reading the Bible to them, such a loving Father.'

They were both teachers, both women Kitty looked up to and respected. Kitty knew that some of the girls didn't like Sister Evangelista, but Kitty did. Both women, just like her own mother, revered, respected and adored Father James. Father James was untouchable. Kitty was lost.

There was no one and nowhere she could go to for help with this blight on her life. This miserable torment, which robbed her of her sleep, her peace and her innocence, was something she would have to bear and could not share. This shame that made her feel disgusting, dirty and unwhole was hers alone. Kitty was quite sure that if she did confide in someone, they would think it was Kitty who was to blame, not the saintly Father James. She could not cope with that on top of what she had to bear now.

'Kitty!' shouted Sister Evangelista. 'What is up with ye, girl, get away with ye now and make Father James his tea, he is waiting for it in the office.'

'Yes, Sister,' said Kitty dutifully, as she made her way to the kitchen.

As she walked into the office, she did not look up. Her eyes were focused on the table in front of her, fixed on the dark wood grain of the desk. She didn't even know if he was there and listened for his breathing. He was there. He watched her carefully, as she moved towards the table where he was sitting, waiting, with the Bible in his hands open at the New Testament.

'Ah, Kitty. Thank ye for the tea. I just wanted a quick word. I wondered, was ye interested in stamp collecting?'

She didn't know how to reply. Even if she had known what to say, the fear in her stomach would have prevented her and stopped it coming out. How could he talk to her so normally? He was the man who did strange things over her, when she lay in her bed and her parents were downstairs. How could he talk as though none of that had happened? He had put his cold, smelly, wet, fish-like hand over her breast and felt it.

Her most difficult days of adolescence and embarrassment were being violated. Only this morning one of the twins, Declan, had burst back into the bedroom unannounced, as she was changing, which she now did when the others had gone downstairs. She closed the bedroom door, which was unusual, and dressed in private, such was her shyness around even her own sisters. Declan was curious as to why the door was closed and had satisfied his younger-brother nosiness.

Then he ran down the stairs yelling, 'Mammy, Mammy, Kitty's growing titties!'

From upstairs Kitty had heard the sharp slap and then Declan's screams, as had probably the whole street.

That was the first time she had ever known her mother hit Declan. She was protecting Kitty from her annoying little brother. Maybe she would protect her from the priest? That morning was the first time Kitty had considered the terrifying possibility of telling her mother. If Maura slapped Declan for peeping into her room, surely she would give out about the priest and what he did?

Father James noted her silence, but carried on anyway. 'I have a wonderful collection, Kitty, left to me by my own father, and I wondered if ye would like to drop by the Priory to have a look. Yer mammy tells me ye have a thirst for knowledge and different countries of the world, and when I suggested it to her, she thought it would be a grand idea.'

Kitty still could not speak. He was talking about her to her mother? Her own mother was colluding to send her to him in his house, where she would be unsafe. For the first time in her life, Kitty hated her mother.

She was flooded with a feeling of intense anger towards Maura, which gave her a courage she didn't know she had.

'I cannot come to the Priory, Father,' she replied. 'I have to help me mammy with the kids. It would be too selfish of me altogether to take time away; and Daddy would wonder why I had done it, as the arthritis is beginning to get into me mammy's knees, now making them very sore.'

She didn't know how she had found the strength to say the words and defy him. She had no idea that self-preservation was kicking in. She could have been fighting for her life.

Father James looked surprised but Kitty stared at him defiantly. 'Be that as it may, Kitty, 'tis your choice. Maybe I'll ask yer mammy another day,' he replied very slowly.

Kitty closed the office door behind her. She stood with her back to the door with her arm behind her, holding tightly onto the brass knob. It was an involuntary attempt to keep the children safe from him and to keep him locked in the office. She stood there for a few seconds whilst she gathered her breath and then, feeling stronger for having thwarted his ploy to get her to the Priory, went back to her classroom.

Kitty had won one over on Father James. What she didn't know was that it had happened only because Father James was slightly afraid of Tommy, in whom he had always sensed a lack of respect. If it weren't for Tommy, if Kitty had a more compliant daddy, Father James would have called round to her house that night and told Maura to send Kitty to the Priory after evening prayers. But as it was, she was Tommy's daughter, so he would let it rest.

It was a warm May and Maura thought, sure, why not, when Kitty suggested throwing a party for the twins' birthday. Kitty was always looking for ways to make people happy, even though she wasn't too happy herself these days. She had become so miserable that Maura jumped at the chance to do something to please her.

Kitty's suggestion for the twins' party had been brought on by the arrival of a hessian sack of flour, which, as far as the children were concerned, had appeared out of nowhere in the corner of the living room. The children were often amazed at the things that turned up in the house during the night.

'It was a magic leprechaun,' Maura would reply if the children pushed for an explanation. A leprechaun was as good as they were ever going to get. Maura had morals.

The sack was eventually moved upstairs into Maura and Tommy's bedroom, because she simply couldn't keep the children from jumping on it and filling the room with a white powdery fog, which settled in a fine dust upon everything in its way.

'As though there wasn't enough dust to deal with from the docks, without it being created indoors as well,' Maura grumbled, helping Tommy negotiate the narrow stairwell as they dragged the sack up the stairs.

The sack of flour had fallen off the back of a ship in the docks, which Tommy had helped unload the previous night. Odd arrivals into the houses on the streets often happened at the end of a shift.

'Split it between Brian's, Paddy's and Seamus's missus' was Maura's only instruction, as Tommy bent backwards and let the sack fall with a thud from across his shoulders onto the floor in the corner of the room, letting out a cloud of white smoke.

It was a case of who wins, shares. Tommy had been working in a gang of four on the dock last night and as soon as they spotted the opportunity to lift the flour, they did so. It involved big Seamus lifting two bags at once from the hold of the ship, as though the weight were only one. Jerry took the bags at the gangway, but passed only one to Brian who, as quick as you like, ran to the entry gate where the security guard was fast asleep. When he raced back into line, Tommy then fell out and ran to the perimeter wall. The gate was closed, but not locked as it should have been. The guard had taken a mug of rum at midnight, once all the dockers were in through the gate to unload the latest arrival, and had fallen into a deep sleep, before relocking the gates.

Tommy had noticed the guard was asleep and pointed it out to the others with a nudge and the nod of his head in the direction of the guard's wooden hut. No words were spoken. Everyone knew the drill. At the first opportunity, a bag would be dropped. It was a high-risk strategy. There were twenty-five thousand dockers working on the Liverpool docks, mostly Irish Catholics, and although they were all part of the Irish Diaspora, the dock gateman was an Orange Lodge Protestant from Belfast who had no respect for or empathy with the Catholic dockers and navvies. He regarded them as papist left footers and could often be heard singing Lodge songs under his breath. He was a nark, but, thankfully, there weren't many who were. The casual nature of dock work, which meant you were only guaranteed that day's work, created a bond amongst fathers, sons and families who worked on the docks together.

The dockers might have had no long-term security, the Mersey Dock Company may have tried to keep wages low and conditions harsh, but try as they might they could never break the resourcefulness of the Liverpool Irish dockers, who made sure that if a load could be eaten or worn, some of it would end up in the bellies, or on the backs, of their own kids.

Tommy squatted down, took two corners of the hundredweight sack, hoisted it up onto his back and was running up towards the four streets in minutes. He deposited the sack in the living room, hared back down to the docks and slipped in through the gates, in line with his gang, with only seconds to spare before the night guard woke.

It was always much easier to take things that could fit inside pockets or the butty bag. A hundredweight sack was an operation, and operations happened on a regular basis, but it was the smaller gains that kept life ticking over on a day-to-day basis. Tommy regularly came home with his huge pocket full of currants or sugar. Sometimes, if they knew a molasses ship was due in, some of the men would take a bottle of cold tea to the dockside and, after they had drunk it, fill it with the molasses that 'leaked' out of the pipe pumping it from the ship into the tanker. It only took someone to make sure that the connection to the tanker wasn't quite tight enough when the pumping began.

With the flour, Tommy had provided the means for Maura to make a birthday cake for the twins and the party was decided.

'That'll be grand for the boxty bread, too,' said Maura, as Tommy went to slip out of the house, a moment of harmony growing between them.

'Aye, it will that, and no one can make it as well as ye,' said Tommy as he leant back in the door and kissed Maura briefly, before disappearing down the street into the early morning grey miasma. He hadn't even stopped for a mug of tea.

Maura knew that Tommy thought all the time about the well-being of herself and the kids. Knowing it was the twins' birthday coming up, he had kept his eye out for anything on the ships he could commandeer to make it a bit of a day for Harry and Declan, even if it meant a risk. Taking risks was what a lack of secure work forced you to do. Despite the Dock Workers Act of 1948 requiring the dock company to keep a register of workers, the dock company openly flouted the law and continued to keep the dockers keen, impoverished and waiting at the gates each morning.

The dockers knew how poor they were and what a struggle life was with so many children, but they were also aware of how much the world was changing around them. They were aspirational. They wanted more for their children than they had had growing up during the war years. They knew that they deserved better living standards, and that some of their working conditions were downright dangerous. Safety measures amounted to little more than the tweed caps they all wore religiously, in an attempt to protect themselves from a swinging crane or load. In such circumstances – all too frequent – the cap was useless, but it made the dockers feel less vulnerable.

On the day of the party, prams – each of which contained at least one sleeping baby and often two, laid head to toe – lined the entry wall on either side of the tall wooden gate leading into the yard. The prams were safe. The community didn't take from its own. Thieving was reserved for the contents of the ships, vans and trucks parked at the docks and, besides, who would steal a pram with a baby in it? Everyone had enough mouths to feed.

It was a warm and sunny day, and children ran in and out of the yard, squealing with anticipation and spilling over into the entry. They were all dressed in the best they had, which might have been worn, third-hand, home-made or worse, but, on party day, clean. They were excited. A birthday party was a major event. It had been talked about for weeks and now it was here. Harry and Declan would even get a present wrapped up in paper to open in front of everyone.

Mothers sat in the wider part of the Dohertys' yard, just inside the gate, on wooden chairs they had wheeled down the street, balanced across the tops of prams. As it was a special day, they smoked Embassy cigarettes instead of roll-ups, and chatted about the new Hoover that could be bought in town from Blackler's if you had the money. No one on the four streets could afford to buy a machine to lift dirt off a floor. There were enough children to do that.

They had removed their aprons, which signified a special event. Aprons came off for mass, parties and Christmas Day. But none had taken the wire rollers and pins out of their hair, covered by headscarves. Even at mass, Jesus had to put up with those. The hair rollers indicated that something better might be round the corner.

The enduring permanence of wire and pins pricking their scalps was the physical and material manifestation of hope, yelling loudly that every woman on the four streets was waiting for better days to come. One day there would be a reason to take them out and, when that day came, they would have had their hair done and would be at the ready.

In the narrow section of yard outside the back door, Maura now had Bernadette's bright yellow Formica kitchen table which had been set up and was laden with sandwiches, fairy cakes and jelly. The bread for the sandwiches had been lifted from the back of a bread van making a delivery in Bootle, just a mile or so away, at seven that morning, stolen to order by the O'Prey boys, heroes for the day. One wooden tray of soft rolls and one of barm cakes. The non-edible evidence of the theft had already been chopped up and placed in the wood store to be burnt under the copper wash boiler on Monday.

Early that morning, Maura had left her house, accompanied by her brood, to fetch Nellie to the party. As Kitty and the children ran up to the green, Maura had knocked on Jerry's door and told Alice, firmly, that she was taking Nellie with her. This was in accordance with instructions from Jerry, as given to Maura, when he had called for Tommy to leave for work at six that morning. He didn't want Nellie to miss the big event in the street. Alice was difficult and bloody-minded. It was better to collect Nellie in the morning than risk Alice saying no later in the day.

'I've come for the child,' said Maura when Alice opened the door after what seemed like an age. Maura felt very conspicuous, stood in her own street waiting for an answer. She felt as welcome as the rent man after a lean week.

Alice stared at her for a few long seconds, as though she was having trouble understanding what Maura said. 'Wait here a minute,' she replied in a monotone, and closed the front door in Maura's face.

'Jeez, have ye ever known the like,' hissed Maura to Peggy, who was stood at her door puffing on a ciggie and watching. The kids were already impatient and hopping around on the street, eager for Nellie to run about and play. 'A stranger in me own street, in a house I knew and cleaned, long afore she did.'

Maura's blood boiled. If Nellie hadn't been Bernadette's child she would have shouted through the letterbox, in a manner far from ladylike, 'Feck off with yer, ye haughty stuck-up Protestant bitch,' and stormed off into Peggy's to confer. If Nellie hadn't been Bernadette and Jerry's child, and therefore worth the effort, a street war would surely have broken out.

It took every ounce of Maura's willpower to hold her tongue and to keep her hands to herself, as, after what seemed an eternity, Alice opened the door and pushed Nellie out onto the street. Nellie looked dishevelled and as though she had been crying, but as soon as she saw Maura, her face lit up.

Maura knew there was no point in kicking up against Alice. She knew that if she did, she would force Jerry to take sides and he would have to side with Alice. Or 'his bitch of a Protestant wife' as Maura frequently called her.

'I know I'm a Catholic and I shouldn't say this,' Maura had confided to Peggy only the previous morning, 'but if Jerry told me he wanted to get a divorce, I would jump for joy, so I would.'

'Right ye are there,' replied Peggy, 'just don't go saying that in front of Father James now, or any of the nuns, or they'll have ye doing a penance.'

They both roared with laughter, because they knew Maura was joking.

'If my Tommy's words get any sharper, or his arse any fatter and lazier, I'll be divorcing meself,' spluttered Maura.

'Aye, away with ye,' said Peggy, 'yer Tommy's words are only sharp because he's always having to slip them in sideways, ye talk so much. Hush giving out about divorce, for Jerry or anyone, no one gets divorced around here.'

Both women laughed as they worked out how to make the Camp coffee that had appeared in the grocery shop that week. Peggy had been told that everyone was drinking it and it was all the rage, so she had bought a bottle for them to try for a change. They poured the brown glutinous liquid into two cups, added the hot sterilized milk and then drank it, pretending they both thought it was lovely.

They never touched it again.

Peggy and Maura went on their way, with Maura's anger towards

Alice having dispersed. But it was a continuous battle to hold her tongue and one Maura knew she had to keep fighting, to make sure she kept true to the promise of her prayers and was able to keep a watchful eye over Nellie.

It was only because Maura had got the child into the church with Jerry's mammy Kathleen, for a quick baptism the day before the funeral, that Nellie was safe in the light. As Maura was her godmother, it was her job to ensure she stayed there and if that meant keeping on even terms with Alice, so be it.

Nellie was excited to see the Doherty children and Maura, whom she loved so much, and left the house without a backward glance, skipping along, towards the green at the top of the street. She chatted away to the children and Maura all the way without stopping. Her long, strawberry-blonde curls had turned to a distinctive red and bounced up and down, freshly rubbed through with a hair lotion called Goldilocks that her da had bought from an American sailor on the Canada dock. He had applied it last thing the previous night, in preparation for today. Her blue eyes sparkled; she found it impossible to contain her anticipation. She had no idea what a birthday party was.

At the jumble sale at a church hall in Maghull, Maura had snapped up a dress and a hand-knitted pale-pink cardigan for Nellie, which she put on her as soon as they got back to her own house. The pink cardigan had faded from overwashing, but it didn't matter; Nellie still felt like a princess. Jerry had that morning given Maura the threepence the dress and cardigan had cost. He had no idea about clothes and he knew better than to ask Alice to take Nellie shopping.

He depended on Maura for almost everything to do with Nellie, who had found her way around Alice. She had even begun to do little things that she had watched Jerry do in their own home, and Kitty and Maura do in theirs. He laughed so much that he almost cried when he caught her in the kitchen one day, battling with the big broom and trying to sweep the kitchen floor.

When he told Maura, she added her own pearls of wisdom. 'Aye, well, it's because, even at her young age, she can feel the need for a mother in the house. She senses the absence of a caring woman, Jerry.'

Jerry didn't reply. He wished Maura wouldn't let on so about Alice all the time. He knew the mistake he had made, but it was his mistake and he would have to live with it. That would be much easier if people stopped reminding him of what he had done.

Sometimes Maura felt angry with Jerry, as if he had forgotten about Bernadette. She knew he never mentioned her name in the house, or to Nellie, and yet when Maura did so, she saw the lump in his throat and the tears in his eyes. Maura, too, welled up every time she thought of Bernadette. She often spoke of her to Nellie.

'She was a lovely woman, a saintly woman. God knows, why would he take a new mother and so young?' she would gasp, over-dramatically, as she clasped Nellie to her bosom.

Nellie had no idea what Maura was really talking about. She knew Alice wasn't her mother, because she called her Alice and everyone else had a mammy. She had never seen a photograph of her mammy, and yet she knew what she looked like, a lady with long red hair and a lovely smile. She was sure that she had seen her. She sometimes dreamt about her. She thought she had seen her sitting on her bed once, when she was half asleep, but when she sat up there was no one there.

The excitement in the Doherty house on the day of the twins' party was intense. All the kids helped to get the yard ready and move the furniture outside. By the time four o'clock arrived, the children began streaming in through the back gate in their Sunday best clothes, clutching either a bag of sweets or a plate of sandwiches or cakes. Everyone did their bit to contribute to the occasion.

Soon the party was in full swing, the children playing and the adults chatting away, with Maura filling up cups of tea whilst trying to pull apart the boys, who had decided to box each other's ears.

Nellie had eaten enough. Maura had loaded her plate, whispering, 'Fill yer boots, Queen,' as she had sat her down at the table. Now that the plate was empty, and with no one to tell her to get down and play, Nellie knew she should stay put until everyone else had gone home and her da arrived.

Nellie had spent hours yesterday at home alone with little to do and no one to talk to. Maura had been especially busy baking and getting ready for the party, and Jerry had felt too guilty to take Nellie across to Maura's house. Alice never addressed a word to Nellie, so it was hard for her to sit quietly in a yard full of social activity. She climbed up onto one of the kitchen chairs placed around the table to see over the heads of the other children.

All the adults were busy, chatting or attending to children. The sun was shining and the concrete yard floor had been washed clean of coal dust for the party. Nellie stood with her hands in front of her, smiling. With a full tummy and everyone around her chatting and laughing, she felt very happy and content.

Looking up, she spotted the rope washing line running across the yard above her head, strung between the two dark-red brick walls. She could just about reach it, so she raised her hands to the rope and held on. She then lifted her feet up and swung, backwards and forwards, before putting them back down onto the chair. No one had noticed. She raised her hands and did it again, back and forth, back and forth.

Harry spotted her and thought it looked like a fun game. He climbed up onto the table to join her. Two years older, Harry was twice the weight of Nellie. They both swung together, giggling, until the rope snapped and gave way, dumping them both in a heap on the yard floor. They shrieked and laughed so much they were almost out of control. Then, suddenly, Nellie threw up all down the front of her pink cardigan.

As some of the mothers moved over to pick them up, the cry automatically went out: 'Where's her mammy?'

There was an awkward moment, as no answer came back, then Maura rushed forward. Scooping Nellie up, she said very firmly, 'I'm her mammy today, aren't I, Queen?' as she removed the jumble-sale cardigan and wiped Nellie's face.

Maura's neighbour of next door but one, Deirdra, a slovenly woman from Tipperary who had only arrived on the four streets two years ago, tutted and shook her head. 'You have enough with your own to look after, without one more to add to your troubles. Where's that Alice woman? Is she not interested in the child?'

Nellie heard this and a feeling of aching loneliness settled in the pit of her stomach. Maura sensed this and glared at Deirdra, hissing, 'Hush yer mouth, why don't ye, and look after yer own breed, before commenting on others people's.'

Suddenly, a lump came into Nellie's throat. She felt acutely alone. Different from everyone else. Why did everyone regard her with such pity in their eyes? Why did the other mothers look at her and then tut and whisper to each other? Why did she have no mammy to talk to about what she had done that day? She wanted someone to say about her, 'God, that child is driving me mad,' but all day no one spoke about Nellie. No one told her off for being naughty, or praised her for being good. In a confined space full of mothers and children, even as young as she was, she knew she was invisible.

With a pain in her heart and tightness in her chest, she missed the mammy whom she sometimes saw but had never known. She pressed her head tightly into Maura's shoulder. She didn't want Harry, who was staring at her intently, to see the tears that had suddenly sprung into her eyes and that she couldn't stop from pouring silently down her cheeks. For the first time since the day she was born, she cried for her mammy, Bernadette.

They heard the noise first: a wailing on the wind that began to filter through and fragment their conversations. It was an audible static that hurt their ears and sent the dogs yelping down the street. And then, rapidly, the wailing became a sudden fierce gale, rising from the surface of the Mersey and taking the water upwards with it, blasting in across the docks and up the steps. On its way it shifted cranes, rocked ships and knocked over piles of stacked-up timber. It scooped up the dust from the bombed-out wasteland that surrounded the four streets and, like a plague of small flies, the dust swarmed ferociously into the centre of the street.

It wrapped itself around the children playing in the yard, blowing into their ears and up their noses and sending them running to bury their heads in their mothers' aprons. It hit the eyes of the women and filled their mouths with dust, making them choke and splutter, and covered their bodies like a brown shroud. Dragging their children along with them, they abandoned the party and idle gossip to run inside and wash the dust out of their mouths and off their skin.

The storm carried on its crest a dead mother's heartache and whilst Maura rubbed Nellie's back and whispered gently into her hair, 'There, there, now,' it found its way between them both and mingled its tears with Nellie's own.

## Chapter Nine

The morning after the party, Nellie woke and sat bolt upright in bed, worried, bleary-eyed, rigid. She did the same thing every morning. Her attention focused on the noises coming from the kitchen. She listened hard for the sound of ashes being riddled, or a shovel of coal being thrown into the range. If she awoke to silence, she would put her ear flat to the cold wall at the side of her bed, concentrating hard, in order to hear better. Once she heard the falling clatter of coal upon brick which let her know Jerry was downstairs, she threw herself back on the pillow and, with her arms straight by her sides, closed her eyes and breathed a loud sigh of deep relief.

'Thank you, Holy Mary, Mother of God,' she whispered, and crossed herself. Maura said she should do this, every morning, and Nellie had, as always, taken her words to heart.

After her morning prayer, she rubbed the sleep out of her eyes, then, with dramatic urgency, she cast aside the blankets, threw herself out of bed and pattered across the cold red linoleum of her bedroom floor. The lino was patterned with large bunches of white, pink and yellow roses, tied together with a green bow, which Nellie used to hop across like islands in a red sea.

When she was a baby, toddling across the lino one morning to Jerry, he had said, 'Quickly now, before Jack Frost gets ye.' Startled, she looked behind her to see what he meant. There was nothing and no one there. Nellie assumed Jack Frost must live under her bed, as she could see nowhere else for him to be.

She had never forgotten those words and since that day, every morning as her feet first touched the floor, she was done for. Now that she knew where he lived, there was no escaping him. Jack Frost would reach out from under the bed where he hid all night and seize her little feet, freezing her to the spot. He would wrap himself around her calves, making Nellie gasp as, just for a second, not satisfied with just her small limbs, he took her breath away too.

Grabbing her breath back, with a squeal that she tried hard to suppress, she flew lightfooted towards the bedroom door, scared to creak a floorboard or bang a door, thereby waking Alice. The thought of Alice spread icy tendrils up from her calves into the pit of her stomach. She mustn't wake Alice.

It was very important for Nellie to catch Jerry in the mornings. If Alice chose to stay in bed, she would forget about Nellie, who would then have to stay in her room, without food and with a rumbling, empty belly, until Alice fetched her, which sometimes could be very late in the day. This distressed Nellie as she needed the outhouse and often had to sneak out in fear of being heard or caught by Alice. Home was a menacing place when Jerry wasn't there.

From the first day Alice had moved in, almost every minute that Jerry was out of the house was a minute Nellie spent in her room, alone. In the early months, she would be left in her bed all day. Alice would leave her with bread and a drink to feed herself with, and walk out. Sometimes Nellie would cry for hours, until her tears became a whimper. After a while, she learnt that crying was pointless. Crying achieved nothing. It made no difference whatsoever, other than to make her sick, and so she stopped and became quiet. At the end of each day, Alice would bring her down an hour before Jerry arrived home. She would change the soaked nappy and put her straight back into her nightdress, before bringing her downstairs, plonking her onto a kitchen chair with a crust of bread in her hand, just in time for her da to walk in through the door.

When Nellie started talking, Alice laid down the boundaries of behaviour she expected from her stepdaughter. One morning Alice squatted down on the kitchen floor, her face level with Nellie's, and said, 'I just want you to know, little madam, that when your father is out, you don't speak until you are spoken to. Don't ever speak to me first, unless I ask you to. Do you get that?'

Alice spat the words out with such venom that Nellie was speechless. The fire in the range was burning high behind Alice's back, the flames licking and dancing, an orange and yellow burst of light in the otherwise gloomy room. Nellie's imagination ran away with her. She knew she was in danger. The thought went through her mind that if she said the wrong thing Alice might throw her in the fire. She thought she would be all burnt up, like the potato peelings, and her da wouldn't know where she was or be able to find her.

Alice terrified her. She did exactly as she was told and spoke only when her da was in the room, but each and every time she did, she cast a sideways glance at Alice, just to make sure it was OK, and Alice was always, without fail, staring at Nellie with a blank face. Only her eyes carried any expression and they were saying a great deal to Nellie.

Sometimes, Jerry would leave for the docks and work through for a straight twenty-four hours. This was hard for Nellie, although it did mean that even though he was in bed, recovering the following day, her da was at home. His being in the house made an enormous difference, for Nellie lived two lives. The one her da and Auntie Maura knew about, and the one she had to keep secret.

Nellie never really surprised Jerry when she opened the kitchen door in the mornings. He always expected her, although he never woke her, preferring to wait until the fire was lit and the kitchen had warmed. For more months of the year than not, Jerry could see his own breath indoors. It appeared to him as though Nellie had some form of sixth sense, because every morning, just as the fire was lit and the crystallized icy flakes slowly began to melt away from the inside of the window-pane, Nellie would walk in through the door, eyes still full of night-time dreams, clutching her old teddy. Jerry had no idea what a punctual alarm clock his morning routine was.

It made all the comforting morning sounds Nellie loved to hear. It never altered and provided her with a familiar morning song to wake up to.

One morning she had come down and he wasn't there, despite the fact that she had heard all the usual wake-up sounds. She hadn't known what to do. Disappointment washed over her, as tears began to flow and she began to sob. A morning without breakfast and a cuddle from her da was indeed miserable, as she might not eat again until the evening. Suddenly, the back door flew open and her da came in with the coal scuttle in his hand. As soon as he saw her, he placed it on the floor and ran over to her, lifting her up into his arms and hugging her.

'Shush now, princess, what is up with ye?' he soothed. She never replied and he never knew, but now, in the mornings if he went outside for coal, no matter how cold it was, he left the back door open so that she would know where he had gone.

This morning, as Nellie tiptoed down the landing, Jerry opened the first tap for running water, and she heard the cistern clank and the lead pipes play a tune that was more suited to a game of musical railway sidings than a domestic water supply. She stopped dead in her tracks, terrified that the sound would wake Alice and that she would be trapped outside her door. With a sharp inward gasp, she swiftly covered her mouth with her hand so that Alice couldn't hear her breathe. If Alice did wake, she mustn't know Nellie was there. She willed herself to be invisible as well as silent, believing this could be achieved by squeezing her eyes tight shut.

Once the water began to flow and the clanks subsided, Nellie opened her eyes and breathed again. She tiptoed stealthily down the wooden stairs, skipping the next to last one at the bottom, which always yelled out in protest as soon as it was stepped on.

As soon as she opened the kitchen door, her eyes alighted upon Jerry and she took her thumb out of her mouth, smiled her beaming smile and ran across the cold stone floor to hug him.

'Good morning, my beautiful colleen,' he said, swinging her up in his arms and lifting her above his head. 'One, two, three,' he shouted, and then threw her six inches into the air. 'By Jaysus,' he puffed, 'I won't be doing that for much longer, I'll be hitting the roof, so I will, and sending the tiles flying into Harrington Road, yer getting such a big girl.'

She hugged his neck, and he breathed in the scent of her hair, just the same as her mother's. He savoured the moment, as he closed his eyes, rocking her slowly from side to side, hugging her tight. Nellie closed her eyes too. They both remained quiet, locked in their special moment until they felt her join them, as she nearly always did. They both felt the intensity of the love that flowed and wrapped itself around them, holding them tightly together and lasting for just a minute. Then it was gone as quickly as it came. But it never failed them; it was always there.

After crashing the range doors once he had put his rashers of Irish bacon and sliced tatties in the oven, Jerry started dancing around the kitchen with Nellie, as he did almost every morning, holding one of her hands out to the side as if they were waltzing. Some mornings Nellie left after him for school, but her weekends were just like the early years with Alice had been, lonely.

Jerry sang at the top of his voice, accompanying Cliff Richard on the red and grey Roberts radio, as he swirled her around the kitchen, and she began to giggle. He never seemed to be in the slightest bit scared about waking Alice.

When they finished dancing, he filled a bowl with milk and water, dropped four or five cobs of bread into it with a sprinkling of sugar and popped it into the range oven with his rashers. If Nellie didn't have her breakfast and milk with her da in the morning, she might go all day without food, but she would never tell him that, because Alice had told her not to. She might also have a bit of bacon and tatties, if she hurried and finished her bowl first. She made sure she hurried.

Jerry took his breakfast and Nellie's 'pobs' from the range and placed them on the dark wooden table. Jerry had loved the yellow table he and Bernadette had saved for and bought together. Now, he and Nellie sat on Alice's very cumbersome oak chairs with dark brown leather seat pads. Jerry and Nellie called them chairs; Alice called them ladder-backs.

At least the bright yellow table had gone to Maura and Tommy, who had been delighted beyond words. They had too many children ever to be able to afford anything new in the way of furniture. Everything they owned was falling to bits. Maura had cried the day he and Tommy carried the table into their kitchen along with the four modern chairs, with spindle chrome legs and plastic seats and backs, covered in the same pattern as the Formica table. It was bright yellow with a design that looked as if someone had scattered a box of grey matches over the top. Maura wrote to her relatives in Mayo and told them it was time they came for a visit. She wanted them to report back to her relatives and friends in the village how prosperous Maura and Tommy were in England and how good the wages must be, if they could afford a Formica table.

Once Jerry and Nellie sat down to their breakfast together, the chatter began. Nellie's chatter, that is. Jerry could never get a word in edgeways. She talked and rambled non-stop. Sometimes she almost made him late, a disaster for a docker. Work was on a first come, first served basis and it was getting harder to be taken on each day.

This morning, the tide was out and Jerry had an extra half-hour. It was Sunday and there was no school for Nellie. From the upstairs window he could see out across the river. He knew, from having popped into the dock office the day before, which boats were expected in and he could see the tugs and pilots weren't moving out yet.

'Let's play a game, shall we,' he said to Nellie. He didn't often get time to romp about with her. There was no Alice up and making demands on his attention, so why not? Nellie was squealing and jumping up and down on the spot.

Eager to make her happy, Jerry remembered a game Nellie had played at Maura's at the weekend and said, 'I have an idea. Why don't we make a den?'

Nellie could not believe her ears and was beside herself with excitement. Jerry took her into the living room and they pulled out the dark oak sideboard, which was normally flush with the wall, and put it across the corner of the room. Jerry lifted her over the top, so she was in the triangle-shaped space, and then pulled the sideboard away and squeezed in himself.

The sideboard was another of Alice's possessions. Again, it was too large for the room but it was her pride and joy and she polished it every day.

Nellie and her da played in the den, pretending that they were in a cave and that out in the living room were lots of wild animals they had to hide from. They both had to go into the kitchen to fetch essential supplies for the den, dodging the imaginary wild animals.

'Quick, let me in,' squealed Nellie, who did the first run to the kitchen to fetch water. 'The fish are chasing me.'

'The fish?' laughed Jerry. 'Why is ye worried about the fish? It's a big lion I can see chasing ye.'

Nellie squealed and both feet left the floor in shock, as she ran, spilling her water on the way. As she squeezed back in behind the sideboard, she screamed when Jerry once again pulled it across the corner, closing the little gap he had left for Nellie.

After they had been playing for a while, Jerry heard the tugs. 'I have to go, Queen,' he said to Nellie. 'You stay here and play with Alice, I will go and wake her.'

Nellie froze. She couldn't speak or move. Within seconds Jerry had moved the sideboard out, removed himself and easily pushed it back again. Jerry was a docker and his upper-body strength was immense. It was no effort for him. He took his cap from the nail on the back of the kitchen door, along with his jacket, and shouted up the stairs to Alice, 'Come down and play with Nellie, she's waiting for ye. Alice, do you hear me?'

He waited for a 'yes' to come down the stairs and then he was off, out of the back door, down the entry, across the road and down the steps to the dock. He was standing at the dock gate, shouting greetings to the other men and laughing about the football prospects for the Everton team, just as Alice put her feet out of bed and onto the bedroom floor. Alice didn't like being woken. Alice wanted to hide in her bed under the blankets and be alone. She liked being shouted awake even less. What did Jerry mean, Nellie was waiting for her? If the child had any sense she would be back in her room, where she ought to be.

*

Nellie tried to move the sideboard to get out, but it was too heavy and she was trapped. She put her fingers onto the top and tried to scramble up. It was too high. Her feet had nothing to grip onto. Her toes pounded like a dog at the door scraping to come in, with no effect. She could hear Alice's footsteps upstairs and she knew she needed to get out. She lifted her hands higher and tried hard to pull herself up. She heaved her feet off the floor, pressing her knees into the back of the sideboard and the soles of her feet flat against the wall behind, to shimmy herself up, one last time. She gave it every ounce of strength she had. The sideboard rocked towards her as she tipped it slightly up off its front legs, just for a second, and then she heard the crash and froze.

As a terrified Nellie squatted behind the sideboard alone, where, only a few minutes ago, both she and her da had been laughing heartily, she heard Alice's footsteps slowly descend the stairs into the kitchen. Alice didn't say a word. She never did. She walked over to the radio and switched it off. Alice hated noise. She was slightly surprised that the kitchen looked exactly as it always did, and yet she knew something was different; she knew Nellie wasn't in her room. She could sense her, smell her, and she wanted to know what had made the loud crashing noise.

Alice put the kettle back on the range to boil, and then walked into the living room. She saw the sideboard moved from its usual place and she stared, with absolute horror, at her parents' precious ornament, a china dancing lady, smashed to smithereens on the floor.

Alice didn't shout. She never shouted. Hissing was more her style.

'So, this is it, this is the day it all changes, eh?' she spat quietly. She walked to the corner of the room and attempted to heave the sideboard back into its original place. Then she saw Nellie, huddled as far back against the wall as she could be, cowering and shaking. Nellie didn't say a word; she knew that was forbidden.

'You dirty, stinking, foul little bitch,' Alice hissed under her breath. 'Stand up.'

Nellie couldn't. She couldn't even breathe properly, let alone stand up. Her legs were shaking so much she couldn't move. Her throat had closed over and her mouth was so dry that, even if she had wanted to speak, she couldn't have.

'STAND UP!' Alice shouted. Nellie wished she could. She wished she could stand up and run out of the door and down to Maura's house, but she couldn't move a single limb.

'How dare you touch my furniture, how dare you touch my furniture, how dare you?' Alice hissed.

Nellie looked at Alice for the first time. Blotches of red had appeared on Alice's neck and were marching up towards her face. A dribble of spittle below her lip had flown out in anger and stood out bright white against the now very red chin. Alice wasn't looking at Nellie, she was talking to herself. Muttering about vermin and foul children, about her ruined life, ruined because of a brat. Even as she was moving the sideboard, she carried on talking to herself, looking over her shoulder to the door. She was in such a rage that she didn't care if Jerry walked in.

Alice's dark hair was tied back in a tight bun, but a section from the front, which would have been a fringe if Alice had ever had a style, suddenly flew out and bobbed backwards and forwards across her eyes like an overlarge windscreen wiper, distracting her. Alice tried to tuck it back, but the errant strand was adamant. As soon as Alice managed it, it flew straight back out, with such a flop it was as if ghostly fingers had pulled it out, and it landed again in front of her eyes. Nellie knew that piece of hair was saving her.

The sideboard was heavy, but Alice heaved and pulled until the gap between it and the wall was big enough for her to get inside.

'Come here, you little bitch,' she shouted, as she leant down and took hold of Nellie, who was tiny and frail by any measure, by the top of her hair, lifting her off her feet. The pain was excruciating, but still Nellie never made a sound. As her feet touched the ground again, she wet herself. She couldn't help it.

The pain in her head was searing and the amber liquid running down her legs stung. She had no time to register the extent of the pain, it was all happening so quickly. Alice let go of Nellie's hair and grabbed the top of her arm. She dug her fingers and her nails into

Nellie's shoulder and arm so tightly that, despite herself, Nellie let out a stifled scream. She was as light as a feather and as Alice swung her through the doorway from the living room to the kitchen, her shins crashed against the door frame.

Nellie could smell Alice's acrid sweat. Alice was wearing a bottle-green jumper and she could see every stitch in every row as her face was rammed up against it. The smell was overpowering close up and caught the back of Nellie's throat, making her gag. Out of the corner of her eye, Nellie could see her 'pobs' bowl and her da's tea mug on the draining board. Suddenly, the sight of something that was her da's made her cry with lonely desperation. Seeing his mug accentuated the fact that her situation was hopeless; she needed him back now.

As they got closer to the range, Nellie began to breathe so fast she became dizzy. She was crying so hard she was beginning to panic. Her feet kept leaving the floor as Alice jerked her along, gripping the top of her arm tightly, lifting her up and swinging her through the air like a rag doll towards the kitchen. This was it, she knew. Finally, Alice was going to put her in the fire. She was going to burn in the flames of hell, like the priest in church said you did when you sinned. She had broken the dancing lady. She was a sinner. She knew was going to die, like her own mammy.

As they approached the range, Alice picked up the boiling kettle. She was still talking and hissing to herself; about her ruined life and having to change the bed sheets of dirty people no better than scumbags, and now she was expected to pander to a verminous brat. Still holding Nellie off the floor by the top of her arm, Alice poured the boiling water out of the kettle into the sink. Then suddenly, Nellie's arm was set free as she grabbed her hair again, jerking her head back.

Although it hurt her so much, Nellie was relieved. The pain in her arm had been so bad she had felt like it was going to snap. She didn't know that in a few more minutes, her shoulder would have dislocated and that Alice had let go just in the nick of time. Alice pulled her head so far back Nellie thought her neck was going to break. She let out another stifled scream and her breath came in short, fast gasps, as Alice brought the bottom of the boiling-hot, copper-bottomed kettle down close to Nellie's face. She stopped with only half an inch to go.

The heat of the kettle was burning into Nellie's nose and cheeks; paralysed with fear, she couldn't move. Her cheeks were burning with a raging heat and it felt as though silence had descended over the kitchen. She whimpered, 'Please don't hurt me,' each word followed by a tiny sob.

'See this?' screamed Alice. 'See this? Next time I won't stop, next time I will smash it down straight onto your ugly face. Do you get it, do you?'

Nellie tried to nod, but she couldn't move her head because Alice's grip on her hair was so tight.

'Do you?' Alice screamed, spit flying out of her mouth to sizzle where it hit the boiling-hot kettle.

The sudden loud smash of pottery on the concrete floor startled Alice. Nellie was vaguely aware of the noise as it happened somewhere in the kitchen, but it was a mere backdrop to the sound of the pain screaming in her ears.

Alice turned her concentration away from Nellie and looked down at the smashed statue of the Madonna, broken into a hundred tiny pieces, fanned out like broken eggshells across the kitchen floor. Alice slowly placed the copper kettle back onto the range. Turning away from Nellie, she stood and looked at the pieces on the floor and then at the mantelpiece above the range. She couldn't have done that, could she? Alice ran her hand along the shelf, feeling for a reason to explain how the Madonna had moved six inches to the edge and fallen off. For a moment she forgot about Nellie as, in utter confusion, she bent to pick up the larger broken pieces from the floor.

Nellie hadn't taken in what had happened. She could not see through her tears or feel through the pain searing across her scalp and throbbing in her arm. She was quietly sobbing and felt sick and dizzy. The hyperventilating from her fast breathing was having an effect and her legs felt weak, pins and needles pricking her whole body. And then, as violently as it had begun, it ended. Everything went black.

Nellie had fainted in blessed relief.

*

Just at that moment, Jerry moved to take a corner of the crate being unloaded from the back of a newly arrived merchant navy vessel. The other dockers called him Stanley Matthews after the great footballer because he always took the corner. Tommy leapt to take the other corner.

'How's the colleen this morning?' he shouted to Jerry, as with six others they carefully steered the crate away from the ship's gangway.

'Sure she's grand, never better,' Jerry shouted back.

They both knew they were talking about Nellie, not Alice. As he spoke, the image of Nellie, not half an hour since, came into his mind. The thought of her running through their imaginary jungle with a cup of water and squealing that she was being chased by fish, looking and sounding just like her mother, made him chuckle yet again. His heart was warm. When Nellie was excited or happy, he saw his Bernadette. It made a difference to his day. The glimpse would stay with him all day as he still thought about her, often.

His daydreaming was broken by the yells of warning from the men at the front. The side of the butter crate they were moving had come adrift and collapsed. Two hundred and fifty smaller wooden crates of New Zealand butter were spilling out of the side of the crate all over the dock floor. As Jerry heeded the warning and ran, two of the crates hit him hard, square on, one on the top of his arm just below his shoulder, the second on the top of his skull.

He didn't see them coming, which was rare. He was usually one of the fastest to jump out of the way of trouble, making him one of the few men on the docks who had never sustained an injury. Neither crates hurt him badly, but enough to make him scream out in pain.

'Shut yer feckin' moaning,' said Tommy, as he ripped open a lid of one of the smaller crates and started stuffing half-pound packets of butter into his pockets. 'Stop crying like a babby and fill yer fecking pockets, there'll be butter on the table fer weeks.'

Jerry did as he was told. He scooped up the smaller packets and, flinching, rubbed the top of his arm and his head. He felt the pain from the bruises for days afterwards.

*

An hour later Nellie woke, exactly where she had been thrown onto her bed. Her head was at the bottom where her feet should have been and she was shivering, on top of the blankets. As she lifted her head to look around the room and check she was alone, she felt a sharp pain in her arm and as though her scalp was raw. She lay back, face down, on the bed, eyes open, heart closed. She couldn't even sob. Her bed was wet and cold. She knew her room smelt and her legs stung. For hours she lay, staring at her fingers or at the door. The pain in her arm and head throbbed, and she felt so alone, so sorry for herself.

She cried quietly, as she listened to the sounds of Harry and the other children playing outside on the green while the light began to fade. The noise tormented her and emphasized her loneliness. She could pick out the individual children by their voices or their laugh. She thought she could hear them shouting, 'Nellie, where are you, come out and play.'

They weren't and never would. The kids in the street had got used to Nellie being kept inside, and Nellie's was the only house that the kids dare not run in and out of without knocking on the door first – and no one did that. Harry's mammy had said Alice was a witch, they had all heard her, so it must be true. The children were scared half to death of what would happen to them if they did knock on the door and she said, 'Come in.'

'If ye knock on Nellie's door,' said Harry, 'the witch will turn ye into a rat and then she'll tell Jerry, "There's a rat in the yard," and he will beat ye to death with the mop until ye was splattered all over the yard. Sure he would because he wouldn't know it was really ye.'

The others would clasp their hands over their mouths. They imagined all manner of horrors in Nellie's life: that she was locked in a crate in the yard, or that Alice turned her into a black cat and sometimes couldn't turn her back again, which was why they went days without seeing Nellie. The kids on the four streets gave Nellie's house a wide berth, sometimes staying in the centre of the road, for fear that Alice's hand would reach through the front door and pull them into the dark, never to be seen again. They all genuflected and crossed themselves as they walked past Nellie's door. And sometimes Nellie saw them.

Nellie knew she was different. She knew that all the children in the road lived the same life, but one that was nothing like her own. Nellie was odd.

Late that afternoon she tiptoed along the landing and sat on the top stair. She needed the toilet but didn't dare ask. The street lights came on and she heard the children being called in for their tea. She couldn't hear a sound in the house. There was no movement from downstairs. No light. The house could have been empty, but Nellie knew it wasn't. Alice never went out. She could sense Alice, sitting in her chair, staring vacantly into the fire, or standing in the dimness of the bedroom, staring out at the street.

Nellie went back to lie on her bed. She was cold and sore and despite a desperate need for the toilet, which had distended her tummy and made pain wash over her in waves, she still didn't dare ask.

Lost in her thoughts, she didn't hear Alice come into the room.

'Get up,' she barked, hovering in the doorway, reluctant to even step into the room that was Nellie's world. 'Go to the outhouse and then to the kitchen to eat, before your father comes home. Then you can get back into bed.'

Her ominous form disappeared from the frame of the doorway almost as soon as it had arrived. Nellie was so lonely that even the arrival of Alice at her bedroom door momentarily dispersed the sadness, if only to replace it with fear.

Nellie did as she was told. She couldn't object and, anyway, she was so desperate for the toilet, she flew down the stairs, terrified that she would soil herself. God alone knew what the consequence of that would be.

Before going, she looked back at the new yellow street light that had been erected directly outside, casting a warm and comforting glow into her room. It wasn't all bad. If she was in her bed when her da got home, she knew he would come in to say goodnight. She also knew she would be too scared to tell him about her beating.

That she would hide the bruise on her arm away from him. That she would not be able to answer him when he asked her what she had done that day and, even at her young age, she would see the hurt and worry in his eyes when his questions were met with silence. Jerry had not the intuition to realize that if Nellie gabbled with enthusiasm on the days she spent at Maura's, there must be something badly wrong on the days she didn't speak at all.

That evening, Jerry paused outside his back door, reluctant to go in. No other man on the streets knew how Jerry lived. He was the only man who had a wife and yet got his own breakfast. Dockers worked long physical hours, while the women stayed at home and ran the house. That was the way it was. Jerry was thankful that he and Bernadette had only one child. How would he have managed with half a dozen? No other man would know how to begin to cook his own breakfast or dinner. No man on the four streets knew that was how it was for Jerry. To think that everyone once envied him for having the most beautiful, the most loving, the most perfect wife. And look at him now. If they knew how it had worked out for him, he would be a laughing stock. It wasn't only Nellie who lived a double life. Nellie and her father lived in the same house and shared a mutual love, but neither knew how the other existed for most of the day.

In the moments when Jerry allowed himself to dwell on the situation, he knew that a time would arrive when he would have to face facts and do something, but, more importantly, Alice would have to accept that something was seriously wrong. He had spent hours trying to find a way out, but there was none. He was trapped in a loveless marriage, forever. One drunken night of insanity and a lifetime to pay for it. He often reached the conclusion that it was no more than he deserved for having behaved so badly. But how much should a man have to pay for a mistake?

Alice's behaviour had become questionable from almost the minute they had married, although even he recognized it was getting much worse. She appeared to have huge difficulty in relating to Nellie, or to anyone, for that matter, other than Jerry. She had been different when they had first met, but not so much as to raise any real concern. Now, he felt her behaviour was deteriorating by the day. Still, on balance, he reassured himself, at least she was still managing to look after Nellie when she wasn't at Maura's. If he wasn't working, God knows what would happen to them.

When he reached this point, he always comforted himself with the thought that he couldn't have carried on the way he had been for much longer, struggling as a single father. If he had, someone would surely have reported him to the authorities.

Sometimes he thought that if he had managed to survive on his own until now, it might have become easier. Nellie was at school during the day. Her baby days were over, it was all so much easier now. Maura could have looked after Nellie after school and at weekends; he would have willingly paid her for that, if she had let him, and he could have paid Margaret O'Flynn in number eight to do a bit of cleaning. She had offered more than once. Why hadn't his head been clearer at the time? How had he let things get on top of him in the way they had? He had been swamped by grief. Unable to make a decision, or to think straight. What a mess.

Anyway, here they were now, him and his girl, and weren't they just getting on grand. He and his princess shared a lot of laughs and love, and that couldn't be bad.

When Jerry arrived home in the evenings, only Nellie knew that Alice was lying when she recounted Nellie's imaginary day to Jerry. He would often listen, in an absent-minded way, as he was removing his boots or having a wash-down at the kitchen sink. Sometimes Nellie's eyes would fill with tears and her bottom lip would tremble uncontrollably in relief at the sight of him. When that happened, Jerry would almost immediately notice. One evening, though, when he didn't notice Nellie's tears, he was taken by surprise.

He thought he had felt Nellie pull at his sleeve but when he looked, she was standing on the other side of the room by the door, looking at him with eyes about to spill over. He stared at his arm questioningly. He had felt a strong, firm tug on the cuff of his jacket; not once, but twice. Firm and decisive.

Once again, the temperature in the room had dropped. This was something that happened often, without reason. The fire could be blazing hot and yet he would feel the warmth in the room evaporate as though it were icy outdoors, even on a warm and sunny day, and then rise again just as quickly.

Without hesitation, he walked over to Nellie and picked her up. Although she was getting bigger, he lifted her onto the draining board so that she could sit next to him and watch him, whilst he washed away the grime and dirt from a day's dusty hard labour. He didn't ask her why she had tears in her eyes. He didn't dare.

He knew someone had pulled his jacket cuff. He also knew no one else was anywhere near. This wasn't the first time it had happened. He knew it was Bernadette. He felt she had never left the house and that she was there, watching them both.

On a clear night, he would often leave Alice listening to the radio and step out into the yard. He would look up at the sky, pick out his star and talk to Bernadette.

'Hey now, she's OK … I'm looking after her and she's gonna make ye really proud one day. We both miss you … loads and, God knows, I still love you, only you.'

He managed to go on only because Bernadette could still be seen daily, twinkling in the navy sky, reflected in the street puddles and on the Mersey, flowing pink on heavy summer nights.

Jerry sighed heavily, and went indoors to Alice.

That night, Jerry went into Nellie's room and sat on the edge of her bed to say goodnight. Nellie rubbed the back of her da's hand with her finger and traced the blue veins that ran from his arm up to the base of his large stubby fingers. She pressed each thick, knobbly vein down with her finger and pushed the blood slowly out, watching it spring back and fill as she lifted her finger off. She picked up her da's hand and pressed his palm into her face, inhaling the smell of molasses, grain and jute.

Jerry studied her. She had no words for him, but absorbed and distracted herself with his hands. He noticed her bed was damp. He smelt something in the room he didn't like. Was it fear?

When he bent down to kiss her goodnight on the top of her head, she buried her face in his chest and clasped her hands tightly around his neck. She inhaled the smell of toil and labour, sweat and dust. He saw a scalp that, like his own, was red raw.

As Jerry left her room, he knew it was time to act. He was out of his depth. He had noticed her flinch as he tucked the blanket in around the top of her arms. She was too thin. As he held her, he could feel her ribs digging into him. Her eyes looked haunted and had great black shadows underneath them.

Something was seriously wrong.

It was time to put his pride on the back burner.

Later that night, when Alice had gone to bed, he sat down at the kitchen table with a paper and a pen and wrote to the only woman he knew who could help.

# Chapter Ten

A week later, while she was playing out on the green with Harry after school, Nellie stopped in her tracks. A lady walking down the street seemed to be looking over towards them. She looked familiar, but Nellie didn't know why. She was stout and well fed, which made her stand out; most of the women on the four streets were thin. Everyone Nellie knew in her life was right here, within fifty yards. The lady was wearing a black hat, with grey curls poking out, and a long black coat, with three buttons at the top and a velvet collar, that went almost all the way down to the floor and she carried a large bag. Nellie saw her stop and talk to Peggy and Sheila, who were chatting on the front step, then Peggy pointed straight at Nellie.

As the lady turned round, Nellie immediately knew she was kind;

she could tell by her round rosy cheeks and the fact that she hadn't stopped smiling since Nellie and Harry had spotted her.

'Why is Auntie Peggy pointing at me, Harry?' said Nellie. Every parent on the street was known as auntie or uncle to all the children.

'I dunno, Nellie,' said Harry, who automatically walked over and took Nellie's hand. That was Harry's job in life, to protect Nellie. 'That's a big bag, maybe she has some sweets in it,' he said, his voice high with expectation. They both stared as the lady came straight over to the two of them. Harry squeezed Nellie's hand tightly.

'Hello, Nellie,' said the lady. 'I'm your Nana Kathleen and I've come over from Ireland to stay and help you and your daddy.'

Nellie grinned. In her little mind, this meant Alice would be going and she was very excited. Nellie didn't remember Kathleen from when she was a baby, but when they were having their breakfast Jerry always read out the blue airmail letters that arrived every couple of weeks. It was like having a new chapter of a book read, each time one arrived. Nellie dreamt of visiting Ireland. Of riding her daddy's donkey, Jacko, and of meeting her uncles and seeing the river her daddy and her Grandad Joe had poached the salmon from. She could see it all in her mind's eye and she knew she was in love with Ireland, before she had ever even been.

Sometimes, when he'd finished reading out the letter, her da would tell her about her grandad and her nana, and the people who lived on the farms and ran the pub and the shops. Some of the stories made her laugh so much that she made him tell them to her over and over again. She loved to hear how the priest had drunk so much Guinness in the village pub one Saturday night that the following Sunday morning he was found, fast asleep, propped up against a headstone in the graveyard. He was still so drunk, he couldn't take the mass. Cuddled up next to him was Mulligan's pig, which had also been lost and had stuck close to the priest for warmth.

'I'm not sure who smelt the worst,' said her da, 'the priest, from the Guinness, or the pig!'

The story never failed to make Nellie squeal with laughter. Even though she had never been to Bangornevin or Ballymara, she imagined the scene, just as it had happened.

Nellie threw her arms around Kathleen's legs and cried. Nana Kathleen had come. This was the happiest day of her little life.

Nellie hadn't managed to hide her bruises from Jerry. He had seen the fingerprint marks on the top of her arms and noticed that the skin on her bright-red scalp was now the same colour as her hair. It was not an unusual occurrence on the four streets for kids to be given a good hiding for misbehaving, and as a child Jerry had received many a whacking himself from his own da. But with a girl it was different, and Jerry knew Nellie hadn't a bad or naughty bone in her body. Whatever Alice had hit her for, it wouldn't have been deserved. He also shared Maura's concerns at how skinny she was.

'Jaysus, Jerry, I've seen more meat on Murphy's pencil!' she frequently said to him, and she was right. Jerry couldn't understand it, as he had always believed that Alice fed her well.

Jerry had taken Nellie to Maura's every day since the night she had silently traced the veins on the back of his hand and he had seen her angry red scalp as he bent to kiss the top of her head. He hadn't said anything to Nellie, but she didn't complain about being taken. In fact, when he told her at breakfast, she began to cry, but she was laughing at the same time. This disturbed him. Clearly, Nellie didn't want to be in the house alone with Alice. When she arrived home from school, she went back to Maura's with Kitty and he called to collect her.

Jerry had acknowledged that he was sinking.

'I'm just a simple man and I'm struggling here,' he had confided to Maura and Tommy in the past. But now, he had taken action and, when Jerry told Maura what he had done, she also laughed and cried together with relief.

Once Maura knew that Jerry had written to send for Kathleen, she waited 'til Jerry and Tommy had gone to work and the kids were packed off to school, then out came the mops banging like jungle drums on the kitchen walls up and down the street. The women ran like mice up the entry, carrying children in their arms, curlers bobbing under scarves, some in slippers and not yet even dressed, with ciggies thrust into coat or apron pockets, to gather in Maura's kitchen and hear the news and each drink a bucket of tea.

Once Kathleen appeared on the scene, Nellie quickly realized that Alice wasn't going anywhere, after all, but things in the house altered dramatically. Alice accepted Kathleen's arrival meekly, and soon became almost subservient to her. Kathleen had a way with her. It was of no consequence to Kathleen that Alice was a Protestant, or that she had been married in a register office.

'What's done can't be undone, Maura,' she said, when Maura brought it up. 'I want to make progress, not dwell on the past.'

She quickly realized that there was something disturbingly wrong with Alice's basic character.

'God knows how he never saw it,' Kathleen wrote to her son back in Ireland, 'he must have been blinded with the grief.'

Kathleen was up for the battle. She had solved bigger problems than this.

One of the first things she did was to march Alice straight to Dr Brendan O'Cole. Surely there must be something he could do? Alice spent a while in with the doctor, who came out to chat to Kathleen afterwards. His own mammy and Kathleen had attended the same convent school back home.

'It's a personality problem, Kathleen, there's little medicine can do for that. But she's also suffering from anxiety, so I'm putting her on Valium, ten milligrams four times a day. You should see a great change altogether, but don't expect miracles. She wasn't brought up running free on the peat bogs, like we were. She had problems.'

'I thought as much, Doctor,' said Kathleen. She had actually changed Brendan's nappy when he was a baby, but felt it right and proper to award him the respect due to his position.

'Ye will cope, Kathleen, as my mammy would too. Ye will make a great difference to little Nellie's life by being here, I'm sure,' said Brendan, who felt about six years old when he was talking to Kathleen.

'Aye, I hope so. I've never been so wanted in all me life before, which leads me to believe something must have been very wrong.'

Alice left the doctor's surgery with a prescription for medication that meant she now spent much of the day staring peacefully into the fire, rather than standing at the bedroom window, glaring at the street. Every now and then, she even smiled.

Kathleen was relieved to have been sent for. What Jerry didn't know was that Maura had written to Kathleen often and pleaded with her to come back and visit, but Kathleen had always said no. Any request for help had to come from Jerry himself. He had to want Kathleen to be there.

On her first visit, she stayed for six weeks. Then she went home for three and came back again for another six. Jerry's daddy, Joe, had passed away a year since. Kathleen's sons had almost all married, and they and their wives managed the farm and the house while she was away.

Kathleen established a routine in the house, which even Alice managed to adapt to. Having Kathleen around taught Alice how a real mother behaved. It was the first time in Alice's life she had known normality. She still had no love for Nellie, which was obvious to Kathleen, but Kathleen also knew that Jerry had made his choice and it was now Kathleen's job to pick up the pieces. Alice was his wife, in God's eyes or not.

Nellie was in heaven. Kathleen brought everything into the home a mother should and, as time passed, Nellie loved the way that all the women now popped into their house for a chat and to have a fuss with Nana Kathleen. It was as if she was everyone's mammy. Alice never made a word of complaint; she knew she couldn't.

Maura never dreamt it would be possible for things to alter as much as they had. For the first time, Jerry's back door began to open and people walked in. Nellie noticed the women never spoke much to Alice. It was now definitely Nana Kathleen's house. The cuckoo in the nest had been put firmly in her place. But it really didn't matter; on forty milligrams of Valium a day, Alice couldn't have cared less.

'Writing to me mammy was the best thing I have ever done in

me life,' Jerry said to Tommy, one day soon after Kathleen's arrival. 'Even Nellie is putting on the weight now. We all are.'

'What could I say to him?' said Tommy to Maura, when he got home that night. 'I wanted to say, aye, well, what's the use of Alice, why didn't you just send for Kathleen in the first place?'

'Because he's a man and he's proud,' said Maura, 'and, like with all men, pride comes before a fall.'

Kathleen's price for staying was for Jerry to trip down to the off-licence every Friday and Saturday night and bring her back two bottles of Guinness. She would put the poker into the fire and, when it was red hot, plunge it into the Guinness.

'That's me iron, Queen,' she would say to Nellie, who watched this ritual with fascination.

On Fridays, Kathleen went down to the bingo with all the other women and even took Alice with her once or twice. Kathleen was teaching Alice to knit; although she wouldn't touch baby clothes, she had been knitting Jerry a scarf for weeks.

Life settled down into a steady pace. The kitchen was like an advice surgery every morning and Nellie loved listening to the problems that everyone brought to Nana Kathleen.

One morning young Sheila came in, crying, with her newborn baby. She had four now and looked exhausted.

'Kathleen,' she cried, 'this babby hasn't slept a minute since it was born, what am I to do, I'm near at me wits' end.'

It took Kathleen mere seconds to diagnose the problem. 'A baby with cold feet never sleeps,' she said. 'Get some socks and some booties on its feet. Here, give him to me.'

Kathleen sat in front of the range with the baby on her lap and his bare feet facing the fire. She rubbed and warmed his feet between her hands and, slowly, the baby calmed. Within ten minutes, he was sleeping soundly. Nellie sat and grinned, feeling very important in having such a nice and clever nana.

Her life had been totally transformed. She now loved going to school and when she arrived home she ran in and out of the house with the other kids to play, rather than go straight to her room as Alice had made her. Her Nana Kathleen would be waiting for her with a mug of tea and a rock cake she had baked that afternoon, and often she and Harry would sit and eat it together before they ran outside. It was almost as though Alice didn't exist.

It transpired over the weeks that Kathleen was the only woman on the street who didn't have the time of day for Father James.

'He gives me the creeps, that man. Mind, I'll hold me tongue and say that to no one but you, Jerry, but he makes the hair on the back of me neck stand up when I see him walking up the street in his big fancy hat.'

Father James sensed Kathleen's reserve and kept his distance. He knew he had met his match. There was no charming Kathleen or pulling the wool over her eyes. She was polite enough at mass, but he knew not to chance a social visit.

Kathleen tried out her reservations on Maura one morning, when they saw Father James leaving Brigie's house down the road. Brigie had been blessed with eight daughters and not a single son.

'That man should be spending more time in his own church and less in other people's houses, if you ask me,' Kathleen said. 'Back home, the priest calls only for a birth, or the last rites. No other good reason for him to be dropping by all the time.'

Maura looked shocked. 'Kathleen,' she said in a pained voice, 'we are lucky to have the Father and grateful to him for sticking with us. He's so well thought of now, he could be in a cathedral, and Rome was wanting him to go to New York, but no, he stayed with us and we won't hear a bad word against him.'

Kathleen knew better than to argue, with no more than her suspicions to go on. Kathleen just knew. In her older years, she had learnt to size people up pretty quickly and Father James wasn't coming out well.

One day the Granada TV rental van arrived on the street and soon almost all the houses had a TV set, with a grey sixpenny meter on the back, installed in pride of place in their front room. Once a week, the man from Granada would come round to empty the box.

He would count all the sixpences on the floor in front of the TV and then write the amount down in a little black book.

He liked Nana Kathleen, who always gave him a cup of tea and a slice of freshly baked cake, while he told her the business of every house in the four streets. The Granada man was very observant; nothing got past him. It was through the TV man's visits that Nana Kathleen heard a lot more about Father James, and she didn't like much of what she heard. She also knew everything there was to know about every neighbour and what was occurring in every house. A cup of tea and a slice of cake paid enormous dividends.

With television, life altered overnight. Instead of listening to the voices coming out of the radio or staring into the fire, everyone sat and watched the telly. Times were changing. Jerry began to comb his hair like Elvis and in the mornings as he shaved he sang the Beatles song, 'Love, love me, do,' into the mirror above the sink. The Mersey beat was taking a grip and had filtered through onto the streets, where some of the houses were replacing their copper boilers and mangles with new, twin-tub washing machines. Nana Kathleen would not succumb. 'There's nowhere to store the ugly contraption, other than against the wall with a tablecloth thrown over to hide it. Why would I want to do that now? We have little enough room as it is,' she protested whenever the idea was brought up by a thoroughly modern Nellie. No one yet had a cooker, but they weren't far off, and nearly everyone now had a fridge.

On the day the letters arrived informing the residents that the four streets were to be added to a slum clearance list and they might be offered new houses, the jungle-drum mops went crazy. No one wanted to move and not a single letter was replied to. Everyone was happy to stay just where they were. One big happy family.

It was hard to believe that once things had been so bad and unhappy for Nellie and Jerry. That, not long ago, Nellie had been creeping down the stairs to avoid Alice and to sneak food from the cupboard, if she got the chance. Now she was woken by Nana Kathleen, shouting up the stairs, to tell her that her breakfast was ready.

'Skinny miss, get your lazy bones up and out of that bed now, before I send in ye da with a cold flannel!' she would shout, and Nellie loved it.

She was growing up and life had been constant and steady since Nana Kathleen had arrived. Thanks to Kathleen's luck at the bingo, Nellie had even been to Ireland for a holiday, visited her cousins and stayed at the farmhouse where she had become firm friends with her auntie Maeve and uncle Liam.

One Friday night, when she had been fast asleep, she had been woken by Nana Kathleen, sitting on her bed and singing. The landing light was on and Jerry was standing behind her, laughing.

'Come on, Ma,' he said, 'let's get ye into bed.'

'No, Jerry,' she protested, 'I have news for my Nellie. Tomorrow, Nellie, me and you, we is going on a holiday to Ireland, so we is. I've just won the jackpot on the bingo tonight and we are going home to celebrate.'

Nellie sat up in bed, hugging her knees, looking at her da. Could this really be true? Would she really see the church and the Moorhaun River?

'Will I see the salmon jumping, Nana?' she squealed, now wide awake.

'Oh sure ye will, that and more,' said Nana Kathleen as the Guinness took over and she collapsed onto Nellie's bed and was out like a light.

True to her word, the next morning, Nellie had all of her few clothes packed into Nana Kathleen's carpet bag and they took the boat to Dublin, the same boat Jerry and Bernadette had met on. Nellie felt like the luckiest girl in the world. She didn't know anyone else who had been on a holiday.

She was so happy she thought she would burst with sheer joy. Nana Kathleen was her angel.

A few weeks after they returned from Ireland, Nellie came down to overhear a conversation between her da and Kathleen that made her realize all was not well.

'I know the signs sure enough, Jerry, and only you will know if I'm right. I'd say she was about four months' gone.'

The blood left Jerry's face, as he sat down on the chair. 'For feck's sake, Mam, are ye sure?'

'I've seen enough, I'm sure all right,' said Kathleen. 'Alice is pregnant.'

Jerry couldn't help being delighted at the news, but he was also anxious. He had long ago given up hope of having another child and he wasn't at all sure how Alice would cope.

Very soon after the wedding, Jerry had decided that sex with Alice was cold and pointless. She would deploy any number of reasons to avoid it and after the rare occasions when it did happen, she would assiduously sit in the bath and douche herself, using a soft rubber hose and a solution she had bought from the pharmacist, for at least half an hour afterwards to ensure she wasn't pregnant. Jerry would lie in bed, smoking a cigarette and listening to the sound of his would-be babies being flushed down a tube. He would look through the window, listening to the distant tugs on the river, feeling bad and swearing that this would be the last time. He didn't know how Alice managed it, but each time they had sex, he felt more alone than he ever had before.

Whilst Alice slept, he often lay in bed, wide awake and looking at the stars, thinking of Bernadette. It was his way of keeping her in his sight. Bernadette was a star, one he could see each night and talk to. In the weeks following the funeral, he would take Nellie out into the yard, shuffle her up in his arms and turn her face to the night sky for Bernadette to see. Holding her in his large palms, he whispered to the twinkling inky night sky, 'Here she is, just look at her, she's putting on weight every day and just take a look at those big blue eyes, who do they belong to then, eh?'

He would frequently dwell on the issue of his own sanity. He felt as if Bernadette had never actually gone. The unexpected suddenness of her death had left him unable to grasp the reality. In the early days, he thought he could hear her running up the stairs, feel her breath, sense her sadness. At night, when he left Nellie's room, the hairs on his arms stood on end as though someone had swept in as he walked out, brushing close as they passed him. But he knew that was truly mad.

*

Kathleen stayed as long as she could, but she had to go back to Ireland ready for the birth of her third son's grandchild in her own house. She promised to return in time for the birth of Nellie's little brother or sister. Jerry knew that once Kathleen had left, Alice tried everything possible to rid herself of the baby. She soaked her soul in gin and took various concoctions of pills bought from a dodgy nurse on Scotland Road who looked after the girls who serviced the sailors whilst they were in port.

But the baby hung on in and slipped out, with the minimum of fuss, at four o'clock one cold and foggy morning, three weeks before he was due. An early morning star.

They had been woken from their sleep by the sound of Alice's waters breaking, like a champagne cork suddenly popping in the room. As soon as he realized things were happening fast, Jerry left Alice lying moaning in bed, and ran to the pub, the nearest place that had a phone he could use, to call the midwife. Alice had refused to attend a hospital.

Neighbours were well used to the odd hours people ran up and down their street to get to the pub for the phone. Births and deaths never happened conveniently during opening hours. As he ran, not a single set of dentures, soaking in pink Steradent, rattled in their glass on a bedside table. Nor did the sound of boots on cobbles disturb a stray ship's rat, raiding the bins. In the dead of the night, only the feral, hungry cats sitting on top of entry walls and bin lids looked curiously through the smog, with interest, at a man in his boots and pyjamas, frantically trying to knock down the pub door. Quietly.

When Noleen, the midwife, arrived at the house, she asked how Jerry was going to manage the new baby, with Kathleen back in Mayo. Noleen, who had made a few house visits, was fully aware of how much Kathleen carried the house and that there were problems with Alice. Work on the docks was thin and big men like Jerry who could get it were working every hour God sent, to make sure they kept their place in the gang. That way they got to keep their jobs.

'I have no idea, Noleen, but Mammy will be back as quick as she can,' he said as he lit the fire in the bedroom, which had been set ready for weeks, whilst Noleen set to work with calm and authoritative efficiency.

She knew she was chancing her luck when, once the baby was born and she had cut the cord, she lifted him without any warning and plopped him down onto his mother's chest. It was a risk, but she considered it worth a try. As she laid the baby down, his wide open eyes looked into his mother's and begged for acceptance.

'Would you look at him, all knowing,' said Noleen, with forced gaiety, grinning from ear to ear. Like all Irish Catholic midwives, she regarded each birth as a miracle and a gift. It never crossed her mind to wonder why such a good God gave poor women so many babies whose mouths they couldn't feed, and why he chose every now and then to make one of them bleed so much from forcing yet another child out of a tired and shot womb that they died in her arms before the ambulance arrived. Noleen was a kind woman and genuinely took a delight in every delivery she attended.

'Sure, he's been here before, that little fella, so he has,' she trilled.

For just a moment, a tiny moment, suspended in the warmth of a room imbued with the love and magical hope a new baby brings, there was a chance. Noleen's words had penetrated Alice's fog, and caught her up in the expectation heaped upon her. Alice thought she would dig deep inside and try to give motherly love a go. She met her newborn son's eyes, as Noleen and Jerry watched, holding their breath.

She tried. They could see she tried, for a second, but then, just when Jerry and Noleen looked at each other and dared to hope, Alice turned her head away and stared into the fire.

'Take him, will you,' she said to Jerry, 'and call him what you wish.'

This time Jerry's tears were not of joy, but of sorrow, as he knew with total certainty his prayers were unheard.

Jerry and Alice had been sleeping with a brown rubber sheet on the mattress for weeks, in case of this very eventuality, a sudden birth, and so it took the midwife only an hour to clean up mother and baby, change the bed and throw a shovel of coal from the bucket onto the fire, before she sat on a chair by the fire to write her notes.

Jerry woke Nellie, despite the fact that Alice begged him not to, and told her the news. Her reaction to the new baby was something he couldn't predict. He had been too scared to discuss it with her before the event. He had wanted to share his joy with her but she was only a child. He needed to know as soon as possible how Nellie was going to take to the new arrival in the house.

Nellie, dressed in her long flannelette nightdress, rubbed her bleary eyes and, clutching her teddy, padded across the landing to her da's bedroom, her hand in his. His big palm felt hot but the lino was cold beneath her feet. It was the first time Nellie had ever seen the fireplace in her da's room with a roaring fire in the grate. Only a single bedside lamp was alight and the room was warm, filled with a golden glow. The reflection of the flames chased each other as they danced and crackled up the walls and across the ceiling.

Although she was now too big to carry, Jerry lifted Nellie into his arms. Her red curls, now grown past her shoulders, tickled his nose and face as, half asleep, she sucked her thumb, a habit she still couldn't break at night. Her other arm was hooked tightly around her father's neck, as he carried her round to the far side of the bed, to look into the crib. Noleen looked on and smiled at what was an intimate and special moment, when a little girl meets, for the first time, her brand-new baby brother.

Jerry felt sick and tearful with relief when he saw Nellie's face as her eyes alighted upon her baby brother. She took her thumb out of her mouth and lovingly grinned from ear to ear. She kissed her father's cheek hard and took away his tears with her lips, whilst her hand clasped his other cheek hard. His eyes shut tight while he suppressed the pain that had rushed unbidden out of his heart, as he remembered the moments of her birth.

Nellie, barely containing her excitement, squealed and wriggled in his arms, to get down and closer to the baby.

'Let's call him Joseph!' she exclaimed, clapping her hands together and feeling very clever. It was almost Christmas, and that day at school Father James had spoken at mass about what a great man Joseph had been to take on a pregnant single mother, Mary. With her wide eyes gleaming, she turned excitedly to Alice who was neither watching nor listening.

So, Joseph he became.

Alice was untouched by the endearing scene and continued to stare into the flames. She had given up trying to find within herself whatever other women had that enabled them to give a fig about their children. There had been years of arguing and grief from Jerry. Shame heaped upon her by the neighbours she watched from her window, acting like good mothers should. She had become the living proof that a Catholic man had committed a mortal sin when he married a Protestant woman. In the words she had heard Maura speak to Tommy on the day of their wedding: 'Surely, as God is anyone's judge, no good will come of it.'

She lay with both hands on her belly, as though nursing a wound. She was unreachable.

A few days later, once Jerry had returned to work, Nellie answered the front door, with Joseph in her arms. She had been kept off school for the week whilst they waited for Kathleen to return, and until Alice recovered a little from the shock of giving birth. Jerry had not explained this, but they both knew someone needed to be there to look after Alice, as much as Joseph. She knew that when she went back to school, if Nana Kathleen hadn't yet managed to return, Maura was going to come in to help feed and change the baby, even though Jerry hadn't managed to get Alice to agree to this yet. But even without Alice's agreement, Maura had already been in once this morning, as had Noleen the midwife. They had all given Nellie so many instructions that her head felt as if it was going to collapse and fall off her shoulders.

Julia, her classmate and friend from down the road, was going to pop in on the way home from school with her mammy, Brigie. Yesterday morning they had both arrived with a large, navy-blue, Silver Cross carriage pram, already made up with soft white flannel sheets and a net covering the opening of the hood.

'The pram is still warm from the baby in number four, who's been turned out into a pushchair to make way for Joseph,' joked Brigie. 'The little fella won't know where he is when he wakes up!'

There was a little hand-knitted teddy on the pillow, popped into the pram as it went down the street by one of the neighbours with a handwritten card. There were freshly baked scones in a bag with a little note from Mrs Keating and a hand-knitted white baby cardigan that Mrs O'Brien kept handy in the drawer for new arrivals on the four streets. Now that hers were all grown up and she had a bit more time on her hands, it was her job to knit the matinee coats. There was also a pile of pale-blue baby clothes and folded terry-towelling nappies, all of which had already been through a number of little boys in the street, washed and pressed ready for use, contributed to by almost every house.

Finally, there was a triangular paper packet full of tea leaves. The four streets were never short of tea. At all times, in one of the back-yards, kept dry in a coal house, there was always a wooden tea chest full of leaves, courtesy of a dock gang catching it off the back of a hull.

A brown earthenware pot with the Pacific Steam Line logo embossed on the lid, wrapped up in newspaper, sat under the pram canopy. It was full of an Irish stew for the evening. There was also a loaf of bread and three sausage rolls, the pastry still hot, and three vanilla slices from the corner bakery.

The pram contained all that was needed for a new baby, plus a feast. Nellie wasn't aware of it, but there had been a collection of halfpennies down the road for the extra meat for the stew and the pastries. She certainly felt the weight of responsibility on her shoulders with the new baby, but she knew she wasn't on her own; there was an entire community to help and support her and her da.

Later in life, as a young woman living amongst those who became obsessed with the material value of their house, car or next holiday, Nellie often looked back in wonder at the resourcefulness, compassion and love that existed in such a poor community, which had nothing to call its own. It didn't often know how the next meal would arrive onto the table, but it took comfort and pride in knowing it had everything of any real value: family, good neighbourliness and friendship.

As she opened the front door, thinking it would be one of the neighbours and grateful with expectation, her heart sank to see Father James standing on the step. She noticed his hands were empty.

'Saints preserve and save us,' he exclaimed when he saw the child straining with the effort of holding a baby. 'Where's ye heathen mammy?'

Nellie had been told not to answer him, and so she didn't. The priest knew her father was at work and launched into a tirade of instructions for Nellie.

She caught bits about Alice needing to be 'churched'.

'The baby needs to be brought into the light and absolved of the original sin. Do ye hear me, Nellie? He needs to be brought up as a Catholic and not a Protestant, as your sinful self has been,' he spluttered.

Nellie didn't reply.

'Do ye not know your own mother would spin in her grave if she knew what the ways of your father have become, since the poor woman's passing?' he went on.

Nellie stood and stared. The hallway of the house was long, narrow and dark. Although tiny, the baby weighed heavily in her arms. She looked over her shoulder to the door of the kitchen and waited, expecting Alice to come through it and save her from this angry priest. But nothing happened.

She had struggled to open the door and not drop the precious baby, who needed her so badly. Closing it was easier. She shuffled forward and, without looking up at him, lifted her foot slightly and kicked the door shut in the priest's face. As the door swung to, his shouting became louder, as though he thought the increased volume would prevent its closure, and the baby began to cry.

Once the door had safely banged shut, she could see his shadow, still silhouetted through the two mottled sheets of opaque glass. His hat made his profile look more like that of a gangster than a priest. He wasn't going to give up that easily although the closed door muffled the noise. She wished hard that he would just go away. She shuffled over to the foot of the stairs and sat herself down on the bottom step, taking care not to trip over the long shawl her father had brought home – it never failed to surprise her how much fell off the back of a seagoing liner – and had left out to be wrapped around the baby to keep him warm.

As she lifted Joseph onto her knee and adjusted his position, he turned his head towards her chest, pecking frantically like a little bird in the nest looking for food. She had no idea what he was doing. Light and warmth flooded the hallway as Alice opened the kitchen door. Her footsteps sounded, slow and heavy, on the linoleum as she walked down the hallway.

She made no mention of the priest as she handed Nellie a bottle and said, 'Here, give him that. It will shut him up.' She turned on her heel and walked back into the kitchen and the warmth of its fire, closing the door behind her as she went.

The previous evening, Nellie had sat and helped her father feed the baby when he got home from work. She had watched him change the disgusting nappy, full of his black and dark green meconium. She had held the baby's head whilst her da splashed water on his bottom and she had shaken the Johnson's talcum powder over him, creating a cloud that made them both splutter and laugh. She helped to fasten the nappy pin, terrified she might put it through his wiggly bits. Her father showed her how to put the back of her hand on the inside of the nappy, flat against Joseph's abdomen, as a shield, to stop that happening. And Nellie had giggled as little Joseph decided, once again, to empty his bladder, which went straight into her father's face as he bent to fold the new nappy over his son.

How she wished her da was here now and not at work. How she wished Nana Kathleen would hurry back. She was still shaken from the priest's visit. He had finally moved away from the door. She nervously put the teat of the bottle into Joseph's tiny mouth. He helped her out by latching on immediately and suckled frantically while his wide-open eyes stared gratefully into hers.

She was overcome with love for him. She knew Alice's coldness better than anyone and that her job would be to protect him, whilst her da or Nana Kathleen couldn't be there. She shifted her arm under Joseph's back and brought her hand up to support his neck. As she cradled him in her arms, she whispered into the side of his face, 'Don't worry, Joseph, I will look after you.' Her tears fell from her cheeks onto the floor. Lonely and lost, she never felt the ghostly arms slip gently around her shoulders, or the tender kiss on her own cheek, but she did suddenly feel much better.

## Chapter Eleven

It was a normal morning on the street. As Nellie crossed the road to 'run a message' to the shop on the corner, she heard Peggy shouting at the school welfare officer.

'I have five feckin' pair of shoes and nine kids, would ye like to choose which feckin' kids stay at home, come on then, come on in, will ye, King Solomon, and choose.'

Peggy stood back and held the front door open, to usher the welfare officer into the house, at which point he banged his book shut and fled down the street. He was no stranger to being shouted at but Peggy scared him more than most.

'Do ye think I want four feckin' kids hangin' round me neck all day, eh? You don't come here, mister, and complain about my kids not being in school until you bring some feckin' shoes with you. Can you 'ear me?'

He was already gone, speeding away in his Morris Minor up the Vauxhall Road.

'There, he won't be back in a hurry,' said Peggy to no one in particular, before she went back inside and carried on shouting, this time at the kids.

He would be back, without the shoes. Peggy would shout at him, again. He would flee to his car, as always, and on it went, a well-rehearsed, recurring drama.

'Jeez, can you hear Peggy giving out,' said Maura to Kitty, who was on her way out of the door to school. 'She will be giving this street a bad name, the way she's carrying on, so she will. I'm going to ask Kathleen to talk to her.' Kathleen was back and settled into number forty-two. Her son Liam and his wife Maeve were running the farm back home so Kathleen had decided to stay put in Liverpool, until her job of bringing up Nellie was done.

Maura had made the same comment to Tommy the previous evening, although he didn't appear to be convinced it was a good idea.

'Why don't you have a chat with her yourself?' Tommy had said, thinking that it would surely be a useless exercise anyway. A letter from the Pope wouldn't stop Peggy shouting.

'Because I don't want to fall out with me next-door neighbour and she has respect for Kathleen, her being older and all that,' said Maura.

'Maura, me love, our street is on the list for slum clearance, how much worse a name can we get than that, I ask ye?' Tommy said reasonably.

Maura had muttered on under her breath, that the only way she would be taken out of her house would be in a box, but Tommy had stopped listening. He was studying the form of the horses for the three-thirty at Kempton, his newspaper laid out on the kitchen table. The children were growing and the sanctuary of the outhouse was no longer his; there would always be one or the other knocking on the door for him to get out.

Tommy didn't really mind. He had never raised his voice to any of his offspring and they all regarded him as a big softie, compared to every other da on the street, other than Jerry. Their peers often felt the belt or the slipper. All Maura's children knew how lucky they were to have such a gentle man as their da and he was adored by them all.

Tommy took the pencil from behind his ear, ready to draw a circle round the name of his favourite filly, and became aware that someone was standing next to him. He looked up to see Kitty by his side.

'Hello, Queen, where's your mother?' said Tommy, in sudden surprise.

'She's gone next door to see Kathleen,' said Kitty, as she pulled out a chair and sat down at the table next to him.

'Jaysus, thank God for that, I thought I'd gone deaf there for a minute, Kitty.'

He looked sideways at Kitty and they both burst out laughing, something they used to do all the time, but getting a laugh out of Kitty these days was much harder work than it ever had been when she was little.

Tommy folded the paper, a natural subconscious gesture, which he had no idea he was making, in order to show Kitty she had his full undivided attention.

'Is everything all right, Queen?' he asked.

'Aye, Da, not bad. I'm taking the kids out for a picnic to the Pier Head to see the ferry.'

Kitty always spoke in the same tone these days. No ups or downs, no stream of chatter, interspersed with giggles. Tommy thought to himself that Kitty was like half the child she once was. A bright burning lamp turned down to dim. It was a long time now, years even, since he had seen the old Kitty.

'Grand,' said Tommy, 'but have ye been afflicted with a blindness, Kitty? Have ye not noticed, it's fecking freezing and there's snow on the ground? What kind of picnic is that?'

They laughed again as Kitty explained, 'Da, there's been snow for months. I'm going crazy being stuck indoors.'

Then she became sombre, as she came to the real reason she had sought out Tommy, just as soon as she could get him on her own.

'Da, will ye do me a favour?' she said, quietly, glancing nervously over her shoulder and out of the kitchen window to see if Maura was returning.

'Aye, Queen, what is it?' He had already reopened the paper, but now looked up and closed it again. He could sense Kitty was about to ask him something serious.

'I don't want to be confirmed, Da. I don't want to go to the Priory for me confirmation lessons and I'm too scared to tell me mam,' she said in a rush.

'Jaysus, Kitty,' spluttered Tommy. 'Why don't ye ask me to tell her ye is joining the circus, it'd be easier.'

'I know, Da, but I just don't want to and I know she will give out so much.'

Tommy smiled. This was the daughter Maura still hoped might one day become a nun. He was secretly pleased. It was the last thing he wanted for his precious Kitty.

For a man who only ever wanted a quiet life, breaking this bombshell to Maura was not something he would look forward to, but he wouldn't let his princess down.

'Come here and give yer da a hug. I'll find a way, Queen. I don't know how right now, but I will do me best.'

'Thanks, Da,' said Kitty as she hugged him tight. She closed her eyes and wished she could be honest with him, but the shame wouldn't let her.

Nellie had arrived at the corner shop.

'Two ounces of red cheese, please,' she said as she handed the money over to Sadie, the shopkeeper, to ring into the till.

'OK, Nellie love, here you go, and tell Nana Kathleen to grate it now, as it will go further. And don't forget to let her know I will be over on Saturday morning for me tea leaves now, will yer, Queen?'

Nellie loved the fact that everyone wanted to pass a message to Nana Kathleen, even the teachers at school. Nana Kathleen had become everything from a Sunday school teacher to a marriage guidance counsellor, and she was the fount of all knowledge. No one knew how she did it, but nothing got past Nana Kathleen and there wasn't one bit of gossip she didn't already know by the time she was told it. She wasn't a gossip herself, but the keeper of all secrets. Nana Kathleen's friendship with the Granada TV man was paying dividends. It was amazing the rewards she could reap, for nothing more than a cup of tea and a slice of cake.

Kathleen read the tea leaves and her reading day was on a Saturday. The house became like Lime Street station as every woman from miles around came to have their tea leaves read. She sat at the head of the kitchen table whilst Nellie and Kitty made cups of tea and the women went in and out all morning.

Her palm had to be crossed with silver, which meant everyone paid sixpence, and it was the sixpences that paid for the two bottles of

Guinness. But if Nana Kathleen thought someone was stretched for the money, as they went to give her the sixpence, she would press an extra one back into their own palm so they came out sixpence up, as well as feeling better for hearing a bit of good news in the tea leaves.

'Kathleen's so good,' said Brigie to Peggy, one morning as, having left Kathleen's kitchen, they were walking down the entry to their own back doors. 'How could anyone have known I had a letter from America last week? I've told no one and it's been sat on the mantelpiece next to the telly since it arrived.'

'Sure, it's a mystery, so it is,' said Peggy, 'and no wonder she gives Father James short shrift, she wouldn't want him spoiling our fun, now would she.'

'I'm amazed Maura hasn't kicked up, her being so religious an' all that, but even she's getting her tea leaves read, can ye imagine and their Kitty's even making the tea!'

Both women roared with laughter on their way home, one thinking there was a windfall on its way, and another expecting a surprise visitor from overseas and a letter from a tall government building. No one ever questioned that there was never any bad news from Nana Kathleen on a Saturday morning. Bad news was as rare as Irish sunshine in Mayo on an April morning.

Kitty ran up to Nellie, as she left the shop.

'Nellie,' she called, 'let's collect up Joseph and the kids and walk them down to the Pier Head and watch the ferries, do ya fancy that?'

Nellie dashed back home with Kitty and began the process of packing Joseph into his pram for the trip. They were going to take Harry, but he had just fallen over on the entry cobbles and skinned the top of his knee. Maura was liberal with her brown iodine on cut knees and it smarted like nothing else.

'Blow, blow, BLOW!' they could hear her shouting, as far as three doors away, while she sloshed the pungent-smelling liquid onto Harry's knee. It stung like hell, as his screams ripped the morning air.

They collected Peggy's latest baby, to pop into the Silver Cross with Joseph, and sat a couple of toddlers on the navy-blue apron.

Another was so desperate to join in, she lay on the wire shopping tray underneath. There were six little ones from various houses on the streets, holding onto various parts of the chrome frame and the handles, all trotting along beside Kitty and Nellie. They looked like travellers moving a caravan to a new destination.

Tucked down either side of the pillows to keep them warm were bottles of formula for the babies when they woke. Two empty glass pop bottles full of water were pushed down by the side of their legs for drinks for the other children during the day, along with a pack of Jacob's cream crackers, sandwiched together with jam and wrapped up in greaseproof paper. The closest Liverpool had to a delicacy.

They would be gone for only a few hours. The wind down at the Pier Head was biting, but Kitty didn't care. She had wanted to escape the four streets, to look out over the wide expanse of water. She felt for the first time in years as though she could escape the stress. Her da was going to stick up for her. She had been terrified at the thought of having to go to the priory for her confirmation lessons and being in the building alone with Father James. Her da was going to save her.

Maybe, if her ma was all right and didn't kick up a fuss, she could tell her parents about Father James and his visits to her bedroom. Even as she thought it, though, she knew she would never have the courage to take that step. She still couldn't risk not being believed, of having to justify what she was saying. She would have to live with the shame until she could get away altogether, but she was worried about Angela. Would he move on to Angela next?

The little ones had enjoyed the change of scene and the adventure, but were starting to tire. As they headed back, two of Peggy's boys began misbehaving, and getting home took much longer than reaching the pier. The snow had begun to fall again and Kitty and Nellie were relieved to turn the corner at the bottom of the street. If only they had turned the corner either two minutes later or two minutes earlier, if only they had done lots of things differently that day, then disaster might never have struck.

*

Callum O'Prey had brought the car round to the house to show off to his mammy. Callum had spent his life searching for things to show off about and impress his mammy with. He used to be the fastest runner in the street, and for that he had the privilege of robbing the bread vans every time there was a 'bit of a do'.

Callum could cater a party for twenty out of the back of a bread van making a delivery. He stole to order. The more he stole, the more respected he felt. The van driver never knew where his sausage rolls and custard tarts ended up.

The car was a shiny, brand-new, grey Ford Anglia. No one else on the street owned a car. Neither did Callum. It was stolen.

People like Callum didn't own cars. The idea of stealing one to keep was just too fanciful; he wouldn't have known what to do with it. He fully intended to take it back to Dale Street, where he'd found it. He didn't even have a driving licence. Callum wasn't that much of a rogue; he was just an underprivileged boy from a loving home in desperate need to be someone, even if just for one day.

He wanted to be a big man, one his mammy could brag about, like Mrs Keating from next door did about her lad, who had become a sergeant in the army. Callum had tried to sign up, but had failed the medical on account of his chronic asthma, made worse by the roll-ups he chain-smoked each day.

'Sure,' Callum had said to the friend who was walking with him as he stole the car, but who refused to get in, 'yer man is inviting me to take a spin, or why would he have left the keys in it now?'

He had driven a few bangers before around the wasteland at the back of the garage where his pal, Michael, worked, and it had been easy. Callum was fascinated by cars and engines but, in his world, people from the four streets would never own a car. He wasn't very brave and hoped the owner was having a very long lunch so he could get the car back before anyone had noticed it had gone.

Today, he loved the smile on his mammy's face as he spun her the line about how a man in town had asked him to run a few messages in his car for him. He stayed just long enough to drink a cup of tea with his mammy, eat a cheese sandwich and have a show-off. He loved the fact that as he enjoyed his fifteen minutes of fame, every child on the street was hanging around the car, looking in through the windows and yelling through the door of the house, 'Callum, is that car yours, will ye give me a ride?'

'Oh, Callum,' his mammy trilled, 'fancy that, you driving round in a smart car. Yer man must know ye to be a trustworthy person, brought up the right way.'

She was even bragging at the door, as she saw him off to carry on with his errand, and shouted down the street to her neighbours, 'Would ye look at our Callum now, would ye,' her face flushed with pride and pleasure.

'Did ye not need lessons to drive that, Callum?' shouted Peggy from across the road, having known Callum since the day he was born.

'I can drive all right, Peggy, but I have to get back to yer man now,' Callum called as he dived back into the driver's seat, not wanting to answer any probing questions.

As Callum left the house, he felt like a hero and six feet tall, rather than the five foot two caused by a lack of meat and poor nutrition. He revved up the engine to impress everyone, as he let out the clutch. But the car went nowhere. It was winter and the road was frozen hard with packed ice. It had been cleared in town by the snowploughs, but in the four streets, as no one had a car, the area hadn't been touched. Callum's knowledge of driving was rudimentary and he pressed down harder on the accelerator, thinking that it would make the car move.

Fear crept into the pit of his belly and settled in, as he began to panic. He had to get the car back, before he was caught. His brother had already been sent down for thieving and Callum knew it would kill his mammy if the same happened to him. She would die with the shame. He now regretted, more than anything in his life, having taken the car. He heard a police siren in the distance, racing along the road, and imagined it was coming for him. It wasn't, but it made his heart beat faster in terror, nonetheless. The wheels began to spin on the ice and the car quickly gathered speed. Callum lost control and slammed his foot down hard on the brake, which made the spin worse.

He froze in fear as he saw people running down the street shrieking. He could hear a screeching noise coming from the engine, but didn't realize it was because his foot was now pressed down hard on the accelerator. It was all over in seconds, but, for years to come, Callum would play the scene out in his nightmares over and over, as though it had lasted for many minutes.

His mammy, as well as every child on the green and in the street, saw the car heading towards the girls, the pram and the children, and screamed hysterically for them to get out of the way. Suddenly aware of what was happening, Kitty pressed down hard on the handle of the pram, lifting the front wheels off the ground, and turned it round quickly to get round the corner, out of harm's way. Both Nellie and Kitty were in control and yelling at the kids to hold onto the pram, but the bigger ones had all scattered, terrified, as the car spun out of control. They had only just turned the pram round and moved it a few feet when they heard the screech of brakes.

As Nellie looked back over her shoulder, she and Kitty wailed with fright and ran, dragging the little children, still holding onto them.

That was when Nellie saw her again. Her red hair flew out behind her as she put both her arms out towards them and urgently whispered, 'Run, my darling, run.' At that moment, Nellie felt as though their feet left the ground and they were propelled twenty feet forwards, just before the car hit them – straight in the back – and then came to an abrupt halt.

Callum saw the look of horror on both of their faces as they went down like rag dolls, and the Silver Cross pram, with both the babies inside, lurched violently forward, before slowly meandering up and down over the cobbles, stopping only when it reached the kerb, taking itself home, like a trusty old nag. And, just for a tiny moment, all was silent.

Harry, even though he was in a state of shock, raced in through the back entry door to the kitchen, for his mam and for Kathleen, and then ran with Peggy to bang on the pub door, in order to use their phone to call for an ambulance. Maura ran screaming like a banshee to Nellie and Kitty.

Once Nellie hit the cobbled ground, the blood from the back of her head soaked into the snow to form a large, bright red halo around her, making her look like a figurine in the Russian icon that hung on the altar at St Mary's church. Kitty was out cold, lying with her arm flung out to the side.

The street erupted into chaos. The screaming and crying could be heard along all four streets and beyond, as people began running out of their homes and gathering round, huddling together from the cold and shock.

In a matter of moments, Nellie's face became paler and her lips turned blue, until the colour of her skin blended with that of the snow on which she lay. Flakes were settling on both girls' hair and remained frozen. A dusting of fallen crystals.

Kitty came round quickly and began to cry with the pain in her arm, shrieking for her mammy. But there was no sound from Nellie. Unconscious and hurt, with no lively spirit to offer a defence or protection, her vulnerability and frailty were exposed for all to see. She looked closer to death than life. A tiny and beautiful bird, broken in the snow.

One of the boys had been dispatched to the dock to fetch Jerry and Tommy. The women were whispering amongst themselves that even though the accident had happened only three doors down from Jerry's house, Alice had not appeared. Nana Kathleen was on her knees next to Nellie, stroking her arms and whispering soft words interspersed with prayers fearing the worst, while Maura tried to calm Kitty down.

'She has the energy to scream, Maura, that's a good sign, she will be all right,' said Kathleen, but the wise words did nothing to stem the flow of Maura's tears or silence her wailing.

Jerry and Tommy ran up the steps from the docks and collapsed onto their knees in the snow next to their girls. Jerry grabbed Nellie's hand and sobbed at the sight of his small scrap of life. The life he was supposed to protect and care for. This couldn't be happening. No God would be this cruel, he thought. His mind was frozen, not by the icy wind, but by fear, as he looked at his baby and felt his mother's arm slip across his back. Nellie opened her eyes, slowly, blinked and then closed them again. Blood was coming from the corner of her eye, which was badly cut.

Her cold blue lips suddenly moved as she said, 'Da, I can't open me eyes.'

Jerry sobbed with relief when, at that moment, they heard the ambulance bell as the van itself screeched and slid round the corner. Within minutes the drivers had the girls loaded onto stretchers and into the ambulance.

'Get back inside now, all of you, it's too cold to hang around out here. They will be well looked after in the hospital,' they told the anxious crowd.

Maura and Kathleen were allowed into the back along with the patients, before the drivers leapt into the cab and sped away.

Silence descended on the street while everyone stared at the retreating ambulance. It had all happened so quickly.

Callum was already in the Anchor, out of harm's way and close to passing out. Tommy and Jerry would likely want to kill him with their bare hands. Everyone now focused their attention on how to get Callum out of this hole and return the car to its rightful owner. The street looked after its own. Michael from the garage was sent for, then the police were telephoned and told about a mysterious car that had suddenly appeared on a garage forecourt.

As the ambulance pulled away, Jerry looked up to see Sheila with the pram, looking after the babies, and Peggy coming towards him and Tommy with mugs in her hand. As she walked up the road towards them, Brigie was shuffling along the ice with a bottle of Irish whiskey in her hand and a wake of little girls trotting after her.

'Hot sweet tea for ye both, for the shock,' Peggy said kindly.

'Here ye are,' Brigie said, as she poured the last drops from the bottle into both mugs. 'That'll help with the shock.'

Tommy, standing at Jerry's side as he knelt in the snow, said, 'Thanking ye, Peggy, and ye, Brigie.'

Jerry was speechless.

'C'mon, mate, we can't lose a day's pay,' said Tommy, trying to break into Jerry's thoughts. 'Let's get back now. They will be all right with Maura and Kathleen.' They both drained the mugs of sweet whisky and tea.

Tommy turned and walked towards his house in order to give instructions to the kids and to hand the mugs back to Peggy, who was talking with the other women. Jerry slowly got up from the ground and stood upright, wiping tears from his eyes that he could never have let Tommy see. The hot tea and whiskey burnt into his stomach and brought him to his senses.

Where was Alice? Why wasn't she here at his side? He looked at the road in front of the houses. The grit had been churned by fear and shock. The ice and snow stained with Nellie's blood.

As Jerry rose, he didn't see the extra, almost indiscernible, imprint of another pair of knees in the snow, alongside his own.

Upon admission to hospital, both girls were dispatched straight to the operating theatre. Several hours after the accident, they had been operated on and admitted to a cheerful children's ward, where they found themselves lying in beds, side by side.

The walls were painted white halfway up and then a pale blancmange pink to the top. Starting six feet above the ground so that no one could see in, huge Georgian windows reached up to the high ceiling. White iron-framed bedsteads were lined up against the walls in a regimental fashion, placed precisely six feet apart. Each top sheet was turned down over the pink counterpane by exactly eighteen inches. The rigorous attention to detail imposed exacting standards on the nursing staff and left no room for sloppiness.

Long, highly polished oak tables ran down the middle of the ward on which sat tall jars of flowers, books, cards, board games and the occasional toy. Around each bed stood a set of curtains on wheels, decorated with white bunnies playing in green fields, interspersed with the occasional bunch of yellow flowers. On a fine day, beams of sunshine tumbled in through the high windows and fell down onto the beds, radiating warmth, calm and innocence, in what was often the setting for high drama and despair.

The busy nurses' office, situated at the ward entrance, offered a clear view of the young patients almost to the very end of the ward, but not quite. The last bed, the 'night before home' bed, was tucked away around the corner. It was every child's aim to sleep in that very grown-up bed and to be on their way home the following morning.

Poorly and post-operative children slept in the beds nearest to the office and, as they recovered, were moved further down the ward. Recovery was measured in a daily physical progression, as beds were wheeled into new positions. Each morning, nurses would walk onto the ward in multiple pairs, like a small army, and cheerfully announce, 'Musical beds time, children.' It was the highlight of the day for those who were recovering and eager to go home.

Maura and Kathleen sat on long wooden benches in the corridor leading to the ward, waiting for the two girls to be returned from the operating theatre. Every time the ward door swung open, Maura would crane her neck to catch a glimpse inside.

Kitty's arm was broken and Nellie needed surgery, having caught one eye with force on the pram handle. Maura and Kathleen huddled together, talking in whispers and looking exactly how they felt when in the presence of authority: invisible and inferior. The antiseptic smell of the Lysol disinfectant, used to clean the hospital floor, left a distinctive aura that hung heavily in the air and added to the sense of fear and the unknown.

A sweet young nurse approached them, carrying a wooden tray. Her hair was swept into an immaculate bun, which provided a throne for her tall starched cap. She had brought them a metal pot of tea and two sage-green national issue cups and saucers, a little milk jug and sugar bowl, and a plate with four biscuits. She rested the tray on the bench beside Maura and Kathleen and then squatted down to be at a reassuring eye level with them both.

'Don't worry, they won't be much longer,' she said. 'Sister says you will be allowed to see them for five minutes but then, I am afraid, visiting is from two to three in the afternoon and six until seven-thirty at night.'

She smiled gently, almost apologetically, as though she could recognize mothers who would be torn by leaving their children in such a scary place as a hospital.

Maura was so overcome with relief at the nurse's kindness, she began to weep.

'Shush now,' said the nurse, 'there really is no need to cry. We are moving the beds around so that when they arrive back from theatre, we can put them next to each other for company and they really will be very well cared for and looked after.'

She put her hand in Maura's and squeezed it, as Kathleen put her arm round her shoulders. The resolve that had kept Maura calm and upright for the last three hours was disintegrating.

Kathleen was well aware that, even though she loved Nellie, she wasn't her mother. She was her nana and it was different. Maura had the right to be the more upset, the one who needed to be cared for, and the thought crossed her mind: poor Nellie. Kathleen loved her granddaughter and would do her best for her, and she would always be there for Nellie for as long as God spared her, but no one could replace a mother's love. Kathleen comforted Maura, knowing that, of the two of them, only Maura had an irrational fear sleeping in the pit of her stomach.

They thanked the nurse for the tea and then both stared at her straight back and precise walk as she glided back through the ward doors, her crepe-soled white shoes squeaking on the highly polished wooden floor.

'She was nice, considering she probably knows we are Irish,' said Maura matter-of-factly, wiping her eyes. 'Peggy's cousin is working on the roads in London and he says the boarding houses have signs in the window that say, no dogs, no blacks and no Irish, can ye imagine that?'

'Well, we could have been a pair of monkeys for all that nurse cares,' said Kathleen. 'She had a good heart and it helps to know she works here, where the girls will be.'

Kathleen poured the tea and handed a cup to Maura. They drank it gratefully, waiting to be summoned, and discussed how difficult visiting was going to be. No one on the four streets owned a car, and the route involved taking three buses. To be at the hospital for two o'clock would take up the whole day in travelling and the fare would seriously eat into the housekeeping. It was hard enough to make the money stretch until the Friday-night pay packet as it was. Everyone lived hand to mouth, week to week.

'If he's not dead already, I will kill Callum with me bare hands,' said Maura coolly. They both considered the possibility, and drank the remainder of their tea in silence.

Nellie could hear voices around her in the dark. The strong smell of Lysol from the operating theatre had got up her nose, causing her to cough and panic. As she lifted her hand to touch her eyes and felt the crepe bandage wrapped around her face, fear took over. Kathleen had never known her granddaughter scream before, but she recognized it was Nellie just as soon as she heard it.

Kathleen didn't wait any longer to be invited in; she ran through the ward doors and followed the scream. Nellie was in the first bed; in the second, lying quietly and half asleep with her arm in plaster, was Kitty. Three nurses stood round Nellie's bed, two holding her down to stop her from thrashing around, whilst one tried to refasten her bandages. Nellie was furiously trying to kick her legs free from the nurses who were holding her down, either in pain or in terror, fighting to break free from their grip.

As Kathleen approached the bed with Maura in her wake, she saw something that made her stop dead in her tracks. The nurse holding Nellie's leg lifted her hand and slapped her hard across the thigh.

'Stop your thrashing about, you little bog jumper,' she hissed.

For a moment, the child's screaming stopped dead, both from the shock of the new pain in her leg and the insult. Confused by the throbbing in her eye, she was stunned by the fact that she was unable to see who had slapped her.

In that moment, Maura grabbed hold of Kathleen's hand. 'Steady, Kathleen, we want to stay and see them both, say nothing.'

The smack turned Nellie's crying into a desperate whimper, as Kathleen shouted, 'I'm here, Nellie, I'm here.'

Kathleen ran to the end of the bed, her face red with suppressed anger. When Nellie should have been cared for, at her most vulnerable, she had been slapped and hurt. But Kathleen, who, as a 'bog jumper' herself, felt the insult keenly, had not the confidence or the ability to challenge someone in uniform.

Swallowing both her pride and her boiling rage, she noticed the name badge: Nurse Antrobus. At the sound of Kathleen's voice, Nellie's cry became more urgent and needy. Kathleen unceremoniously pushed past the nurse. Nellie threw her arms round her nana's neck and cried her little heart out.

Maura and Kathleen were allowed only ten minutes but managed to leave with both girls settled. The ward sister, who had looked at them over the top of her spectacles and straight down her large, upturned nose, spoke to them both as though English were not their first language. She explained that the bandages would be taken off one of Nellie's eyes that night and the other a week later. Kitty would also stay in hospital for a week and would be sent home wearing the plaster cast.

Both women were left in no doubt that they were expected to leave immediately and not return until the following morning. As they travelled home on the bus, they thought they were at least leaving their girls in a place of care and safety. If they had known the truth, they would rather have taken their own lives than knowingly leave Nellie and Kitty exposed to the danger that faced them.

# Chapter Twelve

Thankfully, the majority of nurses on the ward resembled kind Nurse Lizzie, who had brought the tea to Maura and Kathleen. From the very first morning after their operation, free from pain and reassured by each other's closeness, Nellie and Kitty began to absorb their new environment.

They relished food they had never eaten before, such as mashed bananas and ice cream. The kitchen lady, Pat, who was also Irish, had a soft spot for the girls and heaped up their plates at mealtimes.

Nellie adored the nurse's tall stiff hats and the white starched aprons they wore over pink-striped uniforms with white frilly cuffs. She loved the shiny fob watches pinned onto the front of their aprons and the big, shiny, gleaming buckles on their deep-pink petersham belts. She would let her hand slowly drift across the pale-pink counterpane and crisp white sheets, after the nurses had made her bed in the morning. This spotless, happy, hospital ward was luxury.

Her immediate thought on seeing Nurse Lizzie was how beautiful she looked.

'God, they are like angels,' she exclaimed to Kathleen.

'The one who smacked ye wasn't such an angel,' replied Kathleen under her breath, not so convinced. But Nellie had no recollection of being smacked by Nurse Antrobus.

It was only a nurse's uniform, but she had never before seen anyone wearing anything so clean and pretty. She became swept up in the romanticism of the profession. Nellie quietly observed Lizzie soothing poorly children and helping the doctors, and she secretly knew: one day she wanted to be like Nurse Lizzie.

Nurse Lizzie was also Nana Kathleen's favourite and she always popped over for a chat when she saw Kathleen visiting.

'I haven't seen Nurse Antrobus since the day the girls were admitted,' said Kathleen to Nurse Lizzie on one of these occasions – only just managing not to betray herself and preventing outrage from flooding into her voice.

'Oh, gosh no,' said Lizzie, 'and you won't either. The poor woman went off duty that night, slipped on the wet floor in the kitchen and broke her own arm. She won't be back at work for a while.'

Lizzie walked on to take the pulse of the child in the next bed, as Nana Kathleen turned to Nellie and said, 'Well now, who says there isn't a God, eh?'

'God doesn't have red hair,' laughed Nellie.

'Doesn't he now?' Kathleen laughed with Nellie, but didn't ask her what she meant. She didn't need to. She had seen the flash of red hair hovering over Nellie as she struggled on the bed that night.

Nana Kathleen visited every day and brought tales to Nellie of how Alice was coping with Joseph.

'I know it's often an ill wind that brings bad luck,' she said to Nellie, 'but Alice is doing really well with Joseph. In fact, Nellie, fingers crossed but if you ask me it seems that she is finding it hard to resist the little fella's cheeky face.'

Nellie was open-mouthed, hungry for every detail. 'How, tell me how, what is happening?' she demanded to know.

'Well, I kid ye not, but when I got back from the hospital yesterday, they were both asleep on the chair in front of the fire. Him lying full across her chest and she looking as contented as ye like with her arm across his back. It's her mother's love, sneaking out whilst she is asleep, so it is.'

Nellie gave Kathleen a hug. Her nana was a miracle worker.

Both children, but especially Nellie, loved the daily life of the ward – the hustle and bustle, the comings and goings of the cleaners, porters, doctors, kitchen staff and nurses – and it wasn't very long before they knew everyone by name.

But not everyone and everything was as it seemed …

Stanley had worked as a hospital porter at the hospital since he had been demobbed from the army at the end of the war in 1945. He had seen the job advertised in the *Liverpool Echo* four days after he returned home and applied immediately. His old mum, who was alive at the time, wasn't happy.

'Try and get on the buses,' she said. 'It's not bad money and free travel, you won't ever have to pay a fare again, and neither will I, when they get to know I'm yer mam. Or what about the English Electric on nights, that's good money?'

Stanley needed to look after his mam. His father had been killed in what was supposed to have been the war to end all wars and she had spent every day of World War Two in fear of a telegram arriving. Stanley was her only son and had been wrapped in cotton wool since the day he was born, eight months after his father had volunteered for Kitchener's army and been dispatched to the Somme, where he survived for just two days. When Stanley's father left, he had boarded the train at Lime Street with his head held high.

When Stanley's own dreaded call-up papers had arrived, he had burst into tears.

His mam had a point about the money at English Electric, but Stanley wasn't interested in money. The buses weren't a bad option. Lots of children used the bus to get to and from school, so there would be plenty of opportunity for the illicit contact he sought. He would be able to look at and talk to them and, if he was lucky, make friends with some. However, the hospital job was calling him: vulnerable children in a hospital bed who might need his help in some small way. Stanley closed his eyes when he read the job advert. Could there possibly be a more alluring option?

He also knew he couldn't be the only one. There must be others who thought like him. And if there were, then surely they would look for exactly the same kind of job and maybe he would recognize a kindred spirit, someone he could share his dark and secret thoughts with. Maybe Stanley could find a friend.

It took him only months to realize that in Austin, another single porter who still lived with his mam, he had a mate. Austin looked at the younger girls in exactly the same way Stanley looked at young boys. Stanley had looked for the signs when the porters were gathered in the X-ray department to be allocated children to take back to the wards.

A number of conversations were taking place between X-ray staff, parents and porters, but, like Stanley, Austin found it hard to concentrate on the adults talking, because his gaze would rest on a particular child, sitting in a wheelchair, waiting to be returned to the ward. Stanley knew that gaze. The gaze that lingered on the bare legs or the soft blond hair.

Stanley saw that Austin always carried sweets around in his pocket. Stanley went one better. He asked his mam to knit him a little glove puppet teddy to put in his top pocket. The kids loved that.

They couldn't wait to jump into his arms to see if the teddy was asleep. His mam came round to the idea of her son as a porter and thought he was a hero. When he got home after a shift at the hospital, he was treated like a prince.

'I hope they know how lucky they are at the hospital to have a man as kind as you working with them children?' she would say, at least once a week. Stanley thought it was he who was the lucky one. His decision to apply for the hospital porter's job had been a stroke of genius.

Once he had plucked up the courage to make the connection with Austin, letting him know that he and Stanley had a shared interest, his life transformed overnight. It wasn't an easy thing to do, and Stanley had to wait for the right moment to come along, but, sure enough, eventually it did.

One busy theatre day, they were taking a little girl from the operating theatre directly to the nurses' station. Only five years old, she lay on the theatre trolley semi-conscious, naked, and with tubes and drips everywhere. Stanley saw how long Austin's gaze lingered on her exposed limbs.

Even when Stanley spoke to Austin, his eyes kept darting back, until the theatre nurse placed a gown and a sheet across the child's body, for the journey back to the ward.

'OK, lads, quick as you like. They are waiting for her right now on ward two,' snapped the theatre nurse, in a businesslike tone, as she moved on to receive the next child coming through the operating theatre doors.

As they walked down the centre of ward two, with the empty trolley, having delivered the poorly patient to her bed and the care of the nurses, Austin came out of his trance and said, 'What did you say, mate?'

'Nowt,' replied Stanley, smiling to himself.

On the way they passed a child, aged no more than three, crying, sitting alone on the edge of her bed. Stanley watched Austin look around the ward to check if there were any nurses nearby, but they were all busy with the child they had just brought back from surgery. Having made sure that he was not observed, Austin moved over to the little girl.

'Eh, eh, Queen, what's up?' he said, picking her up and swinging her into his arms. 'What do you think is in my top pocket, eh? Go on, look.'

Her tears began to subside and immediately turned to giggles when she put her hand into Austin's top pocket, and he pretended to growl and bite at her hand as she brought out a sweetie. Having stopped the tears, Austin moved on to the next stage.

'Come on now; give Uncle Austin a big cuddle.'

She put her grateful arms around his neck and her legs around his waist. She was wearing only a loose hospital nightdress. Facing him, with each leg around his middle and her arms around his neck, Austin put his hand on her tiny bottom and pressed her body into his stomach.

'There, there, Queen, Uncle Austin is always here for a cuddle.'

Stanley was talking to the child in the next bed, but he hadn't taken his eyes off Austin. He saw the tear in Austin's eye and the look of ecstasy cross his face, before they heard a nurse's footsteps approaching. Austin put the little girl hurriedly back onto the bed.

As they walked away, they put on an exaggerated clowning act for the children, Austin pretending to beat Stanley for being slow, making the children roar with laughter.

'Oh no,' the men squealed, 'Nurse Helen will tell us off, now what are we going to do?' They winked at the nurse walking past, who laughed and shook her head.

As they made their way back to the porters' hut for a cup of tea, Stanley plucked up the courage and said to Austin, 'I like the little lads, myself.'

Austin looked at him sharply, Stanley winked, and that was it: a whole new world of opportunity and delight opened up to him from that day on.

Years later, very little had changed. Austin had introduced Stanley to others who had the same predilection.

'There is nothing wrong with us,' said Austin to Stanley, 'we just like something different from others, that doesn't mean it's wrong.' They all felt the same.

Austin had introduced Stanley to the Sunday meeting that took place in secret at Arthur's house on County Road.

'Homos will be in the law soon,' said Arthur, often. 'We will be one day too.'

Stanley supposed that, as he liked boys, he was a 'homo' too. The difference was, he liked them from the age of two to twelve. Once they reached puberty, they were of no interest to him.

Every week they paid to have pictures sent to a postbox delivery address. Each person in the group took it in turns to collect them before meeting the others at Arthur's house. They circulated the envelopes of photographs amongst themselves, most of which came from abroad and were of varying quality, but they paid the money happily. This was the darkest of secrets and those that shared it were well practised in keeping any knowledge hidden. The code was that if anyone was caught collecting the pictures, the rest were protected. They all knew that one day maybe one of them would have to take the rap, but they also knew the others would be safe.

Over the years, Austin and Stanley had learnt a new technique: to make friends with the families of children they liked. Today, Austin had gone to a child's birthday party and he had been invited to sleep over. The last time he had done that, the father had caught him taking a photograph of the daughter in the bath and had asked him to leave. Austin sailed too close to the wind sometimes. He had been out of his league with that family. After that incident, they spent two nervous weeks being extra careful, wondering if the father truly suspected anything and had written to the hospital.

Stanley was always telling him, 'Stick to the poor kids. They are the ones whose parents are too busy or neglectful to notice. They are the kids who don't get any affection and always need a cuddle. No one buys them presents or sweets. They are always more grateful and if they squeal, no one will believe them or be bothered anyway. Do as I do, stick to the poor kids.' That was Stanley's fail-safe.

Austin loved his new Kodak Brownie and couldn't stop taking pictures to sell on. It was so easy in the hospital. The children thought they were smiling for the camera alone. Sometimes, they were sitting on their parent's knee. Stanley was amazed that never once did a parent ask why a hospital porter was taking a photograph of their child.

Poor people were unused to, and lapped up, attention.

A camera was a novelty. It paid attention.

Stanley was on nights, he had his usual job to do for one of Austin's mates. He thought it was probably the priest, but he was never told whom he was helping. They all preferred it that way and he knew that if someone was helping him, they never knew who he was either. Secrecy was king. What you didn't know, you would never be able to tell.

Stanley's job tonight was to ring one of the children's wards at midnight and tell the nurse someone would have to go to the pathology department to pick up some test results for the doctor who was coming on night duty, and that they needed to hurry because the pathologist had to leave. He would say that he was sorry, the porter would have done it but he was run off his feet.

It took a good ten minutes for a nurse to walk to the pathology department from the ward. Five to work out what was going on and think they had missed the pathologist, ten to walk back and then another five for the cigarette she would smoke outside the ward door before going back in. That was thirty minutes when it was guaranteed there would be no ward round. If there was only one nurse on the ward, she usually stayed in the office until her colleague got back, in case the phone rang. It always did. That was the second stage. To ring the ward again, seven minutes exactly after the first call.

If it was the priest, he hardly needed help because he was known on all the wards as a regular visitor. According to Austin's instructions, Stanley had already checked that the fire-escape door to the car park was unlocked and left slightly ajar, a spanner in his hand in case a curious nurse popped over to ask what he was doing.

Before he pulled the curtain across, he took a peep at the bed closest to the door. Lying there was a young thin girl, barely into her teens. Stanley found that a bit odd. Austin liked them younger even than Stanley, as did most of the men in their group. Age two to eight was Austin's preference. Ah, thought Stanley, then it must be the priest; he seems to like them from quite young to right into their teens. Dirty bastard, he thought, as he put the door back with the bar not quite catching the lock. The irony was totally lost on him.

As soon as they were recovering and up and about, Kitty and Nellie begged to be put in charge of the night-time drinks trolley, while they helped the night nurse settle the younger patients down to sleep. The trolley had jugs of hot chocolate and Horlicks with plates of biscuits. They had never had anything other than tea at home. Hot chocolate was a luxury to be marvelled at.

Nellie and Kitty asked the nurses to keep their beds together and they moved progressively up the ward each morning. They pulled the curtains round to make their two beds into one when the doctors did the ward round. They had been like sisters before and, even with the age difference, they were more so now. Everyone loved them; they brought joy into a ward that could often be a heartbreaking place for staff.

They became so close they even got into each other's beds where they would chat for hours. When the nurses came round they made them squeal with laughter, as Nellie would lie flat on her tummy and hide in Kitty's bed under the covers. They were such a happy and pleasant pair, the ward staff would be sorry to see them both go, even Sister, who never laughed.

Kitty was very happy until, on the third day, Father James paid them a visit. Without warning, he suddenly appeared at the foot of Kitty's bed, where Nellie was also lying, and offered them a jelly baby out of a crumpled white paper bag, which he took out of his cassock pocket.

'Say no,' Kitty whispered urgently, as he approached.

Nellie looked at Kitty in amazement. She was expecting Nellie to say no to sweets?

'Do as I say,' said Kitty, with such urgency in her voice that Nellie didn't dare defy her, even though she loved jelly babies and didn't get sweets very often.

Father James sat on the end of the bed in which they were both lying.

'Your mammy asked me to pop by, Kitty, and say prayers with ye both for a speedy recovery, even for ye, Nellie,' he said, looking at Nellie sneeringly. Father James had not forgiven Nellie for having the cheek to kick the door shut in his face just after Joseph was born.

Kitty said nothing. Nellie turned sideways and looked at her in amazement. Kitty was being rude in not speaking to Father James and Nellie knew that wasn't allowed in the Doherty house.

Father James turned to Nellie. 'I would like to have a quiet word with Kitty on me own. Nellie, would ye like to go and see if the nurses need ye for anything? Do ye not have your own bed to go to now, whilst Kitty has a visitor?'

Nellie immediately threw back the corner of the counterpane, ready to dive out of the bed and dash to the nurses' office. Anything to get away from a strange and uncomfortable situation.

'No,' said Kitty so loudly that Nellie pulled the counterpane back in shock and didn't move. Nellie always did everything Kitty told her.

Father James made small talk on his own for five minutes and then, after offering them the jelly babies again, took his leave to talk to another child at the top of the ward who went to the same school as the girls.

For the rest of the day, Kitty hardly spoke. Nellie had noticed that whilst Father James had been sitting on the bed talking, his hand had been pressed against Kitty's thigh. While he spoke, Nellie stared at his hand and, when he became aware of it, he pulled it away sharply. Nellie watched Kitty's face and thought she looked scared.

As he walked away back down the ward, Nellie took hold of Kitty's hand and said, 'I hate Father James so much.'

Kitty put her good arm round Nellie's shoulders and hugged her.

'God, I love you, so I do, Nellie Deane,' she said and they both laughed.

Nellie asked Nurse Lizzie why Father James was in the ward so much.

'He comes to pray over all the poorly children,' said Lizzie. 'Do you know him? Isn't he just fantastic, he's always popping in.'

Nellie didn't know what this information meant, but she knew it wasn't good. She knew the people she trusted the most in the world didn't like Father James and that included Kitty and her Nana Kathleen. If they didn't, neither did Nellie.

Each evening there was excitement on the ward, as the name of the child going home the next day was written on a board. Kitty and Nellie both cried when they discovered that Kitty was going home the day before Nellie.

Nellie wanted to go home. She desperately missed Joseph and Nana Kathleen and her da. Her da brought Joseph into the ward some nights, but she could see he was missing her too. Suddenly, now that Kitty was going home, everything had changed; she was very keen to leave herself.

Nellie and Kitty parted to sleep in their own beds on Kitty's last night, after discussing how they would live in the same street when they grew up, become wedding-dress designers, or famous actresses, and marry two brothers so that they could become properly related.

They had lots of hugs from the nurses, but Kitty was nervous. She didn't want to sleep alone in the going-home bed at the end of the ward. She begged the nurses to let her sleep with Nellie, but they wouldn't agree. The two children finally parted when the nurses came to give Nellie a sedative, in preparation for her visit to theatre in the morning, to have the final bandages removed from her eye. As she left Nellie's bed, Kitty wept. She told Nellie she was frightened, but Nellie couldn't reply; the sedation had worked on her like a sledgehammer and she went out like a light.

Even though the ward was mainly in darkness, above each bed a nightlight dimly illuminated the faces of the sleeping children.

In the early hours of the morning, Nellie woke to see the curtain pulled round Kitty's bed. She thought she had heard the fire-escape door click open. The drugs had made her very groggy and she tried to say Kitty's name, but her tongue felt huge in her mouth and no sound came out. Kitty was in the going-home bed, tucked into the L-shaped bay at the end of the ward, the only bed away from the nurses' line of vision. But it could be seen from Nellie's bed, the last in the row running down the ward.

From the bed were sounds Nellie had never heard before. Desperately trying to fight the fog in her brain, she looked down the ward to the nurses' office and then, unable to sit up or speak, she managed to roll herself onto her side to face Kitty's bed, prop herself up on her elbow and rub her eyes.

Below the curtain, she saw what looked like a long black skirt and a pair of men's boots.

Almost at the end of the ward, she could hear the low hum of female voices, as the night nurses, who had worked together for years, exchanged news and chatted in muted tones. Tonight was Sunday, which brought with it a nocturnal atmosphere of calm. No operations, no distressed relatives and no one's child about to go to an early grave. The nurses were making the most of a quiet shift.

The telephone in the office suddenly rang and the sound glided down the ward, bouncing off the dreams of thirty sleeping little ones. It was quickly answered, before anyone woke, and Nellie heard the whispered tones of the night nurse swiftly followed by the ting of the bell, as she replaced the black Bakelite receiver.

Nellie heard the sound of the ward door swishing open and shut, followed by crepe-soled footsteps retreating down the corridor. She realized they would now be down to one nurse.

Nellie heard a new noise coming from behind Kitty's curtain. The bed began to slowly creak as though a great weight were pressing onto it. The shoes and the black skirt had vanished.

Nellie couldn't lift her head and her gaze seemed to be fixed down to the floor. She considered calling the nurse, but her tongue wouldn't work properly. She knew she was desperately fighting a battle with the drug to stay awake. She also knew instinctively that Kitty needed help.

Suddenly she froze, seeing the wheels on Kitty's bed moving slowly, backwards and forwards, straining against the brake on the wheel at the foot of the bed. Was someone taking Kitty's bed away?

The noise of something falling caught her attention. She saw a red jelly baby plop onto the floor, and then straight after it, a green one. The bed began creaking rhythmically, faster and faster. Nellie stared in groggy amazement as brightly coloured confectionery rained down from Kitty's bed and then, with an abrupt thud, a white paper packet of jelly babies fell and spewed its contents across the polished wooden floor. Just as the bed suddenly stopped moving and she heard a muffled gasp, she could fight the sedation no longer; her eyes closed as the drug did its work. She slept deeply and didn't even hear the second click of the door.

The following morning, Kitty appeared quiet. Her sparkle had gone and Nellie, still groggy and having been given more sedation to prepare her for theatre, couldn't remember what had been odd about the previous evening.

She and Kitty hugged tightly as the trolley came to take Nellie to theatre. When she returned to the ward, with all her bandages gone, Kitty's bed was clean and made up. Maura had been to collect Kitty and left a note on Nellie's bed.

Nellie's eyes were still blurred and she couldn't read the note.

'God please, ye will be back with us tomorrow. Daddy coming to see you tonight, Maura XX.'

The nurse who read the note to Nellie said, 'Well, there is no need for you to stay now, Nellie, your eye is healed beautifully and if your daddy is coming tonight, he can take you back home with him. You will be able to read in the morning and back to school on Monday.'

Nellie didn't know why, but she cried with happiness. She no longer felt safe with Kitty gone. She wanted to go home to see Joseph and get back to her own world on the streets where she felt as if she was related to everyone.

That afternoon, Father James came to say hello. He told her she was a naughty little girl going home early. That he would have liked to come and give her a special goodbye that night, one that was reserved for little girls in the end bed. He had been looking forward to giving her the treat he said he saved for all the pretty little girls on the ward.

'Why don't you ask the nurse if you can stay until tomorrow and then I will come and see you tonight, with a goodbye surprise?'

He put his hand on the top of her leg and she stared at it, not knowing what to say. There was a note of desperate conspiracy to his voice, as though he was discussing something that Nellie already had knowledge of, something they had already talked about together, a plan she was already a part of. She looked on in silence. She knew something was very wrong, but didn't know what.

'Go on,' he said, 'it will be our special secret.'

Nellie looked to the ward door for her da, who was coming to collect her after work. She prayed sincerely, for the first time in her life, asking God to please not let anything stop her da from coming to get her. She saw Nurse Lizzie, taking the temperature of a child further up the ward, holding onto her fob watch to count out her minute.

Nellie suddenly shouted, 'Nurse Lizzie!' very loudly, and, like a black serpent, Father James gradually uncoiled himself. Whilst Nellie's heart beat in terror at something, she did not know what, he rose and moved slowly away from her bed.

# Chapter Thirteen

Once the girls were both home from hospital and Callum had done his penance, which was to clean the windows of both houses inside and out, life settled back to a normal pattern.

For everyone except Kitty.

For the last few years Kitty had been in an ever darker and more threatening place. She knew what Father James had done at the hospital. Stella McGinty had told Kitty the more specific facts of life in the playground only weeks earlier. It wasn't a discussion that had taken place in Maura's home, but Kitty knew Stella had been telling the truth.

Everyone made such a fuss of her when she came home from the hospital. Even Alice, who as a result of the accident had learnt the basic art of caring for others. Alice had imbued the raw concern emanated by Kathleen and Maura, and, on occasion, had found herself being needed and useful.

It didn't happen automatically. She made a conscious effort on some days to look for something positive to do for someone else, but when she did she was well rewarded. After years of living within her own lonely capsule of solitude, she sometimes found herself smiling with pleasure.

Alice wrote Kitty a handmade card. It was the first she had ever written and it took her an agonizing hour to write her message. Kathleen watched Alice, sat at the table bent over her card, but offered no help. Ironically, Alice had to do this alone. Kathleen knew that the second time would be easier. When Alice put her pen down and folded the card, she felt exhausted.

'A cuppa tea, Alice, for a job well done,' said Kathleen, as she put a cup and saucer down in front of Alice and gave her a gentle hug as she walked away.

Peggy brought Kitty an opinion.

'Jeez, Kitty, ye look so pale. Are ye sure she should be home yet, Maura?' Peggy had demanded, when she came to the house to see Kitty for herself.

Her friends from school called round to visit and brought her handmade cards, letters from the teachers and home-made gifts. Her best friend Julia had made her a pincushion in the sewing class and had embroidered her name across the top in a pretty chain stitch.

'It took me forever and a day!' said Julia, as Kitty opened the little parcel.

'Oh, Julia, 'tis so beautiful indeed,' said Kitty, without a hint of enthusiasm in her voice.

Julia looked at Kitty oddly. As the girls walked home after their visit, they commented that Kitty was still not well.

'Knocked the stuffing right out of her, that accident, if you ask me,' said Julia thoughtfully.

She had noticed a huge change in Kitty of late and, although she couldn't put her finger on it, she knew that there was something more than a stay in hospital and a broken arm upsetting Kitty.

Kitty felt as though she lived in a parallel world to everyone else. Between her and those she knew and loved there was an invisible screen. Her family and friends spent their days rooted in reality, whereas hers were rooted in fear. They lived ... she existed.

Up until now she had found clever ways to thwart Father James and stop him finding opportunities to be alone with her. She had been permanently on the run from his zealous pursuit and had outfoxed him. But now she was done for. That was it. He had won. He had turned her into a repulsive sinner and there was surely no one who lived on the four streets as disgustingly dirty and unworthy as she was.

Kitty didn't feel glad to be home. Kitty felt nothing but shame and self-loathing. It was all she could do to put her feet onto the floor each morning, once she had woken and realized, with acute disappointment, that she was still alive. She knew she had no choices and, as if she were an actress, it was a role she had to play each and every day.

Life on the four streets was getting tougher for the families who lived there. There was less work on the docks for the dockers, and little or no money. Boys who would have followed their da onto the docks were now heading into the big factories, such as Plessey's and Ford. The winter had taken its toll on industry everywhere. It was now March and the ice had only just begun to thaw.

For those houses on the four streets that had kept the ranges ticking over, water hadn't been too much of a problem. In other parts of Liverpool, in homes that had replaced ranges with cookers, and lost their back boiler, they had the misery of burst pipes to contend with. Kathleen wasn't able to keep the range lit all through the night. She filled the bath with water before she went to bed so that if her pipes did freeze, as they sometimes did, they were never short. The bath quickly formed a layer of ice that she cracked each morning to fill the kettle. The danger of frozen and burst pipes was a constant source of worry and anxiety. They tried their hardest to avoid catastrophe by putting extra coal on the fire before they went to bed.

Each night, Kathleen took a secondary precaution and left the kitchen tap dripping to keep the water moving to help prevent the pipes from freezing. There was nothing more miserable and difficult to cope with than a burst pipe in freezing weather. As if life wasn't hard enough. The weather was just another hurdle to overcome for those who were used to dealing with adversity on a daily basis.

Today was only Thursday, the day before pay day, and everyone had already run out of money. For many families on the streets, this meant going hungry. But Kathleen had a plan. She knew Peggy had a big ship's catering pan on her landing under the eaves and she sent Jerry round to collect it. Then she popped in to see Maura.

At the Doherty house, Tommy was fed up. The dockers had been laid off for yet another day and it was not a situation he liked, although it was no fun working in below-freezing temperatures. They had been dipping into the bread-bin 'back-up' money over the last few weeks and it was now running low. This always made Maura nervous and irritable.

Tommy was never miserable for long, though; it took only a neighbour or a fresh face to pop in through the door and he was a happy man again.

'Ah, Kathleen,' he said as she walked in. 'Ye are a sight for sore eyes, come over here and cheer me up.'

Kathleen sat down at the table with Tommy, smiling at the sight of his paper spread out in front of him.

Was there ever an Irishman more proud that he could read, she thought to herself.

If Tommy had read the paper by the afternoon, he would go back to the beginning and start it again. Reading the trivia of Liverpool life in the hatched, matched and dispatched columns gave Tommy somewhere to put his mind, whilst the hullabaloo of a house with well-loved and noisy children carried on around him.

The back door opened again and everyone looked up at Alice, nervously standing in the doorway. For a fraction of a second, the room was silent. This was the first time Alice had stepped inside another house on the four streets.

Alice had no idea why she had followed Kathleen. She was driven by new feelings and emotions over which she had little control. She wanted to belong. When Kathleen left the kitchen after sending Jerry to collect the pan and had thrown over her shoulder, 'I'm away to Maura's,' Alice had wanted to shout out, 'Take me with you.' But she hadn't. She had stood there and thought to herself, I want to go too. And so, that was what she had done.

Walking up Maura's back path was one of the most terrifying things she had ever done in her life. Her fear was overcome by the desire to be with Kathleen. To be like Kathleen. She wondered, should she knock?

Before she lifted the latch she took a deep breath. Perspiration had formed on her top lip and her brow, yet her mouth was dry. She looked at the pale blue, cracked, painted door and stepped inside. Just like everyone else.

Maura looked straight at Alice. She had been touched by the card she had written for Kitty when she came out of hospital and, since that day, her heart had thawed towards Alice.

Tommy, himself shocked for a moment, broke the silence.

'Jeez, how lucky a man am I, with the three best-looking women in the street all in me own kitchen. Alice, come and sit down with me at the table and save me from Kathleen and Maura naggin' at me, will ye?'

Everyone laughed, as much with relief as at Tommy's joke.

'Maura, it's going to have to be a pan night,' said Kathleen, in a resigned voice, as she picked up the tea Maura had placed on the table for both her and Alice. With her other hand, she reached under the table and gave Alice's hand a gentle squeeze. 'If I don't do it, some of the kids in this street will go to bed hungry tonight and we can't have that, so. I will do it in our kitchen, Maura, but if I'm doing the cooking and serving, ye need to do the organizing.'

Kathleen had spoken. It was more of an instruction to Maura than a query.

'Aye, Kathleen, I will that,' said Maura, drying her hands on her apron and sitting down at the table to take instructions. 'How much do we need from each house?' she asked.

'Threepence will do it, but if they don't have it, Maura, don't push it. We will have enough for everyone, so don't make anyone feel bad. Some of these women have been away from the bogs for too long and aren't as good at managing as they would be if they were back home with help.'

'And that's the God's truth,' Tommy chimed in.

'It's not just the women, Kathleen, some of the fellas are straight into the Anchor from the dock after work, spending the food money. The shorter work is, the more they want to drink the money away.'

'Aye, thank God for the family allowance,' said Maura. 'I don't know how we would manage without it, ye drinking as much as ye do, Tommy Doherty.'

She shoved Tommy on his arm, laughing as she spoke. Tommy always put his kids first and the only time he called into the Anchor was on the odd occasion when times were flush and Maura had given him a few bob extra. Every Friday night he walked into the house and put his pay packet on the kitchen table in a small brown envelope. Maura opened and checked it, then gave him his paper, betting and ciggies money. It was all Tommy needed; he didn't ask for any more; he worked for his wife and his kids, not himself.

The family allowance, which was paid out from her book at the post office on a Tuesday, gave Maura over two pounds a week extra, which usually got them over to Friday if things were harder than usual, but this week she had been helping everyone else out, with the odd bit here and there, and now she was shorter than usual herself.

Tommy got his pencil out and they counted up the number of children on their street. Kathleen knocked on the kitchen wall with the mop end for Jerry to come in from Peggy's, and promptly dispatched him down to Mrs Keating, Mrs McGowan and Mrs McNally, the keepers of the ship's catering pans on the other three streets, to let them know what was happening. Jerry came back and confirmed the other women would follow suit. They had done this before and they would no doubt do it again.

Maura went out to collect the money from each house on the four streets. Kitty and Nellie went with her, together with Harry and Angela, wheeling Joseph's empty pram to the shops. There were eighty-three children on the four streets, of varying ages. Maura needed forty pounds of potatoes, twenty pounds of carrots, fifteen of the large Spanish onions, which, to everyone's excitement, had just started appearing in the greengrocer's, and thirty pounds of neck end of lamb from Murphy's.

'Don't ye be giving me no spuds with black eyes in now,' said Maura sternly to Bill, the greengrocer. 'I don't want none of ye rubbish dumping on me, because I'm buying for everyone today.'

The greengrocer was English; if he could, he would palm the rubbish off on Maura and they both knew it. The greengrocer felt bad, knowing what Maura was doing and as she had done many times in the past. Once he had taken her money, carefully counted out in threepenny bits, he said, 'Hang on a minute there, Maura, I've got something for you.'

He disappeared into the back of the shop and came out with a wooden box full of uncooked beetroots.

'I will have to throw these out at the end of today, so if you can get them cooked quickly, you are welcome to them.'

'Aye, so we can and thank ye, Bill, ye aren't all bad.' He and Maura exchanged a grin.

The cheeky mare, he thought. He had a soft spot for Maura, though. She had been Bernadette's best friend and, like every other man who had been blinded after laying eyes upon her, he had been in love with Bernadette.

Maura placed the box of beetroots across the top of the pram and walked on to the homes in the other three streets that would become communal kitchens for the day. When she reached the door, she called out through the back gate from the entry, 'I've an extra treat,' and handed over to each one their share of the vegetables and meat, plus eight big beets. 'Chop them into slices after you've boiled them, that way everyone can have a share.'

'Ye got beets for free from that thieving git?' said Mrs Keating. 'Well, ye never know, maybe pigs do fly.'

Now, everyone was happier. They might have had nothing. They might all have been poor, and this morning they had been facing misery and hungry bellies. Some were smoking what was left of old fag ends in dirty ashtrays and, as a result, they were bad-tempered. Now, everyone was pulling together and an atmosphere of something close to joy had settled on the four streets, as the kids played together, wrapped up against the March wind, aware something close to a party was about to take place.

Kathleen's kitchen became a hive of activity, as did the three others. As a result of Kathleen's thinking, each child would go to bed on a full belly of Irish stew. The women tripped in and out of each other's houses, sharing out the vegetables to be prepared and chopped. Once the beetroots were cooked, they were peeled and put into a large bowl, another gift from a ship's kitchen, and then the ingredients for the stew were put into the pan to cook. The neck end of lamb needed to simmer all day to soften and then break down into stringy lumps. The carrots were put in at midday and then the potatoes in the last hour before the stew was thickened up with flour and gravy browning. The women had also made soft floury bread, which was still warm and ready to be dipped into the gravy.

At suppertime each child brought a bowl and a spoon into Kathleen's kitchen, where she and Alice were dishing up. On the top of each bowl of Irish stew they laid slices of beetroot and on top of that a warm floury cob. You could hardly hear yourself speak for the excited chatter of children sitting on the stairs, as well as all over the kitchen and living-room floors.

'Thank ye, Auntie Kathleen, thank ye, Auntie Alice,' they all shouted, after they had taken the first mouthful, before getting down to the serious business of eating. As each child slurped and ate, silence descended on the house.

This was thrilling for the children. They had none of the worry of making ends meet. To them, this was an adventure, a break from the usual routine, underpinning the fact that they were all one big family and would always look after each other. Mothers wove their way among the children, helping the little ones to eat, making sure they were safe and could manage to spoon the food without spilling any. The women exchanged happy smiles with one another. This was a job well done. This was what their community was about. Together, they could beat anything.

*

Kitty did her bit to help, but she was feeling ill and the smell of the stew turned her stomach. She had helped to look after Joseph and, earlier in the day, once the pram was empty of vegetables, she and Nellie had taken him for a walk. They both kept looking over their shoulders for runaway cars as they ambled along the cold streets, wheeling Joseph to sleep after his lunchtime feed.

Nellie had noticed Alice was helping out in the kitchen, peeling carrots, which she thought was nice. Alice didn't see that Nellie and Kitty had taken Joseph and they didn't bother to tell her. Nana Kathleen knew where they were, that was all that mattered.

Nellie knew Kitty wasn't very happy. She didn't talk much and she didn't laugh at Nellie's jokes. This was unusual and confusing, but then Nellie had a grand idea.

'Kitty, did you know that Nana Kathleen makes everything better?' she piped.

Kitty laughed for the first time. 'Aye, she does that,' she replied.

'So, why don't you talk to her and tell her what's wrong?'

'Who says there's anything wrong with me?' said Kitty sharply. Nellie noted that her eyes had filled with tears.

'No one, Kitty, just me. But I knows ye better than anyone and I know summat's up.' Adversity had gifted Nellie with wisdom way beyond her years.

Silence descended upon the girls.

Kitty wondered, would she dare tell Nana Kathleen? Her mind toyed with the idea. It was a ray of hope. She looked troubled again. How could she tell her, though, if she really would badly hurt her mammy and daddy by telling them what had occurred? Even if they did disown her, maybe a life alone in a convent would be better than feeling like this?

Last week Tommy had read out a story from the paper to Maura, whilst she was at the kitchen sink. Tommy often did that, now that he was better at reading. There was a time when he could only read the horses. He progressed onto the names and dates on the hatched, matched and dispatched and now he was full of himself and read at least one story out of the paper to them all at least once a day. Kitty had been teaching him and he read her school books with her, when she had brought them home. When she was younger, and Tommy used to put Kitty to bed, she would read him a goodnight story and test him on his letters. No one knew from outside the house and no one ever would. He liked to read items from the paper out loud to show off, especially if Jerry came into the kitchen. Jerry was visibly impressed by Tommy's reading skills and assumed he must be much cleverer than he was.

'Would ye listen to this,' Tommy would always begin and waited for silence to descend on the kitchen, for effect. 'A young woman aged seventeen was found in a house in Boswell Street, Toxteth, hanging from a rope attached to the ceiling, where she had remained undiscovered for approximately eight hours. The police have said that it was an unlawful act of suicide and no one else was involved. Now, why the hell would a young girl, with her whole life in front of her, do that, eh?'

Kitty had listened intently. She wanted to tell him that she knew a reason, but she couldn't. She wasn't sure what was right and what was wrong any more. If it was so wrong to tell her parents about Father James and what he did to her, what on God's earth was right?

Her own life was becoming blurred and she knew she wasn't doing as well with her schoolwork. She no longer had any self-confidence and was snapping everyone's head off. She knew that, but she couldn't help it. She carried around with her the darkest, dirtiest secret, which made her feel horrible and sick every day, but if she told someone, she would be a bad person. Nothing that happened any more could make her happy whilst this was the life she had to lead.

What Father James had done at the hospital had shocked her. She hadn't seen him since, but she knew if he tried to do that once more, she would rather kill herself – she couldn't let that happen to her again. She would rather be dead, like the girl from Boswell Street. That would be preferable to carrying round a guilty secret. Over the last three years, he had become bolder and bolder, and now he had done *that*. Every time she thought about it, she wanted to cry. She was so desperately alone.

After feeding the entire street Maura and Kitty were helping to clean up Jerry's house. Jerry had put Nellie and Joseph to bed. Alice had gone up hours ago and Jerry himself was turning in. He and Tommy would be down at the docks early tomorrow, in the hope of a ship coming in and them both being taken on. They wanted a fatter pay packet next week.

Kathleen put the kettle on for the final cup of tea, while Maura finished scrubbing the big pan with a Brillo pad. Kitty startled Kathleen as she flew past her and down the path to the outhouse, yet again.

'That kid's not well,' said Maura to Kathleen, nodding her head towards Kitty as she ran.

'Really?' said Kathleen. 'What's up with her?'

'She has a stubborn tummy bug, which I think she picked up in the hospital weeks ago, and it won't leave her.'

'I'd take her to Dr O'Cole if I were you,' said Kathleen, opening the back door and looking down the path to see that Kitty, who hadn't managed to close the outhouse door, was throwing up in the toilet.

Kathleen was amazed that Maura hadn't cottoned on. She herself had, days ago, but then there wasn't much that got past Kathleen. She thought she had better make a joke of it, since Maura was obviously blissfully unaware.

'If I didn't know better, I'd say she would be pushing that bug around in a pram in six months,' said Kathleen, studying Maura's face for a reaction.

Maura looked up from the pan and laughed. 'I know, me too, just shows we aren't always right, eh?'

I know I am, thought Kathleen, and you will be too before long, Maura.

*

On Saturday night, everyone on all four streets had a wedding to attend at the Irish centre. It was an excuse for a big get-together. Half of Dublin had come to Liverpool for the celebration and nearly every house on the four streets had a guest sleeping over. Mrs Keating's daughter, Siobhan, was marrying the son of a Dublin republican who owned a pub overlooking the Liffey River and he would inherit the pub from his da.

The men saw it as one of the most fortuitous matches any child from the four streets had ever made. The blissful thought of it … a free pint of Guinness always ready and waiting on a bar in Dublin, should they ever turn up. It didn't get much better than that. The four streets buzzed with excitement and those who couldn't fit into the church lined the path to St Mary's and the road outside, armed with rice and confetti to throw at the happy couple.

Early that morning, a crate of Guinness and a bottle of Irish whiskey had been delivered to every house on the four streets so the guests could begin celebrating with the happy couple at breakfast, along with a box of boxty bread and a whole peat-smoked salmon. Tommy thought he had died and gone to heaven.

Everyone was giddy with a happiness that can be found only in an Irish home where, for every stranger, there are a hundred thousand welcomes.

The wedding breakfast began at three o'clock in the afternoon, straight after the church ceremony, and carried on into the early hours of the morning. Nellie loved a party. She loved Irish dancing and she and Kitty were part of a group of girls who had put together a number of dances for the wedding party. They had been practising on the green for weeks without any music and had no idea how fabulous the dancing would be on the day, with the band playing behind them and the huge audience stood in front, cheering and clapping them on. As the girls left the dance floor, everyone pushed money into their hands.

'Oh my God, we're rich!' shouted Nellie, as they passed through the crowd, and they were indeed. Nellie had never seen so much money before. She put it straight into her pocket to give to her da the next morning; he would put it in the tin in the bread bin where all the savings were kept.

This was Nellie's first ever contribution to the tin.

By ten o'clock, Kitty was feeling dreadful and decided to take some of the little kids back to the street. Nellie offered to help. When she heard they were leaving, Alice said she would walk back with them and put Joseph to bed.

Jerry was thrilled that Alice had not only agreed to come but had even seemed to enjoy herself, in her own way. He hadn't even needed to persuade her. One word from Nana Kathleen was all it had taken and when he saw Alice laughing and clapping along to the girls dancing, his heart felt warm. His mother had worked her magic.

When they reached their own street, Alice took Joseph indoors. Kitty and Nellie put Paddy and Peggy's kids to bed and then said goodnight with a hug.

'Get a good night's sleep, Kitty, and ye will feel better in the morning,' said Nellie.

Kitty could barely smile as she went in through her back door. Sleep was not her problem; she could hardly stay awake as it was.

They were all tucked up in their own beds and fast asleep within fifteen minutes, while the adults carried on partying.

Kathleen might have been a grandmother, but she had staying power. She loved to watch the young ones enjoying themselves and having a dance. The Guinness was flowing, the craic was wild, and she had caught up with some of her friends from home who had come over for the wedding. But having had five glasses of Guinness, she was now beginning to feel exhausted herself. The big feeding operation on Thursday had taken its toll and she thought about heading back home.

Kathleen couldn't stop worrying about Kitty, but for the first time in her life she was stumped. The two families were close. She knew Kitty's movements as well as she knew Nellie's. What the hell had gone on? Because there was one thing she knew, for sure: Kitty might have only been fourteen, but she was pregnant all right. It's not a bloody immaculate conception, she thought. Someone put that baby there and I cannot for the life of me think who.

She had no idea how to approach Maura and Tommy about it.

They could tell me to get lost, she thought. An accusation like that, especially if she were wrong, could spoil many years of a good close relationship. To be pregnant out of wedlock carried the biggest stigma. It was a shameful thing. Maura's children were like brothers and sisters to Nellie. Kathleen would have to tread carefully or, even better, say nothing at all, just be there to catch the pieces and clear up the mess the day it did all become clear to Maura and World War Three broke out across the street.

Kathleen put on her coat and took so long to say goodnight to everyone that it took her half an hour to get out of the door. As soon as she stepped out of the club onto the street, the heavens opened. Kathleen crossed herself and thanked God Nellie had got home with Joseph and Alice before the rain had begun, while cursing herself for having stopped so long and had the extra glass of Guinness.

She pulled down her hat, tucking her hair tightly in, and then pulled up her collar to stop the water from running down her neck. With hands thrust deep into her pockets, she began to walk the half-mile home. There was no wind and the rain was heavy; the cobbles were black and drenched within minutes. Kathleen's path home was lit by the yellow sulphur glow from the street lights reflected off the glistening black of the wet path.

She could smell the river on the air as she lifted her head and breathed in. That mist has washed over Ireland on its way here, she thought, I can smell the peat bogs on the edge of it.

She could hear the band playing a folk song from back home. It got her in the back of her throat when she recalled that it was a song Jerry and Bernadette had danced to at their wedding. They had all stood in a circle and clapped and cheered while the besotted couple, who couldn't leave each other alone, danced and held hands. Tears began to escape from Kathleen's eyes and mingled with the rain as she walked along.

'God, I'm getting soft in the head as I get older, so I am,' she said to herself, as she took a hankie out of her pocket and wiped her face.

She missed Bernadette and thought to herself that, if things had been different, she and Bernadette would have been walking home together now, laughing and joking as they used to all the time. She knew her Jerry still went into the yard and talked to Bernadette. She smiled to herself as she thought, maybe she would give it a go and try it herself.

'Bernadette, I need a bit of help,' she said, into the wet night air. 'I'm worried about Kitty and I've no idea what to do, perhaps ye can show me the way, my lovely?'

Kathleen smiled. Holy Mother, she thought to herself, I've only had five glasses of Guinness and I'm as bad as me son. I'm losing me head already.

Suddenly, Kathleen knew she wasn't alone. She hadn't imagined Bernadette gently slipping her arm through hers. Bernadette was walking beside her, but she wasn't happy. Bernadette was urging Kathleen to hurry. Kathleen felt as though she were being implored and pushed to move faster and faster, as though she were being propelled along.

'Oh my God, Bernadette,' gasped Kathleen, 'I'm an old woman, my lovely, I can't catch me breath, slow down.'

Kathleen felt as though she had been flung round the top corner of the entry when suddenly, blinking in the dark and through the pouring rain, she saw a man in a black hat and cape lift the latch to Maura and Tommy's back gate. She stopped dead in shock.

'Holy Mary, Mother of God, what's going on?' Kathleen whispered to Bernadette, but almost before the words left her mouth, she realized she was once again alone.

The feeling of a presence, of someone she knew and loved being right with her and by her side, had gone, as had the intense feeling of urgency. She was now truly alone as she slowly walked down the entry and in through Maura's gate.

Kathleen didn't rush, she was too afraid. Her limbs felt like lead and she wanted to move in the opposite direction. Her throat and mouth had become dry with fear and her heart was racing, as adrenaline surged through her veins. The penny had suddenly dropped.

'Poor Kitty, the answer was under me very nose.'

She lifted the latch and crept into the kitchen. The main light was off, but the lamp had been left on for Maura and Tommy returning.

Kathleen noticed that the door at the bottom of the stairs was slightly open and off the latch.

'Oh my Holy God, little Kitty,' she whispered, feeling like screaming.

She put her hand over her mouth, frozen to the spot. What should she do? Should she run back to the Irish centre? Should she wake Alice across the road to come? She heard a floorboard upstairs creak heavily and she knew she had no time. She looked frantically around the room for something to help her and picked up the poker, leaning up against the range. Far slower and quieter than the faintest heartbeat, she opened the door wide and crept very carefully up the stairs.

He never saw her coming, so engrossed in his own lust that he didn't hear a thing. Kathleen stood still for a moment to let her eyes adjust. The bedroom was pitch black and the only light reflected off the whitewashed wall. She could see his black shape in relief against it and hear Kitty whimpering in terror.

'Please don't, ye will wake Angela, please don't do that again.'

Kathleen felt as if she had no strength in her arm. The poker suddenly felt so heavy she thought she would drop it, but she knew what she had to do. As she raised the poker, she screamed to give herself strength. Just before it came down on the back of his head, he suddenly turned round and, for one second, looked at Kathleen with utter shock on his face before slumping across the bed.

Kathleen couldn't tell who was screaming now, there was so much of it. She dragged Kitty out of the bed by her arms. Kitty was crying and wailing as she tried to lift Angela, who was yelling about being woken up as she was pulled from under Father James, out cold on the bed. Kathleen picked up Niamh and woke the boys in the next room and got them downstairs. Then they ran, carrying the half-asleep twins and Niamh between them, out of the front door and leaving all the doors open behind them, fleeing across the road into Jerry's house.

'Lock the door, lock the door,' screamed Kathleen, when they got inside. 'I'm going back to the club for the others, hold on till I get back, Kitty.'

Kathleen was scared to death at what she had done to Father James. Had she killed him? If she hadn't, surely to God, Tommy would.

Just as she turned the corner at the top of the entry out onto the street, she saw the three of them dancing along. It was raining stair rods and yet they were laughing and singing without a care in the world, Maura linking arms with Tommy on one side and Jerry on the other. Kathleen almost fell to her knees with relief as she put her hand out and held onto the wall to support herself. She had run so hard, she could hardly breathe. Jerry saw her first, then all three of them stopped dancing and broke into a run.

As soon as they got into Jerry's house, Kathleen made Maura and Tommy sit down whilst she held onto Kitty and told them how she had just caught Father James in Kitty's bedroom and what he was attempting to do.

The impact of Kathleen's news was so devastating that it was received in a shocked silence while it sank in. Maura clung to Tommy's hand, both with the same thoughts racing between them. They needed to hold onto each other for strength.

Kitty never spoke. The tears ran down her cheeks while she clung onto Maura, dreading that she might be rejected and shaken off. She felt a huge relief that Father James had been caught, but was sure that now she would be punished.

Then Kathleen added very calmly, 'And, God help me, I think I've killed him.'

Jerry tapped Tommy on the shoulder, picked up the poker from his own fire and rushed ahead of Tommy through the door and across the road, into Kitty's room. Jerry knew that he needed to keep control of the situation, while Tommy's anger burst forth as they ran, not one word intelligible.

'The fuckin' kiddie-fiddling bastard fucking cunt face fucking …'

His insults were in vain. When they reached Kitty's room and switched on the light, there was no sign of Father James. Tommy ran into the boys' room, but again there was nothing. Father James didn't even have the decency to be lying on the bed, injured. He had slunk off into the cold, wet night.

Jerry picked up from the bedroom floor the poker Kathleen had dropped, took it downstairs and put on the kettle.

'What the feck are ye doing?' said Tommy, already on his way out of the door.

'The police can tell who has touched things, Tommy, so they can. Let me do the thinking, man, you go and see to Kitty,' Jerry said.

When the kettle boiled, he poured the hot water over the poker and scrubbed it with the scourer from the kitchen sink. Then he plunged it into the hottest part of the fire where it would remain red hot until the embers burnt down in the morning. Jerry was worried. How injured was the priest? How hard had Kathleen hit him? Father James was powerful. When it came to his word in law against Kathleen's, an uneducated Irish immigrant, Father James would win every time.

Tears, tea and recriminations were flowing in Jerry's kitchen when he returned. Slowly and nervously Kitty told them everything. Jerry courteously stood in the background, facing the fire. Kitty's story was almost too painful to listen to and his stomach was knotted. He could only think how he would feel if this was Nellie sitting here, recounting to them all a story of living hell.

He turned round, about to suggest that he and Tommy go down to the police station, when he noticed that Tommy was no longer there. He felt a chill run down his spine. Tommy was no different from Jerry and Jerry knew exactly what he would want to do right now. He ran to the sink where the meat knife had been resting on the drainer ever since it had been used to cut up the lamb on Thursday. He didn't need to ask where it was now.

'Where the hell is Tommy, Maura?'

She looked up at Jerry as though she had seen a ghost.

'Tommy!' she screamed, when she realized he was no longer at her side. She leapt up from the arm of Kitty's chair and ran back into her own house. Jerry was right behind her.

'He isn't here, he's gone!' she said, as she came back down the stairs and went to grab a coat from the hooks on the back of the kitchen door.

'Oh no you don't,' said Jerry, taking hold of her arm firmly and steering her down the path. 'Go back in to Kitty; this is man's work, leave this to us.'

Maura shook in fear. 'Jerry, what's happening, I'm scared!'

'Well, don't be. This may be a test, Maura, but we will all pass it if we are strong. Go away now back indoors and look after Kitty, that's ye job. The rest is ours.'

Paddy's son, little Paddy, stood at his bedroom window, half asleep and rubbing his eyes, and watched Jerry disappear down the entry. The rain hadn't let up and there were no street lamps in the back alleyways. It was pitch black outside, but it was definitely Jerry.

Little Paddy had been woken earlier by the screaming from next door. He was a light sleeper. When he first woke he had thought it was his da choking. He wondered where Jerry was going at this time of night before he took himself back into bed. He was asleep again within seconds.

## Chapter Fourteen

It was four in the morning before the two men returned.

Maura had put Kitty to bed with Nellie, holding her in her arms as she rocked her to sleep. She was her mother and she needed to know what her daughter had been through, but there would be time for all that. Now, the poor child needed sleep. It still hadn't dawned on Maura that Kitty was pregnant.

Later, Maura and Kathleen sat by the fire in the kitchen, waiting. Kathleen did her best, but Maura was distraught and in shock. They both were. Kathleen had never before almost killed anyone and the realization was beginning to dawn on her of what she might have done.

As they walked in through the back door, the men didn't say a word to the anxious women.

Jerry pulled out the copper boiler from the shed as he came through the yard and then shouted at Tommy to go into the outhouse, strip off naked and to throw his clothes out into the yard floor. Maura noticed blood on Tommy's jacket, which he was unnaturally holding tightly closed across his chest. She put her hand to her mouth and stifled a scream. She was shaking uncontrollably and her legs could barely hold her up.

Kathleen, no stranger to a crisis, flew into action. She dragged the mop bucket in from the outhouse, filled it with hot water and Aunt Sally liquid soap and then ran outside and doused the water over a naked Tommy who was shaking as much as Maura. He began rubbing blood off his body with the floorcloth that Kathleen gave him. Now was not a time for modesty.

She fetched a clean sheet to wrap Tommy in and sent him indoors, then she washed down the outhouse and the yard, forcing the red rivulets down the drain with the yard brush. Jerry submerged part of Tommy's jacket in the boiler as he scrubbed it down. If he fully washed it, someone would notice. He then put Tommy's trousers and underclothes in the boiler, and his blood-soaked shirt on the fire. No one would notice a missing shirt even if it was his best.

No one said a word, but the looks that passed between Maura and Tommy were agonizing. Both were incapable of speech. Maura stood and rubbed his arms vigorously through the sheet, in an attempt to warm him and halt his violent shivering. They had been ripped from their ordinary lives and plunged into hell within minutes and they were struggling to cope.

Jerry unwrapped the blood-stained meat knife, which he had bundled in his own shirt, dropped it into the sink and poured boiling water over it. Then he threw his own shirt straight onto the open fire in the range with Tommy's.

Filling the sink, he plunged his arms in and began scrubbing. Kathleen, having put everything back in order in the outhouse, helped him.

'Thank the Holy Lord it's raining hard,' she whispered to Jerry. 'The rain will have finished off washing the yard by daylight.'

Kathleen was now calm. This was about strength in adversity.

The four streets looking after their own. The crime was irrelevant. The poor would always look after each other; they had to; they had the strength of a judgmental society to beat. And now they had this – an evil that stalked their homes and threatened their children.

'Give me ye boots,' said Jerry to Tommy. He dunked both pairs into the boiler, by now bubbling furiously, and then laid them by the fire. It was a wet night. Of course the boots were wet.

Kathleen opened the whiskey that had arrived yesterday morning, although it already felt like weeks ago, as so much had happened in a short space of time. They had been going to keep it for a Christmas treat.

'Feck Christmas,' muttered Kathleen, filling four mugs and pressing one into Maura's hand.

Jerry took his mug and looked up. 'None of us will ever mention this night again,' he said firmly. 'We will not speak of it to anyone. Do we all understand?'

Tommy, Maura and Kathleen nodded.

'Tommy and Maura, away home now to bed. We will be safe as long as no one knows. Don't be seen as you go. We will decide what is to be done with Kitty tomorrow, when we are calm and have all had some sleep.'

Maura and Kathleen had no idea what had been done with Father James, but they knew better than to ask. They were all now shaking violently with shock, even Kathleen. Now that her jobs had been done and there was nothing to focus on, the trembling took its hold.

Between chattering teeth, she said, 'If you had just put the evil bastard in a room full of young mothers, he would have got his punishment.'

'Sh, Mammy,' said Jerry, who, despite his shaking, was thinking with absolute clarity.

They each picked up their mugs and knocked the whiskey back, to stop the tremors before they parted from one another. Kathleen had filled the mugs to the brim and the amber liquid scalded as it slipped down, flooding them with warmth.

Tommy and Maura staggered back into their own house, having first checked that the street was quiet, Tommy still wrapped in the sheet, carrying his soaking clothes, with Maura clinging onto his arm.

The following morning, Alice woke early. As she came through the door into the kitchen, she saw the meat knife still on the draining rack. Thinking it best to put it away, she ran the knife under the tap and noticed a spot of blood on the end. She boiled the kettle and poured boiling water over it, then dried it and popped it in the knife drawer, before making herself a cup of tea.

She had heard every word that had been spoken last night, but had lain in bed, still and quiet. To Alice, it was normal to observe events from a distance.

The rooms upstairs were full of children sleeping, four girls top to tail in Nellie's bed and two sets of twins on the floor. The air was heavy with night breath. Alice tiptoed over sleeping children and opened the window on her way down to let in some of the fresh damp morning air.

Jerry was still sleeping off the Guinness and the whiskey when there was a knock on the front door. Alice took a breath, smoothed down her skirt and opened the door.

'Morning, miss, can we ask you a few questions?' enquired a young, fresh-faced policeman, one of two standing on the scrubbed doorstep.

Alice looked him straight in the eye and answered as cool as a cucumber. She told the policeman how everyone had been at the wedding party, then come home and gone to bed at about two in the morning.

'Was that just you, miss?' asked the policeman.

'Oh no,' said Alice calmly, 'it was all of us.' She reeled off the names of those living in Maura and Tommy's house, as well as their own.

She asked the constables why they were asking, but they wouldn't tell her.

She smiled sweetly, offered them a cup of tea she hoped they wouldn't accept, which they didn't, and then went back inside.

The policemen – Howard, originally from Wales, and Simon, a

little older and second generation from Belfast – marked both house numbers in their little black book with the words 'alibi for all occupants' and went on their way. The lady in the house was English. She had a very nice accent. One of those proper types, upright and honest. 'Definitely not a bog jumper and obviously telling the truth,' said Howard, as they walked away. He didn't notice Simon flinch at his words as he snapped his notebook shut.

When they went down the other side of the road and came to Maura and Tommy's door, they didn't even bother to knock.

'Leave that one,' said Simon. 'They came home with number forty-two.' If they were friends of the well-spoken lady, they were probably proper English types too.

'You sure?' asked the new and very keen Howard.

It was almost time for a brew and Simon wanted to get inside the car and head back to the station.

'Yes, I'm sure,' Simon replied. 'When you have been around as long as me, you get a nose for these things.'

Inside the house, Alice was feeling an unfamiliar rush of excitement and pride. For the first time in her life, she felt as though she had fulfilled a purpose. She was now relevant, important even. Her moment had come and, without conscious pre-thought or planning, she had risen to the occasion and shone. Even she knew that.

Jerry and Kathleen had looked after Alice. They had been good to her. Over time she had learnt the significance of her differences from most other people and had begun to realize that, as someone who lived on the four streets in the home that she did, she was very lucky indeed. For the first time in her life this had been her big chance to do something for someone else. Kathleen's ways had rubbed off on her. She wasn't going to let them down.

Every member in every household on the four streets gathered round their small black and white television sets that evening, from the youngest to the oldest, and watched the report of the gruesome murder of a priest in Liverpool. They listened in silence as the solemn newsreader described how he had been found on the path to the Priory with a stab wound in his chest and a significant body part dismembered, which had been found later in the day, mauled by a cat, ten yards away in the graveyard. No murder weapon had been found and the police had no clues.

'The local community has been paralysed by the news, because the priest was a well-known figure around Liverpool. He had a particular calling to aid children who were suffering in poor communities, as demonstrated by his work at local schools and the children's hospital.'

On Monday morning, while Kathleen had her cup of tea with the Granada TV rentals man and sliced him a piece of fruit loaf with the meat knife, he told her all the fanciful theories that were flying around the four streets about who had done for Father James. Naturally, not one of them included Maura and Tommy's house, where the Father had been treated like a saint. Or their own house, where the Father never came. They were all safe in their secret. And a secret it would remain, she hoped.

Meanwhile, over at the school, the police were talking to the children in the morning assembly, asking questions about Father James.

'Did any of you see anything unusual on the night Father James was murdered?' asked Howard of the rows of children sitting cross-legged on the wooden parquet floor in front of him.

A complete dead end to their inquiries had driven him, under pressure from their Chief Superintendent, to try a more novel approach to gathering information.

Simon had moaned and groaned and resisted as much as possible. He was not keen on change. He also felt embarrassed. Sister Evangelista was openly crying. Simon had been taught by the nuns when he himself was a boy. He didn't like to see women weep. Nuns were a special breed of women, so he hated that even more.

Howard had considered this a smart idea when he first thought of it; at the very least it would look good when he reported back to the

Super and help him on his race to become a sergeant. But now that he was here, standing in front of so many sombre faces, he wished he was anywhere else.

One little boy was wriggling and enthusiastically thrust up his hand.

Nondescript, slightly dirty, wearing a sleeveless pullover with no shirt underneath, despite the cold, and with a huge hole in the front, with what looked like half a ball of wool unravelled and hanging down in long loose threads exposing his skin underneath, he had been squirming on the floor since the police officers walked in. The tide mark across his neck was as black as the leather on his shoes, which were three sizes too big and only just still attached to the soles.

'Here we go,' said Simon disdainfully, 'he saw Donald Duck going into mass.'

'I did, I did!' shouted little Paddy, punching the air with his hand excitedly – innocently trying to curry favour with Sister Evangelista, who scared him so much he would do anything to be in her good books. 'I saw Uncle Jerry running up the back entry in the middle of the night.'

Simon and Howard both stared at the scruffy boy, wriggling about on the floor with the unwashed hair and grubby face.

'Paddy,' said Sister Evangelista in a stern voice, 'the officers have no time for your nonsense. Shut up, boy, and sit straight in your line.'

By the time she had reached the word 'line', Sister Evangelista was almost screaming. Sister Evangelista had no time for dirty children and must have told Peggy a hundred times, cleanliness was next to godliness. The boy smelt and had head lice, and she had no patience with him whatsoever.

The shock and horror of Father James's death had affected them all. The unanswered questions, along with revulsion at the manner of it, had set their nerves on edge.

When the police officers had told Sister they wanted to speak to the children at assembly, she had almost refused. She had barely slept, as confusing thoughts and questions to which she had no answer kept her awake well into the small hours.

Simon and Howard looked at each other. 'May we borrow your

office, Sister?' asked Howard, who was already motioning to Paddy to join him at the front.

The children sat still and unspeaking as they watched the policemen hold open the large wooden and glass doors for Paddy to pass through from the hall on the way to Sister Evangelista's office. There was no need for the teachers or nuns to remonstrate with those who wriggled as though they had ants in their pants. Everyone was silent and still as they stared at the departing backs of the tall policemen.

Alice was taking her knitting out from behind the cushion on the comfy chair, which was where it lived, when she heard three loud, ominous knocks on the front door.

The Granada man was packing away into his case his little black book and large grey bag of sixpences, and Kathleen was on her way to the sink with the cups and plates, when they all stopped dead in their tracks and stared towards the front door.

'Blimey, that's an important knock,' said the Granada man. 'It'll be a vacuum cleaner salesman. I saw the Electrolux men on Vauxhall Road yesterday.'

Kathleen and Alice looked at each other without a word. Alice slipped her knitting back behind the cushion and walked purposefully to the front door to open it. She was growing in confidence every day.

Down on the docks, the men were unloading the merchant ship, the *Cotopaxi*, which had sailed in from Ecuador early that morning. As he was one of the shorter and tubbier men on the docks, Tommy's feet had left the quay as he jumped up to catch a guide rope for a bag of jute, just above his head and out of his reach. Tommy travelled through the air for the twenty feet it took him to reach Jerry. It was time for their ciggie break and Tommy thought it was about time Jerry knew. As his feet touched the ground again, he looked up towards the jute sack and his eye was caught by two policemen talking to the guard at the top of the steps.

He saw the guard point in their direction, as both policemen tipped their helmet peaks in a gesture of thanks and began to descend the steps.

As Tommy landed, he pushed the rope into Jerry's hand and squeezed it tight, pushing his nails into Jerry's skin, forcing Jerry to look at him in surprise.

'Let go of me hand, you homo,' Jerry said in annoyance as he tried to take the rope from Tommy.

'The fecking bizzies are coming down the steps, Jer,' Tommy almost spat at him. 'If it's us they is after, neither of us say a fecking word. If we don't say nothing, they don't have nothing.'

There was an urgency to Tommy's voice. They both knew which was the guilty of the two, but Tommy also knew they would never let one another down.

Jerry didn't glance at the steps, but looked Tommy straight in the eye as he said, 'Aye, right, to be sure I will say nothin' now, neither of us, nothin'.'

They took a long hard look at each other, as they heard Howard's voice ring out behind them, 'Oi, Jerry Deane, we want a word with you.'

Jerry and Tommy clasped thumbs briefly, then Jerry let go of the rope and turned round.

Alice walked up Brigie's path with ease. Her heart no longer beat faster when she stepped out from her lonely world. She was still not one for small talk and she knew that no one would ever seek her out for a shopping trip to St John's market, or indulge in baby chatter, but she did at least feel as though she was somewhere she belonged.

Brigie had been pacing up and down the kitchen floor all morning with a teething baby daughter who screamed louder than the rest put together. She didn't hear the back door open and could have dropped the baby when she saw Alice walk through it. Alice smiled conspiratorially in greeting, closed the door and then, from under her skirt, produced an almost empty whiskey bottle.

Brigie walked over to the kettle. This was going to be interesting.

*

Simon and Howard had pounded Jerry with repetitive questions for almost two hours, and yet he had remained silent.

The police station, old, large and forbidding, with its distinctive blue light over the door, was in Whitechapel. The cells were small and noisy and, on a Saturday night, full to overflowing with the same prostitutes who had spent so many nights in the cells that they called Whitechapel station home.

Jerry had been held in one such cell for four hours and, so far, hadn't said a word. He was trying the patience of Howard and Simon, who decided to take a break.

They took themselves off to the station canteen for a drink and a game of billiards, to help them decide what to do next. They were coming up against a brick wall. With the best will in the world, no judge was ever going to accept the word of a filthy, witless little boy who obviously wasn't the sharpest knife in the box. And what did they have anyway? Under questioning in Sister Evangelista's office, the kid had moved from having definitely seen his Uncle Jerry to possibly having seen his Uncle Jerry.

They were holding Jerry in the cell on spurious grounds, but once they had him in the cell, he suddenly reeked of culpability for no other reason than he wouldn't speak.

'If he was innocent, he would talk and tell us why he was running down the entry,' said Howard.

Simon, who rarely got anything right, pulled on his cigarette and, as the smoke swirled around his face, replied, 'Aye, I smell a stinking great rat all right. That man is as guilty as hell. The problem is, how? Why? What's the motive? The Sister said he didn't even go to the church.'

'We need to at least pin a motive on him soon or we will have to let him walk,' said Howard, who was not looking forward to the prospect.

The Super had been delighted that at least they had someone in the cell to question for the mystery murder of the priest. Simon and Howard had been feeling pressure as if it was coming from someone much higher up in the force.

'Let's go back in,' said Simon. 'Let's start the good cop, bad cop routine and see if that makes him start talking.'

'We will,' said Howard, 'but I will tell you this: we may have no motive and we may have nothing other than that feckless kid but all the same, that man reeks of guilt.'

## Chapter Fifteen

By the time Tommy arrived home from work, the four streets were buzzing with the news that Jerry was being held by the police. It had been the longest day's work while he had counted down the minutes until he could run back up the steps and confer with Maura and Kathleen. When Maura told him what Alice had done, he felt a shiver run down his spine – and then, 'Jeez, Maura,' he shouted, 'why didn't ye wait for me to get fecking home?'

Tommy was having trouble weighing up the consequences of Alice's actions. Maura had never known Tommy to swear as much as he had since the worst night of their lives; in fact she had heard him shout on only a handful of occasions during their married life. Maura needed reinforcements and sent Kitty across the road to fetch Kathleen and Alice.

'Calm down, Tommy,' said Kathleen with authority, as soon as she came in. 'It's a grand idea if Brigie and Sean will play along with Peggy and Paddy, but you need to get your head together and go and see Paddy. It will work only if ye all agree.'

'Let me get this right,' said Tommy. 'Ye are all asking Sean, Paddy and meself to go down to the police station and say Jerry was sneaking down to Sean's house for a card school and to drink up the wedding whiskey, whilst ye lot was asleep in ye beds?'

Maura, Kathleen and Alice nodded. When it was put into Tommy's words, coldly and with an edge of scorn, it didn't sound so good.

Tommy exploded. He and Jerry had a pact, to talk to no one.

'Ye just couldn't keep ye's gobs shut, could ye,' he shouted. 'Me and Jer, tell no one, we decided. If we can keep it that way they have nothing and nowt, and youse have told the whole fecking four streets. I'm done for, Maura, I'm a fecking goner now.'

Tommy was losing control. Maura felt scared. Normally, Tommy was putty in her hands; she had never seen him like this before. His anger seemed to have erupted from nowhere. She felt the blood drain from her face as she began to think Alice had done something very, very stupid.

Both sets of twins and Angela began to cry, setting Niamh off too. Kitty had no idea what was going on, but she gathered up the children and took them across the road to Nellie, who was sitting in front of the TV on her own. Joseph was already in bed.

Kitty felt a pang of jealousy shoot through her. She had never in her life had a room to herself. As one of seven, she could only dream of such a luxury.

Nellie had no idea what was going on either, but the whispering between Kathleen and Alice had set her on edge. She knew something was badly wrong.

They had told her Jerry was helping the police, but Nellie couldn't understand that. Helping them to do what?

Nellie got up from her chair and took the biscuit tin out of the cupboard. She and Kitty gave a biscuit to each of the little ones to encourage them to stop crying. Kitty felt jealous again. The biscuit tin was rarely full in her house.

When the children had calmed down, both girls sat in a comfy chair together, with their arms round each other. The rest of the Doherty brood sat on the mat and they all stared at the TV, which offered an escape from the frightening atmosphere around them. Nellie felt more settled than she had all evening, now that she was no longer alone, but in the company of her lifelong friends.

*

Sean, who was over six feet tall, had had to remove his cap as he bent to enter Tommy's kitchen. He was a mystery to every man on the street. Sean was as broad as he was tall, a fine specimen who spent his weekends at the boxing club. He worked on the docks by day and was in the boxing ring by night.

'Ye can't blame him,' Tommy had once said to Maura. 'If I had that many daughters, I'd be on a ship to Mexico, never mind the bloody boxing club.'

Sean had a formidable reputation and it went back as far as his street-fighting days in Tipperary. The word on the four streets was that Sean had arrived in Liverpool whilst on the run from the Gardai for having nearly beaten a man to death in a Tipperary pub brawl. No one dare ask Sean if the rumour were true.

'He beats the shite out of anyone who dares go near him in that ring,' laughed Tommy, after he and Jerry had gone along to a match to support their friend, 'the big man'.

And yet he and Brigie had produced only daughters, and lots of them. Eight little red-headed females in one house. Sean was living proof of the street folklore that it was the women who decided the sex of the baby. Unless, of course, she produced boys – and then it was all down to the virility of the man.

Sean hadn't liked what Brigie had told him about Alice's visit earlier in the day. It had perturbed him greatly.

Sean liked to take his wash-down upstairs at the press. The first thing he did every night, when he came home, was to carry his jug upstairs and strip off.

Every one of his daughters had been conceived during the end-of-day wash-down. Brigie looked at the other men on the streets and, with the exception of Jerry who was known for his good looks, she knew how lucky she was in Sean.

She didn't like the number of young girls who hung around the boxing club, and she was no fool. As exhausted as she frequently was, she kept her man happy and paid for it with a lifetime of pregnancy and breastfeeding.

Tonight, whilst Sean was washing down, Brigie had stopped downstairs. He thought over what she had told him and remembered times that Father James had visited his own house. Images flashed into his mind of the Father holding his daughters in his arms. He had often fleetingly questioned why Father James called round to the house so often.

Sean had no idea what had happened on that night or why Jerry was being questioned. He only knew what Alice was asking him to do. There were plenty on the four streets who revered Father James.

Sean told Brigie it was very important to keep her mouth shut. Some would find what they were doing difficult to understand.

'If I do what Alice has asked, Brigie, we need to keep safe.'

Brigie didn't need to be told. The people she lived amongst were as good as her family, but she knew that many were devastated by Father James's death. The Dohertys and the Deanes were good people. She would tell no one.

When Sean stepped into the kitchen, Paddy was already there. The women had left and the men sat down.

The women had talked Tommy round and, the more they had talked, the more he realized their plot made good sense. They were in greater danger without an alibi for Jerry. They needed to source one quickly, get him out of the police station and safely home as soon as possible. They needed help from their friends.

The kettle began to whistle on the range and, as Tommy stood to take it off and mash some tea, Paddy roared, 'Feckin' hell, imagine that, lads, no women and just us men living in one house now, how grand would that be, eh?'

Despite the seriousness of the situation, all three burst out laughing.

'Yeah, but I'm not going to bed with you, Paddy,' said Tommy, carrying a pot of tea over to the table. 'Ye snore.'

They laughed again and the atmosphere lightened momentarily.

'Now, lads, you don't need details, trust me, but Jer needs our help and we all need to be singing out of the same bloody hymn book to do that. Are ye with me?'

Sean and Paddy picked up their tea and looked at each other. They had both moved onto the four streets at around the same time and between the two families they had attended too many baptisms to count. They had both clasped their arms together and held Jerry upright underneath Bernadette's dead body as she lay in her coffin on the day they buried her. One of Sean's daughters was running around the street right now in Angela's old shoes, and the two girls were best friends.

Sean took both sets of Tommy's twins down to the boxing club with him on a regular basis and they had all pooled their resources together on many an occasion to make sure the kids were fed. When Paddy had run out of money before the end of the week, Jerry had often slipped him half a crown.

It didn't matter what Jerry had done. They were his mates and they would do whatever was needed, regardless of the danger to themselves.

'I'm in,' said Sean.

Paddy felt guilty as he looked at his two friends and drank his tea. Peggy had told him what little Paddy had done and big Paddy had taken his slipper to him. He wouldn't open his mouth again, the stupid little fecker. Too much like his mother at times. Spoke rubbish before putting his brain in gear.

He had been home for a full half-hour before Peggy told him what had happened, and the stupid woman had told the lad to hide in the outhouse, out of his da's way.

It took Paddy a full minute for what Peggy was telling him to sink in.

'He did what?' Paddy roared. 'He did what? Are ye telling me Jer is sat in a police cell, being questioned about the priest's murder, because that gobshite of a kid wanted to look clever?'

Shame and anger convulsed Paddy in equal measure. The men had talked about nothing else on the docks other than how ridiculous the police were. They had laughed at the ridiculous notion that Jerry could have anything to do with it.

'Stupid feckers, the bizzies are. Jer didn't even go to fuckin' mass since the day he buried Bernadette,' Brian, his gang mate, had said. 'He's even married a Protestant. God knows when the last time was that Jer even spoke to the priest. What a fuckin' laugh it is.'

Paddy ran up the stairs as quickly as a man could run who

smoked forty a day and had worked nine hours straight. There was no sign of his son.

He ran back through the kitchen, picked up his slipper from in front of the fire and went out into the yard. Now he could hear little Paddy whimpering in the outhouse.

Maura could hear the shouts in her own yard as she took down the washing. She stopped unpegging and held onto the line with her eyes closed. Neither Maura nor Tommy ever hit their kids and it made her feel sick to hear poor little Paddy's pathetic pleas for Paddy to leave him alone.

'No, Da, don't hit me with the slipper,' he screeched, as the outhouse door flung open.

It was too late; his pleas were followed up by loud thwacks, screams and even louder crying. Paddy must have slapped his son at least a dozen times. Maura heard him swear as the slipper flew out of his hand, but that didn't stop him; he then resorted to his fists. The guilt she felt at hearing little Paddy take a beating made her stomach turn sour. Maura loved little Paddy. She often fed him at her own table and had deloused his hair as often as she had the twins. He was one of life's innocents and he never failed to make them all laugh with his antics. 'What has little Paddy done today then,' she would ask her boys at some stage of the evening. She often pulled him to her for a quick hug each time he said 'I wish I lived with ye, Maura.' She wished he did too. Never more than today.

Maura wanted to lean over the wall and plead with Paddy to stop, but she didn't dare. The four streets survived in harmony on the basis of unwritten rules and one of them was: you never interfered or stuck your nose in when it hadn't been asked for.

'I'm in,' said Paddy, relieved to have the opportunity to compensate for the perceived stupidity of little Paddy.

Jerry had been in the police station for eight hours and the police were getting nowhere.

Howard and Simon should have gone home three hours since, but they didn't want to leave this to anyone else. Neither could say why, they had no evidence other than a witness statement from a ten-year-old, but both knew they were on to something.

Their trained noses could smell it. They could taste it. The aroma of guilt filled the station. It was at its strongest in the cell in which they held Jerry and yet they didn't have a single fact to go on.

'Maybe we should let him go, put a watch on him and call it a night,' said Howard, who was imagining his tea, which was always on the table at six-thirty sharp, sitting there congealing.

'Are you joking?' said Simon. 'Look, mate, we both know we are on to something here. That man is playing us like a fiddle. He hasn't said one flaming word since we handcuffed him. We have to keep going until he cracks first.'

'We are running out of time,' said Howard. 'We will have to let him ...'

His words trailed off as, from the window, they saw Tommy, Sean and Paddy march in through the station doors.

Brigie had just got the youngest off to sleep when Howard knocked on her front door. She looked surprised to see him and with a warm and welcoming smile, invited him straight in. He made no small talk and looked as though he was in a foul temper.

He opened his notebook and took out his pencil. 'Would ye like some tea?' said Brigie sweetly. Howard appeared not to hear and got straight to the point. 'Did you, on the sixteenth of this month, receive a bottle of whiskey as a gift from the wedding family?'

'Aye, we did,' replied Brigie. 'And so did everyone else.'

'Can I see your whiskey, madam?' said Howard, feeling more officious than usual.

Neither he nor Simon believed the card-school story. Now they needed to check whether or not the whiskey bottle had been opened. If it hadn't, it would be their only lead. And a big one too. They would be able to prove that Jerry's neighbours had been lying and that was a serious offence indeed.

Brigie looked at Howard questioningly and slowly moved to the sideboard in the front room. Howard followed her.

Brigie bent down to open the cupboard door, looking sideways at Howard and, as she lifted the bottle of whiskey out, she let out a high-pitched squeal and gasped, 'Oh Jaysus, someone has drunk the bleedin' whiskey, there's nothing here.' She turned and faced Howard with the empty bottle in her hand. A look of pure amazement sat on her face and took a bow.

Howard snapped his book shut and stormed out of the kitchen.

At exactly the same time in Kathleen's kitchen, Simon was asking the same question.

'Sure,' said Kathleen as she went to the kitchen cupboard, 'we are saving it for Christmas mind, here ye are,' and she took out a full and unopened bottle of whiskey.

Within an hour, Jerry walked in through his own back door. Everyone had gathered in his kitchen, even Brigie, as once again Kathleen poured out whiskey for all. 'Bugger Christmas,' she laughed as she cracked open the seal. 'Easy come, easy go,' said Sean.

He and Paddy had both told the police that there was a card school, playing for money, in Sean's house that night, well after the women had gone to bed.

They had embellished the story with the admission that they had drunk almost the whole bottle of whiskey between them. They were both prepared to sign a witness statement to that effect. When Paddy said firmly, 'Aye, and my lad wants to withdraw his, so he does. Now he thinks it was me he saw leaving the entry, not Jerry,' Howard's heart sank.

Gone was his promotion.

Simon and Howard knew they were back to square one. With no evidence they had to let Jerry go. He had an alibi with two witnesses. He was safe.

Nellie and Kitty were back together on the comfy chair. Nellie had refused to move from Jerry's arms until Kitty came back in through the door.

Everyone lifted their glass to drink in relief, when Kathleen tapped her glass with a spoon and spoke.

'Before we drink,' she said, 'we need to say thank you to someone. To Alice.' Everyone turned and smiled at Alice.

Alice beamed, feeling swamped by a sense of pride. Her face flushed red and tears pricked at her eyes when everyone lifted their glass and said loudly, 'To Alice.'

It was the happiest moment of her life.

Nellie and Kitty hugged each other, grinning. They had no idea what they were grinning at, or what had just occurred, but everyone was happy and so were they.

Suddenly, without warning, Kitty leapt from the chair and raced through the back door to the outhouse.

As Kitty leant over the pan to throw up the first time, she felt someone holding back her hair from the vomit and stroking the back of her neck. She could hear the voices wafting down the yard from the kitchen, laughing and chattering away. Celebrating. Everyone joyous and happy.

Another shot of whiskey, she thought, and they will be singing next and pushing the chairs back to dance around the kitchen. They wouldn't miss her. She was shaking with cold and felt clammy as she knelt on the floor and clung onto the wooden seat, a long, polished plank that stretched across the top of the toilet. Next to the seat stood a large pile of cut-up pages of the *Echo*, to use as toilet paper. The smell from the printer's ink made her heave again.

The soothing, ethereal whispers calmed her panic. She knew everyone was in the kitchen, and there could be no one with her in the outhouse, but the nausea made her feel so deathly that she was beyond thinking or caring.

Just as she leant over to vomit for the second time and felt her own hair being lifted clear, she saw a long strand of red hair sweep past the side of her face.

Kathleen looked at Maura to see if she had noticed Kitty dashing out of the back door to the outhouse. She had.

Maura went white. She put her hand to her mouth and held onto the back of the chair to steady herself as the realization hit her with the force of a truck.

Kathleen moved over to her side and put an arm round her waist.

'Oh my God, Kathleen, 'twas before me very eyes and I never knew. Jesus, Mary and Joseph, what next? What will we do?'

'Sh,' Kathleen replied. 'Let's enjoy tonight, Maura. That problem is ours to share, tomorrow.'

# Hide Her Name

*For my late father George, the gentlest and kindest of all men, and my inimitable and beloved Irish nana, Nellie Deane, who stole me away from Liverpool in order that I would love Eire as much as she.*

I went out to the hazel wood,
Because a fire was in my head,
And cut and peeled a hazel wand,
And hooked a berry to a thread;
And when white moths were on the wing,
And moth-like stars were flickering out,
I dropped the berry in the stream
And caught a little silver trout.

When I had laid it on the floor
I went to blow the fire a-flame,
But something rustled on the floor,
And someone called me by my name:
It had become a glimmering girl
With apple blossom in her hair
Who called me by my name and ran
And faded through the brightening air.

William Butler Yeats
selected verses from
*The Song of Wandering Aengus*

# Chapter One

'Stop lying on his pyjamas now, Peggy, and let yer man out to earn an honest crust!'

Paddy's next-door neighbour, Tommy, impatiently yelled over the backyard gate as he and the Nelson Street dockers knocked on for Paddy. They stood, huddled together in an attempt to hold back the worst of the rain, as they waited for Paddy to join them.

Much to her annoyance, Peggy, Paddy's wife, could hear their sniggering laughter.

'Merciful God!' she said crossly. 'Paddy, would ye tell that horny fecker, Tommy, it's not us at it every five minutes.' She snatched the enamel mug of tea out of Paddy's hand and away from his lips before he had supped his last drop. There was not a second of silence available for him in which to protest.

'The only reason he and Maura have two sets of twins is because he's a dirty bugger and does it twice a night. I'll not have him shouting such filth down the entry, now tell him, will ye, Paddy?'

Peggy and Paddy had spawned enough of their own children, but Peggy had never in her life done it twice on the same night. Every woman who lived on the four streets knew: that sinful behaviour got you caught with twins.

'I wonder sometimes how Maura holds her head up without the shame, so I do. Once caught doing it twice, ye would know what the feck had happened and not do it again. He must be mighty powerful with his persuasion, that Tommy. Answer me, Paddy, tell him, will ye?'

'Aye, I will that, Peggy,' said Paddy as he picked up his army-issue canvas bag containing his dinner: a bottle of cold tea and Shippam's beef paste sandwiches. Rushing to the door, he placed a kiss on Peggy's cheek, his shouted goodbye cut midway as the back gate snapped closed behind him.

Each man who lived on the four streets worked on the docks. Their day began as it ended, together.

It took exactly four minutes from the last backyard on Nelson Street, down the dock steps, to the perimeter gate. The same amount of time it took to smoke the second roll-up as ribald jokes and football banter rose high on the air. When the sun shone, their spirits lifted and they would often sing whilst walking.

The same melancholy songs heard in the Grafton rooms or the Irish centre on a Saturday night sunk into a pint of Guinness. Melodies of a love they left behind. Of green fields the colour of emeralds, or a raven-haired girl, with eyes that shone like diamonds.

The Nelson Street gang was often delayed by Paddy at number seventeen and would pause at his back gate and stand a while.

Each morning, wearing a string vest that carried the menu of every meal eaten at home that week, Paddy sat up in bed, picked up his cigarettes and matches that lay next to an ever-overflowing ashtray on the bedside table, and lit up his first ciggie of the day.

Paddy smoked a great deal in bed.

He would often wake Peggy in the middle of the night with the sound of his match striking through the dark, providing a split second of bright illumination.

'Give us a puff,' Peggy would croak, without any need of the teeth soaking in a glass on the table next to her. Not waiting for nor expecting a reply, she would warily uncoil her arm from under the old grey army blanket and, cheating the cold air of any opportunity to penetrate the dark, smelly warmth beneath, grasp the wet-ended cigarette between her finger and thumb, put it to her lips and draw deeply.

'Ah, that's better,' she would say. 'Me nerves are shot, Paddy,' and within seconds she would drift back to sleep.

This morning, the squall blew across the Mersey and up the four streets, soaking the men waiting for Paddy. They stood huddled against the entry wall, trying in vain to protect their ciggies from the downpour.

Paddy appeared through the gate, Peggy's words at his back pushing him out onto the cobbles.

'Yer fecking bastards, ye'll get me hung one day, so yer will,' said Paddy only half seriously to Tommy and the rest of the gang.

'I was only joking, Paddy, I've seen a better face on a clock than on yer missus,' said Tommy. 'I knew ye was just stuffing yer gob with another slice of toast.'

'Leave Peggy alone or I'll set her on yer,' joked Paddy. 'She was kept in a cage till she was five. Ye'll be sorry if I do.'

They all laughed, even Paddy.

Tall Sean, a docker by day and a boxer by night, joined in as he struggled to light up.

'Never fear, Paddy,' he laughed. 'Yer a lucky man with your Peggy, her titties are so feckin' big, ye could hang me wet donkey jacket off them with a bottle of Guinness in each pocket and it still wouldn't fall off.'

They roared with laughter and with lots of matey reassuring pats on the back for Paddy, they continued on their way down the steps to face another day of hard graft on the river's edge.

Boots on cobbles. Minds on the match.

From an upstairs window in the Priory, Daisy Quinn, Father James's housekeeper, studied the dockers marching down the steps towards the gate, just as she had done every single morning since she herself had arrived from Dublin during the war.

In an hour, once she had cleared away the breakfast things, she would take her damp duster and move to another room, across the landing and look down on the mothers and children from Nelson Street as they walked in the opposite direction to that of the dockers, towards the school gates.

The Victorian Priory, large, square and detached, stood next to the graveyard and from each of the upstairs windows Daisy could alter her view: of the docks, the graveyard, the school and the convent, or the four streets. Daisy had her own panoramic view of life as it happened. There wasn't very much about anyone or anything Daisy didn't know. They all turned up on the Priory steps at some time, for one reason or another.

'Daisy, have ye any coal to spare? We have none and the babby is freezing.'

'Do ye have any potatoes or bread? A coat for the child to go to school?'

They were always wanting something and, sure enough, Father James could often solve the problem. They had cupboards in the Priory stuffed full of the clothes people donated for him to hand out to the poor.

But the father never gave. Mothers had to ask.

'I am here to do God's work, not the corporation's,' he would often boom in a bad-tempered way when Daisy asked should he take a coat or a pair of shoes to a family, after she had noticed the welfare officer knocking on their door.

But pride never stood in the way of a mother needing to warm a child, so beg they often did.

Occasionally people came for happy reasons – to ask for the father to perform a christening or a wedding – and when that happened, the father would take them into his study and Daisy would carry in a tray of tea and a plate of her home-made biscuits, just as Mrs Malone had taught her.

She almost always took back an empty plate. Hardly ever had Daisy returned a biscuit to the kitchen.

If ever a mother was too polite or too scared to allow her children to take one, Daisy would press a few into her hand at the front door, wrapped in greaseproof paper and tied up with string.

'Go on now, take it,' she would say. 'Have them for later.'

Daisy would have loved to have had children of her own.

She had arrived in Liverpool from Dublin to take her position at the Priory whilst still a child. She became an assistant to the fathers' cook, Mrs Malone, and like most young girls she had a head full of dreams and plans.

Father James had disposed of those faster than a speeding bullet.

'You will have one day and one night off per month,' he told her, within moments of her being summoned to his study.

Daisy was a little disappointed by that news. She had been told by the sisters at the orphanage in Dublin that she would have one day a week to herself and a week's holiday each year, during which she could travel back to Ireland and visit the only place she knew to be home, the orphanage where she had been raised since she was a baby.

Now, all these years later, Daisy could count the days off she had taken on one hand.

'You must work hard and help Mrs Malone in the kitchen,' the sisters at the orphanage had told her. And, sure enough, working hard was what she had done every day since.

Without a moment's pain or illness and certainly without any warning at all, Mrs Malone had dropped dead, almost ten years to the day following Daisy's arrival.

Mrs Malone had often told Daisy what a good worker she was.

'I don't know how I would manage without you, Daisy,' she said, at least once a day. 'The sisters may have said you were simple in the head, but I didn't want you for brains, brawn was what I was looking for and you have plenty of that.'

Daisy smiled with pleasure. Being told that she was simple was not news to her, sure, she had heard it so often before. But the sisters had also said, 'You can hold your head up with no shame, you were born to a very good family, Daisy Quinn.'

Daisy never thought to question why she was in an orphanage and not with her family. She had no real understanding of what a family was.

Being a good girl and coming from a good family must have been why she was sent to take up such an important job in England and for one of the fathers too.

'You have simple ways, but they can be put to good use if you can be protected from the sin that preys upon girls like yourself,' the sisters had told her. Daisy had no idea which sin would prey upon her or what it would do, but she was grateful for the protection.

Neither the sisters nor Mrs Malone had ever mentioned to Daisy the other reason that she had been sent to the Priory.

Daisy presumed that they could not have known, because Father James forbade Daisy to speak to anyone about it.

'To speak of anything that occurs in this Priory would be the greatest sin for which no forgiveness would ever be forthcoming. Ye will be left to burn alone in the eternal flames of hell and damnation. Do ye understand, girl?'

She was asked this question on a regular basis and her answer was always the dutiful same: 'Yes, Father.'

Daisy took over the housekeeper's role in full. She coped well and never took nor was offered a day off.

However, there had also been a number of welcome changes following Mrs Malone's death.

Neither Father James nor any of his friends had bothered her again, and the nuns began to invite her over to the convent for tea.

She had only the bishop to tolerate now.

She sometimes wondered if Father James would have preferred someone other than herself as housekeeper, but on the night of Mrs Malone's funeral, on her way to her modest room, she had overheard raised voices coming from the study.

'The money for the Priory would stop if she left. It must follow her wherever she is and, anyway, the sisters in Dublin would have too many questions to ask should she be moved.'

That was the bishop speaking. A fat man, distinguishable by his thin, weedy whine, which as it whistled into the air struggled past the blubbery folds of lard gathered under his chin.

'I suppose we are safer if she is here,' said Father James in a tone loaded with disappointment.

'Aye, we are that, but anyway, she is simple. No one would ever believe a word she said. I will write now that she is happy and improved. That she is running the show and, sure, isn't that the truth? Wasn't that just the grandest bit of rabbit pie we ever ate for supper?'

Daisy grinned from ear to ear with pleasure. They had loved her rabbit pie.

On this wet morning, Daisy padded across to the south side of the empty house. Sister Evangelista had popped a note through the door late last night to let her know she would be visiting the Priory this morning to help Daisy pack up the father's room, ready to send his belongings to his sister in America.

The murder of Father James in the graveyard had taken place only feet away from the Priory and everyone was still in a state of profound shock.

Everyone except Daisy, that was.

Daisy wasn't sad and didn't miss the father at all. Not in the way she had missed Mrs Malone when she died.

In fact, Daisy missed Mrs Malone a great deal. She had always told Daisy what she could and could not do, and with no one to guide her, Daisy was lost.

Father James had told her what she could and could not say.

What should she say now and who to?

Her mind was in torment.

Daisy pressed her forehead against the cold window and, looking down, watched the children walking to school. She saw Sister Evangelista close the convent door, make her way down the path and turn right along the pavement towards the Priory. The Reverend Mother waved to Kitty Doherty from number nineteen, who was making her way towards the school steps on the opposite side of the road to the convent. Kitty was herding along the two sets of twin boys and that lovely girl, Nellie Deane, from number forty-two was helping her. The girls waved back to Sister Evangelista, all smiles.

The Kitty girl. Daisy had often seen Father James visit her house, very often at night, but he never visited Nellie's.

Nellie, whose mother, Bernadette, had died so tragically young and whom Daisy still saw sometimes in the dead of the night, running up and down the four streets.

It was Nellie's Nana Kathleen who had woken Daisy late on the night the father was murdered. She had been talking to Bernadette as she left the Keating girl's wedding and followed the river, down towards Nelson Street.

Daisy wasn't scared to see the ghostly Bernadette with Kathleen. She often saw her in the graveyard and up and down Nelson Street, as she flew straight through the wall into what had once been her home, number forty-two.

Daisy, uneasy, had been unable to return to sleep on that particular night. She had wandered out of her bedroom, the static from her peach, brushed-nylon nightdress crackling and snapping at her feet as she walked. She had leant over the dark, swan-necked banister that swept away steeply, and gazed down the long stairwell. The hall light was still on. The father had yet to return home from the wedding. He would switch the light off when he returned to the Priory.

From the window, Daisy had watched Nana Kathleen and Bernadette, and waited. And then she had seen the father in his large hat and cloak, turning the corner into the back entry just ahead of them both. He hadn't come back to the Priory as ususal that night.

Daisy knew she should tell someone what she had seen. But Daisy wasn't allowed to tell anyone anything.

'I might be simple,' she had said to herself as she got back into bed on that fateful evening, 'but I'm not an eejit. There's no way I am spending eternity stood in the fires of hell.'

When the bell pull rang, Daisy almost fell down the stairs as she ran to open the Priory door for Sister Evangelista. She had been unhappy sleeping in the huge house on her own since the murder. Today she would beg Sister Evangelista to take her to the convent right away. She would be safe there, just as she had been at the orphanage.

'Morning, Daisy.' Sister Evangelista sounded brighter than she felt.

She was dreading this job but the bishop had been very strong indeed on the telephone.

'Make sure you clear up every single thing that belonged to Father James, Sister, and I shall be with you later in the morning in my car to cart it all away to send on to his sister in America, everything, do ye understand?'

Of course Sister Evangelista understood. Did the man think she was witless?

'Yes, Father, there will be no problem. The housekeeper Daisy will help me and it shouldn't take long.'

'Ah, yes, Daisy, the girl is a bit simple, is she not, Sister?'

'She is, Bishop, but she is a good housekeeper, Mrs Malone trained her well.'

'I am sure she did, but she is bound to be very upset indeed and may be prone to rambling. We must be careful to protect her, as she has no family of her own, except for us. I wonder if a spell in the peace and quiet of the convent might be a good idea?'

This had never crossed Sister Evangelista's mind and she was far from happy. Disruption in the convent always upset the nuns' routine and, sure, didn't she have enough to do with a school to run as well?

However, even she dared not argue with the bishop.

'Aye, well, I'll see how she is, Father, when I get there, shall I? She will need to prepare the Priory for the father's replacement.'

No sooner had the words left her mouth than her throat began to thicken with emotion and tears swam across her eyes.

'I mean, what are the arrangements, Bishop? Where is Father James to be buried? We need someone in authority here. Everyone is dreadfully upset. Will you definitely be coming soon?'

The bishop had promised to visit days ago. But something both mysterious and urgent had occurred daily to prevent him. Sister Evangelista had carried the entire burden alone and now she felt exhausted.

She had almost broken down earlier in the morning when speaking to her friend, Miss Devlin, a teacher at the school.

'Our own Father James, found murdered in the graveyard, and the bishop still hasn't arrived to help deal with the police or bring some authority to the church, and now, here I am, about to pack up all his personal possessions in the Priory with only simple Daisy to help.'

Into one of her hands Miss Devlin had quietly placed a hankie, and into the other a cup of tea with a couple of Anadin on the saucer.

Tea and Anadin, hailed as a miracle cure by all of Liverpool's women. A headache? Take a cuppa tea and two Anadin. A toothache? A cuppa tea and two Anadin. A priest found murdered in the graveyard? A cuppa tea and two Anadin. Anadin sat on the wooden shelf next to the Woodbines in the local tobacconist's and they sold almost as many of one as the other. Acknowledged as an effective alternative to gin to help with the pains of afterbirth, mastitis, monthlies and the constant headaches brought on by looking after a dozen unruly children.

Miss Devlin had spoken in her customary gentle tone. 'It has been very hard indeed on yourself. Drink the tea and take the Anadin now, Sister, and it will all be easier to face. The bishop will be here soon.'

Sister Evangelista's distress on the telephone had been apparent. Sensing that she was losing patience, the bishop had tried to pacify her as an adult would a three-year-old child.

'I will be there this afternoon, so keep calm now. Everyone must remain very calm. We cannot bury the father until the police release his body, but we know how the police can behave. Remember how pushy they were about coming into the school and upsetting the children. You must say nothing to them about anything. They will be looking for someone to blame and we mustn't let that be us, Sister. Of course when I say us, I mean the Church. This is all a dreadful mess but be sure, Sister, we have a responsibility to protect our work.'

Sister Evangelista was speechless. She had no idea what the bishop was talking about. The police didn't have anyone in their sights? He was right. In fact, they had taken themselves down a few embarrassing blind alleys, but none of them had led towards the school or the convent.

She replaced the receiver with a prayer that the bishop would make haste. As God was her judge, if she had to deal with much more on her own, likely she would go mad.

Now at the sight of Daisy's relieved face, she was glad she had come.

'Hello, Sister.'

Daisy grinned from ear to ear in that inane way she had. Her dark hair with its thick fringe was kept short and tidy with the help of a pudding basin and the kitchen scissors. Her nose dribbled slightly, as though she had a cold, but she seemed not to notice and her eyes always appeared bright, as though full of tears.

Sister Evangelista sighed. Her heart suddenly felt very heavy. Daisy would be of little help.

'The bishop is arriving this afternoon to remove Father James's belongings, Daisy. We need to pack up the father's room and all of his personal possessions. I hope to God he sends another priest to us soon to take charge. Everyone is in such a state.'

Daisy's heart sank into her boots. Whenever the bishop visited, he slept over at the Priory and often popped into Daisy's room before retiring for the night. Father James had accompanied him the first time, but ever after he had visited her alone.

Daisy's expression never altered, and she didn't speak.

'Have you any sacks, or the father's suitcase, Daisy?'

Sister Evangelista's mind was already focused on the task ahead. Daisy nodded. 'We have hessian flour sacks folded up in the scullery and there's a suitcase on top of Father James's wardrobe in his room,' she said.

'Good girl, bring them to the study, we will start in there. And, Daisy, you had better bring a tray of tea for us both, we could be a while.'

Daisy disappeared into the kitchen, as Sister Evangelista walked across the highly polished parquet floor of the square hallway and, in a businesslike manner, threw open the study door.

The gust of a breeze created by her sudden entry sent a cloud of dust particles flying upwards where, trapped, they swirled and glittered in columns of weak sunlight. It took her eyes a moment to adjust. She caught her breath and dragged the courage from somewhere deep within her to take the next step.

The courage to walk over to his desk. To begin the process of parcelling up the life of the man she had known well and worked with for over twenty years. This was daunting, even for someone as efficient and strong as she was. The father, whom she had loved and who had had such a passion to help the poorest children in the community. She silently vowed he would never be forgotten and that a mass would be said for him every day at St Mary's, for as long as she was alive.

As Sister Evangelista approached the murdered priest's dark-oak desk, she crossed herself.

As she surveyed the surface, she noticed his diary was open on the day he had died. Pushing her thin wire-framed spectacles to the top of her nose with one hand, she placed the other on the open page and let it travel across the words, as though they were written in braille.

The police had not yet gained entry to the Priory. They required permission from the bishop, which was one of the reasons he was arriving today. Everything was just as it had been on the day the priest had died.

It now crossed her mind that maybe Father James's belongings held a clue as to who had murdered him and that maybe packing away his personal effects might not be the right thing to do after all.

But the bishop had been most insistent. 'We must protect the Church,' he had said. What had that meant exactly?

Father James would have done nothing other than protect the Church, surely?

'Oh, Daisy, you and that tea are a welcome sight. Bring the tray here, dear,' she said, as she looked up to see Daisy standing in the doorway, the sacks rolled up and tucked under her arm. Daisy laid the tray on the table.

'Who was Austin Tattershall, Daisy?' Sister Evangelista enquired. The name glared up at her from the diary page. Four o'clock, Austin Tattershall. The diary entry had jumped out as the name wasn't Irish and was certainly one Sister Evangelista had never heard before.

'I don't know, Sister,' Daisy said. 'He came here sometimes to see the father.'

Daisy was whispering, almost into her chest, as she poured the tea.

Sister Evangelista looked squarely at Daisy, who avoided her gaze as she handed over the cup and saucer, keeping her eyes fixed firmly on the desk as she did so.

'Did the father keep his appointment with him at four o'clock?' she asked.

Daisy still kept her head down as she replied, 'He didn't, Sister.'

A silence fell between them.

Sister Evangelista had spent her life being lied to.

The reasons given for why children came to school with no food in their bellies, shoes falling off their feet and lice dancing on their heads had to be heard to be believed. Sister Evangelista could smell a rat a mile away and she smelt an enormous one right here in this room, right now. Either Daisy was lying, or there was something she wasn't telling her.

She flicked over the diary pages, feeling worse than a thief. Father James was dead and these earthly possessions were of no use to him now, but, even so, she felt extremely uncomfortable. She had always been an intensely private woman herself, raised to have impeccable manners.

Now she saw that there was a diary entry on the same day each week with names she didn't recognize. Arthur, Stanley, Cyril, Brian. Who were these men?

'Manners won't get his belongings to his family, I suppose.' She suddenly spoke her thoughts out loud as she snapped the diary shut, making Daisy jump.

'No, Sister,' said Daisy, unfolding one of the small sacks.

Sister Evangelista placed the diary carefully in the hessian sack.

On top she laid his silver letter opener and a leather-bound volume containing his precious stamp collection, which he often brought children into his office to view.

'The stamp collection is so beautiful. The children would never have seen anything like it before,' she had often said to Miss Devlin.

Sister Evangelista had always thought Father James the most patient of men. She had repeatedly said so to Miss Devlin.

'He is so busy, with barely a moment to spare, and yet he always finds the time to share his knowledge of the world with the children through his wonderful collection of stamps. He never minds them visiting him in his study. I just don't know where he finds the patience.'

Sister Evangelista surveyed the contents of the bookcase on the opposite side of the room and realized she couldn't place the precious stamp collection in a sack along with the books.

'Daisy, I think we are going to need some newspaper. Are there any old rag sheets we can rip up to wrap things in? I would like to protect his stamp collection, at the very least.'

As Daisy left the room in search of dust sheets, Sister Evangelista slowly lowered herself into the father's chair behind the desk. Tears that had never been far from the surface since the murder now threatened once again to pour down her cheeks.

She felt a hum. A sizzling static in the air.

Daisy's receding footsteps had taken her downstairs into the kitchen and could no longer be heard. Sister Evangelista felt as though the father were standing in the room, objecting to the use of his chair. It was a real presence.

The air smelt of the last time it was occupied. An odour trapped by locked windows and doors.

Musty. Ink. Hair grease and man.

He was there.

There was another smell too. Faintly familiar, of lavender floor wax and polish. Daisy may have been simple, but Sister Evangelista acknowledged that the Priory was spotless.

He was there.

'Don't cry,' she whispered to herself, clasping her hands together in front as though in prayer. She was a nun, unafraid of ghosts. She was protected by God's light. 'Just get through this as quickly as possible,' she whispered, defiant, challenging the empty space. Father James might have been a saint in her eyes, but he was no Lazarus.

Distracting herself, she glanced down at the desk drawers. Each one was locked. A small bunch of keys lay on top of the desk next to the open inkwell.

There was still no sign of Daisy. Should she wait for Daisy to return before opening the drawers?

Picking up the keys, she tried first the top right-hand drawer.

The key turned easily. Feeling bold and moving quickly before she could think about what she was doing and hesitate, not waiting for encouragement from Daisy nor permission from the bishop, she swiftly opened the drawer and pulled it out as far as it would extend. It was stuffed full of bundles of white envelopes stacked in three neat rows and tied with string.

She lifted the first bundle and flicked her fingers down the side, revealing the addresses printed on the front. All of the envelopes, she noticed, were addressed to people she did not know and had been sent to a PO Box number. Some coincided with the names in the diary entries. The first one was addressed to Austin Tattershall.

Sister Evangelista took out the envelope and lifted the flap, revealing a wad of black-and-white photographs.

What she saw made her feel as though she had been punched in the heart.

Winded and breathless, in a state of acute shock and creeping numbness, she examined the photographs, one by one.

When she considered the events in her mind later that evening, she wondered to herself how in God's name she hadn't fainted. How had she managed to behave as though she was looking at photographs of a beautiful rural landscape, instead of the most vile and depraved images of young girls and boys she had ever seen?

Some of the photographs had been taken abroad, that much was obvious by the name stamped on the back. Most were of men with children, girls mostly and the occasional boy. Some were obviously taken in a hospital setting. Others were of very young girls. With horror, she realized that one picture had been taken in the father's study and it was of a child she recognized from the school.

She furtively glanced at the door to see if Daisy had returned and hurriedly slipped the pictures back into the envelope, scooping the remaining envelopes in the drawer onto her lap.

Daisy walked into the room with what had once been a large sheet now torn into squares for dusting cloths.

'Thank you, Daisy. I think maybe there are some things I had better take to the convent for the bishop to deal with. Could you begin lifting the books down from the bookcase?'

Sister Evangelista felt as though her head were spinning but she knew she had to remain calm.

Daisy noticed that the Reverend Mother was breathing faster, that perspiration stood out on her top lip, and that her forehead and her cheeks were burning red. Daisy was not quite as simple as people thought.

All the sister could think about was how much she and the entire community had loved Father James and yet all the time this filth was sitting in his drawer. She was out of her depth and had no idea what to do. She had to speak to the bishop as soon as she could, ask him to finish the remainder of the packing up himself. She felt as though the ground were shaking beneath her. She must ask the bishop, should they show this to the police?

'*We have to protect the Church*,' he had said.

She placed the diary and the envelopes on a square of white linen and tied up the four corners.

'Daisy, I don't want to do this just now, I have to speak to the bishop. We will finish all of this later.'

Daisy had never seen the sister so agitated. This upset her. She didn't like to stay at the Priory. She wanted to be at the convent and had hoped to talk to Sister Evangelista about maybe leaving with her when she had finished the packing. Daisy had only ever lived with nuns or in the Priory with the priest, and she knew she preferred to live with the nuns. There were no men in the convent.

'Who came here to visit the father, Daisy?' Sister Evangelista spoke rapidly. There was an impatience and roughness to her voice that hadn't been there before. 'Who visited him here that I wouldn't know of?'

Daisy remembered what she had been told by the father. Her lips were sealed. She looked silently down at the floor. Daisy always did as she was told.

'Daisy, tell me, who did the father see that I do know? He used to visit lots of people on the streets, didn't he, Daisy? Sure, I know he was mad busy, always calling in on the sick and the poor. Was there anyone he saw more often than others?'

Sister Evangelista was running on instinct. She recognized the child in the picture as a little girl from Waterloo Street who had been in Miss Devlin's class last year. She was no more than six years old. Her mother had been seriously ill and when she was bedbound, Sister Evangelista knew the father had visited daily to take mass at home at her bedside.

'Well, I cannot say who came here, Sister, but where the father went is a different question altogether. He liked to visit the Doherty house a great deal, Sister. He visited lots of folk but he was regular to the Doherty house.'

The Doherty house.

The image of Kitty Doherty, one of Sister Evangelista's star pupils, crossed her mind.

Ten minutes later, Sister Evangelista ran down the street towards the convent, hugging a large parcel to her chest with Daisy at her side. On the way she almost bumped into Nellie Deane with her arm round Kitty, leaving the school gates.

'Nellie, where are you off to?' she said, alarmed.

'I have to take Kitty home, Sister. Miss Devlin sent for me. She doesn't feel too good.'

Then, without any warning whatsoever, Kitty threw up all over the pavement.

Sister Evangelista stared at the child who had turned a ghastly shade of grey.

Kitty had been sick in the playground yesterday morning. As she grappled with the realization of what may be happening, she felt as though the vomit-strewn pavement was opening up beneath her.

She needed to help Kitty, but she was frozen to the spot.

She could hear Kitty's voice somewhere in the background, as she said, 'Sorry, Sister, I'm so sorry,' but she couldn't reply. The world as she knew it and all that was familiar to her was collapsing around her and she along with it.

Daisy, a forced keeper of secrets, was staring at her. Her expression was unfathomable.

Sister Evangelista focused her attention on what Nellie was saying.

Kitty's innocence with her wet eyes and pale skin brought her to her senses. Only yesterday Miss Devlin had said how sickly Kitty had been in the mornings.

'If the child wasn't so young and an angel herself, I would swear she was pregnant.'

Oh Holy Mother, this cannot be true, she thought, and then suddenly, pulling herself up, she addressed Kitty.

'It is all right, child, you go home for the rest of the day. I will send the janitor out to clean the pavement. Are you sure you are all right, Nellie?'

Nellie put her arm round Kitty once more and smiled weakly at Sister Evangelista, who realized she could no longer wait for the bishop. This was beyond either of them. She knew what she had to do.

Howard sat at his desk, drumming his fingers and staring at the array of police notebooks before him. It was only ten o'clock and he was already lighting up his fifth cigarette of the day. Not one of the notebooks held a single clue.

They had no witness or a shred of motive but they did have the superintendent breathing down their necks, urging them to find the priest's killer as soon as possible.

Simon walked into the office with two mugs of tea and a message that made Howard feel weak.

'The super wants a meeting at twelve and an update on the priest's case.'

'Have you any bright ideas?' Howard threw across the table to Simon as he picked up his mug.

'Apart from the fact that we both have a gut feeling Jerry Deane knows something, we have absolutely fuck all to go on. Not a single frigging lead. The whole lot of 'em are either ignorant or stupid. No one knows owt,' said Simon unhelpfully.

Howard picked up his tea and groaned.

'Well, sergeant clever dick, we have got two hours, so what do you suggest?'

The black Bakelite phone on the desk between them began to ring.

'There you go, it's a message from the dead priest.' Simon began to laugh to himself. 'He's sending you a little clue from above.'

'Shut the fuck up,' said Howard as he flicked his cigarette stump at Simon. Picking up the handset, he turned to face the wall before speaking into the mouthpiece.

Less than thirty seconds later Simon almost spat out his tea as Howard spoke soothingly into the phone.

'Now, now, Sister, you must not upset yourself. We will be at the school in less than half an hour. I can assure you, you have done exactly the right thing calling me and we will make sure the bishop knows that.'

Howard replaced the receiver with far more enthusiasm than he had picked it up.

'That was Sister Evangelista, she's got news, good news, full of clues news. It sounds as though she has got our motive, mate. Drink up, one very upset nun seems to want to tell us all.'

They both banged their mugs down on the table and two minutes later were whizzing through Liverpool city centre in a pale blue and white panda car, heading up towards Nelson Street school.

# Chapter Two

Life on the four streets had very slowly returned to a normal routine. After all, the women could only last so many days without baking bread.

From the second the news had broken, floor-mop handles had banged constantly on kitchen walls, summoning the women to a conference in whichever home had the freshest piece of gossip first.

As they ran up and down the entry and in and out of one another's homes, with babies on hips, holding half-full bottles of sterilized milk for the tea or a shovel of coal to keep a fire burning, they became engrossed by the most intense speculation. Who on this earth could have done such an awful thing and why?

The women talked of nothing else and almost wore themselves out.

Even the children playing on the green huddled into groups and repeated the whispered conversations they had heard at home. Rehearsing for the future. Dealing in the currency of the streets.

'The Pope is in such a rage, so he is, he is coming from Rome to Liverpool to kill whoever did it with his own bare hands,' said Declan, Maura and Tommy's little rascal, to his rather serious twin brother, Harry.

'No,' said Harry, shocked at the thought of the Pope strangling someone. 'That cannot be true, ye liar, where did ye hear that?'

'It is so, I heard Mammy say it to Sheila in the kitchen this morning.'

If his mammy was telling Sheila, then it must be true for sure. Harry gasped and put his fist in his mouth before he ran off to tell his mate Little Paddy, who had been a bit down of late, having caused such a fuss himself.

He had been at the very centre of his own storm in relation to the murder and was now maintaining a low profile.

As a result of what Little Paddy had blurted out, the police had taken in one of their own, Jerry Deane, for questioning. Everyone agreed this was a fanciful notion on the part of the police, who must have been desperate indeed. And all on the back of Peggy and Paddy's stupid Little Paddy, looking to make a name for himself as the clever one at school. Claiming he had seen Jerry Deane running down the entry on the night of the murder, skulking like a thief in the night.

As if anyone would ever believe anything Little Paddy said.

Jerry Deane had been back at home within the day. Following the beating he took from his da, Little Paddy struggled to sit down for a week.

'That is one child who will never be described as clever,' said Molly Barrett to Annie O'Prey, just loud enough for Little Paddy to hear, as they both stood on the pavement to sweep their front steps.

'As if any child from that family could know anything,' Annie O'Prey replied, not breaking her stroke with her broom.

Little Paddy's da might have thrashed the living daylights out of him, but Little Paddy knew what he had seen, and he knew it was true, and no matter how many thrashings he was given, he knew he was right. He had seen Uncle Jerry running down the entry in the middle of the night. How was he supposed to know that he was only off to Brigid and Sean's house for a card school and to tuck into the wedding whiskey they had all been given as a present by Mrs Keating's publican in-laws on the morning her daughter got married?

Not that he would ever say it again, mind. Next time his da might use his belt and Little Paddy idolized his da. He didn't want that to happen. Little Paddy would keep his gob shut in future.

The reaction of the families on the four streets to the murder of their own priest had been powerful and all-consuming.

Some of the women had cried almost constantly since hearing the news. Others had become so upset that Dr Cole had to be sent for to administer a sedative.

'Sure, it must be the mystery of the century, so it is,' said Annie to Molly, as they both swept away.

Annie was as skinny as Molly was fat. Both wore the traditional uniform of the four streets: a wraparound floral apron and hair in curlers tucked away underneath a hairnet. Annie possessed no teeth and had long since given up pretending to own any. Like many others, she had dentures that lived in a glass on her bedside table, but one morning, instead of putting them in, she decided to leave them where they were. With her husband long dead and both of her precious boys inside Walton gaol, who was there left to put the teeth in for?

'Sure, I never liked him meself,' replied Molly with a flick of the broom as she swept up the dust, across the pavement and into the gutter.

This was the same Molly who had baked the priest a batch of

scones every Sunday morning and had dutifully delivered them to the Priory for eighteen years.

As she knelt to pray, the scones would sit on the pew next to her, filling the church with an aroma of fresh baking, competing with the smell of incense.

Some weeks, she barely had enough flour to make a decent batch, or enough coal to heat the oven on the range. Her own children had often gone hungry and didn't see fresh baking for weeks on end. But she never missed her gift for Father James, her bribe in exchange for a place in heaven.

Now that he was dead, it had all been in vain. He was years younger than she. Who would ever have thought this would happen? Eighteen bloody years of scones, all in vain, she was heard to mutter to herself more than once a day.

'The biggest mystery to me is what was me cat doing with the father's langer in his mouth? Now that truly is a riddle – he had been fed twice that day.'

'Who had? Father James?' asked Annie quizzically. 'How do ye know that?'

'No, Jesus, Mary and Joseph, not Father James, me bloody cat. I have no notion at all what he will bring me next. Sends the shivers down me spine, so he does, every time he wanders into the kitchen. To think, he saw it all. If cats could talk, so.'

Molly had yet to recover from the fact that her cat had proudly returned from his nightly graveyard prowl with a murder trophy.

The news of the priest's death was already speeding round the streets when Molly realized what the cat had deposited on her kitchen floor. Her screams could be heard as far as the butcher's and beyond.

'Aye, true, Molly, if Tiger could talk, we would know who had murdered the priest and ye would be a very rich woman indeed, so ye would.'

They both laughed as they finished sweeping into the gutter and walked back to their respective front doors.

'Well, Annie, now the cat can't talk, but I will tell ye this for nothing. There is one woman on this street who I thought we would see being carted off in an ambulance with the grief when she heard that the priest was dead, and yet I saw her more upset on the day Rita O'Neil's lad was made altar boy and not their Harry.'

Mrs O'Prey shuffled closer to Molly's step, crossing her arms and looking around furtively before she spoke. 'Do ye mean Maura Doherty? Because I was thinking the very same thing meself!'

Both women huddled in close.

'Aye, I do. She looks upset all right, but given that the father was never out of her house and she being all pious, high and mighty so, I thought she might have taken to her bed an' all, but not a sign of it. Kathleen Deane is the same, but I never would expect her to be upset. It was no secret she didn't like the priest and never went to mass. She always took herself off to confession with Father Donlan in Bootle.'

For a brief moment, they both lapsed into silence as, leaning on their broomsticks, they watched Kathleen Deane, with her daughter-in-law Alice and the baby Joseph in his Silver Cross pram, head across the cobbles towards the entry, to Maura Doherty's house.

Once Kathleen and Alice had disappeared from sight, Molly examined her broom head with the bristles almost worn down to the wooden block.

'Well, Mrs O, a rich woman I am not. But I know this, if I don't buy a new broom head today, ye'll be sweeping me step tomorrow along with yours.'

'Wouldn't be the first time,' Annie replied, 'and ye has done mine often enough, Molly me love.'

Molly sniffed in acknowledgment and, without another word, wobbled across her step and closed the front door.

'If ye ate a bit less, ye fat lump, ye could afford a broom head no trouble at all,' whispered Annie to herself as she closed her own front door.

The police car glided round the corner of Nelson Street almost unnoticed. Just a few short weeks ago, the police had been virtually mobbed by neighbours asking one question after another with children constantly circling every policeman and car.

Howard and Simon each took out a fresh cigarette and lit up, squinting through the haze of blue smoke to survey the houses on both sides of the road.

'Where shall we start?' said Simon.

Both men were feeling more confident than they had first thing that morning. That hadn't been difficult given what little information they had and despite their initial optimism, the sister hadn't given them a huge amount to go on.

What they didn't know was that as soon as Sister Evangelista had put the phone down on Howard, she had picked it up straight away and spoken to the bishop, who had been very, very angry when she told him she had called the police. So strong had he been in his opinion, regarding what she should and should not say and do, that he had left Sister Evangelista shaking in fear and in desperate need of something much stronger than a cuppa tea and two Anadin.

Sister Evangelista had no choice but to obey. She answered to the bishop and, much as it went against her better judgment, she would be obedient. Almost. She would not keep to herself her suspicions regarding Kitty. She was fond of the girl and she felt sure that at least must be her godly duty.

It took more than a few slugs of the holy mass wine before she could face Howard and Simon, having hidden the disgusting photographs in her office safe, as the bishop had ordered.

Simon fixed his gaze on Maura and Tommy's house as Howard spoke.

'Well, as Sister Evangelista was worried about the eldest Doherty girl in number nineteen and as the priest spent more time in number nineteen Nelson Street than any other, we should visit there last and question all the others first. Let's not mention the Dohertys or the girl,' he said. 'Just ask, did the priest have any favourites around here, that kind of thing, and let's see what happens. I had no idea priests did home visits, so we have something we didn't have yesterday. And then if that bloody bishop arrives today and we finally gain entry into the Priory, maybe we will find another clue. If we keep shaking the tree hard enough, Simon, something will eventually fall.'

Before they left the car, they both took another long pull on their cigarettes as they watched Mrs O'Prey and Mrs Barrett bang the dust from their brooms and waddle back indoors.

# Chapter Three

Nellie's bedroom window, at forty-two Nelson Street, overlooked the backyard. Earlier that morning, as she had drawn back the curtains, she had spotted her Nana Kathleen and Auntie Maura down in the yard, whispering furtively over the gate. They were too engrossed to look up and see Nellie, so she pressed her ear to the cold glass window to catch what they were saying. Their behaviour was unusual and Nellie supposed it was yet more gossip about the priest.

Nellie had never attended Father James's church, but always took the bus into Bootle with her Nana Kathleen to attend the mass held by a friend's cousin from back home in Bangornevin.

She felt a strange detachment from the upset, but the fact that someone had committed a murder was truly shocking. None of the mothers had allowed their children to walk to school alone since.

So much had happened of late, it was as though someone had thrown a hand grenade into the midst of their lives and they were all still flying through the air.

Since that awful night when all the Doherty children had piled into Nellie's bedroom in the dark small hours and she had heard crying and talking downstairs, she had felt as though Nana Kathleen and her da were holding out on her and keeping secrets.

She was especially worried about Kitty who was more of a big sister to Nellie than a best friend. For the past few days she had been so ill and this morning had even thrown up all over the pavement, in front of Sister Evangelista.

She had dropped the poorly Kitty back at Maura's and had popped home to tell Alice and Nana Kathleen what had happened.

'Well, glory be,' shouted Kathleen as Nellie walked in through the back door. 'Is school on a half-day now or what? Why are ye back home so soon?'

'It's Kitty, Nana, I have just taken her to Maura. She is so sick, the poor thing.' Nellie had leant against the range as she talked and helped herself to a chunk of the hot barm brack freshly removed from the oven.

Nana Kathleen playfully whacked her hand with the end of the tea towel. 'Away with ye,' she half shouted. 'Off to school and stop shirking. There is nothing wrong with ye, miss.'

Nellie's stepmother, Alice, was sitting on a chair next to the fire with Nellie's little brother, Joseph, on her knee. 'How are the sisters this morning, Nellie? Are they still as upset as they were?'

'Oh my gosh, you should have seen Sister Evangelista,' Nellie exclaimed through a mouth full of the hot fruit bread. 'She was running from the Priory with Daisy, clutching a parcel to her chest, and she looked as though she had seen a ghost. I don't know who looked the most sick, her or Kitty. In a right state, she was.'

Kathleen and Alice exchanged a worried glance, which Nellie missed as she made her way to the door with a sneaky slice of the brack in her hand.

'See yer later, alligator,' she shouted as she closed the door and headed back to school.

'Put Joseph in his pram,' said Kathleen to Alice, 'and let's get over to Maura's.'

Kathleen sensed that they were running out of time. They might need to act more quickly than she had thought.

Maura and Kathleen had already decided between them that Kitty should be told that she was pregnant, before they told her own father, Tommy. After all she had been through, she had the right to that.

Once Tommy had been told, a decision would have to be made. What in God's name were they going to do about the dead priest's bastard child?

Maura had hoped that maybe one day she would wake up and it would all have been nothing more than a nightmare.

As she walked into Kitty's bedroom each morning, she crossed herself and prayed to the Virgin Mary for a miracle. The first thing she did, once Kitty was out of bed, was to pull back her blanket and look hopefully for a sign of blood on her sheet.

Father James had not destroyed her faith in her God. Father James was the devil himself. This she had recognized. Satan had tricked his way into her home.

Maura's faith was the stronger for it. She would not let the devil win.

But the Virgin Mary never answered her prayers and as Maura pulled back the blanket every day, her heart sank into her boots.

There was a murdered priest, and his baby was growing in her daughter's belly.

Could there be much worse to wake up to than that?

Wasn't life hard enough as it was, trying to make ends meet and keep everyone happy? Declan wore his shoes out every week and Maura had no idea how she was going to manage to keep him in school. The sisters had asked to see her to talk about Malachi's demon behaviour in class. Angela needed glasses. Niamh had what looked like the beginnings of Harry's asthma. She had lent Peggy some of her family allowance and now might not have enough for her own family. Tommy would go mad indeed if Declan went without shoes because she had been too quick to lend to those who did not manage their money as well as she did.

And on top of all this, she now had something to deal with that eclipsed everything else. A problem so big, so vast, it was almost incomprehensible, so she pushed it firmly to the back of her mind each morning before her feet had even touched the floor.

Tommy would often wake and find her staring at the ceiling. Without speaking he would pull her into his arms and they would hold onto each other tightly.

Maura would weep into his chest and Tommy, blissfully unaware, had no idea that each day his wife was saving him from further heartache and anguish than that which already tormented him.

'God, Tommy,' Maura sobbed, 'I was happy he took himself up the stairs to the kids' bedroom to bless them, I even encouraged him. How can I live with meself, what kind of mother have I been? How could we have known he would follow her to the hospital?'

It was the same question every day. She knew the reassuring answer off by heart.

'The very best, queen, the very best,' Tommy would reply, swallowing down his resentment of Maura's unquestioning acceptance of a priest he had never much liked.

The image of a gallows and a swinging noose burnt into his mind as he lay awake, holding Maura, and stared at the stars through the bedroom window.

Kathleen was all too well aware of the power of the Church and the impending crisis of Kitty's pregnancy. No matter who had put that baby there, it was still a sin of the highest order. The fact that it was a priest's bastard made the situation doubly worse and it would be Kitty who would be labelled the sinner.

There was no separation between the Catholic Church and the local neighbourhood. They were one and the same. The control of the community by the Church was absolute.

Maura had cried each time the subject of Kitty's pregnancy was raised. Kathleen knew she had to allow her time to come to terms with what was a living nightmare, but now she would have to put her foot down. She was finding it hard to believe that Maura was unaware of the danger Kitty's condition presented to them all.

'If we don't act quickly,' said Kathleen to Alice as she took her coat down from the hook on the back of the kitchen door, 'the hounds of hell will be chasing after us and I am not about to allow that to happen when we have other options.'

She fastened a headscarf over her curlers and held Joseph, whilst Alice reached for her own coat. Alice was a Protestant. The power and the ways of the Catholic Church were all a mystery to Alice, but she had learnt enough over the last few years to know that you didn't argue with Nana Kathleen.

Sister Evangelista and her sisters of the Sacred Heart convent ran the school and sustained the children with messages of faith, obedience, guilt and fear.

Whilst the children were in school praying, each mother on the four streets attended mass at St Mary's every single day, some twice, morning and evening. The hold of the Church and its grip on the community were unbreakable. A forgiving exterior hid a steadfast dogma. There was no escape.

Kathleen was relieved to find Maura alone in the kitchen with her latest baby and she appeared to be happy to see them both.

'Oh, thank God it is ye two. I have told everyone I feel unwell, to try and stop the knocking on. I swear to God I am terrified of being in the company of the others and blurting out something that shouldn't be said. My nerves are in pieces, Kathleen.'

Maura didn't need to tell Kathleen that; she could see it for herself. She walked over and took the baby from Maura.

'Is she fed?' she asked, lifting the baby up to her face and blowing a raspberry at the same time.

'Aye, she is,' Maura replied, 'and Kitty is in bed feeling like death.'

Kathleen shifted the baby onto one arm and, with her free hand, picked up the baby's shawl from the top of her sleeping box. Expertly wrapping it around her, she took her outside to the pram in the yard. Moving Joseph over a little, she laid the baby next to him and then covered them both with the blanket.

'Alice, love, take them both for a walk to the shops and give me a while with Maura, will ye now?' she said.

Alice nodded. 'Of course I will. How long shall I be?'

'Give me half an hour and bring me back a packet of five Woodbines. I think we may all need one soon.'

As Alice passed through the back gate with the pram, Kathleen looked in through Maura's window and saw her wiping her eyes with a handkerchief.

Holy Mary, there is more to come. How is she going to cope? thought Kathleen as she closed the gate behind Alice and moved back indoors to Maura.

When Maura was sitting down with a cup of tea, Kathleen began. It wasn't often the Doherty house was quiet and Kathleen had to seize her moment.

'Listen, Maura, Kitty's abuse at the hands of a man of God will present us all with a terrible threat, so it will.'

Kathleen looked at Maura as she spoke, leaning forward so that she could lower her voice. Even with just the two of them in the room, Kathleen still felt the need to whisper.

'Kitty's pregnancy will lay bare Father James's hypocrisy, Maura. It will reveal the truth, that our priest was an impostor, a despicable human being, not a man of God. But who will listen, Maura? Imagine if it weren't Kitty, but Mrs Keating's daughter. What would happen? Who would ye and Tommy have thought was to blame? Your precious Father James? Or the Keating girl? Would anyone talk to the Keatings again? And what would the Church do and the nuns? Would they support her, or do ye think the Keating girl would be labelled a liar and a whore overnight? Would the Keatings even stand by her or would they throw her out? And by God, Maura, here's the worst of it. When Kitty's belly starts to show weeks after the priest was murdered, Kitty becomes a liability. She becomes a motive. Do ye understand me? Kitty's belly will point the finger at you and Tommy. Do you see what that means?'

Maura hadn't said a word. She sat at the table looking at her hands, then began to sob.

'My poor Kitty, she doesn't stand a chance, does she? What in God's name can we do?'

'Maura, when that child's belly starts to show, people around here are going to put two and two together. That's not a baby, it's a motive, and we have to get Kitty out of the way before anyone guesses.'

'Oh my God,' said Maura as she sank back into the chair. 'Oh, Holy Mother, of course it is, I had not realized that.'

Kathleen now put her own arms round Maura's shoulders.

'Aye, two events of such an extraordinary nature would have to be linked, Maura. Once Kitty starts to show, the police will be round here in a flash. We have to get her away, and for now, something is pulling me back home to Ireland. I must leave and take her with me.'

'We cannot put the shame on either of our families in Ireland, Kathleen, are ye mad? They would be scorned and become outcasts themselves. No one would speak to them. We cannot do that.'

'I know, but there has to be somewhere for the poor child to go and, God knows, no one round here must know what is going on. I have to think, Maura, and I cannot do it here. That kid needs a rest, she looks so sick. I'm taking her with me and I'm going to take Nellie, too. Make it look like a grand little holiday now, in the middle of all the upset and all that. What could be more natural, with us all distraught by the priest's death? It is just the sort of thing a nana with a nice farmhouse and family in Ireland would think of doing, especially as I won a handsome amount on the bingo last week.'

Maura smiled for the first time in days.

Kathleen was a legend down at the bingo; she won more often than all the women on the four streets put together.

'Before I take her, Maura, we need to tell Kitty she is pregnant. And we will do that as soon as Nellie gets home from school. She hasn't got a clue. Best to tell them both at the same time.'

Maura nodded. She could not trust herself to speak. Both women turned their heads to look at the flames flickering around the coke cinders in the grate and became lost in their own thoughts. Upstairs, Kitty rolled over in her bed, exhausted and sickly, deep in her second sleep.

Kathleen mused that if it was this difficult reasoning with Maura, how could they even begin to explain it to Kitty?

Kathleen felt a huge sense of responsibility. She was in it up to her neck and it appeared to her that she was the only person who had a plan to save Tommy and Jerry from the hangman's noose.

She had discovered the priest in Kitty's bedroom, about to carry out his wicked deed, and had smashed him over the head with the poker. She hadn't killed him, but she felt as though she had.

'I hated that evil man with his vain and pompous hat and cape from the day I arrived on the four streets. He made the hairs on the back of me neck stand up on end, so he did.'

She had said the same thing to Jerry, every day since the morning Father James had been found as dead as the corpse on whose grave he had been discovered.

She should have known. Why had she not acted on her instincts?

He had been in and out of every house on the four streets that had daughters. It was staring them straight in the face.

Every night since, when she gave Jerry his tea and Nellie was in bed, she vented her spleen.

'Why had not one of us ever noticed that he never called on the Shevlins, with a house full of boys, eh? They're so holy, Maisie Shevlin's knees are rheumatic with the praying she does, and yet it never occurred to us. We never even questioned why the filthy priest did not once knock upon their door or why his vile shadow never darkened their doorstep. Jesus, we must all be bloody eejits.'

Kathleen had barely stopped punishing herself since that fateful night.

'Shush, Mammy, what's done is done now. He'll not be harming any other child,' said Jerry, trying to calm his mother down.

Jerry, who gave the same reply each time, wondered when his mother would stop beating herself up.

'Mammy, how were ye to know? How could ye possibly have known what he was up to? No one knew, not even Maura and Tommy, and he was at it under their very noses in their own home. Shush now or ye will make ye'self ill.'

Aye, but ye don't know all the facts, thought Kathleen as she placed his steaming bacon ribs and cabbage on the table in front of him. When ye do know that Kitty is pregnant, ye will be feeling as bad as I do. Kathleen would not be pacified.

'When I saw him coming out of Brigid and Sean's house, a home full of little red-headed daughters, I should have known. The dirty bastard.'

Kathleen probably should have known because she had the gift. A gift that was aided and abetted by the Granada TV rentals man, and his comings and goings in and out of every house: that was the truth of it. Nevertheless, she did have the gift of prophesy, manifest via reading the tea leaves.

Most of the women on the four streets visited Kathleen on Friday mornings to have their teacups read. Kathleen knew things. She could tell the women what their future held. She knew when most women on the street were pregnant before they did themselves. And yet the biggest danger of all had slipped past her. She had suspected Father James was a bad man, but she had kept her own counsel.

She was convinced she had let them all down and none had been more let down than little Kitty, who would have to be told the worst news of her life.

Early that morning, unable to sleep, Kathleen had tiptoed down into the kitchen to put the kettle on what was left of the heat in the range embers, before stoking up the fire. She looked up at the statue of the Holy Mother on the shelf above. Kathleen often talked to the figurine. They were both mothers. She thought, as she often did, of Bernadette, the woman who had loved the home Kathleen cared for.

Beloved Bernadette. Still thought of and missed every day.

Kathleen set the kettle down on the black range and, with her hand still gripping the handle, bent her head in prayer.

'Bernadette, ye will be in heaven, queen, and so, please God, don't ye mind if I pray to ye both. Help us today with little Maura and Kitty. I know that man wasn't a man of God, he was a man of the devil, deceiving us all. Don't let him win. Holy Mother, the mother of all innocence, be with us today, for the child's sake.'

It seemed fitting to Kathleen, halfway through, that it should be the Holy Mother she prayed to. Having had an unusual pregnancy herself, she might understand.

As Kathleen and Maura drank their tea and stared at the fire, each lost in their own thoughts, the back door flew open and Alice, breaking the silence, rushed in. Rushing was a new experience to Alice. Kathleen was worried that she was rushing a bit too much.

Alice, her difficult daughter-in-law, who had tricked her son, Jerry, into marriage following the death of his wife, Bernadette, had come on in leaps and bounds over the last few years.

Alice had been the reason Kathleen had left the family farm in the West of Ireland to live with Jerry and Nellie in Nelson Street, to save them from the horrors of living with a woman who was obviously, as a result of her own abnormal upbringing, mentally unwell.

Alice, who had been the housekeeper at the Grand hotel until she had married Jerry, had known their Bernadette. When Bernadette had first arrived in Liverpool, she had been a chambermaid at the hotel. That was how Alice came to set her cap at Jerry. As soon as she heard of Bernadette's death, she had her feet under the table before any other God-fearing Irish lass stood a chance.

Alice was now almost entirely weaned off the Valium tablets and each day she felt more alive.

She knew that Jerry and Kathleen, and even Nellie, were watching her closely, but she would never slip back to the dark years. Nana Kathleen had rescued her. It had taken years of patience, but she had got there. And then Alice had rescued herself. Which had felt even better.

'They are both asleep in the pram and I have got the Woodbines. Shall I make a fresh mash of tea, or shall I reuse them tea leaves again?' Alice trilled, without pausing for breath.

Kathleen didn't know why, but today Alice's voice grated.

Alice had proved her worth in recent weeks. She had dispatched the police from their door with a flea in their ears and provided an alibi for Jerry when the police had taken him away for questioning. As an innocent man at the scene of the crime, doing nothing more than trying to protect Tommy from himself, Jerry had needed one.

Kathleen rose from the chair to help Alice make the tea.

The normally happy, laughing, vivacious Maura didn't move her vacant gaze from the fire.

'I've just seen the police on the street,' said Alice cheerfully.

Now Maura stirred. Both she and Kathleen looked at Alice, neither speaking, both waiting for her to continue.

'It looked like Molly Barrett was inviting them into her house. The poor woman must be feeling lonely if she wants a cuppa with the coppers.'

It seemed to Nellie that she was the sick-duty child today because she was now on her second journey out with an ailing pupil.

This time it was little Billy from the Anchor pub. He was so poorly he wasn't fit to walk and Nellie squatted down so that Miss Devlin could lift him onto her back, then she carried him in a piggy-back all the way to the pub.

Billy's da was grateful. 'Come and have a glass of sarsaparilla before ye walk back to school. Our lad is heavy, so he is.'

'I'd love one, thanks very much,' said Nellie.

She liked drinking sarsaparilla. Sometimes, when the pop man brought it round with his horse and cart after church on Sundays, her da would buy a bottle to have with their Sunday lunch. It was sweet and black and made her feel grown up, as if she was drinking a glass of Nana Kathleen's Guinness.

Gratefully drinking the whole glass full almost at once, Nellie handed it back empty with a polite thank-you and made her way down the pub steps to run back to school.

Just as she turned the corner at the top of the road, she saw Alice, standing outside the shop with the pram, in what looked like a deep conversation with Sean, Brigid's boxer husband. The only man Nana Kathleen had said was nearly as good-looking as Nellie's da, Jerry.

Alice threw back her head and laughed, as Sean bent down to look inside the pram.

As Nellie watched, Alice placed her hand on his arm, chatting all the while.

The women on the four streets never really talked to the men. They talked to one another.

Men talked about football and sex.

Women talked about the other women on the four streets and sex.

Nellie didn't know this. She knew only that the warm feeling of happiness that had arrived with the sarsaparilla evaporated, faster than the bubbles that had danced on her nose as she drank.

# Chapter Four

Alice was a new woman, so much so that she was often flooded with feelings of exhilaration, partly due to her growing love for her baby boy, Joseph. The baby she had never wanted.

These days, Alice laughed out loud.

When Jerry commented upon it, she announced proudly, 'I have opinions now and everything.'

Jerry laughed and said to Kathleen, 'Jesus, Mary and Joseph, between you and Dr Cole, you have worked a miracle, Mammy.' As he spoke, he glanced at the unopened bottle of Valium tablets, standing on the press.

'It's like Alice has broken free and now we have no idea where she will end up. Each day I wake up to a bolder Alice.'

Kathleen wasn't as impressed as Jerry by Alice's transformation.

It had all been very gradual and welcome to begin with, but lately Alice was presenting Kathleen with cause for concern. She had moved from moody to giddy in no time at all. Sometimes, it appeared as though Alice couldn't sit still, or stop talking.

Alice and Kathleen were now both returned from Maura's to their own house, waiting for Nellie to arrive home from school, when they would pop back over to Maura's and break the news to Kitty.

'I have given the floor a mop and washed the dust off the sills,' Alice announced as she bustled out through the door to Kathleen who was now in the yard.

'Aye, well, 'tis just a novelty now. I'll enjoy it while it lasts,' said Kathleen, but she had laughed, despite herself. They both had. And Kathleen counted their blessings. As little as a year ago, no one would have imagined that Alice could laugh.

Kathleen turned Joseph's nappies in the copper boiler, using the long wooden paddle.

Electric-mangle washing machines and twin tubs were all the rage now, but in a two-up, two-down there was nowhere to put one. It mattered not a jot to Kathleen. She thought the copper boiler and the big mangle, kept in the outhouse, did a grand job anyway. It was her routine and Kathleen didn't like change.

As Nellie came through the gate from school, Kathleen wiped her hands on her apron and announced, 'Right, we're off, so we are, Nellie, no need to step on Alice's clean floor,' and within minutes, with Joseph once more tucked up in his pram, they were on their way back across the road.

Molly Barrett twitched her net curtains and craned her neck to take a clearer view of the top of the entry.

She had just made a cuppa for Annie and given her chapter and verse on her conversation with the two police officers. Both had said that her scones were absolutely delicious. She had given them an extra one each for later.

'Well, what would ye know,' she said to Annie, 'they are off again. Now tell me there's not something bloody funny going on with that lot. They were all over at the Dohertys' not hours since.'

Annie O'Prey jumped up to look through the nets herself.

Most families on the four streets lived in the back of the house and used the back entry and gates. Not Annie and Molly. They both preferred the front. They liked to see what was happening and just who was visiting who, and this was by far the best place to do it. Molly had placed a folded-down dining table in front of the net curtain, with an aspidistra pot plant in the middle and a chair on either side providing an excellent and unhindered view of who came and went. This was where they both had a cup of tea whilst they did an hour's knitting, most afternoons. On fine days, they took the chairs outdoors and sat on the pavement underneath the window.

'Oh, my giddy aunt,' exclaimed Annie, putting her hand over her mouth in shock as she watched Alice pushing the pram, with Kathleen and Nellie behind, crossing into the entry again. 'Do you think they killed the father, Molly?'

'What? Kathleen? No, you silly cow. How could she do that? It would have taken more than a handbag or a hairpin to take his bloody langer off. No, I don't think she killed him, but there is something very suspicious about the comings and goings at number nineteen and that's a fact.'

'Did you say that to the policeman when he was here?' Annie's voice was loaded with suspicion.

'I might have done,' said Molly in a tone that invited no further questions.

Both women picked up their knitting. There was nothing more to see, but the fact that Molly Barrett's cat had played a part in detecting the murder imbued in her an inflated sense of responsibility. Molly, via her cat, was now involved. She had told the police she would tell absolutely no one, not even Annie, of the fact that she was now officially helping them with their enquiries and had promised to maintain a vigilant watch on the comings and goings across the road.

As Kathleen, Alice and Nellie walked in through Maura's back door, the kettle began to whistle on the range. Maura jumped up to fill a large metal teapot that she placed on the table, along with the milk jug and the cups and saucers. She had been dreading this moment, but she knew there was no alternative. Kitty had to be told.

Kathleen was glad to be getting on with what they had to do. She couldn't explain it with any degree of meaning to any of them but she was weighed down with an overwhelming sense of urgency. It was her gift, helping her, and she knew she had to move fast. The appearance of Bernadette in her dream last night, doing exactly what she had done on the night of the murder – urging Kathleen along, pushing her, faster – had not left her thoughts throughout the day.

As they drank their tea and sat round the table chatting, Nellie looked out of the window over the kitchen sink, steamed up from the boiling kettle.

There she was. Nellie knew she was somewhere, she could sense it. She could see her outside, standing in the yard, looking in. Nellie knew it was her mother, Bernadette. She had seen her often since she was a child and the visions didn't scare her. She never told Kathleen or Alice.

She felt Bernadette's love so strongly that she could have scooped it up in her arms and held on to it.

Bernadette never missed her birthday. Nellie would enter her bedroom and be overcome by a heady smell of flowers. There were no flowers anywhere in the house. None even within a mile of the four streets. Nellie knew it was her mother, the woman no one ever talked about, not even her da.

Nellie didn't always see Bernadette. Sometimes she could only feel her. On the night Nellie had been discharged from hospital following the accident when she and Kitty had been knocked down, she had been curled up on her da's knee, reading the paper with him in front of the fire, when Bernadette came, or at least the feeling did.

As she arrived, her presence washed over them, gradually at first and then wrapped around them both. As Nellie rested her head on her da's chest, she looked at Jerry and they smiled. They hugged one another tightly and watched the flames leaping in the fire, not making a sound nor moving a muscle, not wanting to scare Bernadette away. And then she left slowly, in gentle waves, just as she had arrived, until she was with them no more.

Jerry softly kissed the top of Nellie's head and she felt his hot tears drip through her hair onto her scalp.

Nellie knew her da still missed Bernadette and that, when she joined them in these special moments, it was painful for him, even though she had died on the day Nellie was born.

Nellie knew that if she looked away from the kitchen window now, Bernadette would disappear in a flash. Her eyes began to water – she was scared to blink.

'What are ye gawping at, miss?' said Nana Kathleen, swivelling round on her chair to see what it was that Nellie was staring at.

She blinked. Bernadette left, leaving Nellie alone again.

Maura, timorously, began to speak.

'Kitty, we have a problem, child, and it is something we need to talk about and sort out before we tell Daddy. He will be distraught when I tell him the news and so we must be well prepared, so we must.'

Maura began to cry. She was never going to get through this.

Her Kitty. Maura had dreamt of her daughter taking the veil. Kitty, who was like another mother in the house, so good was she with all the little ones. With two sets of twin boys, Maura found life hard and Kitty had eased her burden by half.

But Maura wasn't selfish. She didn't want to keep Kitty to herself. She wanted to share her with God and thereby elevate the status of the Doherty household above that of her neighbours. Maura craved status; in fact she craved anything that would reward the family for her endeavours. She longed to be looked up to and, indeed, many a less holy neighbour already did look up to Maura. If there was a problem on the streets it was Maura or Nana Kathleen they went to. But that wasn't enough. Maura wanted one of the Doherty clan to do something, to be someone. She yearned for her household to be set above and apart from the others. What could achieve this more than having a child become a nun or a priest?

She had prayed about sharing her children with God. About giving God back some of the issue with which she and Tommy had been blessed.

Kitty had been shared with God.

Just not in the way Maura had prayed for.

Maura knew that what she now struggled to say to Kitty flew in the face of every motherly instinct. Earlier in the day she had questioned Kathleen.

'Once I have spoken those words, there will be no going back, Kathleen. Are we sure?'

'Aye, Maura, we are sure, queen. I wish to God we weren't and

I have prayed that every day you would run up this entry to tell me Kitty was started, but you haven't. There is no use us putting it off any longer or denying it: the child is with child, God help us, so she is.'

Now that they were here and the time had come, Maura lacked the strength to speak. Her mouth felt as though it were stuffed full of wool and the words she had rehearsed so well were lodged somewhere deep in her throat. The tears began to pour uncontrollably down her cheeks.

Everyone round the table stared at her expectantly, but she couldn't make out their alarmed expressions as their faces swam in a blurred haze through her tears.

Maura was weak. She was lost. Events had knocked the stuffing right out of her and she was as close to done for as it was possible to be.

Nana Kathleen decided it was time to take over. Twenty years older than Maura, Kathleen had also been crushed by events but it was not her daughter who was about to suffer. They were her closest friends facing a problem to which there was almost no answer.

Nellie sensed something utterly catastrophic was about to take place.

Had they all stopped breathing? They had. They had.

Fear gradually wrapped its icy tendrils around Nellie's heart and slithered down into the pit of her stomach. Under the table, she slipped a hand across and met Kitty's, searching for her own.

For a heartbeat of a moment, a drumroll of domesticity filled the silent kitchen.

Maura's gentle sniffling into her hankie.

The click of Alice's knitting needles.

The tick-tock from the clock and the slow, repetitive drip from the tap pinging onto an enamel bowl in the sink.

As the coal burnt in the fireplace, it hissed and spat in accompaniment to the slow bubbling simmer of a pan of broth, warming on the range.

Kitty looked at Nana Kathleen and knew that whatever she was about to say had something to do with the night the priest had raped her in her hospital bed. Nothing had been the same since. Then, after years of abusing her, he had elevated his depravity to a new level and was about to do it again in her own bedroom when all were at the Irish centre and dancing at a wedding. But Nana Kathleen had caught him and then the priest was found murdered. He had never bothered her again.

Kitty had been stunned by the reaction of her da. She thought he was going mad with the rage. Tommy, normally mild-mannered and gentle and who loved them all to distraction, had been torn apart by the knowledge that the priest had been helping himself to his precious daughter, in his own house.

The man they had trusted above all others – the Holy Father of the community, whom everyone revered as though he were God himself – had abused their trust. And Tommy, whose only job was to protect and provide for his family, had let down his first-born and closest in a way he could never have imagined, not in his very worst nightmares.

Just when Kitty had thought the horrors of the past were about to fade, she had now begun to throw up every morning and most of the day.

Kitty really couldn't remember normal any more.

Kathleen found the words hard. Kitty was still only fourteen but she looked just twelve and, sure, wasn't that the reason Kitty and Nellie got on so well? Kitty was still an innocent little child, hesitant to embrace her teenage years, while Nellie, having faced adversity at such a young age, was older and wiser than most.

'Kitty, my lovely one,' said Kathleen in a soft voice.

She rubbed the top of Kitty's hand, a thin, pale hand of innocence, held in a plump, warm hand of wisdom.

Kathleen raised her gaze and looked her straight in the eye.

She wanted Kitty to fully understand each and every word she was about to say. There was no room for ambiguity once it was spoken out loud.

All eyes rested on Nana Kathleen.

Kitty waited. Mouth open. Licked dry lips. Heart beating.

Tense expectancy cast a spell and drew them in closer.

'Kitty, we have to tell ye important news, my darlin'. Ye need to know now. We cannot keep this in the dark any longer. Yer mammy and I, we are very sure ye is having a babby.'

She held Kitty's hand more tightly.

'Ye is pregnant with the priest's child and we have to decide what we are going to do about it.'

All eyes were on Kitty and silently they witnessed the moment when her childhood died.

'No,' she screamed loudly, as she dropped Kathleen's and Nellie's hands, pushing the chair away and staggering backwards towards the range – desperately needing to put as much space as she possibly could between herself and what Kathleen had said.

Space, so that the words would not touch her, but would fall to the floor and shatter before they reached her. Space, to protect and save her.

But the words had been spoken. They were crawling all over her, already inside her, screaming in her head, piercing her heart.

It was too late. No escape. She had become what the words had made her.

'A baby? Oh God, Mammy, no, not me. I can't!' She looked to Maura with her hand outstretched.

And then they all died a little as Kitty howled with both her hands clutching at her abdomen as though testing to see if Kathleen were telling the truth.

Everyone in the room began to cry, even Alice.

But Kitty knew. As the words slowly filtered deeper and settled into place, she knew. She had seen Maura and other women on the street in the same situation often enough. Her mind was recoiling. Her heart sank and the fight, which had quickly flared up in her, took its leave and left.

It was true. Really, she already knew.

Within seconds, Maura was at her side, shaken out of her stupor by Kitty's distress. Her child needed her.

Kitty made a sound like that of an animal in pain as they stood and rocked together, Maura absorbing Kitty's agony, holding her upright.

Kitty, in her torment, provided Maura with a reason not to fall apart.

Nellie hadn't moved from her chair and had begun to cry quietly to herself, stunned by the news and shedding her own tears for the loss of Kitty's childhood.

Alice had jumped up and was making another pot of tea while Kathleen began washing the pots in the sink. Ordinary tasks, ushering normality back into the room.

Kathleen could hear Joseph stirring in the large box Maura used as a baby basket. Kitty's crying had woken him. Time to put things back on an even keel, she thought, as she watched Alice pick him up to change his nappy. Now, as she dried the wet cups and saucers, Kathleen felt a sense of relief that Kitty now knew.

Kathleen had won at the bingo twice this month. The money had been placed straight into the bread bin with the money she was paid for reading the tea leaves at her kitchen table on a Friday morning.

She was not short of money. Joe had been a clever and hard-working farmer and they had done well, because they were careful and had saved. Now Kathleen spoke again.

'Sit down now, Kitty,' she said kindly. 'Nothing can alter the facts, but we have to find a way to deal with them.' She gestured towards a chair at the kitchen table. 'Ye may be pregnant, Kitty, but really, 'tis our problem too. We will sort it and don't ye worry about a thing. This is one for the grown-ups.'

Kitty's crying subsided and an expression of desperate gratitude flooded her face.

'Maura, pull yourself together now. It could be worse, the child isn't dying.'

Kathleen knew the worst was over. Now they had to plan.

Nellie jumped up to help her nana and put the teapot on the table. Alice had Joseph in her arms. His little face lit up at the sight of Nellie and Kitty, now sitting next to each other at the kitchen table, with Nellie's arm round Kitty's shoulders.

Alice walked over to the range to fetch Joseph's bottle, which she had placed to warm on a range shelf. She pulled up her sleeve and shook the milk onto her bare elbow to test it was the right temperature and then sat amongst them to feed him.

The atmosphere was subdued. The only noise was the sound of Joseph sucking and the snuffles of his blocked nose.

Kathleen began to talk.

'Kitty, I have an idea if ye can just hear me out. I don't think we should tell the men just yet. I don't think we should tell anyone. What we need is some time to think about how we are going to manage this. What about if I take you and Nellie away back home to Ireland to the farm for a little holiday and try to think of a plan from there? What do ye think, girls? Would ye like that? We can go when the school breaks up for the holiday in a couple of weeks.'

Amazingly, both the girls smiled. Even Kitty. The excitement of a holiday together had for a few seconds wiped out the shock of Kitty's pregnancy.

Kitty had never had a holiday. It would be her first.

'Let's run upstairs now,' whispered Nellie to Kitty. Nellie had visited the farm many times. She wanted to share every detail with Kitty, in private.

'Holy Mother, Kathleen, would ye look at them smiling,' said Maura. 'It's a fairground ride of emotions all right.'

Alice began to pack up the pram. She had her own ideas about what to do.

'Have ye thought of an abortion?' she whispered to Maura and Kathleen, so that the girls upstairs didn't hear. 'You can get one easily. The chambermaids at the Grand used to go to a woman on Upper Parliament Street.'

No sooner had the words fallen from her lips than Alice felt bad. When first pregnant with Joseph, she had visited the same woman, though she had baulked at the offer of surgery. She had witnessed some of the chambermaids return to work in agony and be laid up for days. One girl had been taken into the Northern hospital after having an abortion and had never been seen again. Alice had no idea what had happened to her, but she knew she had been very ill. That was the old Alice.

The Alice who couldn't have cared less.

Alice, shamefully, had taken various concoctions and potions. But to no avail. Joseph was determined to make his entrance and look at him now. None of them could remember life before he had arrived.

However, this was different. Kitty was a child, and Kathleen was right. Her growing belly was a danger to them all.

Maura turned pale at the mere mention of the word abortion. Maura, who had wanted her daughter to become a nun, was now having to discuss whether or not Kitty should commit the biggest mortal sin imaginable, that of taking a life.

A second life.

A second murder.

My God, what and who had they become?

'Do ye think I want two murderers in the family, Alice? Do ye not think one is enough?' she hissed back coldly. The old animosity between Alice and Maura was never far from the surface.

Neither of them could quite forget the closeness there had been between Maura and Bernadette.

'I'm sorry,' whispered Alice. 'It just seemed like a good idea to me. And a quick solution too.'

'Aye, well, I think not. It only seems a good idea to you, Alice, because ye don't have the faith. No abortionist is sticking a dirty coat-hanger up my daughter. That's the path to three lives lost.'

Maura wanted to stop this loose talk of an abortion as quickly as possible and shouted up the stairs for Kitty to come down.

Alice looked to Kathleen, who put her finger to her lips.

The recovery of Alice had been a welcome one, but Kathleen could see that, with each day, her new boldness brought a fresh challenge.

'The offer of a holiday for Kitty is a kind one, Kathleen,' said Maura, walking back to the table, 'and one I will accept gratefully.'

Maura turned to Alice, guilty for her harsh tone a few seconds ago, when she knew how much Alice had done to help them. Alice had done her bit. She was on their side.

'Some way, we will sort this out and, Alice, I know ye think I am wrong, but I can tell ye now, there will be no meat for anyone in this house this week. I'm off to buy some Epsom salts and a bottle of gin. I'll be trying a few methods of me own.'

Alice smiled. She couldn't work out why that would be acceptable, but her suggestion of an abortionist wouldn't. She had heard that all the girls in Liverpool were doing it.

Kathleen felt lighter. Despite the reason why, the thought of returning home to Ireland had cheered her. The school holidays couldn't arrive soon enough, so that she could get on that ferry to Dublin. It wouldn't have been possible a couple of years ago to leave a baby of Joseph's age in Alice's care.

So much had changed.

There was also another dimension to the holiday. While they were away it would be the first time Jerry, Alice and the baby had been alone in the house together. Maybe that wasn't such a bad thing.

Kathleen put on her coat to head home. She would call in at the Anchor pub to use the phone and ring the pub at the back of the butcher's in Bangornevin. Days ago she had already let them know they would be coming home. Kathleen had known all along that it was the only thing they could do. She just had to convince everyone else.

They had made the decision to return to Ireland, she felt they had no time to lose and that feeling was exhausting her.

'I know the answers will come to me in me own kitchen,' she said to Alice. 'I'll get everything sorted from there. Just a few weeks to wait.'

Nellie and Kitty were now standing next to Alice, stroking baby Joseph's feet whilst he bounced up and down on Alice's hip. Nellie was now comfortable in Alice's company. A miracle, considering that, only a few years ago, Nellie had been terrified of her.

Simon and Howard had finished knocking on all the doors in the four streets and had retired to the car. They both lit a cigarette whilst they drank tea from the thermos flask provided by Howard's landlady.

'So,' said Howard, 'the sister's magnificent revelation is that the father spent a lot of time in number nineteen and now the eyes and ears of the world, Molly Barrett, tells us Maura Doherty should be knocked out with grief, but she isn't.'

'Fantastic, solid, wonderful leads. The super will be so pleased,' Simon replied in a voice dripping with sarcasm.

'They may not be strong leads, Simon, they may even be weak, but they both come from different people and both point to the same house. Something is better than nothing and, anyway, was it just me, or do you think the sister was hiding something?'

'Bloody hell, was she?' Simon replied. 'She looked like a scared rabbit. Didn't look me in the eye once, and her hand was shaking, did you notice that?'

'I did. Something or someone had taken the wind right out of her sails in between her calling us at the station and our arrival at the convent.'

Howard wound down the window of the panda car and shook the remaining contents of his cup out into the gutter, then screwed it back onto the top of the flask.

'Come on then,' he said to Simon, who was in the process of rolling up a cigarette, 'let's knock on number nineteen and give that tree a good shake.'

Alice covered Joseph with his blanket just as the Doherty kids burst in through the back door, looking for their tea. Maura's second daughter, Angela, was the first in and began to strop about the fact that Kitty had had yet another day off school. This was nothing new. Angela found a new subject to strop about at least once a day.

'I have had to sit in that classroom with Sister Theresa all day long,' Angela yelled, pointing at Kitty, and they all stopped dead as they heard a knock on the front door.

A loud knock. Three long, fierce bangs on the front door. They sent a shiver of fear like a trickle of iced water straight down Maura's spine.

Alice had heard the knock before. She knew exactly who it was.

Even the twins, in the midst of helping themselves to a plate of biscuits, were frozen in mid-raid and looked towards their mother.

The three knocks came again a second time and made each one of them flinch.

As deafening and as threatening as a death knell.

## Chapter Five

Stanley wheeled the empty oxygen cylinder into place, on the end of a long line of huge spent cylinders waiting for the truck to arrive with full replacements.

He looked across from the hospital stores entrance to the large door of the kitchens on the other side of the yard to see if Austin was about to emerge. He would have to hurry. Stanley wanted a ciggie and they couldn't have one here without blowing themselves up.

Stanley had been a wreck since he had read the news of the priest's murder. He had hardly slept since. His mother had commented over breakfast that morning that he was looking sickly.

'They work you too hard at that hospital. Look at the state of youse. Mind you, I always say it must be harder working with them sick kids. Why don't you see if you can transfer to the Northern hospital or somewhere where it's adults, like, rather than them poorly littl'uns?'

Stanley stared at his mother. What would happen to her if she ever knew the truth?

The thought churned his stomach as he pushed away his plate of bacon and eggs.

'I've just got a bug, Mam, I'm OK,' he said with a hint of irritation.

Last night Stanley had walked into the kitchen to find his mother standing in front of the television with a tea towel in her hand, staring at the screen.

'I'm just plating up yer dinner, lad,' she said, without even turning round to look at him. 'They've got no one for this murder of the priest, yer know. Bloody shocking it is. I reckon there's more going on in there than they are telling us.' She nodded at the television, as though the investigation were taking place somewhere inside.

Stanley looked at his place set at the table and the folded-up copy of the *Liverpool Echo*, which his mam left for him to read as he ate.

The headlines glared at him. 'POLICE SHOCKED BY EXTENT OF INJURIES IN PRIEST MURDER AND APPEAL FOR WITNESSES TO COME FORWARD.'

The now-familiar hand of fear caressed his neck and shoulders as he shivered slightly and took his seat. It slithered down his spine and lay heavily on his chest, pressing down hard, making him work to draw breath.

Not again, he thought, as his face became hot and flushed, and pins and needles ran down his arms, but this time he was spared. His breathing slowed and he didn't pass out. His mother had walked in and, with one eye still on the TV, placed his supper in front of him. She had noticed nothing.

Eventually, Austin ran across the yard, the tan-brown tails of his porter's coat flapping in the wind. His round, dark-framed glasses were as opaque and as greasy as his grey Brylcreemed hair, which was slicked back and hadn't been washed for weeks.

Not for the first time, Stanley wondered how Austin could see where he was going.

'Come on, there's no one in the porters' lodge now,' said Austin, 'let's have a brew.'

Stanley tipped up the sack trolley, shuffled the next cylinder into place and ran across the yard into the wooden lodge with Austin, who placed the kettle on top of the electric ring.

'Have you seen last night's *Echo*?'

'I have,' said Austin.

Stanley stared at his back. Was the man mad? How could he be so calm? Did he not realize the danger they were in?

'What are you being so fucking calm about, eh?'

Stanley had almost shouted at Austin, who now turned round with a look of anger.

'I'm not fucking calm, I'm fucking working hard to make sure no one knows I am terrified of looking up and seeing the coppers walk in through the door, which is more than you are doing. All you need is a fucking sign on your head saying kiddie fiddler, priest's friend, police, please arrest me.'

'Have you collected the photographs?' Stanley asked as he handed Austin a mug of Bovril.

'Yes, of course I have. Did you want me to leave them sitting there, you stupid twat?'

Austin put his hand into his top pocket and handed Stanley a white envelope with his share of pictures inside. Tailored to his taste.

'Arthur is in a bit of a state. Wants us to see him after work tonight. I don't reckon that is a good idea. We need to disperse. It is only a matter of time before they get to us. We can sit here and deny everything or do a runner. I am going to stay put. I'm too old to run.'

How could Stanley run? Austin thought to himself. It would kill his old mam.

'I will stay put too,' Stanley croaked. He took a sip of the steaming-hot Bovril, which burnt his insides as it went down.

'I think Arthur is taking off tomorrow. Locking up the flat and visiting his sister in Cornwall. He will stay away until everything dies down. The PO Box is registered to him. They have nothing on me or on you. We will be all right, Stan.'

Stanley took another sip and then, taking a deep breath, looked up at Austin. He almost cried with relief. He had been the one who had let the priest into the children's ward at night, but only the three of them – the priest, Austin and himself – knew that and now one of them was dead.

'Do you really think so?'

'I do. They have nothing that can lead to us and we didn't bloody kill the priest, so stop acting as though we did, soft lad.'

Stanley felt much better as he opened the envelope and began to look at his pictures.

'There's a new little girl arrived on Ward Four this morning,' said Stanley to Austin. 'She's really lovely.'

Austin smiled. 'Is there now? Well, me and me Kodak Brownie need to visit Ward Four today, to check the oxygen cylinders, eh, lad?'

# Chapter Six

Tommy walked back up the steps from the dock to Nelson Street with a lighter heart than he had for days. The men were often louder on the way up than they were on the way down.

Whilst the others chatted about football, Tommy made plans in his head for the weekend.

Since the dark night, he had been planning non-stop.

'Got to keep busy,' Tommy had said to Maura. He had to ensure his brain was occupied, holding at bay the images he would rather not see, suppressing them somewhere in the back of his mind.

He had already taken the boys to the baths in Bootle. They were the only boys on the four streets ever to have tasted chlorine.

Little Paddy was sad that his best friend Harry was deserting him. 'Learn to swim?' he said to Harry. 'Why would I want to do that? I'm never going to need to swim. Are ye not playing footie on the green, then?'

Harry would much have preferred playing footie on the green. Everyone at home had been behaving in a very strange way and this thing Tommy was doing, taking them to the swimming baths and then to the shore for a walk afterwards, was odd behaviour indeed.

It was no different for the girls. Maura had taken them to the jumble sale at Maghull church, Maura's own secret shopping haunt. She had cannily obtained, for nothing more than a shilling, the entire contents of a new brown-leather holdall, including the holdall itself, which the kindly stallholder threw in for free to pack the clothes in, so that they could carry them home on the pram.

The jumble sale was at a Protestant church, but Maura didn't care.

'I like going to the Proddy church, the women in there don't look down their noses at ye like the women in the pawnshop do. They can be very superior indeed and who knows what for? I have no need to work in a shop.'

Maura had spent years hiding from the other women, and from Father James, the fact that she went to the Proddy church sale in Maghull.

Now that the priest was dead, she no longer cared a jot.

Besides, Maghull was a posh area and some of the clothes in the jumble sale were very decent. Maura was particularly pleased with the coat she had bought for Kitty, which was cream with large wooden buttons and a wide belt around the hips. It looked almost brand new. Maura thought it would do for Kitty later on, too, although she wouldn't mention this to her just yet.

Kitty also had two skirts, a pair of brown boots that were exactly her size and fitted well, which Maura had promised she wouldn't have to share with anyone else, two jumpers and the coat. It was a couple of sizes too big, but Kitty didn't care.

'I will keep this all me life, Mammy,' said Kitty, as she tried it on. ''Tis is the grandest coat I have ever seen, it is so gorgeous.' Kitty stroked the coat across the front and up and down the arms.

Maura laughed.

Angela had a fresh pair of leather boots in shiny leather that was all the rage. The heels and the soles were worn down, but Maura knew the boots would be as good as new for a trip down the cobbler's. They were slightly too large, too, but Angela could put on a second pair of socks.

'And, sure, won't ye grow into them in five minutes now,' said Maura to hush Angela's grumbling.

After the jumble sale, Maura had taken the bus with the pram wedged onto the front platform and then walked Kitty and Angela the rest of the way into town. The twins were out with Tommy and they had no rush with time. As they alighted from the bus, Maura had what she thought was a brainwave.

'Let's make it a really special day and stop at a café for our lunch shall we?'

Neither Kitty nor Angela had ever heard the like or ever been to a café before.

'Why is Mammy acting so crazy?' Angela whispered to Kitty.

Kitty shrugged her shoulders and made no comment, causing Angela to look at her strangely.

Angela drooled as the meat and potato pies that Maura had ordered for them, with bread and butter and a large pot of tea, arrived at the table.

Whilst they were eating, Maura announced that they would be buying new underwear for Kitty.

'God almighty,' said Angela so loudly that everyone in the café turned to look at her. Kitty had taken the first mouthful of her pie at just that moment and it hit her stomach like a hot rock. The familiar feeing of nausea gripped her. She stopped eating and stared at the table in shame.

'Why is she getting all this stuff and clothes and the like, and I'm only getting a pair of boots?'

Angela had yet to be told that Kitty would be taking a holiday to Ireland with Kathleen and Nellie. Maura felt her temper snap.

'Hush now, ye cheeky article, and if ye don't, I'll make sure ye won't sit down for a week. Only a pair of boots? They are of the highest fashion and ye are damned lucky to have them. Now shut ye big ungrateful mouth.'

Then she turned towards the window. Kitty watched Maura take out her handkerchief and wipe her eyes.

Maura cried.

Maura smiled. Maura laughed. Maura cried.

No one knew these days what Maura was going to do next.

Kitty stared at Angela. They had never seen Maura so mad. Angela looked scared stiff. She didn't utter another word of complaint for the rest of the shopping trip.

Woolworth's on Church Street was bright and busy and the perfect place to buy toiletries.

As they walked in through the door, Kitty was amazed to see display after display of lipstick and hand cream, perfume and a huge variety of different soaps.

Maura bought Kitty a pale pink washbag and soap box, patterned with sprigs of white and darker pink carnations with delicate green leaves. This was almost more than Kitty could take in. She felt incredibly grown-up, having her own possessions.

Inside was a bar of lilac soap that smelt like lavender, a toothbrush, a pink facecloth, toothpaste and a tin of talcum powder.

Maura's spirits had lightened. She had become overcome with sympathy and love for her eldest daughter. She wanted to spoil her. To shower her with treats in order to cushion the blow of the knowledge she had to carry.

Maura went mad in Woolworth's and bought Kitty a small tub of lily-of-the-valley scented hand cream and a bottle of Pears shampoo. Kitty left the store with a bag full of belongings, never before owned by anyone else. What was more, they were hers and she didn't have to share them with Angela.

Back at home, Kitty had sat on her bed and looked again and again at her fancy possessions.

When the twins and the girls arrived home from school, Kitty made them sit on the bed with the baby propped up between them, as she took everything out to show them, one gift at a time. The four boys, who could not have been more bored if they tried, began to make their own amusement.

'Look at me, oh la-di-da, I am a very posh English lady,' said Malachi, the most mischievous of the four, as he grabbed the talcum powder, opened it and shook it all over himself, filling the room with a grey cloud that smelt of peaches.

'Mammy,' screeched Kitty down the stairs, 'Mammy,' as she chased Malachi round the room to grab back her beautiful white tub of talc.

Malachi, throwing the cannister down the stairwell, took the stairs two at a time all the way down and burst into the kitchen as Maura tried to intercept him on his way to the back door.

'Malachi, would ye come here now, you little divil, while I slap yer legs, ye horrible child, ye. Leave Kitty alone, do ye hear me, now leave her alone.' Maura was screeching down the back entry as Malachi was long gone and already sprinting across the green.

'God, that lad will be the death of me,' she said to Peggy, who was in her own backyard, putting her sheets through the mangle.

None of the children knew why Kitty was being treated so and Maura couldn't explain.

On her return from town Maura had said to Tommy, 'I'm plain worn out, Tommy. We don't have to keep filling every minute with things to do because of what happened. We will both be exhausted and broke at this rate.'

Tommy sighed. 'But I do, queen. I do.'

Tommy couldn't rest in the house. He hadn't placed a bet on his precious horses or read the *Echo*. He couldn't concentrate long enough to read past the first few lines.

He had to keep busy.

Daisy Quinn stood at her window that night, watched the lights extinguish in number nineteen and then slipped into her own bed. It had been a long and tiring day and she was exhausted.

The bishop had arrived as promised and had brought with him all manner of activity to the Priory.

Daisy couldn't help thinking that she had never in her life heard the sister talk so much in one day nor with as much agitation as she now did. She had always liked Sister Evangelista, who had been an efficient but kind Reverend Mother.

Daisy knew what had made the sister mad. It was the photographs in the drawer. Daisy had seen them too, lots of times.

She was sitting outside the sister's office, when she heard her on the phone to the bishop, asking him what she should do.

'I have already called the police, of course I have. These pictures are the devil's own work and surely they must have something to do with his murder. How can they not? Bishop, ye need to get here, fast.' Daisy heard the sister lower her voice even further as she hissed, 'They include one of our own children, taken in his office, so help me, God, it is a depraved picture. Ye will not believe it or understand what I am talking about until you see for yourself.'

Again, there was a long silence before the sister replied.

'Yes, Bishop. I will say nothing to the police until you get here and see the pictures for yeself, but what will I say to the police? I will always protect the Church, Father, yes, Father, I will, Father. I have to speak with you, though, urgently.' Her voice dropped even further to a rasp. 'I will send them to the Dohertys'. Daisy says the father spent a lot of time there and I swear, as God is true, the daughter Kitty is pregnant, but I'll not tell the police that, now, shall I?'

Daisy heard the sister replace the receiver and let out a big sigh, just as the police car pulled into the drive. Daisy peeped through the door and saw the sister wiping her eyes on her hankie, just as both doors of the police car clicked shut.

An hour later, when the police had left, Daisy boldly and nervously asked her own question.

'Can I stay here, please, Sister, at the convent?'

'Stay here, Daisy? Are ye mad, girl? The bishop will need somewhere to stay. He has to be looked after. Do you think it would be proper for him to stay at the convent, now?'

Crestfallen, Daisy looked down at her hands folded in her lap and replied with a voice loaded with sadness, 'No, Sister.'

'No indeed, Daisy,' said Sister Evangelista. 'Now, off ye go back over to the Priory, there's a good girl, Daisy, and I will pop back myself later with the bishop.'

Daisy was in the Priory kitchen, peeling potatoes for the bishop's supper, when he and the sister rushed in through the front door.

There had been a great deal of banging of doors, and of drawers and cupboards opening and closing.

The sister had brought the convent car, a Morris Traveller, to the front and she and the bishop ran in and out, loading up the back with one box after another.

Daisy couldn't help noticing how anxious they appeared and that there was little conversation between the two. They were very brisk with Daisy, shouting at her to go away when she went into the room to offer them tea.

Before the sister left, they told her that tomorrow the bishop would be receiving the police at the Priory and that they might want to ask Daisy questions, like the ones the sister had from time to time since the other day, and hadn't Daisy found that all very easy now?

Well, the truth was, she hadn't.

Daisy's head was hurting with the amount of questions she had been asked today and she thought it was funny no one had asked her any that she could answer without breaking the rules. Daisy saw a lot of what went on outside the Priory, but no one had asked her about that.

Whilst the sister and the bishop banged and clattered about the Priory, Daisy made the bishop his supper, and dusted and aired his room.

Later that evening, when the bishop returned from mass, the police were waiting for him. After they left, he had asked for his supper to be served in the small sitting room, on a tray in front of the fire, which Daisy had lit for him, with the television news on very loud.

When she entered the room with his tray of hot lamb scouse and steamed jam pudding and custard, he did not even look at her, fixing his gaze on the television screen. He said, 'Thank you, girl.' He said thank you, girl, often.

Just as she always had every meal since Mrs Malone had died, Daisy ate her dinner alone, in the vast basement kitchen at the big wooden kitchen table.

The bishop thought Daisy hadn't seen the bottle of whiskey on the floor, hidden down by the side of his chair, with the glass half full of the amber liquid tucked behind it.

He was wrong. Daisy saw everything.

As she nestled into her pillow and closed her eyes, Daisy heard his footsteps climbing the wooden stairs, slowly and heavily, towards her room on the top floor. The bishop was so fat, he struggled up the four flights, but Daisy knew he was coming to her and with every step she flinched.

She had thought that maybe, tonight, she would be safe.

As always, he sat on the edge of her bed whilst he struggled to catch his breath and, once recovered, he began to speak.

'Girl, the police will be here tomorrow and I am going to tell them that you are simple, do ye understand?'

Daisy nodded, but she didn't speak. She never spoke when he was in her room and he never called her Daisy, always 'girl'.

'If they ask you questions, girl, questions such as, has anything been removed from the Priory, you say no, nothing has. Do you understand?'

Daisy nodded.

'And if they ask you did any men ever visit the Priory you say no. Do ye understand that?'

Again, Daisy nodded.

'And as Father James told you, girl, it would be a grave sin to tell anyone what takes place in this room, even the police. You know that, don't you, girl?'

The bishop stopped talking and looked at her for a long, long time, as though a battle raged inside his head. Then, with a look of anguish, he pushed back the blankets covering Daisy, just as he always did.

## Chapter Seven

As Tommy opened the back gate he could see Maura through the kitchen window, standing at the sink; on her face she wore a tense and warning expression. His heart sank. Something was wrong.

The first thing he saw as he came in the back door was Howard and Simon, sitting at his kitchen table, each with an enamel mug of tea.

'Evening, Mr Doherty,' said Howard, as Tommy removed his jacket and hung it on the back of the kitchen door.

Tommy didn't speak but touched the peak of his cap in acknowledgment and looked over at Maura.

'That cuppa for me, love? What can I do for ye, gents?' With a smile that took every effort, he looked at both men and beamed.

When Tommy finally closed the front door on Howard and Simon, he and Maura peeped through the parlour window nets and waited for them to drive away.

A group of children had gathered around the car. Howard and Simon stopped and spoke to Little Paddy. Tommy watched as Howard raised his hand, waved a greeting and exchanged pleasantries with Molly Barrett, who was standing on her front step, hairnet in place and arms folded, chatting to Annie O'Prey.

As Maura and Tommy looked up and down the road, net curtains furiously twitched back at them.

'Look at that hard-faced Deirdre knocking on Sheila's door,' hissed Maura to Tommy. 'When did you ever see that slattern out on the front street pretending to look for her kids? They wander loose and free from dawn to dusk, without a crust in their belly, and suddenly she's all Mary good-wife, finding any excuse to see why the coppers are at our house. The nosy fecking bitch.'

'Hush,' Tommy replied. 'Don't let the children hear ye. We did all right. They have bloody nothing. I gave exactly the same story I have before. They have nothing, Maura.'

He put his arm round Maura's shoulder.

Deep inside, he was truly worried as they observed their neighbours, people he thought of as his friends, openly gossiping in the street. He no longer felt safe.

There had to be a reason the police had called again at Tommy's house. Something had put a spring in their step and a note of confidence in their voices, leading them straight to his door.

Maura knew Tommy was trying to protect her, but she was too canny to be fooled. She had to act fast. They had to spirit Kitty away from here and as quickly as possible.

Maura returned to the kitchen, wrote Kathleen a note and called Harry down the stairs to take the message across the road right away.

Maura didn't want to be seen outdoors. She knew she wouldn't make it far before a nosy neighbour called her across for an inquisition.

She could hear Peggy already shouting over the back wall, 'What did the police want, Maura? Getting mighty friendly with you and Tommy, they are now,' as she walked back into her own house. Peggy was a harmless friend, but Maura knew that even her idle gossip could be dangerous.

Later that evening, Jerry stepped into Maura's kitchen, just as she put the bread dough onto the side of the range to rise. Tommy had settled down in front of the television and opened the paper on his lap for a night-time read. He had decided it was time to make an effort. Having learnt to read only a few years ago, he didn't want to forget. It was one of the few things he had in his life to be proud of.

He leant forward and shifted the cinders around in the fire with the poker as he motioned to Jerry to sit in the chair opposite.

'Hello, Jerry, what's brought ye over here, mate? Has Alice whipped ye with her tongue then?'

Tommy began to giggle. He always laughed at his own jokes before anyone else did.

In months gone by, Jerry would have burst in through their kitchen door, cracking his own jokes as he came. But that was before.

When Kathleen had told Jerry Maura wanted him to pop over to the house, his heart had sunk. He felt sick and couldn't eat his supper. As soon as it was dark, he made his way down the entry to number nineteen. The sooner he knew what was wrong, the better. There had been too many nasty surprises of late. Kathleen promised she would follow him a few minutes later.

'Hello, Tommy.' Jerry lowered himself into the chair and held both of his hands out in front of him to warm before the embers, which had begun to glow with the heat. 'Apparently, Maura wants to talk to me.' Jerry rubbed his dry, crackling hands together, looking from one to the other.

Tommy looked surprised and glanced over at Maura as she took down from the press the tea caddy and the best, large, earthenware, blue-striped cups.

'Well, 'tis a mystery to me, Jer. Maura, do we want to talk to Jerry?' he said.

Tommy tilted his head to one side as he spoke, as though trying to see around Maura, to pick up a clue from her face.

'Aye, we do, but both of ye just sit while I make us a cuppa, and wait for Kathleen. We need to talk.'

Maura still hadn't turned round to face Tommy. She didn't dare. Without realizing it, she was allowing time for Jerry's presence to settle in the room.

'Well, this sounds serious altogether,' said Tommy, standing up and tipping the last of the coke from the scuttle onto the fire.

Maura felt calmer than she had earlier. Jerry was like a brother to her. In fact, he was closer than her own brother. She genuinely loved Jerry. They both did. Just by being here he had made the atmosphere lighter. She was glad she had asked Kathleen to send him over.

For a few moments, in hushed and whispered tones, the two men talked about the visit from the police.

'It is all just guesswork, Tommy,' said Jerry, leaning forward with his elbows on his knees and his hands clasped together, as if in prayer. 'No one saw us, no one was there, we are safe. You can't hang a man on the back of guesswork.'

Jerry had spoken the word no one else dared to. Hanging.

'No one would think hanging good enough for the murder of a priest, Jerry,' said Tommy, his eyes filling with tears of fear.

Jerry saw the distress on Maura's face. There was a moment of silence, until Jerry deftly moved on to a lighter subject, one guaranteed to alter the mood of the room. Football.

Tommy handed Jerry the *Echo*. The Liverpool football team manager, Bill Shankly, was all the talk in the football world.

'He's a Scot, a Celt. He will never stop being a problem for Everton, mark my words,' said Tommy.

'Aye, so everyone says,' Jerry replied.

Maura was pleased they were discussing football. She loved to hear the two of them natter. It made her feel warm inside. If Tommy was happy chatting football, she was happy. That was how it worked with them both. Maura took as much pleasure from Tommy's enjoyment as he did from hers.

It worked both ways. Each felt the other's pain and pleasure.

Or so Maura had thought.

The depth to which each had sunk into their own private world following the priest's murder had surprised her and added to the trauma. At the time when she needed Tommy the most, they had been the least able to communicate.

Touch, not talk.

Neither wanting to hear the other's opinion.

No analysis. The answers to unspoken questions burnt inside them, too painful to articulate. The knowledge and silence creating a vacuum.

But they had survived the first shock. The aftermath. The adjustment. Now they had to survive the second tsunami. As it rolled towards their kitchen, Maura took one of the hard-backed chairs from the table and dragged it over to the fire.

Jerry and Tommy looked at Maura. She was behaving strangely. Both felt their hearts sink as they waited for her to speak and they jumped when Kathleen burst in through the door.

'Thought it less obvious if we walked over separately,' said Kathleen. 'Molly Barrett's curtains have been twitching like a feckin' ferret all day. What did they want, Maura, what did the police have to say?'

'All the same questions we have been asked before,' said Tommy. 'They have nothing new.'

'Right,' said Maura, feeling much stronger now that Kathleen had arrived. 'I have to tell ye something and, Tommy, ye must not kick off, because Kathleen has the answer to the problem and I need ye to be strong. We all do, especially Kitty.'

Tommy's eyebrows knitted together. He lifted his backside up from the chair ever so slightly and, picking up the dark-green, flattened cushion on which he sat, slipped his newspaper underneath, for reading later.

'I'm ready,' said Tommy.

'I knew it,' Jerry said. 'As soon as Kathleen said you wanted me over here, I knew something was wrong.'

Tommy was suddenly fearful. He felt the change in the atmosphere and wanted time to stand still. He didn't think he could cope with anything else on top of all that had happened. Things were improving. Moving forward. Getting better. Why couldn't it stay that way?

He felt resentment brewing inside towards Maura. A feeling that was a stranger to the man who thought no ill of anyone.

He didn't want Maura to speak.

The coke in the fire was by now a red glow. They waited.

Maura took a deep breath. She spoke the words.

'Kitty is pregnant with the priest's child.'

She had said it. The words were huge, the biggest she had ever spoken, filling the room and polluting the air they breathed.

Before Tommy or Jerry could react she added, 'Before either of you think of gobbing off with an opinion, hear what Kathleen has to say, because she has more sense than all of us put together, so she does.'

Tommy couldn't have given an opinion. He was in shock. His bottom jaw had dropped and there it remained, gawping. Jerry rubbed his hands through his hair and was the first to speak.

'The fecking bastard. He's still here tormenting us. The fecking bastard.'

Maura didn't know where she found her strength. It came from nowhere and surged up in her. As she began to speak, she hardly recognized her own voice.

'Before either of you say another thing, I have children upstairs, and the baby is asleep and I will not let her be woken. They are not going to hear either of you raise your voices and they are not going to know what is going on, just because neither of you two can control yourselves. Do you both understand?'

For a split second, Tommy wasn't quite sure what had shocked him most. The news that Kitty was carrying the dead priest's child, or the fact that Maura was laying down the law when, as Kitty's father, he was more than entitled to kick off. He instantly understood why Maura had asked Jerry to come over.

'Whilst Kathleen explains, I will take some money from the bread bin and buy four bottles of Guinness from the Anchor. Not a word until I get back. I want no argument over this, it is too important.'

Neither man spoke. Jerry watched Maura as she put on her coat and fastened her headscarf over her curlers. The back-door latch clicked shut and Jerry listened to her feet tip-tapping over the yard.

Not for the first time, he admired her. She would fight for her family and here she was, laying the law down in her own kitchen to calm the two men she was closest to.

Tommy tipped his head backwards, stared at the ceiling and let out a large sigh.

His eyes focused on a stain that spread outwards from the light bulb in the centre. Within a dark-brown outline, shaped like a perfect cloud on a summer's day. The type you see drawn in the children's books from which Kitty had taught Tommy to read.

He remembered the first book they had read together. *Janet and John*. When he had told his five-year-old princess that he had never really attended school and had spent all of his childhood with his father, helping him with the horses, she had set her goal: to teach Tommy everything the sisters had taught her at school.

'Come on, Da, up,' she used to say to him when it was time for her to go to bed.

They had decided that it would be their secret. Sometimes, if he was tired after a hard day, he would make an excuse but she would stand there, one hand on her little hip and the other pointing up the stairs, her face set into what Tommy called her school-marm expression.

'Oh no you don't, Da, up you come right now,' she would say and it was all he could do not to burst out laughing. She was the image of Maura.

Sometimes he fell asleep on the bed next to her as they practised their letters. One memorable night, he opened one eye and saw her serious little face right next to his as she pulled the blanket over him, clambered back into the bed and, putting her little arms around his neck, fell fast asleep.

His first-born. His princess. His favourite.

Kathleen, who had not wanted to intrude on his personal grief, began to speak, softly.

'Tommy, we have to move her away from here. Her belly is trouble, a straight link in time to the priest. Two major events in one street would have to be connected. It is another reason for the police to visit your house. I don't know what has brought them here today, but I have a feeling that I just have to get her away. I have already rung home. I'm taking her and Nellie to Ireland for a break while we try to figure out what to do, but I do know this, Tommy: no one around here must have even the slightest notion that the child is pregnant.'

He still couldn't speak. His child was pregnant with the child of a man he had murdered with his own hands. How much worse could it be?

He made no attempt to halt the tears. He didn't care that he was breaking the unspoken code that real men didn't cry.

Jerry didn't speak. He offered no words of comfort. To do so would be to acknowledge Tommy's distress. Jerry had shed many tears of his own and knew that the best thing to do was to let Tommy cry them out.

It seemed only moments before Maura arrived back in the kitchen and was handing each of them a bottle of Guinness.

With a nod of appreciation to Maura for the bottle, Jerry asked Kathleen, 'When are you leaving, Mammy?'

'Tomorrow night, Jer. Well, at three in the morning, when it is at its darkest. We will leave the street without anyone seeing us go.'

'Tomorrow?' Maura almost shouted. 'I thought we were planning for the school holidays?'

Kathleen continued, 'Once we have left, you have to put the story about that my sister is ill. I had to rush back home and the girls came with me to help. I've made enough phone calls from the Anchor and given that story to Bill on the bar. I also used the phone tonight and told them we were leaving soon. I called Maeve the other day when I already knew in my mind what I was planning and she knows what's what.

'We have family in Ireland we can trust, Tommy, we all do. The streets here are on fire with the chinwagging and we need to be out of it. If we aren't here, we can be forgotten. Out of sight, out of mind. If they see us all leaving together with bags in hand, moving off for a sudden holiday, the gossip will run riot around the four streets and might reach as far as the police station.'

They were silent with shock at what Kathleen had planned. Each raised their bottle at exactly the same moment and took a long gulp of the Guinness.

But Kathleen hadn't finished; there was more.

'Now, Maura, we have to put on the act of our very lives, like we have nothing to hide and the fact that we have gone away is just a coincidence. Bring all the girls in tomorrow, even Peggy. Let's have a hair night. We need everyone to think all is fine and dandy in the Doherty house and that we haven't a care in the world. Don't even tell Kitty that she is being taken the following morning. The less she knows, the better.'

The following evening, after a few knocks of mops on kitchen walls, Sheila arrived in Maura's kitchen and transformed it into a hairdressing salon. Nellie had her hair washed, with her long locks tied tightly in rags ripped from an old nappy, which the following morning would leave her a head adorned with beautiful red ringlets.

Brigid had brought with her a jam tart she had made to accompany the copious cups of tea, as well as a baby tucked inside a blanket sling tied across her chest.

In her bag she had a pair of eyebrow tweezers and a jar of Pond's cold cream. This she had smeared thickly over everyone's eyebrows, in preparation for her session of plucking and shaping.

Peggy had settled herself by the fire with a packet of ciggies and an ashtray.

The kitchen was a buzz of activity as Kathleen, Kitty and Brigid took it in turns to have their hair washed over the kitchen sink by Alice as Sheila set about transforming them all into visions of beauty.

Nellie and Kitty were enjoying the excitement. Hair nights in the kitchen happened about once a month, in one house or another. It was the only time Peggy ever washed her hair. Very few could afford a hairdresser and Sheila was a dab hand with a pair of scissors. The shillings she earned from her scissor skills made a difference to her life. Sheila also owned a rubber hose, which divided in the middle and connected to the kitchen taps, just as they did in the hairdresser's. They all loved the atmosphere of the girls' night in. For the first time in weeks, Kitty laughed at Peggy who grumbled and shuffled as usual as she came in through Maura's back door.

The smell in the kitchen changed perceptibly as Peggy walked in. They were all well used to the distinct Peggy perfume and managed to ignore it.

'I swear to the Holy Father I was never meant to marry that fat slob and the midwife definitely slipped someone else's kids, which were devils themselves, into the cot, and gave the good ones I had to someone else. What have I done to deserve that lot next door, eh, Maura?'

'We often ask the same question ourselves, Peggy,' said Maura in a sympathetic tone with a twinkle in her eye as she winked at Kathleen. Everyone stifled their giggles.

Kitty knelt on a chair with her head over the sink, a towel wrapped around her shoulders, with Alice using the hose to rinse the shampoo out of her hair. Kitty's shoulders shook and she felt Alice's belly shuddering with laughter as they both leant over, trying not to be unkind and hurt Peggy's feelings.

That happened often enough when sometimes the little ones called her Smelly Peggy out loud and she heard them.

Kitty was feeling better by the minute. The old Kitty was returning, restored by laughter.

The new Kitty was fading, suppressed by denial.

Kitty loved her hair.

Long, thick and just like her mother's.

Brigid had plucked and shaped everyone's eyebrows, and the kitchen had been full of screams and laughter at Kathleen's antics under the tweezers.

Maura had sat Kitty on a chair in front of the fire and taken the curlers out. Then Sheila had backcombed the life out of her hair, piled most of it up on top of her head and swept her fringe dramatically across, almost covering one eye.

When Tommy walked into the kitchen, he pretended not to recognize her.

'Jeez, Maura,' Tommy shouted in mock surprise. 'What is Marianne Faithfull doing sat in our kitchen and where the hell is our Kitty?'

'Shut up, ye great eejit, this is our Kitty.'

'Holy Mary, how was I to know that? We had better be careful, someone might snap her up to appear in a film or something.'

Kitty threw one of the curlers at Tommy, but she was grinning shyly from ear to ear, beside herself with pleasure.

A grand show it was as the kitchen rocked with laughter and women tripped in and out of the back door, just as they always did. Hardly a word was mentioned about the police and when it was, Maura answered with confidence, 'Well, sure, there was no one the priest was closer to than us, now. Only natural so, that they be looking to us to help.'

Everyone nodded as kindly Brigid, who knew almost as much as the Dohertys, said, 'Sure, isn't that the truth.'

No one other than Nellie saw the smile slip from Kitty's face.

It was pitch-black outside and Kitty felt as though she had been asleep for only an hour when she was woken by Maura, gently shaking her shoulders.

'Wake up, queen,' she whispered, 'come downstairs.'

When Kitty staggered into the kitchen, her clothes were ready warming and Maura had poked some life into the fire. There was a candle lit on the mantel, but Maura hadn't switched on the lights.

As Kitty moved towards the switch, Tommy hissed, 'No, don't, queen, leave it.'

'What am I getting dressed for?' asked Kitty, dazed and only half awake, blinking at them both as she rubbed her bleary eyes.

'You are going to Ireland now, Kitty,' said Maura. 'Hurry, your da is taking you down to the Pier Head to meet Kathleen in ten minutes, so you don't have long.'

Kitty checked the clock on the mantel above the range. 'Mammy, 'tis only half two,' she said.

'Yes, and that is why we have to be extra careful and quiet and leave separately, so as not to wake a living soul. It's why we are meeting Kathleen at the Pier Head, do ye understand?'

Kitty nodded, but she didn't understand. Thoughts of her friends and teachers were flitting through her brain. How would they know where she was, if she hadn't had the chance to talk to them and explain what was happening?

She was too tired to talk. Maura forced her to take some tea and toast, which was the last thing she wanted, but as she drank, the excitement of the adventure began to filter through and drag her up through the folds of sleep.

Ten minutes later, with the new, brown, jumble-sale holdall clutched in one hand and Kitty's hand in his other, Tommy was tip-toeing across the cobbled entry, hugging close to the wall, slipping away into the dark night. Kitty's secret, their secret, was at last leaving the knowing, prying eyes of those who lived on the four streets.

## Chapter Eight

Jerry's brother, Liam, was waiting to greet them when they arrived in Dublin.

It was a dark and wet night and the girls kept their heads bent low as they disembarked to keep the driving rain from directly hitting them in the face. They had sat at the Pier Head for most of the morning as one crossing after another had been cancelled due to the choppy Irish Sea until at last, a ferry was allowed to leave.

Now, they were officially on holiday.

Both girls were still reeling with the shock from the suddenness of their departure. It had all happened so quickly.

'Ye'll get used to the rain,' shouted Kathleen who led the way as she bustled on ahead. 'It rains so much in Mayo, Kitty, that people who stay here for too long grow a set of gills.'

'They don't, do they?' Kitty said to Nellie.

Nellie laughed. 'Not at all, it's Nana Kathleen's joke. She tells it all the time. I must have heard it a hundred times, but me and Da, we just laugh so she feels like she's being funny.'

Both girls began to giggle, more from the excitement of setting foot on the soil of a foreign country than Kathleen's jokes, which they could no longer hear above the sounds of people greeting each other and car horns beeping. Suddenly, they thought they could hear Jerry shout, 'Mammy,' but they both looked up and realized it was Liam, who appeared and sounded as much like Jerry as it was possible to.

'Well, well, well, would ye look at the grown-up colleen now,' Liam shouted as he scooped Nellie up into his arms. 'Here, would ye let me take a look at ye. What a big miss ye are. The absolute image of yer mammy with that long red hair. I bet ye don't remember Uncle Liam, do ye?'

Nellie didn't know why, but she was overcome by a strange shyness. Maybe it was because Kitty was witnessing this very open display of affection. Or perhaps because he had spoken of Bernadette. She felt stupidly proud to have been compared to her own mammy, the mammy that no one in Liverpool ever spoke about. She did remember Uncle Liam. He was loud, gregarious and always playing practical jokes.

Nellie loved him. She loved him twice over for speaking about Bernadette as though she were still alive.

He was the funniest man she had ever met. She hadn't seen him for two whole years but she certainly did remember him.

She loved the farm and everyone on it. She often thought about them all. What she loved most was that it was where her daddy was born, and where Nana Kathleen had also been born, and her daddy before her and his before him. Uncle Liam had built a new house on the same land as the old house, so for a long time there had always been a Deane on the farm. The new house had a fully fitted indoor bathroom. That was a novelty on the four streets in Liverpool. It was a novelty in Ballymara and in the main village, Bangornevin, too. Nellie knew there were lots of people in the village and out in the country who were envious of what a good farmer Liam was and of how well the Deane farm fared.

Nellie had also been taken aback by the suddenness of their departure. Last night she had sat on Jerry's knee in front of the fire for a cuddle. Jerry had played with her ringlet rags and wrapped them round his fingers as they both stared into the fire.

Jerry whispered so that Alice couldn't hear.

'Yer mammy, Bernadette, had loved the farm so much, she used to swing on the big five-bar gate to the yard and do nothing more than gaze up the hill opposite and dream of you. Yourself, little miss, were just the twinkle in her eyes back then.'

She gave Jerry a big hug to try to make him smile. His expression was wistful and sad but she knew that wherever it was he vanished to when he mentioned her mammy, it was somewhere Nellie couldn't reach. She could feel the ache in his heart but it was his ache and his alone, untouchable and not one she could heal.

Uncle Liam placed a kiss on her cheek and put her back down as he bent to greet Kitty. 'And you must be Miss Kitty?' he said grandly as he took off his cap and bowed in an exaggerated manner.

Kitty blushed a deep pink and took the hand Liam proffered.

A self-conscious Kitty had never shaken anyone's hand before.

'Now,' said Nana Kathleen, 'if ye would stop play-acting, Liam, and take these bags, I'd be very grateful.'

Kathleen playfully hit Liam across the back with her umbrella. Liam pretended it had hurt much more than it actually had and began to walk doubled over as though he were in great pain, lifting up the bags and howling with agony.

Kitty and Nellie were in fits of giggles.

'Here, Nellie,' shouted Liam as he threw her the keys. 'Would ye drive? Me back is so bad now thanks to that Nana Kathleen.'

Nellie squealed loudly as she caught the keys, but she and Kitty were laughing so much they could barely protest that Nellie was too young to drive.

Liam, affecting a miraculous recovery, lifted up the tarpaulin on the back of the van and placed the bags underneath.

As Kathleen shuffled herself across the van's bench seat to sit next to Liam, she shouted, 'The rain is playing merry hell with my wash and set, so get in quickly, girls.'

As Liam passed the girls to reach the driver's seat, with a wink he slipped them each a brown ten-shilling note. God, how can he afford that? thought Kitty. The reason most of the Irish were in England was to make money, but Nellie and Kitty's first impression was that they had more money in Ireland. No one on the four streets owned a car. A ten-shilling note was a huge amount of money, enough for two days' shopping at home.

'Flippin' heck, we are millionaires,' whispered Nellie to Kitty, as they scrambled along the bench next to Nana Kathleen, to begin the long journey in the rain across Ireland to the west coast.

Kitty had never before travelled in a car, a train or a boat, and in the space of a day, she had experienced all three.

She had never visited the land of her parents' and her ancestors' birth, yet here she was with her feet on Irish soil and, inexplicably, it felt like her soil. The furthest distance she had ever travelled had been to St John's market with her mam at dusk on a Christmas Eve, to buy a fresh turkey and some bacon from the meat hall at the end of the day at a knock-down price.

To date, that had been the most exciting journey Kitty had ever made. She loved the sawdust-covered, wooden floorboards and the Christmas atmosphere amongst the butchers, cheekily calling out to the women from behind their market stalls.

But that was as nothing compared to the last forty-eight hours.

Everything about this trip was a novelty, such as sloping off in the dead of night to the Pier Head to catch the ferry before the buses were even running. The sandwiches Maura had made her for the journey contained tongue. She had never before in her life had anything more exotic than jam or Shippam's fish paste.

Meanwhile, as Liam drove slowly away from the port towards the streets of Dublin, back at number nineteen Tommy and Maura were clearing up the kitchen following supper.

Angela had been in a foul mood, a seamless continuation from her bad temper at breakfast, when she had discovered that Kitty was taking a holiday to Ireland.

'I cannot believe this,' she had screamed. 'Why her and not me? It's desperate, Mammy, that I am being left behind, it is, desperate,' she sobbed.

Angela wailed and cried at the unjustness of it all, adding to the load of Maura's day.

'Every cloud has a silver lining, Angela,' Maura replied. 'Ye become the eldest child whilst Kitty is having her holiday.'

Maura had no idea that that was exactly what Angela was dreading.

'Thank God Kitty's gone,' said Tommy wearily when he and Maura were preparing for bed. 'She needs this holiday. The air on the farm will put the colour back in her cheeks. They say a change is as good as a rest, don't they?'

With a sigh, he pulled up the sash window. The night sounds of the tugs on the river filled the room. Putting his head outside to blow away his cigarette smoke, with a heavy heart he whispered, more to the moon and the stars than to Maura, 'I only wish I was going with her.'

Hardly a day passed without Tommy thinking of Cork and the village where he had been born and raised. He thought now of his own family – his mammy, daddy and those of his siblings – who had travelled on to America rather than stay in Liverpool. Whenever someone mentioned Cork within earshot of Tommy, he always repeated the same comment: 'Aye, God's own county, and there is no finer a place on this earth, so there isn't. No better people, no finer horses, nor more beautiful women.'

Tommy spent some of his day, every day, dreaming of Cork.

'I sometimes wish we had gone on to America, Maura. We both should have done what my brothers did. Maybe this terrible thing wouldn't have happened in America.'

Maura listened to him, all the while keeping her own thoughts close. How glad she was that she had indulged and spoilt Kitty over the last few days.

'Come to bed, Tommy,' she whispered.

Maura was exhausted from having to wake at two o'clock to spirit Kitty away into the night and coping with the demands of her children. Malachi and Declan ran Maura ragged on the best of days and today was no different. Maura was already missing Kitty in so many ways.

'She is with Kathleen and Nellie, and no doubt having great craic while we are here worrying ourselves stupid. Come to bed,' she said softly.

Tommy pulled the window down and the curtains across before he slipped into the comforting arms of the woman who loved him as no other ever would.

Who was not from Cork.

Kathleen and Liam chatted away as they drove across Dublin, with Nellie throwing in the odd comment or question. Kitty could barely understand what they were talking about. She knew none of the names or the places they were discussing. Liam had a list of deliveries to collect, which would make the journey longer.

Kitty stared out at the wide river and the tenement buildings. Had it been only three days since she had found out what was wrong? Now she knew why her period hadn't arrived. She had started only a year ago and had not thought anything of having missed. She'd had no idea what this meant until Maura had explained it to her last night in furtive whispers, as she sat her in yet another scalding-hot bath before Sheila and the other neighbours called round.

On three occasions over the last three days, Maura had almost boiled her alive in a bath while making her swallow a weird-tasting drink. Her nausea had been replaced by the most awful diarrhoea.

'You need to be purged, Kitty,' Maura had whispered. 'Your guts making all that movement in the outhouse will bring your monthly on, so it will. And you have to drink the Epsoms whilst you are sat in the hot bath, it doesn't work else.'

Kitty had been well and truly purged and, heavens, had a cleaner child ever visited Eire? Her monthly had remained stubborn, clinging to the lining of her womb for dear life.

Kitty pressed her face against the window and looked out into the Dublin night at the women gathered on the tenement building steps under an overhead canopy, smoking pipes and wearing headscarves, with black knitted shawls draped around their shoulders. In long black skirts, they sat with their knees wide apart. By the light of the glass-domed street lamps, she saw children walking in the pouring rain, wearing barely any clothes. They couldn't have been more than two years of age. It was late and yet the streets were incredibly noisy. Through open doors she glimpsed long counters of polished dark wood in bars heaving with customers, drinking the black-velvet Guinness.

They drove past a group of men fighting in the street.

'Dublin is the capital of sin now, Mammy,' Liam said to Kathleen. 'No one comes here unless they have to. It is a bad state of affairs all right.'

'Sure, it always was, Liam, nothing has altered there. Dublin has always been a bad place, which is why I never allowed any of you to come here when ye were growing up.'

The capital of sin? Kitty and Nellie looked at each other and then outside with renewed interest.

Kitty had never even been into Liverpool at night and now, here she was, in the heart of Dublin, driving through the capital of sin.

It felt as though each minute there was a new sensation or experience. Kitty felt time shifting. Her foundation of stability, all she knew and understood, was slipping away from under her. This journey, with every mile they drove, drew a line under her life as the old

Kitty. She tried not to think about what was happening but she realized that, from this night on, nothing would ever be the same again.

Already homesick, Kitty wanted to return to Liverpool to her mammy. To sit with Maura and Tommy, just the three of them together, as they sometimes did at night when the younger children were asleep.

Tommy would tell jokes about what the men had done and said on the docks and they would usually laugh about one of the twins' antics. They would worry out loud about Harry's asthma, and all three would have a drink and a bite together before Kitty went upstairs to bed.

Before she did, she would kiss and hug both her parents goodnight. Kitty would walk over to her da and bend to kiss him on the cheek. He would pretend to be reading his paper and then, at the last second, as she bent her head, he would turn quickly and steal a peck on the lips. He did it every night, but the three of them always laughed as though he had never done it before.

Kitty wanted to be there right now, in the warmth of her kitchen with the people who loved her best of all.

She was a young girl, pregnant, in a strange country with people who, kind as they might be, weren't her own.

Exhausted, she leant her head against Nellie's shoulder and slept.

# Chapter Nine

Alice and Brigid had become good friends.

They shared a secret. They had both become bound by events which took place following the murder.

Brigid had helped in her own way to throw the police off the scent away from number nineteen following the murder. Her and

Sean had provided Tommy with an alibi. They were parents of daughters and although they didn't fully know all the details neither did Alice, not completely. The only people who really knew what took place in the graveyard that night, were Tommy and Jerry. Or so they thought. On the night of the murder, they had all raised their whiskey glasses and made a vow. Not one word was to be spoken about that night, to anyone, not even to each other, ever again.

No one other than Tommy knew of the torment that now woke him in the middle of the night and left him staring out of the window, wondering how in God's name he had gone from a peace-loving family man to a murderer in one fateful hour.

Tommy would rewind the evening over and over in his mind, as though on a loop. Images of the hangman's gallows haunted him as he tried and failed to somehow make sense of the extraordinary events that had taken over his very ordinary life.

It was no surprise, really, that the first real friend Alice had ever made, other than her mother-in-law Kathleen, had been Brigid. They had plenty in common, besides the secret. Brigid had daughters around the same age as Joseph.

There wasn't anything Brigid didn't know about child rearing. There was nothing Alice did know.

They both had the best-looking husbands on the four streets, if not in all of Liverpool.

Sean, like Jerry, was able to make even the elderly ladies on Nelson Street giggle in a flirtatious way and both men hammed it up outrageously.

'Evening, Mrs O'Prey,' Jerry would shout if he saw Annie on her step on his way home. 'God, ye look gorgeous today, so ye do. Lock the door tonight or I'll be desperate to get across into your bed if my Alice turns me away and says no.'

Mrs O'Prey would flash her gums at Jerry and disintegrate into a fit of giggles.

'Oh, away with ye, Jerry Deane, ye bad lad, wait until I tell ye mammy.'

Jerry knew there was very little in Mrs O'Prey's life to make her smile.

If Tommy was with him he would shake his head.

'Nothing wrong in making them laugh, Tommy,' Jerry would say.

'Aye, you just made her day all right, Jerry, you did.'

'What about ye, Tommy, will ye be comin' over after he's finished?' Annie O'Prey shouted cheekily across.

'Oh no, not me, Annie, my Maura never says no,' Tommy shouted back.

Sean on the other side of the road would join in the banter. 'Oi, keep yer hands off my woman, Deane, or yer a dead man. She's mine and if ye want her, see me in the ring on Friday night.'

The street was filled with laughter as Jerry whispered to Tommy, 'If Maura ever hears you telling Annie O'Prey that she never says no, you're the one whose feckin' dead.'

Blowing Mrs O'Prey an exaggerated kiss, the three men separated and walked on to their own back doors.

Sean and Brigid weren't as badly off as other families in Nelson Street.

Sean won money at the boxing ring each Friday night, which he put into the bread bin.

Some of it went to buy the meat and eggs Sean needed in order to remain fighting fit.

Some went towards the housekeeping and to feed his many daughters. And the remainder was for the day when they had enough saved to emigrate to America.

Sean had plans and dreams.

He and Brigid received a letter every fortnight from his sister, Mary, in Chicago.

Mary and her husband, along with Sean's brother, Eddie, had established a small building company and, by all accounts, were doing well. In every letter they pleaded for Sean and the family to travel and join them, to work with them because the business was growing so fast. They could barely manage and were having to employ large teams of Irish builders from home. It galled Mary and Eddie that their very own brother worked as he did on the Liverpool docks, when a life of prosperity and opportunity was waiting for him and his, right there in Chicago.

Sean was desperate to set sail and join them. His work in Liverpool was only ever meant to be temporary and a means of saving for the passage to America.

Mary and Eddie, who were both older than Sean, had travelled on ahead of him to Liverpool, worked for three years and went without, so determined were they to save every penny they earned.

Eddie had taken two jobs: for six days a week, Sunday excepted, he worked as a brickie on the new housing estates on the outskirts of Liverpool, and for four nights as a barman.

Mary had trained as a nurse and lived in the nurses' home, eating on the wards and barely spending a penny of her salary. Within two weeks of qualifying, she and Eddie realized they had enough saved and had boldly booked their passage across the Atlantic.

Their single-minded determination had paid off well.

Sean would have left the day after every letter arrived from America, but for two problems.

The first was that Brigid would have none of it.

'England is far enough away from Ireland and from my family and your mammy too,' she said reproachfully, every time he brought the subject up. 'Now that Mary and Eddie have selfishly gone to America, who will be here for your mammy, should she be sick? Ye know the rules, Sean. The nearest does the looking after and that's me and you.'

The second was that, even if Sean could talk Brigid round, he didn't yet have enough fare money for all of them. He was too proud to ask his sister for help.

Mary's last letter had included a black-and-white photograph of their house in Chicago and a picture of Mary and her husband in front of their fireplace.

Sean had placed the picture on the press. He picked it up and looked at it at least once a day.

It wasn't Mary he looked at, nor her husband, despite their clean, wholesome well-fed expressions and fine clothes.

'It was the size of the marble mantelpiece with the gilt-framed mirror above it and the solid brass fender round the fire. Alongside, a small polished wooden table held an oversized lamp with a fringed lampshade. On the mantel stood an ornament of a sailing ship and a shire horse, with photographs in silver frames.

He studied them all. Such fine things.

Sean would not even have been able to afford the large brass coal bucket at the opposite end of the fender, never mind the house.

'They have everything, sure, there's no denying that, all right,' he said to Brigid.

"I desperately want us to be with them. I know we made the wrong decision to stay in Liverpool. I cannot see a way forward out of the four streets for us all and quick enough too."

Brigid never replied or returned his enthusiasm.

'Sure, she never stops giving out about America and how great it is, does she?' Sean said when he finished reading the latest letter.

'She makes me laugh, so she does,' replied Brigid. 'She always signs off, "From the land of the free". Sure, we are free too. Does she think we are all prisoners in England?'

'We are, aren't we, though, Brigid?' said Sean. 'I can't earn any more money than I do. They seem to be free to do whatever they want to over there. If you want to set up a business, you can. If you want to buy your own house, you can get money to do it. America is growing and bursting with opportunities that we just don't have here. No one cares where you came from or what class you are. There is no class in America, don't ye understand? Everyone is the same. If ye can work ye can win.

'We aren't even the same when we go to the grocer's. All the shite gets loaded into our baskets. Ye heard what the grocer told Paddy in the pub when he was pissed. The best potatoes go to the English, the second-best to the pigs and the rest to the Irish.'

Sean walked over to Brigid and put his arms round her.

'I just don't want our kids to live our life and repeat our hardships every day. We have to keep saving, Brigid, and I have to keep fighting to bring the extra money in.'

He pulled away and looked down at her, seeking reassurance.

Brigid broke free of his arms and refused to meet his eyes. She could be bolder when he wasn't touching her.

'I want to be wherever you are and if you think America is better for our kids, when we have the money for the fare, we will talk about it then, but I'm not making any promises, Sean.'

She was holding him off, playing for time. She turned back to the kitchen sink.

Sean put his arms round his wife's waist and hugged her.

He beat the shite out of three men every Friday night in order to earn the money they needed to save. Brigid would never know how that felt. She would never understand that, knowing she was with him, supporting him and sharing his dreams, would make getting into the ring easier to bear.

With Brigid beside him, he could dive over the ropes and see nothing ahead but their future.

Punches easier to take. Bruises quicker to heal.

Brigid continued washing the dirty dishes.

'I do think about it sometimes, ye know,' she said, with a lift in her voice. 'When Kathleen read me tea leaves on Friday, she said we would be visiting foreign shores before long.'

Sean didn't believe in prophecies found in the tea leaves, but Kathleen's endorsement made him feel surprisingly good.

'It won't be long now before we have enough money for the fare. Two more steady years on this lucky winning streak and we can be off, all of us.' His voice was loaded with a false brightness, but dropped as he added, 'Providing we don't have any more babies.'

Brigid didn't reply. She had no desire to move further away from home. She was happy enough, but Sean was always restless, wanting more and better, and looking to see how green was another man's grass. Sometimes it wore her out.

Nothing wore Sean out.

Winning in the boxing ring was a foregone conclusion for him, driven by his personal goal. Every waking hour that he wasn't working on the docks, he was training in the ring. There was no doubt in his mind that he would have the money within two years.

They were fine the way they were, mused Brigid. She comforted herself with the idea that he would soon grow tired of wanting to leave. Sean was someone in the community. He enjoyed his reputation as a big and powerful man. When he walked down the street, the kids shouted out to him, 'Hey, big man Sean, will ye show us how to throw a punch?'

They would run along beside him, begging and chanting. Often he would stop and spend time on the green, showing them how to jib. He truly was the big man and, when he realized that, pride alone would be enough to make him stay.

Better to be a big fish in Liverpool and not a little fish across the other side of a very big pond.

The adults on the four streets were in awe of Sean's size and strength. Even Kathleen, who had wondered at the arrogance and the cheek of Father James, who had often tripped in and out of Brigid's house. Kathleen liked to imagine what Sean would have done to the priest if he had caught him up to anything.

If neighbours on Nelson Street ever thought one of their own had murdered Father James, they would naturally have assumed it was the big and muscular Sean, not the short and kindly Tommy.

Little did they know.

It took rage to kill a man, not strength.

The night before Kathleen left for Ireland, she had popped down to see Brigid, to tell her they were having a hairdo night at Maura's.

'I haven't time to beat around the bush, Brigid,' said Kathleen, breathlessly, almost as soon as she walked in through Brigid's back door.

As Kathleen looked around the kitchen, she was overcome with admiration. A wooden box sat on the floor to the side of the fire, padded with hand-crocheted blankets, and inside, top to tail, slept two babies. In the pram just inside the back door slept two more. The kitchen was spotlessly clean.

'Brigid, I am here to ask ye a favour,' said Kathleen, 'and I didn't want to do it tonight in front of the others, especially nosy Peggy.'

'Oh, for goodness' sake, sit down,' Brigid said, concerned. Kathleen was bright red and panting. Brigid had always thought Kathleen did too much and should be taking things a bit easier.

'Brigid, I need ye to help me, but I also need you to keep it quiet, between the two of us. I am away to Ireland with Nellie and Kitty. Would ye please keep an eye on Alice and the baby whilst Jerry is at work and I am away? But please, Brigid, please, could it be our secret?'

Brigid pressed a cup of tea into Kathleen's hand and sat down next to her.

'I would be happy to, but Alice seems a different woman altogether these days. Sure, I know it was necessary, but remember, after the murder, she came into my kitchen, all by herself.'

'Aye, I know,' said Kathleen, 'and that is grand and a great improvement, so it is, but it would just make me feel better if I knew ye was keeping an eye out. Things aren't quite right, Brigid. I wouldn't worry if I was here, but I have to travel back home for a little while and I would feel much happier if ye was keeping watch for me.'

'Won't Maura be put out by ye asking me?' Brigid enquired.

'Maura has enough on her plate just now and, besides, they never seem to be able to move beyond Bernadette. Alice can't forgive Maura for being Bernadette's best friend and Maura can't forgive Alice for taking Bernadette's place. I don't think either of them will ever move on. What can I do? One minute they are fine, the next, for no reason whatsoever, they flare up like a pair of entry dogs fighting over a scrap.'

Kathleen drank her tea and the two women chatted on until Kathleen realized she had been away for too long.

Brigid gave Kathleen a hug at the back door.

'Have a rest, Kathleen, will ye? Everything will be fine here now.'

'Aye, I will that, but keep your eyes peeled. Alice isn't herself, she's so bold now. Or maybe this is herself, I have no idea, but I can't help thinking that she probably needs to go back on her tablets. I have other things to deal with right now and I don't want to worry Jerry. Oh, and bring yer tweezers and Pond's round tonight. Me and the girls, we have good reason to need to look a little groomed.'

And with a last smile through the back door and another promise from Brigid that not a word would be spoken about her visit to anyone, she was gone.

As Kathleen walked back, she thought to herself that Brigid, with all her kindness, was the one woman on the street they could trust with the news of Kitty's baby. She was the one person Maura could lean on whilst Kathleen was away, but Kathleen wouldn't dare tell her. She couldn't. No one must know.

Brigid dutifully called in on Alice, the following afternoon. She decided that asking had they got away all right was a good opening line. Alice was not known for gossip. She didn't speak to anyone as far as Brigid knew, but she was determined not to let that put her off.

Alice was slightly hesitant; she had never had visitors of her own.

'Hello, Brigid, you know Kathleen has left for Ireland, don't you?' she whispered, as though someone else could hear.

Brigid decided she had to be bold and make herself at home. She could see Alice was not at ease.

'You don't mind if I put these two on the mat next to Joseph, do ye?' she asked Alice, as she lifted her two youngest out of the pram and put them down on the rug besides Joseph.

Joseph kicked his legs frantically and began to chatter in baby language, which made both Brigid and Alice laugh.

'Would ye look at him,' exclaimed Brigid in mock indignation. 'Still in nappies and trying it on with my girls. I will tell Uncle Sean about ye, little man, so I will. Aye, I know Kathleen has gone home. I just thought I would pop in and see yerself and the little fella, in case ye was feeling a bit deserted.'

Alice put the kettle on and the two women chatted about babies until Jerry arrived home.

As Brigid left, she made a suggestion.

'Do the two of youse fancy coming down to the club with us on Saturday? Would Angela look after Joseph for ye? We have Sean's mammy here and Sean has no fight on, so we are desperate to get out and she doesn't mind stopping in to let us go. It would be a break for me to get away from her and Sean talking about how great America is all the time. They drive me crazy, the two of them. They would have us all packed up onto the boat for New York in the morning if they had their way. I need to remind Sean it's good craic around here too and there's more to life than the boxing ring and work.'

Alice looked at Brigid in amazement.

'Do you not want to go to America then?' she asked, almost incredulous. She could think of no prospect more exciting.

Alice had never planned to remain on the four streets. This was not the future she had imagined for herself when she had married Jerry. She knew she had not been well for a very long while but now she was absolutely sure she was fully recovered. She would never again need the little yellow tablets sitting in the glass bottle on the press. Alice was now her own woman. She could be like others and do whatever she wanted to do, whenever she wanted to do it. Alice felt as if she was truly alive for the first time ever.

She was no longer a spinster housekeeper working in a hotel. Even though it had been the most prestigious hotel in Liverpool. Facing the prospect of spending the remainder of her days alone in an old bedsit with only the rats for company was her future no more, but still, she was slightly disappointed that liberation from her old self had not presented more challenges than how to make a packet of butter stretch the whole week.

Alice had dreamt of living in America for many, many years.

'Oh, I will make up my mind if we ever get to that point,' Brigid's voice pierced her thoughts, 'it's what Sean says he wants and so I have to want it too, I suppose, but I will miss everyone and it's so far from home. Anyway, like all men, he's full of big ideas, but when it comes to it, if I turn on the tears he will maybe change his mind.'

Brigid grinned and winked at Alice, who returned a weak and thoughtful smile.

The following night, whilst Jerry was eating his supper and Alice, wearing Kathleen's apron, scrubbed the pans at the sink, she found her mind full of Sean and how lucky Brigid was.

How could Brigid complain about having a man who wanted to be something other than a docker?

Someone who wanted better than to remain in a house listed for slum clearance?

Alice wondered, did Sean feel like an outsider within the community, as she did?

'I'm an outsider because I'm an English Protestant and I was a sick one in the head at that, not that anyone ever mentions it, mind. Sean may feel the same because he wants better than the rest are prepared to put up with and that makes him different.'

'What's that, queen?' said Jerry, looking up from his plate whilst glancing at the *Echo*, which was propped up on the table against the milk bottle.

'Oh, nothing, just thinking out loud,' said Alice as she turned the cold tap on full to rinse the pan and drown her stray thoughts.

That night, Joseph slept in the room Nellie shared with Kathleen.

When it was time for bed, whilst Jerry switched off the television and the lights, Alice popped in to settle Joseph, who had been slightly restless in the new room.

As she stood at the window, rocking backwards and forwards with Joseph on her shoulder, Alice spotted Sean walking down the street, returning from one of his boxing nights. She felt a thrill in her belly and, without any warning, a flame lit somewhere in her heart.

He must feel exactly as I do, thought Alice.

As he walked under her window, Alice slipped backwards into the shadow of her old self.

She hadn't done it for so long. She had been fixed. She was fine. She was totally in control. She was free. Now that Kathleen had left, she felt the feelings of the past return. She was her own woman again.

As Sean passed she noticed how broad his shoulders were and how tall and proud he was when he walked, not like Jerry, who almost slouched along with his head bent.

She would tell Brigid they would love to go out tomorrow night. She wanted to be in the company of a man who thought just as she did, and who made her pulse race because of it.

Joseph fell asleep and Alice laid him down gently in the cot. She walked back to the window to gaze out on the street for another glimpse of Sean's receding back and then, suddenly, she stopped herself and stepped away.

Oh God, Alice, no, you idiot, she thought to herself. What are you doing?

She felt vulnerable, as though she were tumbling. She realized Kathleen was her prop and that, without her, it was going to be difficult.

She needed to make more of an effort. But it was so hard as it was. Every day the bottle of tablets on the press were a reminder that the familiar pattern of obsessive behaviour lurked, waiting for her to slip.

As Alice walked into their room, she could sense Jerry was still awake.

For the first time ever, Alice wanted to have sex, a feeling she had never experienced before. She slipped into the bed and encircled Jerry in her arms. She felt his body stiffen. She was naked. She could hear his brain working, wondering what was happening and why. She had never before come to their bed without her nightdress.

Jerry rolled over onto his side and looked at her. His eyes were asking her a million questions she couldn't answer. How could she tell Jerry that what had excited her was catching sight of Sean walking down the street? Knowing that just down the road lived a man who shared her secret thoughts and who was talking to his wife about the life Alice wanted? That she had never been crazy and that just a few houses away someone else wanted the grander life she had yearned for too?

There must have been a mix-up, thought Alice. I wasn't meant to be here, I was meant to be down the road, with Sean.

The edges of reality were once again becoming blurred. The fact that Sean worked as a docker and a boxer, that he spent every day and evening working hard to realize the dreams he had for himself and his family, was lost on Alice. Once again, she imagined herself dressed just like one of the ladies who stayed at the Grand, the hotel where she had been the housekeeper. She saw herself surrounded by the leather luggage that had belonged to others, waiting to board the passenger steamer to New York.

New York. Just the thought of it sent a thrill down Alice's spine.

Every guest at the Grand who had been travelling on to New York had spoken beautifully and had dressed impeccably. They could barely contain their nervousness or excitement. Why should they? They were leaving for a great adventure. America.

And now, in the bed she shared with Jerry in the two-up, two-down on Nelson Street and with her thoughts full only of Sean, Alice gave herself up willingly. Jerry looked deeply into her eyes as he gently stroked her arms and breasts and then he kissed her, with longing and passion. For the very first time in seven years of marriage, Alice moved with him, but in body alone. In her mind, it was Sean caressing and entering her. And as she quivered and shook in his arms, Jerry felt that at last, for the very first time since the day they had married, they had truly made love.

# Chapter Ten

Maura and Tommy had a tough night settling the children. All were perturbed by Kitty's absence. Malachi had been playing up and Angela hadn't stopped complaining; Harry cried more than usual because it was hard for him to catch his breath. Each one of the children had a problem which at any other time, Kitty would have shared with her mother.

Malachi and Angela could give out enough for a dozen kids and

Kitty knew how to deal with them. Both Maura's arms and belly had been full of a baby since a year after she had married.

Maura left the boys to Tommy and when she had finally calmed the girls, she lay on her bed to calm the baby on her breast.

After half an hour and with the baby still grizzling, Tommy put his head round the door. 'Just popping down to the Anchor for a quick one, Maura,' and with a wink, he was gone.

Tommy was crafty, knowing Maura wouldn't say a word in case she disturbed the baby. He was safe to sneak out when she was feeding.

Maura would never have objected anyway. Tommy hardly ever went to the pub. He was a family man who preferred to spend his nights in with her and the kids. She knew what he was doing.

This was the first occasion, since the day she had been born, that Kitty had been out of their sight. Oh, sure, she had spent lots of nights with Bernadette and Jerry when she was little and they had been waiting for Nellie to come along, but she was only across the road and within arm's reach. Not like now. Not like this. Not taking her first holiday with someone else's family.

Poor Tommy, he deserved a drink. Maura knew the visit from the police and the removal of Kitty to Ireland had worried him sick.

'Oh, Jesus, Mary and Joseph, please keep him strong,' she whispered into the top of her baby's downy head.

The Anchor was quieter than it would have been on a weekday night before the scandal of the priest being found dead without his langer, but the usual regulars were in and Tommy knew them all. As he walked up to the bar, men he worked with all day shouted their greetings. Most were standing round the fire, their backs to the flames, warming their rear ends.

For many of them there were no fires at home and the ranges were cold. Bill, the landlord, benefited from the money spent on Guinness, which would have provided a bag of coke in many a house.

The men were half-cut and had obviously been there since the end of their shift. Tommy had walked past children sitting on the steps outside, looking pale and perished. They were under instructions from their mammy to bring their da home before he had spent all the money.

Children, no more than five years of age, sent to do a man's job. Tommy knew one of the lads, who was a friend of Harry's.

'What are ye doing sat here, Brian?' he asked the lad, who was shivering so much he could barely speak through chattering teeth.

'Uncle Tommy, could ye send me da out to come home, please? Me ma says I can't go back home unless I have him with me.'

'Have ye eaten any tea tonight, Brian?' said Tommy, bending down so that he was at eye level with the lad.

Brian looked down and shook his head.

Tommy felt an anger he was now becoming familiar with burn into his gut. He put his hand in his pocket and took out a coin.

'Here's a sixpence, lad. Go to the pie hut and get a hot meat and potato pie and then go home after ye have eaten it. Don't tell anyone I gave ye a sixpence. Tell Ma I am bringing ye da home with me soon. Now away, lad, quickly.'

As Tommy walked into the pub, he cast his eyes around and saw Brian's da sitting by the fire, playing dominoes for money and nursing his Guinness.

With one hand thrust deep into his pocket and the other holding his own pint, John McCarthy hailed Tommy as he walked past him towards Brian's da.

'What d'ye think then, Tommy?' said John, looking around him furtively and dropping his voice. 'Go on, yer Maura, she and the priest was as thick as thieves. Who did for him, Tommy?'

'Sure, 'twas Molly Barrett's cat,' said Tommy with a forced laugh as he turned towards the bar and put his money on the long, highly polished wooden counter. He was about to order a pint and join John after he had put Brian's da out on the street.

Tommy had felt like a night of talking about the horses and football to take his mind off worrying about the police and missing his little queen, Kitty.

When he had left her with Kathleen at the wooden hut on the Pier Head, it was all he could do to keep his tears at bay, to be the big man and tell her to have a fabulous time.

He had given her an extra-long hug and she had clung to him, with her hands clenched behind his back. He had kissed her forehead and pressed half a crown into her palm.

'Be a good girl, queen, and bring me back the smell of the wet grass, with a rainbow's end sat on it for me as a present, now, would ye?'

As he made his way back up to the four streets, he turned as he reached the last street lamp and, through the window of the lit hut, he watched his little girl press her face against the glass and wave to him and despite the rain beating down, he could see the deep sadness etched on her face.

Tears blurred his eyes as he raised his hand and returned her wave. He wanted to run back to the hut and tell Kathleen it was all a mistake. That the only place any child could be truly safe was at home, with her ma and da. He had let his Kitty down, they had not kept her safe and now he had to pay the price.

As Tommy looked at Kitty he realized that this was the saddest moment of his whole life and he would always remember her face just as she looked tonight. During the day, he tucked under his cap the very thought of Kitty crossing the water on the boats he watched all day. His feelings swamped him, threatening to drag him down, so he kept them at arm's length and he focused his mind on the trivia of dock life.

Knowing she would not be there when he arrived home didn't make it any easier.

The house was quieter. It was darker. A light extinguished.

Her absence left a gaping hole, which the noisiness of all the others put together failed to fill.

He had to abandon his own thoughts and escape to the pub.

The men round the fire had heard Tommy's comment about the cat and sniggered.

John McCarthy whispered to Tommy, 'Aye, Tommy, keep yer fly buttons done up tight. If ye have to go into Molly Barrett's, put a shovel head down yer trousers and over yer langer, the fecking cat's a lunatic, so it is. It should be hunted down and shot.'

Feelings still ran too high for the men to laugh openly about the death of the priest. After all, some of the men still weren't allowed out in case they should meet the same fate. Tommy realized he couldn't stay in the pub. There was no light relief here.

The landlord began to pull Tommy a pint of Guinness.

'Hold it there, Bill,' said Tommy. 'Four bottles to take out, please.'

Whilst the barman descended into the cellar to fetch the bottles, Tommy walked over to Brian's da.

'Aye, Tommy, howaya?' said McGinty, looking up from his dominoes. 'Do ye fancy a game, Tommy?'

'No, McGinty, I don't and I will tell ye this right now, neither do ye. Get your arse back round home and see to ye wife and kids, else pay me back the ten shillings you borrowed from me to pay the rent.'

McGinty looked at Tommy with his mouth wide open and then began to laugh. 'Don't be an eejit, Tommy, I'm in the middle of a feckin' game.'

Tommy moved over to the table, put his face close to McGinty's and held his hand out.

'The ten shillings, right now.'

McGinty slowly rose to his feet, swearing under his breath.

"I have no feckin' ten shillings as well yer know, yer bastard."

Tommy walked back to the bar as the barman came up with the Guinness.

'Well, that's unusual, Tommy, I thought 'twas only the ladies who drank the bottles on your street.'

'Aye, and me and the missus too,' said Tommy, counting out his coins on the counter.

As Tommy turned right towards Nelson Street, he looked left and, through the mist, saw McGinty, staggering down the street towards home with Brian running from the pie shop to catch him up.

Maura couldn't have looked more surprised when Tommy walked in through the back with the four bottles. Her eyes filled with a ridiculous pleasure at seeing him home again. She shared his sadness.

They both ached. She had been sorry that he had gone out to the pub, but at the same time she understood why. She was tidying away discarded shoes and children's cardigans and jackets that had been scattered all around the kitchen, placing each on its own peg on the door to the stairs, when Tommy walked in.

'Sit ye down, queen,' said Tommy kindly, as he put the poker in the fire to heat and took the bottles to the opener that hung from a piece of string next to the sink.

Maura flopped into one fireside chair and Tommy into the other. As she kicked off her slippers, Tommy plunged the poker first into her Guinness and then back into the red embers for his own.

As they lifted the bottles to drink, they grinned at each other for the first time in weeks. Maura left her chair and sat down on the rug in between Tommy's legs, with one arm on his knee. She looked up at him as they chatted and drank their Guinness in front of the leaping flames for an hour before bed.

Not about the evil that had swamped their lives and divided them, but about the things that held them together.

Their families in Ireland and America.

Tommy's work. What to do about Malachi? Who in the family did Angela take after and had someone snuck into the house and swapped babies when they were sleeping? They talked about the things Kitty would see and do in Ireland, and the kindness of Jerry and Kathleen and the entire Deane family to help in this way. For the first time they talked about everything and anything other than that awful night. That night, Maura realized, was beginning to drive them apart.

Night-time chatter had always been a part of Maura and Tommy's routine. Tommy always sat in the fireside chair, or at the table with his paper, while Maura nattered away to him as she cleared the dishes and tidied up. The ritual had stopped abruptly the night Father James was caught in Kitty's bedroom and it hadn't resumed since, until tonight.

'Bed,' said Tommy, draining the last of his second bottle.

'You go up,' said Maura. 'I want to sort the washing for the morning.'

'I bloody won't,' replied Tommy with a huge grin. 'Get ye'self up those stairs, missus, ye are in for a treat tonight. It's been over a week and that's not natural for any man, especially not this one.'

Afterwards, as Tommy slept a sleep of deep contentment, Maura slipped out of bed. The washing still needed to be sorted for the morning. She sat on the edge of the mattress and looked back at the man she loved, who had fathered their beautiful and loving children. He was the best husband. He didn't deserve to be in this position of guilt. Before she left his side, Maura prayed to God to forgive them for defending their child and asked him to bring them peace.

Maura prayed a great deal.

After all, it was not as if she could take confession.

## Chapter Eleven

Howard and Simon had not been able to gain entry to the Priory until the morning after the bishop had arrived.

At first, Howard had been furious at the nuns' refusal to allow them in immediately following the murder. He and Simon had tried to be as gentle as possible, explaining the reason why it was very important that they have free access. As gentle as it was possible for two hard-nosed Liverpool detectives to be.

They had visited the Priory the morning after, but there was nothing to be seen, other than a gaggle of nuns in a state of high distress.

Miss Devlin, the teacher for whom Howard had a soft spot, was in the process of comforting the housekeeper. She told them no one had been near the Priory and that for all of the previous day the priest had been away, along with everyone else, at the church and the wedding breakfast.

The Priory had felt cold and flat, unyielding of what it knew. The wailing and crying of the nuns, uninviting.

'There's nothing to see here,' Howard had said, finding the tears of a nun particularly disturbing. 'Let's concentrate on the school.'

And, sure enough, they had got lucky, or so they thought, when Little Paddy had blurted out what he thought he had seen from the window that night.

Although the lead had crumbled away into dust in their hands, it had kept them busy for days. But although the lead hadn't held firm, both Howard and Simon felt that nothing was quite as it appeared.

'I can smell a great big dirty rat,' Howard said. 'I just can't bloody see it yet, that's all.'

The superintendent had begun breathing down their necks with threats of demotion and castration if they did not solve the case. It was now time to begin turning over even the very smallest stones.

The bishop had led them both into the study and dispatched Daisy to the kitchen to fetch a tray of tea.

Howard had no idea where to begin without causing offence. As he took his notebook and pencil from the inside pocket of his jacket, he cast his eye around, looking for an object of interest in order to stimulate a casual conversation.

But the study was deadly dull with no ornamentation to elicit his admiration nor painting to be commented upon. Heavy drapes hung across the windows as a mark of respect and the only light shone from a standard lamp in the corner, throwing eerie, creeping shadows onto the high ceiling and the tobacco-stained walls.

The murky-brown sofa and chair had seen better days and, apart from a small table in front of the sofa, the only other piece of furniture, in one corner, was the priest's large dark wooden desk, with one tall hard-backed chair behind it and two smaller chairs opposite.

Tall dark-oak bookcases partly lined the walls, the books appearing not to have been read for many years.

Only a circular dark-burgundy rug with a deep-grey fringe provided any colour. Howard sighed. The room depressed him. There was something on the edge of the aroma, in the smell of musty old books and forgotten sermons, that made him feel intensely uncomfortable.

Having been keen to gain entry into the Priory, he now couldn't wait to get out.

Howard ran his finger irritably around his collar, easing it away from his neck.

'May I look through the father's desk, Bishop, whilst we wait for the tea?' he asked.

'Of course, Detective Inspector,' said the bishop, 'but I am afraid it is quite empty. We removed all the private papers yesterday.'

'Really?' said Howard, with a note of surprise in his voice.

Simon raised his eyebrows. Howard's intuition was kicking in. 'What private papers?' he asked.

'Well, there were his sermon notes going back over some years and he had kept all his prayer requests and mass cards and his confirmation lesson notes.'

Howard immediately felt stupid.

'And what about his bedroom, his clothes and personal possessions?'

'Clothes?' The bishop stood before Howard, looking slightly confused, his brow deeply furrowed. Howard reddened immediately, feeling stupid and keener than ever to leave.

'The only personal possessions in his room were his watch and personal bible, with his coat and hat and a few other personal books. They were dispatched today, to his sister in America.'

'That parcel will be a bundle of laughs to open,' said Howard under his breath as he turned away.

Daisy tapped on the door and, once the bishop had shouted for her to enter, crossed the floor with the tray of tea.

Howard felt the familiar feeling of despair. They were heading nowhere fast, again.

The priest walks home from a wedding, is murdered and dismembered in the graveyard, and they don't have a bloody clue why or how. He felt his promotion slipping further and further away.

As Daisy handed the cups round, Simon tried to engage her in conversation.

'Have you worked here long, miss?'

'Oh, yes,' said Daisy, 'nearly twenty years now.'

'That's a long time,' said Howard, smiling at her. 'I don't suppose you saw anything unusual on the night the father was murdered that you think we should know about, did you?'

Daisy looked at Howard with some intensity, as was her way. This was different from any question the sister had asked her and one she had to think about. *Was there anything she thought they should know about?* Well, maybe there was. Maybe she had seen something and it was nothing to do with what happened inside the Priory and so she wouldn't be in any trouble if she mentioned it.

*Would she? Should she?*

While she pondered Daisy continued to stare at Howard, as though her eyes were boring into his very soul. He felt disconcerted and, with an embarrassed cough, sat up straight in the chair, struggling to balance his cup and saucer. He wasn't used to saucers. He wasn't used to a cup that had retained a handle.

'The girl is simple.' The bishop's voice sliced through the loaded silence. 'Very simple. Back to the kitchen now, please, girl.'

She would have to be, to work here, Howard thought, looking around at the dreary room, slightly relieved that Daisy had stopped staring at him.

Within an hour, Howard and Simon had jumped back into the police car and were heading off down the gravel drive. As they turned left towards the four streets, Simon banged the dashboard.

'God, it's doing my fucking head in. I know there is summat we are missing, like it is just there, out of our reach, and yet we can't get a handle on any of it.'

Howard was silent, deep in thought. As he shifted up a gear, he turned back down the Dock Road into town and, looking into the rear-view mirror, he replied, 'We just keep shaking the tree, Simon, or, better still, let Molly Barrett do it for us. That nosy old woman is better than a dozen detectives on that street. If there is something to know, she will lead us to it, I promise you. We need to give her a little encouragement, sit back and wait.'

Annie O'Prey had finished brushing her step and wondered why Molly had been a no-show. Although their front doors were only two feet apart from each other, Annie turned back inside and walked through her house, out of the back door, putting her broom away in the outhouse, then walked through her back yard, into the entry and in thorough Molly's back gate.

The front door was never used for the purpose that it was intended.

Molly was in the kitchen, baking.

'The priest is dead, Molly. He won't be wanting those scones where he's gone,' said Annie in a superior tone, as she folded her arms and sniffed her disapproval of a woman trying to cheat the inevitable reckoning at the pearly gates. Annie felt pleased with herself, having found a weakness and scored a point. Annie was on top.

Molly neither acknowledged Annie's presence, nor looked up from her task.

'I thought I would bake some for Daisy. I'm neither stupid nor senile, Annie,' she replied. 'I doubt a priest whose langer me cat brought home would be wanting a fresh scone.'

She mentally relished the put-down.

'I've always sent her a few in the batch I made for the priest. Daisy and I are good friends and now that a little time has passed, I thought I might as well pay her a visit, just to see how she is getting along. She has no friends as such and, God knows, it took her ten years before she even began to speak to me and I'm the easiest person in the world to get along with.'

Annie raised her eyebrows heavenwards. Only that morning, she had felt the need to discuss Molly's new-found self-importance with Frank, from the fish shop.

'God, that fat lump gets on me nerves something wicked, so she does. Thinks she's very important now that she's having cups of tea in the parlour with the bizzies. Such an interfering busybody she is herself an' all.'

'Don't listen to her, then,' said Frank. 'Leave the woman to her own devices.'

Both Frank and Annie knew that would never happen. Molly and Annie were best friends who complained about each other so often, it was as if they were sisters.

'There you go, Annie, that's a nice bit of fish,' said Frank, handing her the damp and neatly folded newspaper package. 'Give the skin to Molly's cat, keep him happy and away from my front door, for feck's sake. It's a jungle out there on your streets.'

Annie blessed Frank with smile as she left to impart to Molly the gossip she had gathered from the fish-shop queue. All animosity towards her neighbour was forgotten in a flash of her naked gums.

Daisy looked out of the large sash window as she made the bishop's bed to see Alice walking with the pram down to the bottom of Nelson Street, and Molly walking up towards the church with a basket in her hand, covered with a tea towel. She hoped Molly would be heading to the Priory and, when she turned the corner into the drive, Daisy's heart skipped a beat.

She hadn't seen Molly since the Sunday before the priest died.

Daisy's head was hurting with all the things she had seen and heard, and now that the bishop was on his way back to Dublin, she hoped that Sister Evangelista would let her stay at the convent until the father's replacement arrived. Sister had told Daisy to call into the convent after she had cleaned the Priory, but for now she would stop and have a cup of tea with Molly.

Daisy had a visitor. At last, someone she could talk to about all the things burning in her brain.

# Chapter Twelve

Alice and Joseph were on their way to Brigid and Sean's house.

Brigid was sitting in front of the range with her youngest lying across her lap, about to have her nappy changed.

'Hello, come in, come and sit down, and how's our baby Joseph this morning?' Brigid cheerfully greeted Alice. 'Has the tooth come through that was giving him hell yesterday?'

'Morning, Brigid, no, it hasn't and I really wish it would. He hardly slept last night and his cheeks are burning up like mad,' said Alice, lifting Joseph out of his pram.

'Have ye any Disprin?' Brigid asked Alice.

She didn't look up as she deftly removed the pink-topped nappy pin from the white towelling nappy worn by her scrap of a red-headed daughter. Brigid was house-proud. The whiteness of her nappies, as they blew in the breeze, was a source of joy to her. She had seen too many grey nappies blowing on lines around her and had vowed that hers would always be the whitest in the entry.

As soon as the dust from a load at the docks blew up and across the four streets, she was the only mother to dash straight outside to pull her nappies off the line and dry them indoors.

'No, I haven't used anything, to be honest. Kathleen usually deals with most of this. I am really not sure what to do.'

'Hang on, give me five minutes and I'll get him one, I've plenty. I will just change this little madam's nappy.'

Alice thought how much the red-headed baby reminded her of a skinned rabbit. The soaking wet nappy had filled the room with the heavy smell of ammonia.

To Alice's horror, Brigid now folded the nappy over and wiped it across her own face, rubbing down the side of her nose before holding her hair back to wipe her forehead and under her chin. Then she rubbed it across her cheeks and over her closed eyes.

'Oh, my giddy aunt,' squealed Alice. 'Why the hell did you just do that, with that stinking-wet nappy? The wee has been on that all night!'

Brigid laughed. 'Exactly, and it's all nicely concentrated. There's a reason why we Liverpool girls have the best complexions in England, Alice. A wipe-over with the first wet nappy of the morning is the only beauty regime we need.'

'What, you do that every morning?' Alice found it difficult to hide her revulsion.

'Alice, I have a brood of daughters and an endless supply of wet nappies. I have been doing it for years and so does every woman on the four streets and across the whole of Liverpool. Sean tells me the sailors all say the same thing, that there are no women in the world with skin as soft as that of Liverpool women. They say the sailors are so captivated by it, they sing sad songs about Liverpool girls as they leave port, so they do, and happy ones when they sail back in.'

Alice had to admit it. The women who never seemed to wash, and smelt none too pleasant, always had lovely complexions.

Many of the women on the four streets had lost most of their teeth and those they retained were black and crumbling, but their skin remained beautiful. You could even tell that Annie O'Prey had once had nice skin.

'Jeez, Alice, where have ye been living all of ye life?' said Brigid, laughing.

With expert deftness, she picked up the baby and handed her straight to Alice, who was so shocked she almost dropped her. How did she explain to Brigid that she had never even held baby Joseph until he was three months old?

But Brigid hadn't noticed and was still talking as she pulled back the curtain across her kitchen press to look for a Disprin.

Alice stood with the baby in her outstretched arms begging for her not to move or make a sound.

'Was there anything else ye needed?' said Brigid as she rooted around in her cupboard.

'No, nothing, I just thought I would pop in to say hello and to say that we would love to come again to the club with you and Sean, if you are ever going on a Saturday night again.'

Alice didn't take her eyes off the baby while she spoke.

'Wasn't it a grand night!'

'It was, yes, we loved it and Angela was great about minding Joseph. Jerry gave her sixpence when we got back.'

'God, I would have to pay someone a fortune to mind mine, so I would. We have so many, we have to wait until Sean's mammy is here, but she isn't going back for a few weeks so we can do it again.

Will ye stay for a cuppa? Sure, go on, ye only have the one little fella to look after, ye have time.'

Alice was happy to stay for a while. She wanted to ask Brigid questions about Sean and their plans for America. Her golden opportunity came just as Sean's mammy walked in the back door.

'Oh, hello, Alice, how lovely to see ye. Are ye stopping for a cuppa?' Mrs McGuire said, before she had even taken her coat off.

Sean's mother was half the size of her son and a fine-looking woman. On her visit from her village just outside of Galway, she had adopted the Liverpool custom of leaving her curlers in underneath a hairnet. It was not something she did back at home, where they didn't bother with the curlers. A headscarf was good enough.

But now Mrs McGuire was looking worried.

'Brigid, Caoimhe does not like that school, I'm telling ye, she does not. I almost had to push her through the door. If ye ask me, the nuns in Liverpool are different altogether from the nuns in Ireland.'

Brigid said, 'I know, Mrs McGuire, but what can I do? The nuns say she will get used to it soon enough.'

Mrs McGuire was having none of it.

'Aye, she might that, but if you ask me, those nuns are too cruel. One of them slapped her across her little legs because she was crying for me. Dragged her in through the door by her arm, the sister did. She doesn't get that at home, Brigid, so why should she have to take it at school? Broke my heart, so it did, to leave her at the gate. Why won't the nuns let us into the yard to say goodbye? Cruel, so it is.'

Brigid was only half listening as she mixed a spoon of molasses into Joseph's bottle and handed it back to Alice, full of the dark liquid.

'Here, give that to Joseph,' she said, wiping the bottle with a tea towel.

'I will, thanks, but what on earth is in it?' asked Alice, as she smelt the teat of the bottle.

'It's a bit of molasses, nicked from one of the tankers, mixed with a little warm water and a dissolved Disprin, mixed in with Joseph's milk to take the pain out of his teeth. He'll have a lovely morning nap after that.'

Alice nervously tipped the bottle and put it into Joseph's mouth.

His eyes opened as wide as saucers when he took the first mouthful.

'See, they love it,' said Brigid. 'Kathleen will have a jar of molasses in the cupboard; just a spoon and he will be fine, but only a little. You can mix it in with the milk once a day, but be careful he doesn't get used to it now and want it all the time. The tankers don't come in every day and we have to take it in turns as to who gets the drippings from the loadings.'

'My God, that is the first time he has smiled in days,' said Alice, sitting down on the chair to nurse Joseph, who was sucking so furiously that she was afraid to break his stride.

She was also watching Sean's mammy, and waiting for an opportunity to talk to her about America. She leapt in almost straight away.

'So, do you get to visit your daughter in America, Mrs McGuire?'

'I do, Alice, and sure 'tis a wonderful place altogether. They pay for my fare to go and beg me to live there with them, but sure I can't, unless Sean and Brigid decide to go too. I can't leave them behind with all these babies to look after on their own, can I?'

Searching for the molasses had given Brigid an excuse to tidy out the press and wipe out the drawers. She gave Alice a sideways look as she emptied out the contents onto the kitchen table and wiped down the shelves. She had noticed Alice and Sean were in animated conversation about America on Saturday night. The conversation had made Brigid uncomfortable and she didn't want Alice starting to talk about it again to Sean's mammy.

'I have a mammy too, Alice,' said Brigid haughtily. 'And I have an opinion, and I'm afraid America is not for me and Mrs McGuire knows that. If the boot was on the other foot, you wouldn't want me to be dragging Sean away over to America and leaving ye all alone, now would ye, Mrs McGuire?'

The temperature in the room had noticeably dropped and Alice stood to take her leave. She was amazed by Brigid's lack of ambition and thought how much she wished she could change places with her. She would even have a dozen kids if it meant getting away from Liverpool and on a boat to America.

*

Later that evening, Sean won three matches in a row. It had been a good fight and he had pocketed seven pounds and ten shillings from each match. More than he took in a week's wages on the docks.

He was doing better than he had ever dared to hope and his savings were mounting up.

This was a relief. He had to train hard and, what with his job, it meant he was hardly ever at home. Boxing was a means to an end. He didn't enjoy working on the docks, but at least with the boxing he fought for the money and it was his. He wasn't lining the pockets of the thieving bastards over at the Mersey Dock Company.

As Sean walked home, it occurred to him that there were many things in his life he wasn't happy with, other than having to work every moment God sent.

One of them was Brigid's constant reluctance to talk about the day he was saving for, when they could pack up and leave for America, and join his family in Chicago. He wanted to work hard for himself and his family. To be in charge of his own destiny.

In America, he knew his efforts would be rewarded with a better life for them all.

In England, he struggled to save. Each week he made the dock company wealthier and had his head punched in every Friday night. Life had to be better than that.

His sister's letters were full of the most innocent yet enticing details.

His mother could not stop talking about the opportunies for those prepared to take a risk and put in the graft.

Already his sister and her husband were earning a small fortune, enough to buy their own home and pay for his mother to sail to America twice a year. This summer they had been to Florida for a holiday and had sent him a postcard. It made his stomach crunch to think how much easier and more prosperous life was for them.

Sean decided that he would talk to Brigid again when he got into bed. He would wake her up if he had to. Brigid had to stop this ridiculous, small-minded clinging onto what she knew and realize that emigrating to America was for the good of the family.

'Jeez, what is up with the woman?' he said out loud as he shook his head.

He loved home as much as the next Irishman, but even in Galway there was nothing for Sean other than poverty and then more poverty for his kids too. He punched the entry wall with his fist as he turned the top corner and, for the first time that night, his knuckles bled. Lucky that he had another week for the skin to heal over.

As Sean looked up he was shocked to see Alice standing by her back gate. He had enjoyed talking to her at the Irish centre. She had none of Brigid's reserve. They had spoken most of the night about America. Alice had told him she had kept all the brochures she had found that had been left by guests staying at the Grand before taking their passage across the Atlantic, and that sometimes she still read through them.

God, Jerry doesn't know how lucky he is, thought Sean. I wish I was married to someone who had a spirit like Alice.

'Everything all right, Alice?' Sean asked.

'Yes, everything is fine, Sean. I hope you don't mind me asking, but I want to know so much about how to get to America, and to try to persuade Jerry that it would be such a good idea. I wondered if we could talk again some time?'

Alice felt a thrill that came only when she was in her own secret world. Talking out her fantasies with Sean, without Jerry or anyone else being aware, was exciting. She wanted to know Sean better.

'Would you mind not telling Jerry or Brigid that I asked, though?'

'Aye, of course, and don't worry, I won't mention anything. If Jerry is as stubborn as Brigid, I know exactly what ye mean.'

Alice glanced up at the bedroom window, where Jerry had been sleeping for the last hour. As she looked back at Sean, her eyes gleamed in the moonlight. Sean noticed there was something different, unusual about her. Was she wearing lipstick? Unlike the other women, Alice never ever wore a hairnet and she had styled her hair in the fashion of the girls who worked in the offices in town.

Her deep fringe swept almost over her eyes, with the rest of her hair hanging loose on her shoulders.

Alice had experimented with changes every day for weeks. Sean had noted that she was always a little smarter than the other women on the four streets, in a very English kind of way. No one had seen much of her for years and yet suddenly it was as if she was everywhere.

This was the third time he had seen Alice in as many days.

Alice noticed the blood running down Sean's fingers. She reached out and took his hand in hers, examining it and dabbing his knuckles with her apron, making him flinch.

'Oh, my goodness, is that from your fight?' She looked up at him, holding both of his huge hands in hers, her eyes wide, and turned over the damaged hand to search for further signs of injury.

Alice now took her handkerchief out of her pocket and, wetting it with her saliva, began dabbing away at the open graze.

'No, Alice,' Sean laughed. He had knocked three men out cold tonight without a scratch. How could he tell her it was from punching the entry wall? 'I skimmed my hand on the wall as I walked past,' he said, pulling away.

The sensation of another woman holding his hands made him uncomfortable. Not because it was unpleasant, in fact it was just the opposite. It was a feeling he hadn't experienced for a long time.

He had enjoyed talking to Alice on Saturday night. He had noticed that she had become prettier as the months went by. Since Kathleen had moved into the four streets, Alice had filled out and was no longer the skinny wretch she had once been.

There was an air of aloofness, of reserve about her that Sean quite liked. She wasn't like the Irish girls at home who were apt to be overly friendly in their search for a husband. Alice had a detachment, which he now realized was quite exciting.

'It will be fine. I will run it under the tap when I get in.'

Sean gazed down. He could smell the warmth of her hair and was overcome by a sudden compulsion to bend down and kiss her.

The entry was asleep. Dark and deeply quiet.

'Sure, Alice, I am fine,' he said. 'It is no problem, really.'

Alice, resigned, pushed the handkerchief up her sleeve again and, drawing her cardigan across to keep out the night air, lifted her face to Sean.

'Sean, I think I said too much in front of your mother when I visited this morning and I really hope I haven't caused a problem. It's just that nothing pleases me more than talking about the prospect of living in America and Jerry won't even hear about it. I feel very lonely sometimes and would love to talk to someone who feels just as I do.'

Sean looked down at Alice's hand, which she had placed on his arm whilst she leant forward and whispered to him. She had made the same gesture when he had seen her outside of the shop. It was friendly and intimate. The sensation burnt through his coat sleeve. A warm hint of perfume wafted upwards and distracted him. He realized that never, in all the time he and Brigid had been together, had he smelt the feminine scent of perfume.

Alice was no longer the plain Protestant English girl. She was now almost pretty and, to Sean, in the midst of an assault on his senses, she was certainly very sexy.

Not because of what she wore, or how she looked, although that did play a part. But because of what she said.

She was talking his language and it was playing with his mind.

'I am working the graveyard shift tomorrow. Why don't you come down to the café on the Dock Road and we could have a chat, before I walk home?' Sean suggested.

'Great, that's fantastic, I would love to. I will see you there ten minutes after the klaxon then.'

Alice put her hand on the back gate and lifted the latch.

He smiled. She smiled. They lingered.

The moon glinted from the wet cobbled pavement whilst millions of stars shone and bore witness to the silent messages that flew from one pair of eyes to the other.

Nothing either of them could now do would erase those first few moments.

It had begun.

Sean had already had sex once that day.

Brigid was so scared of becoming pregnant yet again that she often slipped into the bedroom when Sean was washing after work and went down on her knees to satisfy her husband, in order to avoid full sex later.

She regarded it more as a daily task to be completed, rather than an expression of love or intimacy.

An act of efficiency. Two jobs in the time of one. Sean sorted. All finished and done in ten minutes.

The women talked openly and graphically about sex. Their jokes were as ribald as the men's. Each knew exactly who had sex and when. Every woman in the four streets often knew when another was pregnant, even before her own husband did.

Sex provided a reason to complain. An excuse to be ill.

The detail of conversations was always explicit and uninhibited.

Brigid was the only woman on the four streets who undertook this ungodly act and she was frequently besieged with questions from the others, appalled by what she did. Following the third child, they would never willingly volunteer to have sex of any description and went to imaginative lengths to avoid it, all except Maura.

Enthralled, they pressed Brigid for details each time they met in Maura's kitchen for a cuppa and a gossip.

'What does it taste like?' asked Maura, more curious than disgusted.

'It surely has to be a sin, Brigid. Do ye pray for forgiveness?' asked Sheila.

'Sure, I do. I never miss six o'clock mass, Sheila. I'm only a sinner for a few minutes. The father is fabulous and kind, so he is. He asks me for all the little details and I mean every one, to guarantee I am fully absolved, because, sure, we both know I will do it again,' said Brigid. 'He always asks me do I enjoy meself and I always answer, not at all, so that makes it all right, I reckon.

'Confessing to the father takes almost as long as keeping Sean happy. I spend longer on me knees praying for forgiveness and saying Hail Marys than I do with Sean's langer in me mouth. But I'd rather that than have another baby in me belly just now.'

All the women laughed at this, some with genuine mirth, others in utter amazement at Brigid's audacity.

'Ye can still get pregnant doing that disgusting thing, so ye can,' said Peggy when they had all calmed down. 'Ye might think ye is being clever, but ye will still end up with another babby. Do what I do. Just tell Sean to feck off and stop bothering ye.'

'Oh my God, has Sean tried it on with you too, Peggy? That's disgustin', the man is a fiend,' squealed Deirdre from Tipperary, who always got the wrong end of the stick.

'Jesus, no,' screamed Peggy. 'Sean may be the big man around here, but he'd know what a fist was, to be sure, if he tried anything on with meself.'

Brigid often wondered if she would ever one day tell them how she had discovered the way to keep Sean happy and to stop herself from becoming pregnant more often than she already was. Brigid knew she never could. It would be a betrayal and, besides, it was a sinful thing to do to speak in such a way of the dead. Bernadette and Brigid had shared many secrets and her special way to keep Sean happy had been one. Let the leaves of the sprawling oak tree, each one as big as a lady's hand, fan the summer breeze across her grave. Let her be in peace, with the daffodils, tulips and wild primroses in the spring. Red roses and lilac in the summer. Burnt-orange chrysanthemums in the autumn. All provided by the old woman, selling her flowers for sixpence a bunch, from a metal pail at the cemetery gate which Brigid placed in the old, discoloured jam jar at the foot of her headstone.

Often, when running back from six o'clock mass, Brigid would notice that the old flower woman had left for the day.

Having taken the remaining flowers from her pail and shaken the slimy water and strings of bright green moss free from the naked stalks, she would lay the tired blooms with drooping, sleepy heads against the gate railings, for the gravediggers to collect and lay on some lonely and forgotten grave.

Brigid would pick up a few of the blooms (she never took them all) and then, running up the path, she would take the flowers to the friend she had not forgotten, Bernadette.

Brigid never confessed to the other women that, when they were all gathered in Maura's kitchen together, Bernadette was sitting at the table with them, too. She was sure of it.

Laughing and smiling with them.

When they banged their mops on the walls to summon each other to a powwow, they were also waking one of the dead.

They would think she was mad.

Maybe she was mad. Maybe it was her mind playing tricks. Over the last week Brigid had felt strongly as though Bernadette was trying to send her a message. It made Brigid uneasy, in a way she could not put into words, nor did she want to.

Maybe she hadn't seen her, but she was sure she had.

At first, Sean had enjoyed Brigid's routine.

An act, provided by his loving wife, thought to be in the domain of prostitutes alone, had been exciting. It had thrilled him. He knew he was lucky and that there were many men on the four streets who would die happy if their wives would do the same just once in their lifetime.

But now it had become robotic. He had his allotted few minutes, amongst her tightly choreographed domestic tasks, and it was the same every single day. His needs were just another item on her domestic checklist, slotted somewhere between dishes, mopping the floor and mass. He resented it.

But not tonight. Alice had stirred him.

Tonight he wanted full and proper sex. The kind that was normal between a man and wife. He would whisper to Brigid that he would jump off at Edge Hill and that she wouldn't become pregnant. He needed her closeness. To feel her in intimacy and warmth, like it used to be. He was desperate for reassurance that they were a team.

Like Jerry, Brigid had been asleep for over an hour when Sean slipped into bed, began kissing her neck and slowly lifting up her nightdress.

She was exhausted. Between teething toddlers and nursing babies, she had achieved only three hours' sleep the previous night.

'What are ye doing that for? Stop it now,' she whispered, as she clambered up through the layers of sleep and looked at him with bleary eyes. She knocked his hand away. 'You've already been sorted today and ye will wake yer mammy, sleeping downstairs below us.'

Brigid rolled over and turned her back to him, pulling her nightdress in tightly behind her knees.

Sean was disappointed but, realizing there was no point in persisting, rolled onto his back and let his thoughts dwell on Alice.

The little Alice whose eyes lit up when she spoke about America.

He tried to sleep, constantly shifting his body weight on the mattress, searching for a limb on which to lay his weight on that wasn't bruised or tender.

His physical discomfort lessened as his thoughts wandered to the prospect of meeting Alice tomorrow. A woman who could talk about things other than babies and housework. A woman who was interesting. A woman who wanted more.

When sleep finally took Sean, he was already lost in the arms of Alice. And in a similar bed in an identical house further down the entry, Alice was lost in his.

## Chapter Thirteen

Kitty and Nellie woke to Kathleen gently shaking them.

'Wake up, ye sleeping beauties,' she laughed. 'We have arrived.'

The first thing Kitty noticed was the smell. Without thinking, she put her hand over her mouth and nose and retched.

'Don't worry, Kitty love,' said Kathleen, 'ye will be used to it soon enough.'

'Aye, that's the smell of the proper earth, Kitty, so it is, and I'm glad to see, miss, that you have now become accustomed to it,' said Liam, gently poking Nellie in the ribs.

Even though Nellie was half asleep, she grinned.

'I'm so sorry,' said Kitty. 'I don't mean to be rude.'

'Not at all, child,' laughed Liam. 'If ye want rude, Miss Nellie can teach ye a thing or two. The first time I got her out of the van, on her first visit, she was as green as the turf, weren't you now, Nellie?'

Nellie looked sheepish. ''Tis true,' she replied, as from the tail of her eye she watched Liam imitating her throwing up and laughing to himself, making Nellie grin, reluctantly.

'Will ye pack it in, Liam,' said Kathleen. 'I am parched and want to move these girls inside to see Maeve and have a cuppa tea.'

Kitty was now standing outside the van, observing her new surroundings, as Liam lifted the bags out from under the tarpaulin. The deep-blue sky was broken by a full moon, illuminating the Ballymara road, a silver ribbon, all the way back to Bangornevin. Light also poured out from the open doorway of the farmhouse while the lamps in the windows beamed a warm orange glow.

Her surroundings could not have been less like the four streets.

To her right, she could make out the dark and forbidding hill that ran steeply up from the roadside and she could smell the tall rhododendron bushes which bordered the edge of the Ballymara road in a deep crimson fringe.

She could hear a gentle trickle of water and noticed an old stone sink standing in the middle of a stream at the bottom of the hill, directly opposite the pathway to the house.

To her left and out of sight, down past the farmhouse, she could hear the faster-running peaty-brown water of the Moorhaun river.

'That's what Nana Kathleen used for water when she was a little girl,' said Liam, nodding towards the stone sink. 'Ask her to tell ye the stories. Our own ancestors carved that and put it in place to collect and store the water from the stream. Come away in now and eat, plenty of time for exploring tomorrow.'

Kitty could smell so many things.

Water and peat. Crops and cattle. Iron and earth.

The smell was so rich, so natural, it stung the inside of her nostrils and caught the back of her throat, but she instinctively knew it was good air. Free from the smog, coal and stone dust that daily blew upwards from the docks and hovered over the four streets in a threatening cloud, coating the houses and windows with a thin layer of dust and grime.

The air here was free from the toxic yellow smoke spewed out by the chimneys of the houses that edged the Mersey and of the foundries set back from the Dock Road. Free from the fumes and chemicals churned out by the processing plants, which Maura was convinced were responsible for making Harry ill.

Kitty breathed in deeply and slowly. She had quickly acclimatized to the stinging purity and freshness of the air. Her lungs took their fill.

'Come away in and meet Maeve,' said Nellie, who was now fully awake and brimming with barely containable excitement. It was eleven o'clock and they were still up and dressed with no school tomorrow. She was bouncing up and down on the spot as she took Kitty's hand.

'You will love Maeve,' she said. 'She and Uncle Liam are so funny together, she gives out to him so badly and he just laughs at her, which makes her so mad. Come on now, away inside.'

Kitty was reluctant to leave the utterly peaceful quiet and the freshness of the night outdoors. If it hadn't been for the midges crashing into the van lights and swarming around her in clouds, she might have stood there for ever.

'Welcome to Ballymara,' said Maeve from the hallway, smiling as she bustled everyone indoors.

Nellie had explained, before they left, that Ballymara consisted of a road that ran from Bangornevin with two farms at the end.

'Bangornevin is a larger village altogether,' said Nellie.

Kitty was in for a shock. Larger meant it had just two hundred residents. She was expecting something the size of Liverpool. She had never been to a village in her life.

Kitty's first impression of Maeve was that she was stunningly beautiful. Her long auburn hair fell over her shoulders in big curls and her huge brown eyes poured out kindness like a tap. She had the bright rosy cheeks of a farmer's wife, and her figure was generous and comely. Kitty longed to fall into her arms and be hugged, but instead she held out her hand in the way Liam had in Dublin, just a few hours before.

Maeve, smiling, shook Kitty's hand. Kitty was taken aback by the coarseness and dryness of her skin. She had brought her new washbag of toiletries and was overcome by an impulsive urge to give her precious new hand cream to Maeve as a present.

'Come here,' said Maeve impulsively and threw her arms round Kitty. 'We don't do your English handshaking in Ballymara, miss.' And she led her towards the warm orange glow of the kitchen. Kitty grinned and looked over her shoulder towards Nellie, who winked and grinned back.

Kitty felt a weight slipping from her shoulders as she walked along beside Maeve. It was as though by leaving the four streets she had also left her problems behind her. She had been exhausted for so long by keeping a dark and draining secret and now she had been told she was pregnant. A baby. A bomb. An explosion of fact in the midst of what had once been her ordinary schoolgirl life.

She was totally unprepared for the next shock, when Maeve walked her straight into it.

Maeve's arm was still round her shoulders as they passed from the hallway into the kitchen. Kitty had only ever seen inside kitchens on the four streets and what greeted her made her mouth gape open in surprise.

The kitchen was huge. On the left a fireplace took up half of the height and half the length of the wall. In front of it stood a square wooden table, crowded with more food than Kitty had ever seen in her life.

In the middle was a hot and freshly roasted whole leg of pork, on a bed of crackling. Next to the pork lay a wooden board with a large sliced loaf of warm white bread and a freshly churned pat of deep yellow butter. In a larger bowl, big enough to bath a baby in, was a steaming mountain of mashed potatoes, mixed with dark green cabbage with butter melting over the top like an ice cap. Whole roasted buttery carrots sat on a plate next to the potatoes. There were pots of home-made apple sauce and chutney, their lids under green gingham mob caps.

Then, as if that weren't enough, there was a Victoria sponge cake bigger than any Kitty had ever seen before and a bowl of thick cream.

'I made the filling today, with the fruit we bottled from last year,' Maeve told her.

Maeve moved to the fire, filled an enormous brown teapot with boiling water and lifted it onto the table.

Kitty couldn't even speak. Never in all her life, even on their new black-and-white television, had she ever seen a table so laden with food or smelling as good as this one did. For the first time in months, she was ravenous.

'How did ye know we would be arriving now and to have everything just ready?' Kitty asked.

'Well,' Maeve replied, 'JT, who lives above the post office in Bellgarett, was watching for ye passing through in the van and when he spotted ye, he ran down into the post office and telephoned Mrs O'Dwyer at the post office in Bangornevin. Mrs O'Dwyer went across the road to the pub that is at the back of Murphy's butcher's and of course she got a drink for her trouble, and wouldn't she just love that, would Mrs O'Dwyer, any excuse, I'd say, and then Mickey from the bar at the back of the butcher's ran down the road to John's house, who of course, ye know, is Nellie's daddy's cousin, to let him know ye had been spotted, and he came down the Ballymara road on his bike to tell me ye had passed through Bellgarett twenty minutes since. 'Twas easy enough.'

And they all laughed at the bewildered look on Kitty's face. Even Kitty.

Once they had all eaten and the table had been cleared, Maeve took Kitty and Nellie to their room. Kitty was feeling relaxed. She had joined in the banter round the table whilst they were eating and was even beginning to find Liam's jokes funny.

As Maeve opened the bedroom door, and Kitty laid eyes on the room for the first time, she gave a loud gasp. 'Is this for us?'

'No, it's just for ye bags,' replied Maeve playfully, 'ye can sleep in the barn.'

'Of course it's for us,' squealed Nellie. 'Didn't I tell you the bedroom was beautiful?'

'Aye, you did sure enough, but you never said we had our own beds!'

Kitty stepped into the room. When he had brought in the bags,

Liam had switched on a lamp on a bedside table with a pink lampshade, which bathed the room in a warm and comforting glow.

On either side of the table stood two single beds with lace bedspreads and Kitty's new holdall sat on the one nearest the window. She touched it, as though checking it was real; all her precious new things contained inside.

Kitty noticed the walls were painted a beautiful, pale, duck-egg blue. Instead of nets, curtains of thick cream lace hung at the windows and the heavy over-curtains were the same duck-egg blue as the walls, with tiny sprigs of cream flowers.

The floor was covered with hand-made rag rugs in pink, pale blue and cream, and the doors and window frames were painted a buttery cream.

Next to the door stood a press, with a lace runner and a huge pink jug in a bowl patterned with blue, white and cream flowers.

Nellie had described the room to Kitty, but she hadn't told her how it smelt. How comfortable it was. How lush were the cream lace bedspreads, which Maeve had been threading herself since she was twelve years old, or how thick the rag rugs felt under your feet. She had never explained that there was a fireplace, which burnt something that looked like blocks of earth and smelt of heather.

Nellie had not told her that she would have her very own bed to sleep in and a beautiful polished press on which to lay out her new and lovely things.

Maeve then took them to the much prized indoor bathroom down the corridor where Kitty and Nellie cleaned their teeth together before they dressed in their nightclothes, ready for bed.

By the time they returned to the bedroom, Maeve had already hung up their clothes and stored their holdalls under the bed.

Nana Kathleen bustled into the room just as Kitty was very carefully emptying the contents of her washbag and laying them out on top of the press. She had never felt so proud or grown-up in her life, nor seen anything as beautiful as her box of talc and hand cream, neatly arranged on top of the lace runner. She stood admiring them until Kathleen spoke.

'Well, look at ye two, all ready for bed, eh?'

Nellie loved how happy her nana was when they came home to Ireland.

Kathleen turned back the bed covers, and Kitty marvelled at the creamy crispness of the thick Irish linen sheets as she slipped into the coolness, despite the fire in the room. She squealed as her feet bumped against something hot and made of stone.

Everyone laughed.

'It's the Irish version of a hot-water bottle, Kitty. To keep the bed from the river air and your feet warm for a good night's sleep. We have the river at the back and a stream at the bottom of the mountains at the front of the house, so it's a constant battle. Even in summer we need the bottles.'

Nana Kathleen kissed them both goodnight.

'We will be exploring and visiting tomorrow, girls, so sleep well tonight.'

As soon as the door closed behind her, Nellie whispered, 'Well, what do you think of Ireland, Kitty? Donchya just love it?'

'I do, Nellie,' Kitty whispered back. 'It's just the grandest place, I had no idea how grand. You told me what it was like, I know you did, but I had no idea it was anything like this and you had never told me how lovely Maeve is. Is this the room you slept in last time you came, Nellie?'

But Nellie was already fast asleep.

Kitty lay on her back, thinking and listening. She could hear the water running outside and the moths beating against the window-pane, trying to reach the light of the candle, which Maeve had left burning in a glass lantern on the press. She could hear the distant, muffled chatter of Kathleen and her son and daughter-in-law, sitting round the kitchen fire.

Kitty couldn't help thinking how wonderful it would be if her family could live in a house like this. She was still in a state of dazed amazement at how much had happened in just a few short days.

Who would ever have believed this? she thought.

She smiled and rolled over onto her side, wriggled into the crisp sheets and breathed in the smell of freshly laundered Irish linen. Her feet nestled around the hot brick and she fell asleep thinking …

sure, aren't I the lucky one? Green with envy they will all be. And she imagined the expressions on her friends' faces when they heard she was taking a holiday.

When Kitty awoke from a deep sleep a few hours later, she had no idea where she was.

The candle on the press had burnt down and the only light in the room came from the thin shafts of moonlight slipping in through the gap in the curtains.

Kitty's heart began to race. She could feel it. She was used to it.

She had been woken in the middle of the night many times before.

She instinctively reached out her hand to feel for Angela and then it dawned on her where she was.

She strained to pick up what it was that had woken her and then she heard it, the sound of boots crunching on shifting pebbles and the deep muttering of men's voices.

Kitty had no idea what time it was but she knew it had been midnight before bed. She didn't dare to look out of the window but she could tell by the light that dawn wasn't far off.

The house was deadly silent. There were no longer any comforting sounds emanating from the kitchen. Everyone in the house was long ago in bed and asleep. The fire in the bedroom must have gone out because the air in the room carried the edge of a damp chill.

She heard footsteps move along the side of the house and then away into the distance, down the Ballymara road. But one pair seemed to be approaching closer to their bedroom window. She could make out the shadow of a man with a cap on his head, slightly stooped and silhouetted against the window. She heard a door open very gently and then click shut.

She guessed from the sounds of the boots on the pebbles that there were as many as five men walking away from the house down towards Bangornevin and maybe one in the opposite direction, to the other farmhouse at the end of the road. Yes, the footsteps had definitely split into three directions.

Kitty thought they must be burglars. But what would they steal?

Even she could work out that you would need a car to carry anything of significance down the long Ballymara road.

Kitty lay, her heart beating loudly with fear.

She wondered should she wake Nellie or one of the adults.

She had no idea of the layout of the house, or where anyone else was sleeping, but she felt very strongly that she should leave her bed and find Liam.

Her hot-water bottle was barely warm as she stretched her legs and turned to look at Nellie.

'Nellie,' she whispered, 'Nellie, wake up.'

But there was not a flicker of response. Nellie was exhausted.

Right, there's nothing for it, thought Kitty to herself. I'm out of this bed.

She swung both of her feet out onto the rug and tripped over to Nellie's bed. Once again, she tried to wake her, but Nellie was having none of it. Kitty had been thrilled at having her own bed to sleep in, for the first time in her life, but now she realized she didn't like it that much after all.

She gently pushed Nellie over and slipped into bed beside her. They had slept together in hospital, except for that one night, which Kitty had never let herself think about since, not even once.

She whispered, 'Nellie,' twice more, but with no response, and before she had the chance to try again, exhaustion claimed her and she once again fell into a deep sleep.

## Chapter Fourteen

'Oi, What are you doing in my bed, then,' were Nellie's first words when she opened her eyes the following morning.

'God, you would never believe it,' said Kitty as she rubbed her eyes and surfaced from sleep. 'There were men outside last night and I thought I heard one of them get into the house. I was right scared.'

Nellie burst out laughing

'That wasn't men, Kitty, that was a nightmare.'

'No, sure it wasn't, I definitely heard them on the pebbles outside and everything.'

Nellie looked at Kitty to see if she was serious. She was. Nellie was younger than Kitty, but recently Nellie had felt as if she was the eldest and that Kitty was vulnerable, but she had no idea why.

Kitty used to be full of fun, but then suddenly she wasn't any more. Nellie was as confused as Kitty about the pregnancy and she didn't want to talk about it. It was a bad thing for Kitty to be having a baby, Nellie knew that, she just didn't know how bad.

'Let's get up now,' said Nellie. 'Maeve's breakfasts are to die for, but before she does the breakfast, she milks the cow, come and see.'

Both girls dived out of bed and Kitty ran straight to the window. She felt alive and full of excitement about the day ahead.

Their bedroom was at the front of the house. A pathway led from the front door to the narrow road, on the other side of which was the stream Kitty had seen the night before, with a mountain rising straight up beyond, and Kitty saw the deep cerise rhododendron flowers she had smelt last night.

'Holy Mary,' she exclaimed.

'We will walk up it,' said Nellie, pointing at what was really just a very large hill. 'The trouble is that it is very wet and boggy below. You have to go quite a way up before it becomes dry.'

Kitty was lost for words. She was used to Liverpool, to concrete and bombsite rubble.

Kitty and Nellie went to the bathroom together but two seconds later they ran screaming down the hallway.

'Oh merciful God, help me,' Kitty yelled, holding onto Nellie's hand as they flew into the kitchen, knocking Kathleen to one side.

Maeve was bent over the fire, loading the second batch of peat onto the sticks in the fireplace. Liam was sitting at the table, drinking his morning tea.

'Oh my God, Uncle Liam, help us, a big fish has swum up the plughole into the bath,' screamed Nellie, as she hurtled through the door and flung herself at Liam.

'Oh my goodness,' gasped Maeve, 'ye have met the salmon then.'

The adults were helpless with laughter while Nellie and Kitty stared at each other.

'I caught it, ye eejits,' said Liam, 'but don't say that to anyone, or ye will have the Gardai knocking on the door and having me up before the magistrate, ye will.'

As Kathleen's glasses had steamed up, she took them off the bridge of her nose to wipe on her apron.

'Uncle Liam is the chairman of the angling club, which is very useful now as we know the gillie rota and when it's safe or not to fish. As the salmon swim up through the farm, we take a good catch for ourselves and, sure, 'tis our land they are on, so why shouldn't we? The angling club think they own the waters God put here. They make me sick.'

Kathleen and Joe had fought many a battle with the authorities over the fact that the best salmon river in the West of Ireland ran twenty yards from their own back door and across land their family had owned for generations. Kathleen wiped her eyes with the corner of her apron as she remembered her late husband Joe. He had worked so hard to make the farm what it was today and had poached many a huge salmon, sometimes with the help of his young sons, from a curragh, teaching them the way, just as his father had before him and his own before that.

'Oh dear!' exclaimed Kathleen. 'Never mind me, 'tis just the tiredness and the journey home, it always gets to me.'

Kitty asked Liam, 'Ah, was that your footsteps I heard in the night? Were there other men with ye?'

'Aye, five of us last night. John McMahon, his nephew Aengus and a few others,' Liam replied. 'Now, away with ye, girls, and get dressed.'

Once both girls were dressed they ran through the kitchen and out to the cowshed at the bottom of the path, where Maeve was now sitting on a stool, milking.

Kitty was nervous. She had never seen a real cow before, never mind stood so close to one, and she had certainly not smelt anything quite like this. She didn't say anything, but this was the first morning she hadn't wanted to be ill as soon as she opened her eyes.

'Shall we carry the bucket, Maeve?' asked Nellie.

It was a sunny morning and the midges swarmed round their heads, stuck inside their hair and flew down the collars of their blouses.

'God, don't they drive you mad,' said Kitty.

'They will be gone by the time breakfast is over,' said Maeve, 'and ye will be used to them by tomorrow. They sleep on the bog all day but, mind, they will be back out as the sun goes down for another bite at ye.'

The girls deposited the milk in the dairy, a concrete shed to the side of the back door where Maeve made her cream and butter. Kitty was amazed that the milk in the bucket was warm.

'Is this what we drank in our tea last night? It smells disgusting,' she whispered to Nellie. 'It smells like the cow.'

'I know, but you will get used to it and you won't know any different soon, I promise,' Nellie replied.

Kitty wasn't convinced and was dreading having to drink the milk at breakfast.

Uncle Liam was heaping bacon rashers from the griddle onto a plate as they walked back into the kitchen.

'Now, girls,' he shouted, 'we have a big day today, we have the harvest to come in. Kitty, I've assigned that job to ye and Nellie. We need the peat cut whilst it is dry and so we have left that one to ye.'

He looked at the girls. Yes, just as he thought, Kitty's expression was bewildered and serious. The harvest wouldn't be ready for a good few days and he was, as usual, fooling around.

He carried on. 'The two of youse can start work as soon as ye have eaten and we will just away down to the pub for the day now. Ye give us a shout when ye are all done. Is that all right there, Nellie? If ye puts yer back into it, ye should be finished by six tonight.'

Nellie playfully punched Liam in the arm.

'What's wrong?' said Liam, rubbing his arm. 'I thought that was why ye had come, to give Uncle Liam a rest. Mammy, I'm shocked. Ye have brought these wastrels here under false pretences.'

He took a sideways glance at Kitty, who was now laughing along with the rest. Getting that child to laugh is hard work, he thought.

'They have a busy day ahead, Liam, sure enough, without help from you,' said Kathleen. 'We are going to introduce Kitty to Bangornevin.'

'Ballymara will take only two minutes,' said Liam, 'so ye may as well or the girls will be driven crazy with the boredom by tonight and begging me to let them stack the hay, so they will.'

Pots of tea now appeared with piles of bacon and sausages cooked with sliced potatoes and heaps of bread. Kitty had never seen or tasted butter like it. It was a thick, creamy yellow and salty.

She thought about everyone at home, who at that very moment would be tucking into pobs. White, stale leftover bread from yesterday, soaked in milk with a sprinkling of sugar and warmed in the range. Or boxty, which was made with potatoes and flour, rolled round and flat, the size of a dinner plate. If there was butter to be had, Maura would scrape it on and then back off again and cut the boxty into quarters.

How could she ever eat that again and not think of this morning and this wonderful breakfast?

'Can you imagine what Angela would be like, if she could see me eating this breakfast?' she said to Nellie. 'If she knew what I was eating right now, Holy Mother, she would give out something wicked altogether. I can't understand why so many people leave here to go to America and England.'

'Well, Kitty,' said Kathleen, 'it's about work and money and being able to live. There is no work around for people and so they have to leave. Most farms can't support an entire family.'

'Aye, Mammy, but the wages in England, now, they are fantastic for working on the roads and the construction trade is roaring,' said Liam. 'That's why everyone is leaving. We have men here every month coming into Murphy's pub, looking for new men to sign up and take on.'

Liam's brother, Finn, who lived with his wife in Bangornevin, had joined them for breakfast. Now he looked irritated. 'Only the fools stay in Liverpool and work for the English. America is the country to be.'

Finn was as serious as Liam was funny.

The atmosphere round the table became tense and Kathleen leapt in.

'Hush yer mouth, Finn. Jerry has made a good life for himself and Nellie. You should be grateful there are jobs there for people to go to, because this farm would struggle to feed all of ye. What would ye be doing if Jerry and Bernadette had decided to return and work the farm, as was their right, him being the eldest, an' all? Jer went to England because he could and you were younger, to give ye a chance because he knew he could get work. Ye may not be in England, Finn, but ye are reaping the rewards because yer brother is.'

Finn looked sheepish. Nellie was surprised. This was the second time she had heard Bernadette's name mentioned openly. She was learning things she never knew before.

Maeve was already on her feet, choosing the moment to end the tension.

'Right, all of ye. I have a home to run, so will ye all away to whatever trouble ye want to make today and leave me to it.'

'Right, five minutes and we are off,' said Kathleen as the girls began to clear the table. 'We will be so busy today, we won't have the time to bless ourselves. The first thing we have to do is pop in and say hello to all the relatives, so they can see we are here, but first we have to use the phone in the post office and to let Maura know we have arrived safe and sound. And watch that nosy parker Mrs O'Dwyer doesn't earwig in. I will keep the nosy bat talking, whilst you girls call the Anchor and send a message home. God cannot have known what he was doing when he gave the nosiest woman on the planet control of the phone in Bangornevin. She doesn't even have to squeeze the information out of people now or eavesdrop in the shop, she just picks up the bleedin' phone.'

'Jump in the van,' shouted Liam from the hallway. 'I'm off to the village for feed from Carey's.'

Kitty again sat by the window in the van and, as they drove down the road, realized she was keen to reach Bangornevin and to explore Ballymara properly. She knew, without hardly having set foot in either, that she was falling in love with a place that a week ago she hadn't even known existed. Tommy had forewarned her.

'I don't know what it is, queen,' he said, 'but home, Ireland, it does this strange thing, it keeps hold of your heart and never lets you go. There is this feeling just here,' and he clenched his hand into a fist shape and gently punched himself in the gut. 'Some say it's grief for all we have loved and left behind. Others say it is the spirit of our ancestors pulling us back and holding onto us. For sure, I have worked with men from all countries on the docks and none have the same longing in their hearts that we Irish have for our home.

'But do you know what I think it is, eh, queen? I think it is the suffering. I think so many Irish hearts have suffered and died on our soil that the souls of those before have joined up into something powerful, which can keep a grip on ye. Ireland needs Irish hearts to keep her safe and to protect her and she feels it when we go. I believe she cries for the loss of those of us who desert her and is always trying to pull us back home. But I know this: I am glad of it, and I would rather have it and know where my heart truly belongs, than not have it at all and be an exile in doubt.'

Maybe it was in the blood, thought Kitty. If it was, it was only in her blood. Neither Angela nor the twins seemed the slightest bit interested. Maybe that was what God did. Maybe he just passed the ache on to the eldest child in each family, to ensure that one day they would return home to Ireland.

Bangornevin was built on a crossroads adjacent to the river. The spur road to Ballymara joined it once it crossed the Moorhaun and hugged the river down to the McMahons' farm, where the road became a dead end. No one had any reason to walk down the Ballymara road unless they were visiting one of the two farms or using the field just before the turning that had been set aside as a football pitch.

"Ah, Jesus, the lads in Bangornevin are mad about the football," Kathleen explained as they passed.

The Moorhaun river was rich with Atlantic salmon and at the crossroads to the village the torrent roared so loudly you could barely hear yourself speak.

The drive into Bangornevin took all of five minutes.

On one side of the crossroads was the grocer's, which sold everything from sweets to sheep-dip. Jerry and Liam's cousin owned the shop and on her last visit he had even allowed Nellie to serve the customers.

On either side of the road stood a row of very small whitewashed houses. Directly across from the grocer's was the church. On the opposite side of the crossroads stood the village school, a tailor's shop, the tobacconist's, the post office, a hardware shop and a butcher's. The back half of the butcher's, which was divided off by a hessian curtain, was a pub. There was also a full-time pub in the village, but nothing sold there was as home-made or as strong as that sold at the back of the butcher's.

People made their own bread and what they didn't make was bought at the market on market day and stored in damp straw in the cold press.

Liam now turned left and pulled up outside the post office.

'Good luck,' he shouted as they all piled out of the van. 'Shall I call back for ye later, Mammy?'

'No thanks, Liam,' Kathleen shouted. 'We can walk back, or Pat will give us a lift.'

All three stood and waved as the van disappeared down the high street, Liam beeping the car horn and raising his hand to everyone he passed.

The post office was full of women gathered round the counter. As the bell over the door jangled and Kathleen and the girls walked in, every single person at the counter ceased talking and turned round.

Kathleen scanned the shop.

'Morning, Mrs O'Dwyer, morning, ladies,' she boomed.

In no time at all the women gathered round Kathleen and began asking questions.

'How much wages are they paying in Liverpool to work on the roads now, Kathleen? Is it true a man can earn a hundred pounds a month?'

'Are ye staying home for good now?'

'How is that crazy wife? Is she a patch on Bernadette?'

The questions came thick and fast, but Kathleen answered none of them.

Kitty was amazed that every person recognized Kathleen and Nellie, and that they even knew who she was too.

As the women kept Kathleen busy with what seemed like a hundred questions a minute, a very shabby-looking lady, dressed from head to toe in ragged black, much poorer than anyone Kitty had ever seen in her life, approached her.

'Ah, now, ye must be Kitty, come to keep Nellie company on her holiday, are ye?'

'Yes, I am.' Kitty smiled.

She noticed that the woman's shoes and clothes were in a terrible condition. What teeth she had were broken and nearly black.

'I know ye mammy's mammy, she's a Fahey from Killhooney, is she not, and her sister and all. I know her too.'

Kitty had heard her mother speak of Killhooney Bay but had never visited and had no idea that her nana's name had been Fahey.

'I'm not sure,' replied Kitty, smiling at the lady and feeling very sorry for her. She glanced nervously at Kathleen, not wanting to say the wrong thing or anything more than she should.

Kathleen was revving up to challenge Mrs O'Dwyer.

'We have come to use the phone, Mrs O'Dwyer,' said Kathleen with an authority in her voice Nellie had never heard before.

The truth was that not many people could walk into the post office and command any degree of respect. The doctor and his wife, who lived in the big house built especially for him and his family on the outskirts of the village, could speak in the same tone as Kathleen, when resisting the nosiness of Mrs O'Dwyer, but precious few managed it.

'Of course, Kathleen,' trilled Mrs O'Dwyer. 'Will it be the pub now in Liverpool ye'll be wanting?' She picked up the phone and began to dial.

'Aye, but not for me. Kitty here just needs to leave a message for her mammy, who will be waiting at ten o'clock for the call.'

Mrs O'Dwyer scared Kitty. She was staring and grinning in a fixed manner that was most disconcerting, all the more so because she had very few teeth. As Kitty moved towards the phone, she smiled slightly nervously back.

Mrs O'Dwyer beckoned Kitty behind the counter and handed her the phone. To Kitty's shock, Maura was on the other end.

'Mam,' she shouted, a little too loudly. She was excited beyond words to hear Maura's voice. She had already missed her mother more than she could say.

Kitty heard Kathleen talking very loudly in the post office and smiled to herself. Kathleen was distracting Mrs O'Dwyer.

Kitty turned to the wall to seek some privacy, as she heard Maura's voice travel down the line.

'Kitty, how are ye? Have ye been sick? Have ye eaten anything? Did ye sleep? Is Maeve being nice to ye? Have you put clean knickers on and given the dirty ones to Kathleen?'

Kitty laughed. 'Mammy, stop. I'm fine, everything is grand and Maeve is just the best woman ever, she's so nice.'

'Oh, heavenly mother, thank God. Your da and I, we hardly slept for worrying about ye.'

'Mammy, how is everyone at home? Is Malachi behaving and has the baby even noticed I'm gone?'

'Well, I would definitely say so now, we have all noticed, Kitty, none more than Da, we all miss ye. The place isn't the same, but the bedroom is tidy and that's a fact. If I hadn't stopped her last night, Angela would have put all your clothes in the twins' room and claimed the bedroom for herself. Yer da gave out something wicked when he caught her tiptoeing along the landing with all of your belongings piled up in her arms. I don't think she'll be trying that again now. She cried louder than the baby and said, "Da, it's only while she's on holiday," but your da didn't care, he was having none of it.'

Suddenly Kitty heard a beep beep beep in her ear.

'Mammy,' she shouted.

She heard, 'Bye, Kitty,' and then Maura was gone and Kitty, stunned, was left with a dead line.

They had had just two brief minutes.

'Was it the pips?' shouted Kathleen.

'It was timed on the two minutes, Kathleen,' said Mrs O'Dwyer officiously. Kathleen glared at her.

'Never mind. I told Maura before ye left that I would make sure ye wrote her a letter every other day and so now, Mrs O'Dwyer, we need airmail letters, please, if ye wouldn't mind.'

Although the call had been short and sweet, Kitty felt better for having heard Maura's voice.

Kitty looked round for Nellie and saw that she was outside the shop, talking to a girl who had rested her bike up against the post-office window. Kitty hurried outside to join them.

This, Kitty learnt, was Rita, who was Nellie's cousin, after a fashion, whose father owned the local grocer's.

Rita seemed very excited to see them.

'Do ye not have to go to school while ye are here? No? How lucky are ye? I would die not to go to school. Look what the witches did to me today.'

Rita held out her hands. Kitty and Nellie gasped in horror to see the red weals across her palms.

'That looks horrible. How did you get those?' asked Nellie.

'It was the dreaded catechisms this morning,' explained Rita. 'Oh God, I tried everything to stop Mammy sending me to school, but what can I do? The shop is across the road from the school. I have no chance. I knew we would be tested this morning and I knew I would get one wrong. I got the stick across my hand all right.

'I'm out now because I offered to run to the shop to get the Connemara donkey her cigs. I couldn't stand having me hands smacked with the stick again. She lifts it up so high and brings it down so hard, so she does.'

Kitty was horrified. They had the cane at her school but only the really bad lads got it and then just across their backsides with their trousers on. Never on bare skin.

'Who is it you call the Connemara donkey?' Kitty asked.

'Her name is Miss O'Shea, she's from Connemara and she looks like a donkey,' said Rita. 'Will ye get on Jacko, both of ye, and meet me in the village after we finish school one day? Everyone will be beside themselves when I tell them that ye are back, Nellie, so they will. I can't wait to tell them, now. Sure makes a nice change for me to be first in the class for once.' Rita roared with laughter.

Kitty already liked Rita. How could anyone have their hands caned and then laugh as much as Rita, only minutes later?

'You need to be ahead on more than village gossip to stop Miss O'Shea thwacking your hands,' said Nellie, looking worried.

Rita jumped on her bike, shouting, 'See you outside the gates soon, or come to the shop.' She cycled back across the road to the school, holding the handlebars very carefully.

Kitty and Nellie looked at each other. 'Well, I won't be complaining next time Sister Evangelista gives out to me,' said Kitty, 'and who is this poor Jacko we have to jump on?'

'He's the donkey,' laughed Nellie. 'I will make the introduction when I find him. Sometimes I have to run up the hill and look down at the farm. Usually, I can spot his ears, sticking up in the oat field. He is the naughtiest mule ever. He never does anything he is told. Sometimes he likes the walk to Bangornevin, but quite often he will just stand in the middle of the road and refuse to move. He really is the most stubborn animal.'

Kathleen walked out of the post office with the closest thing to steam coming out of her ears.

'Mary and Joseph, save me, that woman is the end. She asks so many nosy questions, I swear to God it must be against the law to have a woman so interfering running the post office.'

'Ah, sure, she's very funny,' Kitty replied, already regarding Bangornevin as though it were a fascinating tapestry.

But she knew this much, she was already in love.

The rushing sound of the river was both familiar and intoxicating, as though it called to her. Deep inside, she felt as though she belonged here, and yet she had only just arrived.

The Deane Farm
Ballymara
County Mayo

Dear Mammy and Daddy,

I am so sorry it was so quick on the phone. I had no idea those beeps were coming. We bought airmail paper in the post office so that I can write everything down so that you know what is happening.

I hope you are doing well at home. It feels like weeks already since I saw you. So much has happened that I am bursting to write and tell you all about it.

I am writing this sitting on my own bed, which has the most lovely lace bedspread you have ever seen, Mammy.

There is a press in the room and I have all my own drawers. I have a beautiful lamp next to my bed with the prettiest lampshade. On the top of the press I have laid out all of my new toiletries like ornaments. They look so nice, Mammy, and the new soap smells like flowers when it is wet. I cupped it in my hands and took it to Maeve to smell when I used it this morning and she said it was just the most beautiful soap she had ever smelt, just like fresh lavender.

I don't like to use the hand cream because I want to save it for special, but I took the pot into the kitchen and rubbed some into Maeve's hands. She works so hard, Mammy, her hands are so rough. She just loved it and she said, hang on now whilst I sit in the chair and enjoy this. Everyone laughed because she closed her eyes and put her head back and said, oh my God, aren't I just one of the fancy ladies now, I'll not be milking the cow any more, so I won't, and Uncle Liam said you will have Bella getting used to those soft hands now, Maeve, be careful or she won't want ye to be milking her any more when Kitty goes home and your hands go back to being as rough as a tinker's arse.

Everyone laughed so much. Everyone laughs all the time.

You would really like Maeve, Mammy.

No one seems to work here, Daddy. I mean they do, Uncle Liam works the fields, but they are his fields. There are no men knocking on in the morning and there doesn't seem to be anywhere anyone goes to work. I asked Maeve where the docks were and she said there weren't any and that everyone looks after the land and each other. That's what they do for work.

We are going to the market in Castlefeale where Uncle Liam will sell his calves and lambs, and Maeve is taking her jam from last summer. She says those who haven't made enough last year, because they were lazy, will be desperate to buy now because they will be running out.

Kathleen took us to visit her relatives today and every time we visited someone's house, we left with a present. We had to carry onions and all sorts of things home with us afterwards including a new yard brush called a scoodoo.

It made me laugh because it is made out of twigs, but I didn't laugh when I saw Maeve brushing the cow shed out because it really works.

All the relatives seem very nice and I met one of Nellie's cousins whose name is Rita. I would hate to be in school here because if you forget your catechisms, you get hit over the hand with a stick. Can you imagine that?

I hope everyone is being good at home and, Angela, you make sure you help Mammy with everything until I am back, which won't be long.

Mammy, my sickness is much better. I think I will be well enough to return home very soon indeed. If Nana Kathleen wants to stay with Nellie, I am sure Uncle Liam will take me to the boat in Dublin, if you or Da meet me. I know how the boat works now and wouldn't be afraid of travelling on my own.

It is just fabulous and because it is so, I can't wait to get back and tell you all about it.

The address at the top is all you will need to write back to me.

Nellie sends her love and asks can you let Jerry and Alice know that she does.

I will see you soon. Two weeks at the absolute most, I would imagine.

Don't be crying yourself to sleep at night, now, Angela, because you and the girls are missing me so much. Lads, be really good for

Mammy and I will use the ten shillings Uncle Liam gave me to bring you all back a lovely present.

Lots of love,
Miss Kitty Bernadette Doherty

Kitty wrote her full name. It made her feel like a lady, not a child, and if she wasn't supposed to write the name Bernadette, why had she been given it as her middle name? As far as Kitty was concerned, everyone should use their middle name.

'What's your middle name, Nellie?' Kitty asked as she clicked the top back on the fountain pen Maeve had lent to her.

Nellie looked up out of her book as she spoke. 'Ethelburga, but don't tell anyone. I would hate anyone to know that. I don't know what Nana Kathleen thought she was doing at the time.'

That night, when the girls were preparing for bed, they noticed two ladies arrive at the front door. One was a cousin, Julia, but Nellie had no idea who the other woman was.

'I wonder what they have come to gossip about?' whispered Nellie to Kitty as they heard the earnest muttering of conversation and the kettle being placed on the fire.

'I don't know, but it sounds like a serious chinwag. The kind Peggy would be good at.'

They both laughed at the mention of gossip merchant Peggy.

Ten minutes later, the fresh air knocked them both flat out, and they were fast asleep.

'Thanks for driving out all this way to Ballymara,' said Kathleen to her visitor, Rosie O'Grady. Rosie was spending the night with Julia, Kathleen's sister, and was related by marriage to Julia's husband. She had travelled to Bangornevin following a telephone call from Julia to let her know her help was urgently needed.

No facts were forthcoming. None were needed and Rosie jumped into her car and travelled to Bangornevein as soon as she had finished work as the matron midwife at the hospital in Dublin.

Maeve knew all about Kitty's pregnancy and was helping Kathleen to find a solution. She also knew it was the priest's doing but she and Kathleen had made the decision no one else in Ireland would be told.

'Sure, we heard the news about the murder over here and it was in the paper. Such a scandal, it was. There are so many from Mayo in Liverpool, Kathleen, anything that happens there is news here, too. The only thing anyone has of any interest out here on the west coast is gossip.'

'Aye, Maeve, I know, but I had to tell ye. I have brought the child under your roof. Ye needed to know.'

'It is a problem for both of us now, Kathleen, we will find a way. The child has changed in just a day and it is a grand thing to see. Let's just leave her to enjoy what is left of her childhood whilst she can and not mention anything to her just yet, eh?'

'Aye, we won't. I couldn't agree more. As true as God, her mammy would never believe how much she has altered, so she wouldn't.'

Once they were sitting down with a cup of tea, Kathleen spoke. She was close to Rosie who had been through troubles of her own in the past.

Rosie had been born and brought up in Dublin, and had trained as a nurse before she married and settled in Roscommon, where her husband was a dairy farmer.

There were two types of farming men in Ireland.

Gentle family men, who did well at school, obtained the leaving certificate and put their brains to good use in developing their farms.

And there were those who ruled their homes and their farms with their fists.

The job of a woman who married a farmer was to ensure she chose the former.

Those who weren't so attractive and didn't quite have the freedom to choose in the way others did often ended up with the latter.

Rosie had used both her looks and her brains to make her match.

She was also the head of midwifery at the hospital in Dublin and sat on the midwifery council for Ireland.

'Has Julia explained everything to ye?' asked Kathleen to break the silence, once the pleasantries had been exchanged.

'Yes, she has,' said Rosie. 'Although, I have to ask, why has she been brought over here? Every day the boat is full of girls running from Dublin to Liverpool for just this reason. Why can't it be sorted out in Liverpool, for goodness' sake?'

Kathleen felt herself flaring up inside, but remained calm. She knew that she was on a shorter fuse than usual.

'Well, Rosie, I am afraid to say that the poor girl was taken advantage of by a man who should have known better. It is not her fault she is pregnant. She comes from a good Irish Catholic family. I have brought her here to try to save the family from the shame and the heartache.'

Rosie studied Kathleen over her glasses. It was obvious she didn't believe the story. Rosie might have been kindly, but she was no fool.

This was going to be harder than Kathleen had imagined. How could she tell Rosie, once Kitty began to show, that people would suspect Kitty's father of having murdered the priest? That a baby, growing in her belly, would provide a timeline straight back to the worst night of their lives. That police had never ceased asking questions every day since and were convinced the answer to the murder lay somewhere in the four streets. Like a dog with a bone, they just weren't letting go.

'How do ye know the child didn't lead him on?'

Rosie's words made Kathleen want to grab her by her scrawny neck and throw her out through the front door.

Instead, she curbed her exasperation.

'Because she is an innocent child and we know he took advantage when she was ill and in her hospital bed.'

As soon as Kathleen spoke the words, she wished she hadn't. She knew how incredible they sounded. Who would believe what had happened to Kitty, unless they had witnessed the priest going about his filthy work? She had seen him with her own eyes when she had walked into Kitty's bedroom at home and heard the girl pleading with him to stop.

Kathleen suddenly felt desperate. It appeared as though someone that she had hoped would provide guidance wasn't going to be much help at all.

'Look, Rosie,' said Julia, suddenly butting in, 'the reasons why and how the child got pregnant are none of our business now, are they? We were hoping you might have some useful suggestions, with you being so highly qualified and in the know, with regard to midwifery and all that. The problem is that no one in Liverpool, or here for that matter, must know the girl is pregnant. She has to have this child in deadly secret, Rosie, and we need your help.'

Maeve took the compacted straw plug from the top of the dark brown bottle and filled sherry glasses with the thick, deep purple damson wine that Kathleen and the girls had carried home earlier that day.

Rosie was a woman with a tough professional exterior but she was as soft as butter inside.

'I have no idea why this all has to be kept so quiet but it is not my business if the poor child has to be birthed in secret,' said Rosie, lifting up her glass.

'I am assuming this has something to do with the fact that you don't want to bring shame on this village or your own streets in Liverpool?

'I find that so sad, Kathleen. We have to change the way girls and women are regarded and treated in Ireland and if we keep hiding these girls away, nothing will ever alter. In Liverpool and across in America, women have it so much better than the poor girls here. I am assuming that what you are asking me to do is to place her into the mother and baby home in the Abbey near Galway?'

'I know it exists,' said Kathleen, 'but I have no notion how it works and to be sure, it had never crossed my mind that it would be possible.'

Rosie carefully placed her glass down on the table and twirled the stem around between her fingers. She remained silent as she thought. Something was obviously bothering her.

The peat logs on the fire slipped and sent a shower of sparks flying into the room, distracting Rosie who then spoke directly to Kathleen.

'There is one attached to a laundry run by the holy sisters. She can have her baby in secret there. I can deliver it when her time is due and then the child could be adopted.'

Kathleen let out a huge sigh. There were answers. They were getting there.

Rosie wasn't just offering suggestions, as they had hoped, she was providing a solution.

'Who would adopt it?' asked Kathleen.

'Well, she wouldn't be the first Irish girl to be in this predicament, Kathleen, despite the numbers filling the boat to Liverpool. The children are adopted by American parents only, so that the child never makes contact with any of the mother's family in the future. The nuns who run the mother and baby home take over a thousand American dollars from the American parents and a hundred and fifty pounds from you, for her keep. Kitty will be placed in the home and work for the sisters until the baby is born and then, as soon as her confinement is over, you can collect her, once you pay the hundred and fifty pounds.'

'One thousand American dollars.' Kathleen almost choked on her damson wine. 'My God, the nuns are making a profit out of unwanted pregnancies. Holy Jesus, Mary and Joseph. I have heard it all now.'

'Do ye have a better plan?' asked Rosie, slightly offended that Kathleen wasn't more grateful. "Because if you do, I for one would prefer it. I have never delivered a girl in any of those homes and I have sworn, I never would. I couldn't be more against them and all they stand for. Call me a feminist or any other insulting term you may wish but I think a pregnancy is nothing to be ashamed of.'

Rosie was suspicious, knowing that there was more to this girl's pregnancy than they were letting on. But that wasn't her business.

They had a distance to travel between here and what Rosie was proposing, but Kathleen could see it was an answer they had never considered. They just needed a hundred and fifty pounds and they would all be safe.

'How do we go about organizing this and having a look to see if it is the right thing to do, Rosie?' said Maeve, as she stood and refilled Rosie's glass.

'You will need a priest,' said Rosie.

We had a priest, thought Kathleen. It was a priest that was the problem.

'You can gain access to the home only if a priest either takes you, or sends a letter.'

'Can you not recommend her to the home, Rosie? You being a midwife and all?' said Julia. 'If ye have agreed to deliver the baby, surely they will accept a girl from ye?'

Rosie looked very uncomfortable and squirmed slightly in her seat.

She had never delivered a child in the Abbey and never wanted to. She was a hospital matron who was known for fighting the Irish authorities and their dated and repressive attitude towards women. By delivering a child in the Abbey, she was condoning the practice of humiliation and suppression. But how could she refuse what was in effect a request from Julia? God knew, Rosie had seen often enough how tough life could be for a single mother.

'I will write to the Reverend Mother and see what she replies,' said Rosie. 'When is the girl due?'

'Around Christmas and none of it is her fault,' said Kathleen, who was trying harder than she ever had in her life not to let her thoughts take the better of her tongue. 'Don't mention who she is yet, please, Rosie. Let us try and protect the girl's privacy for now, eh?'

'Aye, well, be that as it may, it is not my decision. When I hear from the Reverend Mother, I shall write to Julia, which will be a safer method of communication. This isn't something for Mrs O'Dwyer to eavesdrop in on.'

'Well,' said Maeve with a smile, as she emptied the last of the bottle into everyone's glass, 'that's something we can all agree on.'

As Maeve closed the front door after waving the two women down the path, she turned to Kathleen.

'I have heard of the Abbey, Kathleen, and I have been told it is very tough indeed. I am not sure if it is right for the child, but then I don't know what is.'

Kathleen's heart sank. She also knew of its existence, and others like it, but had no idea what they were like.

'God, what a mess,' she said. 'You go to bed, Maeve my lovely. I have a letter to write to Maura, which I need to have in the post in the morning. I don't think we have a lot of time. The child will be showing any day now.'

'Aye, but if we take this route, Kathleen, you have to remember the Abbey is only just outside Galway, so there will be girls in that home from hereabouts. You know how gossip travels like wildfire. Someone may have heard of Kitty being a visitor and know who she is. Visitors are so rare it will be known almost straight away and that Liverpool accent of hers doesn't help.'

'I know,' said Kathleen. 'We will have to hide her name. That is another bridge we will cross tomorrow.'

Once Maeve had taken herself to bed and Kathleen had washed up the glasses and cups, she sat down and, by the light of the dying embers of burning peat, wrote her letter to Maura.

The Deane Farm<br>Ballymara<br>County Mayo

Dear Maura,

Well, my lovely, this is not a letter to read out to Tommy or anyone else, so I suggest if ye have opened this in front of anyone, tuck it away in your apron pocket, make an excuse and read it later.

Kitty is having a ball and has taken to the Irish countryside like a duck to water.

Ye have never seen anyone as excited as she is to be rising at five o'clock tomorrow morning for the market in Castlefeale.

John McMahon from the farm next door and Liam are taking two trucks for the cattle, so there will be plenty of room for them all. She will be back at lunchtime and full of it, please God.

Her and Nellie have taken on a list of jobs they would like to do whilst they are here, which includes milking the cow, would ye believe!

She hasn't been sick once since she arrived and I have watched her nerves return to nearly normal in just hours, which is a pleasure to behold, Maura.

Now, to our first problem.

We had a visit tonight from Rosie, who is the sister-in-law of Julia. Rosie's from Roscommon, and she is also the matron midwife at the hospital in Dublin. She has made a suggestion that Kitty remains here and is placed into a mother and baby home near Galway. She is writing tomorrow to the Reverend Mother who runs the home to see if she will accept her.

Kitty would have be moved fairly soon. I saw the first signs of her showing today. It won't be long before others notice too.

She would have the baby at the home and the sisters would place it with an American family for adoption. Hold onto the chair here, Maura. They sell the baby for one thousand dollars. Then we have to turn up with a hundred and fifty pounds and we can take Kitty home.

Now, the second problem. Kitty will be away from home for months not weeks, and there is no way on this God's earth Tommy will be happy about that and so ye will have to find a way of handling that one.

Before ye get carried away with any grand ideas that she can return home and ye can look after her, Maura, just bear this in mind. When she turns up back home with a belly, it will only be a matter of time before the penny drops with everyone. Even thick Peggy will work that one out.

Ye have to write back soon and let me know what ye think.

In the meantime, if the sisters are amenable, I will travel to see the home as soon as ye let me know. Rosie has agreed to deliver her baby in the Abbey and then we can take our Kitty out of there and back home to Liverpool.

I think it is our only choice, Maura. Maeve says not to worry about the money. We can all work the hundred and fifty pounds between us, so we can. We will all chip in.

Write back to me quickly, Maura. I need to move fast if the sisters are agreeable to taking Kitty in so early. There is one other thing, and that is that the events leading up to our holiday are common news around here. Everyone I have met in the village has asked me for the smallest detail.

I am beyond shame, Maura, but even I blushed when the spinster at Carey's corner asked me how big was the langer they found in the graveyard and God alone knows, she must be ninety.

We are going to have to be as secretive moving Kitty from here to Galway as we were bringing her here. Also, Maura, we shall have to hide her name and give her a new one, just to be on the safe side. You never know.

The home is run by the sisters themselves and until her confinement Kitty would need to work in a laundry they run at the Abbey. Kitty has never been idle and I am sure that if she is doing something useful, she will feel the days pass more quickly. The sisters are well used to pregnant women and will keep a good eye on her.

Anyway, Maura, Maeve, Liam and everyone here sends their love and best regards to Tommy and the children.

Let me know if everything is all right across the road. Brigid is keeping an eye on Alice for me. I will write to Alice next but you know what it is like, I am just a bit worried about her being on her own all day, with her not long being better. Call me a witch, if ye like, but I am not convinced that someone can alter so much so quickly and I am a bit worried that she may have a relapse.

Write back soon, Maura, love, please.
Lots of love,
KATHLEEN

# Chapter Fifteen

Molly thought she would sleep on what Daisy had told her. After all, Molly had known Tommy and Maura since the day they arrived on the four streets, when Maura was six months' pregnant with Kitty. Molly had always admired Maura. She was a worker, that was for sure.

Molly was so shocked at Daisy's revelations, she inhaled a sultana from her fruit scone. What a palaver all that had been, thought Molly, as she pulled on her housecoat over her flannelette nightdress to walk downstairs.

It was four o'clock in the morning and, abandoning sleep, she decided to make a cup of tea as she placed the kettle onto the range and lit a candle. She didn't want to switch the main light on, in case Annie O'Prey woke and saw the light in the backyard. Molly nursed a mild disdain for Annie, who felt the need to tell Molly and anyone else who would listen all of her business.

'That woman leaks like a colander,' Molly had told her husband on a daily basis many years earlier, when he was still alive.

Molly maintained a level of one-upmanship, simply by withholding information from the inquisitive Annie.

Whilst Molly sat in her candlelit kitchen, in her hairnet and slippers, surrounded by a haze of blue smoke from her second Woodbine, burning in the ashtray next to her as she munched on a slice of fruit cake between puffs, she chuckled as she imagined the look on Annie's face if she had a notion of what Molly knew following her chat with Daisy..

Just at that moment, Tiger leapt in through the open kitchen window, making Molly jump with fright. He dropped a half-dead mouse at her feet. She never knew these days what the Siamese cat was going to bring in next.

In order to hold the squealing creature in place, he placed his paw on top of its tail and, as it wriggled and squeaked, he looked up at Molly, seeking her praise.

'Who's a clever boy now then,' she said.

The cat stretched his neck upwards in pleasure as Molly stroked his ears. He purred and arched his back, releasing his pressure on the mouse, which seized its chance and flew under the press.

Molly smiled. She had a new-found affection for the cat. Since the day he had walked in and dropped the priest's langer on the mat half an hour after the murder became news, Molly had become a minor celebrity on the four streets. It had all begun when she had bent down with a bit of newspaper to pick up the bloody bit of flesh from the kitchen floor. She might have been a widow for a good few years but she wasn't senile, she knew exactly what the cat had brought home.

There hadn't been a day since when someone or other hadn't begged her to relay every gory detail of the whole sorry event.

Molly secretly enjoyed the attention, but what she enjoyed most was Annie's jealousy at Molly's new-found celebrity status.

'I have to hurry along now, Tiger, lots to do today,' said Molly, as the cat brushed up against her legs, stretching his head to fit snugly inside her cupped hand.

She had made her decision. It wasn't yet five, but she would need to do a bit of baking and start her polishing early. Molly was expecting important visitors. It would be a very busy day indeed.

It was Harry who took the letters to Maura in the kitchen.

Gentle, kind Harry. He was so excited that he almost opened them himself.

Kitty and Nellie had been away for just over a week and Harry missed them both every day.

Kitty was more like a mammy to Harry than a sister but as the eldest boy, of both sets of twins, he also felt like a big brother to Kitty. He felt that it was his job to look after her, especially since she had come out of hospital following the awful car accident when she and Nellie had been run down by Callum's car. Callum had tried to blame the fact that Liverpool was still covered in snow in March.

They all knew it was because Callum couldn't drive and the car was stolen.

Harry was growing up rapidly. A serious little man, he knew well the meaning of responsibility and manners. Tommy had taught him almost every day, just by being Tommy.

Each Sunday, as they attended mass together, Tommy would walk on the outside of the pavement and encourage the four boys to do the same, ensuring that Maura and the girls were on their inside.

'Manners maketh man, Harry, or that's what they say and I don't think it can be far wrong.'

'Why do we have to be on the outside, Da?' asked Harry.

'Well, son, it's so that when a horse and carriage come along and send up a wave of dirty water, it hits us and not your mammy or the girls, so it doesn't.'

'But, Da, the only horse and carriage is the rag-and-bone man and he doesn't work on a Sunday.' Harry liked to be precise.

'Yes, son, but it's manners and so we just do it.'

'But why, Da, if there's no horses and carriages? I don't get it.'

'Harry, ye will get a lashing from yer mam's tongue soon if ye don't stop talking.'

Harry was good at his manners. At school he would knock over chairs and children in his rush to open the classroom door for the sisters and the teachers, and he always carried a school bag home for one of the girls.

He also knew the meaning of chivalry. Harry was a reader. He couldn't devour enough books from the school library. It was in his nature to worry about Kitty and Nellie being so far away. Although neither Maura nor Tommy would answer his questions, he knew the trip had something to do with whatever it was that had happened. They all knew something was wrong.

And Nellie, well, Harry just loved Nellie and had done since she was a baby. He had always felt that it was his job to look out for Nellie on the four streets. Harry missed Nellie a lot.

The day that Callum's car had hit both of the girls at the top of Nelson Street, Harry had been one of the first at the scene and he had truly felt as though he would die with worry when they were taken to hospital.

And now here they both were, off in Ireland, and he found himself wondering every day, were they both all right?

'The post has come, Mammy, shall I open them for ye?' said Harry expectantly now.

Maura smiled and kissed her serious prince on the top of his head.

'If ye don't mind, Harry, I will read them when ye have all gone to school and then tonight, when we aren't so rushed and yer da is home from the docks, we will all sit down and read them together. What do ye think about that?'

Harry had known it was worth a chance, but he hadn't for a moment thought he would have any luck.

He laughed. 'Aw, rubbish,' he said, as Maura rubbed his hair.

'Go on, ye cheeky scoundrel,' she said. 'More like an old man than a boy in yer ways, going on a hundred, ye are. How many books is it ye have read this week then, eh?'

Angela burst through the door at the bottom of the stairs. 'Letters, letters, let me see, let me see,' she squealed, running over to Maura and trying to grab them out of her hand.

'Get away with ye, ye cheeky article. I'll give ye a slap on the legs if ye so much as touch those envelopes without my say-so.'

Maura snatched the letters back from Angela and tucked them into her apron pocket. She missed Kitty so much. Angela was more of a handful and a hindrance than she was a help.

Tommy had left for work half an hour since. He had helped her to get the boys up and organized before the men had called for him and he had the fire lit in the range at six o'clock.

'I don't know how I would manage if ye weren't such a good man, Tommy Doherty,' Maura had said, as she kissed him goodbye that morning.

Tommy slapped her backside. 'Good in many ways, eh?' he roared. He grabbed Maura's hand and pulled her in to him for a hug. The children had yet to charge down the stairs. 'An early night for us, eh, queen?' he whispered cheekily, as his hands roamed across her backside.

Maura pulled away. 'God, what are ye like? Do ye think of nothin' else? I swear to God, ye cannot be pulling your weight down on the docks, ye have far too much energy left!'

Despite her protestations, Maura was smiling. Not as much as Tommy, however, who would make a point of letting the fellas know, when they knocked on, that he was on a promise for the night.

It singled him out, made him different from those who had to plead for sex. Tommy loved to make the others jealous by bragging about his good fortune, in having a willing wife even though that was something she would never in a million years disclose to any other woman on the streets. There was no credibility to be gained in not making your man beg.

Things were slowly returning to normal. The shock of Kitty's absence had diminished slightly, now that the parting was over. Tommy thought about his princess all the time, but his memory conjured up images and memories of his Kitty before, his happy Kitty. Not Kitty as she was today.

Once the children had left for school, Maura hurried through the morning chores, wasting no time. Her desire to carve herself a peaceful hour to read and digest the letters slowly was uppermost in her mind. They were burning a hole, calling to her from the depths of her pocket, the unfamiliar sound of the flimsy, pale blue paper crinkling as she worked.

She found herself extra chores, as though to punish herself and make herself wait, unsure whether she should be excited or nervous about the contents. She cleaned the splashes from the kitchen window and wiped over the skirting boards with the floor cloth. She mopped the floor, scrubbed the table and changed the bedding on the cot.

Maura regarded the arrival of the letters in the same way she would a visitor to the house.

The hour she stole to read them was her guilty pleasure and it must be deserved. She had to have earned it. The kitchen must be spick and span.

Once the chores were finished, she put the baby down for her mid-morning nap, stoked up the fire, made herself a pot of tea for a cuppa and sat in the comfy chair. Still, teasing herself, she looked around and surveyed her handiwork, delaying the opening by a further tantalizing minute. Then, satisfied that she had truly earned her break, she opened both of her letters.

Maura turned to Kitty's first. When she read the last few lines, where Kitty said she was desperate for home, her heart leapt.

Maura wanted her back, too. The fact that Kitty felt she might be back in just two weeks was wonderful indeed. As Maura folded the letter again and painstakingly slid it back inside its pale blue envelope, she crossed herself and looked up at her statue of the Virgin Mary on the mantel-shelf above the range.

'Please, let it be,' she whispered.

Maura then opened Kathleen's letter, slipping the knife under the gummed flap, and realized she was holding her breath. She knew that if Kathleen had written, she would have significant news.

As soon as she had finished reading the letter, she cried.

It held nothing but bad news. Months not weeks without her daughter. The need to find a hundred and fifty pounds, and the impending moment when she would have to tell Tommy that Kitty wouldn't be coming back any time soon.

A desperate sadness washed over Maura.

There was Kitty, looking forward to returning home with all her tales and presents, and Kathleen pointing out that there was no possible way, for all their sakes, that she could before her baby was born.

Maura knew, if the police knocked on the door and someone cracked, Tommy would end up swinging from the gallows. The thought sent the fear of God through her. God alone knew what would happen to them all. And what of their friends who had helped them? Jerry and Kathleen, Brigid and Sean?

She had dreamt of Bernadette last night and although she could not remember the details, she had woken with a feeling of cold dread in the pit of her stomach. Tommy's morning playfulness had banished the fear left behind by the dream, but now that she had stopped working and rested, it washed over her once again.

She had prayed that Kathleen's letter would tell her the Epsom salts and the gin had worked, and that Kitty had started, once she reached Ireland. God knows, she had given her enough. Girls that age were sensitive. It was easy to lose a baby at such a young age, surely? These were the desperate thoughts Maura had harboured all day, every day, whilst she waited for a letter from Kathleen.

Maura's back door opened suddenly and in scuttled Peggy.

There was no privacy on the four streets. No one ever closed their doors and no one ever knocked, either.

'Oh, queen, what's up?' said Peggy, flopping down into the chair opposite Maura.

It was known as the 'not so comfy' chair, because some of the springs under the cushion were broken, and others had been unhooked and stretched to fill in the gaps. It was the chair Maura often sat in, being lighter than Tommy.

There was a strong possibility that Peggy would sink between the springs and struggle to rise again. She could be in for the day.

Peggy reached over, which, given the size of her belly, was an impressive act in itself, to take one of Maura's hands in her own, while eyeing up the pot of tea and the brack, cooling on the wooden draining board.

'Come on, queen, tell me, so. What on God's earth is wrong with ye?'

Peggy had only popped in for a cuppa. She had just enough coal left for two nights, until Paddy was paid on Friday and was, as needs must, economical with the range.

Maura had given up trying to tell her how to manage.

Peggy felt it was her right that she and Paddy each smoked twenty a day and had one or two extra drinks in the club on a Saturday night. Maura had told her so often that she needed to save for a rainy day and how to cope on the family budget.

Peggy was the last person Maura wanted to see, but she would never make her unwelcome. Neighbours on the streets were all as close as family. You couldn't choose your family and when you were an Irish immigrant, your friends and neighbours either. You got on with it and mostly loved them anyway.

Maura wondered if the chair cushion would smell when Peggy left.

She knew it would.

As Peggy leant over towards Maura, an unpleasant odour wafted across from the top of her apron. Maura was used to this. It didn't make her baulk. Back home, baths were looked on as a treat but Maura was very aware that in Liverpool her countrymen were called the dirty Irish.

If anything, her irritation with Peggy was not because of her smell, or her dirty habits, or her lack of housekeeping. It was the fact that every time the welfare officer, the school nurse or the Prudential man knocked on Peggy's door, she reinforced this prejudice and that annoyed the hell out of Maura. Now she could see that the dull, dark hair wound round Peggy's curlers was covered in the telling white flecks of lice eggs.

As soon as she had heard the latch lift on the back gate, Maura had shoved both letters deep into her apron pocket and out of sight.

'Oh, nothing really, Peggy,' she replied now with more chirpiness than she felt. 'I had a letter from Kitty on her holiday with Kathleen and, you know, I just miss her.'

Peggy sympathized. 'Who can ye trust to run a message now? Boys are useless, and she was grand with the washing and cleaning and looking after the babies. I would miss her too.'

Maura almost laughed out loud at Peggy's ability to talk the talk, as if she ever cleaned. Maura's missing Kitty had nothing to do with what she did in the house or how she helped with the kids.

It was the fact that she couldn't reach out and wrap her arms round her. She missed Kitty's gentle little voice and for so long she had missed her laughter.

'I thought she might be so taken with the farm, she would look down on us lot and not want to return home.'

'Of course she wants to come home,' said Peggy. 'You and Tommy are her mammy and daddy, so ye are, that's where every girl wants to be. The farm might be fabulous, but there's no place like ye own bed, no matter how many kids and bugs ye share it with.'

Maura shuddered. There were no bugs in any of her beds.

She put the kettle on to freshen up the mash of tea.

She was regretting letting Peggy think that Kitty was looking forward to coming home. How would she explain it if she had to stay?

God, she thought, why is everything so difficult and secretive?

As soon as Peggy left, Maura decided to share her news with the only person she could. She put on her coat and ran down the entry.

Maura sat herself down in the chair by the fire in Jerry's house and picked Joseph up.

Alice made them both a cuppa, then sat down with a cup and saucer of her own in her hand. Maura silently leaned forward and handed over the envelope.

Alice put her cup and saucer on the floor, tucked it just under the chair, so as not to knock it with her foot, and took the letter out. Whilst she read, Maura sang to Joseph and played a hand-clapping game. Joseph giggled and bounced up and down on Maura's knee.

For a few seconds, Alice stopped reading, looked up and smiled. She knew she could never be as natural with children as Maura was and it made her sad.

She did feel sadness. It was a new experience, but she felt it.

When she had finished reading, she folded the paper and, without a word, put it back into the envelope, handed it straight back to Maura, then reached out to take Joseph.

Alice stood Joseph up on her lap to pull up his knitted leggings. His clothes had become dishevelled during his clapping game with Maura. And then, sitting him back down on her knee and pulling down his pullover over the top of his leggings she finally spoke.

'Phew, I never expected that. I half thought they would have sorted her out in a different way over there. Thought they might have had a few remedies we don't have here.'

Maura's face burnt and the all-too-familiar tears pricked her eyes.

'Well, she is being sorted out in a way, just not the way you thought, Alice. I am going to have to tell Tommy tonight and then I will need to leave for Ireland, although God knows how I am going to manage that, with no Kitty to watch the kids. Tommy cannot miss a day's work or someone else may take his place on the gang.'

'I will help out,' said Alice, 'don't worry about that. Between all of us, we will manage.'

Alice's kindness took Maura by surprise. This time the tears won and Maura cried. Again.

Alice looked hard at Maura, but could not feel pity. It never happened.

It was close. Very close. Pity teased her from the borders of her emotional awareness. Running in and running out again.

Elusive.

Alice decided to take advantage of Maura's weakness.

'Maura, you do know that lots of women have abortions now, don't you? It could even be legal soon, so the talk on the news says.'

Maura looked up from wiping her eyes, but before she could respond, Alice ploughed on.

'Before Kitty left, I made enquiries. It would cost fifty pounds, that's all, and then it would all be over and done with in just a few hours.'

Maura jumped to her feet and screamed, 'Holy Mary and Joseph, I hope to God you didn't tell anyone it was for my Kitty? Did ye, Alice? Did ye? Tell me, for God's sake.'

'God, no, of course I didn't, Maura. Calm down. I said it was for me.'

Maura had knocked the teacup and saucer onto the floor with a clatter. She squatted down to clear up the mess and Alice once again ploughed on.

'I asked the abortion midwife, Mrs Savage, what she did and it all sounded simple and easy to me, and not a coat-hanger in sight. Maura, there never has been, not for a hundred years. The house is in Bootle, it's clean. There were two women who left her house together as I arrived and they both looked happy enough. Mrs Savage explained everything to me carefully and it is so easy.'

Maura was wiping up the spilt tea off the floor.

'*Maura!*' Alice shouted. 'Will you leave the bloody cup and just sit down and listen to me, please.'

Maura was agitated. She couldn't understand how Alice could speak of a mortal sin and the taking of a life so calmly.

Her hands flitted like birds in front of her as she waved away Alice's words.

'I have never had or heard such a conversation, Alice. There are no Mrs Savages in Ireland and there is nothing your Mrs Savage can do that I couldn't do for my own daughter.'

'Yes, there is, Maura.' Alice was almost shouting. 'There bloody is something that can be done but your eyes are so shut with your stupid, pious, left-footing, Catholic ways, you won't even listen. You are being ridiculous, Maura, and obstinate. We have all got into a mess over this. The least you could do is show an interest in what I have taken the trouble to find out. I'm not the one who is pregnant. I didn't drag Joseph all the way to Bootle on the bus for myself, you know. You owe it to us all to hear me out.'

Maura collapsed back down into the chair. Alice had pricked her conscience. She thought again, as she did once every few minutes, that this was all her fault for having believed in the priest. Alice had just said, 'You owe it to us all.'

No one else had said it. No one had pointed a finger at her, but often she could hear Tommy think it, and today Alice had uttered the truth, yet to be acknowledged. The truth everyone knew.

That dirty, stupid truth. It was all Maura's fault.

She didn't look at Alice. She turned her head and stared deep into the coals burning in the fire. She could smell the cake Alice had made, slowly rising in the oven.

Joseph was trying to stand up on his own feet, pushing against Alice, stretching his arms out to Maura. She noticed him out of the tail of her eye and smiled a thin, tired smile, taking him from Alice. Joseph snuggled into her chest as he sucked his thumb and peeped out at his mother from Maura's arms.

Maura was again lost in thought.

For a fleeting second, she went back to better days.

She imagined a wet afternoon in front of the same fire, in the same room, but with Bernadette sitting opposite her, not Alice. She saw again the glass of long-stemmed, deep-yellow buttercups mixed with fireweed that Bernadette had placed on the windowsill to brighten up the kitchen.

Bernadette, the only woman on the four streets who thought weeds were worth picking. And she had been right.

She used to laugh and say that she picked the weeds because they reminded her of the heather and the peat flowers from home. The wild rhododendrons, the blue-eyed grass and the lady's tresses.

Maura missed the flowers too. She missed her daughter. She missed Bernadette.

'I used to sit in front of this fire with Bernadette,' said Maura quietly. 'We used to laugh and chatter and listen to the heartbeat of

Kitty who was growing in my belly at the time, with an upturned glass that we had Tommy file the base off.'

Maura had broken the taboo. She had mentioned Bernadette. Without even realizing, she had taken her revenge.

Maura had reached a depth of despair she had never plumbed before. She almost cried again, this time for the hours she had spent in this very chair, laughing with the friend she had loved as a sister.

But the comparison with Bernadette had not wounded Alice. It had taken her by surprise for just a second, but nothing more.

She could see Maura's desolation and took advantage of her tears.

'Mrs Savage is a properly trained midwife and knows what she is doing, Maura. She would place some dried seaweed sticks into the neck of Kitty's womb. It does hurt a bit, but Mrs Savage will sell us some opium to help with the pain. The seaweed sticks absorb the fluid from around the womb and then the sticks swell and they push open the neck of the womb. Kitty would have a miscarriage and, honestly, it's just like her having a late monthly and no different from what you have been doing with the hot baths, the Epsom salts and the gin. But it has to be done as early as possible, as you well know. Bring her home from Ireland, Maura, and let's take her. It'll cost us fifty pounds, not a hundred and fifty.'

Maura looked at Alice with steely eyes. She didn't like the fact that Alice had spoken aloud about the gin. Alice had exposed Maura's hypocrisy in all its nakedness.

Maura stood up, placed the pieces of broken china on the draining board and with her back to Alice spoke very calmly. Her words were measured, devoid of emotion and bordering on coldness.

'I know what I have tried to do, Alice, but I was wrong and wicked to have even attempted it. I will not take her to any backstreet abortionist. Kathleen is right. Your mother-in-law is a holier woman than all of us put together. I will travel to Ireland and see Kitty into this home. It is the right thing to do.'

She turned round and glanced at Alice with torment on her face.

'Look, I'm sorry. I didn't want to offend you,' said Alice. 'I was just thinking of what's best for Kitty.'

Maura looked Alice squarely in the eye. Reflecting on the times she had spent with Bernadette in this same kitchen had made her feel stronger.

'And ye think I don't, Alice? Ye think I don't know what's best for the child I failed to protect from that wicked man?'

Alice stood at the back door and stared as Maura walked down the yard path towards the gate.

She lifted the latch, then turned and, with a furrowed brow, asked, 'What kind of midwife is it that kills babies?'

And before Alice could say a word in reply, she was gone.

19 Nelson Street
Liverpool
Lancashire

DEAR KATHLEEN,

I am grateful to ye, so I am, for writing to me so quick like, to tell me that Kitty and Nellie are having such a grand time, thanks be to God.

It was a joy to open Kitty's own letter, Kathleen, and to be honest, when I read yours, it was a bit hard on my emotions, but not too bad now, Kathleen. I'm used to the idea of a home for Kitty and, God willing, I will stay that way so that I can be strong for her and help her through.

I feel overwhelmed altogether by what we have to do.

God alone knows why the Epsom salts and gin didn't work, at her age too, Kathleen. I was sure it would all be over by now and that we would be back to normal.

Ye know I trust all ye say and if ye think this is the way it has to be, then so be it.

I feel bad about putting on Maeve with all of this and, sure, isn't she an angel herself to help us out, so she is. I would like to come over and see the home for myself, but first I have to tell Tommy that Kitty is to be away for longer than he thought, although to be fair, Kathleen, I don't think either of us are thinking straight. Tommy says the answer is to just keep moving.

I never knew Tommy to say boo to a goose before, but he's a different man now so he is.

We have thirty-two pounds saved in the bread bin and I will need four to come to Ireland. It has taken us fifteen years to save that money, so I have no notion where we will get the hundred from.

I know ye are right about Kitty. If she returns home and has a baby after all that occurred, then it is sure that everyone will make the connection.

Also if Kitty were here, she is so sensitive that she would never recover from the way people would treat her either. The lamb has no idea.

Sometimes I wonder, Kathleen, if we should have been as cruel as some others are. If Tommy had taken his belt to the kids, or if I had slammed them up the stairs with no food in their insides, would they have been harder altogether and more able to fend for themselves?

Would they not have been as sensitive and would Kitty have spoken out to us about how that man had been doing his bad things to her and what was happening in her own bed while we were just downstairs, only feet away from her?

Kitty has no idea how hard it would be if she were here and people knew she were pregnant.

Those she calls her friends today will become her enemies tomorrow and God knows what the sisters would say or do. If there was a hint of suspicion, all my kids would be thrown out of the school at the very least. I would fear for us all, Kathleen.

It is what we have to do and the more I have thought about it all day, the more sure I am.

As long as the sisters are from a good and kind order and look after her, that's what is important.

Adoption is the right path and that is why I want to visit Ireland to see her, Kathleen. I know my own baby girl and all that she is, a baby still herself. This will upset her, as she has loved every baby I have given birth to as though it were her own. But, sure, I don't need to tell you that.

I need to talk to her about this and explain what is happening.

If ye do it on your own, Kathleen, she will be looking for me and wondering why I'm not there. I want to be the one to explain to her why we have to hide her name and choose a new name with her. I think Cissy would be good. That way, if someone forgets, Cissy sounds so much like Kitty, it could be passed off with no trouble at all.

Everything here is good. We went to the club on Saturday night for the first time since everything kicked off. It was a delight to see Jerry and Alice there too.

Alice is doing fine. I have seen her tripping up and down the street with Joseph in his pram and popping in and out of Brigid's house, and on Saturday night we all sat together at the club.

Alice didn't dance, but she had a grand natter to Sean whilst Brigid danced with Jer.

She is a credit to ye, Kathleen. She looked fabulous and had made a big effort. She gives me hope in my own despair. Who would have thought, a year ago, that we would see Alice pushing a baby round in a pram and tripping up to the Grafton rooms with the rest of us. She had done her hair and looked lovely, so she did.

God has brought her here to show the rest of us that no matter how desperate things appear, there is always hope. I am sure of that now and ashamed of how I treated her in these past years. I loved Bernadette like my sister, but she has gone and if I have learnt anything now, it is that life is short and you never know what is going to happen next.

I will book my ticket and phone the post office to let you know when I will be arriving. I cannot wait to see my girl, so.

See you very soon, God willing.
Your dearest friend,
MAURA

Maura had wanted to write chapter and verse on how full of herself indeed Alice was, but sure, hadn't she offered to help, so that Maura herself could visit Ireland and settle Kitty into the convent. And, anyway, there was no benefit to be had in worrying Kathleen. She had enough on her plate, and they all had more important things to do than fret about Alice.

*

Tommy had turned a corner.

The night in the Grafton rooms on Saturday had been hugely enjoyable. There had been a singer doing a turn and they had all had a laugh and a dance. Things were calming down at home and as time went by the horror of the past receded. He desperately missed Kitty, but she would be home shortly, he was sure of that.

'I'm home,' Tommy shouted an octave too loudly as he walked in through the door, even though all the children could see him. 'Whose the first with a kiss for yer da?' The best part of every day for Tommy was just this, walking into his warm kitchen and the bosom of his family.

The boys and Angela elbowed each other out of the way, pushing forward to be the first picked up by Tommy. Even the baby sitting in her box began to squeal and wave her arms with excitement as she bounced up and down on her nappy and spat her dummy halfway across the room to attract his attention.

Maura was stirring a pot of stew at the range. She turned round and smiled.

With the baby in his arms, Tommy walked over to the range and pulled the ties undone on the back of Maura's apron so that it fell open. Facing towards the children, he placed one arm across his belly and gave an exaggerated laugh.

'For goodness' sake, will ye stop it!' Maura shouted as the shoulder strap fell from her apron and slid down to her waist. She playfully smacked Tommy with the wooden spoon. The children burst into squeals of laughter at her protests. Inside, her stomach churned at the thought of the news she must tell him later.

The light was fading as Maura scurried along the street to the postbox and then on to mass, glancing down the cobbled entry as she walked. Cowed by guilt. Alice had spoken aloud the thought she had kept hidden and now it wouldn't leave her mind. A nagging, constant thought. It was all her fault.

As she pulled up her coat collar to keep out the breeze, she looked up at the top of the street and yet again saw the blue and white panda car pass by, slowly and menacingly. Her heart beat faster. The only thing standing between that car and the hangman was a deadly secret.

As she stepped off the kerb she saw another police car parked, yet again, outside Molly Barrett's front door. It had been there earlier in the afternoon and she had noticed Annie O'Prey, on her hands and knees, scrubbing Molly's step, with what looked like her ear stuck to Molly's front door.

'God, will Molly ever give up feeding them for company and just let them go?' she whispered to herself, as she ran towards the post box.

Alice was settling Joseph down when she looked out of the bedroom window and saw Maura once again running down the road from the pillar box towards the church for mass. The priests from St Oswald's had been covering at St Mary's since the murder and Kathleen had warned Maura not to miss a mass. If she did, it would be a change from her normal pattern that might be noticed.

Running scared. Chased by the bells. Propelled by her guilt. Fleeing from the shadows. Terrified of missing mass.

Fearful of incurring the wrath of the priest for not making God her priority and showing him the devotional respect he deserved, of not taking the half-confession in case she should meet her end that night.

'What difference will it make if she can't confess the worst sin of all? They never learn, do they?' Alice whispered into the side of her baby's face. 'What does a priest have to do to turn them away from his Church, eh, Joseph? How wicked does he have to be?'

Howard had felt his heart begin to race as Molly told him her story. He knew they now had to tread very carefully, or they could lose their murderer and their case.

Howard couldn't help himself. As Molly spoke, he imagined promotion. He could see the silver epaulettes upon his shoulder. A vision popped into his head of being introduced to the young Queen and her husband when they visited Liverpool. He saw his and Simon's photograph on the front page of the *Liverpool Echo* and his name in the headline.

'This is it. All we have to do is charm the old woman, make her feel important and she will help to deliver those goods in a court of law, eh, Simon. We have scored, mate.'

'Do you really think so?' Simon asked. 'You think all it will take is for Molly to persuade Daisy to talk in court? I thought Daisy was supposed to be simple?'

'Well, she is, but if Molly can testify to her character and to be honest, who says the girl is simple, eh? She doesn't seem that bad to me. No, Simon, never fear, Molly Barrett is the step we need to our promotion, mate. She is a canny woman, that one. What judge wouldn't believe her, eh?'

# Chapter Sixteen

Alice asked herself, was it wrong meeting Brigid's husband, Sean, to just talk to him? She instantly decided it wasn't. Alice knew neither pity nor guilt.

Alice and Sean had already met twice in the pub in the Dingle tucked into the corner in the snug, beside the fire, away from the noisy bar where the men gathered to drink when they knocked off work.

Sean ordered a Guinness for himself and a Babycham for Alice, served in a flat champagne glass, with a gold rim and a leaping Bambi on the side.

Alice nursed the glass and twizzled the stem. Just holding it made her feel special. She watched the small, soft bubbles float to the surface. She giggled when they gently popped against her nose as she lifted the glass to her lips.

Alice had never drunk Babycham before. It would have been considered a hideous expense. Guinness was deemed good enough for everyone on the streets, including pregnant and nursing mothers.

The last time they met, Sean had shared with her one of Mary's letters from America and had watched Alice's face light up as she read it, enthralled by her description of Chicago, her everyday existence and the possibility of a different life for Sean.

Mary had written that the previous night, they had been to a drive-through cinema and watched a movie, *West Side Story*.

Alice could not even imagine what a drive-through looked like.

Mary also wrote about how she, her husband and Sean's brother, Eddie, were trying to persuade their old school friends to travel to America and join them, because they so desperately needed men. It broke their hearts to think of how many from home were still struggling, when they had so much to offer in America.

They had been awarded a construction contract to build a high school in Chicago. Mary had written,

> I cannot begin to tell you the work opportunity out here. We work hard and are honest and have a good name. We are turning down well-paid contracts every day because we cannot cope with the amount of work we are being asked to quote for.
>
> If it is the fare ye are concerned about, just tell me. We can and will pay for the whole family to travel out. It won't even be us paying, Sean, it will be accounted as a business expense.

'Can you imagine that?' said Sean to Alice. 'It won't even be them paying, with the business being so big. I don't understand why I am working my guts out day and night when a new world is waiting for us all, yet Brigid won't hear of it or even talk about us going, unless we pay for ourselves. Brigid knows that will take another two years of my having to beat some poor sod's head in every Friday night.'

Sean's voice began to rise in frustration but Alice didn't try to stop him. It gave her pleasure to know that he was venting his anger and frustration with Brigid. That behind Brigid's perfect facade of calm and organization, things were far from well.

They had arranged a further illicit meeting. The unspoken knowledge that they both shared the same dream drew them together. Neither questioned what they were doing but, for the first time, Alice felt a thrill of excitement as she looked at the kitchen clock and realized that, in just six hours, she would be sitting opposite Sean again. Whilst she supped with Sean, Brigid would be minding Joseph. The delicious, double treachery made Alice's eyes shine brightly with betrayal.

Earlier in the day, Alice had pushed open Brigid's back door with one hand, as she parked the navy-blue Silver Cross pram under the kitchen window and shouted through the door, 'Are you sure you don't mind having him?'

Brigid stood on her tiptoes and leant forward to look out of the kitchen window at Joseph in his Silver Cross, the Rolls-Royce of all prams.

'Holy Mary, is he asleep? Is that lucky, or what? Of course I don't mind having him, especially if he's asleep now,' she shouted, as she stacked the baby bottles she had been washing on the draining board and took a tea towel from the hook underneath the sink to wipe her hands dry.

Alice pushed the pram brake down to lock it and stepped into Brigid's kitchen, tucking her always errant wisps of carefully styled hair back into her criss-crossed hairgrips.

Anyone else would have thought twice about leaving an extra baby with Brigid this particular afternoon.

Brigid's youngest was teething. Brigid herself was exhausted, pale from lack of sleep, and the black bags under her eyes made her appear much older than she was.

'Mrs McGuire is at the shop and she will be back to help in a minute. We will be fine. Is he fed?'

'Yes, and he has only just dropped off in the pram on the way over,' said Alice, as she turned to face the mirror to catch a glimpse of herself. She took out some of the hairgrips and then slipped them back in again. 'God, I wish I had worn a hat today. The rain will pour any minute, I can tell.'

When Alice had first asked Brigid to look after Joseph, she had said she was visiting a sick friend whom she had once worked with at the hotel and that she would be gone for just a few hours.

It had been a simple and easy deceit, as long as she wasn't asked too many questions.

'Have ye time for a cuppa, Alice, before ye go? I'm desperate now, so I am. I haven't stopped all day. Shall I put the kettle on?'

Brigid was keen for Alice to stop and talk.

Mrs McGuire was as bad as Sean and had never stopped harping on about America.

Although Brigid would never mention it, she was upset that they never considered her own mammy and daddy in Cork. She missed them every day and the thought of travelling all the way to America, putting so many more miles between them, was more than she could bear to contemplate. Yet Sean and Mrs McGuire kept pushing and pushing.

The previous Sunday, there had been a mass at the cemetery in Cork for Brigid's brother who had died young in a tragic accident, fifteen years before. Brigid had been the only sibling not in attendance and she felt that guilt keenly.

Now Sean and his mammy wanted to take her further across the sea, miles away from all that she ached for, and she couldn't bear it.

Rather than moving away from Ireland, she yearned to return, to be again with everyone they knew and had grown up with. She wanted their daughters to love their country as she did and yet each year went by without a visit. The same excuse was always given.

The need to save money.

Mrs McGuire came to them to visit, so why would they struggle with all those children and the travelling?

Bloody Mrs McGuire.

Brigid thought she had everything under control and she did, most of the time. But when his mammy came to visit, her ability to keep their domestic routine, as well as Sean's levels of expectation, continuing as normal was stretched to the limit.

Alice said, 'I haven't time, sorry, Brigid, but I will later. I shan't be long and thanks again. I really appreciate it.'

Brigid stared at Alice's departing back and suddenly felt close to tears. She was not one for self-pity, which she regarded as a sign of over-indulgence, but she had been looking forward all day long to Alice calling in.

Just to talk about the things that kept every day ticking along in the rhythm of the four streets. Anything that was outside of her own four walls and ten children.

Alice was flying to the bus stop at the top of the road when she almost collided with Mrs McGuire and Peggy. The children followed them like a row of ducklings, bobbing along in their wake.

Peggy instantly sensed that all was not quite right.

'Well, hello, Alice, ye look grand indeed. Where are ye off to, then?'

There was no such thing as a secret in the four streets and what Peggy didn't know about everyone wasn't worth knowing. There was no way she would allow Alice to scuttle past as she was obviously trying to do, without a full explanation.

'I'm off back to the hotel to visit the housekeeper. She's a bit poorly. I trained her before I left and I knew her even before then. She has asked especially for me to visit and I thought it would be a bit peevish not to pop back to see her, seeing as how it's my fault she ended up with the job ...'

Alice was gabbling.

Peggy and Mrs McGuire stared and for a few seconds neither spoke as they digested Alice's words.

Alice realized she was gabbling. They realized she was gabbling.

She thought they could probably tell, just by looking at her, what she was up to.

Mrs McGuire stared at Alice with naked curiosity.

'Where is Joseph?' said Peggy. 'Has Kathleen come back home?'

'Brigid has him and I shan't be very long. I'll be back before he wakes.' And, with that, before they could answer, just as the Crosville bus came into sight, Alice shouted, just a little too loudly, 'I have to go, I don't want to miss the bus,' and then she was off round the corner, onto the bus and disappeared in a flash.

'Sick housekeeper, my eye,' said Peggy, as she and Mrs McGuire turned round and began walking again. 'Wearing stockings and lipstick at four o'clock? She must think we are stupid. That one's off for a job interview, I'll bet.'

'Either that, or she has a fancy man,' said Mrs McGuire, spitting on her handkerchief to wipe the cinder toffee from around her granddaughter's mouth.

Brigid's daughter squealed at her grandmother's saliva being wiped across her sticky face.

'Now shush, don't tell Mammy I bought ye sweets,' Mrs McGuire said to her earnestly. 'What yer mammy doesn't know won't hurt her, now, will it?'

Sean had run up the steps as soon as his shift finished and arrived at their pub in plenty of time. He was already sitting, waiting for Alice, on the studded burgundy-leather seats in the corner of the snug behind a dark-oak partition.

He had bought the usual Guinness for himself and a Babycham for Alice. Sean didn't want to touch his drink until she arrived. He lit a cigarette and, taking another out of the packet for Alice, propped it up against the ashtray, waiting.

It had begun to rain heavily and he wondered if she would still come or if the downpour of rain would make her think twice.

It would be the third time they had met and Sean knew it was now risky. However, it made no difference. The thrill he felt at the prospect of spending more time with Alice was greater than what he felt when the bell rang at the end of a bout to announce that he was the winner.

This was potentially far more dangerous.

He turned his gaze towards the half-frosted snug windows and felt grateful they were hidden. No one came in here before seven in the evening. They would be safe.

Noisy chatter from the bar had spilt over into the snug. Men were arriving in small groups, heading for the first drink of the day, followed by the women from Upper Parliament Street, looking for their first early trick of the night.

The air in the pub was a deep hazy blue from the smoke of Woodbines and Players, which mingled with the smell of yesterday's stale alcohol, soaked into the dark wooden floor. The fire provided enough heat and the apple-wood logs helped to transform smells that were odious in the cold light of morning into the more pleasant aroma of freshly roasted hops and warm beer by dusk.

Sean lit his cigarette and as he threw the match into the fire, he saw Alice run past the half-frosted window. He took a deep breath and tried to calm the knot in his stomach.

He had thought about nothing but meeting her again since the last time. She had filled his thoughts and his mind.

At work he had been unable to look Jerry in the eye and, without realizing, had fallen into a subdued mood, which made the other men on the docks wonder what was the matter with the big man. But a man's thoughts were his alone, so no one pried. Unlike the women.

Alice dashed into the snug, breathless and soaked. She had reasoned that if she ran fast from the bus stop to the pub, fewer raindrops would wreck the hairdo she had spent hours teasing into place.

She was wrong. Her fringe had long escaped her hairgrips and was plastered to her forehead. Drips ran down into her eyes, smudging the eyeliner and mascara she had applied with such precision.

She didn't care. As she ran into the snug, her heart melted. Sean instantly shot to his feet and removed his cap in honour of her presence. He was the only man ever to have done that for Alice and suddenly she felt like the woman she knew she always should have been.

Not like the one who had tricked Jerry into having sex with her to make him propose.

Alice removed her coat and Sean reached out his hand.

'Here, give it to me. I will hang it by the fire to dry. Make sure you don't forget it before ye leave.'

Alice relaxed and began to laugh. It was amazing to her how easily laughter came when she was with Sean.

'Sean, in this weather, only an idiot would forget a coat. Have you seen how heavy the rain is?'

Sean began to laugh with her as he poured her drink and then, both turning to face the fire, drinks in hands, they picked up the conversation where they had last left off and talked and talked.

Sean had never spoken so many words to Brigid in one day, ever.

Alice had never spoken so many words to anyone in her entire life, ever.

For the first time, Alice talked about her childhood.

She told Sean of her panic and need to flee the hotel and how scared she had been of ending her days alone, in a bedsit as the previous housekeeper had. She skimmed over how she had tricked Jerry into marrying her but praised how Kathleen had nursed her back into sanity. She talked of the tablets, the breakdown and her isolation and feeling like an outsider in the four streets. When she had finished, Sean leant across the table and took both of her hands in his.

Neither spoke. Alice stared down at her small hands enfolded in Sean's huge fingers. He rubbed the back of her hand with his thumb, then brought it up to his lips and placed one deeply tender kiss on the palm.

Alice's first instinct was to pull her hand away and she almost did. But Sean held on firmly.

'Don't,' he whispered. 'Enjoy this, you deserve it. You deserve this and more.'

Alice had never cried. She had never felt sad enough to cry. She lived somewhere in a half-world and had looked curiously at others who could.

She had stared at the tears that ran down Maura's cheeks, as they so often did these days, in slight wonderment. She had seen tears brim in Jerry's eyes, on the night Father James had been caught in Kitty's room. It seemed, at one point, as though everyone was shedding tears of one sort or another.

Everyone except for Alice, who hid in her bedroom and listened from a distance.

Now Alice felt her face flush. It was as though a torrent of emotion had escaped from somewhere inside and now swam through her veins, prickling the surface of her skin and forcing the tears into her eyes. She quickly blinked them back.

'God, what is happening, Sean?' she whispered, although they were the only two people in the snug.

Sean smiled. 'I haven't a clue, but I know I have to see you again and soon.'

Alice wrenched her hand away and jumped out of her seat with a yelp. It was dark outside. They had been talking for three hours.

The bubble of warmth burst in a second and was replaced with dread.

'What am I to do? Oh my God, Sean, it's dark. Brigid will think I have deserted her and left her with the children, and Jerry will be sending out a search party.'

Sean had already reached for her coat and was helping Alice into it. He looked at the clock on the snug wall.

'The bus will be here in five minutes, let's run.'

'What, together, are you sure?'

'Aye, no one will see us. It's dark now. Brigid thinks I have been at the boxing club.'

Alice picked up her bag and they both flew out of the pub swing doors and ran down the road, Sean holding tightly onto Alice's hand as they did so.

It was a Friday, which was fish day, and Mrs McGuire had decided Brigid needed a break and to treat the family to a fish and chip supper. She was cross that Alice had left Brigid with Joseph to look after and had let her daughter-in-law know exactly how she felt.

'I don't ever see anyone giving ye a break, Brigid. Seems to me like you're always being put upon by others.'

'I have you here, Mrs McGuire. You give me a break,' said Brigid, who was feeling a little sorry for herself.

Lifting Brigid's wicker basket down from the peg and placing in it a pudding basin still warm from the range, covered by a pan lid, Mrs McGuire tied a headscarf around the curlers Peggy had put into her hair earlier in the day, before heading off to the chip shop.

It was the first time ever she had worn curlers outdoors and she felt as though she looked very conspicuous.

'When Sean sees me in these, he'll be asking me what radio station I can pick up,' she laughed as she tied the scarf under her chin. 'Ye would never see our Mary in these. She visits to a salon every week now, so she does. It is different altogether over there in America, Brigid.'

And with that, much to Brigid's relief, she was gone.

Mrs McGuire loved the chippy. If she was honest, she loved the chippy more than she did Brigid.

There was no chippy back home, although there had been talk of one for some time.

The prospect of a chippy in the village was partly inspired by the envy of Mrs McGuire's neighbours, whom she loved to regale with stories of the rare delicacies to be found at Mr Chan's.

Saveloys. Oh, how she loved the way that word rolled off the tongue.

Was there ever a more exotic word?

'In Liverpool, I often pop to the chippy for saveloys,' she would say to her neighbours.

'God in heaven, s-a-v-e-l-o-y-s. What would they be?' her neighbours would demand to know.

As it was a Friday night, the chip shop was busy and Mrs McGuire felt mildly irritated as she noticed that the queue was almost to the shop door. Taking her place at the end, she stepped into the brightly lit shop full of hot steam and chatter and untied her headscarf to shake away the surface water. As she fixed it back into place with a knot under her chin, she keenly looked around her to see who else could afford to be in the queue.

Some of the women whose families she knew from back home shouted out greetings.

'Is Sean fighting again tonight, Mrs McGuire? He's on a winning streak, so he is, we will all be putting money on him soon.'

The fish and chip shop was a luxury and Mrs McGuire was surprised to see so many people there. Some of these women have more money than sense, she thought to herself.

'No, not tonight,' she replied. 'He's running short of lads willing to take him on. It's a practice night tonight, so don't waste ye money, he will definitely beat himself.'

She wiped a circle in the steam on the window so she could peer out into the street. The sulphur-yellow street lights had transformed the dirty wet black pavements to the colour of golden marmalade.

She heard the familiar ding-ding of the bell on the bus across the street and her inbred nosiness made her squint to see if she knew anyone alighting.

She recognized Sean instantly. Of course she did. She was his mother and there were very few men in Liverpool as tall or as well built as Sean.

She watched his athletic leap from the platform of the still-moving bus and thought, typical Sean, always in a hurry. As he swung down from the pole and landed on the pavement, he reached up to help someone else down. It looked like a woman, but Mrs McGuire couldn't really see. She leant forward, with her face almost pressed against the window, and wiped furiously at the greasy glass until it squeaked.

'What you want, lady?' Johnny Chan shouted. It was the third time he had asked for her order.

Flustered, Mrs McGuire reached into the basket and handed him the pudding basin with the enamel pan lid for the peas. 'Three fried fish, three saveloys, five peas and five chips, please, Johnny.'

She stepped back over to the window to see the back of the bus disappear down the road, but there was no sign of her son.

With the parcel of fish and chips safely wrapped up in newspaper, and resting on top of her pudding basin, she hurried back towards Nelson Street.

As she neared the top of the entry, Little Paddy flew out of the newsagent's, with his da's ciggies in his hands, and crashed straight into Mrs McGuire, almost knocking the basket straight out of her hand.

'Sorry, Mrs McGuire,' Little Paddy apologized, as he ran past.

'Gosh, Paddy, ye are in a dreadful hurry,' she shouted. 'Look where ye are going! Ye nearly knocked me off my feet.'

If Little Paddy looked where he was going, his da would accuse him of dawdling and give him a belt. He hated it if there were lots of people in the shop. It made his breath short with anxiety and then he couldn't run as fast as he wanted.

Only yards away, Sean and Alice stood in the middle of the entry, each fully aware they were playing with fire. The knowledge thrilled them. All around they could hear the familiar sounds of domestic street life: dogs barking, babies crying, mothers shouting, outhouse toilets flushing.

The only illumination was from the moon and stars, plus the reflections on the pavements of light tumbling from kitchens or bedroom windows, across backyards and over the entry wall.

Occasionally a child ran across the entry, like a river rat darting from one backyard to the next, sent from a house without, to borrow from a house that had.

Light to dark. Yard to yard.

The same sounds repeated daily as they had been for generations.

Different children. Different dogs. Same cacophony of life.

Sean and Alice were startled as suddenly, out of the darkness, a young voice shouted, 'Hiya, Sean, hiya, Alice,' making them both jump out of their skins.

They stepped aside as Little Paddy rushed past and they stared aghast at his departing back. Alice came back to reality with a thud.

'I have to leave now. Wait until you see me leave your house before you go in,' she said, beginning to move away.

'Monday,' whispered Sean urgently, taking hold of her hand and pulling her back. 'Say you will come again on Monday.' He brushed the damp hair back from her face with his free hand.

'I don't know if I can. I can't ask Brigid to look after Joseph again, can I?'

She looked down at her wet leather boot and kicked the cobblestones.

Scamp, Little Paddy's skinny, shaggy-haired grey dog, ran past. He had been waiting loyally outside the newsagent's for Little

Paddy and had hung around, sniffing Mrs McGuire's basket, until he realized no chips were flying his way.

Wherever Little Paddy went, Scamp went too.

Alice and Sean, searching for a reason to delay their parting, watched the departing dog until he was swallowed by the night.

Alice had made up her mind. 'If Kathleen is back, then yes, I will,' she whispered, looking into his eyes.

Sean pulled her in to him, gave her one deep, long kiss and then, shocked by his own boldness, stepped quickly back.

Alice lost her breath and thought she might faint. She had been kissed. Without trickery or plotting or devious manipulation. And, swaying, she laid a hand on Sean's arm to steady herself.

Turning quickly, with her hands thrust deeply into her pockets, Alice walked away, looking back once at his grinning face. It was as though he now knew something he hadn't before and whatever that knowledge was, it had made him very happy.

She couldn't keep the grin from her own face and as she smiled back, she felt a heat slowly rise inside her, threatening to erupt into joyous and uncontrollable laughter.

And then, as the terrible fear of being caught once more took hold, she ran like the wind, in through Brigid's back gate.

To Brigid. Sean's wife. To collect her son.

Sean waited and watched. Suddenly, he wanted to tell everyone. He had fallen in love, with Alice.

The thought that she was running to his house to collect her baby from his wife did not make him feel in the least bit guilty.

Guilt and honour had been tackled and beaten by exhilaration and desire. The sense of peril made him feel alive and euphoric, just as he did in the seconds before he was about to step into the ring.

Now the thought that he would not see Alice until Monday made him groan.

How could he wait a whole forty-eight hours to talk to the woman whose passion for life matched his own?

It seemed like an eternity.

As she turned the corner into Sean's backyard, Alice momentarily held onto the latch before she clicked the gate shut.

'Oh my God, this is madness, you crazy woman,' she whispered, leaning her forehead against the wet, cold, splintered wood.

She turned round to look in through the kitchen window and saw Brigid's outline sway as she rocked Joseph in her arms. It was a touching scene. But all Alice could think of was how long it would be until Monday when she could see Brigid's husband again.

Over at the Priory, Sister Evangelista had pulled her car right up to the front door. Switching off the engine, she took the crisp white linen handkerchief which lay on the passenger seat and blew her nose. Through the windscreen, she surveyed the Priory garden well lit by the almost full moon.

Her gaze wandered over the low wall towards the towering monuments and effigies standing in the graveyard. Unable to help herself, she took a moment and fixed her gaze upon the spot where Father James had been found. Fog clung to the gravestone, creating an eerie scene.

The bishop had become concerned by the number of people calling at the Priory to speak to Daisy and had dispatched Sister Evangelista, at this ungodly time of night, to move her across the road into the convent.

The police had said that they would be at the Priory tomorrow morning to interview Daisy.

The bishop had wanted to know why.

'I cannot be sure, Father,' Sister Evangelista told him, 'but I am almost certain it has something to do with Molly Barrett. She's been spending a great deal of time at the Priory. It cannot be a coincidence, surely?'

'What did the stupid fecking girl tell the woman?' he roared. His temper terrified Sister Evangelista.

She didn't like the way the bishop was speaking to her. They were co-conspirators, both doing their best to cover up the evil work Father James had been engaged in under their very noses. Did the bishop not know that Sister Evangelista was in turmoil? She had loved Father James, whom she thought the most perfect of men. She was struggling, finding it all so difficult. When she wasn't dealing with this mess, she was deep in prayer, asking the Lord to give her the strength she needed to cope. The bishop's bad temper was the last straw.

She had cause to spend a great deal of time on the phone to him recently. Her conscience would not let her stray too far into the reaches of fantasy, but of this she was certain: Kitty Doherty had disappeared, allegedly for a holiday. In all her years, the furthest she had ever known a Doherty to venture from the four streets had been to the Formby pine dunes on the church charabanc, to celebrate the Coronation.

She was also certain the girl was pregnant and there was a murdered priest, with the devil's own work hiding in his desk and cupboards, who had been in and out of the Doherty house like a demon's whisper.

All of this, she had discussed with the bishop.

'I have prayed long and hard, Father, and I am very sure that all of this information would help the police. The Lord knows, it is weighing me down badly.'

The bishop was none too happy with this suggestion.

'Sister, we had a bad man as our priest in your church. Do ye know how much damage would be done to the authority of the churches across Liverpool, if not the whole British Isles, should this information become public knowledge? At the very least, the church would be boarded up, and the convent and the school closed. Is that what we want to happen? And as for what Rome might decide to do to us personally ...'

'But what about Kitty Doherty, Bishop?'

'What about her, Sister? A sick child has been sent back home to Ireland for a holiday and a rest. God willing, she will return cured. Sister, ye will keep all of these fanciful notions inside your own head and ye and I, we will give thanks to God that he sent us, people he knows he can trust, to do the right thing. We have made the right decision to put our responsibilities first. Let the police do their job, we shall do ours.'

Sister Evangelista wasn't at all sure that they were doing the right thing. Her heart was in conflict but, as usual, she replied obediently, 'Yes, Father.'

The driveway flooded with light as the Priory door opened. There, framed in the doorway, was Daisy, with her bag, waiting to leave.

Daisy was happy that she would be sleeping at the convent and leaving the huge empty Priory, with its damp, black bricks, hugged by lichen and creeping ivy. The elusive whispers, which began as night fell, had always unsettled her and now Sister Evangelista would save her from it all.

The demons outside and in.

He had been told to ask for telephone extension twenty-four, which was the mortuary, and to say that he needed to speak to the technician about an inquest hearing in the morning.

The time and the place were always the same when one or other of the tight-knit circle needed to make contact with Austin.

Austin stood by the phone and waited for the call. This was the only place in the hospital where he was unlikely to be disturbed. The technician, always keen to leave before he should, at six-thirty, had no objection when Austin told him he would cover for him.

Stanley was in the porters' lodge. He and Austin were both on the late shift and working until ten. Stanley worried Austin. He seemed unable to act as though nothing had occurred.

To carry on as normal.

'Pull yerself together, man,' Austin had told him only yesterday. 'Have the bizzies been? Has anyone contacted us? Have we heard a thing? No, we haven't, now shut yer gob and behave. Nothing has happened other than you looking and behaving as guilty as hell.'

Stanley was no fool and shot back at him, 'Are you fucking joking? One of our own has been murdered in a graveyard, had his dick hacked off and fed to a cat. We have no idea who did it, he's in our group and you say nothing has happened! How do we know that the person who murdered him isn't coming for us? How do we know that the police won't be led to us, when they are looking for whoever murdered the priest? How do we know that the priest didn't keep all our photos in his stupid fucking Priory? Austin, you are fucking mental. We are in deep shit, mate, and you had better find out what the hell is going on or I'm off.'

But Austin was quite sure that the father wouldn't have kept the photographs in the Priory. None of them kept anything at home. All their photographs were in the hospital, in a locker under the name John Smith. No one asked who John Smith was. No one ever needed to know.

The shrill ring of the phone bounced back off the cold mortuary tiles, filling the room and sounding much louder than it actually was.

The voice on the other end sounded troubled.

'Is that ye, Austin? Are ye alone?'

'Yes, I am,' Austin replied.

'The police are questioning the girl, Daisy, tomorrow.'

'Are you fucking joking? Why?'

It was Daisy who let them into the Priory when members of the circle visited to drop off films or pictures, and the priest had even let Austin visit Daisy when she first arrived in Liverpool. Stanley only liked boys and Daisy had been almost too old for Austin, but he had used her for a year or so.

The Priory had been the best cover for them all. No one would have suspected a priest, or so they had thought.

Although he didn't need to, he dropped his voice to a whisper.

'Do the police have the pictures? Can we be identified? Do they know we let the priest into the hospital? Are you running?' His questions chased one another down the line.

'Don't be stupid,' the bishop replied. 'How can I run? Do I not need to find out what is going on? They don't have the pictures. I put them meself into the incinerator at the convent, with the help of the sister.'

Austin breathed a sigh of relief. They were safe.

'In that case, why do the police want to interview the housekeeper?'

'She apparently had a long chat to one of the neighbours, a Molly Barrett, from Nelson Street. The next day, the police were at her house for most of the day.'

'Look, we didn't murder the priest, I keep telling Stanley. That is what the police are looking for. A murderer. Not us.'

The mortuary door clicked open. Austin almost jumped out of his skin as Stanley stepped in.

'Aye, but we don't know who killed him. The sister has a notion the Doherty house is connected and the Kitty girl is pregnant. We don't know if any of that is true. My worry is that their enquiries will lead them to us and the group.'

There was silence for a moment as Austin accepted a cigarette from Stanley and bent his head to take a light.

'Well, you keep finding out what is happening and we will do our bit here. We need to make sure that we shut down any clues that may lead them to us, don't we, Bishop?'

'True enough,' the bishop replied. 'Now I have a plan to move the girl back to Dublin, out of the way as soon as possible and I need your help.'

As Sister Evangelista helped Daisy load her bags into the car, she chatted to her about the police request to interview her.

'Have ye any idea why, Daisy?'

'I haven't, Sister.'

'Did ye say anything to Molly, when she visited, that might give ye a clue?'

But Daisy just stared vacantly out of the window and didn't reply.

Alice saw Jerry first, before he saw her. He was sitting at Brigid's table, tucking into a plate of food. He looked so natural, chatting to Brigid as she washed up at the sink, that a stranger looking in would have thought it was something Jerry did every night of his life. Joseph was now perched on his knee, trying to grab the fork before it reached Jerry's mouth.

'Oh Lordy, what are you doing here?' Alice exclaimed, in a voice far too high-pitched. 'I left a stew in the oven at home.'

Before Jerry could answer, she reached out for Joseph and turned to speak to Brigid. 'Has he been good?' she asked.

'He's been grand, no trouble at all,' said Brigid, moving over to wipe the hands of her own tribe, who sat round the table.

'Thank you, Brigid, you have been fantastic.'

'I had baked a pie, but Mrs McGuire went off to the fish and chip shop. Jerry didn't know if you had left anything for him, so I gave him the pie. Sean will no doubt have that as well as the fish and chips when he finally arrives home, being the greedy pig that he is now.' Brigid was grinning. Jerry was still tucking into the pie.

Joseph was nestled against Alice's chest, half asleep.

Two of Brigid's babies were asleep in the pram, which was where they would stay until their elder sister was old enough to be transferred from her cot to a bed.

Everything is so normal, thought Alice, and yet only feet away I have just kissed your husband.

She wanted to laugh out loud.

'How was the housekeeper?' asked Jerry, who was genuinely interested.

'Oh, well, not that great, I'm afraid. I would like to call again but we will see. It's having the time. Not that easy at the moment.'

'Not at all,' said Brigid, generously rushing in. 'I will have Joseph any time, so I will. It's not a problem at all for me.'

Alice began to fake her protest but Brigid cut her off. Brigid was playing into Alice's hands, beautifully.

'I won't hear a word, now shush. If ye need to go again, just bring him over to Auntie Brigid.'

Alice didn't feel a shred of guilt. Not a flicker of remorse.

What she did feel was jealousy. It had been brewing since the first time she had met Sean alone. And now, at this moment, in Brigid's kitchen of perfect pastry and well-behaved children, it was stronger than ever. Alice was jealous of the Brigid who in just a few moments would fuss round Sean as soon as he walked in and slipped into their ordered and happy family life.

A realization dawned upon Alice. Sean was two different men. There was the man she had come to know, who had sat in the pub with her, and the man he would become when he walked into his own home and sat at his own hearth.

She didn't want to be there when that happened.

Claiming Sean as her own would be easy. Removing him from the grip of his wife, daughters, mother and his comfortable domestic routine would be much more difficult.

'Jerry, I am taking Joseph over to bed, he is almost asleep,' she said, pulling back the pram quilt and laying Joseph down.

As Alice fastened the studs on the side of the pram hood, Jerry spoke while he was still eating. 'I'm coming, I'm coming,' he spluttered, shovelling the last forkful down, and thinking that whatever Alice had prepared for supper would not be a patch on Brigid's pastry.

'Would ye like some on a plate to take home, Jer?' asked Brigid innocently, not realizing that Alice would perceive the offer as a direct attack upon her competence as a wife.

Jerry, desperate to say yes, looked to Alice for approval.

'No thanks, Brigid. He has to eat the food I prepared at home yet.'

Alice locked eyes with Brigid and smiled as she spoke. A thin smile. Her mind elsewhere.

Thinking. Brooding. Plotting.

'Ah, 'tis the only way to a man's heart, making him good food, I can guarantee that, so I can,' said Brigid as she stood with one hand on the back door and the other in her apron front pocket. She cut a lonely silhouette framed in the light, watching them both walk down the path together. ''Tis how I caught my Sean. Once he had tasted my pastry, he didn't stand a chance,' Brigid chuckled.

'Really?' Alice threw the reply over her shoulder, laced with more than a hint of sarcasm. 'I'll have to remember that one for the future.'

Mrs McGuire walked down the entry and stopped as Sean loomed into sight. 'Sean,' she called out. 'What are ye doing, stood there?'

Sean looked at his mother and was speechless.

How could he say, 'I'm waiting for Alice to leave my house so that I can go home'? His mouth flapped open and closed again while he desperately tried to form a sensible sentence. They both heard the back gate click shut and turned together to see Alice and Jerry walking towards them.

'Hello, Alice, Jerry,' shouted Sean. He was playing for time while he thought what to say to his mother.

'Hello, Sean. Hello, Mrs McGuire,' said Jerry. 'Jesus, Sean, ye have the best pie waiting for ye in your house. I almost stuffed the lot down and left ye nowt.'

'Kathleen will be delighted to hear that the best pie you have ever tasted was made by Brigid,' whispered Alice sharply under her breath to Jerry, just as both men roared with laughter.

Without realizing it, Sean's eyes were fixed on Alice.

Hers gave nothing away. Mrs McGuire forgot to ask again why she had found her son standing alone, kicking the entry wall, rather than in his own home.

Little Paddy ran in through the back door, shouting, 'Mammy, Da, I have the ciggies.'

'What took ye so feckin' long, ye lazy article?' grumbled Paddy, as he took the fags. 'I bet ye fecking dawdled all the way, didn't ye?'

'I did not, Da, I ran all the way.'

'Ran, my arse, ye bleeding liar.'

'Da, I did, I ran.'

Big Paddy cuffed Little Paddy across the ear with one hand whilst he snatched the ciggies from him with the other.

He had run out of cigarettes an hour earlier and had been pacing the floor, glancing at the back door every thirty seconds, waiting for Little Paddy to return.

The dog lay on the floor, with his tail tucked in and his ears down, as close to Little Paddy as he could possibly be.

Little Paddy began to whimper.

'Stop crying like a babby, Paddy,' said Peggy as she walked into the room.

'I can't help it. Da just hit me over the ear and called me a liar. He said I didn't run home with his cigs, an' I did.'

'If yer da says ye didn't, ye didn't and don't cheek him.'

'I did, I'm not a liar, Mammy, an' Alice and Sean can prove it, so they can.'

'Alice and Sean?' said Peggy. 'How can Alice and Sean prove it?'

Big Paddy was taking out a ciggie and putting a second one behind his ear, ready to go before the first one burnt out.

'Because they both saw me in the entry and I spoke to them. They saw me running, so they did.'

'Alice and Sean?' said Peggy for the second time. 'What were they doing in the entry then?'

Peggy had begun washing the dishes and was rinsing a dinner plate under the running tap.

'They was kissing,' whimpered Little Paddy.

Peggy had leant over to lay the plate onto the draining board. Paddy had struck a match to light his ciggie. Both looked at each other in shock as the plate slipped from her hand and smashed into pieces all over the kitchen floor.

## Chapter Seventeen

Kitty and Nellie stood anxiously waiting, just inside the open front door, excited and holding hands, sheltering from the midges. The light was fading fast when they spotted the lights of the farm van trundling down the Ballymara road.

As it passed, it illuminated the rhododendrons on the opposite side of the road. Kitty wondered if her mother would be as taken with their size and wildness as she had been.

Liam's younger brother, Patrick, who was driving, teased both girls, slowing down just outside the front gate, then grinning and waving through the window, before speeding onwards towards the McMahons' farm to turn the van round.

Kitty ran to wait at the gate. Patrick and Kathleen had been to Dublin to collect Maura and had left long before the girls had woken.

Kitty could scarcely contain her excitement. Now she and Maura hugged and held onto each other tightly, before walking down the path and in through the front door.

The fire had been stacked high and the flames made the kitchen brighter and warmer than usual. The smells of burning peat and freshly baked bread competed with each other. Maeve, who was moving the dishes of food around the table to make space for the salmon, quickly removed her apron. Glancing in the mirror hanging above the sink, she pushed the stray strands of auburn hair behind her ears and, licking the top of both index fingers, ran them quickly across her wayward eyebrows.

Both of the dogs were fast asleep, stretched out on their sides in front of the fire, paws covered in the softly drifting peat ash. Their legs were twitching in a dream world, chasing rabbits.

'At last,' beamed Maeve, scooping Maura into a hug.

Maeve would never betray the fact that she had been more than a little worried about Maura's arrival. For Maura lived in Liverpool. A city of sophistication. With bright lights and modern ways. With music and culture and fancy clothes. Liverpool had everything Mayo didn't. Maeve had heard there was a clothes store called C&A, stocking every fashion you could find in the magazines, and a Woolworth's bigger than any building Maeve had ever seen. The doctor's wife also came from Liverpool and she had proudly shown Maeve the china she had bought in a store called Lewis's.

But one look at Maura told Maeve she had nothing to fear.

'Bernadette's lovely friend. I have heard so much about ye,' said Maeve, linking her arm through Maura's.

A look of sadness crossed Nellie's face. Then came that familiar ache in her diaphragm. The deep loneliness she could never explain. The longing for a mother she never knew. She wanted to plead with Maeve, *Say her name again. Please, say it like you used to say it to her.*

'The child has been pacing around all the day, looking up the road waiting for ye, so she has.'

Maeve grinned at Kitty, who nuzzled in and tightened her arms round her mother's waist, sheepishly burying her face in Maura's shoulder.

Kitty inhaled deeply the scent of her mother, the familiar mixture of Nelson Street and cigarette smoke. She was calmed. Everything was better than it had been and it would be even better, now that Maura was here.

Nellie watched Kitty hugging her mother.

She had Alice, but Alice had never hugged Nellie.

She looked at the expression on Kitty's face. Nellie knew she had never felt whatever it was Kitty was feeling right now.

Nana Kathleen had been watching too and now she put an arm gently round Nellie's shoulder, kissed the top of her head and asked, 'Are ye glad to see me home, or what, young lady? And where's me kiss, for goodness' sake?'

Almost as soon as Maura walked into the house, Liam's brother, Finn, arrived with his wife Colleen, as did the McMahons from the farm next door. Each had seen Patrick's van pass by or turn at their door. Julia, Nana Kathleen's sister, and her husband Tom, also pulled up in their van outside.

The noise in the kitchen was deafening, as everyone made Maura feel welcome.

Kitty was keen to hear the news from home.

'Has Sister Evangelista said anything about my being away?' she asked nervously.

'Not at all,' Maura replied gently. 'The sister has her hands full, mind. They have Daisy from the Priory in the sick bed at the convent and she has been there for days. No one knows what is up with her, but she has taken to her bed, so she has, and they all seem in much of a dither.'

Maura didn't add that the police had been at the convent every day, wanting to interview Daisy, and were being given short shrift by Sister Evangelista. This news gave Maura some comfort. What on earth could she possibly say to the police that would present any danger to them?

In honour of their guest, Liam had opened the bottle of whiskey, usually kept until after the harvest. The weather had been so good of late that the village was preparing for the harvest to begin the next day.

*

As usual, Kitty woke not long after falling asleep.

She wondered if the night would ever come when she slept all the way through. Now she strained to hear if anyone else was awake.

Maeve, Kathleen and Maura were still in the kitchen, peeling potatoes and placing them in a pan big enough to bathe an average toddler. Their voices were muffled but comforting enough to send Kitty straight back to sleep.

'It was very plush,' said Kathleen, as she plopped another peeled potato into the cold water in the pan. 'I have never been inside anything like it. Polished wooden floors, a big oak press and very smart rugs and curtains. I wasn't allowed to see the bedrooms. The Reverend Mother said no one is allowed to, but she assured me that the beds were very comfortable. If the bedrooms are anything like the morning room and the hall and stairs, it'll be the poshest room Kitty will ever have slept in.'

'Did they seem kind enough, though, Kathleen? I don't care about posh. God, the child is used to nothing like posh, it's kindness she needs.'

Maura sat down, wiping her hands on the clean apron Maeve had loaned her.

'She was the Reverend Mother, Maura, more businesslike, I would say, but the young novices, they seemed lovely, now, and I'm sure they will be the ones Kitty has more contact with.'

'And what is this Rosie O'Grady like, then, who will be delivering the baby? I know she is your sister-in-law, Kathleen, but is she a good woman?'

'She's Julia's sister-in-law, not mine, and a very well-qualified midwife. What is more, she will keep her trap shut.' Kathleen rubbed the top of Maura's arm comfortingly as she said this. 'I wish the boat had come in earlier and ye could have come to see the Abbey with me, Maura, but this morning was the only time the Reverend Mother had free and time is short.'

Maeve looked at both women. Her heart was heavy and she hated the conversation. With no children of her own, she would love to have adopted Kitty's baby but Liam wouldn't hear of it. He was still hoping, even though Maeve was approaching forty, that one day soon they would be blessed with their own son.

'Let Kitty have tomorrow, before ye tell her,' Maeve said. 'Kitty and Nellie have looked forward to the harvest so much and they will have great fun. If ye ask me, I think one or two of the village lads may have their eyes on our little ladies.'

Kathleen poured away the cold water from the two big hunks of bacon in which they had been soaking all day, and put the pan under the tap to refill the pan.

'Aye, well, they may do, but Kitty is just beginning to show. We can't wait too long before she is taken to the convent. She can have the harvest and then I think we have to take her. But we will let her have her last day here without worrying about what the next will bring. She doesn't need to know yet.'

'We can all drink to that,' said Maeve, with a wink, emptying out the remainder of the whiskey into the glasses.

They sat on the settle in front of the fire. Maeve kicked an ember out of the fire, then jabbing the poker into the flaming peat, she lifted it up to light her last cigarette of the day. The heat from the embers almost singed her eyelashes and tears sprang to her eyes. Wiping her face with her apron, she passed her cigarette along to the other two so that they could light their own.

Picking up her glass, Maeve said in a quiet voice, 'Who says it's a man's life, eh?'

In unison, all three lifted their glasses, took a sip of the whiskey from one hand and a large pull on their cigarette from the other.

'I hope bloody Liam is asleep when I get into bed and isn't going to give me a hard time, looking for his wicked way before the morning. I could do without it tonight,' said Maeve as she exhaled a long blue thread of smoke.

'He's his father's son, Maeve, so ye have no chance,' said Kathleen. 'Be prepared.'

All three laughed, took another drink, and stared into the fire.

Maura wanted to tell them that she had seen Bernadette standing at the farmhouse door when she had arrived. That she had felt a cold hand slip into hers as she walked from the van to the front door. Would they think she was mad if she did?

Bernadette, thought Maura, our lovely Bernadette.

In the comforting silence between the three women, Maura felt cold air pass in front of her and rest right next to her. She knew that, joining them, sitting with them, in their motherly, loving silence, was the friend, sister and daughter-in-law they had all loved best of all.

The flaming red sky of the previous evening kept its promise and the sun rose early, burning away the river mist, ensuring that there would not be one drop of soft, west coast rain to spoil the harvest.

Kitty stood at the back door to the farmhouse, the milking pail in one hand, the other shading her eyes, as she strained to look up the hill. This morning's weather would put everyone in high spirits.

Maeve appeared in the passageway and bent to take the pail handle and helped Kitty carry the milk into the dairy shed.

'People will start arriving soon so get your breakfast now, quick, young lady. There will be no chance at all to stop this morning once the cutting gets under way.'

Maeve had been up since five, preparing breakfast early, and had kept it warm on large enamel plates on the range shelf next to the fire, where the big pan of potatoes began to simmer.

'It will take at least an hour for the potatoes to come to the boil,' said Maeve when she saw Kitty looking at the huge pan. 'And still we have the cabbages to cook.'

Maeve was red-cheeked and flustered, but it was all a dramatic effect. She had everything beautifully under control.

The two big hunks of bacon had been simmering on the fire overnight. It had taken all Colleen and Maeve's strength to lift the pan together and heave out the bacon haunches, which were now cooling on the huge wooden table, ready to be carved up for the lunch.

'That bacon looks grand, Maeve,' said Liam, trying to pull a slice off as Maeve walked past.

'Keep yer hands off, ye thieving bugger,' said Maeve, slapping him on his cap.

Liam and the men were tucking into large plates of eggs, sausage and fried potatoes. Kitty's morning sickness had well and truly passed, but she still couldn't eat the sausages.

'God, they smell just like the pig stall. I'll be sick if I eat them,' she said to Nellie.

Now they heard a strange noise coming from outside.

Nellie ran to the door. 'It's the thresher, the horses are pulling the thresher.'

Kitty was amazed by the sight that greeted her.

Men, women and children were walking across the peat, carrying their pitchforks and scythes, following a horse-drawn contraption in the form of a square wooden box on wheels.

Everyone from indoors moved into the fields to greet those who had arrived and, within what seemed like minutes, they were all at work. The cutter moved slowly as others began on the outside edges with scythes. The oats were put through the thresher to separate the grain, then the stalks were gathered up with pitchforks and stacked six feet high.

The women remained in the kitchen, preparing the food to be carried out to the barn at midday.

'Run and put these cloths on the hay bales in the barn now, please, girls,' said Maeve. 'Nellie, you remember what we did last time you were here, don't you?'

The girls ran into the barn and shifted around the bales Patrick had pulled down for them earlier, arranging them into seats, with eight bales in the middle to serve as a table.

'Can we go to the field now, Maeve?' the girls shouted through the back door when they had finished.

'Aye, off you go and help Uncle Liam and the others and, mind, keep yer hands off them lads,' said Maeve with a wink at Nellie, who blushed bright red.

And off they ran to catch up with Patrick who was supervising the building of the straw stacks.

'Can we help, Patrick?' said Nellie.

'Not with this. I have enough lads. I have to round off the tops so that the rain runs off and doesn't wet the straw.'

'What shall we do then?' Nellie was jumping up and down by now, almost taking his pitchfork out of his hand.

'Aye, go on, then,' he said, handing Nellie the fork. 'Gather up the straw from the thresher and pile it up onto the cart Jacko is harnessed up to. The cart will be moving over here in a few minutes. I see yer man, Aengus, is talking to Kitty, then?'

Nellie looked over and saw the McMahons' nephew had stopped work and was chatting to Kitty.

Aengus had spotted Kitty as she ran into the field. He rested on his pitchfork and thought that he had never seen a young girl look so happy.

'Morning, miss,' said Aengus, raising his cap as soon as he was within earshot of Kitty.

While Nellie had run on ahead to talk to Patrick, Kitty had stopped to tie her bootlace and was squatting down amid the freshly cut stalks.

'So, how do ye like Bangor then?'

Kitty straightened and squinted in the sunlight, her hair loose and hanging about her shoulders. His accent was so strong that she could hardly understand a word he said.

''Scuse me,' said Kitty. 'I'm sorry, I'm not from round here.'

'I know,' said Aengus. 'That's why I'm asking, how do ye like it in Bangor?'

'Oh, I'm sorry,' said Kitty, laughing sheepishly, 'you mean Bangornevin?'

'Aye, I do, but no one ever says the Nevin. Unless ye are visiting from Liverpool, of course, and then ye would be daft enough to say it.'

He was teasing Kitty and grinned as he spoke.

Kitty half grinned back and looked down, as though studying the freshly cut field. The smell of the fresh straw made her nostrils flare. The grain dust shone like gold splinters in the shimmering sunlight and, once again, she had need to shield her eyes as her fingers intertwined into an arch above her brow.

'What's ye name then?' he asked.

He had replaced his cap and was leaning forward with both hands on the top of his pitchfork. He swayed gently from side to side as he studied her face, waiting for a response.

She saw that his eyes were as blue as his hair was red and the contrast was startling. His complexion was pale and freckled. Kitty noticed a matt sheen on his skin where the grain dust had stuck to his sweat.

A brown cravat was tied in a neat knot at his throat and his white shirt fell open at the neck, billowing against his braces as the wind pulled it free from his ragged-bottomed trousers. Even after a short time, Kitty was aware that a neat trouser hem was a rare thing in Bangornevin and yet she had seen Maeve, night after night, sewing them up by the light of the lamp when everyone was in bed.

Kitty averted her eyes, aware that she had been staring.

'Well?' he asked again and Kitty noticed he was grinning from ear to ear.

'My name's Kitty.'

'Kitty. That's a nice, normal name. Mine's Aengus.'

Kitty laughed. 'Well, Aengus is normal enough. Aengus.' She let it slowly roll off her tongue. 'We have just learnt a poem in school called "A Song of Wandering Aengus",' said Kitty.

She looked thoughtful as she scampered around inside her own memory in search of the poem, and, unable to find it, instead spoke his name out loud.

Again.

'Aengus. 'Tis a nice name.'

He began to speak in a slower, softer voice:

*'But something rustled on the floor*
*And someone called me by my name:*
*It had become a glimmering girl*
*With apple blossom in her hair.'*

He looked at Kitty and smiled. She felt her stomach flip.

'If ye go to school in Mayo, Yeats is pushed down your throat, or ye can't pass the leaving cert,' he explained.

'Leaving cert? What on earth is that?'

'It's hard work, that's what it is.'

Nellie ran up alongside and took hold of Kitty's hand.

'Time to start putting the food out,' she said.

Kitty was reluctant to move away.

She liked this boy. She wanted to speak with him for longer. Kitty had never talked to a boy. Boys were like another species at school. She never imagined one would specially talk to her. Why would he do that?

'Ah, food. Well, we will need that soon, to be sure. I will see ye at the barn then, ladies.' Aengus raised his cap and walked away.

As soon as he was out of earshot Kitty said, 'Oh God, was he gorgeous or not? Tell me, Nellie, look back, is he watching me walk away? Go ahead, look.'

Aengus was whacking the boys, who were mercilessly teasing him, with his tweed cap. As he looked up, he saw Nellie looking and lifted his cap high in the air in salute.

Nellie turned back sharply. 'Oh God, Kitty, he's looking straight at us.'

Both the girls giggled and, with an audacity she didn't even know she possessed, Kitty turned round and waved back at Aengus.

'Oh my God, oh my God, am I mad or what?' said Kitty as she giggled. With shining eyes and long hair flowing, they ran to the barn, burning onto the skyline an imprint of youth, as they faded through the brimming air.

Within half an hour, the barn was full with villagers. Maeve and Kathleen gave each helper a heaped plate of food.

'No half-measures at Ballymara farm,' shouted Maeve as she dished up the meal.

The fiddler had shown up and began to play for his lunch. Over in the corner of the barn, some of the women were already swishing their tea round in their cups before they tipped them up and handed the leaves to Nana Kathleen to read.

'One, two, three. There must be enough tea left for the leaves to be swilled round a full three times or the luck doesn't come,' said Kathleen to the circle of women gathering round her.

The first young woman to hand over her cup was shaking like a leaf.

'Aha,' said Kathleen. She had already noted that the young

woman's breasts were bigger than they had ever been before. She had also known her mother, who was as flat as a pancake. 'I think that maybe a babby will be on its way very soon,' grinned Kathleen, looking up from the teacup.

'It is, Kathleen,' the girl whispered, leaning in conspiratorially. 'We haven't told Mammy yet, because she's not so well but we will do, this Sunday, after mass.'

Kathleen continued, 'I think there is a move coming soon, I can see open land and a river.'

'Oh, Kathleen, that is just so fantastic. We are moving to Mulingar and have our own farm from his daddy, right down on the river, with fishing too.'

Kathleen had heard that in the post office from Mrs O'Dwyer.

She smiled. 'Well, I never. Ye know, the tea leaves, they never lie, ye can keep nothing from them at all, so ye can't.'

Aengus had studied Kitty all through the lunch. She had been busy helping to serve the food and as she walked up to the house, carrying the empty tin trenchers, Aengus caught up with her.

He fixed her once again with his magical grin and, with his bright blue eyes smiling, asked her, 'Will ye be away to the Castlefeale dance next Saturday?'

'I may be,' said Kitty.

'And if ye are, would I be able to walk with ye?'

'Ye may be,' said Kitty, smiling back at him. 'I'll have to ask my mammy.'

And with that, afraid of making herself look foolish, she ran up the path to the kitchen door to help the others with the dishes.

Aengus, watching Kitty's back, whispered to himself:

*'With apple blossom in her hair*
*Who called me by my name and ran.'*

Inside the kitchen, Maeve was loading the trenchers into a straw donkey basket.

'Girls, would ye take these over to the stream and give them a rinse for me and then bring them back.'

'And come here and give your mother a hug, miss.' Maura grabbed Kitty from behind and hugged her so tightly, she squeaked in protest.

'Mammy, I can't breathe.'

Maeve looked on fondly and laughed.

Maura spun Kitty round and placed a big kiss on the top of her head. For a small second, mother and daughter savoured the moment whilst Maura silently prayed.

Tomorrow would be a very different day.

The girls each grabbed a handle on the basket and skipped outside. Kitty didn't know if it was the music playing that had created an atmosphere of high gaiety, or the gorgeous boy who wanted to talk to her, or the happiness and love she felt whilst she was staying in the farmhouse. She knew only that she felt so happy, she desperately wanted to cry, and as her eyes welled up, she could barely stop herself.

Being pregnant was something she had entirely forgotten until this moment.

They stopped at the stone sink perched on the stream. Kitty knelt down and, for a moment, put her head in her hands. It was the only place she could be alone.

'What's up, Kitty?' said Nellie.

'I don't know. It is just all so much. Everyone is so wonderful and I have never felt this happy, I don't think, ever in me whole life.'

## Chapter Eighteen

Angela hated having to wait for the boys to catch up when they walked to school. The only one who could concentrate on an instruction for more than five seconds was Harry. The rest wouldn't listen to a word she said.

'Ye aren't our Kitty or Mammy, ye know,' shouted Malachi. 'Ye can't tell us what to do.'

He stuck out his tongue at Angela and grabbed the school bag out of her hand so that it fell to the floor. Picking up the bag, Angela swung it round full circle until it walloped him between the shoulder blades with a thud so hard that Malachi fell forward and hit the pavement with a smack.

His screams pierced the morning air and brought neighbours to their windows to see what was happening.

'Don't do that, our Angela,' shouted Declan, bending down to help Malachi up.

Declan had crusty hair and dried pobs in his ears.

Earlier in the morning he had dared to answer Angela back, who had responded by picking up his bowl of pobs and upending it on his head. The warm milk and bread had run down the sides of his face and into his ears.

'I'm sick to death of all of youse,' shouted Angela. 'None of ye does as ye is told. I'm leaving and going to school on me own now.'

She stormed off ahead, just as Little Paddy caught up with them all. Harry had pushed the baby in her pram round to Alice's house before setting off to school. He met up with Little Paddy as he ran out of his back gate.

'Sure, ye look mighty fed up, Paddy,' said Harry. 'Why haven't ye been out on the green playing all weekend?'

'I got a belt from me da, an' I wasn't allowed,' Little Paddy replied, looking very miserable and downbeat. 'He said I told another lie, but I didn't, I know what I saw, but I 'ave to keep me gob shut. I hate feckin' grown-ups, I do. I'm going to run away to sea on a ship, as soon as I'm old enough.'

Harry nodded sympathetically. He wasn't that keen on grown-ups himself. He thought they were very chaotic and disorganized.

'Ye can tell me, Paddy. I won't say a word to no one, I promise.'

'I can't tell ye. I still can't sit down yet, my backside is so sore. I'm not risking it again, but I will tell ye this, Harry, next time I see something, I'm comin' for ye to see it with me. Everyone believes you and no one believes me, so they don't, an' I hate being called a liar, because I have never told a lie to anyone – I haven't.'

For a reassuring moment, Harry put his arm round Little Paddy's shoulders.

Little Paddy flinched. 'Can ye feel the pain?' he asked. Little Paddy's shoulders hurt too.

'Yes, I can, Paddy, it's terrible,' said Harry, and he meant it. He could feel his friend's pain.

The only noise, as they shuffled along, came from Little Paddy's shoes, which were three sizes too big.

Harry had watched Angela as she stormed away. Now he picked out a soggy lump of pobs from Declan's hair.

He hoped his mammy would be home soon. He hadn't known she was leaving for Ireland and the news had been met with an outpouring of tears from the girls and stunned silence from the boys. Tommy seemed flustered and promised them all she would be back in a few days, but not with Kitty. Kitty would be staying in Ireland a little longer.

Harry was thoughtful as he walked. Alice hadn't seemed that happy to look after the baby and it already felt as if the house was falling apart without Maura.

As they passed by Molly Barrett's, her door suddenly swung open and there she stood with a plate in her hand. 'Biscuit, boys?' she said, nodding at her plate. Little Paddy and Harry looked at each other.

'Yes, please,' said Little Paddy, with enthusiasm. Peggy only ever baked on Sundays.

Harry was frightened of Mrs Barrett but he didn't know why.

Tiger pushed past Molly's ankles and with its eyes fixed on the boys, pushed itself up against Molly's legs. The cat hissed softly as it regarded the boys and both little Paddy and Harry involuntarily placed their hands across the front of their shorts.

Molly wasted no time in quizzing Harry, who couldn't take his eyes off the cat. 'I saw yer mammy leaving the house when I was letting Tiger in, Harry,' she said, with a fake smile, which didn't quite reach her eyes. 'She had a big bag with her, she did. Gone away, has she?'

Little Paddy turned round and looked at Harry with an expression of complete amazement. 'Yer mammy's gone away, where?' he almost shouted. 'Mammy said you is coming to our house for yer tea tonight. Is that why?'

Harry had no idea what to do or say without appearing rude. He decided that honesty was the best policy. He couldn't lie, Tommy hadn't told them to lie and that was a big sin anyway.

'She's gone to see Kitty in Ireland, but she will be back soon, Mrs Barrett.'

'Will Kitty be with her?'

Mrs Barrett wasn't giving up and Harry wished Paddy would stop accepting biscuits from the plate.

Harry was no fool, he had told her all a nosy neighbour needed to know. 'I don't know, she might be,' he replied, then, 'Paddy, we will be late, we have to go. Bye, Mrs Barrett.'

It had become apparent to Angela that their mother must have been on the go constantly when she was at home. Angela was exhausted and yet her only job was to supervise breakfast and see everyone safely through the school gates.

'It's a catastrophe in our kitchen, so it is,' she wearily told her friend, as she walked into her classroom that morning. 'Everything falls on my shoulders, now that Kitty and Mammy have taken a holiday. It is truly shocking, so it is, to put on me so.'

In assembly prayers that morning, Harry prayed, 'Please God, bring Mammy and Kitty home this afternoon, because I'm not looking forward to Peggy's tea tonight. Amen.'

Alice had Maura's baby on her knee, ready to feed her a bottle, and was surprised to see Peggy march in through the back door.

'Morning, queen,' said Peggy breezily. 'How are the little ones?'

'They are both fine, thank you, Peggy.' There was a note of query in Alice's voice.

The unasked question. What the hell are you doing in my kitchen?

Alice was instantly on her guard. Peggy was the biggest gossip in the street.

'Brigid tells me ye are away out today. Can I do anything to help?'

Peggy hovered over Alice, grinning and peering. The thought that Peggy looked just like an old crone fleetingly crossed Alice's mind.

'No, thanks, Peggy. I have everything under control and besides, I am only popping into town for a couple of hours. I won't be long.'

'Ah, town is it, then? And what would ye be getting in town?'

Peggy had sat herself down in the armchair and made herself very comfortable. She looked as though she was settling in for the morning. Alice felt herself seething inside. Peggy smelt especially high, which did not help.

'Well, I'm off to see a friend and then I thought I would call into the meat market on my way back,' she said.

'There's good meat in Murphy's. Ye won't get any better in town.' Peggy sniffed.

Alice felt as if she wanted to scream. How could she rid herself of this stupid woman?

'Well, Peggy, I fancy a change, thanking you all the same, and now if you don't mind, I would like to get on.'

Peggy looked shocked. 'Are ye taking both babies with ye?'

'Heavens, no. Brigid is looking after them for me, until I get back. I have enough trouble looking after one, never mind two.'

'Aye, well, Maura will be back before ye know it. She has only taken Kitty to visit her granny,' said Peggy.

Peggy now knew for sure that Little Paddy had been lying and deserved the beating he had got from his da.

Alice was as cool as a cucumber and, sure, wasn't Brigid looking after Alice's kids, whilst she went into town?

No, not even Alice could kiss someone else's husband and then act this calmly under Peggy's laser scrutiny.

Yes, she was sure. Little Paddy had been lying again.

'Oh, well then, I didn't realize ye was leaving so early, I'm sure,' said Peggy, aware that she was not as welcome in this kitchen when Kathleen was away with Alice presiding.

Hurt and wounded that she hadn't been offered a cuppa, she

heaved her huge frame out of the chair on the third attempt and then waddled down the road, to scrounge her morning tea and as many biscuits as she could lay her hands on at Mrs Keating's.

Alice met Sean outside the Railwayman pub, where she slipped a key into his hand.

'What's this?' said Sean, looking down at it in astonishment.

'It's for room twenty-one in the Grand. It is the room kept for overbooking and that never happens on a Monday. I kept it by accident in my coat pocket when I left.'

Alice was whispering and yet they were the only people on the street, or near the pub, as it had yet to open for business.

'The locks haven't been changed and the room will be empty. We can talk without being interrupted. Meet me there in half an hour.'

And with that she was gone.

Sean slipped up the staircase of the hotel unnoticed.

Maids and bellboys bustled about and the reception desk was far enough away from the staircase that entering the room was far easier than he had imagined. He had only been inside for five minutes when there came a gentle tap on the door. He opened it quickly.

Alice had been leaning her weight against the door so heavily that she almost fell in.

Neither spoke. Both were profoundly relieved to be alone together, at last.

'Did you get the bus after mine?' asked Sean, breaking the silence and grasping for something to say.

Alice nodded. They looked at each other. There was no need for words. There was only need.

The room, which was the size of a small school hall, felt cavernous and cold, even though it was full of spare chairs and tables, being stored for use in any one of the meeting rooms.

The Georgian panelling was painted in a dove grey and edged in a white ornate border, which made it feel cooler. The curtains at the tall windows, a faded pale-grey velvet with swathes and tails, dusty.

There was no warmth. No soul. No heart.

But they neither noticed nor cared. They could have been in a cave for all that they were aware of their surroundings.

Once Sean had reached out and pulled Alice into his arms, it took only seconds for them both to move from the door to the bed.

Within half an hour it was all over and, as they lay on their backs, they both lit a cigarette. For the first time in her life, Alice felt alive and liberated.

She stared at the ornate white coving that encircled the gilt light fitting, in the centre of the smoke-stained ceiling. As she exhaled she turned her head to look at Sean and said, 'God, Sean, I'm normal.' And her laughter danced, all over the bed.

Sean leant on his elbow and looked down at her, smiling. 'Alice, adultery is a sin. It is definitely not normal.'

She lifted her slim frame off the bed slightly and stubbed her cigarette out in the ashtray on the bedside table. As she did so, she thought of the number of times she had emptied the same ashtray in this very room.

'It is, if you are me,' she said. Then she took the cigarette out of Sean's hand, stubbed it out into the ashtray and set about committing adultery for a second time.

Daisy felt fine. It was Sister Evangelista who had told her she was ill. Daisy had been keen to stay at the convent but she did not want to be confined to the sick bay.

One of the novice nuns, who was also a nurse at the Northern, brought Daisy her meals and spoke to her as though she were very poorly indeed.

She had been told so many times she was ill that she was beginning to feel as though she really was sick and this morning she hadn't wanted to leave her bed.

What was there to get up for? She was only permitted to sit in the chair at the side of the bed and soon got pretty cold doing that.

She had been told she wasn't allowed to look out of the window, or to step outside.

One of the sisters brought her some books and there was a bible to read, but Daisy could hardly read anything more than a shopping list. Books were no use to her and she couldn't understand them anyway, even when someone else read to her.

Daisy didn't feel like her food today, either. Something was wrong. Things were changing, people were whispering and she didn't like it.

It was evening and they had switched Daisy's light off an hour ago. Daisy began to cry. She wanted to return to the convent in Dublin, where she had lived before she came to Liverpool. It was the only home Daisy had ever known and she desperately wanted to return. Daisy hadn't cried for a very long time. From a very young age, she had learnt the lesson that crying made no difference.

No one heard. No one cared. Nothing changed.

Sister Evangelista burst into the room without knocking, her arms full of what appeared to be freshly pressed undergarments. She placed them on the bed next to Daisy's feet and began peeling clothes from the top of the pile.

'Daisy, get up, get up,' she hissed. 'You have to get dressed.'

Daisy sat upright in bed. 'But it's night-time, Sister.'

'I know Daisy, I know. You have to get dressed. Come on, girl. Quickly, I have news from the bishop. Ye are going back to the convent in Dublin, but you have to go now and catch the night ferry with the bishop.'

'The bishop is here?' Daisy was confused. If the bishop was here, he would be at the Priory and so should she be.

'Not here exactly, not at the convent. Look, please, Daisy, just do as I ask, would you.'

Sister Evangelista had brought with her a case, packed with smart clothes Daisy had never seen before, and in no time she was creeping down the back stairs, with the sister urging her to be quiet.

Sister Evangelista opened a large wooden door that led to the convent garden. In a dim pool of light, on the other side of the tall wrought-iron gate at the garden entrance, were two men, huddled together against the cold air, waiting. Daisy noticed a parked car. She squinted into the darkness to see if there was anyone sitting inside.

Sister Evangelista took Daisy by the arm and hurried her along the garden path.

'These two gentlemen are friends of the bishop, Daisy. They are going to take you to meet him. He is waiting. They will take you across to Ireland on the ferry and then return you to the convent. You will be happy there, won't you, Daisy?'

Sister Evangelista handed the case to Austin. Now she grabbed Daisy by the hand and looked into her eyes. She had been perturbed that the two men had not wanted to tell her their names and had been less than friendly when they arrived,

Daisy shook her head and began to cry for the second time that day. She knew the two men. She didn't want to go anywhere with them. Not even to the ferry.

'No, Sister,' she whispered. 'I don't want to go, please don't make me, I just want to stay here.'

'Daisy, I have been instructed by the bishop and he is very definite in what he says. You may not know that your family pay for us to look after you. The convent in Ireland, where you were brought up, well, that's the best place for you now that Father James has gone. You deserve that for looking after the Priory for all this time. Time for someone else to take over all that hard work now, Daisy.'

Daisy's tears had turned to sobs. Sister Evangelista looked towards the men the bishop had sent to collect Daisy, and, with a shock, realized they had disappeared, as had the case. At that very moment, Miss Devlin, who had stopped late at the convent for supper and prayers, walked down the back steps towards them with the police officer, Howard, at her side.

Sister Evangelista thought they were too familiar altogether.

'Here ye are. I thought Daisy was up and taking a bit of fresh air, didn't I say she would be, now?' said Miss Devlin. She grinned from ear to ear, flushed with the attention Howard had paid her. He had called back at the convent on the off chance, knowing she would be there this evening, and had offered her a lift home in the panda. And as luck would have it they had spotted Daisy in the garden. Before Miss Devlin knew it, Howard was out of the back door and down the steps. She had to run to keep up with him.

Sister Evangelista forced a smile.

The bishop would be furious.

She had hardly agreed with a word the bishop had said since the father had died. She was now coming to the conclusion that the best way to have dealt with this would have been to tell the police everything, hand them all the photographs and pictures. It was as obvious to her as the nose on her face that it was a parent who had killed the priest. Any parent who discovered what that evil disciple of the devil had done to their child would surely be seized with a rage so strong they would kill, without even knowing what they were doing.

Now she was an accomplice. She had helped to burn the photographs and destroy all the incriminating evidence.

'Tell the police Daisy has run away,' the bishop had said, when he issued the latest instructions. 'We need to sneak her out and return her back to the convent in Ireland, where she will be safe.'

Sister Evangelista's heart had sunk. Everything was moving too fast. She was sure there were things the bishop knew and she didn't. Who on earth were those two men, for example? One of them had looked very familiar, but she had no idea why.

Had she seen him in the Priory ever?

God, this was a mess. What did the bishop propose to do about Molly? He couldn't send a couple of men to carry her off to a convent and God alone knew what Daisy had told her.

Sister Evangelista turned to face Howard. From the corner of her eye, she saw that the car the two men had arrived in slipped slowly and silently down the hill away from the back gate of the convent garden.

They knew, she thought. They knew. They must have seen Miss Devlin switch on the cloakroom light and open the back door with Howard behind her, and they had vanished, taking the case with them, so that it didn't look as though they had planned to sneak Daisy away. She remembered where she had seen the familiar one and felt faint and sick. He had appeared in one of the photographs. But the bishop had sent him?

Her mind was screaming, her heart was racing and pounding against her ribs. As she opened her mouth, she felt sure her voice would wobble and crack, and yet out it came, each word dripping in falsehood, succeeding in concealing her inner turmoil and panic.

'Hello, Officer. Daisy has been a little upset. Her nerves are very bad, and we thought a bit of night air would do her good and calm her down.'

Howard looked at Daisy's face. It was blotched and streaked with tears.

'Hello, Daisy,' he said gently. 'Listen, I'm sorry, queen, if yer nerves are bad, like, but do you know, I think the sooner we get this interview over, the better things will be, don't you agree, Miss Devlin?'

Miss Devlin was keen to impress Howard.

'Oh, I do indeed,' she trilled.

Howard thought that if Miss Devlin or Sister Evangelista knew what Molly had told him and Simon, they would be very keen for Daisy to be interviewed too.

'Well, I am sure the morning will be fine, won't it, Daisy?' said Sister Evangelista. 'But if you don't mind, I shall put her back to bed now, especially if you are coming back in the morning. I know how keen you two are, I imagine ye will be here for breakfast.'

Sister Evangelista managed a laugh. It was hard, but she managed.

Not her usual laugh. You would normally have to look at her to know she was laughing or catch her shoulders shaking. Her entire life in a convent, from when she had arrived as an orphan, had trained her to practise a special, silent laugh, cultivated over years so as not to disturb the peace. Tonight it was more like a pebble rolling around in a tin can. But a laugh it was.

As she put Daisy back to bed, a novice joined them with a depressing but expected message.

'The bishop is on the phone, Reverend Mother, and he said he needs to speak to you without delay.'

Sister Evangelista knew that he would be very unhappy indeed to hear Daisy was to be interviewed by the police in the morning. She had done all she could, including convincing everyone that she was ill, to prevent the interview from taking place. It was out of her hands.

The girl was simple. Surely they could see that? As the sister pulled the cover over her, Daisy smiled in gratitude, a woman who still looked exactly like a child.

Sister Evangelista sighed as she left the room. It was all in God's hands now. She had resigned herself to the fact that she had lifted the entire situation up to the Lord and felt a huge sense of relief as a result.

As she moved towards her office to speak to the bishop, she knew she would not, could not, challenge him. She could not be sure that the man he had sent was in the photograph, but curiously she felt bolder. She would be keeping a very careful eye out from now on and would be more forceful with her own opinions.

As was her custom, Molly sat and watched the ten o'clock news whilst eating a slice of warm millionaires' shortbread.

She had made a fresh batch for the police officers tomorrow.

Molly knew they must interview Daisy and hear her words for themselves, but that would happen soon enough. They had told Molly that she would need to be a witness in court and that her evidence would be crucial to the case.

Molly liked that. Nothing she had ever done in her entire life before could ever have been described as *crucial*.

This was an occasion. Tomorrow, she would take out her curlers, put in her teeth and tell the police that Maura Doherty vanished in the middle of the night. No one in that family had ever spent a night away from Nelson Street and now, suddenly, two of them had disappeared.

This was news. Possibly, even *crucial* news.

It infused her with a feeling of self-importance that she was the only person her friend Daisy had told about witnessing the murder. Molly had told the police and no one else.

The police couldn't rush Daisy. Molly had told them that and they agreed. They had already met her, they knew they would have to coax the information from her gently. That was why they were waiting for her to leave the sick bay at the convent.

Molly smiled as she heaved herself out of the chair and bent down to switch off the television. Annie O'Prey will have seven kinds of a fit when she knows what I have been keeping from her, she thought to herself, carrying her cup and plate over to the kitchen sink.

Tiger let out one of his piercing howls from the yard and Molly heard the tin bin lid slip onto the yard floor and clatter across the cobbles.

'That bloody cat,' she said to herself, as she opened the back door. 'The bin will be full of river rats in the morning. Tiger,' she hissed. 'Tiger, come here, here, you naughty boy.'

It was pitch-black outside. The night had settled down and the street slept. There was not a shaft of dawdling light to ease her way to help her find the cat.

Molly heard another noise, this time from the outhouse.

'Tiger, is that you? Here, you daft cat,' she said.

There was no response. All was quiet.

'Ah sure, well, I need to go to the lavvy anyway,' she muttered as she shuffled across the yard and opened the outhouse door.

Molly kept a candle and a box of matches on the ledge and knew exactly where to put her hand. Plagued by a weak bladder, she could have the candle lit within seconds. As she struck the match, she shuffled round to negotiate her way down onto the lavvy seat.

That was when Molly saw him, waiting for her, behind the outhouse door.

The wooden mallet hit her so hard on the side of her temple that it carried her across the outhouse and into the wall. As her skull shattered, the last thing she saw was Tiger, with claws extended, leaping onto her attacker, but he was too late.

Molly was dead before she hit the floor.

## Chapter Nineteen

The straw bales had been restacked, cloths folded and dishes put away. The bales almost reached the roof of the barn. Nellie and Kitty lay on the top, chins in hands, and gazed out over the harvested fields.

The barn retained the heat of the day and their nostrils were filled with the thick scent of straw and hay, mingled with freshly cut oats. The smell from the midden entered inwards as the breeze altered direction and, unwelcome, rested with them awhile.

Oat sheaves, which yesterday had stood five feet tall and swayed in the breeze, were now stacked into rounded mounds, dotted casually across the fields.

The girls could hear the river running in the distance.

The surface of the fields shimmered a platinum harvest gold in the last rays of the red sun as it slowly dipped behind the emerald mountain that rose from the foot of the furthest field.

'That must have been the best day of me life,' said Kitty wistfully, squinting into the middle distance to watch Jacko as he began to lumber slowly across the stones on the edge of the riverbank.

'Aye, mine too,' said Nellie.

Nellie sat up cross-legged and studied her white socks intently. Tiny, bright-red straw bugs were weaving their way in and out of the white threads. Distracted, she attempted to pick them out, one at a time, with her nails.

Giving up, she nudged Kitty.

'What about the glorious Aengus, then, eh? He took a right shine to you, so he did.'

'Oh sure, he did not.' Kitty blushed.

'Oh my God, he so did and ye to him. Ye should have seen your face.' Nellie began to imitate Kitty. 'Oh, I'm so terribly sorry, Aengus, I'll just have to ask my mammy. Now hang on a moment, er, yes, she said yes, a yes, that is. Not that I'm keen now, but, yes.'

Kitty extended her leg and with her foot ejected Nellie straight off the top layer of straw and she landed on the half-layer below. Both girls were laughing as Maura appeared at the front opening of the barn and called to them.

'Come on now, girls,' she shouted up. 'Time to come indoors. Kitty, ye need to have a bath.'

'Why in the name of God do I need a bath?' asked Kitty indignantly. 'I had one on Sunday.'

'Just do as I ask, please.' There was an element of tension in Maura's voice and Kitty picked up on it straight away.

'What's wrong, Mammy?'

Maura immediately reverted to a mask of gaiety. Kitty's last night had to be a nice one. That was all that mattered.

While Maura and Kitty stepped inside and Kitty took her bath, Nellie sat on the edge of the stone sink and watched the back of the truck loaded with oats disappear down the Ballymara road.

A dark cloud had gathered in the sky above the farmhouse and the air was becoming oppressive. Nellie could hear thunder in the distance but as yet there was not a drop of rain falling on Ballymara.

'Eat fast now, Jacko,' she shouted. 'It'll be all wet soon.'

A rumble grew louder in the distance and Nellie took herself inside. She wanted to speak to Nana Kathleen. Something was occurring. She could sense that Maura was tense and a feeling she didn't much like had slipped into her gut.

As Kitty lay in the bath, she guessed people were talking about her, because she heard her name mentioned more than once. Maura had told her to wash her hair, even though it had been washed only two days ago.

She looked down at the peaty-brown bathwater, which was the colour of weak tea. She still couldn't get used to it and marvelled at the colour each time she filled the sink.

'Is this water safe?' she had asked Maeve on her first night.

'Well, at least five generations have been drinking it here in this house and no one dies before their fourscore years and ten, so I reckon it must be so,' Maeve had said.

Kitty looked down at her belly. The mound was now breaking the surface of the warm brown water. She hadn't noticed that a few days ago. She slowly ran her hand over the firm swelling. She pressed gently to see if she could feel anything. It's a baby in there, she thought to herself, a baby girl or a baby boy. In there.

It felt alien and unreal.

She sat up, rubbed herself down with soap, rinsed it away and then quickly stepped out of the bath. She did not want to look at the visible manifestation of that awful night.

When Kitty arrived back in the kitchen, Maeve and Maura had set the tea out on the table and Nellie was sitting in the big chair by the fire.

'Now then,' said Maura, in a breezy tone. 'Come and sit down, we need to have a chat.'

'Oh no,' said Kitty, 'not another chat, Mammy.'

Her heart sank. Last time Maura wanted a chat it was to tell her she was pregnant. She never wanted to chat again.

'Is our holiday over now, is that it? Do we have to go home? Nellie, are you coming with us or are ye staying longer? Oh, Maeve, I will miss ye so much.'

Kitty had jumped to conclusions and also to her feet to hug Maeve, who, with her arms wrapped round Kitty, moved her back over to the fireplace and sat down with her on the wooden settle, winking above her head at Maura.

Nana Kathleen walked into the room, having just closed the front door.

She had met Liam outside and waved the truck down as he drove past to turn round at the McMahons' farm.

'Go back to the village and stay at Colleen and Brian's for ye tea. Don't come back now until as late as ye can. Give little Kitty a bit of space while we tell her what is happening, will ye now?'

Liam's face was covered in grain dust from the thresher and, as he frowned, specks of it fell from his eyelashes. He lifted his cap and wiped the back of his hand across his eyes.

'Jesus, the poor feckin' girl,' he said as he put the cap back on. 'I'll be off then.' And he rammed the gearstick back into first, put his foot down on the accelerator and drove the truck as fast as it would speed back down the Ballymara road. As Kathleen reached the door she looked back and saw Liam had one hand lifted in a wave to her as he passed.

Just the way his father, Joe, had always done before him.

Kathleen smiled and, at the same time, she felt the familiar pain of loss somewhere deep in her heart.

'Shift up now, missus,' she said to Nellie as she tapped her knees with her hand, indicating that Nellie should move over. Nellie jumped out of her seat and then as Nana Kathleen sat, she plonked herself back down on Kathleen's knee, a more cushioned resting place than the chair itself.

Nellie was quiet. Studying Kitty and Maura, she had placed her thumb in her mouth and, leaning her head back on Nana Kathleen, began to suck it for the first time in years. She was exhausted. The heat of the day and the glow from the fire were forcing sleep upon her. She adored the smell of the burning peat in the huge fireplace. The brown bricks, hewn from the earth and pulled on a cart by Jacko, were a novelty after the coal and coke back home.

Nellie had spent each evening she had been at the farmhouse on the same chair as her nana, lost in her thoughts as she watched the flames flicker. She blinked furiously and fought to keep her eyes open but she lasted only moments as, enveloped in the familiar smell of hearth and home, and on her nana's bosom, she fell into a deep sleep.

Maura was much more confident than when she had told Kitty she was pregnant and she wasted no time in getting straight to the point.

'We have found somewhere for you to have the baby, Kitty.'

Maura didn't wait for a reaction. She wanted this to be over and done with as fast as possible.

'Rosie, who is the sister-in-law of Nana Kathleen's sister, Julia, she will be the midwife.'

Kitty didn't speak but turned round on the settle to face Maura full on. She looked to Nellie for support but she was in what Tommy called 'the land of nod'. As she relaxed into sleep, her thumb had slipped out of her mouth and rested on her chin in the midst of dribble. At any other time Kitty would have laughed, but she knew this was not the moment.

'It is a home near Galway, run by the nuns, but there is a small problem. We will have to leave very soon as ye are beginning to show now. Only those of us who know have noticed, mind, but ye are. When ye have the baby, I will be straight back to get ye out, but we will leave the baby behind. It will be adopted by an American family and, please God, they will never know who its father was.'

Maura stopped talking and looked at her daughter who in the last few weeks had moved from childhood and transformed into a young woman. Her face had altered. She had definitely put weight on from being at the farm, apart from as a result of her condition, and it had filled out her features beautifully.

If I took her home today they would all see such a difference in her, Maura thought to herself.

She took a breath.

'And there is another thing, they think your name is Cissy.'

'Why do they think my name is Cissy?' squealed Kitty in a high-pitched voice.

'It's the best way to protect you and make sure the whole thing is kept secret, and then when it is all over, you can move on with your life. Our life. There will never be a record of anyone called Kitty ever having been there.'

Kitty knew that there was no point arguing about the name. It had obviously been discussed and decided long before she was told. She studied Nellie and looked distracted as she spoke.

'Can I come home to Liverpool first?' she asked.

Maura took a deep breath. 'Everyone in Ireland knows someone in Liverpool and the other way round too, Kitty, so if we really want to keep this secret, it would be best that you don't. We cannot risk one person guessing. Once someone knows, there is no way of unknowing it.'

She saw no need to explain that, under normal circumstances, this would be a good enough reason, but for them it was imperative that no one ever found out and connected the extraordinary coincidence of a child pregnancy in the same parish as a dead priest with his langer chopped off.

'Cissy is an obvious choice of name as it is so close to Kitty,' Maura whispered to her gently as she took Kitty's hand.

Kitty rewarded her with a faint if sad smile.

'We have to leave tomorrow. I have already packed your bag whilst ye was in the bath. We will leave after breakfast. Liam is taking us there in the truck and then Kathleen, Nellie and I are travelling on to Dublin and returning to Liverpool. As soon as ye have had the baby, I will be back with the money to collect ye.'

Maura still hadn't worked out how in God's name they were going to raise that amount of money, but she had put her faith in God and expected him to deliver. He owed her, big time.

'With the money?' said Kitty. 'Will ye have to buy me back?'

'No, not at all. It's just the money to cover ye board and lodgings and the adoption papers. I haven't seen the home but Kathleen tells me it's very grand. The thing is, Kitty, they have a laundry attached to the mother and baby home and ye may have to work to help out. They don't normally take in women until much later than ye but this is an exception and so, early on, ye will have to do a bit of work to help towards your keep. I am going to ask tomorrow if ye can be excused from that. I don't mind paying more for ye if that's so.'

Kathleen remained quiet. She hadn't told Maura that she had asked the Reverend Mother if Kitty could be excused from working in the laundry. The reply had been withering.

'Mrs Deane, this is a working abbey, not an hotel.' The conversation had ended there and then.

Like every child in Ballymara, then and now, Kathleen had been educated by the nuns and was still to this day too scared to answer back.

Once again, Kitty was in shock. She was out of control of everything. Where she lived. Who she lived with. And her name, she was no longer even allowed her name. She was hidden. Her name was hidden. She felt as though she were slipping over the edge of – what, she did not know.

Maeve picked up Kitty's hand.

'The thing to remember, Kitty, is that we aren't far away and this may seem like a long time to ye at the moment but ye will soon be out and life will return to normal.'

Kitty looked from Maeve to Maura. 'Mammy, can I not do my schoolwork while I'm there? Why do I have to work in a laundry? That sounds shocking.'

'It's not, my love. It's just something that has to be done to take us to the other side of this mountain. I will tell everyone in Liverpool that my sister is having another baby and that she needs help and ye are staying with her until after her delivery to help out. Everyone at home will believe that because they all know what a grand little helper ye are to me.'

Kitty was in a daze. She knew she had a million questions to ask and yet she had none. Sleep, having claimed Nellie and now looking for a fresh conquest, had passed over to Kitty, threatening to own her too.

She wearily stood up. 'Did ye pack my washbag?' she asked with an element of panic in her voice.

'Don't worry.' Maeve smiled at her. 'I've left all ye lovely things next to the bag for the morning.'

Kitty wanted her bed and to be alone. What had been a lovely day was over. The sky had darkened and the first drops of rain began to fall.

There was nothing left to say.

In a state of growing numbness, she kissed Maeve and Nana Kathleen and took herself to bed. Nana Kathleen rose from the chair, letting Nellie flop into the big cushion and take it for herself. She pulled a knitted shawl down from the back of the chair and placed it over Nellie as she followed Maura and Kitty to the bedroom. Nellie remained oblivious.

The two women fussed over Kitty, chatting about how quickly the time would pass and how much they would miss her. They wittered on about writing and the children writing and making sure Angela didn't claim the bedroom for their own. It all flew straight over Kitty's head. She was too numb to respond.

Eventually, they stopped their fussing and left.

Maura, with anxious looks and damp eyes, a shadow of her former self, kissed her daughter goodnight. Distress was slowly creeping into her voice, at having to leave her daughter in a strange place with unknown people.

Kathleen led Maura away and the door clicked gently shut.

Kitty lay and listened to their footsteps fade away down the corridor, Maura's light and gentle, her delicate weight barely making an impression upon the stone floor.

Unsure. Unhappy. Miserable, little steps, tripping alongside Kathleen's, which were slow. Solid. Heavy. Assured.

Once alone, Kitty let her tears flow. She was more resigned than afraid. She had known that something had to be done. She hadn't realized she would have to do it alone. Nor that for such a long time she wouldn't see her brothers and sisters or be allowed back home to Liverpool. It felt like never. What she would give now to hear the moaning, complaining Angela kicking off and giving out. She swore to herself she would never again feel resentment towards her siblings.

Kitty placed her hands on her belly and let them softly travel over the mound, which, to her astonishment, was still there when she lay flat on her back. She could feel a firm ridge, just below her belly button. She cradled her tiny belly in both of her hands. A baby. Her very own baby. Her flesh. Adopted.

It was now dark with rain falling heavily. A streak of lightning rent the sky apart and flooded her room with a bright light.

She remembered Aengus's face and his offer to walk with her at the Castlefeale fair.

She saw his blue eyes, his red hair and his cheeky smile, and just the memory of their meeting made her feel desperately alone.

She would never see him again and yet he had made her heart somersault and sing, all at the same time, just by the way he looked at her.

She rolled onto her side, pulled her knees up to her chest and hugged them.

The thunder roared and gave cover to her sobs, which were so loud and strong that her body heaved and shook as they went on and on, barely allowing her time to draw breath.

She wanted to scream at her inescapable loneliness, at the pain of there being no comfort to be found anywhere, to scream and never stop, but she knew she couldn't. It was hopeless. It didn't matter how much she screamed, it would change nothing. No matter how much she wished or prayed or asked people for help, nothing would alter. No one could help her.

Maura was returning home without her, tomorrow. Kitty would leave the warmth and welcome she had felt in the farmhouse.

She would be left at an abbey to live with nuns and strangers and to work in a laundry. She would have no family or friends around her and would have no one who loved or cared for her anywhere near throughout the pregnancy or the birth.

This was it.

Her new life.

This was the awful it.

Aengus had taken supper at the McMahon farm before he returned home.

He had arrived to help his Uncle John with the harvest as he had every year since he could remember.

John jumped into his van and offered Aengus a lift back to Bangornevin, stopping on the way at the Deane farm to drop a basket off for Maeve that his wife had made him take with him.

'Are ye bloody mad? It's pouring down, woman,' he had said to his wife.

'Do stop complaining now. Maeve gave all her eggs away today and she needs more for the morning. Do as I say. Go on, away with ye.'

And with that and brooking no nonsense, she had closed the door.

As John ran through the rain towards the Deanes' front door, Aengus left the van and walked down the path with the oilskin to cover John who was already almost soaked through.

When his aunt had asked John to take the eggs, Aengus's heart had skipped a beat. He was glad of the rain and an excuse to leave the van. He stood a few steps behind his uncle in the remains of the firelight radiating out through the front door.

To his disappointment, his uncle refused the invitation from Maeve to step inside as he handed over the basket. The thunder eased and, in the silence that followed, Aengus heard an unfamiliar noise. He looked towards the bedroom window just feet away from where he stood.

His ears pricked as he heard the sound of a wounded animal, which pulled on his heart as if dragging it down deep into his chest.

He stared at the window, looking for a light or a flicker of the curtains, anything to show him where the noise had sprung from.

It stopped suddenly, but Aengus was glued to the spot. While Maeve and his uncle were chatting about the success of the day, he strained to hear the sound again.

But there was nothing.

Kitty's heart had already broken.

There was no sound left to be made.

The Abbey and the laundry lay at the bottom of a shallow valley and were approached via a long gravel driveway.

The drive would have been easy to miss if it hadn't been for the two red-brick pillars, standing proud like two lone effigies, supporting the high wooden dark-green fence that surrounded the Abbey. A thick belt of tall fruit trees grew directly behind as though providing an additional barrier to entry. Torpid branches reclined along the fence top, slipping down exhausted from carrying their weight of green apples.

'The kids from the village will have them apples before they are ripe,' said Liam as they drove through the black wrought-iron gates, which were opened wide.

Nellie was sat on Kathleen's knee, Kitty on Maura's, crammed into the front of the truck. They had left the last village ten minutes since and Nellie was now desperate for the toilet and had been for over half an hour.

'They would have to be brave kids,' answered Kathleen.

Liam nodded. The unspoken truth, suspended in the air of the small cab.

The truth everyone knew.

The nuns were the sisters of no mercy. If you stole from a convent, no matter how poor or how hungry your family, the Gardai would be summoned. Forgiveness was a valuable commodity, the currency of redemption. Not to be wasted on poor, hungry children.

Kitty hadn't spoken a word since they passed through Castlefeale.

She had clung to Maeve when they left her, early in the morning.

Maeve had slowly unhooked Kitty's hands that were clasped round her back. Holding both of them in her own, she looked into her eyes and said, 'Kitty, promise me this, that ye will come back very, very soon. Promise me now. I want ye to know that if you need somewhere or someone, I am here with no need of warning.'

Kitty found it hard to reply. Her throat was tight and the effort required to answer had all but deserted her. She had been morose over breakfast and lost in her own thoughts, her hand never far from Maura's.

She felt herself drag the words up from somewhere deep inside as she answered, 'I will, Maeve, I promise I will.'

Maeve had wanted to give her something to take with her and to hold onto: the knowledge that she was welcome, indeed, wanted, back.

Maeve put her hand into her apron pocket and brought out something gold and glistening. She slipped it over Kitty's wrist.

Kitty was speechless. It was a bracelet, hung with exquisite and beautiful charms.

With her mouth open in amazement, she lifted the charms one by one. A thatched cottage, a milk churn, a lady's boot, a fish, a tiny bird and a teapot.

Kitty felt guilty. She looked from Nellie to Maeve. Nellie was directly related to Maeve, so surely this was Nellie's.

'Sure, now don't you be worrying about that, little miss,' said Maeve, grinning. 'She has me whole jewellery box marked out as her own, that one does.'

Nellie and Maeve both laughed as Nellie came and joined them both in the hug. Nellie's sweet nature would not for one moment allow her to show a pang of regret that Maeve was giving the charm bracelet to Kitty. Nellie instantly felt guilty. She had so much compared to Kitty.

Maeve hugged them both together.

'Well, that's grand, then, and I will be waiting to see ye, so I will. I expect ye back here next year with our Nellie and Kathleen because I have no idea how I will manage another harvest without ye help. I would have given up and sent everyone home if it hadn't been for ye, Kitty.'

Kitty smiled. She almost laughed, for the first and last time that day.

As they drove off down the Ballymara road, Kitty and Nellie turned round to face the small window in the back of the cab and waved.

Maeve walked across to the other side of the road and stood by the stream so that she could remain for longer in their view.

The rain was falling in the Irish way, soft and misty, but Maeve didn't notice. She wanted to do more for Kitty and if all she had left to offer was to show her she cared by standing in the rain, then that was what she would do.

Kitty and Nellie sat forward together as the van tyres crunched across the gravel drive, creating a noise loud enough to announce their arrival. An imposing white building loomed into sight with a short flight of steps leading up to the front door.

Both girls placed their hands on the dashboard and leant closer to the windscreen for a better view.

A smaller building stood a short walk away from the convent with a long windowed corridor linking the two. Manicured lawns bordered the drive.

'The grass looks like it's been shaved,' said Nellie as they pulled up outside the first white building.

As they piled out of the van, the large wooden door opened and a nun stood with her hand on the big brass doorknob.

She didn't speak. She barely moved. She watched, without a flicker of expression. Maura felt uncomfortable.

'Jesus, would a smile hurt? A kind word never broke anyone's mouth, now did it,' she whispered to Kathleen as they lifted Kitty's bag out of the back.

A feeling of cold dread had already lodged itself in Maura's gut and it was going nowhere.

They felt conspicuous under the nun's gaze. Liam lost his usual light-hearted manner and felt as though he was walking awkwardly.

'Feck, does she have to stare like that?' he whispered under his breath as he pulled back the tarpaulin on the back of the van.

'Shush, Liam,' whispered Kathleen. 'She will turn ye into stone with that look. Come inside with us. I forgot to mention, you're Kitty's father. Maura knows, so she does. Just let me do the talking and don't forget, Kitty, yer name is Cissy.'

Liam looked as if he was about to faint. He had been taught by the nuns and still, as a grown man, he trembled in their presence. He hadn't wanted to step foot inside the convent and had hoped he could wait in the van.

They walked slowly towards the nun, who appraised each one individually as they approached. No smiles or words of welcome came their way.

Maura felt as though they were trespassing.

Had they come to the wrong place? Was someone about to turn them away?

Suddenly, from behind the door appeared an older nun, the Reverend Mother, Sister Assumpta, who glided beneath her habit like a butterball on wheels. Maura had never in her life seen nor met such a rotund woman. There was no wobble, no lurching gait.

'Good morning, Mrs Deane.' She looked directly at Kathleen.

Sister Assumpta's small, bright blue eyes were almost totally occluded by her plump red cheeks. Nellie was stunned by her likeness to the butcher back home in Liverpool.

'Come along inside.' Her voice was well suited to her size and sounded masculine, far from the kindly, maternal voice Maura had imagined.

She moved towards a white panelled door on the left and turned yet another large and shining brass knob. She swung the door open and with a wave of her hand ushered them inside.

'Who in God's name cleans all this brass?' whispered Maura to Kitty as they walked hesitantly into the room.

The dark shining wooden floorboards were covered with beautiful rugs and the windowsills were lined with silver ornaments that shone brightly, even though it was a dull day.

'Who cleans all this silver?' whispered Kathleen to Nellie.

'Please, do sit,' said Sister Assumpta as she moved behind her desk and sat herself in an ornate chair of carved wood and leather.

They all did as instructed and sat in chairs assembled round the desk. There were not enough so Liam withdrew into the background and stood against the wall. He ignored the look Kathleen had thrown his way. Still, no one spoke.

Although there was no sun, bright daylight poured in through the tall window behind the desk, transforming Sister Assumpta into a faceless black shadow.

Sister Celia, the nun who had watched them arrive, walked into the room carrying a tray of tea, which she placed on Sister Assumpta's desk and then without speaking a single word, left the room.

'You must all have a thirst after a long journey,' Sister Assumpta said with a false brightness. 'Mrs Deane, would you like to pour?'

Kathleen jumped to her feet as Sister Assumpta smiled at her. It was a brittle and fixed smile, exuding no warmth.

'Thank ye, Reverend Mother,' said Kathleen.

As she stood, Nellie pulled on the back of her coat. Kathleen turned round and knew the look on Nellie's face.

'Mother, could Nellie here please use the bathroom? She has been desperate for some time now, haven't ye, Nellie?'

A look of displeasure crossed Sister Assumpta's face.

Oh God, please don't say no, thought Nellie, who was sure that if she had to wait much longer, she might wet herself.

Maeve had plied her with tea in the morning and now she regretted it.

Sister Assumpta rang a bell on her desk and then put it straight back down again.

'Sister Celia will have returned to the kitchen by now. Come with me,' she said brusquely to Nellie as she rose and opened the door. 'See, down at the end of the floor runner,' she pointed, 'there is a corridor to the right.'

Nellie nodded.

'Turn right there, it is a short corridor and the washrooms are at the end. Be quick now and do not talk to anyone, that is forbidden, do you understand?'

She had pulled the door almost shut behind them and stood with her hand on the brass knob. Nellie instinctively knew she was making sure the others couldn't hear. Her manner was now far from friendly and her look was cold.

'Walk on the floor, not the runner,' she hissed under her breath.

'Thank you, Reverend Mother,' said Nellie and she began to quickly walk down the corridor. As she looked back over her shoulder, she saw the last of the nun's habit sweeping across the wooden floor as she glided back into the room.

There was no one in the corridor and not a sound other than that made by Nellie's shoes on the floor as she walked alongside the Persian runner.

As she turned into the corridor on the right, the opulence of the main corridor instantly disappeared. The walls were painted an aquamarine blue and the only ornamentation was that of grottos to the Holy Mother, placed at regular intervals, and pictures of Our Lord, carrying his cross on the final stations.

Ahead was an opening leading on to a brown-tiled floor. Nellie tentatively stepped inside and looked around. She saw washbasins to her left and cubicle doors to her right.

Nellie felt as though she were not alone and yet she could see no one else. All the cubicle doors were closed. She bent slightly to look underneath, but there were no feet on the other side of any of them. Nellie cautiously opened the first cubicle door and jumped in alarm as she let out a startled yelp. Behind the door, crouched on top of the toilet seat, was a young girl with her fingers to her mouth.

She whispered, 'Sh, please God, please don't make a noise. I need ye to help me, please.'

Nellie, already older than her years, let out a deep breath as she looked at the girl. She instantly noticed her unusual dark hair, which was roughly cut and very short, like that of a boy. Her brown eyes were huge as she stared at Nellie, all but begging her as they threatened to overspill with tears.

Nellie whispered, 'All right then, please don't cry,' as she stepped inside and, with great seriousness, slid the bolt across on the cubicle door behind her.

As she did so, she stared at the toilet door for just a second before turning round.

Nellie knew she was special. She had known for a long time. It wasn't just that she didn't know anyone else whose mother had died in childbirth, or even that from time to time she saw her ghostly mother. It was simply her life. She was different. Things happened to Nellie.

'Can ye help me, please?' the girl pleaded.

Nellie turned round to face her.

'What can I do? What's wrong?' said Nellie.

'I came here to have my babby five years ago. My daddy died while I was in here and my mammy can't pay to get me out. She knocks at the door every day and they don't even let her in. They just send her away. I see her from the window and for months I didn't even know she was trying, I thought she had forgotten about me. I have to get to Dublin. Can ye please help?'

'How did you know we were here?' said Nellie.

The girl was whispering hurriedly as she wiped away her tears with the back of her hand.

'I was cleaning the floor in the hall when the lady with the silver hair came to visit. I heard her say she was coming back today and so I thought I would clean the toilets and hide in a cubicle in case anyone came. If they find me, I will be punished so bad.'

Her panic mounted as she spoke the last few words and she began to cry again in a way that was so heartbroken it grabbed Nellie's heart.

'We are travelling to Dublin straight from here, but I don't know how we would get ye away.'

And then suddenly, the tarpaulin came into Nellie's mind.

'If ye can get to the front, can ye get under the tarpaulin on the truck?'

The girl began to laugh and cry at the same time.

'I can, oh God, thank ye. The last time I got away, I waved down a car on the road and it was the priest who stopped and brought me back. I was so desperate. I will go round the back and I will crawl out from behind the bin in front of the truck, if ye can help me.'

'I can and I will,' said Nellie. 'But before I do, what is your name?'

'It's Besmina.' Besmina grinned at Nellie.

'Before I go, Besmina, I have to use that toilet.'

*

Kathleen had poured the tea and handed a cup to Liam, Kitty and Maura. Kitty noticed how Sister Assumpta looked straight at her with an expression of astonishment when Kathleen handed Kitty the tea. Maybe Kitty wasn't supposed to have any tea. Maybe the tea was just for the adults. For an awkward moment the atmosphere froze, as Kathleen and Maura had exactly the same thought.

'So, Cissy.'

Kitty stared at her tea.

'Cissy,' the voice boomed.

Kitty's head shot up. 'Yes, Reverend Mother.'

'You will be sharing a room with eleven other girls and working in the laundry until the day of your confinement. You will rise at five in the summer and five-thirty in the winter. First mass is at six and then we take breakfast each day, during which one girl takes the readings. Can you read, Cissy?'

Maura and Kathleen tried not to look shocked.

'Yes, I do, Reverend Mother,' said Kitty quietly.

'She reads very well, in fact,' said Maura, feeling her hackles rise. 'As soon as she comes home, she will be continuing with her education.'

Sister Assumpta gave a small, almost imperceptible snort.

'I'm quite certain she will, Mrs Doherty. It's a shame her education ever had to be broken, some would say.'

Sister Assumpta was now wearing her small reading glasses and shuffling papers around on her desk.

'However, we are where we are. Many girls who end up here can neither read nor write.'

As she spoke, she peered over the top of her glasses at Maura. Her look was almost provocative. Tempting Maura to talk more. Testing her.

Kathleen jumped in quickly before Maura could. 'Will it be possible to speak on the telephone on occasion, Reverend Mother?'

There was no time wasted in the delivery of a response.

'No, it will not. We run an abbey and a workplace here, Mrs Deane. We reject, wherever possible, interference from the outside world.

We seek peace and quiet in which to worship Our Lord and honour our total obedience. Telephones are a distraction from prayer.'

As she spoke, both Maura and Kathleen stared at the black Bakelite phone on her desk.

Sister Assumpta continued. 'The girls have three meals per day and two hours off after lunch each afternoon, for the nursery, recreation and devotion. Bedtime is at nine o'clock. Do you have any other questions?'

The words 'if you dare' hovered in the air.

Kathleen and Maura were silent.

Sister Assumpta looked over her glasses at them both. They could only just define her facial features against the bright light.

When neither replied, she lifted up a paperweight from the desk.

'I have the adoption papers here for you to sign, Mrs Deane. We usually keep the babies until they are three years of age. However, in this case, upon the request of such an eminent midwife, we have agreed to arrange for the baby to be adopted almost immediately. We have many American couples desperate to provide a child with a good Catholic upbringing along with letters of recommendation from our priest, Father Michael, from the church of the Blessed Sacrament in Chicago. He arranges everything at the American end. This way, Mrs Deane, ye can be sure that the paths of the child and yourself never cross.'

Sister Assumpta barely acknowledged or addressed Kitty. It was as though it were Maura having the baby.

'As soon as she begins her labour, we will inform the midwife, by telephone, and she will contact yourself in good time.'

She stopped in mid-flow and peered over her glasses at them yet again, as if expecting there to be an objection.

But both Maura and Kathleen were too dumbstruck by the nun's cool and authoritative manner to utter a word.

'The midwife has told me that you wish to remove the mother from here almost immediately. Is this correct?'

Again, the look.

'Yes, that is quite right.' Maura now spoke in a voice that was little more than a squeak.

'In that case, we will require another thirty punts, making a total of one hundred and eighty punts. Is that acceptable?'

Maura felt as though the floor was opening up under her. Why had Kathleen brought her here? How in God's name would she ever find that kind of money? It was impossible. She would end up in a debtors' prison if she carried on with this. They would have to find some other way. God knew what, but they would.

Suddenly Liam's voice boomed out from what appeared to be nowhere.

'Here is a hundred punts, Mother, and we shall bring the rest when we collect, er ... Cissy here.'

Maura and Kitty stared at Liam as though he had gone mad, but Kathleen looked down at her teacup. Maura realized that Kathleen had known about this all along.

Liam walked over and, peeling off fifty pounds from a large wad of notes, placed the money down on Sister Assumpta's desk, then took his cap back out of his pocket and wringing it in his hands returned to the shadows once again.

Kathleen broke the silence.

'May we take Cissy to her room now, please, Sister, and help her unpack?'

She wanted to leave the study as soon as possible. This interview was far more difficult than the one she had previously undertaken. It was as though the shame of Kitty's pregnancy were heavy in the room and hung around them like a smell.

Sister Assumpta rose from her desk and glided to a dark-oak chest of drawers, from which she removed a heavy metal money-box. She selected a key from a cord around her waist and opened it, placed Liam's notes inside and slid it back into the drawer.

'No, I am afraid not,' she replied, closing the drawer and turning the key.

There was not even a note of regret nor a hint of an apology in her voice.

Sister Celia had baked a delicious fruit bread that morning and Sister Assumpta was keen to try a buttered slice whilst it was still warm from the oven. It was almost two hours since she had eaten.

She glided towards a thick golden cord hanging by the side of the fireplace and pulled it twice. In the distance they could all hear the gentle tinkling of a bell.

'I think it is time now for the girl to settle in and begin her first day. She cannot do that whilst you are still here. God has no patience with idle hands. It is time for you to leave her.'

She smiled yet again, a false and brittle smile. Her rapidly blinking eyes delivered her words as though they were flying steel tacks, pinning Maura to the chair.

Time to leave her.

Kathleen sprang up as though touched by lightning.

The moment was here. It could not be delayed. They could not invent excuses to hold onto Kitty.

'Get up, Maura,' hissed Kathleen.

Maura wanted to scream at the nun: her name is Kitty, not Cissy or 'the girl'. She is a person, she has a name, she is my daughter. Maura stood and reached out to take hold of Kitty's hand. Kitty was cold and rigid with a look of terror on her face.

'Mammy, please don't go.' She stared into Maura's eyes imploringly. 'Mammy, please, please don't go and leave me, please.'

But suddenly, from nowhere, two nuns silently entered the room and, before Maura could intercept, each took hold of one of Kitty's arms and almost lifted her, crying, from the room. Kathleen grabbed hold of Maura's arm and pulled her back, as she moved to run after Kitty. She had known it would be bad. Her sister, Julia, had warned her. She just hadn't thought it would be this bad. Kitty's screams of, 'No, Mammy, Nana Kathleen, please,' echoed down the hall. The pain in Kathleen's heart was bad. God knows what it must be like for Maura, she thought to herself.

Kitty's screams for help became fainter as she receded into the distance. Maura sobbed into Kathleen's chest and Kathleen held her tightly, in case she should make a break for it and run after Kitty. Liam, not knowing what to do, placed his hand on Maura's back. A gentle reminder that there was someone else who would prevent her from reaching Kitty.

Sister Assumpta stood with her hand on the door, waiting for them to leave, her body language all but ejecting them from the room, when Liam suddenly spoke. 'Where's our Nellie?'

He eventually found her standing at the side of the truck.

'Where did ye get to? All hell's broken loose in there altogether. Did ye not want to say goodbye to Kitty?' Liam said.

He was talking for the sake of it, upset and agitated by Kitty's distress. Yesterday, he had watched as she and Aengus had flirted and laughed together. From the top field, he had seen Aengus raise his cap and smile as the girls ran. Was that only yesterday?

Kathleen walked down the steps with Maura, virtually holding her up.

'Jeez, she's torn with the grief, so she is,' said Liam to Nellie.

Sister Assumpta had closed the convent door before they were even on the second step.

No wave. No smile. No goodbye.

'That nun is one fuckin' scold of a woman,' Liam whispered to Kathleen. 'God help Kitty in that place, because she won't.'

As they drove through the convent gates, Nellie turned to gaze out of the back window. The cab was silent apart from Maura, who was quietly sobbing.

Nellie checked the tarpaulin and saw the girl shift slightly underneath. She hoped she would be safe in there until they reached Dublin. Nellie realized this was the worst of days. She had lost Kitty and in her place, lying under the tarpaulin, she was smuggling her new friend, Besmina, out of the convent.

'Have ye ants in the pants?' said Kathleen to Nellie, exasperated. 'Ye haven't sat still since we left. What in God's name is up with ye?'

'Nothing, Nana, are we nearly there yet?'

'Aye, ten minutes more,' said Liam.

No one had spoken very much at all since leaving the convent, each imagining a different version of what life there would be like for Kitty.

In Maura's thoughts, Kitty was sitting in a dorm with girls similar to herself. They were laughing and joking, and kind novices were laughing with them. She had eaten a good supper and was laying out her belongings on a press, as she liked to do. She imagined

Kitty placing her freshly ironed nightdresses in a drawer. Maura knew Kitty would feel lonely but at least she would have other girls her own age around her and, surely, they would have a bit of fun and get to visit the village in the afternoons when the laundry was done.

She tried counting the days until she saw Kitty again.

'I will make a chart on the wall at home, to mark off the days till she comes home.' Maura hadn't really meant to say this out loud but once she had done so it made her feel much better.

'That's a fantastic idea, Auntie Maura,' said Nellie. 'I will too, an' I will draw a picture every day of things that happen. Can we write to her?'

'God, I hope so,' said Maura. 'It's not a prison. Liam, I need to talk to ye about what ye did.'

Maura thought it would be better to tackle Liam than Kathleen about the money. She had made the decision not to approach her own family whilst in Ireland. There was too much to explain. They had even less than she and Tommy. Too much to keep secret.

'Maura, we don't need to talk. There are times people need to look after each other. Don't worry about us and, anyway, it's been a good harvest, we are fine.'

'That's kind, Liam, but we will find a way, one day. We will pay ye back.'

'Ye already have, Maura, ye paid us in advance. Ye picked Jerry up off the floor, when Bernadette died, and Mammy says she doesn't know how Jerry would have survived without ye and Tommy. Ye have already paid, Maura. It's time for us to pay ye back.'

Silence fell once again in the cab. Nellie knew this wasn't a conversation she should be involved in. She knew her place.

The light was beginning to fade as Liam decided to pull up outside a café. 'There's two hours until the ferry. Time to fill up on some grub before ye leave, girls.' He jumped out and, as he went to lock the door, noticed one of the ropes on the tarpaulin was loose.

'Bloody hell, this could have blown off if there had been a wind. Mammy, I need a pee. Will ye tighten this rope?' said Liam.

'I'll do it, please, I can,' said Nellie.

Kathleen laughed. 'Go on then, madam. I'll go and get ye some food. Will egg and chips be all right now?'

'Aye, that'll be grand, thanks,' said Nellie, as she pretended to tighten the rope.

Nellie heard the café door close, quickly undid the knot and lifted the corner of the tarpaulin.

'Quickly, get out now,' she whispered.

The tarpaulin shuffled and shifted; Nellie saw a crop of dark hair as Besmina appeared. Grabbing Besmina's arms, Nellie helped to drag her out from underneath the tarpaulin. As soon as Besmina's feet hit the pavement, Nellie was already tightening the ropes.

'Oh God, I cannot believe I am free,' said Besmina, looking around her. She began to laugh and cry at the same time. 'What street am I on? Which street is this? Where is the river?' She was talking fast as she spun round, trying to take her bearings. 'My nanny lives on Faulkner Street, I have to get to her first. My mammy's moved and I don't know where she has gone to.'

'How do you know your mammy has moved?' asked Nellie.

'I got the laundry van driver to post a letter for me, with his address on for the reply. He told me the letter came back saying, "No longer at this address," so I need to get to Nanny to find out where Mammy is.' Besmina was still looking around her, trying to see the street sign.

'How do you know your nanny is still in Faulkner Street? She might have moved too.'

'No, she will not have moved, I was born in her bed and she was born in that house, as was my mammy. She will still be there.'

'Why couldn't ye get away?' asked Nellie. 'Please tell me, it's just that we have left Kitty there. Will she be OK?'

'Will she be OK? Are ye fucking mad? It's worse than a prison. It is worse than hell. Will she be OK?' Besmina began to laugh incredulously.

The café door opened and Kathleen put her head out. 'Come on, Nellie, your meal is ready. What are ye doing?' Kathleen looked at Besmina curiously.

'Nana, do ye know where Faulkner Street is near the river?' asked Nellie. 'This lady is lost.'

'Ye couldn't be closer, love.' Kathleen laughed. 'Go to the end of this street and it's there, right in front of ye on the other side.'

'Thanking ye, missus,' Besmina shouted back. She looked at Nellie. 'Ye saved my life, Nellie. I might have grown old and died in that hell if ye hadn't been brave. Some get transferred to the asylum when they go mad with the frustration of being locked up. If ye have left your Kitty in there, for God's sake make sure ye go back and get her out, will ye. Don't leave her there, thinking them nuns is nice and kind. They become the devil himself in that place.'

And with that, Besmina turned round and ran up the road in the direction Kathleen had indicated.

Nellie stared after her as she watched her disappear into the dusk, feeling sick and heavy-hearted. How could she walk into the café and tell them what she knew? She had helped to smuggle a girl out. She might have got Nana and Maura into trouble. Nellie didn't feel afraid. She knew she had done the right thing. But she also knew it was a secret she would have to carry alone.

## Chapter Twenty

Alice was bathing Joseph in the kitchen sink, whilst Jerry sat in his armchair, reading the paper, when Tommy walked into the kitchen.

As the back door opened, Joseph's expression altered to one of wonderment. He put both of his hands onto the front of the sink and leant forward to see who had arrived, expecting Kathleen.

'Evening, Alice, Jer,' Tommy shouted as Joseph yelled and kicked his legs frantically in order to attract Tommy's attention.

'What ya doin', little fella, eh?' laughed Tommy as he stepped over to the sink and playfully splashed small waves of water over Joseph. 'Would ye look at him now, growing bigger every day. I don't know what ye feed him, Alice, but sure, he'll be the size of Sean McGuire and joining him in the ring before he starts school at this rate.'

Jerry laughed.

Alice, not so much.

'Here, Tommy, do something useful for once, would you, and hold this towel, please.' Alice sounded mildly perturbed.

She scooped Joseph out from the sink, clear of the water, his wet, elongated and slippery body making him look more like a skinned rabbit than the bonny baby he was. Then she placed him onto the waiting towel.

Well practised, Tommy quickly wrapped the towel around Joseph and, after placing a kiss on the top of his head, handed the warm fluffy bundle back to Alice.

'Have ye news, Tommy?' said Jerry.

'Aye, I have. Albert called in on his way home from the pub. Bill sent him over with a message from Maura. She and Kathleen will be back with Nellie tomorrow.'

Jerry was pleased; he missed his Nellie.

'What about Kitty?' asked Jerry.

Tommy frowned. 'Not a word. I wondered if ye had any news from Kathleen or Nellie?'

'No, we have none. I'm relieved they are coming home. It's often very hard to get Mammy back over here, when she's been visiting home, and Nellie is just as bad. I think they would both live there, given half the chance.'

His friend Tommy was worried. Maura had been very secretive about Kathleen's letter and had herself slipped away to Ireland under the cover of darkness. Tommy could well imagine the inevitable questions, should she walk down the streets in daylight, carrying a bag.

'Where are ye off to then, Maura, with no curlers in and yer lipstick on?' someone would be bound to ask.

'What's up with her?' one neighbour would say to another.

'She's been right odd, so she has, since all this business with the priest,' would be passed down the line in the butcher's shop.

'Aye, she has that. She hasn't washed her nets since it happened and I haven't seen sight nor sound of their Kitty,' Mrs O'Prey would mention to someone in the grocer's.

'That Tommy's been acting like a mental bastard, threatening to bash McGinty's face in and giving pies to their Brian. The man has never in his life even taken a belt to his own kids, so he hasn't,' the men would say down in the Anchor.

'Angela Doherty has never stopped giving out about how she has to work now that their Kitty has done a moonlight flit,' the kids would say in the classroom.

And on it would go. Gossip, which would lead someone somewhere to jump to a conclusion.

'Would ye like a cuppa tea, Tommy?' asked Jerry as he rose from the chair. Tommy looked exhausted.

'Aye, thanks, Jer, I will. If I leave them little buggers long enough, they'll kill each other before I get back and that'll make things a bit easier in the morning.' They both laughed.

But not quite as much as they once might have done. Jokes about killing people sounded strangely hollow.

'I'm taking Joseph up,' said Alice, walking over to the fire with Joseph on her hip and his bottle in her hand. Joseph leant his head on Alice's shoulder and sucked his thumb noisily, half smiling at Jerry and Tommy.

'Say goodnight to Da and Uncle Tommy,' said Alice.

Joseph leant forward and bent down for another kiss from Tommy. Then he stretched out his arms to Jerry, who cuddled him and kissed his cheek.

'Night, night, little man. See ye in the morning for breakfast,' said Jerry, bathing his son in the most loving of smiles.

'I can't imagine what it must be like with only the little fella,' said Tommy. 'Me and Maura, we love our kids, make no mistake, but this week, Jerry, God, I'll tell ye this, I never knew my missus worked so hard, so I didn't, an' I never realized how much our Kitty did either. If Maura wasn't coming home tomorrow, I don't know how much longer I could cope. I've burnt the bloody letter from the nuns, complaining about Declan going to school with his ears blocked up with pobs. Jeez, Maura would have a fit if she saw that.'

He looked up at Jerry and, after a moment's hesitation, they both began to laugh as they imagined the sight of Declan with a bowl of pobs on his head.

The men sat and drank their tea, their anxiety gradually draining away. Once Tommy's mug was empty, he walked to the door to pick up his coat and said, 'Well, Jerry, I feel a million times better than I did when I arrived, so I do, and now I'm off to knock all their bleedin' heads together and get them into bed.'

The back door was closing and Tommy departing just as Alice returned to the kitchen.

Jerry was still grinning at the thought of Declan's ears being blocked with pobs as he grabbed Alice round the waist and pulled her to him.

'I think it's about time we went to bed and got an early night, don't ye think? We haven't had a chance yet to enjoy it, just being us in the house.'

'You go up and I will follow when I've cleared Joseph's bath things away.'

'I don't think so, Mrs Deane. Do ye realize, this is the last time we will have the house to ourselves before Kathleen and Nellie come back tomorrow? I think we should get in that bed now and make the most of it, don't you?'

As Alice walked up the stairs ahead of him, she realized this must be the last time. She would have slept with two men in two days, which was a recipe for disaster. As Jerry undid the buttons on the back of her dress and slipped his hands inside and cupped her breasts, she closed her eyes as a thrill of wickedness shot through her. She imagined it was Sean not Jerry who was caressing her. She focused her mind on Jerry's hands, which became Sean's, and the pleasure she felt as they roamed.

She either had to stop seeing Sean, or leave Jerry, she knew that, but for now, she would enjoy tonight knowing that when the morning came, she would have no idea which one she would choose.

*

The following morning, Harry popped his head round the kitchen door. 'I've left the babby in the pram by the outhouse, Auntie Alice.'

'Thank you, Harry,' Alice replied quickly, so that he could hear her before he closed the door.

From the sink, Alice watched Harry, serious little Harry, with his purposeful walk and his head slightly bent. As he reached the pram, he straightened his cap and then lifted his green canvas army bag from the pram apron. He gave the pram handlebars a quick wiggle and slipped though the gate. As he closed the gate behind him, he saw Alice at the sink and gave her a smile before the latch clicked.

The Silver Cross pram bounced up and down in a gentle rhythm famous for sending babies to sleep within seconds.

The baby must be restless, thought Alice. She looked at Joseph, who had drifted back to sleep a half-hour since, and slipped into the yard. She pulled back the fly net and there was the baby with eyes wide open, blowing bubbles.

'You little tinker,' said Alice, smiling. 'Your mammy will be back later. Back to sleep now, or I'll be having a word with your daddy when he gets home from work. I have things to do today, miss.'

At that moment, Mrs Keating walked in through the gate, followed by a young woman Alice had never seen before.

'Morning, Alice,' said Mrs Keating, 'this is my niece from Cork, Finoula. She is staying with me while she writes after jobs. She's trying for work looking after babies, so she is, and I thought that, as Maura is away, she could get some practice in with the babby and could be a grand help to ye, an' all?'

Alice noticed that Finoula's hair was an unusual colour for an Irish girl. It was strawberry blonde, instead of flaming red or black. There were usually no in betweens; the Irish were one or the other.

'Well, that would be fine by me and I'm sure Maura wouldn't mind,' said Alice. 'But we are expecting Maura back tonight and I'm sure she will want the baby all to herself. You know what Maura is like. Would you like a cup of tea?'

For the first time in her life, Alice reached for the mop and banged on the kitchen wall for Peggy to come and join them. A visitor to the street was news.

Alice was becoming more Irish by the day.

Within half an hour, the kitchen was full. It was hard for Alice to concentrate on what the women were saying and she was glad that the conversation focused on Finoula, who was answering a barrage of questions about the news in Ireland.

Peggy had knocked on for Sheila and Deirdre. Alice began to understand that it was a very different gathering without Kathleen and Maura.

Her thoughts were wandering above the babble, not to last night with Jerry, but to the hotel, with Sean. As she remembered every second, a thrill of intense excitement shot through the pit of her stomach.

Where was Sean now? she wondered. Was he at work?

Brigid arrived at the back door with Mrs McGuire. Alice's heart sank. She had been avoiding them, not wanting to face either wife or mother.

The women round the table chorused, 'Brigid, Mrs McGuire, come on in, sit down for a cuppa.'

Alice felt resentful. She couldn't help it. She was uncomfortable with people treating her kitchen as though it were their own.

Peggy jumped up. 'I'll go and fetch a couple of chairs from mine,' she said. Then, 'Holy Mary,' she shouted from the yard, 'there are so many prams out here, I can hardly get back to me own house.'

'Shall I put the kettle back on, Alice?' asked Sheila, who didn't feel entirely comfortable doing so without asking first. She wouldn't have thought twice had Kathleen been there.

'Yes, of course,' said Alice, dragging her thoughts away from Sean. She could not erase him from her mind and she could not for the life of her stop thinking about their lovemaking. Was it really so different from what had happened with Jerry last night, she asked herself? No, it wasn't. And then, with the force of a train, it hit her.

She enjoyed sex with both men, but only one man dominated her thoughts to the point of distraction.

She was in love. She must be.

The laughter and the babble of the women faded. She had never felt like this before. She had thought of Jerry constantly, from the day she met him, but not like this. That was an obsession. This was love. There was an enormous difference. This made her feel happy and joyous, while her obsession with Jerry had made her reclusive and anxious, devious and mean. She had been cruel to Nellie and resentful, and she had made Jerry's life a misery.

God, I was a sick person, Alice thought to herself and, for a second, the sadness of the life she had led, and the person she had been, clouded her thoughts of Sean.

What am I going to do? she asked herself. What a bloody mess. What is the right thing to do?

'A penny for your thoughts,' said Finoula, sitting next to her.

'Oh, gosh. You don't want to know what my thoughts are,' laughed Alice. 'Even I can't work them out.'

She heard the dock klaxon sound as she finished washing the kitchen floor.

Jerry was working an extra half-shift, because the bar was full. Ships were waiting for a pilot to bring them into a berth. The pressure was on to unload as quickly as possible.

Finoula had taken both the baby and Joseph back to Mrs Keating's in the same pram. She had offered to feed them and take them for a walk. Alice was grateful for the break.

She loved her freedom and she wanted, more than anything, to be alone with her thoughts. To have space to dwell and think, without any interruption, about Sean and the time they had spent together.

At what point had she fallen in love with him? She had no idea, but she did know that, right now, her heart ached to see him.

As though she had willed him into her presence, the back door opened and Sean walked in. He looked round the kitchen. 'Are ye alone?' he asked.

'I am, yes.'

Within seconds they were in each other's arms. Within minutes, Sean had lifted her skirt up to her waist, and his hands, wild to feel every inch of her, were all over her body, down the tops of her stockings, across her back and over her breasts, seemingly at the same time. As he entered her, he had only one reckless thought: that he desperately, beyond any notion of reason, wanted either Brigid or Jerry to walk in at that very moment and catch them both – just as he claimed Alice as his very own.

There was no school for little Paddy. It wasn't his turn for the shoes. He was watching *The Flowerpot Men* on the black-and-white television when Peggy shouted to him, 'Paddy, go and get my kitchen chairs, there are two of them in Alice's backyard next to the gate. Go on now, do as I say.'

Little Paddy groaned.

Scamp sat up and looked at Little Paddy keenly, wagging his tail. He placed his paw on Paddy's back and whined.

'OK, OK, I'm coming,' said Little Paddy, jumping up. 'Mam, I have no shoes to put on, so how can I?' he grumbled.

'Here, put my slippers on,' said Peggy, slapping margarine on the bread and then scraping it off again, for the meat paste sandwiches they would have for their lunch. Little Paddy wasn't the only one not at school; there were four of them watching TV, but he was the only one that Peggy and Big Paddy ever sent to run a message.

Peggy kicked off her slippers, the only footwear she possessed, and slid them across the floor to Little Paddy.

'Here ye are,' she said. 'Butties ready when ye come in with the chairs.'

The damp slippers were dirty and even Little Paddy could tell that they stank. He screwed up his face as he slipped them onto his feet.

Scamp ran ahead of him to Alice's back door. Scamp loved Kathleen, who, like Brigid, always saved him stock bones and strips of bacon rind.

Little Paddy found the chairs next to the outhouse and began to carry them both to the gate.

'Come on, Scamp,' he said.

Scamp stood with his back to Little Paddy, looking up at the closed back door, wagging his tail furiously.

'Come on, Scamp,' shouted Little Paddy again, this time

impatiently. It had been raining and the damp was soaking through the holes in Peggy's slippers, making his feet cold and wet.

He put down one of the chairs as he lifted the gate latch. Pulling the gate wide open, he leant against it as he attempted to pick up the chair and struggle through.

'Scamp,' he shouted again, angrily. The chairs were difficult to carry and he didn't want to have to put them down again.

Little Paddy looked up towards the kitchen window, to see if anyone had noticed him taking the chairs.

What he saw made him so scared, his knees felt weak.

Little Paddy went white and hissed under his breath as loudly as he could, 'Scamp, get here now, ye fecking eejit dog.'

Just at that moment, Scamp, growing impatient, scratched at the back door and barked loudly.

Paddy looked back to the window, but no one indoors had heard. Paddy saw that Alice's breasts were bare and that she was pulling her dress back over her shoulders. And Sean McGuire was helping her.

'Oh, fecking hell, I'm dead,' groaned Little Paddy, putting his hand over his eyes.

## Chapter Twenty-one

It was almost midnight when Maura and Kathleen turned the corner of Nelson Street. They froze with astonishment at the sight that greeted them.

There was not a family in bed on any of the four streets.

Every parlour light was switched on. Front doors stood partially open, as light bled out onto the pavement. Children and women stood in the shadows, in huddles, whispering, and the men, having hurriedly left the lock-in at the pub, stood silently at the opposite end of the street, pint glasses still in hand.

As Maura and Kathleen stepped into the circle of street light, everyone turned to look at them. For a moment, frantic, panicky thoughts whirled through Maura's brain. She imagined her neighbours knew the truth about Kitty and were waiting for her, to scold and shout at her, to wag their fingers and to chase her off the street.

'*Where have you taken your whore daughter then, eh? What have you done with her? Ye all so high and mighty and ye can't even teach yer own daughter to keep her knickers up.*'

Kathleen took Nellie's hand and gently drew her close. Kathleen sensed danger and death running hand in hand, wild on the wind.

Maura's panic gave way to alarm when she spotted a large Black Maria police van outside Molly Barrett's house. Three more blue and white panda cars were parked in front of the Black Maria. A man with a camera in his hand stood on the opposite pavement.

'Hiya, love,' he shouted. 'Do you live on this street?'

'Yes, we do,' replied Kathleen. 'What's going on?'

'There's been a second murder,' said the man casually. 'An old woman, apparently, who lives in that house.' He pointed towards Molly's. 'She was found only a couple of hours ago. Do you know what her name was?'

Stunned into silence, neither Kathleen nor Maura could speak.

The man with the camera carried on. 'Seems like we've got a madman living around the dock streets. That's two murders. I'm from the *Echo*, queen. Anything you can tell me about the old woman?' He took his pencil from behind his ear and his notepad out of his pocket, conveying an air of expectancy.

At that moment, Harry and Little Paddy, with Scamp at his heels, came running up the street, wearing their pyjamas.

Maura said, 'My God, it's nearly midnight and Harry is not in his bed, *and look at Little Paddy's nose.*'

Kathleen slipped Maura a sideways glance. There had been a second murder on their own street and yet Maura was more worried about the fact that Harry was still awake and Little Paddy had been neglected.

Kathleen realized Maura's reaction was odd and inappropriate. She needed to move her indoors.

'How could any of the kids sleep?' she said, in a matter-of-fact voice. 'With a spotlight rigged up outside Molly's front door, how could anyone sleep?'

'Mam, Mam,' yelled Harry, throwing his arms round Maura. 'Molly is dead, her head has been smashed in. Annie O'Prey found her. Molly had been missing all day until Annie found her in the outhouse.'

The man from the *Echo* wrote down every word.

'Me ma says we aren't safe in our beds tonight, Auntie Maura,' said Little Paddy.

The end of his nose was cased in many days' worth of hard dried snot. Maura made a mental note to take him into her kitchen and soften it overnight with Vaseline, then she would help him clean it off in the morning.

Molly was dead. The street was in chaos and yet Maura fixed her attention on the things that kept her sane and grounded. The trivia of domestic life.

In the seconds that followed, an ambulance almost knocked them over.

'Molly might be alive,' said Maura, nudging Kathleen.

The man from the *Echo* dispelled that notion in a flash of the light bulb on his camera. 'Nah, that's the body trolley,' he said, matter-of-factly.

More adults moved out into the pool of light and joined the children, carrying cups of tea, smoking cigarettes and wearing their nightclothes. The boldest came first, with others following nervously, taking their cue.

An hour earlier, the entire street had been alerted by Annie's screams when she had found Molly. Anyone who hadn't heard Annie would have been woken by the sirens, not fifteen minutes later, as they fired down the street, announcing the arrival of the police. But by that time everyone already knew, on the four streets and far beyond.

A row of heads in curlers and hairnets began to line both sides of

Nelson Street in a guard of honour. The lit upstairs windows filled with the faces of smaller children, not allowed out into the misty night air.

Silence fell upon the crowd as neighbours ceased talking in order to show their respect to Molly.

As the ambulance departed, a new feeling of fear descended upon the inhabitants.

Molly had been bludgeoned to death. Old fat Molly who made cakes and gossiped.

As the ambulance trundled down the Dock Road towards town and the siren faded into the distance, taking Molly further from the place where she had spent every day of her life, the women began to cry. The first and the loudest was Peggy. Then others followed suit until the air became choked with the wailing of frightened women.

Tommy and Jerry were walking up the street towards Kathleen, Maura and Nellie.

'Two murders, Tommy,' said Sheila to Tommy, as he passed. 'Are any of us safe in our beds, eh?'

Tommy couldn't answer. He touched his cap and walked steadily towards Maura, whose dark eyes radiated fear.

The only sound he could hear was that of Molly's cat, Tiger, howling on the back-entry wall.

## Chapter Twenty-two

The taciturn nuns led a sobbing Kitty upstairs to a room in the eaves. The floorboards were bare and each wall was lined with a row of wooden-framed beds. Upon each lay an uncomfortable looking ticking-covered horsehair mattresses.

On one of the beds lay a dark blue pair of long shorts, a dark blue top and a white apron.

'Put the clothes on, please, Cissy,' said a novice.

'I don't want to,' sobbed Kitty. 'I want to see my mammy.'

'You don't have that choice, I'm afraid.'

Kitty noticed that Sister Celia carried her leather bag. Kitty didn't want anyone else touching her precious belongings and so she leant down to take the bag from her.

'Ah, not so fast, thank you,' said Sister Celia. 'We take this. You can have it back on the day your family collect you. You are very lucky, young lady. If it weren't for the midwife, you might never see them again.'

Kitty was speechless. No one had ever spoken to or looked at her with such unkindness.

Sister Celia continued, 'There are rules here. You will speak to no one, ever. Do you understand?' Kitty could not believe what she was hearing. 'No one. Not a soul. We don't want the poor girls who won't be leaving to be upset by your good fortune in having the midwife as your relative. No one here is allowed to speak. Do you understand that? We have penitents here who will have no one to collect them. They atone for their sin fully and so we don't want them upset, now, do we? *Do we?*'

Sister Celia shouted and Kitty visibly jumped. 'Now, get those clothes on and we will take you over to the laundry.'

The nuns stood and watched her. Kitty stared back, waiting for them to move away and allow her some privacy. They didn't budge.

'Hurry up. Have you something different from the rest of us, Cissy?' Sister Celia sneered. 'Pity you weren't so shy when you were dropping your knickers for your five minutes of fun, eh? Not so shy then, were you? Get dressed.'

Kitty moved over to the bed. With her face burning and tears streaming, she removed her own clothes and put on the blue calico outfit that had been laid out for her.

The nun snatched Kitty's clothes from her aggressively as Kitty held them out in her shaking arms. To Kitty's utter horror, Sister Celia turned Kitty's still-warm knickers inside out and, holding them almost at the end of her nose, inspected them through her thick wire spectacles, squinting as she did so. She sniffed the gusset and, looking up at Kitty with a smirk on her face, she hissed, 'You dirty sinning whore. Not your fault, eh? Well, we've heard all that before and these knickers tell us differently, eh?'

She turned away with everything Kitty could call her own in her arms.

Kitty didn't know how she survived the day.

The work in the laundry was hard and there was no food until evening. She thought she would faint.

There were girls of her own age and many much older. Not one dared speak a word. Silence reigned the entire time whilst she plunged dirty sheets into the large sinks.

The laundry was filled with the sound of hissing steam and the noise of rollers and trolleys being wheeled in and out.

The only distraction arrived in the afternoon when the nuns, seemingly on the verge of hysteria, ran round the washrooms, demanding to know where a girl called Besmina had gone. No one knew, but Kitty noticed the looks that passed from one girl to the next.

Hours after she began work, a girl who seemed to be about her own age, with short red hair and freckles, passed her a wicker basket of dirty clothes. As she did so, she whispered, 'Don't cry so. Ye will make yourself sick. We will have a natter tonight, after they put out the lights.'

She gave Kitty's hand the gentlest of squeezes.

Kitty had finally lain down on the dormitory bed, having carefully watched and followed what the other girls did. Minutes after the nun had said a prayer and put the lights out, Kitty became aware of the noise of rustling sheets and feet pattering on the floorboards.

Then a kindly voice whispered, 'Come on then, shift up so we can get under yer blanket and have a natter.'

Kitty opened her eyes to a circle of girls standing round her bed.

They told Kitty about the routine and how they survived it. She learnt about the missing Besmina, who had been in the laundry for years. Her family had never returned to collect her, but every day she used to imagine that she saw her mammy, who had died years earlier, walking up the steps and knocking on the Abbey door.

'God knows where she is now,' said Aideen, the girl who had spoken to Kitty in the laundry. 'She was mad to escape and has tried so many times. She always ends up being brought back and then she gets punished so badly with the stick, poor Besmina.'

'I know my family will come for me,' said Kitty quietly. 'I counted the days today when I was washing. My mammy will be back for me. I know she will. I will count them down every day.'

They talked on Kitty's bed for over an hour.

'Not all the nuns are scolds,' said Aideen. 'We have new ones every now and then. They all start out nice.'

'Aye, but once they've been here a few months, they turn into fucking witches,' said an older woman on the end of the bed who had hardly spoken until that point.

Some of the girls had already birthed their babies, but had to stay, working without pay in the Abbey until the children were three years old, because they couldn't raise the one hundred and fifty pounds without which they couldn't leave. Kitty could hardly believe what she was hearing.

'I had my little lad two years ago,' said Maria, in a quiet voice. 'I have one more year with him and then he will be adopted and live with an American family. I pay my way here by working in the laundry and the parents in America will pay for his adoption. It's a win all round for the nuns. They use our baby money to buy their grand silver and Persian rugs, so they do.'

'Is Cissy yer real name?' asked Aideen.

Kitty was shocked. How did Aideen know?

Before she could reply, Aideen elaborated. 'We were all given different names on the day we arrived, and we can only be called by saints' names but, sure, it doesn't happen anyway. We are only ever called by our last names. No nun has ever called me anything other than O'Reiley since the day I arrived.'

'My name is Maria but on the day I arrived they told me that my name is now Frances.'

'They can't take away your name,' said Kitty as she sat further up in the bed. She felt enraged at the notion that someone could have their name removed. She was only hiding her name; it wasn't being taken from her. She was still Kitty.

'Aye, they can and they do,' said Maria.

The older woman spoke again. Kitty thought that she looked the saddest. She later discovered that she had been in the Abbey for five years and that her baby had long since gone but that she had no home and no money. Ever since, she had remained in the Abbey, working twelve-hour days every day for no pay and at the mercy of Sister Assumpta's whim and temper.

'Just be sure to never speak,' she advised Kitty. 'Even if you are at the rollers in the laundry and ye think the noise will drown out what ye is saying, it won't. The witches have fuckin' good hearing, now they do. They will hear and ye will be sent to the Reverend Mother and when ye are, she will beat ye with a stick so bad … See this.'

She pointed to a thin, bright-red weal down the side of her neck.

'And these.'

She held out her hands to Kitty, who inhaled sharply at the sight of the cuts across the older woman's palms.

'I got the stick because Besmina disappeared, like it was my fault. Besmina was put with me on the corridors and the bathrooms this morning. I'm just warning ye …' She tailed off as she saw the look on Kitty's face. Kitty was appalled at the idea of a woman, the age of her own mother, being beaten.

The light from an oil lamp at the bottom of the stairs crept under the door. In seconds, everyone had fled to their own beds.

Kitty lay awake. The footsteps, belonging to the lamp-carrying nun, clipped away into the distance.

The gentle breathing of her roommates became deeper as they succumbed to exhaustion. Kitty heard the unfamiliar creaks and groans of the building as it moaned in objection to the wind buffeting it from all sides. Her eyes adjusted to the starlight shining in through the skylight opposite her bed, illuminating the faces of the sleeping girls.

She thought about the harvest, which might almost have happened weeks ago. Could it have been only yesterday that she met Aengus? She felt for the charm bracelet Maeve had given her. It was still there. She removed the bracelet and tucked it underneath her mattress in case a nun saw her wearing it and took it away.

As the faces of Tommy, Maura and her siblings filled her mind, she thought about home. She wondered, would the baby even know who she was by the time she returned? Everyone and everything felt as though it belonged to another life, a life she had left. Was it only this morning that she had arrived?

As she closed her eyes, she heard Sister Evangelista praising her English essay and remembered her pride when she had won a bar of Cadbury's chocolate, the class prize for reading. A feeling of utter homesickness overwhelmed her. Tears ran silently down her cheeks. She had never slept in a room with so many people nor ever felt so alone.

'Not long,' she whispered, as she scrunched the bed sheet tightly in her hand, as though it were a rope holding her onto the edge of sanity.

After breakfast the following morning, a novice instructed Kitty to visit the Reverend Mother's office before she began work in the laundry.

There had been no talking at breakfast. Everyone remained silent while the nuns ate their bacon and sausages, and the girls their milky gruel.

Once the ordeal was over, the girls sat straight-backed on their wooden pews, hands folded in laps, waiting to be dismissed to the toilet before work. Kitty closely watched what they did and copied them, exactly.

Once the bathroom call was over, they were sent straight down to the laundry. Some were issued with house-cleaning duties, which meant having to scrub long corridors on their hands and knees.

This was regarded as light relief after washing other people's dirty linen.

Kitty knocked on Sister Assumpta's door, the biggest she had ever stood in front of in her life, painted a glossy white with six tall panels. She stood with her hand resting on the large brass knob and strained to hear the instruction for her to walk in.

The word 'Enter' boomed towards her from across the vast room and penetrated the door with no difficulty whatsoever.

Kitty turned the knob and nervously stepped inside. The fading aroma of Kathleen's 4711 eau de cologne lingered behind the door, and ushered her across the acreage of pastel-green Persian carpet.

Kitty's heart leapt and then sank again. There was no one in the room other than Sister Assumpta, seated at her desk. As before, she was but a silhouette against the light flooding in through the window behind her.

Kitty hovered, not knowing what to say.

From what she could make out, Sister Assumpta was scrutinizing a letter. On her desk lay a long-handled, bone-and-silver letter opener.

In the absence of any acknowledgment or instruction, Kitty acted upon her own initiative and walked to the same chair in front of the desk on which she had been instructed to sit only yesterday. The dark wooden seat was upholstered in a beautiful, cream damask silk. Before she sat down, she glanced out of the window behind Reverend Mother and noticed that, on the front lawn, a long row of heavily pregnant young girls were on their hands and knees, picking at the grass with their bare hands.

Kitty watched for a moment, amazed that this was how the vast expanse of lawn was maintained. The girls crawled backwards as they shredded the grass, harvesting daisies. Following behind them were two more girls, pushing an enormous metal roller that was at least twice the size of them both, flattening the freshly picked grass.

'*Did I tell you to sit?*' the Reverend Mother roared with such ferocity, it made Kitty spring back to her feet.

She cupped her hands in front of her and stood looking down

at them, for no other reason than she felt it would be impertinent to look directly at Sister Assumpta and she didn't know where else to look.

'Would you like me to send for tea, would you, Cissy?'

Sister Assumpta's voice was laced with sarcasm. Kitty lifted her eyes and could just make out that she was peering at her over her spectacles. She was not smiling.

'No, Sister, I have had my tea, thank you,' she replied with more confidence than she felt.

Sister Assumpta laughed. A hollow, unkind laugh.

'Have you, girl? Then, that's just as well, isn't it? I wouldn't like you to be thinking you could wander in here for a cup of tea at any old time of day, would I?'

Kitty knew she was being laughed at and remained silent.

'*Would I?*' Again the roar. Kitty was close to being afraid.

Her words wobbled on the edge of tears as she replied, 'No, Sister.'

Sister Assumpta stared at Kitty for what seemed like an eternity.

Kitty listened to the seconds ticking by on the grandfather clock in the corner and, with each second, her fear grew.

A fierce heat slowly crept upwards from her neck, under her chin and onto her face, as she looked down again, afraid of causing offence if she turned her eyes elsewhere.

'I have received a letter this morning, Cissy.' She stopped. '*Cissy*.'

Kitty's head jerked upwards. She looked bolder than she felt. In truth she was terrified.

'The midwife has written to say that she will be calling to see you. Now, that's very special treatment, isn't it, Cissy?'

Kitty didn't know how to answer but her heart skipped a beat.

She knew the midwife, Rosie, was a relative of Nana Kathleen.

'She will be here a week on Wednesday. I will see you again before she arrives. However, the reason I have asked to see you today is that I need to ensure that you always remember that many of the girls here are penitents. Just like yourself, Cissy, they are fallen women and have been placed in my care to help them find salvation through obedience and work. They do not have an esteemed midwife in the family, money, or indeed relatives gagging to take them out when the time comes. They will end their days here, seeking salvation and forgiveness from the good Lord. If you lived in Ireland, and had none of the privileges you do, you would likely be one of them, as you surely have their sinful ways, girl.'

She stopped talking and again stared at Kitty, waiting for a reaction.

Sister Assumpta was not happy that she had agreed to take in this girl. She had been given no back story and she didn't like that at all. She had not even received a letter from the girl's priest in Liverpool, which would have been the usual means of introduction. Something was not right with this situation. Kitty and her family were hiding something.

The Reverend Mother was no fool. However, she could not ignore the midwife, Rosie O'Grady. Since the hanging incident, it had been hard indeed to persuade a midwife to work at the convent under any circumstances. Rosie O'Grady was the matron at the women's hospital in Dublin where she had made a name for herself as the most senior in her profession in Ireland. She was not someone to be refused.

The most recent hanging had cast a grave shadow over the convent. The nuns had tried to keep it quiet, but bad news travels faster than any other. 'If only the stupid girls hadn't shouted out of the window for the laundry van drivers to help, we would have stood a better chance of keeping it quiet. We had managed it every other time,' Sister Assumpta often complained to Sister Celia.

She had to repair what damage had been done to the convent's good name.

News like this could stop the prison and the hotels sending their laundry out to the Abbey and that would be a catastrophe. The nuns would receive little help from Rome if their income dried up.

Refusing to take a referral from Rosie O'Grady would infer they had something to hide.

The Reverend Mother focused her attention on Kitty and noticed her tremble.

'I don't want you upsetting things and so you must not discuss your situation with anyone, do you understand me?'

Kitty nodded.

'*Do you understand me?*'

Kitty began to shake. She tried to not to, but she couldn't stop herself. The trembling began in her hands, travelled upwards through her arms and soon took over her entire body. Her teeth began to chatter uncontrollably. She could not stop them. But something unexpected washed over her. The knowledge that she was loved.

She was not alone. She was not friendless. She had people who cared about her who had brought her here out of kindness and, seemingly, at great expense.

A confidence she didn't know she possessed forced her to lift her head to look at Sister Assumpta straight in what she took to be her eyes.

'Yes, Reverend Mother,' she replied defiantly and almost slightly too loudly. 'I have committed no crime. I am not a penitent. I am here of my own free will, because this is the place my mammy and Kathleen chose for me, on Auntie Rosie's say-so. I'm glad Auntie Rosie is coming to see me next week. I shall be able to send a message home when she does and let them know I am all right.'

Sister Assumpta peered over her glasses in surprise at Kitty. Her mouth opened and closed like a fish and then, with a wave of her hand, she shouted, 'Oh, get out of here, girl. Get out and just remember, you are forbidden to talk. Everyone is forbidden, but you even more so.'

With a new-found and growing confidence, bordering on reckless, Kitty forced a smile to her lips. She looked straight at the blurred dark form in the midst of the light and said, 'Thank you, Reverend Mother,' and, turning on her heel, she moved towards the door.

Just as she pulled it closed behind her, she heard the voice booming impatiently behind her. 'And don't walk on the carpet.'

Once safely out of the room, Kitty whispered to herself, 'This must be what hell is like. I've been sent to hell. I'll bloody beat it, though.'

And, for the first time since she had arrived, she strode with her head held high.

# Chapter Twenty-three

Howard knew he would have to be especially kind when questioning Daisy. He was also keen to impress Miss Devlin.

'Have a heart, Howard. What can she possibly know? Sure, Daisy is a bag of nerves most of the time. This is freaking her out altogether, so it is,' she said.

Howard had popped into the school office to have a word with Sister Evangelista and afterwards had lingered, making pointless small talk, until Miss Devlin offered him a cup of tea.

Had he but known it, Miss Devlin was delighted to see him again.

She had taken to wearing her newly lightened hair in a fashionable short pixie style, in place of the ponytail tied up in a bow that she had sported since she was six years old.

Miss Devlin had recently celebrated the universally acknowledged spinster age of thirty. Alone. Reading *Madame Bovary*, with a pot of Earl Grey tea and a lemon puff. As far as she and most of the people around her were concerned, she was well and truly on the shelf. Howard's attention was an answer to her prayers. He wasn't a Catholic, but she was so keen, she was prepared to overlook this previously non-negotiable requirement.

Howard loved to stare at her soft powdery face, drowning in her liquid blue eyes with the first signs of crow's feet appearing at the corners. And now, as he became transfixed by her gently moving, cherry-red lips, he had trouble concentrating on what she was saying.

'Pardon?' he asked, as she finished speaking.

'I asked you, what could Daisy possibly know? She is simple and has been in the care of the sisters since she was born.'

Before he could answer, a loud metallic crash followed by a violent ping echoed across the room as the school secretary frowned over the top of her prim and proper, horn-rimmed spectacles.

She was a click of a letter away from informing both Howard and Miss Devlin that she did not approve of flirting at work.

Miss Devlin frowned back. She made a mental note to inform the school secretary that in future she could take herself and her solitaire diamond engagement ring over to the convent for half an hour and leave them alone.

Howard could not tell Miss Devlin what Daisy was supposed to have confided in Molly. They needed to hear it for themselves. It was no use to them as hearsay and now that Molly was dead, they had to move quickly. They didn't want to be made fools of, yet again.

'We will be very careful with Daisy, you needn't worry.'

'What is it like down on the streets? Are the women anxious about the murder whilst the men are out at work?'

'It is bad,' Howard replied. 'Everyone is jumpy and who can blame them? They are all safe enough, though, we have officers everywhere.'

Howard didn't mention to her that he and Simon had a major headache. There was nothing he would have loved more than to have discussed it with her, but secrecy was a fundamental part of his job. In police work, he had to keep his own counsel.

They had been watching Tommy Doherty like a hawk since Molly Barrett had told them that Daisy saw Tommy murder the priest. But they knew it could not have been Tommy who killed Molly. He had been in his own house at the time.

Howard's superiors were convinced that whoever had murdered the priest had also murdered Molly.

Howard and Simon knew that, if what Daisy had told Molly was the truth, this just couldn't be the case and, besides, who would believe that? There had never been so much as a burglary on any of the four streets before. This community looked after its own, and yet he would be asking everyone to believe that there had been two random murders committed by two different people in a short space of time in one community. Even Howard knew that sounded incredible. Over and over again, he had quizzed the officers who had been on duty. Their stories were faultless. Not a crack in any of them.

Tommy had left Jerry Deane's house the evening of Molly's

murder. He had returned home and walked in through his own back gate. He was seen closing his bedroom curtains and switching off the light an hour later. He never left the house again until the men knocked on for him the following morning.

Tommy Doherty had not murdered Molly Barrett. This was one of the very few facts in their possession. There had been a police officer in a parked car at the end of the road, close to Tommy's front door, and another car parked by the end of his entry all night. They had not stopped watching Tommy since Molly's confession over the lightest sandwich cake Howard had ever tasted.

Molly's house was on the other side of the road. Whoever had murdered her had been calculating and audacious. Not one of the officers had seen or heard anything, but they did have one solitary clue. A Pall Mall cigarette filter had been found on the outhouse floor. Congealed in blood, but definitely a Pall Mall. They had taken good note. Tommy smoked roll-ups. Molly smoked Woodbines.

Until Molly's murder, Howard and Simon had thought that they had a solid lead. They had been waiting for Daisy to recover from her attack of nerves in the convent.

Now Molly was dead. And someone did it right under the noses of twelve of Lancashire's finest coppers.

There was a gnawing feeling in the pit of Howard's stomach that, somehow, he and Simon were responsible for Molly's death. That if they hadn't spent so much time in her parlour, drinking tea and eating cake, she might still be alive today.

There was only one person Howard knew who smoked Pall Mall and that was Simon. He made a mental note to ask Simon where in town he bought them to try and draw a link between someone in the streets and the filter.

Howard placed his empty cup on the desk beside Miss Devlin.

'I have to go. I'm off to brief Simon down at the station and run through the questions we have to ask Daisy.'

'It's a good job Sister has given permission for both me and Daisy to jump in the car with you at six tonight,' said Miss Devlin. 'I think Daisy will find it helpful having me there to hold her hand,' she added with a smile.

Howard grinned. ''Tis you who will need the chaperone if you are in a car with me,' he replied cheekily.

The typewriter carriage crashed and pinged and Howard flinched.

'Does she fire tin tacks out of that machine or what?' he whispered as he walked towards the steps.

'You cheeky thing,' Miss Devlin whispered back, tapping his arm playfully.

Howard's blue and white panda was parked at the iron gates. As he opened the door, he turned round and winked. She looked at him and they both smiled. A nervous smile. A smile that wished they were both in a different time and place, far beyond the four streets and the double murder investigation. A smile that made a promise. Soon. When this is all over.

Soon.

The interview was difficult from the start. Daisy had appeared nervous as they stepped into the large police station at Whitechapel, and now she had become quiet and non-responsive.

Even though the nuns had told her Molly was dead, she didn't appear to have taken in what it meant.

'It would have been better to do this in the convent,' Miss Devlin whispered to Howard as they descended the dark stone stairs to the interview room.

'We can't,' he replied. 'It has to be done on a tape recorder.'

To prove his point, Howard wound a thin ribbon of brown tape round one of the two wheels on the front of the machine that sat on the interview desk.

Simon, who had asked to lead the interview, came into the room behind them.

Howard reflected on how neither he nor Simon had ever before been involved in a case with so few clues and so little motive. This was the seventh murder case they had worked on together. Howard had been called up for yet another meeting in the superintendent's office that morning. He had explained that he could not find a single motive for either the murder of a much loved priest or that of an old woman, whose only crime was to have been in possession of a wicked sweet tooth.

The case had hit the news headlines yet again and put Howard's superiors in a bad mood. 'Police clueless over double dock street murders,' the *Daily Post* headline taunted them from the paper-sellers' stalls along the streets of Liverpool.

'No clues anywhere,' Howard said to Simon when he came back into the office. 'A motive is where our investigations usually begin. We have no motive. We have no beginning. All we have is simple Daisy.'

Simon removed his silver cigarette case from his trouser pocket and held it open in offering to Howard. A fountain of tobacco fell out over the newspaper Howard was reading. Despite their intense disdain for the press, they read every word of the article.

'Thought you smoked filters?' said Howard, flicking the tobacco away with one hand as he eased a Woodbine out of the case with the other. 'You are the only person I can think of, other than the murderer, who smokes Pall Mall. Where do you get them from? Where is the closest baccy shop to the four streets that sells them?'

'Dunno,' Simon replied. 'I decided filters are for queers and moved onto Woodies,' as he snapped the slim case shut and slipped it back into his trouser pocket. 'I gave myself a hernia tugging at the filters. I'll ask around the baccy shops, see if anyone knows, but you do realize, don't you, thousands of people in Liverpool smoke Pall Mall.'

Howard nodded. 'I know, that's why I say we have no leads.'

They both lit up. Enough said. Once again they both leant over the newspaper.

The basement interview room at the station was high and gloomy, lit by one light bulb, shaded by a bottle-green, glass pendant lightshade, and a single window that was protected by four vertical iron bars, sunk into the concrete.

The brick walls were painted brown to halfway up, then cream the remainder of the way up to the ceiling. The cream had turned a murky shade of brown, thanks to dense cigarette smoke, which, due to a lack of ventilation, hung around in the atmosphere, refusing to leave.

Grey light stealthily slipped in between the iron bars, but failed to reach even the table round which the four now sat. Daisy was constantly distracted by the sound of footsteps as people on the pavement outside walked past the window.

Howard bent to sweep a carpet of cigarette ash from the table with the cuff and lower arm of his jacket, and laid down two notepads and pencils.

'Gosh, seven o'clock already,' said Miss Devlin, with a false brightness.

'Yes. The time is moving on, sorry,' Howard said.

'Did you have a busy day today?' enquired Howard as she looked around.

'No more than usual,' she said.

Making small talk in a big space. That was what they were doing now. That and waiting for whatever Daisy would say to make a difference.

The tape recorder was ready. The table was ready. Everything was ready to begin.

Miss Devlin took a deep breath.

She felt as though they were sitting in a hospital waiting room, expecting a doctor to walk in and announce some life-altering news.

'*It worked, he lives.*'

'*It failed, he died.*'

Only no one would live. They were already dead and whatever Daisy revealed wouldn't alter that. Miss Devlin knew that what Daisy was about to say could possibly place someone's neck in a noose.

Someone else might die. Someone she may know.

She felt slightly nauseous.

It had begun to rain and the footsteps of passers-by became hurried. In a sudden downpour stilettos clicked rapidly alongside the steady clomp of solid brogues as in the twilit street the gutters filled. As they passed, cars sent up small tidal waves that splashed the pavement and soaked ankles, but never quite reached the basement window.

Daisy stared at the window and at the stockinged legs running past.

Simon had asked Daisy a number of the most subtle of questions but it was obvious, they were getting nowhere.

'So, what did you and Molly talk about?' asked Simon, gently, for the fourth time.

'Go on, Daisy,' Miss Devlin said, as she squeezed Daisy's hand, 'you aren't in any trouble. You're here because you are a grand help and a very important person.'

Daisy grinned. She didn't think anyone in her whole life had ever been as nice to her as Miss Devlin was, except maybe Molly.

'Go on, Daisy,' said Simon, 'we are all ears.'

The only noise in the room was that of the background hum of the tape recorder as the metal wheels swished round and round. From the street outside came the sounds of footsteps and trailing voices, the incessant patter of rain and beeping car horns. Life was moving on, whilst down in the Whitechapel basement they waited.

Daisy giggled at Simon. 'All ears! You aren't all ears, you only have two ears, doesn't he, Miss Devlin?' Her expression had softened. Daisy was beginning to enjoy the fact that they were interested in what she might have to say. They were interested in talking to her about her friend, Molly Barrett.

Daisy found her courage. She remembered that there were things she could say about Molly.

The memory of Molly sitting with Daisy at the Priory kitchen table came back to her. She was encouraged by a gentle pat on the arm from Miss Devlin, who with her delicate painted fingers lifted Daisy's fringe and pinned it back into her cross-clips.

'We talked about making cakes, me and Molly Barrett, and she always gave me some of the scones she had baked for the father and, oh gosh, she told me such funny stories about Tiger. That cat, he was the divil himself. Molly never knew what he was going to bring in through the door next.'

Daisy began to laugh. They laughed with her and then, as the laughing subsided, Daisy continued to smile at each one of them in turn. They all smiled back.

She had made them smile. She couldn't have been more pleased with herself if she had imparted a nuclear code. Daisy continued.

She talked about the neighbours. Especially Molly's nosy neighbour, Annie.

Simon shot Miss Devlin an earnest look.

She looked at her watch. Surely, something must happen soon.

Miss Devlin gave Daisy a big, false smile and nodded enthusiastically. 'Yes, go on, Daisy,' she said.

'She talked about all the people on the four streets because she knew them all, she did, every one of them. She didn't like Deirdre very much, because she never paid her bills and she said Sean McGuire was flirty. She even told me that once she saw Little Paddy nick a bottle of sterilized milk from Mrs Keating's doorstep. Can ye imagine? She was such good fun, was Molly Barrett, so full of stories. She used to make me laugh, so she did. I only ever laughed when I was with Molly. She was so nice and always said nice things to me, like, Daisy, you are the only person around here who can keep a house and a secret as well as I does. I used to love her coming, so, I really did.'

Daisy began to look sad and her voice cracked with distress.

'Molly was the only person who was really nice to me. I miss Molly now. I wish she was here and she could tell you all the things we talked about better than me. She was my only friend in the world, Molly was, and I miss her.'

Daisy began to cry. Miss Devlin began to cry. Howard took out his hankie.

Simon put his head in his hands in exasperation.

Things were not going well.

Howard rang the bell and a young officer carried in a tray of tea. He also brought a clean ashtray and removed the full one from the interview table.

'Have a cuppa, Daisy,' said Miss Devlin, pouring tea into the pale blue cup and saucer.

Howard decided to have a try himself and nodded to Simon to

indicate as much. He had nothing to lose. He would have to put the words into her mouth and see what happened next.

'Daisy, did you tell Molly that you saw someone murder the priest?'

Miss Devlin was in the middle of wiping Molly's nose with her own lace hankie as Daisy answered.

'Oh, yes I did, I did see who did that,' said Daisy, 'and I'm not talking about the Priory, because I know I'm not allowed to talk to anyone about anything that happens in the Priory, but that was outside, an' so I told Molly when she came.'

Miss Devlin stopped wiping Daisy's nose.

Howard and Simon both put down their cups at the same time and leant forward. Howard gently asked, 'Who murdered the priest, Daisy?'

It was now almost dark outside. The Victorian street lamps lent their aid to the single bulb illuminating the room. The long shadows, banished to the corners by the central light, clambered up the walls and hovered over them all. Waiting.

Miss Devlin noticed that the rain had stopped falling and that the footsteps were now few and far between. The workers were home. She imagined her sister putting the key in the door, switching on the lights, picking up the post from the mat. Doing the normal things they did every day, sometimes together, and here she was, Miss Devlin, about to hear who had brutally murdered the priest. She was trying hard not to shake.

'It was Tommy Doherty, from number nineteen Nelson Street,' said Daisy. 'I saw him with me own eyes.'

Miss Devlin slumped back in the chair.

It was over. The suspense.

'*It failed.*

*He dies.*'

Simon motioned for Howard to follow him outside the cell.

'I just need a word with Howard, Miss Devlin. I will ask them to send you some more tea. Will you be all right with Daisy? We will only be a few minutes.'

'Of course,' Miss Devlin replied.

She was in shock. She knew everyone in the Doherty family and would even count Maura as her friend. This was a terrible mistake. It could not be true. She looked at Daisy who was tucking into an arrowroot biscuit with no idea of the bombshell she had just dropped.

'We will be all right, won't we, Daisy?'

'Eh, what?' Daisy said, looking up.

'Nothing, Daisy,' said Miss Devlin. 'It's fine, really, it's fine.'

'Right,' said Howard, 'do we arrest him now?' He had closed the interview door behind them. Simon paced up and down in front of him, rubbing his fingers through his hair. He appeared anxious.

'No, we bloody can't arrest him. There are just a few things here, Howard, that you may have forgotten. Tommy Doherty has an alibi. He was a witness for Jerry Deane and his alibi is the rest of the card school. Remember that? They were all at the card school, together with the rest of the fucking street. Have you seen the man? He wouldn't say boo to a goose. We have been watching him since Molly Barrett told us what Daisy said to her. We know he didn't murder Molly Barrett. The super is very sure that whoever murdered the priest also murdered Molly. There is no way two entirely different psychopaths would have chosen the same street to have their fun on in such a short space of time. Add to that the fact that Daisy is simple and would be a nightmare in the witness box. Do you really think you should go to the super and get him to arrest Tommy Doherty, a man with a cast-iron alibi, on the back of that?'

Howard looked confused. 'I don't understand. When Molly told us what Daisy had seen, you were excited, you thought we had nailed him, and yet now you are telling me we haven't got anything?'

'No, Simon. What I am saying is that, until we began questioning Daisy, I didn't realize how simple she was. She is a sandwich short of a fucking picnic. With Molly Barrett alongside her, to stand testimony to Daisy's character and to what Daisy saw, we had half a chance. Without Molly and with Daisy that flaky, I'm not sure we have any chance at all. How was I to know that someone was going to come along and murder the old biddy? For fuck's sake, Howard, she was a harmless old lady and our only credible witness.

'Go and take them both home. I am off upstairs to phone the super to make sure he is free first thing in the morning, so we can ask him what he thinks. Go inside to those two and I will join you in a minute. Whatever we have, it has to hold water in a court of law and I don't think we have that here.'

Ten minutes later, when he went back into the interview room, Simon noted that Howard was deep in conversation with Miss Devlin, and Daisy was working her way through the biscuits.

'Well?' Howard enquired.

'I am seeing him in the morning. We can have a good night's rest ourselves beforehand.'

As they were gathering up their things to leave, Howard said to Simon, 'I will run the ladies home now, in the panda, if that's all right with you?'

Simon winked at Howard. 'That's fine by me,' he replied and then asked, thoughtfully, 'Daisy, what made you look out of the window that night if the place where the father was murdered isn't under your bedroom window?'

Howard fleetingly wondered why they hadn't asked that question when the tape recorder was running. How did Simon know which window was Daisy's?

'Oh, 'twas Bernadette,' replied Daisy cheerfully.

'Bernadette?' Howard looked at Miss Devlin. 'Who is Bernadette?'

'Well, I know of only one,' said Miss Devlin, holding on to her hat with one hand and removing her hatpin with the other, 'but she died a few years back now. She was Nellie Deane's mammy, so it can't have been her.'

Miss Devlin picked up her gloves and handbag from the table, ready to leave.

'Oh yes, 'twas,' grinned Daisy. 'She's there all the time in the graveyard. I often watch her. I see all the ghosts. I was never afraid of them. I am now, though. I don't want to see the priest. I don't want to see his ghost, ever.'

Miss Devlin was speechless. Howard and Simon groaned in unison.

## Chapter Twenty-four

Harry didn't tell Maura he had been picked to play Joseph in the school nativity play. She heard it from Angela. Despite the churlish way in which Angela imparted the news, Maura thought her heart would burst with pride.

'Our Harry is playing Joseph, is he? Our Harry? Well, isn't that just the best bit of news we have had for a long time now, eh, Angela?'

Angela looked at her mother as though she had gone mad.

'No, it isn't,' she replied. 'If I had been picked for Mary, now that would be the best news. Harry's a boy, so who cares what part he has in the play? All he has to do is put a tea towel on his head, wear the coat the sisters will make and carry a toy lamb.'

Angela continued to grumble, despite the fact that she could tell Maura had long since stopped listening.

'At last,' said Maura, flushed pink with pride, 'this is something we can hold our heads up and smile about.'

It had been too long. Excited at the news, Maura knocked on the wall for Peggy to kick off the jungle mops. This was something to crow about, although Maura knew perfectly well that it would last only minutes, compared with the constant speculation about who had murdered Molly Barrett, the question that had now eclipsed the previous one, who murdered the priest.

The news about Harry's starring role did not have the same joyous impact on Tommy, who fretted every single day about their Kitty.

'Try and be pleased for Harry,' Maura said to him that evening, once all the children were in bed.

'I am, Maura, I'm trying. It would be easier to be happy for Harry if we could write to Kitty and tell her that her brother is to play Joseph. That would help.'

'I know, but it is a long time off, Tommy. The school term has only just begun. There may be a chance, surely to God, somewhere between now and Christmas to get news to our Kitty. Rosie has written to say that, once Christmas is out of the way, Kitty will be back with us soon after. It will all fly past, Tommy. Our Kitty will be home soon, so she will. That is what I am holding on to.

'Holy Mother!' Maura shot up from the arm of the chair. 'With all the excitement, I haven't marked off today on the chart.'

She walked over to the range and picked up the pencil hanging from a piece of string, tied to a nail next to a chart she had made with the days marked off until Kitty returned to the fold.

Not one of Maura's neighbours had questioned this, or even thought it was slightly odd. Maura was known to be a devoted mother and most of the women found it endearing how much she missed Kitty.

'Just so typical of Maura, it is, to send Kitty to look after her poorly sister in Mayo, when she is missing her so much back here. God, she is the paragon of virtue, that woman is,' said Peggy to Mrs Keating.

Standing on the doorstep, she leant out and snatched up two of her boys by the scruff of the neck as they ran past. She slapped both of them across the backs of their legs and ordered them into the house for their tea, never breaking her stride as she spoke. Mrs Keating didn't bat an eyelid.

'Aye, she is that, always has been,' said Mrs Keating. 'Any news, Peggy, about the murder? Did you get a chance to speak to that policeman, as you walked past? What did he say?'

'Well then, now.' Peggy leant in, folded her arms and lowered her voice. 'It definitely wasn't the bloody cat. Apparently, she had taken a chocolate sandwich cake out of the press and left it on a plate with a knife next to it in the kitchen. She didn't expect to die, did Molly.

She thought she was going back in for a slice. The only clue they have is a ciggie butt on the outhouse floor, which isn't the brand Molly smokes. A Pall Mall it was. Who in God's name smokes Pall Mall? They don't even sell those around here.'

'A Pall Mall?' said Mrs Keating with a note of disbelief in her voice. 'They only sell baccy, Woodies and Capstan Full Strength in the tobacconist on the Dock Road. Pall bloody Mall? 'Twasn't anyone from around here, then?'

'Aye,' said Peggy, 'I know that's what I said, and a policeman wouldn't lie to me. It was definitely a Pall Mall.'

At the same moment they both spotted Sheila running towards the entry.

'Powwow in Maura's,' Sheila shouted down to them, as she shifted her toddler back into position on her hip.

'Maura has been knocking for ye, Peggy.'

'This is more like it, things getting back to normal,' Peggy said to Mrs Keating as they both wobbled along, Peggy's slippers squeaking and Mrs Keating's nose wrinkling at the rising smell.

'Only ye could describe gossip about a murder as getting back to normal, Peggy, shame on ye. I'll see ye in mass tonight,' said Mrs Keating as they both pushed in through Maura's back gate.

Later that evening, as Maura drew another line through another day on her chart, Tommy stood from his chair at the table and walked over to his wife. He put his arms round her and hugged her deep into his chest. 'I am proud of Harry, I am. I know it's Harry and the others keeping the show on the road. If it weren't for them kids, I'd be a dead man, Maura. Thank the Lord for our kids.'

'It has been a struggle, Tommy, but we are doing all right now. Things are getting better. We have more money to find and despite the promise from Kathleen and Jerry that they will provide when the time comes, we must pay it back.'

'We will, queen,' said Tommy. 'We will be paying it back for the rest of our lives, but pay it back we will, every half-penny.'

Maura kissed him on the lips and, putting a hand on either side of his face, looked into his eyes. She was now the stronger of the two. The news that Harry had been selected to play Joseph had picked her up more than any tonic could have. For Maura, the essence of her life was pride in her family.

'Not long now, Tommy,' she said. 'Tomorrow will be a busy day and then, soon enough, the days will fly by and she will be back home. On the day the children go back to school after the Christmas holiday, she will be nearly home. The Christmas holidays will whizz by, they always do.'

Tommy nodded. The way Maura put it gave him hope. It sounded not far away at all.

Tommy had never worried about a thing in his life, other than whether or not the horse he had placed a shilling on would come in for him. He now spent hours of every day worrying about the future. He was convinced a new and unforeseen disaster was heading their way and nothing Maura could say would disabuse him of this notion. His fear was rooted in guilt.

Changing the subject, he spoke again of the thought that constantly nagged him and which, in the darkness and privacy of their bedroom, he and Maura discussed every night.

Tommy lowered his voice.

'I can't stop thinking about poor Molly Barrett. Me guts tell me that her murder was connected with ours.' He dropped to a whisper. 'But we know it can't have feckin' been. What is going on, Maura?'

'I don't know. The women came in this afternoon after school. Peggy talks to the policemen, wouldn't she just! One told her they found a Pall Mall cigarette stub on Molly's outhouse floor.'

'A Pall Mall? Well, that means Molly's murderer was a bloody queer, or a woman. No man I know smokes feckin' Pall Mall!'

The back door latch clicked and Jerry stepped into the light of the kitchen from the black night outside.

Maura withdrew her hands from behind Tommy's neck and slipped them back into her front apron pocket.

'Eh, behave, put him down.' Jerry winked at Maura. 'I fancy a pint at the Anchor, you up for it, mate?'

Tommy looked at Maura who smiled her approval.

As he moved to take his jacket from the back of the door, Tommy said to Maura, 'Don't wait up, queen, you go to bed. I'll wake you when I get in, though.'

Maura winked back at Tommy and grinned. She heard the familiar, 'Ye lucky bastard,' from Jerry, as they walked down the back path.

Shortly after Jerry and Tommy had left for the pub, Kathleen arrived in Maura's kitchen.

'How are things?' she asked.

Casting her eye around, she could tell Maura had been hard at it, as usual.

The indoor washing pulley was suspended across the ceiling and from it hung a row of hovering white ghosts, wafting in the heat thermals from the range, masquerading as school shirts. As Kathleen looked up, she saw an array of children's clothes and nappies, steaming in the rising heat.

'No worse than usual,' smiled Maura.

She couldn't tell anyone of the horrible guilt she held deep inside. She was now happy to have left Kitty in the convent, happy that not a gossamer shred of shame would touch the family and that they had survived, intact in the eyes of her neighbours. She knew it would be tough for them all and she missed Kitty every single day. But hadn't she, Maura, been the one revered above the others as the wisest woman on the street? Wasn't hers the one house from which a child was likely to enter God's service? Wasn't it bad enough that everything she had striven for, all her married life, had been stripped from her by that man of the devil, without having to be publicly disgraced in front of her neighbours?

With the help of Kathleen, who was as good as family, she had come through and they were all safe.

Kitty would be home and then everything could be forgotten. Yes, she was relieved that she had left Kitty well cared for and looked after at the Abbey, but she knew Tommy would never understand. The Doherty family had not slipped from its pedestal. That was important.

'I am still in shock about Molly,' said Kathleen. 'What the hell has happened there, Maura? Everyone is saying it is the same person who murdered the priest. What the bleedin' hell is going on?'

Maura shook her head. If she had a pound for every time someone had asked her that question, she would be able to pay to take Kitty out of the convent on her own.

'Here,' said Kathleen, taking a bottle of Guinness out of each coat pocket. 'Put the poker in those coals and let's have a ciggie, too.'

Maura took two glasses down from the press and then shoved the poker into the fire, ready to plunge into the Guinness.

'Jerry nipped to the pub and picked them up before he came back for Tommy,' said Kathleen, nodding at the bottles. 'He's a good lad, is Jerry.'

Kathleen turned her head to watch the end of the poker turning bright red from the heat. She let out a huge sigh.

'Jesus, I'm worried about Alice, Maura. Do ye know where she is tonight, by any chance?'

'Alice?' Maura said with surprise. 'No. Is she not at home with ye lot?'

'She's not,' Kathleen replied. 'She went out after she put Joseph to bed at seven and said she was slipping down to Brigid's. But I just passed Mrs McGuire and told her to pass a message on to Alice, when she got back indoors, to say that I was nipping over to see ye and that Nellie was watching Joseph. Mrs McGuire looked confused. She said Alice wasn't there.'

'Well, maybe she went to the off-licence for some cigs on the way?'

'Aye, maybe, but she had a full packet before she left. I know, because I ran out and she gave me four Woodies from hers, to put in my packet.'

Maura opened the bottles, which let out a familiar welcome hiss, and slowly began to pour the Guinness into the glasses, which at one time had been the property of the Anchor.

'Where was Mrs McGuire off to?' asked Maura. 'Not the bloody chippy again? That woman is never out of there.'

Maura took the poker from the fire and plunged it into Kathleen's glass first. The sizzle of scorched Guinness filled the kitchen air, replacing the ever present smell of chip-pan fat.

Kathleen continued talking as Maura sat back in her chair. The dishes were done. The washing was drying. The boys' shirts were made of the new Bri-Nylon drip dry and didn't need to be ironed. She could relax without guilt.

'She said she had been to the boxing club to fetch Sean. Had a bee in her bonnet, she did, about how much training he is putting in. Said Brigid did too much and she was going to fetch him out, to come home and spend some time with his wife and kids. She's a tough woman, that Mrs McGuire. Mind you, there is no such thing as a soft woman from Galway. They don't put up with any nonsense. Not like us daft bats from Mayo.'

Both women laughed. Neither was daft. Both were back in control.

'But, Jaysus, she was giving out something wicked, she was. Had Little Paddy and Scamp to walk with her to the club, she said, being scared after Molly's murder an' all that, and Sean wasn't even there. She then started asking me, had I seen Sean? I thought, Holy Mother of God, here we are, two grown women, out in the streets, worrying about two kids who are supposed to be grown-up. I said to her, tell you what, if you find Alice first, send her home to me, will ye, and if I find Sean, I'll do the same with him. Kids!'

Maura and Kathleen both shook their heads and took a sip of their Guinness.

'Did ye walk all the way across yerself?' asked Maura. 'Because I don't think it's safe, so I don't. We don't know who the hell did that murder. It must have been a madman. Ye shouldn't come down the entry alone in the dark.'

'Are ye kiddin'?' said Kathleen. 'There are police cars everywhere out there tonight. The entire Lancashire police force must have come back from holiday, or summat, because I've never seen so many police cars in one street as there are tonight, other than on the night we got back from Ireland.'

'No?' exclaimed Maura in surprise as she rose from her chair and moved into the parlour to look out from the nets. Kathleen followed her and they stood together at the windows in the dark.

'I know it's weird and it's just all in me mind, but I feel as though they are all watching my house,' said Maura.

The two women walked back into the kitchen. As they passed through the hallway, both dipped their fingers in the holy water they had brought back from Ireland, which sat in a small ornamental bowl on a table under Maura's sacred heart on the wall, and crossed themselves.

Kathleen didn't want to confirm Maura's worst fears, but she felt the same. The police were indeed all looking at Maura's house.

'They say the cat's distraught,' said Kathleen. 'Annie has taken it in and is feeding it, but it keeps sitting at Molly's back door, making that crying sound, it does. I heard Annie shouting last night, "Tiger, come on, big boy, come and be good for Annie now, I have a nice treat for ye." Good job we know she's talking to the bloody cat. The police probably think she's some kind of wanton woman.'

Both women roared with laughter at the image of toothless Annie, as far from a wanton woman as one could imagine.

After a moment had passed, Kathleen smiled at Maura as she lifted her glass to drain the last drop of Guinness. The police might have been watching the house, but there was no way they could nail Tommy or Jerry for this. They would be all right.

Life was, in a very strange way, getting back to normal.

Jerry talked to Tommy all the way to the pub. Tommy hardly spoke at all, except to tell him he missed Kitty. His own, his favourite, little Kitty. She had patiently taught him to read and, in return, he had let her down so badly. His little Kitty was sleeping in a place where no one loved her best of all and that broke Tommy's heart in two.

'It's the last leg now, Tommy mate.' Jerry's words penetrated Tommy's thoughts. 'Once Kitty is home we can really begin to move forward and get back to where we were.'

They bought their drinks at the bar and took the table for two next to the fire.

The bar was busy and the noise and smoke erupted out onto the street as they opened the door.

Tommy picked up his pint of black nectar, closed his eyes and, tipping his head back, slowly let the balm pour down his throat, soothing his fractious mood. Putting his pewter pot down with a thud, he wiped the foam from his lips with the back of his hand before he spoke.

'Jerry, two of the McGinty kids are sat on the wall outside, again. That's the second time I've seen them out there. Is that man a fecking eejit? I told him what would happen if I ever found those kids shivering outside. I'm going to take them a couple of bags of crisps. They don't look like they've been fed tonight.'

Jerry wasn't surprised. The McGinty kids had a tough life. Their father, an alcoholic, was never out of the pub. They could be without coal for a week, if his wife didn't manage to catch him on a Friday night and rescue his pay money before it had all been drunk or gambled away.

Jerry watched as Tommy walked back out through the pub door. He could just make out Tommy's blurred form through the frosted windows, bending down to give the grateful and hungry kids their crisps. McGinty was in the bar, already half cut, and it was only eight o'clock. The children had been sitting on the wall since their mother had sent them down to retrieve their father, and what was left of the housekeeping, two hours since. They were still waiting, unable to extract him and too scared to return home without him.

Tommy strode back in through the revolving door, a look of fury on his face. He glared over at McGinty, who was propping himself up on the end of the counter.

McGinty saw Tommy looking at him and raised his cap in greeting. 'All right, mate?' he called across the bar nervously.

Tommy strode purposefully towards him.

'Tommy,' Jerry shouted, trying to avert any trouble, 'your pint's here.'

Tommy didn't hear him; his anger towards a man who would leave his children sitting on the pub wall, hungry and half frozen, was rising rapidly.

While he had been speaking to the McGinty kids, he could see his Kitty. The McGinty girl was half frozen, her hands were almost blue, with bright-red chilblains running down her fingers. Her large eyes were filled with tears from the biting wind. The lad, Brian, wore no coat and the girl had nothing more than her mother's shawl pulled tightly around her shoulders.

'Aye, I've asked everyone whose gone in to tell him, so I have, but he still hasn't come out,' Brian had said to Tommy when they walked past.

McGinty's reactions were too dulled by alcohol and too slow to anticipate what happened next. Tommy took him by the scruff of his neck and, marching him across the sawdust-covered floorboards, propelled him out through the door.

'How many times do ye need to be told to look after your feckin' kids?' he hissed.

McGinty's protestations were more of a squeak. 'What the feck are ye doing, yer mad bastard? Me pint, I have me pint on the bar.'

'Too fecking bad,' said Tommy, not wanting to raise his voice and scare the kids. 'Get fecking home to yer missus and take yer kids wit' ye.'

The two children were nervously walking across from the wall to their da.

'And if ye lay one hand on them kids, I'll smash yer bleedin' face in. Do ye get that, eh, McGinty?'

McGinty was nodding furiously.

'He had it feckin' coming,' said Tommy to Jerry as he re-entered the pub, picked up his pint again and downed what was left in one.

As he slammed his pint pot back down on the table, he looked at Jerry and said, 'I did that for our Kitty.'

## Chapter Twenty-five

Stanley and Austin met in the Jolly Miller. It was darts night and the pub was full.

They were downing a quick pint after work and then heading off to meet Arthur in a house in Anfield, an empty property belonging to a landlord friend of Arthur's.

Their instructions were not to drive, but to take the bus and alight at Lower Breck Road, then walk the rest of the way, down a small entry at the side of the house and in through the back door, which would be left open. Stanley assumed the landlord was in the ring, but he couldn't be sure, because he didn't even know his name.

Secrecy, and information that was shared on a need-to-know basis only, ensured they all remained anonymous and safe.

'Why does Arthur want to see us?' Stanley asked Austin, as he set his pint pot of mild down on the bar. The drink made Stanley feel better. It wasn't until he had put the drink to his lips that he realized how badly he had needed it.

He had told the doctor that his nerves were worse again. He couldn't stop the bouts of shaking.

'I'd have bad nerves, if I lived with your mother,' the doctor had said, writing him out another prescription. 'I've seen mothers like yours before. They keep a grip on an only son. You need to break free. It's not too late. Get yourself a wife.'

Stanley promised he would.

The only people who knew Stanley preferred little boys to girls were Austin and Arthur, plus some of the men they met up with, to exchange pictures and photographs. Quite excitingly, last month there had been a cine film on a camera and projector that Arthur had acquired, which they had all paid towards. But there had been no gathering since the priest, one of their ring, had been murdered. That had put the fear of God into them all.

The priest had been one of the few people running the group that were known to Stanley. He had been told there was a bishop too and some very high-up and important people, a politician even, but he didn't know who they were.

Stanley kept himself to himself as much as possible and only targeted the poor kids. They were easier to deceive, along with their pathetically grateful parents. Unlike Austin, Stanley took no chances.

'Right, drink up,' said Austin, 'and try to stop the fucking shaking.

You will make the others nervous. They'll think you are unreliable. Here, I'll get us a chaser.'

Austin moved to the bar while Stanley took another of the pills the doctor had prescribed for him. He didn't want anyone to be worried about him. The circle was the most important thing in his life. He had to remain a part of it. It stopped him taking risks and kept him safe and out of prison.

Austin put the two shorts on the bar. 'Here you go, mucker, down in one,' he said.

Stanley had never drunk whisky before and he spluttered as it burnt all the way down into the pit of his stomach.

Feeling much stronger, they slipped out of the pub and into the dark, moonless night.

As instructed, they stealthily took the steps into the back of the large town house. It was almost pitch-black, apart from a trembling light provided by one flickering candle wedged into the top of a sterilized milk bottle, placed in the range grate.

Arthur was waiting, as were the others, hugging the shadows on the wall. Dark, sinister figures.

Stanley could not make them out. He pulled his cap over his brow and looked at his feet. 'No idea who the hell is here,' he whispered to Austin.

'I have,' Austin replied, 'but you don't fucking want to, believe me.'

Stanley nodded. He already knew one was a politician. He could hear him talking. He knew his voice from the news on the telly. Stanley and his mother watched the news together every single night.

A man began to speak. Stanley did not recognize the voice. His accent was refined, but mingled with a colloquial edge, Stanley couldn't tell what. It wasn't Irish. He guessed the man was attempting to disguise his voice, due to the scarf tied across his mouth.

Stanley and Austin squatted down with those who were sitting on the floor.

The man who was speaking stood next to Arthur. He was tall and, in addition to the scarf across his face, he wore a trilby hat, the kind worn by the men on Water Street as they strode towards their offices each morning. The collar of his long, beige gabardine mac was upturned, hugging his face and adding a further layer of disguise.

The mac provided some kind of illumination, as though it had absorbed the sun's rays during daylight hours and in a ghostly way was emanating a faded light back into the darkest of rooms. As the man moved, the gabardine static crackled and snapped.

'I know you were all nervous following the murder of the priest,' he began. 'That has made you dammed jittery because he was one of our ring. And there has been the additional murder of the old woman.'

He stopped for a moment as though he was weighing up his words very carefully.

'Arthur has told me that you all have questions. He is worried that any change in your behaviour as a result of your nervousness could make you vulnerable and therefore pose a risk to the rest of the ring. Now, listen to me, all of you. Everything has been taken care of. There will be nothing to lead back to the group. You have to trust me on this. I know what I am talking about.

'It was a parent who murdered the priest.'

There was a sharp intake of breath from everyone with the odd 'Fucking hell!' hissed into the dark.

The man had voiced aloud a consequence that threatened them all. Their worst nightmare was to face the revenge of a parent. Give them the police, any day.

Stanley's eyes were adjusting to the light and he could just make out that there were about fifteen of them in the room.

The man continued speaking.

'The priest had become greedy. Too damned full of himself, and as a result he became slapdash and careless. A lesson to you all. I have no idea how the parent caught him, but I can tell you this: he doesn't want to hang for his actions and therefore won't tell anyone.'

The shadowy figures sitting on the floor tried surreptitiously to look at one another, natural curiosity getting the better of them. All they could see were the whites of eyes. It was enough.

'We know the parents have been very careful and have shipped the girl away. We believe that she may be pregnant, so they have done the right thing, going to great lengths to hide their connection to the murder.

'The old woman had to go. She knew who murdered the priest and, unfortunately, that could have opened an infernal can of worms, which may have been very difficult indeed.

'You may hear on the news tomorrow that a man has been arrested. Stay calm. I can assure you, you will be protected. He has a young family and has no intention of becoming acquainted with the hangman. He will not be making any confession and will be released without charge. You have our assurance of that. Now, any questions?'

There must have been ten of them sitting on the floor and five standing, in the darkest corner of the room. Stanley assumed the five were the group leaders.

Stanley shuffled his foot to a more comfortable position. With a nervous cough, Austin struck a match to light up his cigarette and, for a second, all of those seated round him.

The sudden squeak of a mouse shattered the silence as it scuttled across the floor through discarded and crumpled newspapers, disappearing into its nest at the base of the range. An owl hooted in the large garden at the rear and, from the road, they could hear the occasional car and the squeal of brakes on the bus, as it stopped outside the front of the house.

No one moved. The candle in the milk bottle began to splutter and spit as the wax reached the end of the wick.

Someone spoke, but Stanley had no idea who.

'What about the girl, Daisy? She was in the police station tonight, being questioned.'

The man who was speaking turned to another disguised man, who was rounder and shorter, as if asking for permission to comment.

'All organized I tell you; there is no need for concern. She will be sorted in an orderly way. The man who will be taken into custody will be released and, as soon as he is, she will be taken care of. You are all protected.'

A sigh of relief swept across the room.

They all believed him. He was right. One significant breakthrough in the investigation into the murder and it could all come tumbling down. The parent would talk. His child would talk; her friends would talk. There would be digging around and they would all be in danger.

Thank God, no one would know who they were, or what they did. They were free to continue as before.

Stanley wondered what 'taken care of' involved. It gave him a thrill. How normal everything sounded and yet, here they were, in a dark and dirty room, discussing a double murder. In their world, this was big time. Now that Stanley was reassured they were not in danger, he found the events exciting rather than threatening.

Austin punched him on the arm and with a grin said, 'Come on, mate, let's go. Time for a quick one?'

On the way out Austin whispered to Arthur, 'Back to our usual time on Saturday, Arthur. I've been saving up a stack of camera film I need developing.'

'Aye,' said Arthur. 'Back up and running. We have some great cine film on the projector for you, Stan, see you Sat'day, lads.'

As they turned the corner of the house and walked towards the bus stop, Stanley noticed that two of the men slipped into the back of a car, parked up the road, driven by the chauffeur.

'Don't look,' snapped Arthur. 'You know that's not in the rules.'

Ten minutes later they were back in the warmth and bright lights of the pub. Two happy men.

## Chapter Twenty-six

Simon knocked on the door and waited to be admitted.

He could hear the super talking on the telephone but couldn't make out what he was saying. He then heard the click as the Bakelite handset was put down and the super called him in.

'Ah, Simon, my good man. How are things progressing? I take it no one is aware the ladies were downstairs?'

'No, sir,' Simon replied. 'The only people who know are Howard and myself, and one uniformed officer who I believe has received instructions directly from yourself, and the chaperone, Miss Devlin, who is also aware of the need for confidentiality.'

'Jolly good. Now, what has she said? Is it true she becomes very confused from time to time?'

Simon briefed the super on the interview with Daisy.

When he finished, the super swung round in his new swivel chair and, with his back to Simon, looked out of his window onto the noisy Liverpool street below.

It was rush hour and the traffic was heavy, he noted. People thronged the pavement, rushing and bustling backwards and forwards across the road like mice on the bottom of a cage. Buses queued and jostled to turn the corner. From his window he could hear bells ringing and bus conductors shouting. A constant source of irritation. He loathed the noises of the street. They reminded him of his wartime service, of the distant sound of enemy fire. He loved the peace and quiet of his garden in West Kirkby and resented every hour he spent in Whitechapel.

He turned back to face Simon.

'All right,' he said. 'Bring the fellow in for questioning, but don't arrest him. However, unless he drops an absolute corker, you had better let him go once you have a record on tape. Frankly, an unreliable witness is ten times worse than no witness at all. Neither of us needs the humiliation. We both know that whoever murdered the priest murdered the old woman too, and we know it cannot have been Doherty.

'If the housekeeper from the Priory struggled when being questioned by you and a chaperone, with kind words and tea, how would she cope with a Liverpool silk, far tougher than any silk from London and that's a fact?'

Simon nodded. He hadn't even told the super about Daisy's ghostly sightings, which would be laughed out of court. If he did, likely he would be laughed out of the super's office.

'Go and bring him in now. Do it with the minimum of fuss, there's a good chap. I will need to speak to the assistant chief constable over this. I'm playing golf with him today and will do it then. Keep the cars on the streets until I report back to you.'

Maura fed the baby in the kitchen while Tommy, in his string vest and long johns, took his shave at the kitchen sink, humming along to the Beatles on the radio. The fire in the range roared its morning high, as if waving its arms in fists of flames at the smog that huddled against the windows.

Only half an hour earlier the kitchen had been quiet and still.

The early light, thick and grey.

Maura thought how this first fire was the best of the day, the strongest, laying down the bed of hot ash for the remainder of the day's fires to simmer on. She could hear Peggy's voice through the kitchen wall, shouting to big Paddy to wake up.

She thought how normal everything looked and sounded.

Why then did she feel so restless? What had brought on this feeling of breathlessness? Although the fire roared, she felt cold.

'Them lads are doing well, aren't they, queen?' Tommy said with a nod of acknowledgment at the radio, as he rinsed out his shaving brush under the running cold tap, before shaking it carefully into the Belfast sink and rubbing it hard onto the block of pure white shaving soap in an old chipped cup. 'Remember when we saw them play in the pub, when Bernadette was alive? They was just kids then.'

'They still are,' Maura laughed, lifting the baby onto her shoulder to wind her.

Maura could smell flowers. Strong and heady. Definitely flowers. She put her hand out and pulled it back sharply. Despite the heat from the fire, it had passed through an icy breeze.

In half an hour exactly, she would walk up the stairs to rouse the kids for school and she couldn't wait to fill the kitchen with the melee of their routine.

'Aye, I remember that night in the pub with Bernadette,' she replied in a distracted manner as she rocked the baby from hip to hip. 'That was the best night out we ever had. The craic, it was fantastic. They were the days, eh, Tommy? What a laugh we used to have. We will never see the Beatles in the flesh again though, never.'

'We will again, queen. They will be going for years yet, those lads, and will be sure to play in Liverpool loads of times,' said Tommy, lathering his face in soap. ''Tis their home crowd, to be sure they will.'

This time there was no knock on the front door.

Neither of them heard a thing until suddenly the back door was quietly opened by a uniformed officer and Simon stepped into the kitchen. Both Tommy and Maura were stunned.

Simon wasted no time, as the officer took the razor out of Tommy's hand and passed him the shirt that was hanging on the chair next to the sink.

'Tommy Doherty, we are taking you down to the station for questioning, in relation to the murder of Father James Cameron.'

Maura tried to put the baby back into her box, but she couldn't. Her legs wouldn't move. Within seconds, they had gone. Tommy grabbed her hand as he went past and said just two words: 'Get Jerry.'

They had left the back door open and the wind howled round the kitchen, lifting Tommy's newspaper up from the table. Maura watched as it floated back down onto the floor.

The wind suddenly slammed the back door shut, startling both Maura and the baby, who began to cry.

'Sh,' she said, as she gently rocked her. They stood in the kitchen alone, with only the sound of the radio and the tap still running, pouring cold water all over her day.

Maura ran upstairs, told Angela to wake the kids up and ready for school, then she plopped the baby down on her bed and ran out of the house, down the back entry.

At Peggy's back gate, the men stood waiting for Big Paddy. Maura just managed to reach Jerry before her knees gave way and buckled beneath her.

'What the hell is wrong?' Jerry asked her urgently, but realized at the same time that he already knew, as he shouted to Sean and Big Paddy to run with him to the police station.

'Pull yerself together and don't panic,' Jerry whispered harshly in her ear, as he escorted her back to the gate. 'They can't break us or our alibi. Ye have to laugh hard in the face of this, Maura, do ye understand? This has to be the most ridiculous notion the police have ever had and ye have to look as though nothing could bother ye less, because ye know he is an innocent man.'

Maura nodded. 'Aye, right. I will do that. The feckin' bastards, how dare they take my husband in.'

Jerry turned back to Maura; he almost laughed at the irony but thought better of it as he made his way to rescue his pal.

And, as if by a miracle, before teatime Tommy walked back into the kitchen with Jerry.

'They had nothing,' said Jerry.

'Aye, he's right,' said Tommy. 'Nothing. Same questions as before with the same answers. Nothing.'

As Maura felt the tightness she had carried around in her chest all day long ease away, she began to cry.

'Look, Maura,' said Jerry, 'stop fretting. If someone saw Tommy murder the priest, or they had a murder weapon, or a motive even, we would worry. But they haven't, they have nothing.'

'I have a feeling they will be knocking on for Big Paddy, to take him to the station next,' said Tommy. 'Maybe they just need to be seen to be interviewing every male on the street. 'Twas the queerest thing I have ever been through, to be sure. It was as if they wanted not to book me. Some queer posh nob with silver ropes on his jacket shoulder came in and asked me a few questions, but nothing I couldn't answer. He was more interested in how well I knew Molly and Daisy. Stop crying now, queen,' he said as he handed Maura the mop. 'Knock on for the women. If ye don't, it will look funny. Keep everything normal.'

And Maura did. Within minutes, her kitchen was full.

The neighbours had almost laughed when they heard Tommy had been arrested, assuming the arrest was in connection with the murder of Molly. Each and every one of them knew Tommy Doherty was the softest man on the street. He wouldn't harm a hair on a dog.

''Tis a joke and an act of desperation, all right,' Peggy had said to Sheila.

'Tommy Doherty? Even his own kids aren't scared of him!'

No one knew of the whispered conversation between Maura and Tommy in bed that night.

'Why did they call you in?' Maura had asked, terrified of earnest little Harry hearing her. 'They must know something, so they must, or why have they waited all this time?'

'I don't know, Maura, but I do know this. They had nothing, because if they had, I would have been arrested and in front of a magistrate. I don't want to be bold now, but I'm saying we are safe.'

And from that night on, each day had been lighter.

## Chapter Twenty-seven

Rosie did pay a visit to see Kitty, just as Reverend Mother had said she would.

One of the nuns collected Kitty from the laundry in the middle of the morning. Kitty was delighted beyond measure to remove her hands from under the cold tap of the huge long sink, in which she rinsed out the carbolic from the dozens of sheets she washed each day.

She walked along the corridor with the nun, rubbing her red hands dry on her calico apron.

Kitty had no idea where she was being taken and assumed it was to Reverend Mother's office, but as they turned up the stairs to where the girls slept, she realized she was wrong. She was being led to the labour room to be examined.

Sister Assumpta had initially objected to Rosie undertaking a prenatal examination. She held no truck with such things. The Holy Mother had managed without, so why should penitent girls and those with incontinent morals deserve more?

However, Rosie had put her foot down.

'It is important for Cissy to be familiar with the surroundings she will be birthing in, Sister. I am afraid I must insist.'

Sister Assumpta was keen that Rosie leave with a good impression of the Abbey and laundry, and so with very little grumbling she agreed.

Kitty had never before entered a room that truly terrified her, but this one did. The smell of Lysol assailed her nostrils as soon as she opened the door, reminding her of her hospital stay following the accident. It was the place where the baby in her belly had been conceived, in agony and humiliation.

White and stark, the room was cold, clinical and unwelcoming. It contained no feminine comforts whatsoever. A bed with no headboard stood away from the wall, in the middle of the room, with a pole on each end, with leather straps attached.

Almost at the base of the bed was a hole cut away and tucked underneath, out of sight, was a white enamel bucket with a navy-blue rim. Apart from a white enamel trolley covered with a small snowy-white sheet, and a fully stocked white enamel cabinet with glass doors, the only ornamentation was a plaster sacred heart attached to the wall and a wooden cross above the sink.

The sheets were white. The room was white. Virginal and cold.

Along one wall ran a long and shallow sink with elongated brass taps. Piled on the wooden draining board, folded and ready, lay half a dozen or so grey-looking towels. Not white.

The large small-paned window let in almost too much light and draught. The wooden floor was bare and the air was freezing cold. No Persian carpets in here.

Rosie avoided looking at Kitty as she set down her Gladstone bag on the only wooden chair and took out an apron and some gloves.

She snapped the brass clasp shut and turned round with a look of irritation.

'That will be all now, thank you, Sister,' Rosie said to the nun. 'I will examine Kitty, er, sorry, Cissy, and then call you in when the examination is over.'

The labour room was tucked away in what had been an attic, far away from the rest of the house. No nun wanted to be disturbed by the screams of girls in labour, which regularly filled the corridor outside. The only room anywhere near was the girls' dormitory across the hall.

More often than not, babies were delivered in the middle of the night and it was a short step to the labour room, without inconveniencing the nuns.

There was a midwife who lived in. Her room was on the other side of the dormitory, with a wooden hatch connecting the two. If one of the girls went into labour, they would lift up the hatch and shout through to let her know.

It was a fact that most would rather have given birth alone than in the presence of the dour and unfriendly resident midwife, who most of them doubted was even qualified at all.

Fortunately, today she had taken herself off on her bicycle into town. Rosie wondered whether that was deliberate. Maybe she didn't relish the prospect of being questioned by a midwife tutor about her training or qualifications.

The nun, with Rosie's smiling stare fixed on her, backed out slowly and quietly, hovering outside the door for what felt like an eternity. Rosie placed a finger on her lips, mouthed a 'Sh' and smiled at Kitty. After a few seconds, the nun's footsteps could be heard gently descending the wooden staircase.

'Jesus, Mary and Joseph, that was hard work,' said Rosie, turning a warmer smile towards Kitty. 'Now quick, take off your shoes, stockings and knickers, Kitty, and jump onto the bed. Shuffle down so that you are comfortable and while I am examining you, you can read these letters I have smuggled in my bag. I will have to take them away with me, so you do need to read them quick now.'

Kitty looked at Rosie with eyes wide in shock, wondering whether Rosie had already read the letters.

'Don't panic, Kitty. I will speak to no one. Your secret is safe with me. I will take it to my grave, so I will. I see lots of girls and ladies in a difficult position. I am only here to help you.'

Kitty relaxed, her fear at the prospect of an examination being replaced by the sheer joy of reading a letter from home.

'Come on,' said Rosie, in a fractionally louder and slightly urgent voice. 'They won't give us all day, you know.'

Kitty slipped off her stockings and shoes and then carefully slipped down her knickers, without revealing any of herself.

Raped and pregnant, she knew the meaning of shame.

Rosie smiled kindly and once again thought to herself: poor, desperate girl.

'Jump up,' she said, 'and make sure your bottom is about here.' She tapped the middle of the bed and helped Kitty up.

'Pull your legs up like this,' she said, as she lifted Kitty's knee up, 'and now we let it flop, down to the side just a little.'

It hurt Kitty. The muscle on the inside of her thigh, unused to being stretched in such a manner, twinged with pain.

'I know this is hard, Kitty, but I need to examine you to see how far on you may be, so that I know when to expect this baby to arrive. I have to come from Roscommon if I am at home, so it will take me a little while. I could even be at the hospital in Dublin. Once I know when your due date is, I will spend some time at Julia's and if your waters broke when I was there, well, wouldn't that be a dream now, but in my experience, no baby ever arrived when it was wanted to.'

Rosie didn't want to tell her that it was imperative she reached to the Abbey as quickly as she could. She had no intention of leaving Kitty to the mercy of the sisters, or the resident midwife.

'Do you understand what I'm saying, Kitty?'

Kitty looked up at Rosie's face, which blotted out the single bulb hanging from the centre of the ceiling. The white lampshade appeared as a halo around Rosie's head, shining in a perfect circle.

The word 'angel' flitted, unbidden, across Kitty's mind as she stared at Rosie's moving lips. She felt vulnerable and scared but she trusted Rosie and she had letters in her hand to read. She had to do what Rosie told her and repress her panic. Tears prickled the back of her eyes. Rosie's kindness, fear of the impending birth, the mixed emotions that hounded her about the life growing in her belly and the letters: all overwhelmed her.

'This is how we do this,' said Rosie. 'Breathe in and out, deeply, and let your muscles relax. Then read as fast as ye can. They won't give us long before one of them is back.'

Kitty wiped her eyes with the back of her hand and, pulling herself together, began to read the first letter. It was from Maura and Tommy, but there were others, from Maeve, Kathleen and Nellie.

She pulled out Maura's letter first.

Kitty felt Rosie's hand slip inside her and, with a sudden, sharp intake of breath, she clenched the side of the bed. She dropped her precious letters, which slowly fluttered down onto the floor. Every muscle in her abdomen tensed. She was terrified.

'Breathe,' said Rosie, 'in and out, just breathe, come on, sweetie. In and out, in and out.' She pursed her lips and made a sucking and blowing noise. As Kitty copied her, she felt her abdominal muscles begin to relax.

Rosie picked up the letters from the floor and handed them to Kitty. 'God, child, ye will have to read fast now, to be sure.'

Within seconds, Kitty was transported back to Liverpool, to her home and her siblings, to her life on Nelson Street. There were messages from her school friends and even a little note from Harry, written across the bottom in his perfectly formed, neat hand.

Maura's letter was full of ordinariness. No mention of Molly Barrett, or the events that had shrouded the four streets in fear.

Kitty stopped for a second as once again she tensed and grabbed the side of the bed.

'How do my mother and the other women on the four streets go through this so often?' she gasped and then continued to puff and blow her way through the letters.

They heard footsteps ascending the stairs and the door gently opened, just as Kitty finished dressing.

Rosie was at the sink, washing her hands and arms.

'I'm thinking the beginning of January,' she sang out, pretending she hadn't heard the nun enter the room.

The letters had been well and truly packed away, back into the Gladstone bag.

'Were you around when your mammy had her babbies, Cissy?' Rosie asked, briefly looking over her shoulder at Kitty, as she rinsed her hands under the tap. God help her if she hadn't been, she thought.

Rosie didn't know how this girl had become pregnant in the first place. She had been so shy, so nervous and tense, throughout the examination. Surely it was as obvious as the nose on anyone's face: Kitty was no child of the world. Whoever had made her pregnant had done so with force.

Kitty nodded.

'Well, I suppose we must be thankful for small mercies. So you will know then what happens and that you will bleed for a little while afterwards?'

Again, Kitty nodded.

'I will bind your breasts until your milk dries up, so there will be no problem there. I imagine the sisters here are used to spotting the signs of labour, aren't you, Sister?'

Rosie threw a professional smile at the nun, who nodded without any hint of a smile in return.

'I think you will be calling me around the fourth of January, Sister, or thereabouts.'

Rosie had no intention of putting this shy girl through the embarrassment of asking when her last bleed had been. The examination told her early January and that was good enough for her.

Kitty looked at Rosie, who was now writing in a foolscap notebook. Kitty dare not ask her the question now burning inside her brain. She felt a sense of bitter disappointment that the nun was there and had returned so quickly. She knew if she did ask Rosie her question, it would get straight back to the Reverend Mother, who would not be happy.

Rosie, replacing her notebook and snapping the clasp of her bag shut, immediately understood the look.

'We will have you on your way back to Maeve for a few days, to recover almost straight after the delivery. She is expecting you. Then you'll be back on your way to Liverpool, a week or so later, just as soon as you finish bleeding and your stitches heal.'

They were both shocked when the nun's timorous voice piped up, 'We don't stitch here, midwife.'

'You don't stitch?' replied Rosie in a shocked voice. 'Why ever not? What about bad cuts and tears?'

'Reverend Mother thinks the tear is God's just punishment…' Her voice trailed off.

'Punishment?' said Rosie.

'The resident midwife is not allowed to stitch. Reverend Mother won't entertain it. They all heal, eventually.'

For a short moment, Rosie was speechless and then she retorted, 'Dear God, of course they heal eventually, but we don't live in the bogs a hundred years ago, Sister. Sutures are a fine way to improve healing and to prevent the woman from suffering unnecessarily. Tears should be repaired hygienically and efficiently.'

Rosie pursed her lips. Kitty had turned a shade paler than she had been a moment ago.

'Don't worry, Cissy.' Rosie put her hand reassuringly on Kitty's arm and winked. 'It will all be fine and well. You have seen Mammy deliver often enough.'

By God, she thought, this would be her delivery and she would manage it how she liked. She took a deep breath and decided she would not pick an argument now, but would wait until the moment came.

'Reverend Mother has tea waiting for you in her office,' the nun said to Rosie. To Kitty, she said, with slightly less grace, 'Sister Celia is waiting for you in the laundry.'

Rosie smiled at Kitty and said, 'Take it easy now and I will be back in a month to check up on you again.'

Kitty almost laughed. Take it easy! The hours in the laundry were long and hard. So hard. Every day, Kitty saw heavily pregnant girls who had been on their feet for nine hours, crying in pain. But there was no reprieve. Not from the sisters of no mercy. There was only more work to be done.

They shoved and wheeled in heavy piles of dirty washing, and they washed, dried and pressed until it was placed in the large wicker baskets, mounted on wheels, and taken out to the vans that arrived from Dublin to collect them. For six days a week there was no let-up and no one finished work until the day's laundry was done. On Sunday, the nuns made the girls clean out their own dorms, change their bedding and wash their own laundry, as well as feed the nuns and clean their rooms.

And all day long, the arduous toil was undertaken in silence.

It occurred to Kitty that the nuns must be earning a great deal of money for the laundry that the girls heaved in and out through the doors.

Even knowing what she did about the Abbey, Kitty didn't imagine for one moment that the Reverend Mother would find reasons to refuse Rosie entry to the Abbey until she was due. Her biggest fear was that they wouldn't tell Rosie when she went into labour. She knew that was a possibility.

Kitty was scared.

# Chapter Twenty-eight

It was the night before Christmas Eve. Tommy and Maura made sure they arrived at the school over half an hour early. They wanted to be at the front of the hall and bag the best seats, those behind the reserved rows at the front, which were a constant source of irritation to Tommy, especially if they were behind the seat reserved for Mrs Skyes.

Mrs Sykes lived on Menlove Avenue in the posh houses and provided regular donations to the sisters. Her husband, a shipping merchant, had died many years ago, since when Mrs Sykes had discovered that loneliness was the preserve of the poor. She quickly learnt that the gentle and careful disbursement of funds bought respect, position and somewhere to go. In a hat. To a seat marked 'reserved'.

Tommy never failed to grumble when he visited the school. He began the moment he walked in through the big double doors.

As he had spent his childhood in the shadow of his stablehand father, schools made Tommy feel uncomfortable and inadequate.

If it hadn't been for their Kitty, he wouldn't even be able to read. The school reminded Tommy of all he had failed to achieve. His neck burnt red and itched.

As they walked into the hall, which smelt of lavender wax, Maura heard Sheila call out to them both through the open hatch of the cavernous kitchen beyond. The two giant-sized Burco boilers were starting to steam and simmer. Huge dark-brown teapots stood waiting to be filled, just before the interval. Sheila was laying out cups and saucers at the hatch and pouring milk into the copper jugs.

A smell of stale mashed potato and gravy from lunchtime hung in the air.

'Keep us a seat, Maura,' Sheila called across, as Maura and Tommy walked down the hall between the rows of chairs that Harry and the other boys had taken down from the tall stacks and placed into position, ready for the nativity play.

'I will, queen,' Maura shouted back, as she and Tommy headed straight for the best seats at the front.

Under his breath Tommy muttered to Maura, 'If Mrs bleedin' Sykes has no kids at the school, why does she have a better view of our kids than we do?'

Maura was mortified.

Far too loudly, Tommy added, 'Jaysus, the size of that woman's hat. Is no one here going to ask her to take the feckin' thing off, eh, eh?'

They trotted down the hall in their rush to reach the front.

'Get behind the bishop, Maura,' Tommy said, 'at least he's bald.'

All four twins had a part in the nativity play. As Joseph, Harry was one of the stars of the show. The other Doherty boys were two sheep and a goat.

Little Paddy was in charge of the lights. He skilfully manned the dimmer switch as parents and children began to filter into the hall. Having looked up at the ceiling to check all was in order, he proudly scuttled back to his seat. Tommy gave him a wink as he passed.

'Good lad, Paddy, well done.'

Little Paddy grinned from ear to ear.

The lights on the Christmas tree at the side of the stage twinkled brightly, casting an iridescent glow across the hall. Watching them sparkle in the dark for the first time, the children gasped, their excitement beyond containment.

They were just hours from Christmas Eve and the hall was infused with an air of anticipation. Children who were used to behaving in an orderly manner, within the confines of the school, were now wriggling on their seats, whispering in loud voices, articulating their hopes and dreams for Christmas morning. Most of them were aware that an orange on the end of the bed would be their only luxury.

Kathleen arrived and sat down in the seat next to Maura. 'Where's Alice?' asked Maura.

'Not feeling too well,' Kathleen whispered back. 'Says she will come along in a while if she feels any better.'

The programme on the seats informed them that Brigid and Sean's daughter, Grace, was playing Mary.

Both Tommy and Maura felt their hearts crunch. They knew that Kitty had been Sister Evangelista's favourite. This year would have been her last year at the school. If Kitty were home, she would be Mary.

'Grand,' said Maura, in a falsely jovial manner, 'isn't that wonderful, Grace being Mary and our Harry her Joseph? Them knowing each other since they were babbies, like?'

She wanted to be pleased for Brigid and Grace, and fought with every ounce of good nature she had to sound more delighted than she felt.

'Are Brigid and Sean here?' Maura asked Kathleen.

'No,' whispered Kathleen, 'not Sean, he is in town for a match tonight. It's a big one, apparently, good money if he wins. Brigid is on her way.'

'How good?' Maura's curiosity knew no manners.

'Five hundred pounds. Can ye imagine?'

Maura couldn't. She had never even seen that amount of money. The remaining money needed to free Kitty seemed like a mountain to climb to Maura at the present, and there was Sean, who could be walking home with five hundred.

'Imagine that,' Maura half-whispered thoughtfully, more to herself than Kathleen.

Maura knew Jerry, with only one child, had saved a great deal and Kathleen had money from the farm, but it was obvious that even Kathleen was impressed by such an amount.

'Aye, imagine,' said Kathleen. 'And all he has to do is to beat the shite out of someone. My lads did nothing else when they were at school. If I had only known there was money in it, I'd have had Joe encourage them. Oh, here you go, sh,' she said, 'here they come.'

She waved to Brigid and Mrs McGuire, and pointed to the seats next to her. Brigid had the youngest baby tucked in her arms, wrapped in a crocheted blanket of many colours. Behind them was Peggy, ushering her brood into the seats. Big Paddy didn't attend school plays or parents' evenings. He had no interest in his offspring's activities and had viewed the nativity play as a good opportunity to escape down to the pub for a sneaky hour or two.

'Thanks for keeping the seats, Kathleen,' whispered Brigid, pulling a face at Mrs Sykes's hat, directly in front of her.

Peggy squeezed along and sat next to Kathleen, just as Kitty's teacher, Miss Devlin, appeared. Leaning forward, she whispered down the row, 'No more smoking now, please, ladies.' Lifting her hand up to her mouth as though to channel her words in a straight line: 'Mrs Sykes doesn't like it.'

Peggy turned to the others. 'Merciful God, she has to be fuckin' jokin', doesn't she? It's at least an hour until the break, once it starts. If yer allowed to smoke at the filums, why can't we smoke here? That's desperate.'

Mrs Sykes's hat wobbled in indignation. She had obviously overheard Peggy.

Maura put her finger to her lips and made the sound of a silent sh.

Peggy was having none of it.

'Mrs McGuire,' Peggy said, 'would ye mind swapping seats with me so that I can get out quick, like, in the break. I'm not even allowed to smoke in me own children's school now, so I'm not. Did ye ever hear of anything that took such a liberty?'

Anticipation fizzed through the air as Sister Evangelista appeared at the front of the school hall.

As she scanned the assembly before her with steely eyes, the children nudged each other sharply in the ribs. Like a gentle wave washing over the gathering, the chatter began to subside, starting at the front with those closest to her, until only Little Paddy's voice could still be heard.

'Me da will be here in a minute, he will, Declan, he's just gone to get his ciggies, he has so. Mammy, isn't me daddy on his way?'

The realization that the entire audience was listening to him dawned only as Sister Evangelista spoke. 'See me after the play, Paddy, and not another word now, boy.'

And then, as if by magic, her face broke into the brightest smile.

'Parents, ladies and gentlemen, special guests.'

'I suppose if I'm a parent, that means I'm no lady then,' said Peggy under her breath.

Maura and Kathleen looked at each other and smiled.

Kathleen reached across and gave Maura's hand a squeeze.

Kathleen hoped that Christmas would mark a turning point for Tommy and Maura.

Maura looked at Kathleen as she squeezed her hand, the best friend in all the world. Maura smiled back.

Sister Evangelista continued, 'Welcome to the St Mary's nativity play acted out by your children, in honour of the birth of our Lord, Jesus Christ. Before we begin, I have a little announcement to make. Many of you will know Daisy from the Priory.'

Everyone turned to look at Daisy who was at the hatch, quietly helping Miss Devlin to fold Christmas napkins for the interval.

'Well, tomorrow morning Daisy will be leaving Liverpool and returning to Dublin, to live with her family.'

For a second the hall fell quiet, apart from the odd sharp intake of breath, and then without warning or planning the audience erupted into applause.

Sister Evangelista beamed as she joined in, as Daisy flushed bright red and grinned from ear to ear. Miss Devlin gently placed her arm round her as the applause continued.

It had been a shock indeed when the bishop had called to see Sister Evangelista in a very agitated state.

'I have a letter from Daisy's family,' he announced indignantly. 'They are stopping the money and want her back.'

'Well, praise be,' Sister Evangelista had said, 'isn't that wonderful news? I thought her parents wanted her cared for all of her life?'

'They did,' said the bishop, who was sweating profusely.

It crossed Sister Evangelista's mind that he was heading for a heart attack.

'The parents have died and the elder brother, a state solicitor, found out about the arrangement when sorting through the estate. He wants Daisy back. Here, read the letter.'

He thrust the letter into Sister Evangelista's hands. As she read it, her heart filled with warmth and happiness.

Her prayers were being answered: prayers for God's love and light to shine into their darkness, to banish to the shadows the evil that had lived amongst them for so long. Poor Daisy, she thought, she had been living in the midst of it all and none of them had known.

'But this is a wonderful outcome, Bishop,' she said, handing the letter back to him. 'He is a good Catholic, ashamed that his parents felt they couldn't raise Daisy, and they want to make amends. Surely this is wonderful news.'

The bishop grunted. 'He wanted to collect her from the convent but I have told them we will put her on the boat tomorrow,

Christmas Eve. That way they can have their precious Daisy back for Christmas Day. I wonder if they have asked themselves where she would be if it hadn't been for us caring for her all this time?'

'Where would we have been without all that money, Bishop?'

Sister Evangelista asked the last question quietly. She knew how much they were paid. The family had obviously been very wealthy. She had often wondered to herself whether or not Daisy's family knew that their daughter was working as a housekeeper for so many years. She suspected not.

'Well, we shall send Daisy off with our blessing, Father. Only you and I know what that poor girl was living with in the Priory.'

In the midst of the clapping, the children began to cheer for Daisy.

And tears began to roll down her cheeks.

She couldn't believe what was happening to her.

She had made Miss Devlin read over and over again the letter her brother had written to her.

They had both laughed and cried together the first half-dozen or so times they had read it. Now she didn't need anyone to read it to her, because she could hear Miss Devlin's voice and the words. They were fixed in her mind. She wandered round in a daze as she went over and over them.

'*I am your older brother, and my wife and I want you to be back in your home and in the heart of your family, where you were meant to be, with your two sisters, your nieces and nephews, and me.*'

Daisy had barely been able to sleep since reading those words. She had a home and a family who loved and wanted her. She would never again see the bishop and never again have to endure him. She was going home to be safe.

Her only sadness was that she couldn't tell Molly, and so Daisy told her in her prayers instead.

Now, Sister Evangelista walked towards Daisy, with a present wrapped up in Christmas paper. All the children began chanting, 'Open it, Daisy, open it, Daisy.'

In front of two hundred children and their parents, and with the help of Miss Devlin, Daisy unwrapped the present and took out of a box a delicate hat. It was the most beautiful thing she had ever seen in her life. As everyone clapped again, Miss Devlin, who was trying hard not to cry, reached up and placed it onto Daisy's head.

'Spare hatpin, anyone?' Miss Devlin shouted over to the parents who were all sitting hatless, in curlers.

Every pair of eyes turned on Mrs Sykes who, for the first time that night, smiled as she took a pin from her own hat and passed it along the row.

'We hope one day you will come back and visit us, Daisy,' said Sister Evangelista. 'We would all love to hear your news, once you have settled in Dublin, and you know that we will always be your family.'

Brigid leant over to Maura. 'Would Jesus have allowed reserved signs on chairs in a church, Maura? Would he?' she whispered, nodding towards the great and good in the row in front. 'And would he not have said big hats were barred altogether?'

Maura nodded and grinned. Sister Evangelista's voice faded away into a blur as Maura took in the scene around her.

For a second, her gaze alighted on her own children's shining faces. Sitting on their hands, wriggling in their seats, they fixed their eyes upon the stage, waiting, with pent-up anticipation, for the play to begin.

The lights dimmed further and their eyes, reflecting the bright spotlights shining on the empty makeshift stable in front of the stage, sparkled with excitement like stars sprinkled in a dark night sky.

Maura's gaze found Angela, sitting with her younger sisters, her arms folded. She was the only one not smiling, or covertly whispering and fidgeting. But even her normally grumpy expression had softened. Maura remembered what Kitty had been like at her youngest sister's age, barely able to keep still. Maura's love for her children was, as always, brimming under the surface. She took immense pleasure from watching them, when they didn't know she was looking, something she did all the time.

As she watched Angela and her sisters she thought to herself, no harm will come to any of ye. I have eyes in the back of me head now.

Six little ones from the primary class now took their seats at the side of the stage and picked up their triangles and tambourines ready for the carol singing.

As they tinkered with their instruments and Sister Evangelista peeped behind the curtain to see whether everyone was ready to begin, the spirit of Christmas swept through the hall and touched all in its way. Maura noticed Angela smile as one of her sisters took her hand and stretched up to whisper in her big sister's ear.

She looked at Peggy, who was checking for ciggies in her pocket, so that she could make a run for the door in the break.

Maura, who had thought that this Christmas would be a miserable affair, unexpectedly felt a nostalgic pull from all the Christmases past, familiar and comforting.

Nothing any of them said or did tonight was out of the ordinary or unexpected, and that was just how she wanted their lives to be forever more. Ordinary.

Everything was as it always was and always had been. Almost.

Tommy squeezed her knee and smiled at her. The spirit of Christmas had touched him, too.

Suddenly, the hall burst into applause. Sheila's eldest was pulling hard on a big rope at the side of the stage and the curtain began to lift slowly. Maura watched as her precious Harry walked into the pool of light at the front of the stage.

The tea towel was his headdress.

A striped dressing gown his cloak.

A pared branch his staff.

Maura's eyes filled with tears of pride.

Kitty wasn't here. Things weren't right, but they were better.

They were still in the darkest tunnel, but she could see the light at the end and there was her Harry, standing in the middle.

It was seven o'clock sharp as the curtain went up. Miss Devlin walked from the back of the hall to the front foyer and closed the large wooden doors to the school, prohibiting further entrance. Lateness was intolerable, both in children and in adults. Pity the parent working late.

There would be no room in the hall.

As the large bolt slid across the door, Alice emerged from the shadows of the high convent wall opposite.

A few moments earlier, she had felt an overwhelming urge to walk towards the light that poured out of the school doors and tumbled down the steps to the playground.

She felt an ache, deep in the pit of her stomach, that made her long to be a part of the warm laughter. The temptation to belong was almost irresistible.

For seconds, she teetered on the brink of running into the school hall and confessing everything to Kathleen. Kathleen, the older woman who had saved her. The mother she had dreamt of having, all through her childhood nights, and whom she now truly loved. The only woman who for years had ever shown her kindness.

Kathleen had ripped away the memories that tied and bound Alice to her past.

Kathleen, her saviour.

Alice wondered if she would ever be forgiven for what she was about to do, but she knew the answer was probably not, ever.

Tall Victorian street lamps lined both sides of the road that sloped gently down towards the town.

Alice moved to stand underneath one, imagining that some warmth might penetrate her frozen bones. She looked again to catch sight of the bus. Maybe he wouldn't catch the bus to the school. Maybe he would alight at the stop before, so as not to be seen, and walk the rest of the way.

Alice laughed out loud. What would it matter?

'Oh, please let him win,' she whispered to herself, noticing her frozen breath hanging in the air and wondering at how dramatically the temperature had dropped in the past hour.

The wide cobbled road had been built to accommodate shire horses and carriages, pulling flat-bed loads from the docks to the processors. It was quiet and eerie now. Nothing had passed by for the past ten minutes.

From the shadows cast by the wall, Alice had silently observed the sisters as they crossed the road from the convent to the school, excitedly chattering to each other as they bustled in to see the nativity play, a highlight in their calendar year.

The biting cold now cut through to the bone as Alice pulled her coat tighter. Her eyes began to water as, full in the face of the icy northerly that lifted up from the river, she stared down the hill, willing him to come quickly.

Flinching from the rising wind, she turned towards the classroom windows.

Inside would be the desk and chair where one day soon Joseph would sit. She conjured up an image of his dark hair and his freckled face as he looked at a blackboard and then wrote earnestly in his notebook. Alice knew, she could tell already, Joseph would be bright. He was as inquisitive as he was funny. Joseph, the little man she had come to love.

She imagined his short legs dashing down the steps with his brown leather satchel flying in the air behind him and his face beaming as he ran to someone. Who is it? Alice thought, looking eagerly at the gate, now shrouded in darkness, where during the day the mothers stood waiting and chatting. Many arrived early to engage in the school-gate gossip. Whom will he run to? Who will it be? There was someone at the gate, she thought, moving back into the deeper darkness – but she couldn't make out who it was, waiting to greet the excited, laughing Joseph.

The icy wind slapped her across the face and made her eyes sting. She closed them for a second.

In her own darkness, she saw herself in Joseph's bedroom. He was fast asleep, his little head lay on the pillow, Nellie's old and threadbare teddy tucked under his arm. One thumb, half in his mouth, having slipped out as he had fallen into a deep sleep. His soft, flannelette, blue-and-white striped pyjamas kept him warm. As always, he had kicked off the pale blue cot-blanket that Kathleen had knitted and the beautiful, hand-made, white lace cover his Auntie Maeve had sent across from Ireland.

She could smell his powdery, sleep-filled room.

Her heart felt as though it were in a vice as in her mind's eye his angelic face softened with the laughter of a dream.

She saw her boy, waking up on Christmas morning, every room in the house smelling of the turkey Kathleen had slowly roasted in the range overnight.

She saw Joseph running into the bedroom to wake everyone, in his haste to open the presents under the tree.

The previous Christmas, Jerry had made Nellie wait on the stairs as he held the door to the kitchen closed, pretending that Father Christmas had forgotten her.

'Has he been?' said Jerry, peeping through the door, opening it just a crack, pretending he could see the tree. 'Oh, no, I don't think he has, Nana Kathleen. I think Miss Nellie can't have been a very good girl this year.'

They drove her crazy as she playfully pummelled Jerry's back with her fists, in an effort to push past.

Alice replayed the scene in her mind. She had stood at the top of the stairs, watching, smiling, not really a part of what was happening. Observing in her usual way, from the edge.

Will he think of me? she asked herself. Will he remember who I am? Will he run home from school with the others and wonder where his mammy is?

She began to shiver with the cold and then she felt it on her skin, the first snowflake of Christmas. She looked up into the wind. It was as if the angels had opened a trapdoor. The snow fell heavy and fast. In less than a minute, the pavement on which she stood was white, her shoulders were heavily dusted and, despite the swirling wind, it began to settle.

Once more, she glanced directly down the road, into the wind and through the snow. Still no sign.

When she had explained her plan to him, he hadn't wanted her to wait at the school.

'Don't go out, Alice,' he had said. 'Just say you're unwell and stay at home. I will come straight there.'

But she couldn't. She was compelled to leave. She hadn't wanted to see them getting ready. She couldn't bear to kiss Joseph goodbye. He would have been full of excitement at being taken to the big school for the play. Joseph was always beside himself with delight when in the company of other children.

Alice had made an excuse about having dreadful toothache and said that she would take herself off to the dentist in town.

'Oh, that's just desperate now, ye poor thing.' Kathleen's face had instantly become a picture of love and concern.

'I will be fine, Kathleen. It's happened before. I may be a while, though, and I won't feel like going to the school afterwards. I will just come home and go straight to bed.'

'Best thing, queen,' Kathleen had said as she busied about making an early tea before they left.

Alice had hidden in the shadows and watched them all arrive. Nellie had pushed the pram up the hill and Kathleen had held onto Nellie's arm.

'Ooh, I'm blowing for tugs,' she had heard Kathleen gasp.

Alice had felt like a ghost. She could see and hear all but she was invisible.

She had seen Peggy, smoking as she walked, with a gaggle of children round her, nervously squealing and jumping up and down, running ahead of Peggy, up the steps to the entrance. It seemed as if every young woman from the four streets had filed into the hall, chatting in that companionable way that had always eluded Alice.

She knew that Joseph was now inside the school hall, happy and warm, sitting on Nellie's or Kathleen's knee, and here she was, back where she had begun, on the outside looking in.

She had tried to explain her feelings to Sean.

'My marriage to Jerry was a symptom of my illness and of the person I had once been. I want to leave that person behind. I am whole now. I have fallen in love all by myself, without manipulation or deceit and it feels the most amazing thing. I cannot stay and live a lie and nor can you, but what is worse is that if we do, we have to carry on with our old lives and see each other every day. I could not bear that.'

Alice looked down at her shoes. They were buried in snow. The school door and the windows of the classroom opposite had taken the full force of the wind and both were plastered in the white powder.

On each pane of the sash windows, a hand-made paper Christmas decoration peeped through the snow. Soon, one of them would have 'Joseph Deane, Class 1' written on the back.

But Alice would never see it.

She felt her insides crunch. The school gate was still shrouded in darkness and yet the feeling that she wasn't alone was stronger than before.

Applause suddenly reverberated through the school doors and then, after a short time, she heard voices. Children were singing the beautiful haunting first notes of a carol she recognized from her own unhappy school days. 'Silent Night'. And it was. A very silent night.

She doubted now if she could do it. Maybe Sean was right. Maybe meeting him at the school had been the wrong thing to do.

Already the pain of missing Joseph was intense. She would never hear or see him sing 'Silent Night' with his school friends.

The strains of 'Little Donkey' followed, pouring out into the snow-filled air. Was Joseph trying to sing? He would be looking up at his Nellie and trying his best to join in. A child in a hurry to grow up. His world was perfect, his routine stable. He was surrounded by people who loved and adored him, but she wasn't there. She knew he would be looking for her. He would turn his little head to the door when he saw a fleeting shadow pass. He would look seriously at Nellie when she said to him, 'Mammy may be here soon, if she's feeling better.'

Pain and doubt ripped through her heart.

She turned and saw his figure emerge over the brow of the hill, walking slowly towards her, his head bent against the driving snow. His hands were thrust deeply into his pockets and his long overcoat kicked out before him.

When he reached her, she saw his face in the lamplight. One eye was closed and filled with blood. She had never seen him look so bad.

'Sean,' she whispered, 'oh my God, are you all right?'

Sean looked at her frozen face. Her hat was covered in snow and if he hadn't been in so much pain, he would have laughed. 'I'm fine,' he replied. 'You won't even know I've been in a fight a week from now.'

'Did you win?'

Alice almost didn't want to know. If he hadn't won, nothing would have altered. Half of her felt a sense of relief at that prospect, the half that wanted to stay with her son and to watch him grow into manhood. The other half, that loved Sean to the point of pain, willed him to have won his fight. If he had, they would take the morning passage to New York.

'I won,' he said, placing his hand on her elbow and looking around. 'I have put an envelope with money on the mantel for Brigid and I have already left both our bags at the hotel. We can do it, Alice. We can sail to America in the morning.'

Conflicting emotions tore through Alice. She wanted to shriek with excitement at the prospect of realizing her dream and also to cry with grief at all she was leaving behind.

Tears poured down her cheeks.

'Have ye changed your mind?' asked Sean.

Their future hung on her answer.

They had agreed that if they didn't take passage to America together, then their illicit affair must stop and they would both spend the rest of their lives in agony, each knowing the other was only yards away, under a different roof, married to someone else.

Neither of them could bear that thought. It would be impossible. Alice thought she would rather die than have to live through that kind of misery.

Sean put his arm round her shoulder and turned her towards the brow of the hill. 'Come on, Alice,' he said, kissing her on the temple. 'We have to, before anyone leaves and sees us.'

They both turned and walked into the wind and drifting snow. Alice was now sobbing quietly. Sean understood. The pain he felt at leaving his daughters was intense, but he thought that Alice's heartache as a mother must surely be worse.

'As soon as we are settled, we will send for them to visit us, or we will sail back and see them. We aren't leaving them for ever, Alice.'

She turned her head to look back at the school.

'Little Donkey' was reaching an end. She could hear applause yet again and laughter, and then she saw a movement at the gate. Someone else had been there all along. Who could it be?

The snow was driving into her eyes and forcing herself to blink, but she saw her. It was definitely her.

Against the frosty whiteness, Alice could not doubt the wild red hair swirling in the midst of what had become a blizzard. Bernadette. The dead wife and mother whose place Alice had stolen, with deceit and lies. Bernadette looked at Alice and her gaze was one of deep sadness, deeper than anything Alice had ever known.

She stood rigid in shock.

'Alice, come on, we have to hurry,' said Sean urgently. 'Come on, queen, what's up? Ye look like you've seen a ghost.'

The moment the the singing stopped and the clapping began, Peggy took herself to the front of the school and tried to push back the bolts on the wooden door.

Little Paddy had done his job of turning up the lights and everyone was gathered round the school hatch for their mince pie and cup of tea.

One of the classrooms had been opened up and orange squash and mince pies were being served to the children. For some of them, those whose parents often skipped mass and spent their wages in the pub, it was the only treat they would enjoy all Christmas.

Once Little Paddy had finished his chore, he ran to help Peggy open the door. Sliding back the bolt, they both gave a gasp of shock as they saw the snow, already over an inch deep.

Little Paddy grabbed the sleeve of his mother's coat. 'Do ye see that?' he yelled in surprise. 'It's snowing!'

'Merciful God, we could do without that, all right,' said Peggy, grudgingly putting her foot onto the first step. 'Here, Paddy, give me yer hand.'

Little Paddy put out his arm to help his mother down the steps.

Peggy was wearing her usual old slippers with no stockings. She had neither the time nor the money to be fussing with stockings and suspender belts.

'Just another thing to wash,' she would say to anyone who troubled to ask.

Within seconds, the cold had made the varicose veins around her ankles protrude like bunches of black grapes.

'Holy Mary, it's fecking cold out here, Paddy,' she muttered, as they negotiated the steps. 'I'll stand here, lad,' she said, once they got to the second step. 'It's far enough away from precious Mrs Sykes.'

Little Paddy left his mother as quickly as he could and ran into the classroom, yelling, 'It's snowing outside!' Within seconds, Peggy was engulfed as children flew down the steps on either side of her.

'Oh, would ye look at that,' said Nellie, running to Peggy's side. Peggy smiled. The front yard was full of children shouting and throwing snow into the air.

Nellie crouched down beside Peggy to make a snowball, but the snow just crumbled into powder in her hands. Peggy looked up and down the road to see if there were any buses running.

It took her a minute to make out what she had seen, but once she was sure, she knew.

As Nellie stood up, Peggy spoke to her. 'Nellie, would ye run back inside, queen, and ask Nana Kathleen to come outside to me.'

'Now?' said Nellie.

'Yes please, queen,' said Peggy, 'now.'

Peggy knew they would be over the brow by the time Kathleen reached the front door, but she wanted to protect Nellie. Fetching Kathleen had been a ruse.

'Well, well, well,' said Peggy, out loud. 'My lad's not a liar, after all.'

Peggy pondered as she watched Alice and Sean disappear into the town; what should she say and to whom.

They were walking briskly down the candlelit corridor to Compline. Kitty felt uncomfortable. She had been lost in her own thoughts, recalling Rosie's words. Some time in January. She could be home in just a few weeks. The tightening round her waist now began each time she walked, but the girls had warned her, it was just her body rehearsing, preparing her muscles for the delivery.

As she looked closely at Aideen walking along beside her, it occurred to Kitty that she would soon miss her friend. How could she help her to leave this horrible place? she wondered. Surely there must be a way? Her thoughts were distracted as, once more, her abdomen clenched.

Later the following morning, Aideen and Kitty were both in the laundry, ironing shirts. Sister Celia, who watched over them to ensure there was no talking, had taken herself away for a moment, reprimanding Aideen as she went for not pressing the collars crisply enough.

'Probably gone to stuff her face with another slice of cake,' Aideen grumbled as the laundry-room door closed. 'God, that woman is a scold. She never stops bellyaching at me. We will see that cake sat on her fat arse when she comes back in.'

Kitty laughed, but she didn't know how she had done it. The baby she carried was so heavy and she had been on her feet for hours. She felt as though the baby would just drop out, so great was the pressure.

'Will ye be able to get out of this place soon, Aideen?' she asked, looking up from her ironing. Beside her stood a large wicker basket on wheels, only half empty. Kitty's job was to iron the whole lot before the day was over.

'Well, I would, if I had the money to buy my way out.'

Once again, Kitty felt lucky that she had people who cared for her. Aideen was looking at spending at least three years of her life in the laundry. It was worse than a prison sentence.

Aideen was not going to waste the advantage presented by Sister Celia's absence. When the opportunity arose, the girls spoke twice as fast as normal, making up for lost time and hours of imposed silence.

'Sure, some who've been sent by the government are here for ever, so they are, and some lucky ones leave when they have paid with three years' work in the laundry and have somewhere to go to. The bitches still charge the Americans for the adoptions, though. The poor kids get taken from their mammies when they are three. The tears and the wailing on those days would rip yer heart out, it's shocking, so it is.'

Kitty knew, she had heard it. At first, as she was one of the girls who was never allowed to visit the nursery and, as there was no conversation permitted, she had no idea what was happening until it was one of the girls in her own dormitory who had her little girl taken.

Kitty folded her shirt neatly, placed it on the pile and then took another out of the large wicker basket.

She was wondering why the girls didn't escape like the one called Besmina.

The Gardai had been to the home twice. The girls had gathered from the whispering nuns that Besmina had not been found.

'It's the reason we aren't allowed to speak. The girls who are here for ever, who have been sent by the government, have done nothing wrong. Some are just orphans and, God knows, one was sent here because she was so gorgeous, the lads in the village kept whistling at her. She's in the asylum now. I saw them take her myself in a van, strapped up. Some of them even get pregnant whilst they are in here. Now tell me, how the fuck does that happen?'

Kitty whispered back, 'They can't have done nothing, they must have done something wrong. It's illegal to lock someone up for nothing.'

'Oh, sure it is, Kitty, yer right about that,' said Aideen. 'This place is feckin' illegal. That's why we aren't allowed to talk. The nuns are getting bloody rich on the back of girls who are sent here by the authorities and ending their days here as slaves, for nothing more than being raped by their own brother or the feckin' priest, which was beyond their own doing.'

Kitty almost dropped the iron. She stood for a second and put her hands inside the pocket of the apron she was wearing. There were other girls here who had been raped by a priest? She wasn't the only one?

Aideen, who hadn't noticed Kitty's shock, continued, 'Some of them are got pregnant by the priests whilst they are in here and no one says a fucking thing. It's as though they are invisible. One of the older women in here has had three babies in twenty years. Either the immaculate conception is common in places like this or Father Samuel is having his end away and no one gives a fucking flying shite.'

Kitty put her hand on to the side of the ironing table to hold herself up.

'Are ye all right?' asked Aideen.

'I'm OK, I just felt a bit weird, like,' said Kitty.

'Sit down then, for feck's sake, ye look as white as that shirt.'

Kitty could hardly believe what she was hearing. She had been sent here because of a priest. She had thought he was the only one in the world to behave in that way and yet here she was, being told by Aideen that, even in the Abbey, no one was safe from a predatory priest.

At that moment, Sister Celia walked back into the room. The telltale signs of cake crumbs clung to the front of her black habit.

'Are you two talking?' she shouted. 'What are ye staring at, girl?'

Kitty was wearing an odd expression. Her mouth was open and her eyes looked wild, but she made not a sound.

Kitty thought the room suddenly seemed much brighter and hotter than it had before. And then it came. A pain that felt as though someone had placed a band of metal round what was once her waist and was slowly, slowly, tightening it, relentlessly, in a painful contraction.

Kitty heard a piercing scream coming from somewhere in the room. And then she realized the scream was her own. Without warning, a gush of warm water cascaded down her legs and formed a large puddle on the floor. At the same time, the metal band began to slowly, slowly loosen its grip.

Kitty began to sob. She had no idea what she was saying, but she knew she was crying for help.

Aideen rushed forward and took both of her hands.

'Get the disgusting thing out of here,' Sister Celia screamed at Aideen.

They both knew, without asking her to explain, that the disgusting thing was Kitty.

Sister Celia then shouted to one of the girls from across the room, who were now looking over the top of a sink, 'And stop yer gawping, you filthy lot, and get this mess mopped up.'

Sister Celia hated it more than anything else on earth when the girls went into labour in the laundry. She would avoid it at all costs. Sometimes she even pleaded with the nuns who worked on the other sections of the laundry, not to send her the girls who were far gone. She had had no choice with Kitty.

God alone knew why they had accepted that girl. The Reverend Mother had been on pins since the day she had arrived and Besmina had escaped. Reverend Mother hated anyone knowing the Abbey's business. Sister Celia had been stuck with the girl. And now her worst fear had been realized and, God knew, she hated it.

The screams, the pain, the mess: they were the audible and visible manifestation of sin. Sister Celia became agitated. She was surrounded by sin, breaking free and setting itself loose in her laundry. It leaked, it oozed, it ran and it smelt. Sin escaped.

And, God forbid, now sin was laughing at her, sat in a puddle on her laundry-room floor.

## Chapter Twenty-nine

The women stood just inside the school entrance, whilst the children ran and screamed in the playground, full of excitement at the arrival of snow. And on the night before Christmas Eve.

Sister Evangelista would normally be irritated by the delay. Tonight was different. She even huddled up with the rest of the women, an unlikely member of the gang. The icy wind whistled in, bringing with it light dustings of snow lifted from the playground. Once in through the door, they dropped and immediately melted. Even in the short time that the women had waited and despite the appearance of muddy puddles on the highly polished, parquet floor, Sister Evangelista remained in a good mood.

She was happy with how the evening had gone.

Brigid and Mrs McGuire moved tentatively down the steps to the playground, and began rounding up the McGuire children and shook the snow off the pram apron. Brigid carried the baby in her arms.

'Holy Mother, would ye look at this,' she exclaimed, brushing the inch of snow from the pram canopy and lifting out the pillow to give that a shake, too.

'It'll not last long, it never does in Liverpool. Sean says it's because of the Gulf Stream. I've only ever seen the river meself.'

'It was still here in March last year, Brigid. I hope this isn't it for another three months,' said Mrs Mcguire.

'Will I go to the chippy, Brigid?' Mrs McGuire asked hopefully. She saw the frown on Brigid's face. She knew Brigid had mashed potatoes and gravy waiting for supper.

'Oh, go on, it'll be a little snow treat for the children now. It's not every day it snows and you know I like to treat them, when I'm here.'

'I'd rather that the children looked to your heart, Mrs McGuire, not your hand,' chided Brigid, but they both knew Mrs McGuire would win. 'Oh, go on then,' she said. 'Take Patricia with ye. I will start getting the others changed and ready for bed. Don't forget Sean, he might have something to celebrate tonight.'

Mrs McGuire was feeling confident. If Sean won tonight, he would surely persuade Brigid to move to America and join their Mary and Eddie, wouldn't that be just fantastic. With his own money and not dependent on others, he would be free to travel over first and then send for his family very shortly afterwards.

Mrs McGuire had it all planned out. She would travel over with Brigid and the children, and they would all settle in Chicago together.

Sean had always agreed with her but, over the past few weeks, she had found it impossible to engage him in conversations about America in the way she used to.

She had put it down to the big fight he was having tonight.

The big Liverpool Christmas fight, on the same night as the nativity play.

Mrs McGuire knew her son. He was a secretive one, all right, always had been. Only she knew how desperate he was to reach Chicago. Liverpool was too restrictive. The tales of big wages he had heard about in Ireland before he arrived were out of all proportion to the reality.

In Liverpool, if you arrived poor, you stayed poor. This was not the case in America, as their Mary and her husband had demonstrated. America was full of opportunity.

Mrs McGuire linked arms with Patricia, so that she didn't slip in the snow, and they strode off together towards Jonny Chan's, smiling and happy.

Jerry took hold of Nellie's arm and Kathleen shuffled in beside Nellie, wheeling the pram. Nellie thought she would attempt to ice-skate, like she had seen on the black-and-white television last week, and within seconds was flat on her back on the pavement. Jerry and Kathleen roared with laugher and Joseph, with his face peeping out from his hand-knitted balaclava, clapped his hands in excitement.

Kathleen smiled. 'I've never, in my entire life, seen a baby laugh and smile as much as he does, Jer,' she said.

'It warms my heart every day, so it does, to see how great Alice is with the little fellow.'

Jerry put his arm round his mammy's shoulder and placed a kiss on the top of her head.

'Get away with ye, Jerry, are ye going soft altogether?'

Nellie laughed. They were all three full of Christmas cheer.

Kathleen held onto the pram; Nellie held onto her nana; Jerry, on the outside, held Nellie's hand.

A warm glow wrapped around them.

The deep companionship of the three. Virgin snow that sparkled like glitter on the pavement. The sound of the children's breathless laughter. The crisp freshness of the air. The promise of a white Christmas Eve to wake up to. The beautiful, loving baby boy grinning at them from the warmth and comfort of his pram.

They walked in companionable silence aware that they would remember this night for ever.

When they reached Nelson Street, Maura and Tommy turned and waved goodnight to them.

'Nana, it won't be long until Kitty is home, will it?' said Nellie.

Kathleen squeezed Nellie's hand and smiled at her. Trust Nellie to be always thinking of others, she thought.

'Aye, I know, queen, and a blessing that will be, for sure.'

As they reached their door, Malachi ran past, screeching at the top of his voice, as he chased Harry and Little Paddy, with a ball of snow in his hands, ready to shove down the back of both their necks.

Older neighbours, who hadn't been to the school, were peeping round their net curtains to see what all the noise was about. The news of snow was heralded by excited cries.

'Da, Da, save me,' Harry squealed as he ran past.

Maura had stepped indoors. Tommy stood in the middle of the road, not daring to run, yelling at the top of his voice, 'Malachi, get here now, or I'll give ye a good hiding!' Everyone who heard him knew that was a lie.

Jerry reached out and caught Malachi by the collar, lifting him clean off the ground.

Malachi's legs pedalled furiously as his temper flapped at his heels.

'Put me down,' he screamed, 'put me down.'

'Come on, Malachi,' said Jerry, laughing. 'Come on, Harry. Yer safe, lad.'

'Mam, put the kettle on, and tell Alice I'll be two minutes, if she's up. I'll just help Tommy, the big soft lad, with these little scamps.'

Kathleen and Nellie, both laughing out loud, turned into the entry.

*

When Brigid stepped in through the back door, she was surprised to see that the main light had been switched on. She knew she had switched it off when they left and she wondered, was Sean home?

Relief flooded through her as she realized that he must be.

She had regretted letting Patricia accompany Mrs McGuire to the chippy and wished she had sent one of the younger ones instead. It was difficult, though. Mrs McGuire and Patricia had a special bond.

Brigid was the youngest of fourteen and so the notion surprised her that Patricia, as the eldest, had a different place in the family from all the rest.

Sure, wasn't she the most organized of any of her siblings? Didn't she run her house with absolute order and control?

Her house was immaculate.

Brigid had a great deal to be proud of. She still wished she had told Patricia to stay, though. Having to get five under the age of five ready for bed, never mind the others, was hard work and Patricia was a grand little help. Brigid was exhausted. However, she hadn't told Sean yet she was pretty sure there was another McGuire baby on the way.

This one made her more tired than she ever had been before and her face was flushed and burning, not signs of early pregnancy that she remembered from her previous babies. She could hear her heart beating in her eardrums and had fallen asleep during the nativity play. Never mind, she thought. If Sean has a win tonight, a pregnancy will hold off any talk of a move to America for a while.

As soon as she took off her coat, she put the kettle on and reached for the nappies she had left to warm on a shelf next to the range.

'Ooh, warm as toast,' she said to one of her toddlers, pressing the warm nappy on her ice-cold and bright-red little cheek.

Brigid shouted up the stairs to Sean. No response.

That's funny, she thought to herself.

She filled a small enamel bowl with warm water, took down the towel and pyjamas, and began changing the toddlers and the baby.

When she had finished, they jumped up and, one by one, piled onto the sofa in front of the TV. The older girls came down into the kitchen, all changed and ready, carrying their shoes with them.

'Clothes all folded neatly on the press for the morning, girls?'

Each one nodded.

'Shoes by the back door now,' she said. 'Was Daddy upstairs, Emelda?'

Emelda shook her head as she slipped onto the sofa with her siblings.

Brigid sat at the table and looked at the row of red heads, watching *Coronation Street* on the television. They didn't really understand it but they all knew that being up this late was a treat and not one of them was about to complain or misbehave. Besides, Nana and Patricia were gone to the chippy.

'Isn't this just the best night of the year?' little Emelda said. 'We've had the play, treats at the school, snow and the chippy too. This is the happiest night in me life, Mammy.'

Brigid felt her heart fill with love. Making her children happy was a bonus. Keeping them clean and fed, and running an orderly home, was her job. None of Brigid's children missed a day from school, ever, not unless they were truly poorly. Brigid was a good mother. She and Sean did things the right way.

'Is it now, you gorgeous thing?' Brigid's face suffused with a warm and loving glow as she looked at her daughter's toothless grin. 'It's mine, too.'

At that moment, they all heard Mrs McGuire and Patricia walk up the path and the back door opened.

'Mary and Joseph, would ye close that door,' Brigid shouted, rubbing her arms to counter the cold blast.

The kitchen filled with the smell of newsprint soaked in vinegar.

'Here we are, all,' said Mrs McGuire, 'chips and a saveloy each.'

Mrs McGuire loved pronouncing the word 'saveloy'.

'Pass the big plate down from the mantel, would ye, Brigid. It's nice and warm and we can put it all in the middle of the table for them, what do ye think?'

'Aye, that's grand, thanks, Mrs McGuire. I think maybe Sean nipped back earlier, but he's not here now,' Brigid replied thoughtfully with a hint of concern in her voice.

The children had dived off the sofa and were dutifully piling onto the chairs round the table. Grace fetched forks out of the drawer, and the plates from the neat and tidy row along the back of the press.

Emelda had removed the muslin used to keep the flies away, taken the breadboard and knife from the press and placed it on the table. Now she began helping the smaller ones up onto the chairs. They were all chattering away excitedly, salivating at the smell of the chips. Chair legs scraped across the stone floor, cutlery and plates banged loudly on the table, and the kettle whistled impatiently on the range while Emelda set the table.

Little Paddy's dog, Scamp, scratched away persistently at the back door. He had followed Mrs McGuire all the way home from the chippy and was now letting Brigid know he was there. Brigid was begrudgingly kind to Scamp. She felt for him, having to live at Peggy and Paddy's, and often threw him a bit of raw sausage.

Brigid reached up for the big meat plate from the mantel-shelf above the range and immediately saw the envelope. She recognized the handwriting as Sean's. He had never, in their ten years of marriage, written her a letter.

A feeling of dread crept slowly into the room and her expression became one of fear, as she ripped open the envelope and extracted the single sheet of notepaper. It had been torn from Patricia's school book and with it was a wad of ten-pound notes. Brigid's first thought was one of irritation at his having taken paper from Patricia's school book. Brigid kept her own pad of usable scrap paper, with a slip of string through the corner to hold it together, in the press drawer.

On the television, Ena Sharples was giving out to Minnie Caldwell. Someone took the kettle off the range to silence its persistent whistle.

Brigid couldn't hear what they were saying. The noise from the television and the children's chatter had merged into a low background buzz.

She felt her blood drain into her boots within seconds, as happiness, laughter and hope for her future left.

Mrs McGuire bent down to turn up the television and the closing theme music from *Coronation Street* began to fill the room.

'Merciful Mary, it was that flaming queue, Patricia. We've missed it,' she exclaimed in a bitterly disappointed voice.

Brigid stared at the letter. The meaning of the words washed over her slowly in rhythmic waves, becoming stronger and more painful with each second. Her mind, shielding her soul, refused to absorb the truth at once, but held at bay the realization of all the things she had suspected – had known, really, but had suppressed and ignored in the midst of her busy life.

No morning kiss. Distracted. No talk of America. No desire for sex. Already gone when she awoke. Never home when she went to bed.

Her heart began to race and pound in her chest as the adrenaline swam out to shield her. Tears swarmed in her eyes, blurring the words, washing them away, saving her from the pain of reading them again, for now.

Mrs McGuire turned from the television to look at Brigid and saw it happen.

The moment when the words seeped through, hit Brigid's heart and, shred by shred, tore it apart.

Kathleen thought it was very unusual that there were no lights on in the house and that the fire had gone out.

'Jesus,' she cried, as they stepped into the kitchen. 'I didn't bank the fire up, because I thought Alice would be back to do it and the flamin' thing has gone out, on the very coldest night of the year. Would ye believe that? Nellie, Alice must be feeling very poorly indeed. Let's get a pot of tea mashed and then we can take her one up and see how she is. You see to Joseph, while I get the fire going.'

'I'm going up to the cot, Nana, to fetch his pyjamas,' said Nellie.

Kathleen had dropped to her knees, raking the range fire and muttering to herself.

'Aye, there's enough life left in here,' she said with relief, whipping an *Echo* out from underneath the seat cushion and screwing it up tightly. Within a minute, the kitchen glowed orange and the reflected flames danced up the walls. Kathleen carefully placed one piece of coke after another on top of the burning paper and then closed the range doors.

The crêpe-paper garland decorations that Kathleen, Alice and Nellie had patiently glued together over a week of evenings, and then strung across the ceiling, shuddered and crinkled above her as the heat rose from the fire, lending the festive decorations a life of their own.

Kathleen leant back onto her haunches and wiped her hands down the front of her apron. 'Thank the Lord for small mercies,' she whispered, looking up at the statue of the Virgin Mary, and crossed herself.

It wasn't the statue Jerry and Bernadette had bought. That one had mysteriously broken some years back, when Nellie was just a toddler. Nellie had asked her only the other day where it had come from.

'The first one was bought before Jerry and Bernadette were married. I remember, they bought it from a lady in the little shop in Crossmolina, when they were at home on their holidays. This is the second one, though, and I have no idea where that came from, or even how the first one broke.'

All that seemed such a long time ago. As she stared at the holy figurine, Kathleen murmured, 'Ah, Bernadette, ye loved Christmas like no one I have ever known before or since.'

Kathleen crossed herself again. It must have been the emotion of Christmas, of having a moment here on her own, in front of the fire, in an empty kitchen, because as she waited to see if the coke had truly caught, something suddenly touched her. They hadn't switched the lamp on yet and, apart from the fire, the room was dark. She thought about life and its ups and downs. How different her life would have been if their Bernadette had lived, if she had been here with them tonight at the school. The pain of her memory and the acuteness of her loss stabbed Kathleen straight in the chest. It always did.

Kathleen took her handkerchief out of her apron pocket.

'Ah, get away, ye daft old sod,' she said, wiping her eyes and lifting up the poker, ready to open the range doors.

She suddenly felt cold and yet she was kneeling in front of the range, with the flames already roaring up the chimney. She held her hands out to the door to feel if it was hot. Yes, of course it was, she could see that, couldn't she?

An icy shiver passed over her. She rubbed her arms and looked around, confused.

'God in heaven,' she said to herself, 'have I a chill?' And leaning back, she pressed the back of her hand to her forehead, which felt normal.

Nellie walked slowly down the stairs. She had dressed Joseph in his pyjamas as if on automatic pilot. Her inclination had been to scream and to run down to the kitchen, but she didn't. She held on.

She had thought that they had been burgled. The press drawers were open, along with the wardrobe door. Alice's apron, and a few of her clothes, were strewn around the room. Everything else that had belonged to Alice had gone.

Everything, except for Joseph.

She had looked in the wardrobe first. The hangers on the side that belonged to Alice were empty. The drawers in the press, likewise, and her few bits of make-up, her hairbrush and curlers, which lived on the top, had also disappeared.

Her shoes. Her boots. Her coat. Her hats. Her gloves. Her everything. Gone.

As Nellie came through the door at the bottom of the stairs, holding Joseph in her arms, she stopped dead in her tracks.

Joseph put his thumb into his mouth, silently laid his head on her chest and stared at the scene in front of him, sucking slowly and steadily. The kitchen was still dark. The fire had now reduced from its initial roaring blaze to a softer, quieter flame.

There was Kathleen, kneeling in front of the fire, and next to her knelt Bernadette. There was not a sound in the kitchen. When the coke in the fire slid down onto the grate with a sudden crunch, Nellie almost jumped out of her skin, but nothing altered.

Bernadette's hair had absorbed the warm light from the fire and radiated a red glow that wrapped itself around them all.

Kathleen wiped her eyes and Bernadette put her arm round her shoulders. Nellie heard Kathleen talking to Bernadette, but she couldn't hear what she was saying.

Nellie wasn't scared at all of Bernadette, her mammy, whom she loved without ever having known her. But she knew something was shifting, altering, that she was in their midst and that whatever was happening was beyond their control. Something was very wrong. Why else would Bernadette appear, and so openly too? But this feeling, in the kitchen, this was special. It was like magic. It felt like heaven.

Nellie kissed the top of Joseph's warm head and as he nuzzled in deeper, she hugged him. She felt an ache, very deep inside. A yearning. A longing. A need to be the one her mammy was hugging. A desperate loneliness flooded her and her eyes filled with pain, as she quietly sobbed and, for the very first time in her life, she cried the word 'Mammy' out loud.

After what seemed like many minutes but was in fact only seconds, the spell was broken by the sound of Jerry lifting the latch of the back gate and the noise of Peggy and Little Paddy, shuffling along behind him in the snow, urgently shouting, 'Jerry, Jerry, will ye wait. Come here while I tell ye.'

Before the back door had even opened, Kathleen was on her feet and Bernadette had vanished.

It was Christmas Eve.

Daisy wanted to stand on the deck of the boat and stare as hard as she could until she saw the coast of Ireland and her family waiting for her.

She had so many images in her mind of what they would look like and what they would say when they saw her. She had been told that her older brother, his wife and his eldest son and daughter would be there to greet her. Miss Devlin had said that when Daisy's sister-in-law had spoken to Miss Devlin on the telephone, she had become so full of emotion and excitement at the prospect of Daisy being with them at Christmas that both she and Miss Devlin had been blubbing like a pair of eejits.

They had made Miss Devlin promise that she would visit in the school holidays and, of course, she had said she would.

After all she had been through, Daisy now had a family of her own and a friend in Miss Devlin.

Miss Devlin had put Daisy on the boat and asked two elderly sisters who were also boarding, and whose names she discovered were Edith and Elsie, to keep a watch on Daisy. They assured her that they would and Miss Devlin explained that Daisy's own family would be right at the gate when they docked, waiting and ready.

She had asked the ladies if they would show Daisy where the toilet was, and help her to buy a cuppa and a biscuit to settle her stomach.

The ladies, who were both from Dublin, were as kind and friendly as any Irish grandmother would be.

'Of course,' they had said, 'no problem at all, you just stick with us, Daisy.'

But Daisy hadn't wanted to sit in the café inside. Daisy had spent almost her entire life inside. She wanted to gaze at the sea and watch for her family.

The ladies had brought Daisy a cup of tea on deck. 'We will be back out with another cuppa in half an hour,' said Elsie kindly.

Daisy had smiled and thanked her. Daisy knew her manners. She could count on one hand the number of times anyone had ever made her a cuppa, but that didn't mean she didn't know the right thing to say when someone did.

She hadn't stopped smiling since Miss Devlin had first read her the letter from her family. Tonight, she didn't mind being alone. She had so much to look forward to. Daisy would never be alone again. She reached her hand up and stroked her felt hat, which had been presented to her at the play. It felt so soft. Daisy could barely believe her luck.

It was as she bent to place the empty teacup onto the bench behind her that Daisy saw the man approach.

'Hello,' she said with a big friendly grin, as she stood upright. She recognized him immediately. 'Are you going to Dublin too? Well, fancy. I am off to meet my family. I have a family, you know. My brother, he's the state solicitor and he wants me to live with him and his wife. Can ye imagine that? I don't want to go inside. I want to wait here. I don't care about the cold tonight. I don't really.

I want to be the first to see my family waiting for me when we arrive in Dublin. Miss Devlin tells me they will be at the very front, waiting for me at the gate.'

Daisy looked over the rail and across the sea as she giggled at her own words. She was beyond excitement. For the past twenty-four hours she had been seized by a euphoria that manifested itself as a new calmness and radiance. Everyone had noticed.

'She cannot keep the grin from her face,' Miss Devlin had said to Sister Evangelista.

'I have noticed!' the sister replied. 'Sure, she is radiant indeed. Let's pray to God that smile stays there forever because if anyone deserves to be happy, Daisy does.'

Daisy felt the man's hand on her back and turned to face him. 'Will someone be waiting for you, too?' Her smile was open. Friendly, happy, questioning. Simple.

'Yes, they will. Daisy, your family, they have asked me to escort you. I am taking you to meet your brother, Daisy. You have to come with me now. Let's move down to the front of the boat to be ready, so that we can be the first away.'

Later that evening, Simon was on duty and had arranged to meet the super at his golf club where he was hosting a family celebration.

The bobbies were becoming agitated. They wanted to be at home with their families, not sitting in police cars, doing absolutely nothing at all on the four streets.

Simon stood in the glass foyer and lit a cigarette. He watched the doorman enter the restaurant and inform the super that Simon was outside.

The super half stood, waiting for the waiter to remove his chair, and patted his mouth with his napkin. He cast a glance through the door to Simon and then, seeming to apologize to his guests, walked out into the foyer.

'I'm sorry, sir,' said Simon, 'but it's Christmas Eve and the men . . .

'Not at all, I am delighted you are here,' said the super. 'Look here, this is a good time to shut things down. The papers are on holiday and everything and everyone has gone terribly quiet. I have spoken to the chief, who agrees that we should keep the file open and stand the men down until something or someone comes forward. Best thing to do. Let the men go home.'

'Thank you, sir,' said Simon. 'I will tell them straight away and let Davies know.'

'Good man. Merry Christmas.' And without another second wasted, the super walked back into the club dining room and returned to his party.

'Yes, thank you, sir, Merry Christmas,' said Simon to his retreating back.

Simon left the club via its large revolving door and lit another cigarette. It was his last. As he slipped into the driver's seat, he threw the red and white packet onto the ground.

On his drive back to the four streets he called in to the station to make a call.

'Investigation abandoned,' he said in a low voice into the phone.

'Are you sure?' came the reply.

'I'm certain,' said Simon. 'We are all safe.'

As he replaced the receiver, he took a packet of Pall Mall out of the top drawer of his desk and headed back down to the four streets to send the officers home for Christmas.

As he sat in his police car, he looked into his rear-view mirror and, flinching, he ripped off the Elastoplast dressing on the back of his neck, squealing as he pulled away some of the downy hair.

'Bleeding cat,' he hissed as he turned the key in the ignition.

As Simon drove past the Grand on to Lime Street, he stopped at the pelican crossing outside the Shamrock pub to allow Alice Deane and Sean McGuire, their heads down, to run across the road. Sean was carrying two suitcases and they were both heading down towards the Pier Head. Neither noticed as they passed in front of his car. The snow on the main roads in town had turned to slush and his rear wheels slipped slightly as he accelerated away.

As he drove down Church Street and then onto the Dock Road,

he wondered how long it would be before he was summoned to investigate a missing passenger on the Dublin ferry.

And then, letting out a deep sigh, he grinned as he turned left and headed up towards the four streets.

Christmas morning.

She had only Aideen to comfort her when her son made his arrival into the world. The snow had begun to fall at exactly the moment Kitty's labour pains seized her. Within no time at all, the solitary overhead telephone cable fell and lay buried under a carpet of crystal-white snow. They were stranded from the outside world.

Aideen almost chased the nuns out of the room when they arrived to impart the news that there was no telephone to contact the midwife and no way of getting a message into the village. She felt that, for some reason, the nuns were nervous, almost scared of what they said and did around Kitty. Aideen, who was sharp as a knife, took full advantage of this.

Kitty was the only girl anywhere near her due delivery date and the resident midwife had taken herself home to Dublin for the Christmas break. As she slammed the front door behind her, her last words had been, 'That girl's not my responsibility.'

Despite having chased the nuns from the labour room and having witnessed plenty of her own mother's births, Aideen was terrified.

Pain wrapped itself around Kitty's waist like a metal band and each time its grip became longer and harder to bear. She heard screams filling the room but was too far gone to feel shame or embarrassment.

'God, help me,' she screamed over and over. 'Mammy, help me.'

Aideen held Kitty's hands and walked her round the room. She sat next to her on the bed when she could persuade Kitty to lie down. She mopped her brow with cold water and gave Kitty sips of water. And all through the evening and into the night, the baby showed no sign of making an entry into the world.

The girls from the dorm had sneaked bread into their apron pockets and slipped into the labour room to hand it to Aideen.

'Fucking hell,' said Aideen. 'Did not one of them mean bitches think one of us could do with the disgusting slop they give us as soup? She has no energy. How is she going to push this thing out?'

Juliette, one of the older girls, looked concerned as another contraction took hold of Kitty.

'Would ye like me to take over for a while, Aideen? Maybe we should take it in turns to stop with her?'

Aideen looked at Kitty, soaked in sweat and almost delirious.

'No, thanks, I will stay and see the job done. I feel close to this poor girl.'

Juliette nodded and left the room. She understood. They all felt close to her. She was a sweet kid and, God knew, the faces she had pulled at the nuns behind their backs had all but creased them up with laughter at times.

'I'll see ye later then,' whispered Juliette from the door with a glance at Kitty who was oblivious, in a world of intense torment.

By four o'clock in the morning, following hours of pain and screaming, Kitty had given up. She felt calm and no longer tried to respond to Aideen's instructions to push. 'No,' she whimpered, 'I can't, I don't want to do it.'

It was now Aideen's turn to begin to scream.

'Push, ye fucking bitch,' she shouted at Kitty. 'Do ye think I'm wasting my night in here for you to decide you can't be bothered to push? *Push*, now.'

There was no response from Kitty. She wanted to die, in a place of her own, somewhere distant from the room and Aideen. She had had enough.

'It is the perfect thing,' she muttered in her delirious haze. 'It is the perfect answer if I die. There will be no trouble for anyone and no problem. I just so want to die.'

The slap across Kitty's face hurt almost as much as the contraction that quickly followed. Aideen was yelling into her face to push.

She had climbed up behind Kitty, dragged her up the bed and forced her to sit upright, resisting Kitty's urge to lean back and lie down again.

'Don't let the fucking witches win. Don't let the child's bastard father beat you. Don't let him win.'

Aideen was now scared. She could see Kitty had disappeared somewhere and she didn't know where. She was terrified that Kitty was indeed about to die.

'Do you want the bastard father to win, do ye?'

Kitty could hear Aideen. She was aware of her hands prodding and pushing her heavy, flaccid body. She was aware of Aideen's words penetrating though her fog.

The bastard father beating her? Was that what Aideen had just said?

Kitty began to laugh.

'For fuck's sake.'

Aideen climbed back down from the bed. 'What in God's name? Why are ye laughing now?'

Kitty snapped back from the place where she wanted only to close her eyes and sleep. She didn't want this baby. She didn't want to be here. She didn't want to work in the laundry. She hadn't wanted to be raped. But none of that mattered. Kitty didn't want to live, she wanted to die, but she didn't even have that. Aideen wasn't going to let her. Aideen was going to make her live and have this spawn of the devil himself. Aideen thought that, in this way, Kitty would be winning. She wasn't even going to let Kitty choose whether or not she died.

It made Kitty laugh again, almost in hysteria.

'Push,' yelled Aideen, as the pain once again seized Kitty's abdomen with an intense ferocity and made it harden like a rock. With all that she had left, Kitty pushed again.

Following sixteen hours of screams and chaos, the labour room suddenly fell silent, apart from the tiny snuffles from deep within a white knitted blanket, which Aideen had found in the layette of baby clothes Rosie had left behind when she had visited to examine Kitty.

An hour later, once she had managed to clear up the afterbirth mess and had washed down Kitty and the baby, Aideen suddenly felt giddy and sat down on a chair, before she fainted herself with exhaustion.

Although Aideen had switched off the light, hoping that both she and Kitty could catch an hour's sleep before morning, the room was lit with a vivid bright whiteness, reflected from the snow-laden sky and the newly covered trees.

'Would ye look at him,' said an exhausted Kitty as she lifted her new baby up to show Aideen. 'Isn't he just gorgeous?'

Kitty now had no recollection of not wanting to have this baby. As she first laid eyes on him, no thought of rejection crossed her mind. He had brought his own love with him.

As Aideen had finally delivered his thin and slippery body, without warning Kitty had been swamped by emotion. Since the second he had been born, she had been unable to take her eyes off him.

Aideen gave her a look of concern. 'Aye, he's sweet enough, all right, but in days he will be the child of a rich and fancy American couple, so don't forget that and go getting all attached.'

Without speaking a word, Kitty brought the bundle up to her face. She felt the warmth of his body lying against her own and nuzzled her face into the dark downy hair on his head.

'He looks like me da,' she whispered to Aideen in the dark. 'Can I give him a name?'

Aideen looked at her. 'Aye, but I'm sure his new mam and da will want to choose his own name. What were ye thinking?'

'John,' Kitty whispered into her baby's warm cheek where she had laid his first kiss, 'his name is John.'

There was a tap on the door as the girls from the dormitory tiptoed in one by one.

'Would ye believe it,' said Juliette as she came into the room. 'Sister Virginia is first up. I told her about the awful night with no midwife an' all and she gave me the key to the kitchen and said go and fetch the girls a tray of tea and some toast. Ye have certainly spooked them, having a Christmas baby, sent them all of a dither, that has, and it being you an' all, Kitty. Would a sinner give birth on Christmas Day? In a right state they are!'

Kitty looked up as the girls slipped in. The room filled with the smell of hot buttered toast and Juliette began to pour the scalding hot tea into cups.

One of the girls, who, like Aideen, had to stay at the Abbey for the full three years and had already had her baby, handed Kitty a bottle of formula milk.

'Did ye forget about the baby?' she smiled at Aideen.

'No, not at all, he just hasn't bothered looking for a feed yet,' Aideen replied. 'I was just getting over me shock. I swear, God was holding my hands through that because I had no idea what I was doing.'

Kitty was no stranger to feeding a baby a bottle and she expertly fed John, who latched onto the teat in a split second.

'Look at him,' Kitty laughed, 'he nearly has it drained already.'

The laundry-room girls cooed over John and Kitty, and chattered quietly, something they were never, ever allowed to do.

Kitty had noticed that some of the girls, who had been in the Abbey for a longer period than most, spoke almost like the deaf little girl on the four streets. So unused were they to talking that, when they did, it was as if their tongues had forgotten how to form a word. When they did speak, it was slurred and difficult to understand.

One of the girls sat on the edge of Kitty's bed, smiling at her and gently rubbing John's back. 'A Christmas baby, can ye imagine? That will make him very special indeed.'

Kitty didn't know what to say. He would be special, but she wouldn't see it. Dawn was breaking and there was an atmosphere in the room. The Christmas baby and hot buttered toast were having an effect.

'I'm not wasting having the key,' whispered Ann. 'I'm off to make more tea and toast. There was enough bread in that kitchen to feed a fuckin' army.'

And she giggled as two of the other girls tripped down the steps with Ann to make a further raid on the kitchen. 'It's a blessing that ye are here, Kitty, ye have made Christmas for us with the toast.'

As Kitty sat up in the bed, with her baby laid on her chest and a cup of tea in her hand, she looked round at the other girls chattering. Letting no thoughts other than those needed for that moment come into her mind, she smiled the first smile of happiness since the day she had arrived at the Abbey.

I will remember this, she thought to herself. My days of imprisonment here are nearly over.

And then as though he could read her thoughts, her little bundle wriggled his tiny feet in objection and kicked her tender tummy of raw jelly and, once again, she bent down to kiss his head.

Breathing in deeply, she allowed her nostrils to fill with his smell and held on to it, not breathing out, willing her mind to remember. She rubbed his back slowly, aware of her every move. She bent to look at his face and his blue eyes locked onto her own. She burnt the image onto her memory and into her heart. This was all she would have to remember. These moments, bathed in snow and dawn light.

Aideen began to pour the second round of tea. There was no laundry work today; none of them would return to bed now. She looked at Kitty and worried. Kitty, just a girl and full of motherly love.

'Maybe it's better that we get three years with them,' Aideen whispered to Ann. 'That way we have more to hold onto and remember.'

'Three years or three days, it's all cruel,' Ann replied harshly. 'One day these witches will get their comeuppance and I for one cannot wait.'

They turned back to look at Kitty. The dawn had broken as the first robins perched on the snow-covered branches of the plum tree outside the window. The Abbey bells began to ring. Kitty's son lay in the crook of her arm with his head tucked under her chin. Both were fast asleep.

Sister Assumpta was relieved that Kitty had given birth. The sooner she could get that child out of the convent, the better. The nuns, all of a fluster that a baby had been born on Christmas morning, had been almost beyond her control. She could hardly believe her ears when she had been informed that the girls had been handed the keys to the kitchen.

'God in heaven, what next?' she had screamed at Sister Celia.

'He's a baby born in sin and out of wedlock, he isn't Jesus Christ and she is certainly no Holy Mother!'

As she silently climbed the stairs to the labour room, the Reverend Mother had already decided to send a message to Rosie to collect Kitty as soon as was physically possible. Although how she was going to do that in the snow, God alone knew.

The girls scattered when she opened the labour-room door and stepped into their midst. She noted that the electric fire had been switched on without permission and the detritus of breakfast lay scattered on the tray.

'Get down to prayers, all of you, they started ten minutes ago,' she spat at them in a voice that contained no hint of Christmas cheer.

The girls flew out of the room and down the stairs towards the chapel. Aideen kept her eyes lowered and cheekily snatched the last piece of toast from the tray as she hurried past.

The noise woke Kitty, who opened her eyes. Aware of the baby lying across her chest and the old rolled-up nappy Aideen had placed between her legs, she shuffled herself painfully up the bed, using just one elbow as she gripped the baby with her other hand. Sister Assumpta watched in stony silence and offered no assistance. The cramps sweeping across Kitty's belly and her breasts, although nothing compared to the labour pains, were bad enough to make her wince as she attempted to move. Aideen said she had torn quite badly and she knew the warm feeling between her legs was blood oozing out onto the rags with the effort of moving.

Sister Assumpta showed not the slightest concern, only irritation, as she glanced at the baby. The more attractive the baby was, the happier the new parents in America would be when he was handed over. This one would be leaving soon and he definitely was very attractive. She would not keep a baby born on Christmas morning in her convent for a day longer than necessary.

'The snow won't be here for long,' she said crisply as she walked to the window and cast her glance over the carpet of glistening white lawn. 'It will be just a day or two before the midwife is here and I am sure we all agree it is for the best if she takes you back to your family as soon as possible. You can stay up here in this room.

There are no other deliveries due and I will have food sent up to you. You have no further work to do. Just stay on this floor and don't come down into the Abbey until the midwfe arrives.'

Despite her huge discomfort, the tiredness, the burning pain in her belly and the fact that her legs felt as though they wouldn't work even if she tried to walk, Kitty felt a huge relief. It would be at least two days before Rosie would reach her. Two whole days with her baby. Two days of memories. Two days in which to smother him with a lifetime of love.

Regardless of her best effort not to, Kitty's face broke into a loving smile as she shuffled her baby up into her arms.

Sister Assumpta turned away from the window and she saw the smile. She blinked. Within seconds, she had assessed the scene. Her face set, hard. In a voice devoid of emotion, she spoke.

'I will send up a novice directly to collect the baby. He will live in the nursery now until his new parents land at Shannon airport.'

Before Kitty could utter a word in protest, she glided out of the room on the wave of her own destruction.

Kitty had only minutes with her baby as she heard the bells peal the end of prayers. There was no time to think or plan, no point in pleading. She knew the coldness, the evil, that resided in the heart of the Reverend Mother. Evil was no stranger to Kitty.

'Wake up, little fella,' she whispered urgently as her tears ran onto his downy hair. 'Wake up.'

And he did. He woke and scrunched up his newborn red face. Lifting both of his tiny clenched-up fists to his cheeks, he scratched his own delicate skin with a papery fingernail and began to whimper in complaint.

Kitty held him out in front of her and shook him gently as she heard heavy footsteps ascend the stairs and knew this was it. Her last moments. Sister Assumpta had wasted no time.

'I love you, do ye hear me?' she whispered to him urgently. 'Can ye hear me?'

He opened his deep-blue eyes, level with her own, and, once again, stared deeply into hers. His perfect lips, tinged white with milk, opening and closing. He knew her. Her smell. The sound of her voice. He ceased to whimper. She had all of his attention. He knew her as he knew himself. The physical cord cut, but the bond remained intact.

'I will find you one day, I will. I will find you,' she whispered desperately between her sobs. Her salty tears fell onto his newborn face and his eyes narrowed as if in concern.

Her lips were pressed against his soft and warm temple as she spoke, holding him tight. Repeating the words, 'I will find you, I am Kitty. I am your mammy, only me, no one else,' pressing them deep into his soul. Hiding them there. For ever.

# The Ballymara Road

*For Clifford*

*1959–1991*

*It's a long way to Tipperary…*

# Chapter One

It was early on Christmas morning at St Vincent's convent in Galway.

'Frank, wake up, did ye hear that?' Maggie O'Brien prodded her sleeping husband in the back, in an attempt to wake him. 'Frank, 'tis someone knocking on the lodge gate. Wake up now.'

Frank O'Brien was not in bed with his wife. Deep in the heart of a dream, he had just won first prize for his best onions at the Castlefeale show. All around him, people clapped and cheered as he stood at the front of the produce tent, holding high a bunch of onions so big, brown and sweetly perfect that it aroused naked envy in the eyes of the assembled gardeners and farmers.

'Frank, will ye fecking wake up, 'tis the gate. Who can it be, knocking at this ungodly hour? 'Tis the middle of the night.'

Frank woke with a start, as his ethereal body entered its earthly form with an unpleasant jolt. Startled, he begrudgingly opened one eye and viewed the world of the living. His first-prize elation faded within seconds. Blinking in the darkness, he rolled over to face his wife, but she had already leapt out of bed and nimbly hopped onto the wooden bench under the high, arched, mullioned window that looked down onto the main gate.

As the bench rocked back and forth, precariously and noisily, on the uneven stone floor, Maggie reached up to draw the heavy curtains and, in doing so, exposed her plump and naked backside beneath her old and tattered nightdress.

This is no ordinary morning, thought Frank. It feels special.

'Ah, 'tis Christmas,' he said, smiling as he focused his gaze on his wife's round buttocks.

Maggie was blissfully unaware of her husband's burgeoning arousal as she attempted to peer out, carefully peeling the curtains back from the thick layer of ice that coated the inside of the window.

'Merciful God, it has snowed heavily overnight. I don't know how that car has made it here. Maybe it has trouble, that's why they is knocking,' Maggie hissed as she rubbed her eyes, blinded by the car's headlights reflected in the window.

''Tis odd, indeed, to be knocking on a convent gate at this time,' said Frank, swinging his legs out of bed to place his feet on the cold stone floor.

All thoughts of an early romp between the sheets with his Maggie disappeared as she finally managed to draw the curtains, leaving behind thin threads of fabric stuck fast to the ice.

Frank squinted as the car headlights flooded the small lodge with their brilliance. 'Fecking hell, I can't see a thing, 'tis so bright,' he said furiously.

Frank and Maggie worked as the gardener and cook at St Vincent's convent, on the outskirts of Galway. It had been in existence for just a few years, having been hurriedly established by local Catholic dignitaries and busybodies to meet what they believed were declining moral standards amongst the local female population. It was five miles away from the more established Abbey, which was run by the same order of nuns and so full to the rafters with sin that it couldn't possibly take any more.

The convent chiefly comprised the large main house and an adjoining chapel, connected by a long passageway. A mother and baby home occupied the top floor and the girls – mothers and penitents alike – slept in the attics. Closest to the elements, they froze in winter and boiled in summer. A chapel house in the grounds was home to a retreat, used mainly by visitors from Dublin. An orphanage lay on the outskirts of the convent, almost entirely concealed from sight by an overgrown hedge of juniper trees.

Maggie and Frank, who also doubled up as gatekeepers, lived in the tiny lodge at the entrance to the grounds, which was as near to the main house as any man was allowed after dark, unless he was a priest. Frank maintained the grounds and grew enough produce to ensure that the convent remained amply supplied. Maggie ran the kitchens with the help of the orphans, who, as she constantly grumbled, were used as nothing more than slaves by the sisters, even though they were paid for by the state.

Maggie and Frank had grave misgivings about both the mother and baby home and the orphanage, but they were wise enough to keep their own counsel and, with it, the roof over their heads.

'Jesus, Mary and Joseph, it is not yet five o'clock in the mornin',' said Frank, as he pulled on a donkey jacket over his nightshirt. Then, placing his cap on his head, he stepped out through the front door into the snow, making for the pedestrian gate set into the green iron railings attached to the lodge.

'Have ye trouble?' he asked, shining his torch into the face of the tall man outside the gate.

Frank felt as though ice-cold water drizzled down his spine as the man's eyes met his. He wore a trilby hat, not usually seen in the country and certainly never before on any visitor to the convent. It was pulled down low, obscuring his face, and his overcoat was buttoned up to the neck, with a scarf wrapped around his mouth.

'No, no trouble. I think I am expected,' the man replied through the scarf in a muffled English accent.

'Not here,' said Frank. 'I have no message to expect ye and I'm the gatekeeper. Is it the Abbey ye want? If so, 'tis a further five miles towards Galway. Ye do know it's Christmas morning, don't ye? We aren't expecting anyone at the retreat today.'

As soon as Frank had spoken, he heard Sister Theresa's voice behind him.

'I will deal with this, thank you, Frank.'

'Reverend Mother, what are ye doing out in the snow at this time in the mornin'?'

Frank was incredulous. Life at the convent followed a very strict routine. No one ever caught sight of Sister Theresa before she began prayers at five-thirty and never, since the day Frank arrived, had she walked down to the gatehouse to meet a visitor. Not in fine weather, and very definitely not in the snow, at four in the morning.

'That will be all, thank you, Frank,' Sister Theresa replied curtly. 'You can step back indoors now. I will deal with this.'

Frank turned to look at the stranger once more. He didn't like him. He said later to Maggie, 'He was shifty-looking, all right, and something about him made my skin crawl.'

'Well, who will lock the gate then, Reverend Mother? Sure, I can't leave it wide open.'

Frank was not as keen to move indoors as Sister Theresa would have liked. He did not like disruption any more than she did.

'Wait then, Frank, and lock the gate when we have finished.' Sister Theresa, distracted, had already begun talking to the man directly. 'It's impossible. You can't drive the car up,' she said. 'She will have to walk. There is no guarantee you would make it, either there or back again. The slope leading to the house is very steep.'

The man appeared relieved. 'I would rather just hand her over here, if it is all the same to you,' he replied. 'The bishop said he didn't want her to be seen, so I hope everything is as discreet here as it should be.'

Frank noted the sideways glance the man threw in his direction.

'There is only one return ferry to Liverpool today and I need to be on it.'

Frank watched as the man opened the back door of the car; to his amazement, a young woman stepped out. She was very well dressed, wearing a smart hat, and although the man had clearly woken her from sleep, she appeared quite content.

She also recognized Sister Theresa. 'Hello, Reverend Mother,' she said enthusiastically. 'Are they here?'

'Hello, Daisy,' said Sister Theresa, who, it appeared to Frank, was less than pleased.

The man lifted a small suitcase from the boot of the car and placed it on the frozen ground, next to the girl, saying, 'I will be off now.'

And Frank, with his mouth half open in shock, watched as he jumped into his car and drove away. Sister Theresa turned on her heel and marched up the driveway, with the young and tired woman following along behind.

'Well now, it never broke anyone's mouth to say a kind word and yet no one out there had one, not even for the young woman, although she looked as though she could do with one and as likely give one back, it being Christmas morning an' all.'

Frank made this speech at the back door as he removed his coat and cap, shaking snowflakes onto the floor, before he hung them both up to dry.

He gratefully took a mug of tea out of Maggie's waiting hand. Much to Frank's disappointment, she was now dressed in a long, black quilted dressing gown, decorated in bright red roses as large as dinner plates. Her hair was wrapped in a turban-style headscarf and her eyes twinkled, alight with curiosity concerning their early visitor.

'Was she a postulant, maybe?' she asked eagerly. 'Although, sure, 'tis an odd time to be arriving, on a Christmas morning.'

'I have no notion, Maggie, but no postulant arrives wearing a hat as nice as that one. We know from your sister's girl that anything half decent they leave behind for the family to wear. What use is a fancy hat to a postulant? I know this much, the Reverend Mother recognized her and called her Daisy.'

'Well, I know of no Daisy who has visited here before,' said Maggie thoughtfully.

'Me neither, but then they keep so much secret up at the house, what would we know anyway? They told me the nuns was digging that land for medicinal herbs and yet there's not a sign of anything green put into the ground, but they keep on digging.'

They both stood and looked at each other.

'Is it blasphemous to say what I think is happening?' whispered Maggie.

'Aye, I think it probably is,' Frank replied. 'When I asked the priest what they had been digging for, he near exploded in front of me eyes and ripped the tongue right out of me head, so he did.'

Maggie and Frank both made the sign of the cross and blessed themselves.

'Well, I'm sure the nuns and the priest know what they are doing and, sure, 'tis none of our business. We're here to grow food, cook it and answer the gate. We should remember that.'

Frank sipped his tea. He hadn't told Maggie that he had seen babies and children being carried out from the orphanage and laid in the earth. No coffins, no prayers, no headstones. Just two stone-faced nuns with a couple of shovels.

The nuns had used older girls in the orphanage to help dig the huge burial plot, for those unfortunate enough to succumb to any one of the diseases that stalked the cold, damp building, to claim the malnourished and broken in soul.

Frank couldn't tell Maggie about that. It would be the end. Every day she threatened to leave, but where would they go?

'No point in getting back to bed now, is there, Maggie. The cold has woken me for good.'

'Please yerself. There's another hour waiting for me under that eiderdown and I'm not wasting it.'

Maggie slipped under the covers, still wearing her dressing gown, and soon filled the room with her snores, seconds after switching off the lamp.

Frank smiled at his wife. He couldn't have slept even if he had wanted to. He had never slept well since the eviction. Reaching up to the mantelpiece, he took down his dudeen and, pushing in a new plug of baccy, he slowly lit up, drawing the air in through the long clay stem.

A proud and hard-working tenant farmer, Frank had made his farm so productive over a period of twenty years that it became highly attractive to potential buyers. Never one to miss an opportunity to line his pockets with gold, his landlord had sold the fields right out from under them at auction, giving Frank and Maggie twenty-four hours to pack up and leave. It was a shock so huge that neither of them had fully recovered even to this day.

By a fortuitous coincidence, just as Frank and Maggie were made homeless, the sisters arrived and took up residence in what would become St Vincent's.

Their arrival had been announced at mass at their local church, the day before Frank and Maggie were evicted from their home. It had been a Sunday just like any other, when they had lit the fire, milked the cows, had rashers and tatties for breakfast and walked to mass.

Frank could remember every single second of that last Sunday on the farm and he frequently replayed each one in his mind as he went about his work.

The landlord had not even had the courtesy to inform them he was putting the farm and their home up for auction. Their only clue came in the form of a tall man in a scruffy suit, who had arrived unannounced and began strutting around the farm on the Friday afternoon.

'Landlord sent me,' was all he said to Frank as he left his car parked across the gate and then strode out along the bottom field, peering into the ditches.

Frank had worried all weekend.

'If there was anything to worry about, the landlord's agent would have told us,' Maggie had protested. 'Stop fretting, ye panic when there's nothin' to panic about.'

Yet all the time she had felt so sick with anxiety herself that she was unable to eat or sleep. A cold hand of fear had rested on her shoulder and there it had remained ever since.

The priest in the local church had been overly excited about the nuns arriving and the establishment of St Vincent's. Nuns spoilt priests and that was a fact.

'The sisters are here to protect your loose morals. The bishop has recognized that I, being the only man of Christ's teaching in the area, am indeed struggling,' he had announced in a scathing tone.

'Who is he talking about, Frank?' Maggie had whispered.

'I've no idea, Maggie, but they say 'tis free love all over the world, especially in Liverpool. They have the Beatles and everything. Maybe they's worried we will be next, all lovin' each other.'

Maggie knew it wasn't funny and she tried hard not to laugh. One of the daughters on the adjoining farm had become pregnant without any notion of free love and she had been sent away to the Abbey. It had been a shock to Maggie, who had thought the girl a beauty, both in looks and in nature, and Maggie failed to understand how she had become pregnant at all.

''Tis beyond me. She has never set foot away from her own farm and family. How in God's name could she be pregnant?'

Four years later, the girl had still not returned, and she wasn't the only one.

The sisters had moved into an old manor house that had been deserted by an English lord following the potato famine and had been purchased, via the Vatican, at a knock-down price. It didn't take long for the nuns to realize that their order had bitten off far more than they could chew.

The gardens and land had not been tended in many years and were as wild as any jungle. With men and young boys from the village leaving for Liverpool to join their friends in building homes and laying roads on the mainland, labour at home was scarce.

As soon as the priest heard what had happened to Frank and Maggie, he had taken them straight to St Vincent's. The newly established sisters needed considerable assistance with the overgrown and rundown manor, and the priest became a hero in their eyes for finding it in the shape of the rotund, married, middle-aged Frank.

Frank had not been truly happy since the day they had arrived. Although he loved working in the large gardens, there were strange goings-on up at the convent that made him feel very unsettled.

'I would love to know that the potatoes and vegetables I grow find their way onto the plates of the children in the orphanage,' he said to Maggie, 'but how can they? Them kids look half starved. The skin is hanging off their bones.'

Maggie was equally perturbed.

'I cook only for the nuns and the retreat. The orphanage has its own kitchen. I don't know what the orphans eat. Almost nothing is delivered up there. I have no idea where our slops go. They don't go to the pig man, but they disappear from the bucket, sure enough. I hope to God the orphans aren't fed that. It would taste too disgusting for anyone to eat. Surely not, Frank?'

Frank shook his head. The truth was, neither of them knew and they dared not ask.

Frank and Maggie knew very little of the convent's business. Their hours were strict and their routine rigid. They simply provided and cooked the food. That was their role, nothing more nor less, other than manning the gates.

Frank pulled on his pipe and inhaled deeply. Something in the eyes of the man who had dropped the woman off that morning had made Frank feel uneasy.

When Maggie rose an hour later, Frank was still on the settle, nursing his empty mug in one hand and his extinguished pipe in the other.

'Are you still sat there? That mug won't fill itself by you looking at it now. Why don't ye put the kettle back on. And as the ground is frozen today, ye can help me in the kitchen this morning.'

Frank didn't reply, still deep in thought, holding in his mind the image of the young woman, Daisy. There was something about her that perturbed him, a sweet, trusting innocence. He trusted no one.

Yesterday he had picked the vegetables for the Christmas lunch. They lay in flat wooden trugs on the stone floor of the kitchen cold store, waiting for Maggie to prepare and cook them.

'Frank, what is up with ye, cloth ears? Will ye help me or not?'

'Aye, Maggie, of course I will, love.'

Frank leant forward and placed his elbows on his knees. Maggie knelt down in front of him to stoke up the lodge fire.

'Ye know summat, Maggie,' he said to her back, pushing baccy into his pipe with his thumb. 'I know this sounds fanciful, and I know ye is going to say I is mad an' all, but even though 'tis Christmas morning, I think today I met evil for the first time in me life. It was dressed up as a man in a hat, but 'twas the divil himself, all right, and of that I am sure.'

'Well, if ye did, that doesn't bode well,' said Maggie.

Her husband wasn't fanciful by nature. She sat back on her heels.

'There was a time when we woke on our farm on Christmas morning to the sound of a baby singing,' she said as she looked wistfully into the fire. There were many things Maggie had yet to recover from and, Frank knew, the death of their child would always be one of them. Their only son, lost to diphtheria, had been born on a damp night, on a straw-filled mattress at the farm in front of a roaring fire. They had been two, alone. He had arrived in a hurry and then in the wonder of a moment, they became three, complete.

She dealt with life by keeping busy, but he was aware that memories pained her every day.

For a moment, they sat in companionable silence. Frank knew that, like himself, Maggie had returned in her mind to the last Christmas morning they had spent with the only child they had been blessed with.

Frank put his hand on his wife's shoulder. His clumsy gesture, well meant, was intended to ease her pain. She patted the top of his hand with her own.

'I have to leave for the house. God knows how many busybodies they have coming for lunch today. Councillors, doctors, priests, the bishop, his bishop friend from Dublin. There's been so much fuss, I wouldn't be surprised if the Pope himself pops in for a cuppa.'

As Maggie entered the convent kitchens, she flicked on the light and almost immediately jumped with shock at the sight of the young woman sitting at the end of the long wooden table.

'Well, hello,' said Maggie. 'I near jumped out of my fecking skin then. Who might you be?'

The girl, her face streaked with tears, looked tired.

'My name's Joan,' she said softly. 'Reverend Mother says I have to work down here with Maggie. Is that you?'

'It is me, and there is no other, so ye are in the right place,' said Maggie. 'Have ye had any tea?'

The girl shook her head.

'Did ye get any sleep?'

The girl shook her head again.

'Have ye been sat there since ye arrived, in the dark?'

The girl nodded. 'The Reverend Mother took my clothes and then gave me these.' She looked down at the regulation serge-blue calico worn by all the girls and orphans.

'Well, that's the first thing we have to do: get a cuppa tea and some breakfast inside ye. And when we have done that, ye can start telling me how ye ended up here at four o'clock on Christmas morning. I also know yer name's not Joan, 'tis Daisy.'

Daisy looked afraid. She had been told her new name was Joan and to forget that she had ever been called Daisy. She knew how strong the wrath of the nuns in Ireland could be if you disobeyed an order.

'Don't worry,' said Maggie. 'I know the name of everyone here is altered from the moment they arrive. I've yet to work out why in God's name that happens. 'Tis a mystery to me. Are ye pregnant?'

Daisy looked stunned. 'No, I'm not.'

'Well, ye aren't on a fecking retreat. Are ye an orphan then?'

'I had thought I was. When I was a child I lived in an orphanage in Dublin, with Sister Theresa, because they thought I was simple, but then I went to Liverpool to work as a housekeeper. A few weeks ago, my brother and his family made contact. He wanted me back with himself and his wife and children. They was so upset. He knew nothing about me or that I had been given away to the nuns when I was a baby. Miss Devlin, the teacher at the school in Liverpool, told me that my mam and da had even paid for me every year to be looked after – that was how I came to be in service.

'I was supposed to be with my brother now, at Christmas. We were all so excited in Liverpool; Miss Devlin bought me a hat and they gave it to me at the school nativity play. My brother was due to meet me at the ferry, but then it was such a surprise to see the policeman on the ferry. I don't think anyone can have known he was there or they would have said and he brought me here. Now they have told me I have to stay and work in the kitchens. I thought my brother would be here, waiting for me. That was what the policeman told me.'

'Whoa, whoa, steady on. Ye lost me back at the orphanage in Dublin,' Maggie said as she tipped up a bucket of coal into the oven burner. 'Tell ye what, Daisy, we have a Christmas dinner to cook for every sod and his wife today, so why don't ye help me do that for now? But there is going to be lots of time for us to talk so don't cry any more tears. Me and my Frank, we get upset when we see people cry, now. Ye saw my Frank when ye arrived and he is worried about ye. Don't tell the Reverend Mother we have spoken, but me and Frank, we will help ye to get things sorted.'

Daisy smiled for the first time since saying goodbye to Miss Devlin in Liverpool before she boarded the ferry.

They were interrupted by the sound of footsteps as the nuns who helped prepare breakfast ran down the worn stone steps towards the warmth of the kitchen.

'Shh, now. I will call ye Joan, in the kitchen, but to me an' my Frank, ye will be Daisy.'

That night, sitting on the settle in front of the fire, each with a mug of poteen, holding hands, even after all their years together, Maggie and Frank discussed Daisy.

'There's something not right there, Frank. The bishop from Dublin came down to have a word with her and she burst into tears right then and there in the kitchen, in front of everyone.'

'What are ye thinking of doing, Maggie?' He knew Maggie had a way of getting to the bottom of every situation.

Frank leant forward to poke the fire, sending a fresh shower of sparks up the chimney and out onto the hearth. Maggie instinctively drew her feet in closer.

'I don't know yet, but she shouldn't be here and if it is my job to find out where she should be, then so be it. Maybe we were sent here for a reason. Maybe God put us through what he did, when they took our farm away, because he could make use of us here to help others.'

'Well, we have nowhere else to live. If we cross the nuns, no other convent or church anywhere would help us, so for God's sake be careful.'

'Aye, I will, but that poor lass is sleeping on a mattress in a store in the kitchen. For some reason, Sister Theresa doesn't want her mixing with either the other girls or the nuns. It doesn't smell right, Frank. I will bring her down here tomorrow night. She can sleep in front of our fire and, that way, I can find out more.'

Frank stood and filled Maggie's mug. He loved her best when she was plotting. When her interest was keen. The sparks from the fire reflected in her eyes as he lifted her to her feet with a smile. Then he led her to the bed, to finish that which, given half a chance, he would have begun, at five o'clock that morning.

## Chapter Two

'Do you want to know a secret?' Little Paddy whispered to his best friend Harry four days later, as they sat on the small squat lump of red sandstone known as the hopping stone, positioned on the edge of the green.

Snow had fallen heavily in Liverpool, on and off since before Christmas. Crystal-white pillows nestled on the lids of metal bins and windowsills while the cobbles lay buried under a glistening, dimpled blanket. Soot-stained bricks and chimneys that spewed acrid smoke had, for a short time only, taken on an aura of purity and cleanliness.

The boys were shivering on the cold, late December evening. Harry drew his thin coat tightly around him in a feeble attempt to shield himself from the brutal wind blowing up from the River Mersey.

Little Paddy didn't own a coat. He shivered the hardest and the loudest. Harry had loaned him the overly long scarf, which Nana Kathleen in number forty-two had lovingly knitted him for Christmas, although now Harry wished he could have taken the scarf back from Little Paddy and wrapped it around his own exposed neck.

It was the school Christmas holidays and, although it was much warmer indoors, neither boy wanted to be inside a cramped two-up, two-down that was jam-packed full of siblings, babies and steaming nappies, drying on a washing pulley suspended from the kitchen ceiling.

Harry, the more sensible and sensitive of the two, shuffled on the cold stone, trying to secure a more comfortable position. Its carved surface was undulating, as though to actively discourage anyone from loitering around for long.

Harry ignored Paddy's question and began to speak, more in an effort to distract his mind from the biting cold than from having anything interesting to say.

'You know that if you're running from the bizzies and you jumped onto this stone, the police couldn't arrest ye until ye fell off? Did ye know that?'

Harry was right. The stone was no man's land, a stubby oasis of temporary refuge on the four streets where petty pilfering was essential, in order to survive.

'Yeah, me da told me. The O'Prey boys were always jumping on and off it before they went down. It never saved them,' said Little Paddy, feeling very clever indeed to have been able to impart this information to Harry, who was the cleverest boy in the class. Little Paddy jumped up and stood on top of the stone.

'But I suppose it's hard to balance, when yer hands are full of a tray of barm cakes you've just robbed out of the back of the bread van.' Little Paddy hopped from foot to foot, as though testing how difficult it would be to balance on the stone.

Harry smiled as he remembered the O'Prey boys, the over-indulged sons of Annie, who lived across the road. They had been a great double act. What couldn't be sourced from the docks when it was needed, the O'Preys would acquire. From a pair of communion shoes, to a wedding dress or even a wheelchair, for a small fee the boys could be depended upon to provide anything within reason, or even without, for anyone on the four streets. They thieved to order and were paying the price at Her Majesty's pleasure.

'D'you wanna know my secret, or not?' Little Paddy was becoming disappointed with Harry's apparent lack of interest.

'Paddy, ye always have a secret. Does gossip just fall out of the sky and land in your kitchen?' Harry replied, exasperated but interested, despite his determination not to be.

Harry was still in shock at having discovered Little Paddy had known all along that big Sean, who was married to Brigid, and Alice, who was married to Jerry, had been blatantly carrying on right under everyone's noses. To add insult to injury, his mammy, Peggy, had even seen them running away together the night before Christmas Eve, when everyone else had been watching the school nativity play. Gossip about the runaway lovers raged through the four streets, and everyone buzzed to distraction, all over Christmas.

Harry's mammy, Maura, had been mad about Peggy's role in this and had given out something wicked to Harry's saintly da, Tommy.

'Gossip carts itself to that woman's door, so it does, because it knows it will get a good hearing and then a good spreading after.'

Tommy had looked across the table at Harry and winked whilst Maura ranted. It was taking her some time to adjust to the fact that Peggy had known – long before even Maura herself or Jerry's mother Kathleen – about the devastation that had torn apart the lives of Maura's closest friends. This was a thing of shame. Both Maura and Kathleen would have difficulty holding their heads up amongst their neighbours for some time to come. Their credibility as the wisest, holiest women on the four streets had been shot to bits. And who would now visit Kathleen to have their tea leaves read, when she couldn't even foretell the catastrophe that was occurring under her very nose, in her own home?

Maura was not happy.

'To think, the shame for Kathleen, with Alice married to her own son and living under the same roof, and neither she nor Jerry had a clue. Can ye imagine the lies, and the stealth? God, what a wicked woman that Alice surely was. The cut of her. Didn't I say so all along? Was I not the one who was never happy with such a union? Didn't I say this would happen, eh? Eh?'

Maura banged her rolling pin on the wooden table and then waved it at Tommy. Flour flew from the end, dusting Maura and transforming her raven hair in metal curlers into an even, rolling, snowcapped range.

Tommy didn't dare say that, since the day both of them had been witnesses at Alice and Jerry's wedding, Maura had never even intimated that Alice would have an affair with Sean, the husband of another of Maura's closest friends on the street, and then have the audacity to run away to America with him. When Maura was in this mood, there was only one thing to say and do.

'Aye, Maura, ye did sure enough,' he said, nodding sagely.

'Did Jer never so much as say anything to give yer a clue as to what was going on? Did he not? He must have said something, Tommy. How could yer miss summat like that? Was Sean not acting different, like? Holy Mother, Sean was one of yer mates and he has run off with yer best mate's wife. Ye work with them both all day, every day, and yer never knew a thing. Jaysus, Tommy, ye are a useless lump sometimes.'

Tommy, the meekest of men, forgot his own rules of engagement and took mild exception to this latest criticism.

'Me? For feck's sake, Maura, Kathleen runs an industry reading the bleeding tea leaves every Friday and she read fecking Alice's every week. If she couldn't see it coming, how did ye expect me to? On the docks we don't talk about such things as women. We talk about the horses and football, so don't blame me.'

'Bleedin' football and horses, when there is really important stuff going on under yer very nose. Ye amaze me, Tommy Doherty, ye really do, so.'

Maura undid her apron, throwing it onto the table. Then she flounced out of the back door, crossing the road to Jerry's house to speak to Kathleen. There, once again she would offer solace and comfort, in the midst of the shameful tragedy that had befallen both of their houses.

'Put the boxty in the oven,' she had thrown over her shoulder as she left. 'Do ye think ye can manage that? Have ye brain enough, eh, Tommy?'

Maura hadn't waited for a reply. As the back door slammed, Tommy turned to Harry, who throughout his exchange with Maura had been watching his da intently.

Watching and learning.

'Always agree with women, Harry, 'tis the only way to a quiet life.'

And with that, relieved that Maura had left to vent her irritation elsewhere, Tommy extracted a pencil stub from behind his ear and continued to mark out his horses in the *Daily Post* for the two-thirty at Aintree.

'Put the boxty in the oven, lad,' he said as he shifted his cap back into place. 'I'm fancying "Living Doll", a nice little three-year-old filly at seven to one. What do you think, Harry?'

Slamming the oven door shut, Harry rushed to sit next to Tommy to continue his education in how to be a man, whilst his twin brother, Declan, ran round the green, kicking a ball and pretending to be Roger Hunt.

Scamp, Little Paddy's scruffy, grey-haired mongrel, ran across the green towards the boys and flopped down into the snow at their feet, grinning proudly. From his jaws hung the carcass of a steaming-hot chicken, one leg hung by a sinew, dripping hot chicken juices onto Harry's shoe.

'Fecking hell, where has he nicked that from?' said Little Paddy as both boys stared at the dog, their own mouths watering.

In truth, Little Paddy was acting. On the four streets, no one locked their doors. The always hungry and artful Scamp had returned home, on more than one occasion, carrying a joint of hot meat. Just last week, Peggy had snatched a shoulder of lamb from his jaws, rinsed it under the tap and then thrown it in to the pot with their own meagre meal, a blind stew, which until that moment had comprised of potatoes and vegetables. Once the stolen shoulder of lamb was in the pot, all evidence of Scamp's kill was concealed and they were safe from any neighbor who chose to burst through the back door yelling, 'Have you seen me joint?' Which was exactly what did happen only moments later.

'That'll do nicely and, ye lot, keep yer gobs shut,' Peggy had said to her wide-eyed children, once the kitchen had returned to normal, as she dried her hands on her apron, which had been in desperate need of a wash for almost a month.

The boys only occasionally saw a roast chicken on Sunday and not always then, either. Quite often a Sunday roast would be without meat of any description. Instead it would consist of two types of potatoes, roast and mash, with mashed swede and carrots, topped with a great deal of fatty gravy. This was made with dripping and surplus meat fat left from previous meals that had been saved in an enamel bowl. Amazingly, here was Scamp, with half a steaming chicken in his mouth. As good a piece of meat as either had ever eaten on Christmas Day.

Both boys were by now salivating as they wondered who on earth on the four streets could afford to cook a chicken on a Tuesday.

'Maybe we should run home, before whoever it does belong to runs down the street, looking for it. I'll get the belt from me da, without wanting another from somebody else an' all,' said Little Paddy as he looked up and down the street nervously. But there was no sign of anyone.

Harry felt sorry for Little Paddy. Tommy had never so much as raised his voice to any of his children. They often heard Big Paddy next door laying into his kids and Harry knew it pained Tommy. But there were rules of survival on the four streets and one was that when it came to matters of children being disciplined, you didn't interfere.

One evening, Little Paddy's cries were so loud that Harry had begged his da to save his friend.

'Da can't, Harry,' Maura had said, pulling him to her and giving him an almighty hug, while she shielded his ears with her hands. 'We can't interfere. It's the law.'

*

Little Paddy, made nervous by the arrival of Scamp and the stolen chicken, was now becoming impatient with Harry. 'Do you want to know a secret or not?' he demanded, hands on his hips.

Harry's stomach was rumbling at the sight and smell of the chicken and his attention had wandered from Little Paddy's secret. Always mild-mannered, unusually for him, he was not in the best of moods today. He didn't really want to know. He was more interested in reading than in gossip. School didn't begin for another week and he had read every book he had been allowed to bring home for the holidays. Without another world to disappear into, he felt adrift.

Tommy had promised that tomorrow he would take him into town on the bus, to the second-hand bookshop on Bold Street, to see whether there was anything suitable for him. The new library, being built alongside a new children's nursery on the bombed-out wasteland, was only halfway through construction. Harry was possibly the only child on the four streets to have lost sleep with excitement at the thought of having an endless supply of books at hand and no longer having to beg them from the sisters, or explain why he wanted something other than the bible or a prayer book.

'Make sure you choose the biggest book they have, if they are all the same price. It will last longer,' Maura had said when Tommy had made the suggestion early that morning.

Maura had never read a book in her life.

Neither Harry nor Tommy commented, but Harry saw the little smile reach the corner of his da's mouth as, once again, he gave Harry that wink. The wink that told Harry: they were united, father and son. A team. Together.

Paddy had persuaded Harry to watch him playing footie on the green with his brothers and the rest of the local boys. Harry's asthma meant that he couldn't join in, but he enjoyed watching. Harry looked up at Little Paddy and nodded.

'Go on then. You look as though you will explode if I don't listen to whatever gossip it is ye have now. Although God knows, Paddy, it always gets you into trouble with ye da and I have no notion how it is ye get to know all these things.

Little Paddy needed no further encouragement. He was now

unstoppable. He jumped from foot to foot on top of the stone and spoke at double his natural speed.

'There's a new priest arriving at the Priory. His name is Father Anthony and he has said that he is going to get to the bottom of who killed Father James, so help him, God.'

Little Paddy roared the 'so help him, God' bit, and raised his fist to the sky and dropped his voice an octave to mimic an older man.

Little Paddy continued, 'Mammy went to the Angelus mass last night at St Oswald's and she heard it herself from Annie O'Prey. Sister Evangelista has asked Annie to give the Priory a good dusting before they arrive and to be the new cleaner, now that Daisy has gone. She's to help the new father's sister, Harriet, who is coming to look after him and protect him from murderers. Annie is taking over from Daisy, so she is, and she's right pleased about it, too. And there's more. They think Daisy has gone missing, so she has, and never got off the boat in Dublin, or met her brother.'

Harry was now impressed. This was serious news, but he also knew his mother's chagrin at Peggy's having heard first would know no end, especially as it concerned the arrival of the new priest.

His mother was always the first with gossip from the church, her being so holy. Before the murder of Father James, followed by Kitty leaving so suddenly to visit Ireland on her far-too-long-for-Harry's-liking holiday, his mammy had never missed the Angelus. With her being the most religious mother in the street, she would surely have had that gossip first.

Twilight was falling. Both boys lapsed into silence as they looked across the misty graveyard towards the Priory. Harry felt an icy shiver run down his back as the lights in an upstairs window flicked on and then off again, as the night closed in.

Downstairs, in the Priory basement kitchen, Annie O'Prey was almost on the edge of hysteria. Sister Evangelista was trying her best to calm her down.

'Jaysus, it was there, so it was, on the kitchen table. I went upstairs for no longer than five minutes to light the fire in the study. I came back down and the chicken was gone. What am I to do if I have no food ready for the new father and his sister? What kind of welcome to the streets would that be, now?'

Sister Evangelista was relieved that a new priest was arriving and that his spinster sister was accompanying him to act as his housekeeper. They had left Dublin that morning and were expecting to be welcomed with a quiet supper at the Priory, with a full meal at the convent with the sisters the following night.

Sister Evangelista had been glued to the phone since Christmas Eve. As yet, she had told only the few nuns she could trust that the previous housekeeper, Daisy, had failed to meet her family at the port in Dublin. Daisy's brother and his wife were convinced that Daisy had never boarded the boat at Liverpool. But Sister Evangelista knew better. Miss Devlin, a teacher at the school as well as a good friend to the convent and to Daisy, had put her on the boat herself. She had even asked two elderly ladies to look after her, until they berthed in Dublin, so they knew she had caught the ferry. Neither of them had a good Christmas, worrying about Daisy's whereabouts.

What was more, the bishop had been less than sympathetic. He had even shouted at Sister Evangelista down the phone and since then she had refused to talk to him again.

'Take a hold of yourself, Sister, you are like a hysterical farm girl from the country,' he had said. 'Take charge of your senses and stop yerself from turning everything into a crisis, when none exists, will ye? I am fair exhausted with the carryings-on at St Mary's. Father Anthony and his sister will arrive shortly, so just leave it all to him. And remember, ye tell him nothing of what ye found in the Priory, before Father James was murdered by whoever it was who savaged the poor man, do ye hear me?'

She had heard him all right. Having discovered in the Priory, following his death, the father's dirty secret and a heap of filthy photographs of young children, she wasn't so sure she would describe him as a poor man any longer. She had also heard the bishop singing a different tune altogether regarding the arrival of Father Anthony, who had been sent directly to Liverpool from Rome via Dublin.

The Pope was none too keen on his priests being murdered and their private parts dismembered. So the Vatican had taken Father James's replacement out of the hands of the bishop, who had been incensed from the minute he was told the news.

'Apparently, Father Anthony has been at the Vatican for a number of years and is very well known and trusted. Seems to me the Pope knows exactly what he's doing and, regardless of what the bishop says, I am mightily grateful for the Vatican's intervention,' Sister Evangelista had told Miss Devlin, the teacher at the school.

Sister Evangelista had been made very angry by the bishop's tone. There had been two murders, not one: Father James and their neighbour, Molly Barrett, who had been found in her own outhouse with her head caved in. Sister Evangelista had had to beg the bishop to visit Liverpool and take some responsibility, but had been bitterly disappointed. He had been no help at all, leaving Sister Evangelista to deal with the police single-handed. It was not until she found the disgusting photographs in Father James's desk that the bishop had bothered to visit the Priory. As she had confided to Miss Devlin, this was all very strange behaviour indeed.

'Sure, he was never away from the Priory when the father was alive. Now that he is dead and we need the bishop's assistance, I'm having to beg. That is a sad situation altogether.'

Miss Devlin had agreed, but the bishop had been put there for one purpose only, to be obeyed, and neither of them felt inclined to challenge his authority.

Sister Evangelista once again felt a familiar sense of helplessness and isolation. Father James's housekeeper, Daisy, was missing and the bishop just couldn't care a jot. And after all the trouble she had taken to follow his precise instructions for Daisy's safe journey to Dublin.

So much had happened in the aftermath of the two murders that Sister Evangelista had found herself struggling yet again. When she heard that Father Anthony and his sister Harriet would be arriving to lead the church, she had dropped to her knees in relief to give thanks to God.

Another welcome pair of shoulders to carry the burden of upholding the authority of the Church in the parish of a murdered priest.

The devil had brazenly strutted down their streets and Sister Evangelista was convinced that she was possibly the only person in the whole world who knew why.

Maura let herself in through Nana Kathleen's back door, to find Nellie washing the dishes, Kathleen rolling out her boxty on the kitchen table and Joseph snoozing in his pushchair.

Maura smiled at Nellie, the child whose birth had taken the life of Bernadette, Nellie's mother and Maura's best friend, and who was up to her elbows in soapsuds.

'You all right then, Nellie?' Maura asked.

'That poor Nellie,' Maura had said to Tommy in bed only the night before. 'First her mammy dies and then her stepmother runs away with the father of one of her best friends, leaving the little lad behind for her and Nana Kathleen to look after. What child deserves that, eh, Tommy? What next? Nothing, God willing, because that child can't take much more. She has lost enough.'

Tommy pulled Maura to him. 'No one was closer to our Kitty than Nellie, that's for sure. She will be missing Kitty badly, so she will. Ye can't worry about everyone, Maura. Once our Kitty is home and Nellie has her friend once more, they will both be back to normal.'

Within seconds Tommy had fallen into a deep sleep, but Maura lay awake into the small hours, worrying about everyone and everything but most of all about Kitty, whose secret baby was to be delivered at the Abbey mother-and-baby home in Galway. Almost no one, other than those closest to her, knew.

No one on the four streets, not even nosy Peggy next door, had suspected what had really happened to Kitty, or why.

'I'm grand, thank you, Auntie Maura,' Nellie had replied without her usual bright smile. 'Would you like a cuppa tea?'

'Aye, put the kettle on, Nellie,' said Kathleen as she slapped the big round potato-bread onto a tray and slid it into the range oven at the side of the fire. Every woman on the four streets baked in the morning, using the roaring heat of the first fire of the day, before they began to simmer the stock.

'Any news?' Maura asked Nana Kathleen as she pulled a chair out from under the table.

Kathleen knew exactly what she was talking about. Both women had been waiting for some kind of fallout since the night Jerry's wife had left him for his workmate and neighbour, Sean. But Jerry had barely reacted at all. The emotional tempest anticipated by the women had never arrived.

'No, not a dickie bird. I have to say this about our Jer, I've never seen a man recover from a broken heart as fast as he has, so I haven't. Seven days they have been gone and this morning, he didn't even mention her. Nothing like when Bernadette died and he was beyond any consolation that I, or anyone else, could give him.'

'What about little Joseph?' Maura whispered, so as not to wake him.

'Well now, that's different altogether. He's asleep now because he's been awake all night. The poor child has no idea what is going on. When he is in my arms, he pulls me to the kitchen window and I know he is looking down the backyard for his mammy. Maura, what can I do? I cannot even say her name, so I can't, or I will risk setting him off. Thanks be to God for our Nellie. She can really distract him now, much better than me, can't you, Nellie?'

Nellie looked across at them from the range and nodded. Maura noted that she looked sad-eyed, as though carrying the weight of the world on her shoulders.

'And what about poor Brigid?' said Maura.

Maura was referring to Sean's wife: the wronged woman, deserted without the slightest inkling that anything had been amiss and left with a house full of little red-haired daughters to keep and care for. A woman who was both extremely house-proud and very much in love with her husband and her perfect family. Perfect, that is, until the moment on the night before Christmas Eve when she had opened a note she found propped on the mantelshelf, informing her that Sean, the husband she had devoted her life to, had run away to America with Alice, the wife of her friend Jerry.

That was the moment when everything had altered. When her love had turned to hate. In one tick of the clock, her life had gone from light to dark. All she believed was true in their world had washed away before her, in a river of tears.

'We should call in and see her this morning,' said Kathleen. 'The poor woman is distraught.'

Nellie was pouring boiling water into the tin teapot when she saw Bill from the pub burst through the gate, run down the yard and in through the back door.

'Maura,' he panted. 'Maura, ye have to get to the pub now, yer relative from home, Rosie, she will be calling back in thirty minutes. She says to tell ye she is phoning from Mrs Doyle's in Bangornevin. She needs to speak to ye as well, Kathleen. She said I have to take ye both together 'cause she won't have the chance to call back again, she needs to speak to ye both and that I had to make sure of that.'

With that, Bill ran back down the yard to the pub where the draymen were in the middle of a delivery. But that mattered not a jot. News from home was the most important kind and not to be kept waiting.

Kathleen, Maura and Nellie looked at each other, but no one spoke until Nellie whispered into the silence, 'Can Kitty have had the baby?'

She put down the kettle and moved closer to the others. They were in their own home and no one could possibly overhear them, but they were the only females in Liverpool who knew why Kitty was in Ireland. She had slipped across the water, in the dead of night, with Kathleen and Nellie for company.

The baby growing in her belly had been put there by Father James, and Tommy had ensured he paid for it. A priest's murder, dismembered of his langer, coinciding with a child's pregnancy would surely have guaranteed that Tommy would have been hanged once the police realized he had been defending his daughter's honour. The connection was too obvious.

Kitty had awaited the birth in Galway, hiding in a convent and working in a laundry. Waiting out her pregnancy and delivery.

Sister Evangelista and Kitty's school friends believed that Kitty was visiting Maura's sister who was poorly and needed help, but on the four streets only three women – Maura, who was Kitty's mother, and her closest friends, Kathleen and her granddaughter, Nellie – knew the truth. Or so they had thought.

'She's not due for three more weeks, but it is possible,' said Maura.

'If it's Rosie wants to speak to ye, then that baby has been born and if Rosie is at Mrs Doyle's, it's her way of letting us know Kitty is at Maeve's farmhouse and safe,' said Kathleen.

Maura was already standing at the back door, holding it open and waiting impatiently whilst Kathleen tied her headscarf and fastened her coat, ready to run to the pub and reach the phone to hear news of her daughter. She had counted the days, one by one, since Kitty had been dropped off at the Abbey. Thoughts of her daughter were the first to enter her mind as she woke in the morning and the last as she closed her damp eyes at night. The pain of missing Kitty was almost more than she had been able to bear.

But Maura knew that the existence of Kitty's baby would have provided the police with a motive and a direct line to the murdered priest.

The only way Maura had been able to maintain any degree of normality, after she returned with Kathleen from Ireland, was to believe that Kitty was happy and being well looked after. That she would have made friends with the other girls, and that the nuns would not have made her work too long, or too hard, in the laundry as her pregnancy progressed. These thoughts had sustained her throughout the months of missing her daughter.

'As God is true, I have been counting the days to this news, Kathleen,' Maura said as they ran down the entry together.

'I know, Maura. Jeez, can we stop a minute. I'm pulling for tugs here.'

Maura stood and waited for the older woman to catch her breath. Kathleen, red in the face and panting, reached into her pocket for her cigarettes. 'It helps me breathing,' she said to Maura, offering her the packet to take one.

The phone rang just as they pushed through the wooden doors and Bill smiled as he waved them over.

'Aye, they are both coming through the door right away. Ye can speak now …'

His words trailed off, as Maura grabbed the phone from his hand.

'Rosie, have ye any news?' Maura hissed, her heart beating wildly.

Rosie was a relative by marriage and a midwife. She had been due to deliver Kitty's baby at the convent, in the middle of January.

'Is she at Maeve and Liam's? Shall we come to fetch her?'

There was silence at the end of the telephone.

Kathleen didn't want Bill to hear the conversation between Maura and Rosie. There had been too many people interested in one another's business since the murder of the priest, and then there had been poor Molly Barrett, bludgeoned to death in her own outhouse. That one had stumped even Kathleen.

She knew who had murdered the priest all right but Molly Barrett, that was a mystery, which had perturbed them all.

'It's freezing out there, Bill,' said Kathleen. 'Any chance of a couple of ports before we run back? Not often we get news from home in a phone call.'

'It's more often than not a birth and sometimes a death, Kathleen. Has your Liam got Maeve with a babby on the way, then?' said Bill, grinning as he took a bottle out from underneath the bar and began pouring the ruby-red liquid into two glasses.

Kathleen grinned back uneasily and, taking the glass of port, used all her willpower not to down it in one.

'Ye have been through a bit of bad luck, with Alice and all that business there over Christmas,' said Bill to Kathleen, leaning on the bar.

'Rosie, can ye hear me?' said Maura, her voice louder this time.

'Aye, Maura,' came the reply down the crackling line. 'I have just asked Mrs Doyle if I could speak in private and had to wait while she moved into the back of the post office.'

Maura could visualize the hovering Mrs Doyle, who looked as much like a crone as anyone who hadn't met her could possibly imagine and a crone with more than her fair share of rotting teeth.

Rosie's voice crackled down the line again.

'Kitty has had the baby, Maura, but I'm afraid I was not in attendance. The snow brought the Abbey telephone lines down and they couldn't get through to me, until yesterday morning.'

'Oh, Holy Mother of God, is she all right?'

Maura's eyes filled with tears. The longing to be at her daughter's side clutched at her heart, robbing her of breath and dragging her down, till she was bent double over the counter with her free hand involuntarily clutching her abdomen.

'The baby was born on Christmas morning. It was a boy and his adoption to an American couple was arranged even before he had filled his first nappy, so it was. I got her to Maeve's as quickly as God allowed me. I have news, Maura ...'

The line crackled and hissed as Rosie's voice faded.

'Rosie, Rosie, are ye there?'

The line was totally dead. The crackling had stopped.

Maura cared nothing now of what Bill could hear. Rosie had just said that Kitty had had the baby and then – nothing.

'Rosie!' she yelled down the line.

'Is everything all right, Maura?' asked Kathleen, concerned.

'I don't know. She said she had news and then she disappeared.'

With her hand outstretched and shaking, Maura handed the receiver to Kathleen.

'Hello, hello, *hello*!' Kathleen said loudly, and then she heard Rosie's return.

'Kathleen, thank God you are there.'

## Chapter Three

It was two days after Christmas. Within a second of her opening her Dublin office door with her Yale key, the black Bakelite phone on Rosie O'Grady's desk rang. It was as though it had been patiently waiting for the first familiar sound of her return following the long Christmas break.

'Oh, Holy Father, would you believe it,' Rosie muttered to herself. 'I'm not even through the door yet and it's started already.'

The previous evening Rosie had doubted that she would even make it into work after a sudden and very heavy Christmas snowfall, which had covered Ireland from coast to coast. The roads in Roscommon, where Rosie lived, had been impassable in places, but she was relieved to see that, in Dublin at least, some effort had been made to clear the main roads.

Rosie had not missed a day of work in her entire life and there was no way she would allow the weather to defeat her now, despite the ploughed walls of snow on the roadside standing as high as six feet in places. As the head midwife at Dublin's maternity hospital, senior midwife tutor and the chair of the Eire midwifery council, Rosie took her responsibilities, as well as her reputation for high standards and reliability, very seriously indeed.

The midwifery block was reached via four red sandstone steps that led up to an imposing, semicircular entrance hall, complete with parquet floor, whose windows overlooked the car park. The administration office doors flanked a wooden arch beyond which lay the wards and the main hospital. Rosie occupied the most impressive office, in accordance with her status, for she also had responsibility for the training school from which she proudly turned out twenty well-trained midwives each year. The majority of Dublin's babies were delivered at home, but a growing number of women were choosing to give birth in hospital, especially those who were likely to have complications.

'Morning, Mrs O'Grady.'

As Rosie passed through the revolving glass doors into the hospital foyer, Tom, the head hospital porter, greeted her from behind his high, glossy, dark-wood desk, tipping the brim of his cap as a mark of respect. She stamped the snow from her boots on a large coconut-hair mat before stepping onto the freshly polished wooden floor.

The hospital caretaker had taken advantage of the Christmas lull to buff every floor in the hospital. Rosie stood for a moment as she removed her headscarf and shook the last of the snowflakes onto the mat, inhaling deeply the familiar smell of fresh lavender floor wax. It had a calming effect on her.

'I said if anyone makes it in today, it would be you, with you having travelled the furthest an' all. On ward three, there's a midwife not turned in for her shift yet and she only lives across the river. You have put her to shame, so you have, struggling all the way in from Roscommon.'

'Well, it wasn't easy, Tom,' Rosie replied as she searched in her handbag for her office keys. 'It took the help of a tractor and a very good husband to see me onto the Dublin road, or I would indeed still be stuck in Roscommon. We had all our animals down on the lower fields to make it easier over Christmas, so it hasn't been too bad for us. I could at least commandeer the tractor without too much guilt, now. But that didn't stop yer man grumbling, and, sure, being as he's a farmer, he doesn't usually need much of an excuse, now, does he?'

Tom laughed out loud, feeling sorry for any man who tried to cross Matron O'Grady.

'Aye, well, you have still made it in and that is to your credit. We can complain all we like but to wake up on Christmas morning to a white Ireland, that was a miracle, was it not?'

Rosie smiled at Tom. It had been very special indeed. The fields and the church had looked magnificent. Even the old prison walls became magical and romantic.

'Aye, Tom, it was a miracle. Deep snow on Christmas Day, who would have thought it?'

'Shall I ring the kitchen, shall I? And ask Besmina to bring up your tea?'

'Oh God, wouldn't that just be grand. I'm parched,' Rosie replied. 'You can always rely on Besmina.'

'You can, that. She will always be grateful to you for the job you gave her. You have a loyal employee for life there, Matron, and that's for sure.'

Rosie's husband had done everything possible that morning, to try to persuade her not to travel to Dublin.

'Are ye mad?' he had said when she had asked him to tow her car out onto the main Dublin road, using his farm tractor. 'Phone lines are down all over the place. No one is driving anywhere. I will be halfway to Dublin by the time I find a decent stretch of road to leave you on, and then how in God's name would I know ye had made it in? And tonight, how will ye travel back if it freezes over? It's a Hillman Hunter ye drive, not a bloody tank.'

'Aye, I know that,' Rosie had replied. 'Calm down for goodness' sake. I don't expect you to take me all the way to Dublin. Just leave me on the first clear stretch and I will manage the rest of the way.'

It didn't matter how much he remonstrated with her, no one could alter Rosie's mind about anything when it was made up. Once she had set herself on a course of action, she was unstoppable.

'Jeez, the mule is less stubborn,' her husband had grumbled as he set about moving the tractor out of the barn.

As she opened the office door to the ringing telephone, Rosie hastily dropped her bag onto the floor and pulled off her leather driving gloves with her teeth. She noted that at least the hospital phones were working. Having removed the second glove, she just had time to lift the receiver to her ear before the caller hung up.

'Good morning, Rosie O'Grady, matron midwife,' she trilled down the line, cheered after her long and cold journey by the knowledge that tea was on its way to her office to warm her.

She secretly hoped that the office kitchen maid, Besmina, would pop a slice of thick, white, hot buttered toast onto the tray, as she often did. It had been over three hours since Rosie had left home to set off for the hospital and the loud rumblings from her stomach were letting her know as much.

The crackling phone line was poor, which wasn't surprising, given the weather, but Rosie could just make out the voice on the other end as that of the Reverend Mother at the Abbey convent and laundry out in the windy west, near Galway.

She had been dreading this call.

Her heart dropped into her boots. There was only one reason why the Reverend Mother would be telephoning her now. Rosie was very careful to keep her distance from any of the laundries or the mother and baby homes run by the sisters. Their very existence made her uncomfortable.

For many years the Irish government had made use of the laundries to imprison women and hide them away. Rosie knew that girls were sent to the abbeys and convents by the authorities, for the most spurious of reasons, and would remain incarcerated there for their entire lives. Many were not, nor had ever been, pregnant. Some were sent for being nothing more than a pretty orphan, assigned to the Abbey for her own protection, away from the lure of temptation and sinful ways.

These girls, known as penitents, were transferred to the Abbey straight from the industrial schools, run by the nuns and brothers. Many were country girls from the village farms, victims of incest and rape, or just a girl carried away at a dance, or a fair. Those who found themselves pregnant outside of wedlock would be deposited abruptly at the Abbey's doors by their parents or by the local priest. In their imprisonment, some went mad from grief and despair.

Many in Rosie's circle knew about the laundries. An industry run by nuns who made vast profits enslaving women deemed to be sinful. The sisters and the government, worked as a team.

This had made Rosie cross herself in shame when she last walked through the Abbey doors. If the penitents were lucky, after three long years of unpaid work in the laundry they might manage to buy back their freedom, provided that their families could supply the necessary one hundred and fifty pounds. However, before they left they would also be required to agree to give up their babies and to allow the Abbey to sell them on to American families.

For the country girls, there was no way to bypass their years of slave labour. There wasn't a farm girl from one end of County Mayo to the other who would ever see that kind of money in her entire lifetime.

For young Kitty Doherty from Liverpool, Rosie's involvement with Sister Assumpta and the Abbey had been necessary.

A necessary evil.

Kitty was neither a penitent nor a country girl but, for her own sake as much as anyone else's, for a short while she had needed to become one.

Rosie had agreed to personally deliver the baby at the Abbey when Kitty's time was due, but, based on Rosie's examination a few months earlier, she had thought that wouldn't be until the middle of January at the very earliest.

Rosie was one of very few people who knew that Kitty's secret arrival in Ireland was in some way connected to the murder of the priest. The news of the murder had been all over the Dublin newspapers for almost a week.

Since it seemed like half the men of County Mayo had travelled to Liverpool, to work on the roads, at the docks or building new houses, anything that happened in Liverpool was news in Ireland too.

Rosie didn't want to know the details of why or how Kitty had become pregnant.. Sure, hadn't she seen enough girls in Ireland in the same position. The priest in Liverpool was not unique. She was delivering Kitty's baby under a cloak of secrecy, at the request of her sister-in-law, Julia, who lived in Bangornevin in County Mayo. Refusal was not an option. A girl was in trouble. It was the job of the women to find a solution to her problem. Kitty Doherty's name had been changed to Cissy so that no one would ever know she had been at the Abbey. It had been drilled into Rosie that no one must know where the girl was, who she was, or that she had given birth. Once she had done so, she would need to return to Liverpool as soon as possible.

Rosie was well aware, without having to be told, that the part she had played – in helping to hide the child at the Abbey to have her baby – had saved Kitty's father, Tommy, a good man, from the gallows.

The justice of the four streets was brutally simple.

An eye for an eye. A life for a life stolen.

The family had altered Kitty's name to Cissy, to hide her true identity from the nuns, and Cissy her name would remain. Unlike the other girls in the Abbey, who had their name removed on the day they arrived.

No one was allowed to use her real name whilst resident at the Abbey. Hair was cut short, personal possessions removed and girls were not allowed to speak of their past. In fact, they were not allowed to speak.

Kitty's case was slightly different. She was to be resident at the Abbey for just a few months, rather than years. Kitty had not been dropped at the door. Nor was she a penitent.

Kitty wasn't even an Irish resident and had been registered under a false name from the very beginning.

'Shall I put the tray on the table, Mrs O'Grady?' Besmina whispered to Rosie.

For a second, Rosie almost lost her concentration and focus on what the Reverend Mother was saying, as her stomach responded to the smell of the hot tea and buttered toast. She winked at Besmina who began to pour her tea from the aluminium teapot. The porter had slipped into the room with his arms full of logs and set about lighting the fire, hoping to warm the cold office, which had been empty for almost a week.

The voice at the other end of the line was as cold as the room.

'The child was delivered in the early hours of Christmas morning.'

There was no compassion in the words of the Reverend Mother.

Rosie felt a sudden chill, which had nothing to do with the temperature of her office.

The Abbey's delivery practices were barbaric. Pain was regarded as an atonement for sin. Stitching was not allowed. The perineal tears were looked on as a continuing physical reminder of the need to seek forgiveness.

'Where is she now?' Rosie had already forgotten about the tea and toast. She knew all was not as it should be.

Besmina, the kitchen maid, arrived at the hospital only a few months previously. It hadn't taken long for the staff, over tea and brack, to discover that Besmina had detailed knowledge of the Abbey, where Kitty had been left to deliver her baby in secret. The moment Rosie discovered that Besmina was familiar with the Abbey, she pressed her for information.

It had been a difficult task. At first she was very nervous but, gradually, she had opened up to Rosie. The staff had no idea why Rosie was so interested and she wanted to keep it that way.

She wasn't the only one keeping secrets. There was much Besmina hadn't told Rosie, or anyone else. She would never confess that she had been an unmarried mother herself or to having birthed her child at the Abbey to save her mother and grandmother from the shame. Or that she had escaped with the help of a child from Liverpool by the name of Nellie.

'Thank you, God, for sending Nellie to me,' was the opening line of Besmina's first and last prayer of every day.

Besmina had informed Rosie that, behind the Abbey, in the middle of a copse of trees, were graves, dozens of them, belonging to girls as young as thirteen. And babies. Lots of babies.

For this reason Rosie had been very glad that Kitty's family, related to her own, had asked her to deliver the baby herself.

Rosie knew that Kitty came from a loving and caring family. God alone knew how that priest had been able to do what he did.

The Reverend Mother had ignored both Rosie's question and the tone of her voice.

'I have given orders for her to be left in the labour room until you arrive. I do not want her working in the laundry any longer. A baby conceived in sin, but born in the Abbey on Christmas morning, is not viewed as helpful, Mrs O'Grady. I don't need to explain to you how unsettled this birth has made everyone. I would like her to be removed as soon as is possible.'

'Right, how is she?' Rosie asked. 'Was the delivery straightforward and is she recovering well?'

'You will be able to answer those questions when you collect her, which I hope will be today. Her baby was a boy. I had him removed to the nursery, immediately following his birth, and I am delighted to say that his new parents are making haste travelling from America to view him. They will take him back as soon as possible once a passport can be issued.'

'View him? Well, goodness me, what an odd expression. That is very quick altogether, is it not?'

Rosie was no stranger to efficiency, but the Reverend Mother appeared to have moved with unseemly haste to have the baby adopted.

'It is our normal practice to keep the children until they are three. Adoption takes such a time to arrange in America. A letter can take as long as six weeks. When a new baby is available, we have the very best Catholic families on standby who will drop everything once they receive a telegram from us. I hope there will be no complaint? The girl has already signed a contract, stating that she relinquishes all rights to the baby and that she will never attempt to make contact with the child or his family, at any time in the future. What time can we expect you?' Her tone brightened as she added, 'Sister Celia would love to bake you a cake.'

In her state of trauma following the delivery, Kitty had signed the contract using her real name. The Reverend Mother, in her haste to have the contract signed, had not noticed Kitty's error.

Rosie was speechless. The journey to Dublin from Roscommon had been an ordeal. Now she would have to drive across country to Galway and then take the girl on to Ballymara.

'I hope to arrive at the Abbey at around two o'clock, all being well, so long as I am able to drive down all the roads, please God. Thank Sister Celia, I am very much looking forward to her wonderful cake.'

Rosie frowned as she replaced the receiver. She felt intensely uncomfortable but she knew that she must make her way to Kitty, as fast as she possibly could.

Rosie whispered a prayer, 'At least the girl is alive, thanks be to God,' and blessed herself. She quickly telephoned Mrs Doyle at the post office in Bangornevin and asked her to send someone across the road to fetch her sister-in-law, Julia, to the phone.

Whilst she waited for Julia to call back, she just had time to drink her tea and eat her toast before making another call to her husband, who was less than pleased by her news.

'Rosie, if the baby has been born, why can ye not wait for the weather to clear? I've been looking at the sky and, sure, 'tis as heavy as a sinner's heart. There will be snow tonight again, I am certain of it.'

'I will be fine. You know me, always the lucky one. Stop fussing now and get back to work. There won't be much light today.'

'Aye, right, well there is no use me arguing now. I will make sure Julia knows to put the watch on from Castlefeale and have them ring me, as ye pass through. Drive with care, Rosie.'

As Rosie finished her last phone call, she once again reminded herself how blessed she had been to marry a man like JT. Never once had she known him to lose his temper, which could not be said for some of the men of rural Ireland. On countless farms, husbands and fathers ruled by the fist.

She set off into the snow once again, this time with her Gladstone bag full of dressings, sutures and useful things she might need for Kitty, as well as a little extra knowledge, which she had artfully gleaned from Besmina as she cleared away the tea tray.

When Rosie turned in through the Abbey gates at three o'clock, the light was already fading fast. At the best of times she thought the Abbey looked like the coldest and most miserable of institutions, but today in the frozen mist it appeared even more forbidding than usual as it loomed up, like a white effigy, against the dull grey sky.

To the right of the main building was a long glass corridor, which led to the laundry; on the opposite side lay the chapel and convent. Rosie knew the girls' dormitories were up in the roof.

She wiped the misty windscreen with her leather glove. From the window on the top floor shone the single, dim yellow light of the labour room, which was where Kitty would be lying, probably alone.

'Merciful God, the poor child,' she said out loud as she pulled up in front of the convent.

As Rosie turned off the engine, she saw a huddled procession of girls shuffling in a straight line down the steps, from the Abbey nursery to the laundry. Rosie wondered if this was the end of the one hour per day they were allowed to spend with their babies and children, and were being herded back to commence another five hours of hard work. Two girls looked directly at Rosie and then began talking to each other. One smiled at her nervously, as though trying to attract her attention, before being sharply prodded in the back by the nun walking alongside.

Rosie had been told by Besmina that whenever a child was adopted, the mother was made to carry it down the long corridor to the door at the far end. There, she would have to hand the baby over to the person who would oversee the handover to the new parents, at Shannon airport.

'’Tis the walk of shame,' Besmina had said, 'and the nuns, they all line up in a row on either side, praying for forgiveness, which, if you ask me, never seems to come. If the mother breaks down, or becomes upset, Jesus, she is punished so bad.'

'How, Besmina, how?'

Rosie had asked this question before but it was not until today that Besmina had answered her, with uncharacteristic bitterness.

'They are taken into the Reverend Mother's office, where they have their heads shaved and painted with gentian violet. Then they are beaten with a cane, tied to a chair and left in a room, alone, for hours. The nuns can be witches, so they can.'

Rosie assumed purple gentian violet would be a physical warning to the other girls, should they dare to shed tears as they handed over their babies.

Besmina, who was a good girl, had told Rosie very little but what she did say had shocked her. Rosie was a good Catholic, but sometimes even she worried at the corruption of her religion, and wondered how there could be a justification for such places as the Abbey.

The Reverend Mother stood waiting, framed in the doorway, a vision in black. By the time Rosie had reached the top of the steps, a flustered, white-veiled novice was also hovering behind her, twittering.

'At long last. I thought you would never arrive,' Sister Assumpta exclaimed impatiently, as though Rosie had travelled from the local village on a dry and pleasant day. 'I have tea ready for you in my office.'

At last, an acknowledgment of the dreadful conditions I have driven in, thought Rosie.

'We saw the lights of your car and had it made immediately. Sister Virginia, show Mrs O'Grady to the bathroom and wait to bring her back. Then you can have your tea and cake, midwife, and Sister Virginia will escort you to the labour room, to collect the girl. Sister Celia has made you the most fabulous sandwich cake and covered the top in melted chocolate. Can you imagine that?'

Rosie followed the novice down the highly polished corridor laid with a green Persian carpet, and lined with heavy, dark wood furniture, with ruby brocade curtains hanging at the windows. Against the wall stood an overpowering statue of St Anthony that had obviously been recently carved. She wondered exactly how much money the nuns were bringing in on an annual basis from their laundry work and baby selling, in order to fill the Abbey with such finery.

The ceremonial tea and cake in the Reverend Mother's room were consumed in minutes. Rosie was keen to see Kitty as quickly as possible, so she stood and picked up her heavy bag. She had to admit, to herself, it was the best slice of chocolate cake she had ever eaten. An unexpected sweetness.

'Er, before you take the girl, I am afraid we have a small problem.' Sister Assumpta's voice, behind her, had now dropped an octave to sound almost menacing.

As Rosie turned back to face her, Sister Assumpta averted her gaze and shuffled pieces of paper across her desk.

'And that would be what, Reverend Mother?' enquired Rosie.

The atmosphere in the room had taken a decidedly frosty turn.

'Do you have the money with you? There is a further eighty pounds outstanding, before the girl can leave.'

Rosie felt her blood boil. She had had a very long day and the last thing on her mind when she had received the Reverend Mother's call was driving to Bangornevin to collect what amounted to bail money. There had been only one idea in her head as she had replaced the receiver and that was to make haste to Kitty's bedside as soon as God and the weather would allow.

Rosie looked the Reverend Mother straight in the eye and spoke with more authority than she actually felt, especially as a painting of the Holy Mother seemed to be staring down at her with a touch of disappointment in the eyes that she had not noticed until now.

'No, I do not, as it happens, because you have given me no time to organize the payment. You appeared very keen indeed to have Kitty removed from the Abbey when you called me this morning, and so I am afraid you will have to wait until I can send someone over. You will have to take my word, unless you would like to hold me for a ransom?'

Both women laughed. A dry slightly shrill laugh, although not one even remotely funny word had been spoken.

Turning on her heel, Rosie crossed the acreage of plush carpet to the office door and almost had to edge the novice aside, to place her hand on the brass doorknob.

'I know my own way, thank you very much,' Rosie hissed as she opened the door with a flourish, almost flattening the simpering novice.

She could feel Sister Assumpta's eyes burning into her back as she made her way down the corridor to the main staircase. Rosie, who held a powerful position and moved in elevated medical and religious circles, knew that, in a direct challenge of authority, Sister Assumpta would not want to cross her. Rosie felt sure that the Reverend Mother would avoid at all costs any situation that encouraged more questions about the running of the mother and baby business.

Rosie's heart began to beat slightly faster, as she waited for a voice to ring out behind her and order her to stop. There was nothing but silence. She let out a deep breath. She had won.

Not for the first time, she detected something malevolent and sinister, cowering in dark corners. Now, it followed her, down the long corridor. Rosie gave an involuntary shiver as she approached the stairs, feeling the hairs on the back of her neck stand up and goose pimples break out on her arms.

'Don't be ridiculous,' she whispered to herself as she hurried up the stairs. 'They can't hold us prisoner.'

Rosie opened the door to the labour room, and was immediately assailed by the smell of stale blood.

'Holy Mary,' she gasped, covering her mouth against the stench.

Across the other side of the room, Kitty lay on her back on the hard delivery bed, looking small and frail. One arm flopped down over the side, almost reaching the floor, like the broken wing of a bird. It was quickly apparent to Rosie that Kitty was in a great deal of pain.

As Kitty's head turned towards Rosie, instant tears of relief ran down her cheeks. She reached out and grabbed Rosie's hand.

'Oh God, it hurts so much,' she cried. 'I feel so sick, the pain is so bad.'

Rosie dropped her bag on the floor and dragged over to the bed a white enamel trolley that stood against the wall. Hurriedly she retrieved equipment and dressings from her bag, placing them on the top of the trolley.

'What hurts, Kitty, where? Is it down below?' Rosie said as she prepared her trolley.

Kitty nodded and put both hands on her abdomen. 'God, it is so bad, and here,' she cried, placing a hand on her chest. Rosie could see that someone had attempted to bind Kitty's breasts, one of the other girls, she supposed, but had not made a very good job of it.

'I need to examine you, Kitty, but when I am done sorting you out, I am putting you in the car and taking you home. Your time here is over.'

Rosie had thought she would drive Kitty straight to Ballymara, to Maeve Deane and her husband Liam, Kathleen's middle son and Jerry's younger brother.

Kitty sobbed loudly, almost screaming and thanking God that she was no longer alone. It was difficult to distinguish her cries of pain from those of relief. Before Kitty had entered the Abbey, she had spent time at Maeve's farmhouse, becoming very close to her and Liam. Now, as Rosie looked down at her chalk-white face, she wasn't so sure Kitty was well enough to travel even that far.

Kitty's cries were heart-wrenching, rising in a crescendo and bringing Rosie, an experienced midwife to the verge of tears herself.

'It hurts, the pain, oh God, the pain,' Kitty yelled again.

Rosie began to palpate Kitty's abdomen and did not like what she felt. It was rigid and hard, resistant to her touch. She pressed her fingers flat against Kitty's uterus and as she did so, Kitty let out a terrifying scream. It was as much as Rosie needed to know.

She lifted up Kitty's knees to examine her, but it took every ounce of her willpower not to allow the disgust to register on her face.

In her twenty-five years as a midwife, she had never seen lacerations so bad. What was worse, they looked seriously infected. However, Rosie knew that the external appearance of an infection was only part of the story. She quickly took Kitty's temperature. It was 104. Rosie was very used to dealing with girls from the tenements, who arrived at the hospital in a similar state, but in Dublin she worked in a controlled environment, with professional colleagues, doctors and midwives. She had never seen a girl in such a post-delivery state, even one who had been brought into the hospital from the country.

'Mother of God, who has been looking after you?' she asked as her own eyes now began to fill with tears. Wasn't this girl going through enough, after all that had happened to her?

'Aideen and Agnes,' Kitty sobbed, holding tightly onto Rosie's hand, as though terrified to let go, lest Rosie disappeared.

And then, as if by magic, as if summoned by angels, the two girls who had delivered Kitty's baby, and done their best to help her, slipped in quietly through the door. Rosie recognized them as the girls she had seen trying to attract her attention when she arrived.

'Thank God you are here,' said Aideen to Rosie, without the ceremony of introduction. 'I'm Aideen, I delivered baby John. The fucking midwife went away on Christmas Eve and she hasn't returned yet. She said Kitty was nothing to do with her and she wasn't coming back just to see to her. There's no baby anywhere near due for another month so we haven't had sight nor sound of her since.'

Rosie was no stranger to bad language. She had heard some of the finest ladies in Dublin use exactly the same words, and worse, when in the middle of a contraction.

'Aideen, can you help me,' she said, with an edge of desperation to her voice. 'Kitty is in a very bad way and I must stitch her before I can move her. Can you fetch me a bowl of hot soapy water from the sink, please?'

Agnes looked alarmed. 'It's not allowed,' she hissed, almost in a whisper. 'The Reverend Mother will go crazy mad, so she will, if you stitch her. She says the rips are put there by God to teach us what we have done wrong and no woman should try to rectify God's own handiwork.'

Rosie felt as if it was now her turn to swear. However, with a great deal of effort, she retained her cool, taking the Spencer Wells forceps and catgut out of the autoclaved pack she had brought from the hospital.

'She is held together by blood clots, Agnes. I cannot move her in this state. Here, can you help and get this tablet down her, and maybe some water to follow? I'm going to give her an injection, to help with the pain, but it may make her feel sick and we can do without that, on a car journey.'

Rosie could tell Agnes was the more nervous and gentle of the two. Life had been harder on Aideen, that much was obvious.

Rosie quickly drew up a vial of pethidine and within seconds had injected a large dose into Kitty's thigh. Rosie noted that Kitty was in so much pain she didn't even flinch.

'We aren't allowed to have painkillers either,' whispered Agnes, who was now in awe of this strong and defiant midwife.

'This is not God's doing, Agnes, but it is the work of the devil himself to leave a poor girl in this state. I will be no part of that,' Rosie replied.

Pouring her antiseptic wash into the bowl of warm water, which Aideen had set on the trolley, she began to swab Kitty.

It took her almost an hour to rectify the damage. Kitty had torn down into her perineum and backwards deeply into her rectum. She bled profusely, as Rosie worked to ease away the huge clots and crusts of blood, which were by now over two days old. As they reliquefied, they filled the room with a sickening metallic smell. At times, both Aideen and Agnes looked pale and nauseous but, dutifully, they held Kitty's hands and remained upright.

While Rosie worked, the girls whispered soft soothing sounds. Aideen had placed a folded rag between Kitty's teeth, just as she did when she was in labour, in fear of her moans attracting the nuns. Like dancing moths drawn to a flame, the sisters always fluttered to the sound of pain.

As Rosie worked, Agnes prayed over Kitty, who had become quiet and drowsy. The pethidine was working at last. She had injected Kitty with one of only four doses of the emergency drug she had popped into her bag as she left the hospital. As the full effect of analgesia worked its magic, Rosie wondered, would Kitty feel safe enough to let go? To relax and sleep?

'Will you girls land yourselves in trouble for being here?' Rosie asked, gently stroking Kitty's hair away from her damp and clammy brow.

Aideen replied with a hint of fear, 'If we wasn't with you, midwife, we would be fucking whipped for coming here, and kept without food for days, but the witches daren't do that because we are with you. They are scared of you, I know that because I heard one of the postulants say so, I did.'

'Yes, but I will be gone soon,' said Rosie, her voice loaded with concern. And then she had an idea. 'I will tell them, when I leave, that I am returning with the money and that when I bring it I have promised to look in on you both, to let you know how, er, Cissy is doing. That should buy you some safety.'

For a split second, Rosie had almost forgotten Kitty's secret name.

Aideen and Agnes looked at each other and smiled. Then, together, they both reached down the front of their calico skirts into their knickers and handed Rosie two warm letters.

'Would you post these for us, please, midwife?' whispered Aideen. By far, the bolder of the two, she had made the decision that Rosie could be trusted. 'You know, we aren't allowed any post in or out and have no contact with the outside world. I need to know, is me mammy coming with the money to get me out of this hell-hole soon, or do I have to escape?'

'Escape?' said Rosie. 'That sounds so desperate.'

'It is fucking desperate. Poor Agnes, she was sent straight here from an orphanage, because the fucking authorities didn't know what else to do with her. That's not fucking right.'

Rosie nodded. She still wasn't shocked. She had once overheard a politician's wife say the word 'fucking' more than three times in thirty seconds when she gave birth, more noisily than at any time before or since.

As Rosie bandaged Kitty's breasts, Agnes gently mopped Kitty's face and washed her hands with a fresh bowl of warm water, drawn from the long shallow sink. Apart from the bed and the trolley, it was the only piece of furniture in the room.

Rosie packed her bag and stowed away the letters. Then she scribbled down her home address and the number of the hospital office on a piece of paper and handed it to Aideen.

'Here,' she whispered. 'Keep this somewhere safe and away from prying eyes. If it reaches the point where you have to escape, contact me and I will help.'

Aideen grabbed hold of Rosie's hand. 'Thank you,' she said, displaying the first sign of gentleness, and her eyes filled with tears.

Rosie watched as Aideen ripped away the surplus paper, leaving only the area on which Rosie had written, and then rolled it between her finger and thumb, over and over, until it was a tight cylinder. She tucked the almost needle-thin paper roll through the stiches in the hem of her baggy calico knickers.

Aideen grinned to Agnes. 'The bitches won't find it there, will they?' The light of hope sprang gleefully into both girls' eyes. 'We do all the laundry, so they will never find it.'

Rosie felt overwhelmed with tenderness towards both girls. Aideen might be a farm girl with little education, rough around the edges, but she had heart and humanity enough to risk angering Sister Assumpta by caring for Kitty, as best she knew how.

'If it comes to that and you do escape,' Rosie's whisper was barely audible so the girls leant in close to catch her words, 'make sure you leave my address behind, for anyone else who may need it. I have a good kitchen maid at my hospital, Besmina. She has told me a great deal about what goes on here and I want to help, if I can.'

'Besmina!' Both Aideen and Agnes looked at one another in shocked surprise.

'That's right. I think she worked in the kitchens here, before her grandmother brought her to me to give her work at the hospital. When I was a district midwife, I delivered Besmina at her grandmother's house in Dublin.'

Aideen smiled, knowingly.

'Yes, that's right, miss. She worked in the kitchens,' said Aideen slowly.

The three women now began to help Kitty to her feet. Dehydrated and with a dangerously high temperature, she was mumbling incoherently as though delirious. Rosie knew Kitty could have a febrile fit at any moment. God only knew how she would cope with that, here in this godforsaken place.

Rosie was eager to get Kitty to hospital. Out in the country, in the rural farms and on the bogs, she had seen girls develop serious infections after giving birth. By the time Rosie reached them, peritonitis had often fatally set in. She would do everything in her power to ensure that did not happen to this child.

Moving as softly as they could, Aideen and Agnes helped Kitty down the stairs. When they reached the bottom step, Agnes suddenly froze.

A ghostlike shadow upon the wall announced that the imposing form of Sister Assumpta was gliding silently towards them, the Persian silk runner absorbing the sound of her inescapable approach.

They were trapped. Motionless, they stood as if turned to stone whilst her shadow turned the corner and enveloped them.

Her mouth dry with fear and her knees turning to jelly, Agnes clung onto Kitty's arm, holding her upright in the process.

She had felt bold, sneaking away to see the midwife, passing on the details of the birth and helping the poor girl. They had guessed by her accent, she must have come from Liverpool and that for some reason she had told no one her story. They had all guessed that Kitty held a secret.

'God knows, don't we all have our own,' Aideen had said to Agnes.

But now, with the wrath of Sister Assumpta bearing down upon them, their boldness fled.

Jeez, we are mad, thought Aideen. What had seemed like a brave idea only an hour ago now appeared reckless and foolish. They had broken every rule in the Abbey, including having spoken to Rosie and each other. Agnes felt as though she would wet herself in fear at the consequences.

Sister Assumpta stood before them, not speaking a word, staring first at Rosie and then at both girls.

'And what, may I ask, are you both doing in the main house at this time of day? Why are you not in the laundry?'

Rigid with terror, neither girl could utter a word of response. Aideen tried, but her tongue stuck to the roof of her mouth in dread.

'*Speak!*' Even the mice shook at the sound of Sister Assumpta's anger.

Neither girl could have responded even if her life had depended upon it. Agnes began to shake.

'Sister Celia!'

Sister Assumpta's voice boomed out again, although her lips appeared not to move, nor her glare to leave the girls. However, she needn't have wasted her breath because Sister Celia almost immediately waddled into view, carrying the leather holdall Kitty had brought with her on the day she had arrived. It contained her own clothes, which had not been seen in months.

'Take these girls into my room immediately and search them, please, Sister.'

With no grace and even less kindness, Sister Celia dropped Kitty's holdall on the floor. Grabbing Aideen and Agnes each by the arm, she marched them both away down the corridor. As Kitty began to slip to the floor, unsupported, Rosie had to move swiftly, placing her arm under her shoulders and round her back.

Sister Assumpta said to Rosie, 'I told them on the day they brought this – this girl,' she almost spat out the words; she had wanted to use a very different term but she had eighty pounds owing to her, and was not going to put the payment in jeopardy, 'that many of the girls here are penitents, placed here into my care by the government. I have a job to do here, midwife, and, as I told you, I would prefer you not to speak to the girls for any reason at all.'

Rosie was not easily intimidated, and she had no intention of apologizing, but right now she just wanted to be out of the Abbey and on the road to Dublin. Stooping to pick up the holdall she shuffled Kitty towards the door.

Sensing the sister's hot breath on her neck, Rosie gave way to rising panic. When she finally managed to open the door, she took a deep breath of the chilled, rejuvenating air. She was nearly there.

'Thank you, Reverend Mother. The girls have been very helpful. I am sure I will have messages of thanks to deliver to them, from the family, when I return with the payment. I hope to see them again.'

As she walked out, she knew that Sister Assumpta still stood in the doorway, rooted to the spot, observing her every step.

And she also knew that she would not be allowed to see Aideen and Agnes ever again.

With an effort, she laid Kitty down on the back seat of her Hillman Hunter. As she closed the car door on her and placed her holdall into the boot, she heard the sound of stifled cries. Rosie felt sick at the thought of the girls being beaten, only a few yards away, but right now she had a sick girl only forty-eight hours post-partum with a temperature of 104, lying on the back seat of her car. She prayed that her contact details were not found in the hem of Aideen's calico knickers, and quickly checked that the letters were safely in her handbag before placing it on the passenger seat beside her.

The sky was darkening rapidly as Rosie left the Abbey. When she pulled away, she was aware that her retreating car lights were being followed: from behind the twitching, heavy curtains by disapproving nuns' eyes downstairs, and by grateful waves from unknown girls through the cold, uncurtained windows of the top floor and the laundry.

As she looked across the vast lawn towards the trees, in the bright moonlight she noticed a gravestone. Rosie shuddered. Each one of those girls in the graveyard would have died terrified, screaming in agony, feeling unloved and alone. Rosie crossed herself as she pulled out of the gate and sped, as fast as the icy road would allow her, on to Dublin.

In less than ten minutes, she realized she would never make it. An abandoned bus completely blocked the road. Rosie left her car and shouted up into the driver's cab, but there was no one inside. The door was locked and footsteps leading away, lightly covered by fresh snowfall, told her that the driver and passengers had long since left.

Kitty slept fitfully on the back seat with Rosie's spare sheepskin jacket laid over her and an Aran picnic blanket rolled up under her head for a pillow. There had been no tea or cake for Kitty. Rosie knew she was weak and in danger. The Kitty she had known before the delivery had been a bright girl. Now she was without the energy even to cry. The only words she had spoken, as the car had pulled away from the Abbey, were, 'Rosie, fetch the baby, fetch John,' before sleep possessed her.

Rosie made a decision there and then. She would drive as quickly as possible – in the opposite direction, to Maeve and Liam's farmhouse on the Ballymara Road.

She would pass the doctor's house on the way and would collect some antibiotics and ask him to put up a drip that Rosie could look after whilst she nursed Kitty at Maeve's. The doctor would trust her. She could provide him with an entirely false name for Kitty and, if he pushed, she would make him aware that no further information would be forthcoming. Not even a doctor would push for information regarding a young girl, with no baby to show for her pains.

The drive to Bangornevin was tortuous. With the coming of night, the temperature had plummeted and what had earlier been the soft snow, during the day, had frozen into solid ice along the narrow country lanes. The road, which was not easy to drive on at the best of times, now felt to Rosie as unyielding as iron.

She knew the route well, but the fog and mist that had rolled down and onto the fields confused her. Every few yards or so, a cow in search of warmth loomed up from the mist in the dim yellow headlights as a ghostly spectre, causing Rosie to yelp with fright.

The moon was full, and the sky ahead appeared to go on forever, an inky-black carpet of glittering stars, interspersed with heavy clouds full of snow. Rosie gave thanks, more than once, for the ethereal, sparkling light, which reflected from the ice, transforming the road into a frosted satin ribbon, winding its way along the riverbank, leading them on.

The moon kept with her all the way, refected in the fast-flowing river beside her, watching and guiding her. Even in her gloves, Rosie's hands were near frozen and the heater struggled to make any difference whatsoever to the temperature inside the car.

On a number of bends, Rosie missed the road entirely when the car jolted frighteningly against the roadside scrub and stones. At one point, she had to get out of the car and push the tyres out of a shallow dip. By the time she was back in the driver's seat, wet and chilled to the bone, she had to scrape the ice from the inside of the windscreen before she could safely continue on her journey.

They had not passed a single car along the way. She felt gripped with terror when she realized that if anything did happen to the car, both she and Kitty would surely freeze to death before they were discovered. She was glad that Kitty was sleeping and unaware of their danger.

Rosie had no idea that since her baby boy had been born and taken away from her on Christmas morning, Kitty had lain awake, day and night, yearning for Rosie to arrive. She had barely moved her gaze from the window, watching for the car headlights. Kitty was now in the deepest sleep. With her pain controlled by the pethedine, her body had surrendered.

Although she was cold, Rosie was sweating with fear and praying out loud.

'Thank you, Lord, for bringing me here. Now, could you just take me a little further, please God.'

Rosie prayed to every saint a day was named after, to every angel whose name she could remember and to the Holy Mother. She barely stopped to draw breath as she did so. She knew that if she stopped to think about their predicament, she might lose her resolve. Rosie was tough, having seen and dealt with most things. Now, however, she was alone. Her ability to reach help was at the mercy of the elements and she had never before felt so out of control, or been so afraid.

Irish winters were harsh and the locals in Bangornevin still spoke sadly of the two brothers who had been discovered in their farmhouse, snowed in and frozen to death, in 1947, as though it had happened only yesterday.

Rosie reached over to the back seat to place her hand on Kitty's forehead. The girl appeared to be more unconscious than asleep. Despite the cold, Rosie knew, with heightened concern, that Kitty was burning up.

'Oh, God in heaven, no. Please, not peritonitis, Lord, please, no,' Rosie whispered to the heavens, putting her foot down and trying in vain to drive faster and more safely.

'God in heaven, help us,' she whispered, crossing herself, as she followed the river round to Castlefeale. Tears of fear filled her eyes, as she began to shiver violently with the cold.

Rosie thought about her husband and their animals on the farm. Maybe he had been right. Maybe she should have listened to him. 'That would be a first if ever there was one, eh, Kitty,' she said aloud and laughed nervously. What she wouldn't give now to have her husband here, giving out to her for not listening to him.

'Ye always think ye knows best, Rosie, but ye don't, not always!' How many times had he said that to her and she had scoffed in his face, right back at him.

Talking out loud to Kitty, albeit it with a trembling voice, helped to calm her fear and made her feel less alone.

'What I wouldn't give right now for you, Kitty, to sit up on the back seat and tell me you are feeling much better. God in heaven, I would gladly give away everything I owned, if that would happen just now.'

But there was no response to her frantic gabbling. Not a sound.

She leant over the steering wheel to scrape away the ice, yet again, from the inside of her windscreen. She could see her breath before her, forming into soft grey clouds. She blew hard on the glass, hoping it would make some difference.

Never in her life had she known a night as cold as this. Never.

As she rounded the bend into Castlefeale, turning away from the river, Rosie's heart sank further. They had lost the moon.

'Well, there goes the moon, so we are on our own now, Kitty. At least it kept us from driving straight into the river, thanks be to God.'

She was talking faster as her fear mounted.

The road became dark as the mountains rose up on either side, casting their shadows, obscuring the torch of the moon that had illuminated their route, but then suddenly, as though in answer to her prayers, it slipped out from between the two mountains and illuminated the way ahead.

'Oh, thank you, Lord,' Rosie now sobbed in relief as once again she scraped furiously at the windscreen.

After what seemed like hours, they passed through Bellgarett and Rosie gave a huge sigh of relief. They were heading towards civilization, such as it was in this part of the world. As she drove past the post office she noticed that they had been spotted. Her husband would now be telephoned and told she had passed safely through. She wound down the window and waved feebly before quickly drawing her arm back inside.

'We've been clocked, Kitty,' she said. 'They will be ringing on ahead now so that they will be watching out for us in Bangornevin. By the time we arrive in Ballymara, they will be waiting for us with a smashing dinner. Won't that be grand?'

As she reached the doctor's house she pulled up sharply in front of the gates but her heart sank. The building was in darkness and the gates were firmly locked. Shaking her head, she quickly slipped back behind the wheel and carried on towards Bangornevin, heading through to Ballymara.

Rosie wondered what reason Maeve and Julia would have given to Mrs Doyle, the nosiest postmistress in all of Ireland, for this visit on the coldest night of the year. She told herself that no one would notice Kitty, lying on the back seat. They would think something was up at the farmhouse for Rosie to be so mad as to drive on a night like this.

'A good meal in your insides is what we need next, eh, Kitty. Sure, we must be the only people in all of Ireland not indoors.'

Rosie could not hear a sound from the back seat. Not even the faintest breathing.

But her fear began to subside as she felt the watching eyes of the home villages, following them on their way. At last, they were safe. No harm would come to them now. The hardest part of Rosie's journey was yet to come: the mile and a half down the bumpy terrain of the Ballymara Road. Although she was used to being in charge during difficult, even life-threatening situations, she felt a huge relief to see Maeve and her sister-in-law Julia running out to meet them when she finally drew up outside the farmhouse.

Through the doorway, a warm light radiated onto the road. She could see the welcoming flames of the peat fire licking up the chimney; she could smell the freshly baked bread wafting towards her. Rosie felt as though she had driven into heaven.

The skies were darker over Ballymara and as Rosie opened the back door of the Hillman Hunter, the flakes began to fall thick and heavy.

'God in heaven,' said Maeve as she saw Kitty asleep on the back seat. 'Julia, get Liam out here now.'

Within seconds, Liam was at her side and between them they slipped Kitty out through the car door. Liam carried her into their kitchen and laid her down on the padded settle in front of the fire.

'She hardly looks like the same girl we dropped off at the Abbey,' he said, with more than a hint of anger in his voice.

'She looks desperate, Rosie,' said Maeve.

'Well now, I'll not hide the truth from you in your own home. It is desperate,' said Rosie. 'I think she may be developing an infection. I called into the doctor's house when I passed through Bangornevin, but there were no lights on.'

'They have gone back to her mother's house in Liverpool for Christmas,' said Maeve. 'They won't be back until after the new year. And even if they were there, no one can know about this. What in God's name do we do?'

'Well, right now I want to give her a proper clean-up and check the stitches I rushed to put in at the Abbey. Have you any chicken stock to get down her, Maeve? It's the next best thing to penicillin. The Abbey girls told me the poor kid has lived off next to nothing for months. It's a wonder she had the strength to give birth to her baby at all. We need to pray hard, ladies. This child is as sick as sick can be. Frankly, if she was on one of my wards I wouldn't give much for her chances, never mind out here in the country without a doctor or a hospital for miles.'

Julia crossed herself. 'I need to drive to the post office and telephone Kathleen in Liverpool so that she can break the news to Maura and Tommy.'

'No,' Rosie said sharply. 'There is nothing they can do. They couldn't even travel here in this weather. Let's leave it for a day. I need a chance to nurse her back to health, if I can.'

'Well, ye don't need to do that alone, Rosie. Mrs McGuffey has the cure for this. Liam, Liam!' Julia shouted, rushing through the kitchen to the back porch, where she knew Liam would be. 'Can ye get the van out and get to the McGuffeys' in Gisala?'

'Aye, I can do me best,' said Liam.

Within minutes, they saw the van lights disappearing slowly along Rosie's fresh tracks in the snow, up the Ballymara Road.

Maeve, who was forty and childless, was filled with sadness at Kitty's return to the farmhouse, alone, without her baby. Maeve would have loved to have adopted Kitty's child, but Liam wouldn't hear of it.

'We still have time for our own yet,' he had whispered to her in the dark when they were lying in bed. Maeve had used every trick in the book known to woman. If she couldn't persuade Liam to let them adopt the baby, when he had a belly full of Guinness in the moments just after sex and before sleep, she knew she never would.

Julia came in to set down a bowl of hot water and a pile of clean, warm towels.

Rosie said, 'God, it is better facilities here than it is in the Abbey, I can tell ye, Maeve.'

Kitty would need to be washed down. Both Maeve and Julia had noticed a smell of stale blood as she entered the warm farmhouse.

'What was the baby?' Maeve whispered to Rosie as she ladled soup out of the pot into mugs. Maeve was sensitive to the fact that even though Kitty was half unconscious, she might be able to hear.

'The girls from the Abbey told me it was a boy. I spoke to the one who was there, Aideen, her name was. She said it was an awful time, but, she swore, God held her hands as she delivered him. She told me he was beautiful, with dark hair and bright blue eyes. Kitty named him John, although, God knows, his adoptive parents will already have altered that.'

Maeve handed Rosie the mug of soup. 'Did she have any time with him?'

'Not long. She was forbidden from leaving the labour room. Apparently the nuns were all of a dither that a beautiful baby boy had been born at the Abbey on Christmas morning, it being a full moon and all. One of the sisters said she had seen an angel rise over the Abbey, when the boy was being born and it sent them all quite senseless. The Reverend Mother had the boy taken straight to the nursery and out of sight at first light, so Kitty had only a couple of hours with him. The girls said she didn't put him down from the moment he was born at about four o'clock until the Reverend Mother had him taken away.

'She was distraught, the girls said. She has been asking for him constantly since he was taken. God knows, the girls who helped were relieved to see me. The chatty one, Aideen, thought Kitty was killing herself with the grief and looking at her now, she may have been right. Her chances of making it to this time tomorrow aren't great, I can tell you.'

'Aye, but ye didn't know about Mrs McGuffey, Rosie,' said Maeve. 'We don't lose many women around here, once they have been given a few doses of Mrs McGuffey's home brew.'

'For goodness' sake, Maeve, I'm a trained midwife and I'm struggling. How can Mrs McGuffey know what to bloody do?'

Rosie was never one to let her professional demeanour slip. A look of surprise crossed her face as she realized she had sworn for the first time in her life. Despite the seriousness of the situation, she found herself laughing. She was only too well aware that in every country home there existed a potion for every ailment known to man.

'I'm sorry, Maeve, it's just that out here in the country, between you, every house has it covered from impotency to impetigo. God alone knows what the doctor does.'

As Rosie and Annie began tenderly to undress Kitty, Rosie didn't notice a tear slide down Maeve's cheek.

The perfect loving wife, the kindest friend and neighbour, Maeve now felt desperately sad. She had never asked her husband, Liam, for anything. She had never needed to but, now, although Liam was a good and loving husband, for the first time in her marriage she felt angry.

In the only thing she really needed from Liam to ease her deep sadness and make her happy, he had refused her. She could have brought up Kitty's baby as her own. They would have found a way and then Kitty could have been an auntie to the baby. Sure, how many families did they all know of in Ireland and Liverpool where that happened? There was a family on every street. It was the widely accepted thing to do. Why couldn't Liam do it too?

'I couldn't love another man's child, Maeve, so I couldn't,' he had pleaded. 'If it isn't ours, how can it be our baby?'

'Because people can and do,' Maeve had replied. 'Ye love that mangy dog that goes everywhere with ye as if it were ye son. Am I wrong? Am I?'

Liam had stormed out of the room. He did indeed love his dog and Maeve's question was a fair one, but he just couldn't answer it.

'Maeve, is that you?'

Kitty had woken as Rosie and Julia began to wash her down, making soothing noises as they did so. Maeve already had night-clothes warming for Kitty by the fire. She had hung them there as soon as she heard Kitty was coming.

Rosie was removing Kitty's blood-soaked knickers and they were both trying to sit her on the chamber pot, which Liam had tactfully placed on the floor before he left for Gisala. Maeve held both Kitty's hands to steady her as she wobbled to one side. Kitty looked as though she would break if she fell off the pot.

'Aye, Kitty. You are back in Ballymara and we are going to look after you here. You will be right soon enough and back in Liverpool before you know it.'

Kitty wasn't listening to what Maeve said. She stared straight into her eyes.

'I have to find him. I have to find my baby.'

Rosie said, 'Kitty, we need you to concentrate on getting yourself better. We will talk about the baby later. Let's just think about you. Here, swallow this.' Maeve held up to her lips a mug of oversweet tea with aspirin dissolved and concealed in the thick, brown liquid.

While Maeve held Kitty upright on the pot, Rosie poured the jug of soapy water over her wounds to clean her stitches. Then, placing a towel under and across her, they lifted her onto the huge padded settle and laid her down on a feather eiderdown covered with towels.

Rosie whispered to Maeve, 'I have to return tomorrow with the rest of the money. Can you believe it? The sisters are charging us to half kill the child. The money from the Americans to buy the baby isn't enough.'

'That cannot be right,' Maeve replied.

'It isn't,' said Rosie. 'I've already made enquiries but you know the Church, all powerful, more powerful than the government, even. It is all a cosy agreement if you ask me. Everyone knows what is happening but it is all kept secret. They have no such institutions for the boys, mind.'

Rosie felt Kitty's pulse; it was weak and thready. Her skin was sallow and hot, her abdomen was distended and hard, and a foul-smelling pus oozed from her perineum. Rosie crossed herself. The pus was as nothing, compared to what might be developing internally.

Rosie sat down on the end of the settle with a sigh.

'Go to bed, Maeve,' she said. 'I will sit with her for the night. She is in my charge. I will need your help in the morning, but for now, you grab what's left of your sleep.'

'I will not,' said Maeve. 'We will have a drink and a ciggie here and wait and see what Liam fetches back from Gisala.'

Maeve moved over to the press and poured two large glasses of whiskey. She winked at Rosie and said, 'Get this down ye. It's amazing how much better ye will feel after and, if ye don't, I'll fetch the bottle.'

Maeve took her rosaries out of her apron pocket, kissed them and wrapped them around Kitty's unresisting little fingers.

It seemed as though they had been sitting for only an hour or so when they heard the sound of the van return. Julia bustled into the room with Liam.

'Well, that was difficult, I can tell ye. Maeve, I had to say it was for ye sister. Thank God she had that little girl last week and ye must remember to tell her what I said. 'Tis a tangled web we are weaving here all right.'

'Well, everyone this side of Bellgarett knows Rosie is here,' said Maeve, 'so it fits.'

Rosie wasn't listening; she was busy removing the straw stopper from the green bottle that Liam had handed her.

'Jesus, what is in this? It smells like pee,' she said, pulling her nose away sharply.

Julia shrugged. 'Aye, well, likely it has a bit in there, but it's mainly plants and things, usually. Do ye have anything better?'

'It won't be human pee,' said Maeve helpfully. 'Most likely from their goat and, anyway, it'll be whatever is mixed with it that does all the good. Stop yer complaining now and get it down her.'

'That goat wins the show at Castlefeale every year, so it does,' said Julia. 'There's so many put out around here by it, I'm surprised someone hasn't slit its throat. It's well known the McGuffeys make a fortune, so they do, from the magic of its medicine.'

Lifting Kitty's head, they managed to pour half of the bottle down her, followed by some soup, painstakingly fed to her by Julia, one teaspoon at a time.

Julia and Maeve retired to bed, more comforted to have seen Kitty settled.

'Everything you will need is in the press,' Maeve whispered, giving Rosie a hug. 'She looks so much better already. The McGuffeys' medicine has done the trick.'

Before Rosie could respond, Maeve left the room, knowing she would be required in the morning to help with the more practical things like stacking the fire, preparing food and persuading Rosie to catch some sleep.

Rosie wrung out a cloth in the fresh warm water Julia had left by her side and began wiping down Kitty's arms with long strokes, in an attempt to bring her blood to the surface and cool her down. Rosie was desperate to take on the high temperature and conquer it. She was experienced enough to know Kitty was on the way down, not the way up.

It would be a long night.

Rosie woke to the sound of a loud knock at the front door.

It was light, the cock was crowing furiously, and through the window she could see that although the sky was loaded with snow, for now at least, it appeared to have ceased falling.

'Morning, Aengus,' she whispered, as she recognized one of the young McMahons from the farm next door standing on the step.

'Morning, Rosie. John asked me to knock and check everything was good, what with your car arriving so late and with the lights having been on all night.'

'I'm fine, Aengus, tell John thank you, would you, but we are all good in here.'

Rosie saw Aengus gazing through the doorway towards the settle, where Kitty was sleeping. He looked straight at Rosie and, in that unguarded moment, his eyes asked multiple questions.

'Ye may be fine, but, sure, the car is not.' The words Aengus spoke did not reflect his thoughts in any way. Rosie saw that her car was half buried by snow.

'Don't worry, it will be gone soon. Tell Liam I will clear it now,' Aengus said, then lifted his cap and turned to walk back towards the McMahon farm at the end of the Ballymara Road.

Rosie moved back inside and found Maeve in the kitchen.

'Sure, I expected that,' she said, nodding towards the door. 'I'm surprised there was no one knocking on last night. If I had seen a car arrive at the McMahons' I would have been out there like a shot to see if all was well.'

Rosie smiled. The farmers in Roscommon liked to think they were a little more sophisticated than those in Mayo, but really it was just the same.

'Aye, I suppose a car is a rare sight on the Ballymara Road,' she said.

'Everyone in the village will know within hours that Kitty is back with us,' said Maeve. 'There will be plenty knocking on soon enough, people wondering why we have a visitor. How is she? Is her temperature down? We need to move her into the bedroom to keep her from prying eyes.' Maeve was talking as fast as her brain was working.

'She has stopped burning and fretting, and seems to be sleeping more peacefully now.

'But if people know it is Kitty, it will be obvious she has been in Ireland all along, else how would she have made it here last night in this weather? I will say she has been helping me out in Dublin, training for something or other, on a secretarial course maybe, and staying with family for Christmas, and that she has taken ill on her way to visit us. Will that do now?'

'It is as good as anything, aye, and no one will be checking up on you, will they, you being so grand and important an' all.' Maeve winked at Rosie as, between them, both women lifted Kitty from the settle and carried her into the bedroom where Maeve had lit a fire.

'Well, the sisters can whistle for their money because I will be driving nowhere today. Good job I rang home before I left for the Abbey to let them know what I was doing or my poor husband would have a search party out on the road by now.'

As Rosie pulled up the covers, Kitty opened her eyes and, for a moment, looked confused as she took in her surroundings.

'Have ye got the baby, Maeve?' she whispered.

Maeve threw Rosie a troubled look. 'I'm off to get ye some tea, miss,' she said, squeezed Kitty's hand and left the room.

Rosie sat on the edge of Kitty's bed. 'Well, ye gave us all quite a scare,' she said, picking up Kitty's thin, trembling hand.

Kitty looked at the face of the speaker, staring her in the eye. She knew this woman, she was sure, but she just couldn't remember.

'Do ye have the baby?' she asked again.

'No, Kitty, I don't. The baby has been adopted by an American family. You signed an agreement, do ye remember?'

Kitty turned her head towards the window and saw Aengus, clearing the snow from Rosie's car.

'Aengus,' she whispered. She remembered him. Maybe he would know where her baby was.

Kitty's room became a hive of activity: Maeve fed her, Rosie washed her, and Julia acted as handmaiden, changing her bottom sheet, bringing fresh water and putting her in a clean, warm nightdress. They all made soothing noises, stroked her hair and threw each other worried glances.

'A few more days and ye will be up and about,' said Maeve.

'We will have you as right as rain in no time at all,' said Rosie.

'With Maeve's cooking, ye will be giving us a dance in a week,' said Julia.

They were almost talking to themselves because Kitty wasn't there. They could see the thoughts flitting across her brain, the questions and the confusion, as she looked at them, unknowing, through narrowed eyes, her brow furrowed. And then she spoke.

'Where's my baby? Do ye have my baby?' Once she found those words, she said them again and again.

No one spoke. There was no answer.

'I think Jacko the mule must know ye are here, Kitty, he hasn't stopped braying. He's hanging around the back, waiting for ye, I reckon,' said Maeve, remembering how much Kitty had loved riding on Jacko.

But Kitty made no sign of recognition. She closed her eyes and laid her head back on the pillow, once more overcome by exhaustion. She tried to lift her hand to tap on the window to attract Aengus's attention.

'Aengus,' she whispered.

Instinctively, he stopped shovelling snow and looked towards her. He could not see Kitty through the net curtains, but he rightly guessed she was there, on the other side. In a wild gesture of hope, he smiled and lifted his hand. He was rewarded when, after just a second, he saw her own hand press the curtain flat against the glass, before it slipped down and the curtain gently swung back into place.

The three women retreated and left Kitty to sleep.

Kitty turned her head from the window and watched the bedroom door close, gently.

'Sleep is mother nature's healer,' said Maeve.

Julia placed the bacon rashers on the griddle and began preparing them all some much needed breakfast.

'I'm worried about her delirium,' said Rosie. 'Her temperature is down but I still must find some antibiotics, somewhere, this morning. Whatever was in that potion has worked a miracle, so it has. It's more her state of mind that concerns me now. She doesn't seem to understand what is going on.'

'She understands she has had a baby,' said Julia. 'Looks to me like she's on the edge of madness. I saw it once with a woman, after a stillborn. Hanged herself in the barn, she did.'

'Jeez, Julia, shush,' said Maeve. 'The girl has had a loss and been very ill. She will be well soon enough. I'd say a week from now, she will be a different girl altogether. She's young, she will bounce back in no time. Liam is ready to run ye to the doctor in Castlefeale, for whatever it is ye want, Rosie, but eat first. It could take a while on these roads.'

From the familiar bed she had slept in while on holiday at the farmhouse, Kitty could hear the muffled voices in the kitchen, just as she had heard them, only months earlier, when they had decided what to do in order to contain her secret. Nellie had been with her then, in the bed on the opposite side of the room.

'Nellie,' she whispered. Was that Nellie sitting on the bed? It was; there was no mistaking Nellie's red hair. 'Nellie,' she whispered again as she reached out her hand, but Nellie had gone.

She was alone again, or so she thought, but not for long.

Turning slowly onto her side with her face towards the window, she saw Aengus digging the snow away from Rosie's car. Kitty remembered their meeting at the harvest, their flirting and her happiness. Her eyes filled with tears. She had thought she would never see him again but she had remembered his name.

'Aengus,' she whispered. 'Aengus.'

She raised her hand again and her heart filled with joy at the sight of his smiling face.

He will know, he will tell me, he will know where my baby is, she thought. But as she saw him walk away, back to the McMahon farm, Kitty felt anxious.

'Don't go,' she croaked through her dry lips. 'Aengus.'

But he had gone. The sound of his feet crunching through the snow faded as the distance grew between them.

Kitty decided to follow him and tried to put her feet on the floor. Maybe he had left to fetch her baby, to bring him to her. That must be it. She would go with him, she must.

'Aengus,' she rasped again, setting her feet on the rag rug at the side of the bed. She felt dizzy and it was difficult to move, but then they came. They filled the room and they knew where her baby was.

There was her mammy, Maura, and her da, Tommy, and Nellie and Aengus were with them, and they were leading her away from the bed and outside to her baby. They knew where he was and she laughed. They were taking her to her beautiful baby boy, to her little prince, her baby John.

They held her hand, helped her across the bedroom floor and swept her down the corridor towards the dairy door. As it opened, the dazzling white glare from the first rays of sunlight reflecting up from the snow almost blinded her and the blast of icy air took her breath clean away, but they were leading her, urging her on. She laid her bare foot on the glistening snow and laughed but, as she looked down, a look of puzzlement crossed her face as drops of blood were falling at her feet, piercing the snow as they dripped. Deep, hot, penetrating red against the icy brilliant white.

Someone held out a hand. It was no longer Maura supporting her, but a man she didn't know, and she smiled at him as the others circled round her, calling her name.

'Mammy,' she whispered, looking for Maura. 'Mammy, I have to find my baby.' She held her face up to the watery sunlight reflected in the glistening snow, so pure and white and cold.

'Do ye know where my baby is?' she asked the man as he took her hands and led her into the deep snow towards the river's edge. And there, he pushed her down into the cold rushing water, and held her still. The last thing Kitty saw was a lady with long red hair and a beautiful smile, who looked just like Nellie, holding out her arms.

'Did ye know Kitty was back?' Aengus asked his aunt and uncle as they sat down to bacon and tatties from the range, before they began their day's work.

'No, I did not. Well, I never, I had no notion,' said his aunt.

'Well then, we will be seeing a lot more of ye around here seeing as ye have such a soft spot for the girl,' said his uncle, laughing.

'I think she may be poorly now,' said Aengus. 'She was asleep on the settle and, later, I saw her wave from the bedroom.'

''Tis unusual for anyone to be ill when it snows,' said his aunt. 'The snow freezes all the sickness solid, so it does, inside and out. There is no cure for any ailment as good as the snow.'

Later that morning, when Aengus was leading the cows back out and taking feed to the pigs, he looked down from the top of the hill. Below him he could see Liam and Rosie, Julia and Maeve, running along the bank of the Moorhaun River, at the point where it passed from their own land onto the McMahons' farm. He saw his uncle run out of the barn and he heard Maeve scream.

And then he saw Kitty in her blue floral nightdress, floating on the fast river, and Maeve and Liam, running to catch her.

He looked to the top of the Ballymara Road, at the point where the road, the river and the village met and, for a brief moment, his eye was caught by a very large black car, gliding out of the churchyard and turning right, across the top of the Ballymara Road, away from Bangornevin and on towards Galway, the heavy wheels cutting through the snow with ease.

'Who the feck?' he whispered under his breath. As he was on his way down the hill, he wondered who was the red-haired woman, kneeling at the side of the riverbank next to Kitty.

Before he reached the bottom of the hill, she was gone and now, all he could see through his tears was Liam, staggering across the white, river-worn pebbles, carrying Kitty, dripping wet and limbs hanging lifelessly, like a broken rag doll.

# Chapter Four

When he learnt that he was to be sent to Liverpool to assume responsibility for the parish of St Mary's, Anthony Lamb had insisted that his sister, Harriet, accompany him. He knew he would need all the help he could find, in a parish where the priest and a respected parishioner had been murdered within weeks of each other.

His wish had been granted. En route he had broken his journey in Dublin to collect Harriet, as well as to help her shut up the house, which had been their childhood home and where Harriet, the remaining spinster of the family, had been living alone.

Although she was only thirty-five years old, Anthony was aware she had sacrificed much of her own life, caring for both their elderly parents until their deaths, and he felt an overpowering obligation to protect her.

'Isn't life funny, Anthony? If Mammy and Daddy were still alive, I would still be in Black Rock, helping to run the house. Daddy just wouldn't countenance giving up the surgery to retire. God knows, he loved all his patients.'

Her parents' deaths had not been a great shock, to Harriet or to any of her eight siblings. Both had lived to a ripe old age and her father had still practised as a family doctor almost up to the day he died aged eighty-five.

Harriet, having been the youngest of nine, appeared to have missed out, as each of her brothers and sisters had carved out their paths in countries and towns too far away from Dublin to be any help when it was needed. Surprisingly, when trouble arose at home, in the places where her sisters lived the postal service often seemed to be struggling to survive. The postmen were always on strike in Watford, Luton, London, Chicago and New York, all at the same time, or so it had seemed.

Harriet occasionally resented them all, every last one of them, apart from her beloved Anthony, and then felt tormented with guilt. Her life had been given over to caring for her parents and she had longed to break free. To move away from Dublin and experience some excitement of her own, if only for a short while.

'It is not so much funny, as the way God planned it, Harriet,' Anthony said gently, smiling at his sister. He sensed she was a Catholic out of duty, not commitment. Harriet smiled back. Her lack of true belief was the guilty secret she would always carry.

Pressing her face up against the cab window as they headed up towards the four streets, she changed the subject. 'Gosh, Anthony, would you look at those shops.'

Anthony had asked the cab driver to take them on a short tour around the city of Liverpool before they arrived at the Priory. It had given him huge pleasure to see the look on Harriet's face as they drove past Lewis's and down Church Street.

'The housekeeper's name is Annie O'Prey. I have already written to her,' Harriet said as she settled back again on the cab seat. 'She said she would have a hot supper ready for us when we arrive and that Sister Evangelista would be waiting for us. Then tomorrow, it's down to work. Sister Evangelista did say we would be rather thrown in at the deep end.'

Father Anthony sighed. He had hoped to begin his time on the four streets on a more positive note, but he was at a loss to find a positive in a double murder. The world was changing fast and holding a community together in England was difficult at the best of times.

As they drew nearer, Harriet became entranced by the docks. When the klaxon sounded, the cranes, which loomed like spectres, ceased to swing and men began to appear at the top of the steps, hurrying home. Each one looked directly at the cab and lifted a hand in greeting as they looked to see who was entering their domain. Harriet felt slightly self-conscious, but Anthony smiled and waved from the window with a smile for each work-weary face they passed. A car on the four streets was an event, unless it was a police car.

As they pulled into the Priory drive, Harriet's heart sank. It wasn't because of the rows of back-to-back houses, the towering, smoking chimneys and the all-too-apparent poverty of the neighbourhood; none of that bothered Harriet in the slightest. Anthony had prepared her well and she knew what to expect. What troubled her was the eerie Victorian tombstones peering at them over the Priory wall out of the darkening mist, and the knowledge that Father James had met his ghastly end just yards from the Priory front door, where the cab now paused. She looked over the graves, down towards the river, and cold shivers ran down her spine.

The Priory door flew open. Sister Evangelista, who filled the brightly lit doorway with Annie O'Prey hovering behind her, sang out in greeting, 'Ah, thanks be to God, ye have arrived at last. Come away in, now.'

After an exchange of introductions and greetings, there was a bustle in the driveway while they tripped over one another, each trying to ease the other's burden and carry the largest number of bags indoors.

The cab had long since disappeared.

'I'll be going now, queen, if that's all right,' the cab driver had said to Harriet, taking the money from her gloved hand. 'It's a bit creepy round here, like, since the murders and I'm a bit of a wimp. I'm not one of youse Catholics.'

Father Anthony, who had carried a trunk indoors, could be heard struggling up the stairs to a concert of instructions from Sister Evangelista and Annie O'Prey. Harriet stood with the remaining bags, waiting for him to return and take her own trunk, which was too heavy for her to lift.

She looked up at the red-brick building covered in lichen and ivy, at the tall sash windows on the top floor and the even taller chimneys. She counted eight, soot-blackened doubles and she couldn't even see over the other side of the roof. She had yet to set a foot indoors, but her heart was already yearning for their white-rendered, sea-facing, welcoming home close to Dublin.

Harriet shivered. The snow-covered ground had frozen. She could feel the mist penetrating her woollen coat as it drifted over the gravestones and onto the Priory lawn, lying at her feet and rolling out a carpet of welcome, all the way to the front door.

Father Anthony's voice boomed out into the damp air.

'I'm sorry, Sister, I think that maybe 'tis a painting now on the floor as I cannot see round this corner on the stairs.'

Harriet smiled. Anthony had never been very practical, always bookish.

'Whaaa!'

Harriet screamed sharply as, apparently from nowhere, a frozen little hand grabbed her cuff. It was the iciness of the fingers that shocked her as much as the unexpected company.

'Sorry, miss, sorry, shh, please don't scream, me da will kill me if I make a nuisance of meself.'

Little Paddy was standing next to Harriet with Scamp at his side.

'Oh, my Lord, you scared me half witless,' said Harriet.

Laughing out loud at the sight before her, her laughter vanished when she saw how cold the poor boy looked. Into the light stepped another young boy, who was better dressed.

The one who had seized her cuff spoke first.

'We came to say hello, miss. Are you moving in today? My mam says you have come from Dublin to live here and you must be relieved to be safe at last. Is that true?'

Harriet instantly warmed to him. How many youngsters would go out of their way to say hello? she thought to herself. Most children were shy, especially boys.

Little Paddy continued, 'Are ye going to stay for long? They sent a priest already to replace Father James, but he spent just the one night in the Priory. He said the place needed to be burnt down and that it was unholy. Me mammy said he was really just scared.'

Harriet was thoughtful. It occurred to her that the dog looked better fed than Little Paddy, not realizing that her own chicken supper was already in the dog's stomach.

Harriet could hear the clumping of Anthony's feet on the hallway stairs.

'Well, I will be too exhausted to travel back tomorrow, so I will be here for at least two nights, that's for sure, and if I know my brother he won't be leaving until there have been definite improvements.'

'Goodness me, who have you there?' asked Anthony as he stepped out onto the driveway.

Sister Evangelista bustled to his side. 'Heavens above,' she exclaimed. 'You will get yourself frozen standing out here and what are you two doing here?'

Harriet wanted to hear more from the boys, to include them in the conversation, but was amazed to discover that they had vanished. Where they and Scamp had stood only seconds before was now empty space and it was as if they had never been.

Less than an hour later, they were all gathered round the fire in the study, chatting to Sister Evangelista after enjoying Annie O'Prey's shepherd's pie and sponge cake. Harriet sat back in her chair, fighting to keep her eyelids open, and smiled sleepily as the conversation buzzed around her.

'That was a lovely supper, Mrs O'Prey,' Harriet had said. 'I have never had cake as good as that anywhere before in my life.'

Annie O'Prey beamed from ear to ear. She liked Harriet instantly.

When Harriet smiled, Annie knew at once that the four streets were going to be lucky with her. She could feel it in her bones and see it in Harriet's eyes.

As the new father and his sister ate upstairs, Annie cleared away the pans in the basement kitchen, while chatting to her dead friend, Molly, whose bloodstained reflection gazed back at her through the kitchen window from the deep, dark night.

'Well, Molly, I can see as clear as the nose on your face they are just grand. The father and his sister, they is just what we need around here now. Yer man, the father, he is nothing like Father James, nicer altogether, if ye ask me, and his sister, well, she knows a good cake when she tastes it. I could always bake a better sponge than you, Molly, and that's a fact.' Annie turned the tap on full and filled the bowl with fresh water.

'But, you know, there are enough families on the docks could do with a bit of her kindness, that's for sure. I'll just finish this pan, Molly, and I'll make us a cuppa.'

Molly had been Annie's closest friend in life. Annie hadn't told anyone, but she knew that, even in death, nothing had altered.

Upstairs, Sister Evangelista spoke in hushed tones as she related the events that had rocked the congregation and the community to its core. While Annie conversed with Molly in the kitchen, in the study Sister Evangelista recounted the details of Molly's violent death.

Suddenly there was a loud knock on the door. They heard the quiet voice of Annie O'Prey and the louder one of another woman, full of anxiety.

'I had better see who that is, Father,' said Sister Evangelista.

The study door burst open. Harriet was lost for words as Annie O'Prey appeared before her, in an obvious state of distress. For the second time that night, Harriet came face to face with Little Paddy, now standing at his mother's side. Both were in tears as, for the first time in her life, Peggy struggled to speak.

Maura knew she was in hell.

Leaning against the bar of the Anchor, she held the phone out to Kathleen and watched the smile on the other woman's face slowly fade as, on the other end of the line, Rosie told Kathleen the news.

Kitty was dead.

'Kitty is dead, Maura. Kitty is dead.'

With no preamble, Kathleen had said it, just like that. And in just the three seconds it took her to tell Maura that her beautiful, precious and beloved daughter had gone, before Maura's very eyes Kathleen was transformed from the upright, proud and bonny almost sixty-year-old she was to a woman who looked nearer eighty.

Maura heard the screams. She thought they came from Kathleen but then realized they were her own.

'Carol, get out here and help me quickly,' Bill called to his wife and, together, they put their arms round Maura and led her to a chair.

'Sorry for your troubles. Sorry for your troubles. Sorry for your troubles,' Carol and Bill repeated, over and over.

Kathleen pushed a glass of port into Maura' s hand, but it was too late. Maura stumbled and as she hit the sawdust-covered floorboards she kept on going, plummeting all the way down, deep into her own living hell.

Tommy carefully guided a pallet of jute across Huskisson dock and took the ropes, whilst Jerry lit up a quick fag. The light was fading and they were minutes from the klaxon ushering them home.

'Oi, Stanley Matthews, get yer corner quick,' shouted Tommy to Jerry as the pallet swung round.

Jerry ducked and then, with the grace of a leopard, sprang back up to take his rope and helped to ease the pallet down. Holding his thumb up to the crane driver and moving his head from side to side, he frantically blinked away the smoke from the smouldering ciggie that dangled from his bottom lip. There was no man alive who could light up as fast as a docker.

'What's Bill's lad doing, Tommy?' asked Jerry. Throwing Tommy his tobacco tin for him to make a quick roll-up, Jerry unhooked the ropes and the pallet rested safely on the cobbles.

'What d'you mean?' asked Tommy. With a quizzical frown, he let the rope and hook swing back to the crane, then followed Jerry's gaze.

They could see Billy speaking to a policeman in the hut positioned halfway down the dockers' steps. The officer waved Billy on as he raised his helmet and rubbed his brow, scanning the dockside.

''Tis bad news,' said Jerry.

He watched as little Billy clambered over a wall of stacked jute and ran up to men who were working. He was pulling on their jackets and seemed to be asking questions. He was shouting, agitated.

'Aye, 'tis that to be sure. I've never seen that kid run before. I wonder what it can be,' said Tommy thoughtfully.

He took a long drag on his ciggie and lifted his cap to wipe the sweat from his head with his sleeve and, as he did so, he noticed a gang of men point towards them both. Tommy instantly knew not only that little Billy was running towards him, but that he carried the worst news.

Tommy, overcome with a desire to turn and run himself, knew

that he would never forget these last seconds as little Billy covered the ground across the dock. He sensed that nothing would ever be the same again.

'Stop him, would ye, Jer,' said Tommy, a note of desperation in his voice.

With a furrowed brow, Jerry turned to Tommy, but it was too late. Little Billy was within hearing distance and he was shouting as loud as he possibly could. 'Tommy, Tommy, ye have to come to the pub, me da says to tell ye 'tis bad news. Maura needs ye, Tommy, 'tis Kitty, your Kitty, she's dead.'

'Tommy is on his way. Tommy is on his way. Tommy is on his way.'

Since there were no words of comfort that had any meaning or could even begin to make sense, Kathleen and Bill continued to reassure Maura with the promise of Tommy's imminent arrival, in an attempt to penetrate her despair. As though Tommy's presence would alter anything.

Tommy was the last person Maura wanted to see. If Maura had known that there was a choice – either your husband hangs or your daughter lives – Tommy would have hanged.

In the blackest days following the news of Kitty's death, Maura could not look at Tommy without wishing he was dead. She hated him. He had killed the priest and, for that, they had paid the unthinkable price.

Tommy couldn't help Maura. As far as he was concerned, the root of all the evil in their lives was Maura's vanity and her desperation to be better than everyone else they knew.

'Why else would she be so pally with the priest?' he said to Kathleen as she tried to comfort him through his anger. 'I always knew what her game was: she wanted one of our lads in the seminary, to be a priest.

''Twas not good enough, now, that a fucking priest was helping himself to our daughter in me own house. She wanted to send more of our kids their way. All Maura has ever prayed for was a son for a priest and a daughter for a nun.'

Kathleen made soothing noises, but even she was shaken by the rift between Tommy and Maura at a time when they needed each other the most.

Day after day the house filled with people calling to pay their respects.

Maura sat and stared.

Tommy was not allowed time off from the docks, for which Maura was glad.

Night after night, Kathleen tried to help.

'Away to bed, Maura, 'tis late. The kids are all sleeping now, and so must ye.'

Maura did not sleep in a bed for weeks on end. She could not engage in any activity that resembled normality.

Switching off the lights and preparing for bed, slipping in between the sheets: that was normal. Normal was what other people did. People untouched by evil.

Maura spent her nights sitting in the chair next to the range, staring at the fire. In those hours when she was alone, she relived her days with Kitty. The first time she had set eyes on her first-born's face. Kitty's first day at school, her funny sayings, the way her hair smelt when she slipped her arms around her mother's neck for her night-time kiss. Night after night, in the hours before dawn when sleep finally claimed her, Maura dipped in and out of Kitty's fifteen years, comforting herself with recent memories as well as old ones, which she forced out of the darkest corner of her mind. As Maura succumbed to sleep, her last vision was that of Kitty, standing before her in front of the range where she used to dress on winter mornings: dripping wet, cold and crying for her mammy.

Exhausted, Tommy slept on top of the covers, fully clothed. Each time he closed his eyes, he prayed into the darkness, 'Please don't let me wake.'

He regarded his children as a curse and he hated them. They were compelling him to carry on, to provide food for the table and a roof over their heads.

They did that to him, just because they were there. It was the obligation to feed his children which drove him from his bed and down to the docks. Every morning he had to wake and know his Kitty was gone. Without Maura, who was mad somewhere within a living hell, he had to cope alone. He hated his family for forcing him to survive. He hated everyone, even the neighbours who left meals warming on the range for him, because their children were still alive.

Day after day could pass without either Maura or Tommy speaking a single word, either to each other or barely to anyone else. Once Kathleen had been able to persuade Maura to sleep in her own bed, for weeks Maura was hardly able to get up again or put her feet on the floor to face the day. Many mornings, she didn't even try.

She lay in her bed, facing the wall, untouched and unaffected by the needs of her family. She was deaf to the cries of her baby, impervious to the sound of Tommy's voice, oblivious to her own basic need for food or drink.

Those were the days when neighbours let themselves into the house, unasked or uninvited, and did whatever had to be done. They had their own code. If Peggy didn't hear the familiar early-morning noises coming from Maura's kitchen, she knocked on the walls with the mop handle, the jungle drums of the four streets, to inform the others that, today, they were needed. That today was not good. And, without fuss or drama, the women of the four streets took over the running of Maura's house.

They did her washing, mopped her floor and left stews on the range. They baked her bread and cleaned her windows, letting her know they were there. Life still went on and, if she wanted, she could absent herself from it for a while but they would not allow her to leave altogether. She had children to care for. She could heal, in her own time, but she would not be permitted to wither.

With the support of old friends such as Kathleen and Jerry, and new friends like Harriet and Father Anthony, Maura and Tommy slowly surfaced from the deepest well of their own black thoughts. Their daily existence now became one of oppressive, scarcely bearable greyness. And still they did not speak.

It was Harry who eventually broke the spell of their despair.

'Mam, Mammy, Da.'

In the small hours, Angela had turned on the landing light and stood framed in the doorway of Maura and Tommy's bedroom.

Maura didn't reply.

'Mammy, 'tis Harry. His asthma has been really bad since yesterday and now he can't breathe.'

Maura sat bolt upright in bed and strained her ears. She could hear the familiar whistle coming from the boys' room, Harry's distinctive and unique breathing: short in, long out. But it was too short in and too long out.

Maura had been so wrapped up in her own misery that she had been oblivious to the fact that Harry was ill.

She shook Tommy awake and, for the first time in six weeks, they spoke as though there had never been a period of silence between them.

'Tommy, 'tis Harry, quick. It's his asthma, something is wrong.'

The thaw came as they sat outside the children's ward at Alder Hey Hospital, just as the first dawn light was breaking.

Tommy realized his anger had dissipated, to be replaced by concern for Harry. As he carried the two cups of tea the nurse had brought him, his love for his wife flooded back at the sight of her perched on the edge of the wooden bench, looking frail and exhausted, a shadow of the strong woman she had once been.

Maura placed the cup and saucer on the bench next to her. Tommy slipped his arm round her shoulder and pulled her into him. She cried and, for the first time in his adult life, Tommy cried too.

'God, I've missed you,' he whispered into her hair.

'I've missed you too,' she whispered back. 'Please God, let Harry be all right. Tommy, I could not imagine ...'

Her voice trailed off as a doctor came out through the swing doors from the wards and made his way towards them. They could tell, just by looking at him, that he was Irish. It wasn't just his red hair, it was his facial features too. He appeared familiar. At his approach Tommy squinted, trying to place him.

The doctor was smiling.

'Harry is going to be fine, so he is,' he said.

Maura's hand flew to her mouth as she let out a sob stemmed in relief.

'We have been using a new trial drug, Salbutamol. I wish we'd had it all the years your little lad has been poorly.

'A year ago, things could have been very different indeed, given the state of his asthma when he was admitted. He has responded better than we could have hoped for. What's more, you can use it at home. It will make a huge difference to how we manage his asthma in the future. Harry is one of the lucky ones. This drug isn't available everywhere yet.

'I would just say, though, Mr and Mrs Doherty, it isn't good to leave him so long when he has breathing difficulties. It makes life very problematic for us when we can't find a vein that we can insert a needle into, to treat him with the drugs we now have that we know will work. When asthma is as bad as Harry's was, the peripheral veins shut down and, even with the best drugs in the world, if we can't get the drugs into him, treatment becomes impossible.'

The doctor placed his hand over Maura's and gave it a squeeze.

'I know you have had a lot on yer plate, but this little lad needs his mammy and daddy to look out for him. In the meantime, we are going to keep him here for a few days to make sure he is absolutely right before he returns home.'

By now Maura was beyond speech. When he spoke, Tommy's throat was thick with unshed tears.

'How do ye know, doctor,' he asked softly, 'that we have a lot on our plate?'

Neither he nor Maura had said Kitty's name out loud since the day of her funeral.

'My brother is the doctor in Bangornevin and he told me about the accident. Harry asked for his sister Kitty and then became distressed, for a short while. When he said a few things I put two and two together. I hope ye don't mind my mentioning it. He is fine now that he is breathing much more easily.'

'No, we don't mind,' croaked Tommy.

Just at that moment both he and Maura turned as they heard the footsteps of Peggy and Little Paddy, their ever faithful friends and neighbours, heading down the hospital corridor towards them.

The arrival of Father Anthony and Harriet had transformed everything, despite the fact that his first mass had been for little Kitty. It could barely be heard above the sobs of every resident of the four streets. They crammed into the pews and the aisles, with many gathered outside the church. They stood, a sombre gathering, not a dry eye amongst them.

Howard – the detective and now the new fiancé of Miss Alison Devlin, teacher at the four streets convent school – had been the first person at the Dohertys' house, following a phone call from the County Mayo state solicitor after Kitty's drowning. It had been his responsibility to take a witness statement from them on behalf of the police in County Mayo.

Howard met Peggy on the way out of Maura and Tommy's back door.

'What the fecking hell do you want?' Peggy asked, dispensing with even the most basic pleasantry.

Peggy had hardly slept the previous night. How could she? The most unimaginable thing that could happen to any mother had befallen the house next door. Howard, afraid that she might thump him, noticed that her right fist was clenched, ready. It was not unheard of for neighbours like Peggy to risk a prison sentence, in loyal defence of their friends. Howard, having served his probation on the beat in Liverpool and now having been elevated to the CID, knew that such communities took loyalty to an impressive but all too often self-destructive level.

'Ye had better not be sniffing round here, to take Tommy Doherty to the station on one of yer trumped-up charges, 'cause if ye do, ye have me to answer to. The man is beside himself with grief. Have ye no fecking respect?'

'I do, Peggy,' Howard replied, softly and meekly. 'I am here to offer my respects and to have a form signed, so that Kitty can be brought back to Liverpool to be buried. I am not here to arrest Tommy. The investigation into the priest's murder is over and we all know Tommy had nothing to do with it.'

'Aye, well, just ye fecking remember that,' Peggy had said grudgingly, 'and, if ye want anything else, come to one of us, don't go barging in there. We will be looking after them, for as long as it takes. Maura is on the floor with grief and Tommy with her. We will make them right again, but we can't do it with the likes of ye sniffing around here, causing worry, so we can't.'

And with that, in her damp, rancid slippers she had shuffled across the cobbles, out of the back gate and into her own home next door.

As he opened the back door to Maura and Tommy's, Howard was greeted by Sheila, who was stirring a huge pan of broth on the stove, and Jerry, who was squatting in front of the fire, carefully stoking the coke. He had been more welcoming altogether.

'Hello, Howard,' Jerry whispered. 'Everyone is lying down with their own thoughts. Can I help?'

As Howard had looked at Jerry, he had been consumed with guilt that he and Simon had ever suspected Jerry of being involved in the priest's murder. Here he was, rushing straight to his neighbour's side in a time of crisis. Howard knew that his own Alison had baked a plate of biscuits and dropped them over earlier. Howard was in awe of how much people cared for everyone else here. How could he and Simon have ever thought the murderer had been so close to home?

The tragedy that had greeted her on her arrival at the four streets enabled Harriet to play her part. She spent a great deal of time with Nellie, as a result of Nana Kathleen voicing her need for help.

'I am at the end of me wits, with nowhere to go, what with Nellie and Maura and Tommy. Everyone is in shock, but I have never known our chatterbox to be so quiet. She's scaring me, so she is, and I have to admit, I'm at a loss what to do.'

Harriet had left the Priory at that moment and accompanied Kathleen home. Whilst Kathleen organized others to help care for the Dohertys, Harriet spent hour after hour sitting with Nellie, holding her hand and slowly trying to coax her to speak.

Nellie barely uttered a word for almost a month and, when she did, it was as an accompaniment to a flood of wretched tears.

'I have never heard nor witnessed such sad tears, Anthony. They sounded as though they were pouring straight from her heart,' Harriet had confided in her brother over supper that evening.

'Maybe that is it now. Maybe she will begin to accept what has happened and improve,' Anthony had replied.

He himself was weary from struggling with Maura and Tommy. He felt that, along with losing their daughter, they were losing their faith, somehow blaming the Church. It was as though they didn't altogether trust him.

'How did she drown, Anthony, do we know? It seems so tragic. One of the women told me that her cousin lives in Bangornevin and that the water where Kitty was found was less than a couple of feet deep. Can that be so?'

'Well, sure enough, if it had happened in England, it would be suspicious, certainly, but it wasn't even in Bangornevin, Harriet. It was on a remote farm just outside, in a place called Ballymara, with no one and nothing around for miles. She must have slipped and knocked her head on a rock. 'Tis a stony river and a famous one for the salmon, so I'm told.'

Jerry and Kathleen would be forever grateful to Harriet.

They were well aware that it was only because of the time that she had spent sitting at Nellie's bedside, soothing, reading and even singing to her, that Nellie had surfaced from her own deep grief.

On one of the rare nights when Kathleen had allowed herself to break down, she had cried to Jerry, 'If wasn't for Harriet, I think we would have lost our Nellie with the grief as well as Kitty. I have never known the like, a child not wanting to eat or speak. I was out of me depth, Jerry, we both were.'

It was only when Nellie had recovered that Kathleen allowed herself to grieve. Once she knew everyone else was out of the woods, in the privacy of her own home, beside her own fireside, when Jerry and Nellie were asleep, she allowed her tears to flow.

Little Paddy and Scamp did all they could. Paddy would step silently into the Dohertys' kitchen each morning, whilst Scamp waited patiently by the back door, to ask both sets of twins the same question every time.

'You all right, lads? D'you wanna game?'

Each time they said yes and the boys slipped out, to escape the gloom within. Too guilty to leave the house on their own, they jumped at the chance when Little Paddy called and offered.

For Harry, his asthma made running difficult and football impossible. Often he didn't play but just sat on the stone at the edge of the green, watching them all and waiting. He sometimes cried as he sat there, for his Kitty. Although by day, the mood of the house had improved, by night, everyone cried their own tears, under the cover of darkness.

## Chapter Five

The winter had passed and it was the first sunny day of the year when Daisy walked up to the large greenhouse with her basket and an order from Maggie for Frank.

'Morning, Joan,' shouted Frank, giving Daisy a wink.

'That girl tells me she is simple,' Maggie had said to Frank on Daisy's second day. 'She is not simple. Daisy has just never had anyone talking to her for any length of time and she's been frightened out of her wits by the priest she worked for. She speaks funny, mind, but 'tis her tongue not being exercised enough, nothing else. I tell you, one week of working with me in that kitchen and she will be talking as well as I do. No one will be calling her simple then.'

'What's she doing here? Have you found out why she arrived in the early hours on Christmas morning?' Frank enquired.

'I'm trying, Frank, but it's hard. I can't help the others if I am caught out so I have to be careful. Here, one of the girls sneaked me a letter. Can ye take it to the post office?'

Frank nodded and put the letter into his large coat pocket. Being caught would mean him and Maggie being turfed out on their ears. They were too old for that to happen a second time, but it never stopped him helping the girls when he could.

Maggie and Frank grinned at each other.

'Come here,' said Frank and, removing the short distance between himself and Maggie, he threw his arms round her.

Maggie was uncomfortable with affection of any description, preferring to display a tough and practical exterior. A front belied by her acts of kindness and the degree of danger she frequently placed herself and Frank in, by helping the girls in the mother and baby home.

'Ger off, you fat lump,' she exclaimed as she pushed Frank away, but he took no offence.

Frank knew his wife's capacity to love. He had seen her face as she held their baby. That was when Maggie had been soft, on the days she had walked out to the fields, carrying his lunch in one hand and holding their son on her hip with the other. That Maggie had never pushed him away. That Maggie had laughed when he threw his arms round his wife and baby son. If he closed his eyes for long enough, he could see her back as they walked away from him in the sunlight, his child, resting on his mother's shoulder, smiling at his da and his small hand waving goodbye.

'Maggie has sent me for greens, Frank,' said Daisy.

'Has she, now? Well, let's grab some of these, then, shall we?'

Daisy followed Frank, whom she liked and trusted, into the greenhouse.

It had taken Daisy her customary while, but she had eventually opened up to Maggie and Frank. Each day, Maggie extracted a little bit more of Daisy's extraordinary history.

'How is it up at the kitchen today then? Is Maggie's temper holding up?' Frank said.

Daisy laughed. 'Yes, it is. She gave one of the novices a right scolding. I thought the girl was about to faint with indignation, but Maggie doesn't care.'

'Aye, that's because she knows they would fall apart if she left. They don't want to be on the wrong side of Maggie or they would all starve, so they would, but I wouldn't dare push it, mind. Me and my Maggie, we don't have too many choices now. Are ye coming down to us for supper?'

'I am, Frank. I have something to ask you and Maggie this evening but I would like to ask you together, if that's all right with you?'

'Of course it is, Daisy,' said Frank.

'Shh,' she said as she looked around. 'You know the trouble we get into for using our real names.'

Daisy wasn't really angry with Frank, and, with a smile, she picked up the wicker basket and headed off back to the kitchen.

That night, as Daisy sat in Maggie and Frank's kitchen, she told them her tale in detail.

She left nothing out. She spoke about her abuse at the hands of the priest and the bishop. It had been the very same bishop who had appeared in Maggie's kitchen and had spoken to her on Christmas night.

'He told me that I was here for my protection. That I should never tell anyone anything at all about my life in Liverpool. He said that there were some very bad people around and I could suffer the same end as my friend, Molly Barrett, who was murdered in her own outhouse. He really scared me when he said that. Molly was the only person who knew I had seen the murder. I know that on the night she was killed, she had told the policeman about it that very same day. It was the same policeman as brought me here to the convent.'

Maggie and Frank both made a sharp intake of breath. They interrupted only to whisper the words, 'Yeah, yeah, go on now,' as encouragement for her to continue.

She told them about Miss Devlin, and how Daisy's family in Dublin had made contact, wanting her home for Christmas. She told them about Sister Evangelista and the school and all the residents on the four streets. As Maggie poured mug after mug of tea, worried that Daisy might stop, she told them about Maura and Tommy Doherty, and about little Kitty, who, she was sure, the priest had made pregnant, which was why he had been murdered by Kitty's da, Tommy.

And the last thing of all that she told them was about the goings-on at the Priory. How strange men came with pictures of children and how she and Sister Evangelista had found hundreds of black-and-white pictures in the dead priest's desk drawer.

'All the children in the four streets are poor and the priest is very powerful. If I or anyone else told what happened to us, no one would believe us.'

'Aye, well, 'tis no different in Ireland,' said Maggie. 'Make such an accusation in any of the villages around here and in no time at all ye would find yerself living as a penitent in a place like this, that's for sure.'

'It is all so wrong,' said Frank, 'and I don't mind saying that I don't understand all that much of it, but I do know this: you have to go back to Liverpool, Daisy, and see justice done. You have to take all of this to the Gardai.'

'How can I?' asked Daisy. 'The bishop knows what I have seen at the Priory and what he has done to me himself. That is why he has me prisoner here. I am trapped.'

'He was terrified of you telling your brother anything, Daisy. That's why you were as good as kidnapped by that policeman, who is obviously in cahoots now with the bishop, wouldn't ye say so, Frank?' said Maggie.

She had no trouble at all in picking up the various threads of life in a city she had never visited and, having never left the countryside, could barely imagine.

'You were sent here to be hidden and to be hushed up,' said Maggie. 'Do ye have the address of your family in Dublin?'

'No, I don't. Miss Devlin arranged everything. They would have been waiting for me at the port, but the policeman took me off the ferry. We passed through what looked like a kitchen and I saw him hand a man who worked in there a ten-shilling note and then we came out of a door and down a ramp different from the one I saw everyone else leaving by. I never even saw my family. They must be worried about me and Miss Devlin will have been out of her mind.'

'Why did ye not say something to someone as he was leading ye off the boat?' asked Frank.

'I was scared and at first I thought he was taking me to my brother's house. I had no idea.'

'Don't ask such stupid questions, Frank,' Maggie remonstrated with him. 'Do ye remember what she was like when she first arrived here? As nervous as a kitten she was. Look at her now, talks fifty to the dozen, she does. 'Tis me that can't get a word in edgeways these days. All this girl needed was for her mouth and brain to be worked a bit.

'Simple, my arse. I'll give ye this, Daisy, the butcher would find ye an easy one to cheat. Yer counting is not strong and yer trust in others is blind, but ye can hold yer own in any conversation and I'll take the credit for that. Frank, pop a drop of poteen in these mugs. Enough of the tea now, we need to think of a plan. Daisy, ye is welcome on that mattress, but ye can't sleep there forever, or in that storeroom the nuns have put you in. They keep plenty prisoner up in that place, but they can't keep ye. We have to find a way to get ye back to Liverpool. I'll tell ye this, it'll be a long time before Sister Theresa notices, so little attention do they pay ye.'

Frank and Maggie's chance to smuggle Daisy away arrived more quickly than any of them had expected. Sister Theresa had taken the decision to compete with the Abbey and convert the old stables into a laundry.

She was swayed by the opulence of the Abbey, which she and her nuns had cause to visit from time to time, and by the luxury of Sister Assumpta's office. She took little convincing that a laundry was what they were missing.

The carpets and silver picture frames ate at her heart each time she visited. Her envy was not unnoticed by Sister Assumpta.

'Did you see the way they were looking at my ornaments?' she asked Sister Celia, following Sister Theresa's latest visit to the Abbey with Sister Virginia in tow to spy.

'Were they?' asked Sister Celia.

'Were they? Of course they were. Are your eyes afflicted all of a sudden? Rome has given them next to nothing. They have a lot of catching up to do. It'll be a few years before they can afford a Persian runner or a set of French doors in the study.'

Sister Theresa, unhappy with running the most recent and the poorest convent in the area, had very different ideas. Rome had indeed been mean.

'There is machinery now that can turn those girls into a far more productive operation altogether,' she had said to Sister Virginia on their return journey from the Abbey. 'We have enough money saved to install washers and dryers. That means the girls we take on can turn round twice as much as the Abbey, at the very least, I would say. The hospital may decide to transfer its custom to us on this side of Galway.'

'Won't the girls become soft altogether if we use machines?' sniffed Sister Virginia, who was driving the new Mini the nuns had purchased from Donegal only the week before.

'No, not at all. They will still have to do all the work, the lifting, the sorting and the ironing. The machines mean that we won't lose a day's drying when it's wet and we can put more dirty laundry through and faster too. The longer we keep that bit of information from Sister Assumpta, the better. They have used their own money to buy fancy ornaments and carpets. We will use ours to buy washing machines and, once we do, we will be secure forever. It's all about making sure there are enough funds to keep the convent running, come what may, Sister Virginia. I think Sister Assumpta forgot that, somewhere along the way back there.'

Within a month, Frank had opened the gates to the delivery of industrial-sized washing machines and dryers.

A week later, he welcomed the fitters who would convert the barn into a laundry. Although Irish by birth, they were based in Liverpool, travelling back to Liverpool every Friday night and returning on Monday morning. It occurred to Frank that this arrangement could be quite handy. He made a point of chatting to them as they unloaded their vans. It took him only a couple of days to strike up a friendship with the works foreman, Jack, who knew the location of Daisy's former home, the four streets.

Thursday was Frank's regular night for a jar at the local pub, a habit of which Sister Theresa was blissfully unaware. When he found out that the workmen were boarding there, Frank arranged to meet Jack in the bar after work. A week after they had first arrived, Frank strolled down to the pub to meet Jack. He needed to take a measure of the man's trustworthiness.

As he walked into the bar, Frank greeted the foreman, who was more than pleased to have someone fund his night of Guinness.

It took six pints before Jack agreed to smuggle Daisy out of the convent. It took a further two to convince him to deliver her personally to the police station and to stay with her until he could be sure she was safe. Daisy had provided Frank with enough details for him to work out the address of the Priory and of Nelson Street.

The decision was taken not to smuggle Daisy out until the day the job finished and the workmen were leaving for the last time. That way, it would look as though one of the workmen was to blame. Frank and Maggie would be free from suspicion.

As the day approached, they became more and more twitchy and Frank worried that Jack would change his mind.

'Jesus, we have helped many in the mother and baby home to hear word from a relative or snuck out a letter. I've even smuggled food into the dormitory for the girls, all of which would see me strung up, but I've never done anything as bold as this,' said Maggie to Frank.

The thought of what they were about to do almost made Maggie shake with fear, but she would not let this deter her.

The night before they were due to put their plan into action, there was a gentle ring on the gate bell.

'Jesus, who can that be?' Maggie almost jumped out of her skin.

Frank had already opened the door from which he could see the gate.

''Tis the foreman, Jack.'

A minute later, Jack was standing in front of the fire with a mug of Frank's poteen in his hand. He looked on edge.

'I'm not sure we should be doing this, Frank,' he said. 'If we are caught, the Reverend Mother may stop our money and, sure, 'tis serious money. I have wages to meet for the week's work on Friday night. I cannot risk the men not taking their pay packets back to their own families.'

Maggie began to speak, but Frank held up his hand and stopped her. Instead, Maggie placed her arm round Daisy's shoulders. She looked crestfallen.

'I understand that now, Jack, sure I do, but how about this? We carry on with the plan and, if we are caught, Maggie and I will own up. We will say that it was us that smuggled Daisy into the back of yer van and ye had no idea whatsoever what was happening.'

Maggie and Daisy both gasped. Maggie was more aware of the consequences.

They would be turfed out of their home there and then. No amount of Maggie's prowess in the kitchen would save their necks from that. Within an hour, Frank and Maggie, together with what belongings they had, would be on the wrong side of the convent gate.

'Well, I'm sorry to say as I know the risk to you now, but that would put a different complexion on things. As long as I could have your word, Frank?'

'As true as God, ye have my word,' said Frank, holding out his hand to shake Jack's.

'Did I do the right thing, Maggie, love?' Frank whispered to Maggie later that night as they lay in bed while Daisy slept on the lodge floor in front of the fire.

'Ye did what yer heart told ye to do, Frank, and that can never be wrong. I'm sure someone or something was guiding yer words as there was no time to think.'

'There will be plenty of time to think tomorrow, if we are caught,' whispered Frank.

Maggie stroked Frank's arm and silently said her own prayer that they could safely survive the next twenty-four hours.

They had helped lots of the girls, but none had presented as great a risk as this.

The following morning, the tension they all felt was palpable.

'What clothes will I wear, Maggie?' said Daisy, who had worn nothing other than her calico since the day she had arrived.

The girls weren't allowed bras and Maggie always thought there was something particularly degrading in the way the nuns dressed them.

'Leave that to me,' said Maggie. 'I know where the linen room is and where the clothes the girls turn up in when they first arrive are stored. I will fetch them later, after breakfast. If I don't find yours, I'll find something better than that outfit ye is wearing now.'

Daisy smiled. The thought of not having to wear the disgusting uniform filled her with pleasure.

'Could ye look for my hat, Maggie? I don't really care about the clothes, but I would really like my new hat back.'

The hat was the only present Daisy had received in her entire life. It had happened on such a special night. She grinned stupidly to herself when she thought of that moment, seeing the mothers and children in the school hall, clapping as Miss Devlin had placed the hat on her head.

The final day of the fitting out of the laundry was one of celebration.

The bishop had arrived and was to bless the brand-new facility with a mass.

From nowhere and with no warning to Frank and Maggie, there had been a fresh intake of girls, with bleakness and sadness in their eyes. At the same time that the laundry was fitted, an attic had been converted into a dormitory.

When Frank saw the Reverend Mother inspecting the gardens, he had the audacity to ask her where the girls had come from.

'Frank.' Sister Theresa talked down to him, her expression disdainful. 'We are here, at the behest of the Irish authorities and the Vatican, to become the guardians of local morals. Where girls do not behave as they should, they are sent to me by the local priest, or the council, and they will live here. They are not girls who abide by the word of the Lord our God, Frank, they are penitents. Sent here to work, in order to seek salvation and to atone for their sinful lives. These girls will work in the new, mechanized, very latest, up-to-the-minute laundry. There is no other like it in all of Ireland, and with the sheets each girl washes, she will be filled with the knowledge that she is rinsing away the stains of sin from her life.'

'Aye, Sister,' said Frank, looking as though he fully understood and agreed with everything she said.

He had once asked one of the girls what had brought her to the convent's door. She told him she had been sent from the convent orphanage in Dublin, where she had been left by her mother when she was barely twelve, to prevent her father from coveting her. The lust she had incited in her father had made her a sinner in the eyes of her mother.

'There is nothing to choose now between ourselves and the Abbey,' said Sister Theresa to Frank, changing the subject. 'In fact, there will be many institutions preferring to use our services. We have dryers. They don't have those in the Abbey now, do they? Our laundry will be far more productive.'

'Yes, Reverend Mother,' Frank replied, 'superior altogether, I would say.'

He had no idea what they did and didn't have in the Abbey, and he cared even less.

The workmen were invited to the mass to bless the sinks and the dryers. Jack, the foreman, said they had better stay, even though the men were kicking off, all hoping to be back in Liverpool for a Friday night in the pubs, which they now saw slipping away.

Jack had also agreed to keep his promise to stop at the lodge to collect Daisy. He would hover on the outer side of the gate while Frank and Maggie bundled her into the back of his van.

When the time came, Daisy stood inside the lodge door with Frank and Maggie.

It had been difficult for Maggie to run back to the lodge, which was half a mile from the convent, since Sister Theresa had wanted to put on a special tea, to bless the laundry.

Local dignitaries had been invited, and the Reverend Mother and the nuns from the Abbey had been invited too, to admire the new equipment.

It was now their turn to be envious.

Frank watched from inside the lodge as the workmen's vans made their way down the drive.

He saw the brake lights of the first van as it slowed down to pass through the wrought-iron gate.

'Jesus, Holy Mother, where the feck is Jack?'

Frank opened the front door to look the other way down the drive. He saw Jack's van turn out of the parking area at the front of the convent at the same time as Sister Assumpta and Sister Celia slipped into their own car to return to the Abbey.

'I cannot wait to be out of here,' said Sister Assumpta to Sister Celia as she placed her key in the ignition. 'I think the bishop needs to provide a few more lessons in the scriptures down here. Are they not aware that greed is a sin? I have no idea why the Holy Father thought there was a need for another convent around here. God knows, 'tis we who take in sin in abundance and who work wonders, converting these girls into something far more holy altogether.

''Tis we who suffer and now the Holy Father rewards Sister

Theresa with the laundry equipment. They have the home and the orphanage and the retreat. Do they not have enough?'

Whilst Sister Assumpta ranted, Sister Celia listened. And then she ranted some more.

'Why is that van stopping at the gate? And that's another thing: this convent employs staff. We do all our own work ourselves. We have never employed gardeners or cooks or kitchen maids. Seems to me as though they are all a little too high and mighty around here, so they are.'

Their car pulled up behind the van, which had stopped at the gate.

The van driver put his arm out of the window and waved Sister Celia to overtake him.

'Sorry, Sister,' he shouted out of the window as she drove past. 'Something wrong with the engine now, sorry, Sister.'

Sister Celia raised her hand in acknowledgment and slowly moved round the stationary van.

She turned down the road and, as she did so, in her rear-view mirror she noticed a woman leave the lodge house and then quickly step back inside.

But Sister Celia's thoughts were elsewhere.

'Do you know,' she said to Sister Assumpta, 'I would love the recipe for those coconut golf balls. Now, where in Galway would sell desiccated coconut? Would we have the time to call in?'

Daisy was halfway out of the lodge doorway when Maggie pulled her back inside.

'Not yet,' she hissed. 'They slowed right down, once they were on the road, and all nuns have eyes in the back of their heads. I don't trust them not to see.'

Daisy threw her arms round Maggie, her eyes full of tears.

'Maggie, will I ever see you and Frank again? I can't bear it if I don't.'

'Aye, Daisy, ye will. I don't know where or when but I do know this, things are changing. I can feel it. This business of locking away for their entire lives girls who have done no wrong, it cannot carry on. The world is moving on and Ireland will be called to account for its sins one day. The biggest of them all will be this, as God is my judge. I know I'm right. God willing, we will meet again, soon enough.'

Daisy sobbed, scared. Caught up in the excitement of the adventure, she had been anticipating this moment with impatience. Now that it was here, she was loath to leave the safety, the company and the comfort provided by Maggie and Frank.

Frank was on the drive, talking though the open window to Jack.

'I've cleared a space, in amongst the tools in the back, Frank, and put some rags on the floor. 'Twas a bit dirty, like, but is all right now,' said Jack.

'Bless you,' Frank replied. 'There will be a place in heaven waiting for you, Jack.'

'Aye, well, I hope so.' Jack laughed. 'That was a close call,' he said, nodding towards the nuns' car.

'Don't leave her until ye knows the police are listening to her, will ye now, and would ye drop me a line to let me know all was well? There's a good man.'

'I will write ye a line on Sunday after mass and before the pub, and post it on the Monday. But, ye and yer missus, have no fear now, I will do all ye have asked.'

Frank looked round to see where Maggie and Daisy were. Looking up at the house, he caught sight of the bishop opening the door of his own car.

'Maggie,' he hissed. 'Get a move on.'

In a second, Daisy was by his side, pulling at his sleeve. .

'Go on now, in the back,' he croaked. 'Maggie, sort her.'

Frank pushed Daisy gently towards Maggie as she began to break down. He bent again to Jack's window.

'Don't let her come back. She will be upset but, sure, she will come to her senses quick enough. And don't stop for the bishop. He will be on yer tail now all the way to Dublin, unless ye can shake him off.'

Frank and Jack heard Maggie slam the rear doors of the van.

Frank looked up and she winked. He banged the palm of his hand twice on the van roof and, within seconds, the van, with Daisy safely stowed in the back, moved away down the road.

Ten seconds later, they raised their hand in farewell to the speeding bishop.

Frank put his arm round Maggie's shoulders and, for the first time in twenty-four hours, they both heaved a sigh of relief.

Frank noticed the tears in Maggie's eyes. 'Come on now, away inside.'

'Do you know, Frank, I reckon we could do that again one day if we needed to. We should try and help these girls more.'

'Let's hope so, love,' said Frank. 'Let's hope so.'

## Chapter Six

Sean shuffled forward on the back seat of Henry's newly imported red Bentley so as to narrow the distance between himself and his sister, Mary. She had shrunk so far down into the passenger seat, it was as though Sean and Henry were the only two people travelling in the car. Sean linked his fingers tightly together, his knuckles shining white through his now all-American tan, while his thumbs rolled over and over. The Bentley was an unusual sight on the streets of Chicago. Henry could have had any American-made car he chose, but that was too easy and did not confer the one-upmanship over the British which he subconsciously sought.

Sean had no idea what to do or say and so, his voice laden with concern, he said the obvious. Being a father himself, he could sympathize to some extent with the pain felt now by his sister and her husband.

He gently laid a hand on Mary's shoulder and said, 'Come on now, Mary, don't cry.'

'I'm not, Sean, I'm not crying. I'm fine, really I am,' his sister responded brightly, as she lied through her hankie. 'I'm just being silly, aren't I, Henry?' She looked sideways to her husband for support as she laid her hand on top of Sean's with a reassuring pat.

Henry didn't reply. His eyes were fixed straight on the road ahead, his facial muscles unyielding and set. The only visible movement was a vein in the side of his broad red neck, beating wildly. Henry never lied.

Sean looked directly into the rear-view mirror. For a fleeting second, his eyes met with Henry's, who quickly averted his gaze, but it was too late. Sean had noticed. The usual, ever-present twinkle of mischief and happiness in Henry's bright blue eyes had been replaced with a deep, desperate sadness, and Sean had seen it.

Sean leaned back and stared out of the side window. Once again, his hands in his lap, he continued rolling his thumbs. It was a habit he had acquired during his boxing days in Liverpool whilst he sat in the back of the arena, waiting to dive through the ropes and into the ring. It had helped him when he was anxious and his nerves had got the better of him, listening to the roar of the crowd, counting down, chanting, yelling for the blood of the poor bloke in the ring. He would rock gently, back and forth. Over and over his thumbs had rolled.

And now here he was, in the back of his brother-in-law's car, having offered to accompany Henry and his sister to the doctor's office to provide some family support. Here he was in a situation so grave that he had no idea what to say or do. Everyone had known that something was wrong with Mary and Henry's little boy.

Alice, who called herself Sean's wife, even though they weren't married, had mentioned it to him many times.

'There is something wrong with that little Dillon,' she said. 'Look at his face, he's as white as a sheet and he hardly wants his bottle. Mary keeps making excuses, but I've seen enough babies born on the four streets to know something is wrong. He's too slow to put on weight.'

Alice had left her own son, Joseph, behind in Liverpool. She hadn't seen him since the day she and Sean had set sail from Liverpool, to join Mary in America.

Sean had ten daughters by his real and only wife, Brigid, a strict Catholic who would see hell freeze over before she granted Sean a divorce. He had neither seen nor heard from his daughters since the day he had left England, and likely never would until they were adults and could meet him on their own terms, free from their mother's bitter anger.

The concern over his nephew had made him think more about his daughters and the pain in his gut was like nothing he had experienced in the boxing ring. It gnawed at his insides at times, making it impossible for him to eat.

Only yesterday, he had confided in his mother.

'I can't eat that, Mammy,' he had said, when she had placed his breakfast in front of him. They were the only two people in Mary's kitchen, which was as big as the school hall on the four streets, where Sean's daughters sat for assembly each morning.

Mrs McGuire leaned across the dining bar.

'That pain ye feel, the pain in yer gut, that's putting ye off breakfast for the first time in yer entire life, it's called guilt, so it is. Guilt and grief. I suppose I should be glad because, to me, 'tis a sign that at least I reared ye to have a conscience.'

Sean had worried that it must be hard for Alice, having left her own son, to live in a house with a baby boy, especially one as angelic as Dillon, Mary and Henry's little son.

Dillon was everything his parents had prayed for throughout the long barren years. Not a day went by when his parents had missed the four o'clock Angelus mass. Wherever they were, at the end of Henry's working day, they gave thanks to the Lord for the miracle that was Dillon.

Mary's happiness was infectious. She was often to be seen dancing around, holding her son.

'I prayed for a little lad and the angels sent me you,' she would sing as she swung him round and round. He spent his life being kissed and cuddled, and only because Mrs McGuire intervened did he now sleep in his own room, instead of tucked into his mother's arms.

The all-Irish team, of Henry and his two brothers, ran a large and successful construction company. They had finally persuaded Sean to take up his rightful place as a member of the family firm, making all four of them wealthy.

Sean had taken the plunge only six months ago. The delay had been a matter of frustration to everyone, Sean having been held back by his wife Brigid, who had no intention of emigrating to America. Always pregnant with another child, she had clung to Liverpool, using guilt and family to hold Sean back for too long. But then Sean had fallen in love with Jerry's wife, Alice, and she, just like Sean, wanted to seize with both hands every opportunity their new country had to offer.

Proud and strong, Henry had arrived in Chicago with his beautiful wife Mary fifteen years earlier. The only luggage he had brought with him that was of any use was his canvas bag of tools and the telephone number of someone in the city who was 'taking on' men. Today, Henry employed the sons and grandsons of the man who had given him his first day's work in the land of the free.

The strength of the Moynihan business was that it was built on the labour of people from back home in Ireland. Henry was a generous employer and looked after his workforce. Henry's two brothers regarded everyone who worked for them as extended family, and those who had been with Henry since the early days repaid his kindness with toil and respect.

Sean was about to be made a partner in the business. He found it hard to wind his head round that one, but Alice managed to do it for him. Henry had deposited fifty thousand US dollars in a bank account, as Sean's first down payment, telling him to find a plot of land where they could build a house of their own.

'Ye can't be living with me and Mary forever,' Henry had said. 'It takes a while, but ye and Alice, ye know what's what now. And I'll tell ye this, divorce, 'tis not the big deal over here that it is back home.

Time you got that sorted and ye and Alice began having children of yer own. We each need a little lad to leave this business to.'

Alice had recoiled in horror. As soon as she and Sean were alone, she tackled him.

'Sean, we have enough children between us. Henry doesn't expect us to have any more, does he?'

'Well, sure he does and I don't think it's such a bad idea. Brigid could produce only girls. Ye already have a little lad so we know ye can do it. 'Twould be grand to be able to hand on what Henry has built up, and which I will be a part of, to an heir one day.'

'Hand it over to your daughters,' Alice had said with genuine amazement. Sean had thought she was joking.

'A lad would have to be born into a business like this, Alice, to understand how it works. You aren't born knowing how to price up the cost of building a shopping mall. It takes experience.'

'Really?' Alice had retorted. 'Well, seems to me that counts you out then, as the only experience you have is unloading hulls and beating the brains out of men.'

Sean had stared at her in a state of confusion. He and Brigid had never argued, not once in all the years they had been married. With Alice, arguments were coming thick and fast and Sean had no idea what to do.

Moynihan's was a name to be seen all across Chicago. It hung on banners at every new roadside and from every bridge, parking lot or school where construction was taking place.

Mary and Henry lived in a large house, drove fancy cars and could have most things money would buy, but in the years before Dillon had arrived, Mary complained loudly and often.

'This money, the house, everything, it all tastes like a brack loaf I forgot to put the sugar in, with no little ones to share it with.'

They had desperately wanted children, especially a son, to make all the hard work and sacrifice worth it. Now that the prayed-for son had arrived, Henry dreamed about eventually handing over his business, and Mary researched the education they would provide him with. They would give everything they had, heart, soul and dollars, into helping their boy achieve whatever he wanted. In turn he would give to them all the kudos and respectability money could not buy. He would have a university education and letters after his name. Dillon would make the sacrifice of leaving Ireland for America worthwhile. Their own flesh and blood could live the American dream.

It made no difference to Mary and Henry that Dillon was adopted. From the moment they heard that the baby boy they had both dreamt of each and every night was available for just three thousand dollars, they slept hardly a wink until he was safely in Mary's arms.

'Tell me if I become too besotted with our little boy and neglect you, Henry,' Mary had said, when they finally took to their bed.

And she meant it, although both of them knew that becoming besotted was unavoidable, given the gorgeous bundle of joy, which had become their very own. And he had been born an Irish Catholic too.

What was not to love?

'She has that baby on a pedestal and he's only been home for five minutes,' Henry had soon complained to his brother, Eddie, although both knew Henry was only joking. 'She leaps out of bed for his feed at two o'clock in the morning and everyone has told her not to. She's a rich woman now and living in a wealthy country. We have maids coming out of our ears, she could have as many nurses as she wants, but no, they can wash and iron my clothes, so they can, but they can't touch our little lad.'

'All women are the same with their first,' Eddie had replied. 'It'll wear off in a few weeks and, sure, definitely by the second, I would say so.'

Henry had roared with laughter. They had waited fifteen years for Dillon. By the time the second child came along, he would be old enough to be a grandfather.

Henry hadn't realized quite how upside down his world would become in the space of a week. To cap it all, he heard the Moynihan business had been awarded a contract worth millions of dollars.

'Merciful God,' he had said to Mary, 'someone is looking down on us all right. We have enough money to do anything we want and a baby on the way, Mary. How much better can life be, eh?'

'I want my mother to live with us, Henry,' Mary had replied.

Even Henry couldn't have predicted that so much good could turn so sour so fast. Henry felt his elation deflate faster than a pierced balloon.

'I want to share our first boy with her. Every woman needs her mother by her side, with a new baby. After all, she's had plenty of her own and helped Brigid raise all of hers in Liverpool.'

Henry didn't argue. He and his Mary were so blessed and happy, nothing could cloud their horizon for long, not even Mrs McGuire arriving to live with them in Chicago.

'When ye speak to yer mammy, tell her to bring Sean out here. Now that I have that contract, Jesus, we need family, people we can trust, more than ever before. Will ye do that, Mary?'

Neither Mary nor Henry were prepared for Mrs McGuire's telephone call with news from Liverpool.

It would appear there was something that could cloud any horizon, if only for a little while.

When Sean and Alice had run away, they had decided to do so by boat, rather than by aeroplane, both realizing the furore they left behind would need time to settle down before they faced Mary and Sean. They also wanted to have days and nights alone together, something they had never known, to spend time getting to know each other better and to become a real couple, before they landed and began their new life.

They had no idea whether anyone would even meet them when they disembarked, whether Mary would ever forgive Sean for committing such a despicable sin. Walking out on his children and his wife for another woman and a fresh start was a scandal few families could tolerate. Mary and Henry might decide they would not associate with nor acknowledge Sean and Alice. The thought haunted Sean during every day of the crossing.

As they stood on deck while the boat sailed into New York, watching the bands playing and the streamers flying, the first person Sean laid eyes on at the customs hall was his sister Mary with Dillon in her arms. Standing beside them were Henry and their mother, Mrs McGuire.

'My sister has a baby?' said Sean.

'Oh no, your mother has arrived here before us,' said Alice, with more than a hint of despair in her voice. 'She must have flown.'

This was the last thing Alice would have wished for and Mrs McGuire was the very last person she would have wanted to greet her in New York.

Sean was equally amazed. As they slowly walked towards his waiting family, his mother chose to dispense with welcoming pleasantries.

'Well, ye is a dark horse all right, Alice, I will give ye that. Never a clue did I have and that's for sure.'

'Mammy,' said Sean, pleading.

'Never you Mammy me, Sean. Ye could have handled things better than ye did. Whilst ye have been cruising, leading the life of Riley, I had to help Brigid and the girls. I was there when she opened yer cowardly letter. Can ye imagine what that was like for me? It was the worst night of me life and I hadn't even a notion of what ye were up to. Ye lied to me and yer kids and everyone else, running off in the night like a pair of thieves, leaving yer children to face the worst Christmas of their lives. The shame was awful, awful, it was. Can ye imagine what Brigid, yer poor wife, went through? And without so much as a word of warning, not a fecking notion did I have.'

Mrs McGuire lifted her handbag and smacked a stunned Sean, straight across the side of his face, and then, just for good measure, smacked him again across the other side.

'An' that one was from Brigid,' she yelled before she stormed away.

Sean stood with his head down, as an equally stunned and shaking Alice linked her arm through his.

'We are here now, Mrs McGuire.' Alice sounded bolder than she felt, as she spoke to the retreating back of Sean's mother. 'And even if Mary and Henry don't want us, this is where Sean and I are making our life.'

Mrs McGuire turned round and Alice looked directly at her. She challenged the older woman using only her eyes as weapons. They were as cold as steel and just as hard.

Mrs McGuire was not so easily beaten. Retracing her steps, she marched back to Alice.

'Well, be that as it may, Alice, it is just as well, for there will be no welcome anywhere for either of ye two in Liverpool. Big as ye are, Sean, Brigid's brothers would kill ye, if they so much as had a sniff of where it is ye are at. There will be no welcome in Ireland for ye, Sean. Ye have both burnt yer boats and that's for sure. Ye have no option but to settle here, Alice. Ye are here and here forever, I would say, so here's praying to God ye like it because ye have nowhere else to go. And, thanks to the sneaky, lying behaviour of ye both, and the shame ye have put me through, neither have I. I can't even hold me own head up in Liverpool now without the gossip following me wherever I go.'

Her voice trembled on the last words. Mrs McGuire loved her granddaughters. She loved her family. Nothing meant more to her than her pride. What Sean had done had put her at the centre of one of the biggest scandals to ever hit the four streets and would be a subject for discussion every time the women piled into Maura Doherty's kitchen.

Mary decided it was time to break the tension.

'You are welcome to live with us and become part of the business, Sean. Sure, the house is big enough. We have twelve bedrooms and will struggle to find you. We need you, so we do, sure, we always have. God knows what has taken you so long. But, Alice, in America you must be Mrs McGuire. I don't want anyone thinking you are both living in sin. I'll not have that shame laid at my door. And as Brigid will never in a million years grant you a divorce, Sean, you have no option, so you don't. Living your life as a lie, 'tis all you have left.'

Nothing else was said as the sombre party made its way towards Mary and Henry's car where a driver was waiting.

For almost six months Mrs McGuire did not speak another word to Alice. All conversation was channelled directly through her daughter or Sean himself. According to Mrs McGuire, it was entirely Alice's fault that Sean had left his family. Her son had never, and could never, do any wrong, as she explained to her daughter.

'Brigid was only waiting for the littlest one to grow up and that is a fact. She was most enthusiastic about bringing them all to America, Mary, that's no word of a lie. That Alice must be a wicked one altogether. I swear to God, no one other than Peggy and Paddy's lad had a notion of what was going on and he knew only because he caught them almost at it and now, sure, I imagine everyone in Liverpool knows every detail. Alice turned his head, she did. She must have bought a mighty potion from somewhere because it just isn't like our Sean, he would never do such a thing as abandon his own family. She cast a spell, I would say. Ye have invited a witch to live under yer own roof, Mary.'

'Aye, well, Mammy, what is done is done. Sean is not a mean man. Now that he is here and part of the business, Brigid and the children, they will want for nothing.'

Mrs Mcguire took comfort from this knowledge. She knew that, back in Liverpool, new possessions would ensure that Brigid rose above the shame. She could do this easily with a new twin tub, an Electrolux hoover and a nice, vinyl, three-piece suite with cushions upholstered in autumnal colours. No one else on the four streets had anything as grand.

Mrs McGuire had made it her business to ensure the money was sent to Brigid to compensate for the behaviour of her wayward son. There would be no secondhand communion shoes for any of the McGuire girls on Nelson Street. They might not have a daddy at home, but, God knew, they would wear the prettiest veils.

The passage to America had been fun for Alice and Sean. The bars, the dancing, the food. Their first night in the cabin had been one of hedonistic indulgence as they made love half a dozen times. Not until they were standing on the deck to watch the famous Liverpool portside buildings, the Three Graces, disappear into the distance, had either spoken of the families they had left behind.

Alice had loved every minute of the crossing, but if she were truthful she had to acknowledge that, as the days wore on, the fierce desire, which had drawn her and Sean together, alongside the intense longing to reach America, no longer existed. The first signs began to appear when they struggled to make normal conversation. Their lovemaking, which at first had been fuelled by greed and passion, quickly waned.

Despite the long journey to Chicago, Sean set to work with Henry six days a week as soon as they arrived. With only Sundays free, Alice was traumatized to discover that the family attended mass, twice, together, every Sunday.

Mrs Mcguire had left Alice in no doubt as to what was expected of her.

'Tell Alice, Sean, she walks with us to mass. All part of the lie ye have to both live out whilst ye pretend to be man and wife. And may God forgive ye, because I never will.'

'I don't want to attend mass, Sean,' Alice had remonstrated. 'I've never even been inside my own church in England, never mind yours.'

'Ye have to, Alice.' Sean was incensed by what Brigid and her stubbornness had denied him all these years. He was now in love with Chicago and all that it had to offer. Anger flooded him when he thought of the years he had wasted in Liverpool, scraping by. There was no place in his life for another stubborn woman. He would have none of it.

The guilt he carried around with him each day had hardened him. Alice could see that the Sean she had known in Liverpool was a very different man from the one he had become in Chicago. She was horrified too at the prospect of spending two hours of her precious Sundays in a church thick with incense.

'Kathleen and Jerry never took me to mass once during the years I was in Liverpool and under their roof, so why would I want to start now?'

'What happened in Liverpool doesn't count any longer. If it did, I would be sitting in church with my daughters. We worship together, Alice, and that is all there is to it.'

'Henry and I flew to England to rescue Mammy from the chaos you left behind, Sean,' Mary had whispered to him when they had a moment alone one morning over breakfast. 'We stopped until Brigid's family stepped into the breach. It was a bad business all right and not something I would want to have to do again.'

Sean felt ashamed for what he had put his children through, but nothing could stem the tide of anger he now felt towards Brigid. He would not allow this opportunity to be wasted. His share of the business would be bequeathed to his girls but, in the meantime, Alice must play her part. He would need a son to carry on the business so that it could continue.

Mrs Mcguire's dockside words had chilled Alice, but Henry's, about her having another child, had chilled her more. Sean's having a son had not been part of the deal.

'I have a son that I have left in Liverpool. Why would I want another?' she had said to Sean.

'Because of this is our new life, Alice. Do you want it to be just the two of us, growing old together? Don't you want us to be able to share our life out here with a family? Even I hadn't realized how well the business is doing. Mary had understated that in her letters all right.'

Alice didn't reply. If Sean thought he was going to make her pregnant, he could think again. What she couldn't tell Sean was that she missed Joseph. So much so that she had trouble sleeping. Deep in her heart, she missed Jerry too, as well as the four streets. She missed the life she had lived before and knowing that it had gone forever made the pain worse. While Sean worked hard all day long, Alice moped around the house or called for the driver, if the car was free, to take her to the mall.

Mary often invited Alice to her coffee mornings and fund-raisers for the church, but they left Alice cold. She had never been one for small talk, and it hadn't come more easily just because she was on a different continent.

Alice had been made responsible for their banking and had been charged with sorting out the new house, with Mary's help, tasks which occupied only the smallest part of her day. But the complaints from Alice faded into the distance following a discovery that altered the course of all of their lives.

'Henry, the baby hasn't woken for his feed,' said Mary, switching on the bedside light. 'It's been a struggle all week to make him take anything. I'm worried.'

Henry sat up in bed and switched on his own light.

Dillon had never taken a whole feed since the day he arrived, always just two ounces at a time, at regular intervals.

'The doctor said not to worry. As long as he was taking something every few hours, he was fine.'

'I know, Henry, but add it up: he had only eight ounces all day yesterday and that is the equivalent of one feed, for a baby his size.'

Mary fastened her dressing gown and made her way to the adjoining bedroom.

But as she opened the door, there was silence. No gurgling, or shuffling of bed sheets, no thumb sucking, no warm breath or blinking eyelids. Nothing.

The light from the main bedroom cast a faint glow over the cot. As Mary approached, she knew something was dreadfully wrong.

'Henry,' she said in a tight voice.

'What is it?' he replied.

'Henry,' Mary said again.

Alarmed, Henry sat up as Mary came towards him, holding the baby. Dillon was flaccid in her arms, his little head lolling in her hand and his legs swinging loose.

'Dillon, darling,' whispered Mary. The baby opened his eyes and looked at her, but there was no light of recognition.

Henry noticed his pale leg, which had fallen free from his nightgown.

'What's that, Mary?' he asked, pushing back the child's white flannelette nightshirt.

An enormous black bruise covered the back of Dillon's calf.

'I don't know, but phone the doctor quick,' Mary whispered, with tears pouring down her cheeks as their son, once again, closed his eyes.

A week later, Sean was trying his best to pay back Mary and Henry's kindness by travelling with them to meet with the doctor. Today they would know the results of the many tests Dillon been subjected to. Sean felt totally helpless.

'Let's stop and get us the biggest rack of smoked ribs when we are all done at the hospital, shall we, Sean?' Henry had said earlier that morning.

They were all three assembled in the hallway, ready to leave for the doctor's.

'And, Mary, you won't have any problem with that now, will you? Not today, Mary. None of your lectures now, d'you hear me? Today we celebrate, because the doctor is going to tell us our little lad will be fine.'

Mary avoided responding by fixing her hat in the mirror.

'Ouch,' she said as she sucked her thumb, after a prick from the hatpin. 'Let's not fly in God's face, shall we? We don't try God and you should know that.'

She dipped her fingers into the stoup on the hall table, full of holy water that had been shipped over especially from the Vatican, blessed herself and pushed forward her husband and brother so that they could do exactly the same.

'What's up with ye both?' she admonished them. 'Are ye both so full of your own arrogance you have no time to bless yourselves today of all days, so help me, God?'

Mrs McGuire was in the kitchen with Dillon, rocking him back and forth on her knee. She had been trying for over an hour to coax him to take his bottle. Worry lines were etched on her face. The situation with Sean had taken its toll, and now this.

'Will you be all right, Mammy?' said Mary, fussing around.

Mrs McGuire waved her daughter away. 'Will I be all right? I'm not Mrs Clampett. I can manage very well, thank ye. Just because ye live in a big house doesn't mean anything to do with rearing a child has altered. Now go, and come back with good news that this little fella is going to be fine.'

Sean noticed how anxious his sister looked. Mary hadn't laughed for a week. Not since their last appointment at the doctor's office, when the doctor had told them that they would need to travel straight from there to the hospital where a Dr Sanjay would remain behind, waiting for them.

'For goodness' sake. Right now? What for? You're joking, right?' Mary's voice was tight. She had spent every moment since she found Dillon making herself believe that the doctor would put everything right. She had done a good job.

The doctor wasn't joking. Far from it. Dr Sanjay, a specialist, was indeed waiting at the hospital, examining a set of X-rays of their little boy.

At that moment, Henry saw his wife's spirit die. She had turned to him and tried to smile, to let him know that she would make this better, but her smile had died too.

'Don't worry, Henry love,' she had said, Mary the fixer. Mary, the mother. Mary, who made everything right.

She grabbed Henry's hand and pulled him closer to her, protecting him from the news that she herself failed to comprehend. 'It's nothing serious,' she said, with no conviction whatsoever.

But Henry had seen hope decay, right there and then.

The smile on her face. The dream in her eyes. Dead.

Their little boy had a form of leukaemia, but one that could be cured relatively easily. The chances were high that the bone marrow of a family member would be a successful match.

'In my years of practice I have never known a family match to fail,' Dr Sanjay had said.

It was all very simple. They had to place everyone on the federal donor bank today and then return to the clinic on Monday. They would have to log in their social security numbers and blood type, and once they had done that, the doctor could start work.

'The sooner we find a donor, the less the disruption to your little man's life,' Dr Sanjay had said. 'Dillon is still a baby and this will be nothing more than a correctional process. We just need to give him another blood transfusion in the next few days in order to turn his cheeks pink again. We have all the cards in our hands. I wish every child's case was as straightforward as yours.'

Sean liked Dr Sanjay. He was calm, matter-of-fact. He had said that the little lad had an excellent chance of a complete recovery. They were the best odds.

Dr Sanjay had answered all Mary's questions honestly. Now they had to return home to Mrs McGuire and Dillon. Sean knew that Alice would be back from the hairdresser's and would be helping Mrs McGuire. The frost between the two women had almost completely thawed in their concern over the baby.

Sean knew Alice missed Joseph. It was something none of them ever mentioned.

'That is the strange thing about America,' Sean had said to Henry. 'It is as though your life before you reached these shores had never happened. When you are an Irish immigrant in a country as proud as the USA, the only thing that matters is today and tomorrow; the past is forgotten.'

Sean was right. It was all about now. You were reborn as an American citizen and you began anew.

This filled Sean with hope. Their life would begin in earnest with a son of his own, a little Sean McGuire, and Alice would have to agree.

'Are you OK, Mary?' Sean now enquired again, this time with more confidence. 'Are you not happy with what the doctor said?'

Henry answered, 'Mary is fine, Sean. She just needs a little time to get used to things, that's all. Isn't it, love?'

Sean almost smiled. He loved the way Henry's accent was an absolute mix of American and Irish when he was calm and collected, and yet it was full-on, one hundred per cent Irish, when he was mad or worried, which wasn't very often. He was obviously worried right now.

'I'm sorry, Sean, Henry, I'm sorry.' Mary turned in the passenger seat and stretched out to take hold of Sean's hand. Her mascara had carved tiny black tracks through her powdery cheeks and the whites of her eyes were bloodshot.

'It won't be a problem, Mary, so don't cry. You just have to do as the doctor said.'

Sean didn't know what he had said wrong but, whatever it was, he had really upset Mary. She began to sob openly. Sean looked to Henry, seeking reassurance, wanting him to say something to halt Mary's distress, but tears were sliding down Henry's cheeks. What the hell was going on?

Henry put his foot on the brake and as they slowed down Sean looked out of the window. They were turning into the parking lot for the new mall that was still only half built. Parked outside, he spotted green construction vehicles with the family name, Moynihan.

'I will be five minutes,' Henry said. 'Look after Mary, Sean. I will stay home with you today, love.'

Mary grabbed her husband's hand as he moved to slide out of the car seat. He hesitated a moment with his hand on the door handle and whispered, 'Just hold it together, love, until we get into the house, OK?'

Sean shifted forward and patted Mary's hand. It didn't matter how much he scrabbled around for something useful or comforting to say, he found nothing. So he decided the best thing to do was to say nothing and just let Mary know he was there for her.

Henry, who had been gone for less than five minutes, ran back to the car.

Sean had never seen a man cry before, but now, unashamedly, with no attempt to wipe away his tears or to halt their flow, Henry wept freely.

'Tell me, Mary, what is it, what is wrong?' Sean's voice trembled slightly. He was not sure he really wanted to know the answer. They were almost home, only minutes away from being able to walk in through their own front door and break down in private. Sean thought, with a huge sense of relief, thank God, Mammy is there. She will know what to do.

Amazingly, Mary appeared to be pulling herself together just as Henry was falling apart. She turned from the front seat to face Sean full on. Picking up his hand, she began to speak.

'Sean, things are not as you think. We have only six months. Six months to find a match for Dillon.'

Mary looked directly at Henry to reassure herself before she spoke. They were words that could not be taken back once said. He raised no objection.

'We never discussed our baby boy with you because so much was happening when you arrived – the upset with Mammy, the new contract to build the flyover. It was all going on and, anyway, you never asked and why would you?

'Little Dillon, he came from a convent in Ireland, near Galway. We don't know who it was who gave birth to him and gave him up for adoption. We don't know who his family is or where we can trace them to find a bone marrow match. We flew straight from here to collect him, it was all so quick, and stopped over in Liverpool on the way back. He flew on a temporary passport. They had it all arranged before we even arrived.'

'Six months.'

Mary repeated those awful words as though they were a death sentence. The car journey had eaten up almost an hour of those six months since the doctor had first given them the news.

As they pulled into the drive, Sean saw Mrs McGuire, who been waiting patiently, struggle to open the heavy oak front door. She was more used to a cottage in the village on the outskirts of Galway, where they had all been born, or the Nelson Street two-up, two-down. Little Dillon was in her arms, looking pale and wan, but he still managed a smile for his parents' return.

Sean was struggling to take in everything Mary had said.

Only his thumbs moved, over and over.

As they stepped inside, Mrs McGuire and Alice stood in the hallway, anxiety binding them together in a flimsy companionship born from a joint concern for Dillon's health.

Mary, as ever pragmatic and fighting for the life of her little boy, knew without any discussion what she needed to do.

'Mammy, Alice, I have to travel to Galway with Dillon. Will ye both come with me?'

The three women hugged briefly and silently. They would do whatever it took, no matter how inconvenient or difficult.

The scent from Mary's jacket made Alice feel nauseous. She slowly breathed out a deep sigh of relief. Galway. It was much closer to Joseph, to Liverpool, to Jerry, and to everyone and everything she knew, than Chicago.

For the first time in her life, Alice uttered a silent prayer of thanks and made a decision to withdraw the full fifty thousand dollars in their joint bank account on the day she left.

## Chapter Seven

'You look like a nervous wreck,' said Simon to Howard, as they stood inside St Mary's church, waiting for Howard's bride to arrive. 'Stop pacing up and down like a demented dog. You are making me on edge and I'm only the best man.'

Howard took out yet another Embassy cigarette from his packet and handed one to Simon.

'Here, have one, go on. Me hands are shaking, I've got to have another to calm my nerves,' he whispered.

Standing on the groom's side at the front of the ornate church, now filling with incense, Howard's nervousness was as much to do with the formality of the church ceremony, as the fact that he was about to leave behind his carefree bachelor life and marry a woman who knew how to organize a list to within an inch of her life.

Howard had completed his conversion to the Catholic faith upon the absolute insistence of his bride, Miss Alison Devlin, spinster of the parish, deputy head teacher at the four streets convent school and all-round holder-together of the community during a time of crisis. The latter quality had been tested to the limit recently. The four streets had been through more than their fair share of drama and crisis.

'Howard, we are forty minutes early. Let's go outside and walk round the church for a fag. Your bride will kill you if she can't see you from the door for blue smoke.'

Howard, a local detective inspector, had first met Alison during the investigation into the deaths of the priest, Father James, and Molly Barrett. Howard still felt guilty about Molly. Molly had given him information about who had murdered the priest. But no sooner had she confided in them than she had been murdered herself. The confusing thing was that Molly must have been wrong. She had told them that the priest's murderer was Tommy Doherty. But that couldn't have been the case. They knew Tommy Doherty hadn't murdered Molly. As he was under suspicion, they had watched his every move that night. It wasn't him and it was impossible to believe that there were two random murderers on the rampage in the four streets.

It had all been one extended nightmare. The very worst of it had been the tragic drowning of little Kitty Doherty during her visit to Ireland, and the fact that Daisy Quinn, the Priory housekeeper, had gone missing since the day she had left Alison's care to catch the ferry, down at the Pier Head.

It had all been too much for everyone to take in.

'Will the day ever come when you can see us getting married?' Howard had asked Alison a number of times. It seemed to him as though the dark cloud that had settled over the community would never pass.

'I would feel better if I could travel to Dublin and look for Daisy myself,' Alison had responded. 'God alone knows where she is. Her poor family, to have been left standing, waiting for her at the port. They must be desperate and I feel so responsible. I put her on the boat. I even asked two old ladies to look after her. She was so excited about being reunited with her family for Christmas. I just need things to become a little more like normal.'

Howard knew she was right. In order to remove all barriers to his nuptials, as well as its accompanying rights and pleasures, he had arranged for them both to visit Dublin so that Alison herself could speak to the police and Daisy's family.

He had hoped as a result that she might be more reasonable regarding his manly needs. It seemed as though everyone, everywhere, spoke about nothing other than women's liberation and free love. Some women were even burning their bras, what for, Howard wasn't sure, but it seemed to him like a great and generous gesture.

But none of it mattered. Alison was a stickler for propriety and was apparently wholly against joining her sisters on any march that would make it easier for Howard to stay the night.

'We will, Howard, when the time is right and things are happy again,' Alison replied, each and every time he asked. This would be followed by four very disappointing words, which achieved their unambiguous purpose.

'When. We. Are. Married.'

The door of illicit sex slammed with finality. Words of steel held it shut.

Bang. Bang. Bang. Bang.

'I would be very happy, if I could go to bed at night and wake up with a wife,' Howard said over and over, but there was little point in complaining.

The nuns, the school and the entire community had become mired in grief. Although not touched by events in quite the same way as his fiancée, Howard realized that to pursue his aim, under such a veil of sorrow, was fruitless.

Daisy's brother had not blamed Alison in any way for his sister's disappearance and had been grateful for the care she had given to the sister of whom he had known nothing until the death of his parents.

The family were still in shock at the news that, after a difficult birth leading to fears that she would be brain damaged, Daisy had been placed in what was in effect a Dublin orphanage, under the care of nuns. As if that were not enough, they had been dismayed to hear that, whilst still a child, she had then been shipped to Liverpool, where she had been pressed into service as a housekeeper to the murdered priest.

Via his own contacts, Howard had arranged for Alison to speak to the police in Dublin. They had then met with Daisy's brother, who was the state solicitor and much respected by the Dublin Gardai.

''Tis is a mystery, so it is,' said the Dublin detective. 'She was seen standing by the boat rails one minute but then, when it came time to disembark, she was nowhere to be seen.'

Alison asked the question that had been preying on everyone's minds since the moment they heard that Daisy had not met up with her family at the agreed rendezvous.

'Could she have drowned?'

'Not impossible,' replied the detective. 'But, if she had, her body would have washed up somewhere by now. The boat had almost docked the last time she was seen on deck. I would say that her drowning was highly unlikely.'

Reassured that there was a strong likelihood that Daisy was alive and with the knowledge that she would most likely be found at some stage, Alison agree to name the day and to put Howard out of his misery.

Howard and Simon now stood at the back of the church in the graveyard, out of sight, but with a good view of the road so as not to miss Alison's approach. Simon held out his silver cigarette lighter to Howard as they lit up.

The top clicked back into place with a cushioned slickness.

Not for the first time, Howard wondered where Simon got the money from for all his fancy bits. The lighter, the cigarette case packed with Pall Mall cigarettes (which, Howard noticed, Simon bought only on days when he thought he might have to offer a woman a ciggie from his expensive case), his smart suits and the new Ford Capri in which Howard had been grateful to be driven to the church.

'You should be careful smoking those Pall Mall,' said Howard.

'That's the only link to Molly's murder. Just because one was found at the murder scene doesn't make it glamorous to smoke them, you know. What happened to your Woodies? Not good enough now, eh?

Although Simon had the same rank as Howard, his manner was bumptious. He always assumed authority over his colleague, yet both were on the same pay scale. Howard had commented on it to Alison only the previous week following the wedding rehearsal when Simon, much to their surprise, had presented them both with a solid silver rose bowl.

'Even accounting for the fact that he has no wedding to pay for and obviously no intention to start a family and buy a home, he seems to spend his money lavishly,' said Howard.

'I'm not complaining at his foolishness.' Alison had smiled. ''Tis a beauty of a rose bowl all right.'

Howard knew better than to pry or ask Simon for an explanation. No other officer in the force was as close to Simon as he was. Howard never asked personal questions, which Simon obviously appreciated. To Howard's knowledge, Simon had no girlfriend and had never had one, in all the time they had been in the force together. He lived alone in his Aigburth house and visited his mum every other weekend. At lunchtime he enjoyed a roast beef sandwich and a slice of the home-made fruitcake which he brought back from his visits home. That was about as much as Howard knew, or was ever likely to know.

Howard, who was less secretive and more down to earth altogether, was more of a sausage-roll-and-a-custard-slice-from-Sayers man. Simon was a member of a rather posh golf club on the Wirrall where, at the weekend, he sometimes teamed up with the chief super and his friends. One of the officers from over the water had told Howard that a politician often played a round with them. Simon never spoke of it and Howard dared not ask.

Howard knew the closest he would get to the golf club would be if he were ever asked to caddy and the chances of that were very slim indeed. Now he smoked his cigarette down to the tip in less than a minute.

'Let's have another,' he said to Simon, 'and then we will move back inside.'

As Simon offered his cigarette case to Howard, they both peered over the church wall to watch the bridesmaids arrive.

Nellie Deane alighted from the car first, followed by the younger Doherty girls and then the page-boys, Little Paddy and Harry. They had been prepared and made ready for the day at Alison's house by her sister. Everything had to be perfect and Alison had taken no chances.

'Strange that not long ago we had both those girls' fathers in the cells, questioning them over the priest's murder, and now their kids are Alison's bridesmaids,' said Howard.

Simon did not reply. He squinted into the sunlight as the girls fussed about their lilac chiffon dresses and white satin shoes. He could hear the voice of the now oldest Doherty girl wafting up to them on the warm breeze.

'Will you get off my shoes, Niamh. You have put a stain on the white satin. Oh God, would you look at that, now.' Angela bent down and rubbed at the shoe like crazy.

'Stop it,' hissed Nellie. 'You are making your white gloves dirty.'

Neither girl had ever been so dressed up in her life. It was making them nervous to the point of nausea.

Alison Devlin had chosen Nellie Deane and the Dohertys for a reason. Not only were they her favourite pupils at the school, but both families had suffered more than most in their lifetimes. Alison had the softest heart.

That could be the only explanation why Little Paddy had been chosen as page-boy.

'Alison, we would have to disinfect the lad before we could put him in a page-boy outfit,' Howard had remonstrated.

'Aye, we will that and won't that give us just a huge sense of satisfaction now,' Alison replied.

Howard was starting to realize that he had as much influence over what happened at his own wedding as he had over the weather. He would have to accept that this was also the beginning of the rest of his life.

'God, I feel so ashamed,' said Little Paddy, as he tried to pull the ruff down from his throat.

'Don't complain, Paddy,' said Harry. 'Ye have a new pair of shoes for wearing a fancy outfit for the day. Ye won't have to borrow anyone else's for ages now.'

Harry patted his friend on the back. Little Paddy smiled. Sometimes he felt as if Harry was more like what a da should be than his best friend.

Wedding nerves had reached the Priory. This was Father Anthony's first wedding since taking over St Mary's church and he knew the turnout would be huge for the most popular teacher for miles around.

'Harriet! Harriet!'

Father Anthony shouted from the top of the stairs down to his sister, who was carefully decorating the two last trifles with silver sugar balls, fanning out from tinned pears which had been placed in a pattern of flower petals, laid on a bed of Fussell's tinned cream. It was all ready to deliver to the Irish centre for the reception. This would take place straight after the nuptial mass. Harriet had stomped round the kitchen, shaking the cream in the tins to thicken it, and was now running late. The whole process had taken far longer than she had anticipated due to the unexpectedly warm weather.

'Shake them above yer head,' Annie O'Prey had told her the previous day. 'It makes them thicken quicker.'

Harriet couldn't see how this could be true, but she had done it anyway.

Harriet and Alison Devlin had become good friends since Harriet had moved into the Priory. Jointly, they had helped to heal broken families and nursed a community back onto its feet. They had become almost inseparable as a result and it seemed only natural that Harriet would play a main role in the organization of the wedding.

Harriet was a helper and a healer, but, despite the fact that she was the priest's sister, she wasn't terribly holy. Something she took care to keep secret.

The fact that her brother was conducting the nuptial mass of her new best friend made the whole thing very tidy, which was just how Harriet liked things to be.

'You would think no one else had ever been married on this street,' Annie O'Prey had grumpily complained a number of times when Harriet had asked for the sitting room to be given an extra polish and a run over with the Ewbank, ready for yet another wedding-planning tea.

'Wedding planning? I've never heard the like. All she needs to do is make a white frock and turn up at the church. I've never known such a palaver.'

In the Priory there had been talk of nothing but the wedding.

The reception, the dress, the food and the endless fittings for the bridesmaids' dresses and the page-boys' outfits. Decisions over colours and flowers and what food to put on the buffet. It had been a huge and never-ending frenzy of activity. Harriet held onto another secret throughout. Never once did anyone see the pain that sometimes squeezed her heart or the odd tear that sprang to her eye at the sad thought that she, so truly now the spinster of the parish, would possibly always remain so.

Most women were married by the age of twenty-one. Any older was seen as being highly unusual. Alison, who was now thirty, had thought she had been well and truly left on the shelf. But no one, not even Alison Devlin, entertained the thought that, at the grand old age of thirty-five, Harriet Lamb would ever be married herself.

'Anthony, stop shouting.' Harriet ran up the wooden stairs from the basement kitchen, closely followed by Scamp, who had quietly inserted himself into the daily running of Priory life and, subsequently, Harriet's affections.

One advantage of the wedding planning taking place at the Priory was the legitimate reason it gave Little Paddy and Scamp to be useful. There were always errands Harriet needed to be run. Little Paddy also got to eat up the leftovers from Annie O'Prey's baking, despite Anthony's constant complaints about the boy and his dog hanging around the kitchen. Anthony might have been the priest but there was no way he was the boss, not even in his own Priory. Alison and Harriet had a lot in common.

'I cannot find the list of family names I have to read out in the service. Have you put it somewhere when you were tidying? Why do you have to polish my office so often?'

'Because I am your housekeeper, Anthony, that is my job. I look after my holy brother. I have told Annie O'Prey to polish in here on Mondays and Fridays. A twice-weekly damp dust and a polish in a big old priory like this is not too often.'

Harriet removed an envelope from his desk drawer on which Alison Devlin had written a long list of names to be mentioned during prayers. At the top of it was Sister Evangelista's, while the bishop's was nowhere to be found. Father Anthony had discovered the bishop had seriously upset Sister Evangelista before his tenure and no matter how many ways he had tried to extract the reason for this, her lips remained sealed.

'Don't ever mention the bishop if you want the cream to stay fresh,' Harriet had told him a few days after their arrival. 'But don't ask me why. I will find out in good time, but it is a tricky one all right. I have never known a bishop to be so disliked. All I know is that after Father James Cameron's death, the bishop was no help whatsoever. In fact, from what I can gather, he was nowhere to be seen. He ignored Sister Evangelista's phone calls, he was unreasonable with her when she did get through to him, he made poor decisions and he was bad-tempered altogether.'

'Blimey!' said Father Anthony. 'Well, here's hoping I'm never on the wrong side of Sister Evangelista.'

'You?' said Harriet. 'Anthony, you have everyone you ever meet eating out of your hand. You are goodness itself, so how could that ever happen?'

'Now,' said Harriet, 'we had better hurry or we will be late and that will not do for the priest. Let me just place a damp tea towel over the last trifles. It seems to me as if half of Liverpool is attending this wedding and that trifle is their favourite dish.'

They both stopped short in the hallway, hearing the sound of organ music as if carried on the rays of sunshine that fell in shimmering pillars, through the open Priory door.

'Look at them all,' said Harriet, smiling up at her brother. 'I have never seen so many people stand outside a church to watch the bride arrive.'

'Aye, well, it's no different from home. We may be in Liverpool, but everyone here is Irish and the ways have just travelled across the sea.'

Father Anthony waited while Harriet pulled on her lemon gloves. She picked up a lemon-and-white hat from the hall table and said, with a flourish and a spin, 'There, holy brother, will I do?'

'You are a vision of primroses, sister. Mammy and Daddy would have been very proud.'

'Come along then, Father Anthony,' she said briskly, gently pushing her brother in the small of his back as they stepped outdoors.

They walked down the path together but could barely make their way through the throng of people assembled outside the Priory walls, lining all the way down to the church gates.

The crowd parted to allow the priest and Harriet through. The words, 'Morning, Father,' rang out from everyone they passed.

For everyone in return, Father Anthony had a smile and a greeting. 'Morning to you, 'tis a wonderful day,' he called to the happy well-wishers.

No one saw Alison Devlin's car, as it passed the top of Nelson Street and then swung away again.

'Go round once more,' Alison urged the driver with an uncharacteristic impatience. 'I don't think they are ready for me. I can see Father Anthony and Harriet walking to the church. I want to make a big entrance. Turn round quickly.'

'Why not, queen,' laughed her father, as he sat in the back of the car and lit up a cigarette. 'You only get married once. Let's make the most of it.'

'Da, watch my veil with the match,' shouted Alison as a profusion of gauze, trimmed with appliquéd white cherry blossom, almost went up in flames.

Alison was aware that not one resident in the four streets had ever before seen a bride arrive at the church in a car. It was a first.

The distance from most people's houses to the church was so short that every bride walked and, besides, cars were a luxury that just could not be afforded. Miss Devlin taught at the school, but she lived in Maghull and her true home was Cork. Her life was so deeply rooted in the four streets and St Mary's church, convent and school that there was never a question she would marry anywhere else.

Alison turned and looked out of the back window as the car moved away. She saw her friend Harriet and Father Anthony, winding their way through the crowd towards the church entrance. Just behind them, Tommy and Maura Doherty, the parents of her bridesmaids, were strolling up to the church with Kathleen and Jerry, Nellie's nana and da. They walked with heads bent, linking arms as if holding each other up. Even though it was her wedding day, Alison's heart turned over in sadness.

Harriet noticed that everyone who could do so had squeezed into the church itself, respectfully leaving four pews empty for the nuns. She grinned at the sight of the sisters pouring out of the convent and making their way towards the church, bustling and giggling like nervous, happy schoolgirls.

She thought to herself how different the nuns in Liverpool were. At her own convent school in Dublin, she had never seen a nun bustle or giggle.

The bells were ringing out in happiness, the sun was shining. Harriet looked about her, amazed at the love and support the community openly displayed for their favourite teacher, Miss Devlin.

Children from the school, both past and present, and residents from the four streets sat scrubbed and clean, in their Sunday best, chattering to each other over the organ music. Rays of sunshine, passing through the stained-glass windows, were reflected by one head of red hair after another, infusing the chancel with an amber glow.

The familiar smell, found in all churches everywhere, of old dark wood, once lovingly carved into pews and altar by hands long forgotten, mingled now with that of fresh flowers and damp moss.

Harriet had attended so many weddings in her lifetime, too many to count and now, here she was, too old even to be a bridesmaid.

'Morning, Harriet, you look lovely, you do. Love your hat.' One of the mothers, Deirdre, edged past her to take her seat next to her neighbour.

'Morning, Deirdre, thank you. You look lovely too. That's a pretty dress.'

'I know,' Deirdre replied with no false modesty. 'I got it in a jumble sale. Isn't it great? And it's got a label that says St Michael, so I did well there. Not just a lovely dress but it's got the name of the Irish centre and a saint on it. Can't be bad, eh? I've got me back covered, me. I'm going to wear it for the bingo, so I am. Reckon it'll bring me luck, Harriet?'

Both women laughed as Deirdre edged her way down the pew.

As she had promised to help Alison with her veil once she arrived, Harriet hovered by the church door and peeped out to see if she could spot the bridal car. The street seemed to be lined with every available officer from the Lancashire Constabulary.

Harriet was amused as she pondered another guilty secret. She had always liked a man in uniform.

Maura was having one of her bad days. Some were merely bad, others were dreadful. Today was just bad. She was coping better than she thought she would as a result of having Kathleen at her side.

'Maybe it's because the girls have been picked as Miss Devlin's bridesmaids, and Harry and Little Paddy as page-boys, that I don't feel so bad today,' Maura had said to Tommy early that morning.

She had packed her excited daughters into the taxi Miss Devlin had sent to take them to Maghull for the bridal preparation rituals, which apparently included lying on the spare bed for thirty minutes with slices of cucumber on their eyes.

Tommy joined Maura on the front step just as she raised her arm to wave goodbye to her daughters.

The daughters left behind. Those who hadn't died. The ones she had been allowed to keep.

'Aye, they will look grand when we see them later,' Tommy whispered into her wire curlers as he hugged her.

'They will and, sure, isn't that something to look forward to?' said Maura, hugging her Tommy back. Today, for the first time in a long while, Maura vaguely remembered what it was like to feel proud. She moved up the brow with her arm linked through Kathleen's and the two men following behind.

Maura still found it difficult to pass through a crowd. She could feel the silent sympathy that flowed towards her from the other mothers and, although she knew it was kind and well meant, she just couldn't handle it, not even now after so much time had passed. Sorry for your troubles. Sorry for your troubles. Sorry for your troubles.

They were the only words anyone had spoken to her for weeks and they still rang in her ears.

Maura and Kathleen stopped for a moment on the way up the hill to exchange words with some of their friends and for Kathleen to have a last cigarette.

'It lasts too long, a nuptial mass, too long to go without a ciggie and it looks rude, stepping out in the hymns for a quick one. And besides, I don't want to get on the wrong side of Father Anthony and Harriet,' Kathleen said, taking her ciggies out of her coat pocket.

'Look at this lot,' she said as she lit up, blinking through a haze of stinging blue smoke that brought tears to her eyes, 'not a curler to be seen anywhere. Doesn't everyone look nice, eh, Maura?'

Maura looked around. She had taken out her own curlers and put a comb through her hair that morning. She had to admit the women of the four streets had scrubbed up well.

'Peggy, how do ye manage to sleep with that beehive?' Kathleen asked, putting up her hand to feel Peggy's hair. The solid tower wobbled to one side as Kathleen pushed at it.

'There's a whole tin of lacquer on it, that's how,' said Peggy, bending her head to take a light from the end of Tommy's cigarette for her own. 'It's like sleeping on a fecking brick some nights.'

'You want to watch that when you light up,' said Kathleen. 'Lacquer is flammable, you know.'

'Flammable, what's that?' said Peggy. 'I use Get Set from Woolworth's. It's the best and costs nearly a shilling a tin. Does the job, though. My hair won't be going anywhere now and it lasts a whole two weeks each time it's done. Jesus, it's fecking itchy, though. Thanks be to God for knitting needles.'

Tommy took another half-ciggie from behind his ear and lit up to join Kathleen. He put his arm across his Maura's shoulders and hugged her to him.

In the past few weeks, they had a newfound closeness, brought about by the realization of how near they had come to the edge of disaster.

Neither would speak of the days when they had almost torn each other apart with blame and hatred. They did not acknowledge that Maura had entered her own temporary world of madness. Tommy, struggling with his own grief, had had to hide the tablets the doctor had given her, as he feared she would wake in the night and swallow the whole bottle. A shiver ran down his spine when he thought of how close they had come to falling apart. Looking at his neighbours all around him today, he knew, without doubt, how they had been saved. If it hadn't been for Harry needing the hospital that night, God alone knows where they would be by now.

Extinguishing cigarettes on the pavement under their heels, they walked into the church where Nellie and the Doherty girls stood at the back, near to the font, in all their lilac fluff and finery, waiting for the bride.

'Not so comfortable with all these bizzies about, are you, Jer,' Tommy whispered to Jerry.

''Tis a great day for robbers today,' said Jerry, 'the lucky bastards.'

Jerry had said as much to Nellie that morning over breakfast.

'They will all be here in the four streets today, every copper in Liverpool. There will be great pickings over at Seaforth on the docks when they know the coast is clear.'

'Eh, pack it in, walls have ears,' said Nana Kathleen, smacking

Jerry across his cap with the tea towel and nodding furiously towards Nellie.

'Eat that breakfast. Ye can go nowhere on an empty stomach,' Kathleen had said to Nellie early that morning. Nellie had spent the entire night in yellow sponge curlers and had hardly slept a wink.

'I'm putting those curlers in a parcel to Maeve,' Kathleen had said as she removed them that morning.

Kathleen sent a parcel from Liverpool back to the farm in Ballymara about once a month, as did anyone in Liverpool who could afford the postage home. In County Mayo, the shops carried very little of interest, their stocks being related directly to the need to survive rather than to entertain or amuse.

Nellie had spent more hours than she could count in the post office queue, holding oddly shaped brown-paper packages tied up with string, ready to be weighed and posted by sea mail to Mayo.

'They are no use here. Curlers to sleep in, my backside. What's wrong with just leaving them in all day for decoration? Who would want to sleep in curlers? Curlers are meant to be worn, not slept in.'

The parcel to be sent home lived in a drawer in the press and its contents grew each week.

Only yesterday Nellie had taken a peep at this month's parcel: Ladybird baby vests for someone in the village back home, Vitapointe hair conditioner and a bottle of Coty L'Aimant perfume for Auntie Maeve's birthday, all these lay on the brown-paper sheets, waiting to be posted.

Now, as Kathleen had scooped up the curlers and thrown them into the press drawer, Nellie found she was not sad to see the back of them.

'Howard has no fecking idea that the fruit in his wedding cake came from a sack off the back of the *Cotopaxi* when it berthed six weeks ago. Sandra Dever doesn't get her fruit or sugar from anywhere else. It's always knock-off.'

Both men sniggered and then Tommy stopped. He always felt guilty when he laughed, feeling he shouldn't. After what had happened to Kitty, laughing must be wrong. He had never, ever wanted to laugh again. It had only been in the past few months that he had wanted to live.

'Howard is all right,' said Jerry. 'It's that Simon who gets to me. When they were questioning us, I always got the impression that he knew exactly what had happened and that, for some reason, he wasn't letting on.'

'That was just yer imagination, Jer. He couldn't have known. How could he? No one saw us.'

Tommy's heart lightened as soon as he saw his girls in church, a cluster of lilac-dipped angels, smiling at him – even Angela. Before Kitty had died, she could rarely raise a smile and she certainly hadn't done so since. Now she stood at the font in her white-satin, T-bar shoes, hopping from foot to foot, beaming.

'Da, hurry up,' she said impatiently. 'The bride is arriving soon. Move, move, Da.'

'I'm not budging until I get a kiss first,' said Tommy, placing his hands on his hips.

The girls laughed and clamoured, more eager to be rid of their embarrassing father than in need of a kiss. He placed a kiss on each of his girls' foreheads as Jerry did the same to his Nellie.

'You all right, Nellie?' asked Jerry, thinking his heart would burst with pride. His little girl was growing through her own personal heartache with dignity, and growing more like her mammy every day with her red ringlets tumbling down over her shoulders.

Nellie grinned up at him. 'I am, Da, but get lost.'

She playfully punched her da in the stomach. Jerry, pretending to be winded, laughed and followed Tommy into the nave.

As he moved down the aisle, a thought struck Tommy.

'Angela gets more like Kitty every day,' he said to Jerry.

'I was just thinking the same thing myself,' said Jerry, patting his mate on the back as they dipped on one knee, blessed themselves and slipped along the pew, taking their seats next to Maura and Kathleen.

Jerry didn't like being in church. It made him uncomfortable and, already, his collar was beginning to make his neck itch. Since the death of his first wife, Bernadette, he had attended only the christenings and communions he could not avoid. Today he had no choice, as Nellie was a bridesmaid. He would be forced to sit and witness another couple take their vows at exactly the same altar where he and Bernadette had knelt all those years ago. Her coffin had lain in front of that same altar a few short years later.

He now struggled to recall those years with the clarity he would like. This often made him panic, feeling that she was fading, which would mean that she was leaving them for good.

It was the same church, the same time of day, the same sunshine. The same people bearing witness. The people of the four streets.

The same shimmering silver ribbon of river flowed past only yards away. Every heart was filled with gladness, just as each had been for Jerry and his beautiful bride, Bernadette.

Jerry and Tommy both knelt in prayer: Tommy, because Maura had prodded him; Jerry, because, for the first time he could remember, he felt compelled to give thanks for Nellie and his mother, Kathleen.

He had lost his Bernadette in childbirth. His wife Alice had run away to America and left him for another docker on the four streets, a man who was supposed to have been his mucker. But he had his mam and his Nellie, both loyal and faithful, and he wanted God to leave them with him forever. For that, he knew, he should pray and ask him for his forgiveness, because sitting next to him was his best mate, Tommy, who had lost his daughter, Kitty. And there was Jerry, with his Nellie, alive and laughing at the back of the church. There, but for the grace of God, thought Jerry as he prayed.

A frisson of excitement swept through the congregation and, without anyone having to turn round or guess, they were all aware that the bride had arrived.

The organ struck up the bridal march and, as everyone stood, the procession began.

Kathleen linked Maura's arm with hers as they left the church, blinking in the bright sunlight. During those first awful weeks

Kathleen had felt as though it was her job to prop Maura up. Now, it had become a habit. A physical reaction to Maura's weakness. She had become a human crutch.

The churchyard filled with the sound of cheers and children squealing as they pushed past each other.

'Well, isn't that just a grand sight,' said Kathleen, smiling at Nellie and Maura's daughters. The three girls, holding Alison's bridal train high off the cobbled path, were giggling and ducking as their school friends showered them with confetti.

As they walked on to the Irish centre, Kathleen shouted out to Maura and Tommy's twin boys, 'Run on ahead, lads, and keep our table. Run now, fast.'

Peggy had caught up with them whilst her silent husband, Paddy, fell into step alongside Tommy and Jerry.

'Aye, keep ours too,' said Peggy to her son, Little Paddy, giving him a cuff across the shoulder. He ran off to join Harry. 'There's nothing going to stand between me and that buffet today,' she said, 'and I want a good seat now 'cause I'm in for the night.'

'Will ye be taking to the dance floor tonight, Peggy?' asked Kathleen, squeezing Maura's arm gently.

Maura smiled. Making Maura smile was something Kathleen knew she could sometimes still make happen and it gave her enormous pleasure. There had been times when Kathleen had wondered whether she would ever see her friend smile again.

'I'll be dancing, all right, so I will,' replied Peggy. 'Michael Kenny is putting soap flakes on the floor tonight so we can dance a little faster. I can't wait! Jer, I'll be coming after ye for a spin as Paddy here, he's feckin' useless.'

Tommy and Jerry exchanged glances of dismay. Jerry couldn't think of anything worse than being forced to jitterbug with the neighbour named by the local kids as 'Smelly Peggy'.

'I have a spare pair of bloomers in me handbag just in case,' said Peggy to Maura without a hint of embarrassment. 'Don't want the same thing happening as last time.'

As they all walked on up the hill engrossed in the midst of comfortable chatter, no one dared ask what that was. All of them were talking, except for Big Paddy, who chain-smoked but never spoke a word. It was impossible to walk and talk at the same time when your lungs provided only enough oxygen for one function or the other.

The bridal retinue stood on the path, posing for the photographer. The tall arched church door provided the backdrop for the former Miss Devlin and her new husband, Howard.

As Nellie watched the departing backs of her da and Nana Kathleen walking up the brow, she felt both alone and very grown up to have been left behind with the wedding party. The girls were bouncing up and down with excitement.

'Would ye look at them flowers,' said Angela yet again, plunging her bouquet straight into her face and inhaling the fragrance. 'Have ye ever smelt anything as wonderful as that?'

Angela spun round and stuck her posy straight into Nellie's face. Nellie's posy was exactly the same and smelt just the same. Nellie fell about laughing as Angela began sneezing repeatedly.

'Girls, girls,' said Miss Devlin. 'Stand still for the photographer now.'

Nellie thought she had never seen anyone look as beautiful as her favourite teacher did today.

'I'm sorry, Miss Devlin,' she said, running up to the bride and grabbing her hand. With her face infused with pride and happiness, she grinned up at Miss Devlin, who slipped her arm across Nellie's shoulder.

Click, click, snapped the camera shutters.

'Smile, girls,' said the photographer.

Click, click. A black-and-white moment, captured forever.

'Look towards me, ladies. Kiss the bride, Howard. Go on, yer allowed, she's yer missus now.'

Nellie and the bridesmaids blushed and giggled at the photographer's friendly taunts. They could hardly believe that Howard was actually going to kiss Miss Devlin, their teacher, right there in front of them, in broad daylight, yet he did just that.

While Howard kissed his blushing bride, Nellie noticed a police car pull up alongside the bridal car that was parked at the church gates.

'Where's Harriet?' said Alison, scanning the churchyard, then spotting Harriet modestly standing back from the main party. 'Harriet, come here. I'm not having my photographs without you in them, so I'm not.'

Harriet walked up to Nellie and, standing alongside her, placed her hand lightly on her shoulder, whispering in a confidential, girls-together way that made Nellie feel as though she wanted to burst with a sense of belonging and pride.

'There are police cars everywhere, Nellie. I've never been to a wedding like this before and that's for sure.'

Nellie smiled up at her. It was not so long ago there were police cars everywhere on the four streets, every day.

'We are used to that around here,' said Nellie in a very matter-of-fact, grown-up kind of way. 'It's how Miss Devlin and Howard met.' Nellie was displaying her life-before-Harriet credentials, her subtext being, not in an unkind way, *we have known her longer than you.*

Harriet smiled down. She knew exactly what Nellie was doing.

'Well, 'tis just a delight that everything has gone so well now. Don't you think, Nellie? A wedding without a hitch, I think we could safely say.'

Nellie laughed with pleasure. Harriet, a woman of indeterminate age, who was beautiful, travelled, clever and was the sister of the priest, was talking to Nellie as though she were her equal.

'Yes, who would have dreamt that,' Nellie said.

She raised her gloved hand and returned her da's wave as he turned on his heel and, for a moment, walked up the brow backwards to check up on his not-so-little-any-more girl.

'But Miss Devlin is special, so she is. She can do anything. There not being a hitch was how it was always going to be. God, she would have let out a roar if anything had gone wrong, so she would.'

As Nellie spoke, she noticed there was something unusual about the police car which had drawn up by the church gate. Rather than the usual blue-and-white panda, it was black and the officer who stepped out of it wore a flat-peaked cap with a very impressive wide black-and-white chequered band around the middle, not a domed helmet like most of the policemen around.

He began talking to people in the street and casually walked over to some of the officers.

Others, who obviously should have been elsewhere, such as on Seaforth docks, and not at the wedding, slunk back to their cars and began to slowly melt away.

'Ooh, who is this?' asked Harriet, following Nellie's gaze.

'I've no idea at all,' said Nellie. 'I've never seen a police car like that on the streets since the night Molly was murdered.'

She whispered the last few words. It felt inappropriate to talk out loud about a murder whilst smiling for the camera at a wedding.

'Howard, have you got a minute, lad?'

One of the officers called out this most ridiculous-sounding question to Howard, beckoning him away from Alison, his bride of only minutes. Her smile slipped from her face as fast as her new husband's hand slid out of hers.

'Howard, what is it?' Alison asked. Her feminine antennae were up.

'Can't be anything to do with me, love. I'm off for a fortnight now,' Howard called over his shoulder. 'Back in a second. I will just see what it is. Smile for the camera, girls.'

His size twelve feet crunched on the gravel of the church path. Nellie realized that you could hear it very clearly because, suddenly, everyone else was quiet. The wedding scene stood in freeze frame. Only Howard was moving and the air filled with an intense expectation.

Alison was the first to break the silence in an attempt to mask the sudden absence of her husband.

'Harriet, what can it be?' she said, putting out her hand to her friend, who moved from Nellie's side to Alison's. Nellie stepped closer in and tucked herself under Alison's arm.

Alison called to Sister Evangelista, who stood at the end of the drive, close to the important-looking policeman.

'Who are they?' she asked.

Since Sister Evangelista had been talking to Annie O'Prey at the gate when Alison had called her, it was a fair assumption that she would have heard every word that had been spoken.

'I have no idea, Alison. They asked Mrs Keating if they could speak to Howard. Annie O'Prey butted in and told them he was getting wed today, but apparently the man said it couldn't wait, and he had to speak to him now.'

As Sister Evangelista finished speaking, Howard was seen talking to the man with the black-and-white chequered band on his hat and frowning.

Howard began to walk back down the path with the important-looking officer, both heading towards Simon, who had moved over to the gravestones without anyone noticing. Simon looked even more concerned than Howard.

'What is it, Howard?' said Alison as they both walked past her towards Simon. Alison sounded agitated. This was not part of her carefully orchestrated wedding-day plan.

'Who are they?' asked Harriet.

She had never seen so many men in uniform in one place before in her life. She felt her face flush; she had never known such excitement occur in one day.

The man in the peaked cap put his hand on Simon's elbow and led him to the back door of the large Black Maria police car, its windows blacked out. Nellie could see that there was someone sitting in the back, but she couldn't see who.

'Alison,' said Howard, shouting back down the path, 'love, they have some news and they are going to need to talk to you.'

'Me?' said Alison, sounding both disbelieving and disappointed all at the same time. 'Why me?'

Suddenly the back door of the car opened and Alison gasped.

'Daisy?' Alison almost screamed her name.

Click, click, snapped the shutters. Click, click.

Wearing the pillbox hat they had presented to her at the Christmas play, and which Maggie had found on a hook in Sister Theresa's section of the linen cupboard, Daisy half raised her hand in a nervous wave to Miss Devlin.

'Oh, thank God.' Alison put her hand to her mouth as tears filled her eyes. 'I thought she was dead.'

Sister Evangelista, Alison and Harriet reached for one another's hands. All three women exchanged glances of relief and happiness that they could not express in words. Harriet knew who Daisy was. How could she not? Alison used to speak of her every day.

'Here, Nellie, hold my flowers,' said Alison, thrusting her bouquet at Nellie. She began to run down the drive towards Daisy, tottering on her high heels while holding up her white satin explosion of a dress.

'Alison, it isn't all good news, love,' said Howard as he put out his hand to help her over the cobbles.

'What do you mean? Daisy being found is the best news I could have on my wedding day. Howard, this is the best present I could have had, ever.'

By now, she was hugging Daisy.

'Alison, love.' Howard was struggling to get through to his new bride, but, in her euphoria at Daisy being found, she was beyond hearing.

It was only Nellie and Harriet who spotted the handcuffs being placed on Simon before he was discreetly slipped into the back of the car Daisy had vacated. The man in the black-and-white cap with the chequered band took the seat next to him and, within seconds, the car had quietly whisked them both away.

## Chapter Eight

'I'm coming, Mother,' Ben shouted down the stairs, in response to her repeated calls summoning him to her traditional morning fry-up. His mother's hearing had been damaged by a bomb blast during the war and, despite the fact he had now replied three times, she hadn't heard him once.

Ben couldn't move down the stairs as quickly as he used to.

During the war he had served as an officer in North Africa and Italy. When in France, he had taken a German bullet that had shattered his right tibia and fibula into many pieces, at the same time that a flying piece of shrapnel took up residence in his cheekbone, leaving a four-inch scar running parallel with his right eye. Ben never complained. How could he? He was one of the lucky ones. His brother had returned home in a flag-draped box and his mother had yet to recover.

Immediately following his injury, Ben had been taken by stretcher to a field hospital to be stabilized and made well enough to travel to a military hospital in Belgium. On the long journey back to his home on Queens Drive, he had spent three months in a convalescence home across the water in West Kirby, where his mother had come to visit once a week. He had managed to see his father just before he passed away of a broken heart. No words had been said but Ben and his mother both knew that the dead son had been his badly disguised favourite.

All the doctors in the world could not have prevented Ben from being left with a right leg three inches shorter than his left. He was awarded a clutch of medals for his endeavour and bravery, which did nothing to ease his pain nor mend his anguish at returning from the war disabled and an only child.

There were some medals he wore on his chest, pinned to his suit when he attended formal regimental dinners. There was also a much larger memorial trinket in the form of an iron leg caliper, which he would wear every day for the remainder of his life. At forty-two years of age, he required a stick to help him walk, very slowly.

A more serious effect of his injuries had been their impact on his self-esteem. Before his facial injury Ben could have been described as handsome, albeit quietly so. He now felt that no woman worth her salt would ever want to look twice at a man as broken and unattractive as he. Since the day he had returned home, he had never once looked a woman directly in the eye. If he didn't see her eyes, she might not see the deeper, hidden scars beneath his own.

This saddened his mother who knew that, at sixty-six years of age, she could not be far from the end of her life. Whenever she felt she could do so, without making him cross, she would raise the subject of marriage with Ben. Her son never became really angry, but his scar would turn a tell-tale red when she had upset him and touched that ever-raw nerve.

The scar spoke for him. It burnt and flamed the message back to his mother: 'Who would take this trophy of war?'

Olive Manning had lost her first son, Matthew, at the outbreak of hostilities and Ben, her second, had been injured close to the end of them. Her husband had died two weeks after Ben's honourable discharge. His last words to his wife were that now Ben was home, injured but alive, and he would look after her. Her husband was quite right. Benjamin did look after her. He was the most dutiful of sons.

Ben often wandered into his brother's bedroom. The telegram, which his mother had received from the War Office, lay folded on the top of the dresser she polished every Friday morning, ready for the weekend, during which nothing of any significance ever took place.

Ben often picked up the envelope, faded to a tea-coloured brown by the bright sunlight that still on occasion slipped into the room, and he read the black ticker-tape words over and over again. It had lain there, in the same place, propped up against the dark mahogany-framed mirror. It was as though his mother had placed the telegram on the dresser to inform any ghostly relative who might pop into Matthew's room that he was dead, that he had joined them already and that he would not be returning to lay his earthly head on his feather pillow with its crisp linen cover. No point hovering here. Matthew has gone. We know this. Read the telegram.

Ben hobbled into the kitchen, ducking his head under the narrow doorway at the bottom of the stairs, and winced, as always, as he managed the last two steps. His mother pretended not to notice.

'What important meetings do you have this morning then?' she asked.

Benjamin worked at the City Corporation offices and was responsible for managing the fund the government had poured into Liverpool. It had taken them almost twenty years after the war, but at last they were building new houses, roads, libraries, nurseries and schools.

Liverpool was about to benefit from a growth spurt and, as the new estates sprang up, private landlords would lose their grip on the poor with their extortionate rents for squalid houses.

'It's a meeting at the Priory of St Mary's, down at the docks, about the new nursery and library we are building. The church want to have a say in running both.'

'And is that possible?' asked his mother. 'St Mary's? Isn't that the church where the priest was murdered? I'm sure it was. Dear me, Ben, you had better take care down there. I would quite like you home in one piece.'

'You're right, Mother. It was that church. Well remembered. If I'm honest, I had forgotten. It was my secretary who pointed that out to me. There is a new priest now, apparently. He is very new school, very nineteen-sixties. He wants the Church to reach out and become more involved in the community. That is why they have asked me to attend the meeting. It is something I am happy to discuss. The more the Church helps, the less it costs the council, but I'm very nervous about the library. We want more than bibles for people to read and that will be a stumbling block.'

'Quite right,' replied his mother with a hint of relief in her voice. 'Don't let the papists take over everything, because they would if given half the chance, Benjamin. That's how they work. It is all about power and control. The more pies they have their fingers stuck in, the more influence they can wield. I'm not saying they are all bad. The Pope seems quite nice as a matter of fact, but they just have too much say in what happens everywhere in this city, if you ask me. This isn't Dublin. It's Liverpool, a different country entirely.'

'Have you finished?' asked Ben with a grin, buttering himself a slice of toast . 'You say exactly the same thing about the Jews. You didn't stop to draw breath there. Anyone would think you ran up the frocks for the Orange Order on march day.'

'Don't be cheeky, Ben. I don't like any religion. They are all trouble, as far as I am concerned. I go to my Church of England service on Easter Sunday and Christmas morning, and that is all that is required from any respectable Christian. All that God bothering. I can't be doing with it. If God existed, he would make sure there were no wars and I would still have my son and ...'

Her voice trailed away. She wanted to say that Ben wouldn't have been injured and he would have a wife and she would have grandchildren and her husband would still be alive and she would make a Sunday lunch for them all and present it on the ten-place dinner service she and Ben's father had bought with love and care for just that day. It had been wished for and spoken about, even longed for. This was not the life they had foreseen in the heady first years of their marriage.

But she didn't say a word. She knew Ben didn't like it when she raised the subject of marriage, even though that didn't always stop her.

She placed in front of Ben his breakfast of black pudding, sausages and fried eggs.

'They've taken over Everton, you know, the Irish,' she said and poured them both tea before sitting down at the table herself, as she did so sliding towards Ben the Royal Albert marmalade pot with its dinky silver spoon popping out from under the lid. 'You can't move for the Irish and Catholics anywhere on the brow now. They even have their own things in the shops.'

'Oh, really,' said Ben, already sounding exasperated. 'Like what?'

'Well, in the butcher's, he has changed the sign from "bacon" to "rashers". It's just the start, Ben. They were all supposed to go back after the famine. It's about time you stopped worrying about all those Irish and concentrated on finding yourself a wife. I will be in a wheelchair by the time I have grandchildren.'

Suddenly, it was as though an icy blast had shot through their little kitchen on Queens Drive. She had uttered the words guaranteed to ruin Ben's day.

For the first five years following his discharge, Ben's mother ceaselessly harped on about his finding a wife until suddenly, without any warning, one day when his leg was particularly painful, Ben had exploded. It was the one and only time he had ever shouted at his mother and now, here she was, poking at his wound once more. Not the one she could see, the visible wound that made her heart ache for the physical discomfort etched on his face when he returned home from a long day at work, but the invisible wound. The raw, lonely, aching wound Ben carried inside.

'Please don't, Mother.' His voice was calm but cold as steel. 'You know the terrible row we had last time you brought this up. Nothing has altered. I don't want a wife.'

Mrs Manning put both of her elbows on the table and leant forward earnestly, nursing her teacup in both hands and speaking across the rim.

'Ben, I will soon have had my threescore year and ten. How can I die a happy woman, knowing you will be all alone?'

Ben carefully returned the marmalade spoon to the pot, replaced the lid and kept his eyes focused on his toast.

'No woman wants to marry a cripple, Mother. It would be a hugely unfair thing to ask anyone and, besides, no self-respecting woman would look twice at this contraption.' He glanced down at his leg.

He no longer felt like eating his breakfast and slowly, with the aid of his stick, rose from the table.

'I have to leave. The meeting at St Mary's Priory begins at nine-thirty. I had better start out now as I need to change buses at the Pier Head and make my way down to Nelson Street.'

'Nelson Street? Heavens above, you are right in the middle of them all down there at the docks. You can't move for bog jumpers.'

'Mother.' Ben's voice rose sharply in condemnation, even though he had heard the expression so many times. It was commonly used amongst those who were not of Irish descent.

Ben took down his coat from the hook on the hall dresser that stood adjacent to the front door. His mother scooped up his plate from the table with annoyance and banged it down on the draining board next to the kitchen sink.

'We need to be a bit less welcoming, if you ask me, and then maybe a few more of them would go back home,' she shouted from the kitchen.

'No wonder the Irish stick together if they have to face comments like that. What would you do in their shoes? I feel obliged now to let the church have whatever they want with the nursery and the library.'

Once outside, Ben let out a long breath. He had closed the front door with unaccustomed force. He hadn't realized how much his mother irritated him when she was mean about others and harped on about their taboo subject, his finding a wife.

'That is never going to happen,' he whispered to himself, leaning on his stick as he began his walk to the bus stop.

# Chapter Nine

'Watch the road now, Mr Curtis, 'tis a good stretch from here to Dublin. A few hours and you will be safe, back home with your good wife. I am delighted, so I am, that all was in order and you will come again, will you? We will be looking forward to it, won't we, Sister Celia? And be sure to give us plenty of notice now as we wouldn't want you to travel all this way and be hungry, not even for a second, would we, Sister Celia?'

Sister Assumpta was bidding farewell to the visiting councillors and do-gooders who had called to inspect the laundry and the mother and baby home.

'Watch the vans on that road, will you. The boys driving the delivery vans from the village are just demons, the way they speed along that road. They can drive at forty miles an hour, some of them, so the man who delivers the laundry from the hotel in Galway told me, and he is a good Catholic, he never misses mass and would never tell a lie, isn't that so, Sister Celia?'

And the car doors slammed. One. After. The. Other.

At the sound of the car engine starting up, she waved to the retreating boot of a Ford Cortina.

Sister Assumpta and Sister Celia were both rather too enthusiastically waving goodbye to the councillors who were visiting from the county offices.

They had asked far too many questions for the Reverend Mother's liking.

She stomped back down the corridor to her office, Sister Celia bustling behind in her wake, struggling to keep up.

'The nerve of them,' she ranted, once she had closed the big double wooden doors behind them. 'Fancy asking me to make sure all *my* tracks are covered. Can you believe they used those words? You would not believe the nerve of them, would you now?'

'No, Reverend Mother,' Sister Celia gasped. Unused to moving so quickly, she was already puffing and red in the face. It had been a hard day, what with visitors probing around her ovens and making her nerves jangle. 'I've felt like a mad woman all day, trying to keep the surliest of those ungrateful girls out of the way. God alone knows, the moon would crack itself if one of them smiled. They were no sight for visitors, so they weren't, and ye just never know when one of them might try something on, like turning on the waterworks.'

'You were right, Sister Celia. This visit must have something to do with the cut of that interfering woman, Rosie O'Grady, that busybody of a matron. She has never stopped asking questions and probing into our business since her family brought that girl here from Liverpool.'

'Well, they did say that their next visit was St Vincent's, so she must have reported them too. Did they say what we have to do?' asked Sister Celia, aware that after such an important visit, there must at least be something required of them in terms of how they functioned. The officials had taken lots of notes.

'We have to make sure that our own records don't reflect the bank transactions, nor identify which payments come from which government departments, nor for which girls the payments are made. We have to keep everything confidential. As if we didn't already. They must think we came down with the last shower. Why do they think we change everyone's names the minute they arrive?'

'Are we still claiming for the two girls who escaped? Aideen and Agnes?' asked Sister Celia.

'We are that,' Sister Assumpta threw Sister Celia a sharp look, 'but we have to be careful. If you ask me, 'tis no coincidence at all that they became very friendly with the midwife and it was they who delivered the baby of the midwife's girl, Cissy. As sure as God is true, I know she has had something to do with their escape. Not for one minute would she admit it, though. Someone outside the Abbey helped those girls get away. They could not have done it without help. There must have been a car at the very least.'

'Maybe someone on the road gave them a lift if they got through the gates?'

'You know, that could be true. Maybe we need to employ a gate man as St Vincent's have done. We can do without runaways and that's the truth.'

Sister Assumpta flopped into her office chair with little grace and began opening her mail. The official visit had put her a day behind and had thrown the Abbey routine into disarray. In preparation, the areas shown to the visitors had been scrubbed spick and span. Many of the girls with children in the nursery would not see their babies for a week, as a result of the extra work made necessary by the visit.

'It will soon be time for lunch, Sister Celia. I shall have mine whilst I see to the bills in the post. 'I will eat in the office today, but first, to prayers.'

Both women bustled off towards the chapel as the sound of bells called them to prayer.

Sister Assumpta, although disturbed and made bad-tempered by the visit, breathed a sigh of relief. They had survived. The officials hadn't asked to see any further than the first few sinks in the laundry.

They had, however, undertaken a very detailed examination of the kitchens. Sister Assumpta was well aware that the councillors had assumed the food being prepared for the nuns was also for the girls. It wasn't for her to disabuse them of that notion.

'Sure, do they think girls eat beef stew when they are steeped in sin?' asked Sister Celia, running along beside her as they walked to mass. 'Do they not understand the job we have here, to keep these girls under control? If we fed them what we ate, they would think they were forgiven and become impossible to manage. For the sake of heaven, why would they think they know better than we?'

The visitors had, in fact, been extremely impressed with Sister

Assumpta's facilities and soul-saving discipline. It served them no purpose to agree with the complaints made by Dublin's most senior midwife. Who did she think would look after such wayward girls if the holy nuns didn't, and at what cost?

'Sure, God alone knows the money these nuns save us and the good they do,' one councillor had whispered to another as they surveyed the spotless kitchens where a rich beef stew was being stirred by a smiling nun.

The officials had understood the need for cleanliness and obedience. They had needed no convincing that redemption from sin was to be achieved via hard work. There was even talk that they would send them more girls, because they felt the Abbey could easily handle an increase in numbers.

More girls meant more money.

'That high and mighty, overeducated Rosie O'Grady will not be happy if she discovers that her interfering has brought us more penitents,' Sister Assumpta had grumbled. 'I wonder if she knows her complaining has made things better for us. I have no notion what it is that woman was trying to achieve by reporting us to the authorities, as she has half a dozen times. Will she not stop?'

As she prayed, Sister Assumpta gave thanks that the councillors hadn't asked to look at her paperwork, nor enquired what happened to the girls or the babies who died. There were no death certificates to show them, only plots of earth in the garden. Underneath the weeping willows.

Disgraced girls who had arrived at the convent from the country were not even given the grace of a requiem mass, nor a name – their own name – to mark their graves. Only the penitents who came directly from the industrial schools run by the brothers or other convents were issued with a death certificate, but, even then, not always. Money came into the Abbey for living penitents, not dead ones. On occasion, Sister Assumpta would delay as long as a year before informing the authorities that a girl had died.

The dead babies and children were laid together, deep in the earth. She had lost count of how many there were or even what their names had been. There must have been hundreds by now. The nuns had begun digging the plot over fifty years ago at the turn of the century. The previous Reverend Mother had kept a ledger in which she entered in ink the name of each child and the date they were buried. Sister Assumpta had thought for a long time now that the ledger needed to be destroyed.

Babies were lost in childbirth. For those who survived, many fell victim to disease and infection.

Their pitiful bodies had been preserved in the gently receiving, peat-rich earth, condemned to purgatory for eternity.

When mass was over, Sister Celia took the Reverend Mother her lunch on a tray: boiled beef left over from the previous evening's supper, with salad leaves that the nuns grew in their own garden, and an apple pie, made by Sister Celia from the apples stored in the straw-layered wicker baskets, down in the dark cellar.

'Put the tray by the fireplace,' said Sister Assumpta as Sister Celia wobbled precariously through the door, 'and stay for your own. I'd like you to join me as I don't feel like eating alone today.'

Sister Celia flushed with pride. She was the only nun the Reverend Mother ever invited to eat with her.

'I'll be right back then,' she gabbled and rushed from the room with the empty tray.

Sister Assumpta took over to the fire the few letters she hadn't yet tackled and, after pouring the tea, she picked up the last remaining airmail letter.

She noticed it was from America, but this was not unusual by any means. Sister Assumpta received such letters every day. Sometimes they were from priests, writing on behalf of families in need of a baby or a child to adopt easily and quickly. Sometimes the families wrote themselves.

Some might be letters containing begging pleas and offers of money from barren parents willing to pay any price to adopt a child of their own.

Shovelling into her mouth a huge bite of salted beef and lettuce, sandwiched between freshly buttered white bread, the Reverend Mother leant back in the chair, flicked open the letter with the ornate silver-and-bone-handled knife and began to read.

'I'm back,' Sister Celia trilled as she waddled through the office door, laden with an ample lunch for her own consumption.

Reverend Mother didn't answer.

'What is wrong?' Sister Cecilia enquired. 'You look a little pale. Is it the beef? Is it all right now? We saved the best cut for you, Reverend Mother.' Sister Assumpta still did not reply.

She turned the letter over in her hand and looked at the sender's address on the back of the envelope. And then she turned it round and read it again.

'It concerns the child who was adopted by the Moynihans in Chicago, the builders who paid us three thousand dollars for the baby if they could take it quickly. The baby is sick and they need to know who the mother is. They are on their way here on an aeroplane to talk to us. As if we need more visitors. We may as well open as an hotel and start charging an entry fee.'

'Ye can't tell them that anyway.' Sister Celia looked shocked. 'It is against the rules, and the authorities wouldn't allow it. Besides, who is the mother? Is she a penitent?'

'No, it was the girl Rosie O'Grady sent and delivered.'

'Oh, Heavenly Father, no.'

The flush faded from Sister Celia's own cheeks. Rosie O'Grady was trouble. Nothing had been the same since the day she had taken that girl. They had even had a reporter knocking at the door last week because Rosie O'Grady had written a letter to the newspaper, calling for an explanation of the role of the laundries and the mother and baby homes.

'What will ye tell them?' Sister Celia asked.

'I will tell them the truth, which is all I do know: that the girl's name was Cissy, and that she came from Liverpool. She kept her own name because of that Rosie O'Grady's involvement. I shall send them straight on to see Mrs O'Grady in Dublin. Let her deal with it. We upheld our part of the bargain; the girl has nothing to do with us. She was neither a penitent in the laundry nor a country girl from the mother and baby home. She was a favour we did for the matron. I hope they aren't after getting their money back just because the child is sick.'

Sister Assumpta gazed into the fire deep in contemplation while

Sister Celia ate. The airmail letter hung loosely in her hand and rested on her knee.

She startled Sister Celia when without warning she said, 'There is no moon tonight, Sister Celia. I want all the ledgers from the locked cupboard to be carried out to the midden. Everything, all the papers dating right back from when the first girl arrived here sixty years ago, except for the contracts each girl signed, agreeing to surrender her baby. Set the lot on fire. We can't be blamed for what can't be proven.'

'Sure, well, we will do that, Reverend Mother. I've plenty of girls to get that done, but then what?'

'No, don't use the girls. Don't even use the novices. Let this be done by the nuns. I don't want the girls' prying eyes seeing this, not that any of them can read. We will burn the lot and, tomorrow, we will pay a visit to the sisters up the road at St Vincent's and suggest they do the same. They have been here only a few years but, sure, they will be keeping good records, I have no doubt.

'That Sister Theresa was always a stickler. I don't want people assuming that what they practise there, we follow suit here. More secrecy is what is needed and, if I know Sister Theresa, that won't even have crossed her mind. Oh, yes, come along in now, she would say to anyone who asked. She always was a foolish woman who could never see what was right under her very nose. They would have her tied up in knots. We will drive over first thing in the morning.'

# Chapter Ten

'Shall I wait, nurse? Will he be long or would you rather I came back in half an hour?'

Stanley was instructed to wait. It was a Monday morning in the X-ray department of the children's hospital. The nurse was obviously keen to finish and empty the department so that she could rush to the canteen and meet the other nurses for their post-weekend, lunchtime gossip.

Stanley sat on one of the hard wooden benches as he waited for the young boy he had brought in a wheelchair to be pushed back out to him. In the meantime, he took the opportunity to roll up two cigarettes for both himself and Austin, then carefully laid them on a bed of tobacco in his tin, which he slipped back into the large pocket of his brown overall.

Stanley always experienced the same frisson of excitement when he took a call at the porter's lodge to collect a little lad from the children's ward. This one had been a disappointment. He was far too young.

Stanley had standards. He regarded himself as above the others in the ring, especially Austin.

Just at that moment, Austin breezed into the X-ray department in his long brown porter's coat and sat next to Stanley, having himself wheeled into the department another child from the same ward.

Austin seemed agitated.

'She's back,' he whispered to Stanley.

'Who's back?' Stanley asked. A puzzled frown sat on his face.

'The housekeeper, Daisy, she escaped and she's back.'

'Jesus, are you fucking joking?'

'Do I look like I'm fucking joking?'

Indeed, Austin was as white as a sheet.

'How? How did that fucking happen? I thought the bishop had sorted it and that she was put away?'

'He did and she was, but she is back and she has fingered the policeman, Simon, the one who took her to the home. I knew it was fucking crazy, sending someone she could finger if she was asked.'

'Jesus, let's hope she doesn't remember you, Austin. She was one of your favourites. You and the bishop had more than your fair share there when she was a kid. Anyway, she's simple, isn't she?

No one will believe anything she says. She's mental, isn't she? That's what you always said.'

'You cheeky bastard,' said Austin, 'don't blame any of this on me.'

'I'm not blaming you, but what do we do now?'

'We do nothing, Stanley. We aren't the main players in this, for fuck's sake. Why do you think everyone's identity is kept secret? You and I only know each other because I took you. We only know Arthur because he took me. The only other people we know are the bishop and that policeman, but I know this, Stanley: there are people way, way more important than you or me in that ring. Jesus, who do you think I sell all my photos to?'

'I don't fucking care,' said Stanley, his voice rising.

Austin lightly placed his hand on his sleeve.

Stanley dropped his voice and continued, 'Who is that Daisy going to finger next if she's named the policeman? This is a disaster, Austin. She knew all about what went on at the Priory, for fuck's sake. She even opened the door and let some of the kids in. The priest was so up his own arse he thought he was too important to do it himself.'

'It isn't people like me and you at the bottom of the pile that they will be looking for. It's the posh nobs, the politician from London with the chauffeur-driven car, the ones who speak like they've got a finger stuck up their arse – those are the ones they will be after. And anyway, like you say, she was fucking simple. She won't even remember our names. It's much easier for her to say, the policeman, the bishop or the politician. That's why the policeman has been fingered. She said a policeman and then probably identified him. She didn't know where we work or what we do for a job. Relax, mate, haven't I always been right, eh? Eh? Haven't I? Every time you've had a wobbly, didn't I always know what was what and that it would all be all right?'

Stanley nodded. It was true, Stanley was always the nervous one and Austin had always been right.

'It's all right for you, Austin, you live alone. I have me mam to worry about. I can't even think how it would affect her, if she ever knew what I did.'

'Relax, mate,' said Austin. 'There's nothing to worry about with your mam, it will all be good.'

Austin's words weren't having their usual calming effect as, Stanley had noticed, his voice shook slightly.

The nurse called out for Austin as she wheeled her child out of X-ray.

'Let's meet up for a fag in ten in the lodge when you are done here,' he whispered to Stanley as he rose from the bench.

It was Austin who had kept Stanley on the straight and narrow when he had the collywobbles, on the days when he was tormented by guilt, fear and worry about his being caught and his mam being disappointed in him. It was Austin who pulled him up sharp and made him see right again.

Not today, though. Never before had Austin failed to reassure Stanley. His guts had turned to water.

Since he and Austin had become involved in the group to which Arthur had introduced them, they often talked about the legalizing of their own inclination. Stanley had even gone by coach with Austin and Arthur to a meeting in London about that very thing. Times were changing. Arthur never stopped saying, 'Homos will be legal soon, we will be next.'

Soon, paedophiles like themselves would be protected by the law just as homosexuals would soon be. This, they firmly believed.

Stanley knew that someone in the ring was involved in all of this progress. He just didn't know who it was, which was how it would always remain. They were each protected by their own anonymity.

Stanley could tell Austin was spooked. The cool, untouchable swagger was gone, replaced by rounded, almost slumped shoulders.

The pretty little girl in the wheelchair was about six years old, Austin's favourite age, but even this hadn't put the usual grin on his face. He carried his Kodak Brownie in his big overall pocket everywhere he went. In normal circumstances, in the lift, he would have slid the little girl's blanket and nightdress up over her knee and photographed her, before she was returned to the ward, laughing and joking as he did so.

It was so easy. The poorer and more impoverished the children were, the more they loved the attention of the camera. Not today, though.

Stanley stood and, through the circular porthole windows, high in the wooden doors leading to the X-ray department, he followed Austin's retreating back. Agitated at the news that Daisy was in Liverpool once more, he then sat down and turned to look through the large window to the courtyard. He could watch Austin cross, wheeling the chair to the ward doors on the opposite side.

It took a few moments for Stanley to register what was happening as, with an action as slick as an uncoiling snake, a policeman stepped out through the ward doors and snapped a pair of handcuffs onto Austin's wrists.

Stanley immediately knew what he had to do. They had been through the drill so many times at their monthly meetings. Slowly, he rose from the bench and, so as not to draw attention to himself, he walked calmly out of the back door.

'Porter, porter, your patient's ready,' shouted the radiographer from within the lead-lined cubicle. 'Would you believe it,' he heard her say to her workmate on reception, 'the porter has only gone and buggered off for a ciggie.'

By the time he reached the hospital gates, Stanley was running. He turned out on to Queens Drive and kept on running. He knew that he had to reach Arthur, the ringleader as quickly as possible. Arthur would know what to do.

The plan had been in place for over ten years and it was always the last thing discussed each time the group met. Secrecy was their modus operandi. People like them were never, ever, caught. Never. They were methodical and careful. They had strict rules. Should those fail, they would resort to long-established and well-rehearsed procedures. Arthur had people who could protect them, contacts who could offer places to hide. Once the others found out what had happened to Austin, Stanley would need just such a place himself.

# Chapter Eleven

'Fancy delaying your honeymoon, Miss Devlin. I can't believe it, I just can't. You should be in the Isle of Man by now. I feel so bad that I have upset everything. Do I still call you Miss Devlin, or is it your married name now?'

It was Monday morning. Daisy was ladling as much marmalade as she possibly could onto her last piece of toast before popping it into her mouth. This meant that, for a brief second, she ceased talking and drew breath.

She had almost finished her breakfast in the convent where she had spent the previous two nights. She talked so much and so fast, it was hard for anyone to slide a word in edgeways. Not only was Daisy talking fifty to the dozen, she was surrounded by nuns and children. Annie O'Prey, Sheila from Nelson Street with her children, and a constant relay of neighbours were tripping up and down the convent steps to visit her.

Alison laughed. 'You do love your food, don't you, Daisy? I want to be here because I want to see your brother again and make sure that, this time, I hand you over personally. Besides, they have asked Howard to return to work and to delay our honeymoon. We don't mind at all. In any case, I will have a much nicer time, knowing that everything is properly sorted here. It would have been difficult, Daisy, trying to enjoy myself, having no idea where you were or what had happened to you.'

Sister Evangelista walked into the refectory and sat down at the table with them both. No longer a stranger to a crisis, she was absolutely certain this time about what to do.

'Will you be ringing the bishop to let him know Daisy is back?' Alison asked.

'Sure, I will not. What use would he be if I did tell him? He was as much use as a chocolate fireguard last time we needed him and with half the backbone. No, thank you. We have Father Anthony and Harriet with us now, sent directly to us by the Lord, I have no doubt. They will be a grand help. I have no use for a weak bishop. Father Anthony will know what to do and, if the bishop needs to know what is happening, Father Anthony can tell him. I am washing my hands altogether of that responsibility.'

The new Mrs Davies was almost sure she heard Sister Evangelista mutter, 'Stupid man,' under her breath, following on from the 'chocolate fireguard'.

'The bishop doesn't need to know Daisy has returned or that the police have already been to the Priory to see Father Anthony, who, I will have you know, Alison, has handled everything in an exemplary manner. The man is magnificent in his ability to project authority and calm. That's what a spell in Rome can do for a priest. We have a different quality in the parish altogether now and, sure, we are very lucky here, we are. Is he not the most fabulous priest? We could do no better at all. No, leave it all to Father Anthony, he will know what to do, not the bishop.' She began to mutter as she poured her tea and from behind a plume of steam, Alison was sure she heard what she said.

There it was again, now Alison was certain: she definitely heard Sister Evangelista say, 'Useless man,' when she had finished speaking.

Alison had not wanted to pass comment, but she was quite sure that at one time, she had heard Sister Evangelista heap exactly the same praise she had for Father Anthony on the dead priest, Father James. She would now no longer discuss him, no matter how much Alison tried to persuade her to do so.

Without knowing it, Father Anthony had shamed the bishop over his obscure and evasive behaviour during the previous investigation.

Sister Evangelista looked lighter and happier than she had in months. 'I noticed Harriet leaving the Priory earlier and I wouldn't be surprised to find she is on her way over here. Everyone else appears to be. I've never known the convent so busy, Daisy. You are quite the attraction.'

'Well, I'm here because I cannot go anywhere else and I don't want to leave Daisy,' said Alison. 'Howard has been called back to work to assist the new commander from today onwards. At least we had the weekend, eh? Anyway, thank goodness it is the summer holidays and the school is closed. I don't want to miss having a few days with Daisy. I think it would be nice for her to get to know Harriet and Father Anthony.

'Ah, speak of an angel and hear the rustle of her wings,' Alison trilled as Harriet swept in through the door.

'Morning, everyone.' Harriet's voice rang out from the hallway. 'Are you up already? Have you recovered from the wedding and all that dancing on Saturday night?'

'You will often hear Harriet coming long before you see her,' Alison said to Daisy with an indulgent smile.

'Aye, she seems to forget she's in a convent and silence is a virtue,' Sister Evangelista said drily.

Daisy smiled. To all who had asked her, she had explained about her having been in a convent in Ireland. From the moment she had arrived back in the four streets she had been besieged with questions. Once the wedding festivities had begun, Daisy knew she was safe and so she had the time of her life.

It was hard for Daisy to find words to express the difference between Sister Theresa's convent in Galway and the one in Liverpool. She could not understand why it was that the nuns at St Mary's were kindness itself compared with those at St Vincent's. It was a mystery to everyone other than Daisy as to why Simon had taken her to the convent.

Maggie had told Daisy to be very careful what she told and to whom she told it.

'Keep your powder dry. Tell no one anything they don't need to know, not even the sisters at St Mary's. The only people you should tell almost everything to are the police. But you don't mention another word about that little girl's da, Tommy. It sounds as if that family have been through enough.'

Daisy had listened very carefully to Maggie. She felt mean not telling everything to Miss Devlin, who she must try and remember to now call Mrs Davies, but she knew Maggie was right and had worked everything out meticulously.

'I loved the dancing,' said Daisy. ''Twas fantastic to see all the girls dancing like that, it was just grand. I know I shouldn't laugh but the funniest thing was watching Big Paddy trying to throw Peggy over his shoulder. She wouldn't give the man a rest.'

They all laughed at the memory of Little Paddy hiding his head in his hands in shame.

'Mam, Da, will ye stop!' Little Paddy had shouted, bouncing up and down with the ruff of his shirt collar muffling his words.

When Peggy and Paddy had ignored him, he had tried to cut in between them both, but to no avail. His mother had then taken his hands and, twirling him round on the dance floor, danced with him instead. An experience which had left Little Paddy traumatized with embarrassment at the memory. That morning, it had been the first thing he thought of when he woke and it made him blush with shame when the boys on the green had shouted, 'Give us a dance then, Paddy,' when he ran to the shop for his da's ciggies. Boys didn't dance but if ever one was so misguided as to try, the last person he would dance with in public, and in front of all his school friends, would be his mother.

'Would ye stop,' said Alison, catching her breath. 'I enjoyed my own reception more than I should have. I thought I would be on pins and nervous, but, Daisy, you made it the best.'

'I would like to visit a few of the women if that is all right with you, Sister Evangelista,' said Daisy. 'I told Annie I would call over this morning. Would ye mind if I leave now?'

'Not at all, Daisy, you go ahead. I am here all day and your room is your own until the police say your brother can collect you. Harriet and I are both off this morning to a meeting about the new nursery, but we will be at the Priory if you need us.'

Maura was surprised when she heard a knock on her front door. It was only just audible, more of a gentle, nervous tap than a knock. As it was the school holidays, everyone was still in bed, catching up on their sleep following a weekend of excitement that included a late night after the wedding. None of the children had made it to bed until the early hours on Sunday, and they were still recovering by Monday.

When Maura saw Daisy on the doorstep, she smiled.

'Well, what a commotion you caused on Saturday, miss,' she said as she opened the door wider for Daisy to step into the hallway.

'You were laughing and talking away on Saturday night with everyone, so you were. I never had the chance to catch a word meself.'

Maura hadn't set eyes on her for six months and she noticed a difference in the girl. She was more grown up, with a worldly-wise look about her. As both women moved into the kitchen, Maura gestured for Daisy to take a seat.

'Sit down, love,' she said, 'and I'll make us a cuppa.'

'Thanks, Mrs Doherty,' said Daisy, sitting on a week's worth of Tommy's *Liverpool Echos*, which lived under the seat cushion and crinkled in objection as she gently lowered herself onto the sofa.

'Miss Devlin told me about Kitty. I'm sorry for your troubles. I really am, I'm sorry for your troubles.'

Maura didn't reply. She couldn't. There were no words to be said.

'You haven't been in my kitchen before, have you, Daisy? You were always too busy in the Priory,' said Maura brightly, wanting to change the subject. 'Although I know Molly used to visit you sometimes, and Annie O'Prey. Did ye talk to Annie last night?'

'I did, Mrs Doherty, I am off to see her in a minute, but first I wanted to talk to ye. I have to tell ye summat.'

Maura stood the pot of tea and the cups on the range shelf and poured milk from the bottle into the two cups.

'Will you drop the Mrs Doherty, Daisy. My name is Maura and you aren't working at the Priory now.'

'I saw him, Maura. I saw him every time he left the Priory and walked down the entry towards your door. I watched him from the window and I was glad he was over here and not bothering me. I'm sorry, Maura. I'm sorry I never told you.'

Maura gasped and lowered herself onto the sofa next to Daisy.

Maura couldn't speak. She could make no response other than to wring her hands in her lap and stare at Daisy as though she had grown an extra nose whilst sitting in her kitchen.

'God in heaven, he was doing it to you too? It never crossed my mind.'

Hot tears sprang to Maura's eyes. God knew, she had cried enough to fill the Mersey but they were always there, just beneath the surface, looking for a reason to flow. She reached out and held Daisy's hands in her own.

'It is me who is sorry, Daisy. Me. That man was evil itself and I don't feel sorry when I say that, as God is my judge, I am glad he is dead.'

Now it was Daisy's turn to well up. There, she had finally said the words she always knew she should share with Maura, so that Maura would know, she hadn't failed Kitty and that there was nothing she could have done. Father James's behaviour had been beyond the comprehension of any decent human being.

The two women looked at each other for a long moment. One was considered simple and vulnerable. The other had thought she was an expert at keeping her children safe and out of harm's way. Maura reached out and took Daisy's hand in her own. They were now keepers of the same secret.

Daisy said, 'You are right, Maura. He was an evil man, a son of the devil, Maggie says, and me and Kitty and the others, there was nothing we could do.'

Daisy didn't tell Maura that he had done the same thing to lots of girls and that she and Sister Evangelista knew this because they had found the photographs in his desk drawer. Daisy didn't say this to Maura, but she was going to say it herself to Sister Evangelista. Maggie had told her she had to. She had written down all the things Maggie had told her she had to do, one by one, and telling Sister Evangelista that she had to tell the police what she had found in the father's desk drawer was number four.

Talking to Maura was number two. Stepping into the police station and giving them the letter from Maggie and Frank, that was number one.

When she had written the list with Maggie, Daisy had thought that she would never be able to do any of it. But now that she was here, seeing Maura had been so easy, and to think she had thought it would be the worst.

'Get the hardest things out of the way first,' Maggie had said. 'The rest will be straightforward then and nothing to be frightened of.'

Maggie had been right.

Now, Maura and Daisy were both crying.

'But, Maura, there's more, there's more I have to say.'

Maura sat back slightly. She realized this was big for Daisy. She could see a battle raging somewhere inside her and that what she had said had not been easy for her.

Maura picked up Daisy's cup and handed it to her.

'Here, drink some tea,' she said. 'It will help calm your nerves. Shall I get us a couple of Anadin?'

Daisy shook her head and sipped the tea. Maura was right. She felt calmer now. Tea cured all ills.

Maura stood and dropped the catch on the back door. It was a thing she had never done before in all the time she had lived on the four streets, but intuition told her that the last thing she needed today was Peggy barging in.

Maura sat down again, closer to Daisy who, in preparation for her most crucial words, placed her cup and saucer on the floor near her feet. She leant back and took a deep breath. For a second, she heard Maggie's voice.

'Just say it out loud, Daisy, you only have to say it once and then it's done.'

Daisy looked Maura straight in the eye. 'Maura, I also saw what happened on the night the father was murdered. I saw how it happened, from the upstairs window in the Priory.'

Maura felt the room spin. Her foundations were moving, as if a chasm were about to open. She had been clinging onto the edge of a precipice for so long, waiting for something unknown to tip her off, and now here it was. It was Daisy.

She grasped the wooden arm of the chair tightly. She was teetering on the edge of her own sanity and she needed to hold on. She had to brace herself for whatever it was Daisy was about to say. Maura couldn't look. She couldn't see Daisy when she spoke the words that would condemn her husband to death.

'Oh God,' she gasped, putting her free hand to her mouth.

'No, don't worry,' said Daisy, placing her hand on Maura's. 'That is why I am here. I am sorry, I told the police once, but they didn't believe me. They thought I was simple and do you know, I was. I was so upset at what was happening to me. The awful secret I had to keep, it made me simple. That's what Maggie says anyway and I think she is right, because I can see everything so much clearer now. Thank God they didn't believe me. I only did it, I told them, because Molly said I had to. Molly is dead now and I am not simple, but I am the only one who saw it happen. I am the only one who knows and it is the thing Maggie said I had to keep a secret and never speak of it again, except to you, to put your mind at ease. That's what Maggie said.'

'Maggie?' said Maura. 'Who the hell is Maggie?' Maura almost screamed the question.

'She is the lady who looked after me and helped me back to Liverpool. She taught me to speak properly. And she helped me to escape and get to the police and told me everything I had to do and say.'

'What did you see, Daisy?' Maura asked, almost in a whisper. 'Did you see Tommy and Jerry and what they did?'

'Me, I didn't see nothing, Maura. Maggie said that, once I told you, I was never to speak about it again and that I had to forget what I had seen. She said you had suffered enough, that we all have, and that the priest got everything he deserved, and that she would have done the very same.' Maura laughed and cried at the same time as she hugged Daisy. The two of them wiped their eyes. Maura poured more tea and, sitting next to Daisy and placing her hand back in hers, she asked, 'Did you know what happened to Kitty, Daisy?'

For the following hour, Maura sat with her arm round Daisy's shoulders as she told her Kitty's story. Simple Daisy, the first woman apart from Kathleen that Maura had talked to about Kitty. It felt good to talk to Daisy. She had shared Kitty's nightmare. She would understand. Maura cried as she spoke and, at times, her words battled with her sobs to be heard. But nothing could stop the outpouring of emotion Maura felt as she sat, side by side in front of the range fire, with Daisy.

Daisy knew at first hand the evil which Kitty had known. They were now sisters. Blood sisters.

Maura had been so engrossed in talking to Daisy about Kitty that she hadn't heard Harry and Little Paddy on the stairs, nor noticed that they had halted their descent. Having heard voices in the kitchen, they were sitting on the bottom step behind the door.

She usually did hear the children. Since Kitty had died, Little Paddy often stopped over for the night, as he and Scamp were great at dispelling the gloom and lightening the atmosphere. Like all Maura's children, Little Paddy was convinced she could see through wooden doors.

Neither of the boys moved a muscle while they listened to every word. Harry's own tears fell softly as he heard his mother speak about his beloved Kitty, something Tommy had told him he was not allowed to do in front of Maura, for fear of upsetting her. He cried for Daisy too. But boys weren't allowed to cry.

Just as Little Paddy put his arm round Harry's shoulders, they heard Malachi dive out of bed, yelling, 'Mam, I'm starving.'

Harry quickly dried his eyes. Little Paddy held out his little finger. Harry held out his and hooked it through Paddy's and their hands shook.

'Secret forever,' whispered Little Paddy. Harry nodded in response. Both boys jumped up and, stamping on the stairs to announce their arrival, they noisily entered the kitchen just as Scamp began to bark at the back door.

# Chapter Twelve

When Ben Manning arrived at the Priory, it was a hive of activity. He took the letter from the inside pocket of his jacket and reread it carefully, checking the name of the person he was supposed to be meeting.

'Here is a very charming letter,' his secretary had said. 'Well written too. Miss Harriet Lamb, she's obviously had a proper education. Look at that punctuation. I bet she's about ninety. This is a woman who knows how to get her way. Little old ladies can be very disarming, Mr Manning. Be on your guard when you meet her on Monday morning.'

Ben had smiled. It would take more than a little old lady with beautiful diction to make him agree to the library being run by the local church.

As Ben stood at the Priory gates and glanced over at the churchyard where, he knew, the murdered priest had been found, he once again checked the address at the top of the letter. He was at the correct Priory, and the name on the bottom was Miss Harriet Lamb. He scanned the people arriving who were also attending the meeting, searching for a woman with a kindly face. He had already imagined Miss Harriet Lamb.

He half expected her to look like every Irish matron in Liverpool: rotund, wearing a headscarf and a black skirt.

When the door was opened by a young woman in a floral dress, with long dark curls, smiling the broadest smile, he fully expected her to direct him to a room in the Priory where Miss Lamb and her committee would be waiting for him.

'Hello,' the young woman said in a beautiful voice. 'I'm Harriet Lamb. Are you Mr Manning from the City Corporation?'

For a moment, Ben couldn't speak.

'I am sorry to be so presumptuous,' she almost sang. 'It is just that, obviously, it is a very tight community around here and, if you don't mind me saying so, a man who knocks on the Priory door in such a smart overcoat sticks out like a sore thumb. And besides, we are expecting you.' She laughed.

He had no idea what she had just said. He was only aware of her lips moving and had no idea what to say in response.

The woman stopped laughing, but her smile remained. Ben noticed that she never once looked down at his leg, unlike almost every other person he had met, since the day he had been discharged from the army.

'Hello in there,' she said, laughing and pretending to look into and behind his eyes.

Ben spluttered and blurted out, 'I am so dreadfully sorry, but I was expecting someone older.'

The young woman laughed again.

'But your accent?' Ben knew he was being incredibly clumsy but seemed unable to stop himself.

'Ah, yes, well, it may surprise you to know, Mr Manning, I was educated in Dublin and my father was a doctor. We don't all speak the same, you know. And, if you don't mind me saying so, I have met many people in Liverpool who don't speak with a strong accent.'

Ben blushed, profoundly embarrassed.

Harriett smiled. She had already realized that Mr Manning would be a pushover and that she was halfway to achieving every outcome she wanted from the meeting. She'd had no idea that it would be quite that easy or that the man from the Liverpool Corporation would be so gentle.

'I have to apologize for asking you to come to the Priory. It is just that there are so many of us and your secretary thought it might be better if you came here. Also, I thought that if you did so, you could see the committee in action. I know there was a great deal in the press regarding an unfortunate incident that took place here last year, but I wanted you to see that that is all behind us now. The church is a happy church and the people involved are committed to this community.

'Now, come, Mr Manning, come and meet my brother, Father Anthony, and Sister Evangelista, and my friend who is a teacher at the school, Alison, who was only married on Saturday and should be on her honeymoon now, but that's a different story. You will like them all, I promise you.'

Ben fell in line beside Harriet, unaware that she was deliberately walking more slowly than usual. She had seen the caliper without his having been aware.

Ben, who was painfully shy around women at the best of times, had lost his tongue completely.

'And here is everyone,' she said, leading him to the study where her brother sat behind the desk.

Amid the clatter of chinking china and teaspoons in sugar bowls, Harriet introduced Ben to the people sitting around, beginning with Father Anthony and finishing with Nana Kathleen.

Ben knew nothing whatsoever about the church or its ways. He felt uncomfortable, as though, whatever he said, he would surely put his foot straight in his mouth and show his ignorance.

'Now then,' Harriet said, having introduced everyone, 'I have written to Mr Manning to explain to him that we are delighted that a children's nursery is to be built on the bombed-out wasteland, and the library too. I have explained that we also understand that it is for the benefit of the people living in the tin houses, which, Mr Manning, I know are the prefabs, but everyone around here refers to them as the tin houses. However, as the convent plays such a huge role in the community, including running the school, I am sure Mr Manning agrees with me that there must be ways we can work together to a mutual benefit.'

An hour and a half later, Benjamin Manning made his way back to the bus stop. He had never before spent such a happy time in the company of others.

They were such joyful people. And Harriet Lamb, surely such a beautiful woman could not be single? He smiled ruefully to himself. Miss Lamb. He had granted her every concession she had asked for. He had nothing in his briefcase that could defend him against those bright blue eyes and her lovely smile. All the way home on the bus, he relived every moment, every gesture. He closed his eyes and summoned the sound of her voice.

Benjamin felt sad that his injuries would prevent him from asking Miss Lamb to have tea with him at the Lyons Corner House one afternoon. From living a normal life as most men did. From having a wife. He knew he had to banish her from his mind. A woman as lovely as she was would be ashamed to be seen walking down the road with a man wearing a caliper. Harriet Lamb did not need a cripple on her arm when she could do so much better.

As he looked out of the window on the journey home, he did not see the river, the sprawling warehouses or the ships, waiting patiently at the bar. As the bus turned up the hill into Edge Lane, the familiar terraced houses and the children playing in the streets were just a blur. He was somewhere else, in an imagined life. One he had never dared to visit since the day he was wounded. He could hear the voice of another, one that did not belong to his mother, calling him to breakfast. A voice he had heard for the first time just a few short hours ago.

He did not notice the solitary tear of loneliness that ran down his cheek.

When everyone had left the Priory and only Father Anthony and Harriet remained, she was unusually quiet.

'Has the cat got your tongue?' asked Anthony.

'Don't talk about cats and body parts,' said Harriet and tapped him on the arm.

'Heavens, I forgot,' said Anthony, shuddering.

The murdered priest's body had been discovered, just as Molly Barrett's cat had walked into the street, carrying his langer in its mouth. This was now a source of secret jokes amongst the children on the four streets and the subject of not so secret ribaldry down in the Anchor pub.

'I was just turning over in my mind, who else we should ask to be on the committee for the nursery.'

'May I make a suggestion?' said Anthony. 'Ask Maura Doherty.

That woman needs something to occupy her mind. I think that she could benefit from focusing on anything other than the loss of her daughter. It might just be the thing to bring her out of herself and to help her heal. I feel sorry for the twin lads. Little Harry and Malachi always look a bit lost. I know Declan and Kevin are a different pair altogether, but if something doesn't give to restore a bit of happiness into that home, I can see those two going off the rails before long. Declan runs riot at the school and I know Sister Evangelista is loath to say anything to Maura and Tommy because of all their troubles.'

'Would you like me to have a word, Anthony?'

Harriet loved the Dohertys. The hours she had passed helping to heal Nellie Deane had brought her close to the families affected by Kitty's death. She had spent a great deal of time with Maura when she helped the neighbours to look after Maura and Tommy.

Harriet and Anthony had never met Kitty, but they had heard enough from Sister Evangelista to know that there was something they weren't being told. But that didn't matter. They were here to minister and to love their neighbours and that was what they would do. Harriet might not have been holy, but she was good.

'I don't know, Harriet. Maybe you could have a gentle word about the twins at the same time as you ask her to help?'

Harriet smiled. 'I will find a way. Come here and give me a hug.'

Benjamin Manning came unbidden into Harriet's mind again.

'What are you thinking of, Harriet? You surely aren't this pensive about a nursery committee?'

Sometimes Harriet thought Anthony could read her mind. 'Well, I was just thinking what a nice man Mr Manning was.'

She blushed.

'And what a pity we hadn't met years ago. Useless thoughts, as no man as handsome as he is would want to date a woman my age, so never fear, they were just idle imaginings.'

'Brought on by Alison's wedding on Saturday, no doubt,' said Anthony, looking at his sister with great care.

They told each other everything. They were the closest of siblings, and had been made even more so by the recent loss of both their parents. They were also bound by the fact that it was silently understood, Harriet as a spinster would remain with Anthony. He felt guilty that his sister had spent the best years of her life nursing first his father and then his mother, whilst he had been away at the seminary.

He felt guilty that she had sacrificed her life. He wanted to do all that he could for her. That was why he was determined to take his sister with him in the role of housekeeper. He could not leave her alone in Dublin in their parents' big house. Anthony was the first priest ever at St Mary's to have a housekeeper as well as a full-time cleaner, but he didn't care. Where he went, his sister would go too.

'I suppose thirty-five is rather late,' Anthony replied. 'But you never know.'

A modern priest in the city of the Beatles, Anthony was trying to be helpful, but he realized it wasn't working.

He sat down at his desk to work, and Harriet went into the kitchen to make their tea. As she filled the kettle, Harriet felt a pain stab her in the chest.

She thought of how happy Alison Devlin had been at her wedding. Alison was also old to be getting married. She had complained about it often enough, even confiding that she thought she might be too old to have children. Was it so impossible for someone Harriet's age to find a husband?

As she stood over the sink, her tears fell and not for the first time. They were hot tears of loss and frustration for the life she knew she could never have, that of a wife and a mother.

Even as she cried, she knew it wasn't just because of the wedding on Saturday. It had something to do with that lovely shy man, with the kind eyes and the caliper, which she could see hurt him as he walked. The gentle man who was softly spoken and nervous, and who had told Sister Evangelista he wasn't married.

She looked down and smiled as Scamp licked her feet. At that moment, they heard Little Paddy and Harry banging on the back door.

'Well, look who's here? The boys to take you on your walk, little fella.'

And within seconds, the kitchen was filled with boys and dogs and the noise that Harriet wished had always been a part of her life.

# Chapter Thirteen

Stanley was too afraid to switch on the lights.

The back door had opened, with difficulty and a loud creak, into the kitchen where they had held their crisis meeting after the priest had been murdered. Stanley remembered the men who had sat round the table on that night. Most of them he didn't know, but there were some that he had recognized.

Austin had told Stanley that the key to survival was anonymity. If no one knew who each other was, no one could tell anyone anything.

Austin had now been arrested. Would Austin snitch on Stanley?

Stanley had never touched that Daisy from the Priory, but Austin had and she knew who he was. Austin was fucking mad, always taking risks. He had told Daisy he worked at the children's hospital. He had been showing off, pretending he was a doctor. The priest had Austin's address and details in his diary. Stanley knew that. He had seen it. No one had Stanley's. He had told no one anything. Still, he was taking no risks. If Arthur said this was where he should be, in the safe house, this was where he would stay.

'The bishop will be on his fucking way to Panama now if he's got any fucking sense,' Arthur had said to Stanley.

'Does the bishop know she has come back?'

'He fucking must do, he's the one who had her in hiding. The bishop isn't going to let her fucking escape without doing a runner himself, although how the fuck he let her get away from wherever he had her, I don't know. I would have fucking drowned her myself. All the stupid policeman had to do was push her over the rail. Fucking yeller bastards. Now we are all at risk because the bishop couldn't do his job properly.'

'Bit hard for bishop to get someone topped, I suppose?' Stanley had said.

'What? A bit harder than shagging her when she was only twelve? Yeah, right.'

Remembering there were candles in the hearth of the range, Stanley felt his way across the kitchen. He took the lighter out of his pocket and flicked the flint into life.

The dirty, shoddy room lit up, with images even Stanley didn't want to see.

The floor was covered in newspapers and near the fire a grubby toy doll lay discarded. The flame from the lighter was reflected back to Stanley from the cold, glass eyes.

He lit a candle from the store in the fireplace and began to unpack the bag he had brought with him, placing items one by one on a wooden table that stood at the side of the sink. Corned beef and spam, condensed milk, a packet of tea. He assumed he would be safe to visit the shops. There would be no one looking for him around here. Even if Austin spilt the beans, he wouldn't remember this house, or know that Arthur would send him here and use it as a safe house.

Austin might direct the police to the hospital or Stanley's home, but not here. When he thought of his mam and how distressed she would be, he felt sick.

Maybe he would sneak out in the dark and nip back to see her. He could make up a story, although he knew not what, and tell her he had to lie low for a while. As he sat huddled in the glow of the paltry fire and his solitary candle, he realized he might have to spend many hours doing very little else. He had managed to light the range, using bits of wood he had found in the garden. Some were windfall branches that had fallen way back in wartime, when the house had last been inhabited. The huge tree in the middle of the lawn had shed a pile large enough to keep a fire ticking over in the range for at least a couple of weeks. In the coal store, he had found the best part of a half-hundredweight of coal, which he would use sparingly.

Arthur had sent no message, nor had he called in as promised. This made Stanley feel even more nervous as the day went by.

Days later, he ran short of provisions, and was almost sick with worry about his mother.

'Where the fuck is Arthur?' he said to himself over and over as he paced up and down in the dark back kitchen of the bomb-damaged house. The one trip out that he had made to buy further supplies had alarmed him and he didn't want to have to do it again.

He had slipped out to the shops the day after he had arrived, just before they closed, when shopkeepers were packing up, distracted, thinking of their journey home and putting tea on the table. He had used the big grocery store before the green on Breck Road, just down from Holy Trinity church. The shelves had been piled with good things to eat, but Stanley had no idea how long he would have to make his money last.

His eye was immediately caught by square metal bins with plastic lids, along the front of the long wooden counter, full of every imaginable kind of broken biscuit. He hadn't eaten since the previous day and his stomach growled as the smell of custard creams filled his nostrils. His mouth began to water. He took a brown paper bag and slowly went from one bin to the next, filling the bag. Keeping his head down, he handed it over the counter to the man in a white overcoat to be weighed.

'Anything else I can get for you?' the shopkeeper enquired as Stanley continued to look in the bins, as though fascinated by the contents.

'A quarter-pound of tea, a pint of sterilized milk, a pound of sugar.' Stanley still didn't look up.

Armed in addition with beans, bacon, bread, cheese and twenty Players, he hung around the green until it was dark when he could return to the house, entering through the back door, unseen by neighbours.

Arthur had said he would call on Stanley's mother to tell her that she must not, under any circumstances, contact the police about her son's sudden absence and that she was not to panic. Stanley knew she had never met Arthur and would be out of her mind with suspicion and worry. He was all she had and he meant the world to her. She depended upon him for everything. Without his wages this week, she would be more than a little anxious.

Stanley squatted down on his haunches in front of the range, waiting for the water in the enamel pot to boil. He had found it in a cupboard, covered in dust and cobwebs.

He couldn't stop himself from worrying about his mam. In amongst the mouse droppings and the old newspapers scattered over the terracotta-tiled floor, he made the decision; as soon as it was dark, he would catch the bus back home, just to see if his mam was OK. He would slip in through the back door and stay just a few minutes, long enough to sign his bank-book so that she could take out any money she needed from his savings and to collect a few things.

Then he would take the night sleeper to Edinburgh and, once there, move up to the highlands. He could work as a kitchen porter for a year or so, until everything had died down. When it was safe, he would return home to his mam.

The enamel pot on the range began to bubble softly. Stanley took it off, using discarded newspaper to protect his hands from the heat of the handle. He tipped some of the tea leaves into the pot and stirred them with a stick before adding the sterilized milk. For the first time in days, he felt his panic begin to subside.

He had a plan. He was in control. He would be fine and so would his mam.

Back at Stanley's home, his mother had placed a tea cosy over her best Royal Doulton teapot, after pouring Howard a cup of tea as he charmed her with the tale of his recent wedding.

'Our Stanley never wanted to get married, you know. I tried to persuade him, but he's never been interested. Mind you, I doubt there has been a woman born, who could be as good to him as his mam has.'

The bright blue budgerigar, in the cage inches from Howard's head, had hobbled to the end of its perch and now stared curiously at Howard, with its head on one side.

'He's a good lad, our Stanley. Tips his money out onto the table every Friday night as soon as he walks through that door and no man could be more devoted to his work than our Stan. He makes me knit teddies to take in for them kiddies, you know. There are very few men as good as our Stanley.'

'I've spoken to his employers, who think very highly of him,' said Howard.

'Did they say why they had to send him to another hospital so quickly?' she asked. 'It is all very strange. A man from his work called to tell me what was happening. I gave him Stanley's clean clothes and everything but I can't understand why Stanley didn't come home himself first. The man said Stanley had taken a child in an ambulance to another hospital down south and he would be staying until they returned to Liverpool. Typical of our Stan, that is. I bet no one else would do it. He would have volunteered. That's just what he's like, you know. He loves them kids, he does.'

Howard drank his tea, feeling sorry for the mother of the sick pervert he was determined to catch. Poor woman doesn't have a clue, he thought.

'Well now, the thing is, I am afraid I'm not allowed to tell you anything other than that we need to ask Stanley some questions. He isn't in any trouble, mind. It is all a bit top secret, to do with a case at the hospital. Stanley has been a great help to the police, but we need to speak to him as soon as he gets back. So what I will have to do is leave this police officer here in your house, while you are asleep, to keep you safe until Stanley returns. You must be very nervous on your own with him being away.'

'Well, I am, but what will the neighbours say? They will think our Stan has done something wrong, won't they? Is that really necessary?'

'I am afraid it is. Stanley has been doing some good work for the hospital, but there are a couple of bad lads who work there and we can't catch them without Stanley's help. It won't be for long. I spoke to the doctor at the hospital, and he tells me Stanley should be home any time now.'

'Well, thank God for that. I don't want me neighbours thinking anything is up, here in our house. You had better tell them if they ask when you go out. I feel ashamed having a police car outside me house.'

'There is no police car now. I had it moved down onto Queens Drive. I didn't want you to feel worried about that,' said Howard with all the charm he could muster.

An hour later, Stanley's mother was in bed, having left nothing short of a feast on a tray for the officer whom Howard left behind, with explicit instructions.

'The only thing we have got so far is the name of two of the people who Daisy can confirm visited Father James at the Priory and we know what they were up to. She has given us some shocking details. We also know that Simon worked with them and that it was he who delivered Daisy to the convent. The pieces of the jigsaw are slipping into place.

'Stanley is the next piece. The psychologist at the hospital tells me Stanley will be anxious about his mother and will, at some stage, attempt to return home, if only to reassure himself that she is well. We also know that he is working with someone, because whoever it was called here to spin a story to Stanley's mother. If only the other porter, Austin, or Simon were being as cooperative, eh? Stay hidden and keep your eyes and ears open. If he returns home and you miss him, you will be looking for a new job tomorrow, do you understand?'

The police officer looked terrified. 'Yes, sir.'

'Good, now I'm off to my new home and my new bride. It feels as if I have barely seen my wife since we stood at the altar. Stay out of sight, and make sure the old woman is in bed as soon as possible. If he returns tonight and clocks that the lights are on, he will think she is still up and we don't want her being around when he's nicked.'

'Yes, sir,' said PC Shaw. 'Er, sir, what's that white stuff on your shoulder?'

Howard hadn't heard him. The probationary officer spoke to his retreating back as Howard almost ran towards Queens Drive, where he had left the car parked. The room filled with the squawks of an accomplished budgie.

Stanley's mother lingered before finally taking herself off to bed.

'Are you sure you're gonna be all right now, just sat here in the kitchen on yer own?' she asked PC Shaw at least half a dozen times.

She made one last descent in a hairnet and no teeth, to leave the biscuit barrel on the table and to quiz the officer.

'I don't know what's going on but I've got a funny feeling in me water I have. Is that CID officer all right or what? He kept telling me Stanley was helping the hospital and the police, but with what? He's never said nothin' to me. I don't understand what's going on, like.'

Finally, as soon as PC Shaw heard the bedside light click off, he dived at the food she had left for him, kept fresh between two plates. Corned-beef sandwiches on thickly buttered white bread were piled high, together with a home-made Victoria jam sandwich.

As he munched the first sandwich, he looked round the room.

Who would have thought it, eh? he mused. Normal mam, normal house. So what turns someone into the sick weirdo Stanley obviously was? Shuddering at the thought of a man who desired children, the PC knew what he would do if he ever caught anyone near his own daughter.

'I'd chop his bloody dick off,' he muttered to himself.

His thoughts wandered to the murder of the dead priest and his detached body part. Just as a penny rolled to the edge of his thoughts, about to drop … he heard a noise. It was a key in the front door.

Begrudgingly, he placed the remaining sandwich on the plate, secreted himself behind the door and waited.

'Mam,' Stanley whispered as he opened the door into the kitchen. Only the glow from a small lamp on the sideboard illuminated the room.

'Mam,' he whispered again, this time with more urgency.

He had opened the kitchen door wide and blinked before he knew what had happened. His arm was up his back and the PC, his handcuffs ready, had snapped them on within seconds.

'Never mind your mam, you dirty perv, you're nicked, mate.'

The budgie squawked his greeting from the cage, 'Hello, Stanley,' just as his mother called down the stairs, 'Stanley, is that you?'

While the PC radioed for a police car, Stanley's mam got up, tied the belt on her dressing gown and ran her false teeth under the tap to wash off the Steradent tablet, quickly popping them back into her mouth. Her bedroom was suddenly filled by the blue flashing light of a police car, parked right outside her front door.

'Oh God, Stanley, what have you done?' she muttered as she walked down the stairs. 'Honest to God, the shame.'

## Chapter Fourteen

'I'm back,' shouted Harriet as she burst in through the Priory door, causing it to swing on its hinges and crash against the wall. She continued to shout as she threw her hat on the hall table. 'I am so starving hungry, are you?'

Harriet had never in her life entered a room with any degree of caution. There was simply no need. No fearful shock had ever hidden behind any closed door, nor hit her in the face when least expected. Nothing unexpected or out of the ordinary had jumped up and bitten her. Harriet had never known fear.

She had just finished delivering leaflets to the houses on the four streets. She removed the satchel, slung across her shoulders, that held the remaining leaflets and placed it with a thud on the table, next to her hat.

She had spent the early part of morning at the Priory with the plainclothes police officers while they interviewed Daisy, who was excited beyond all notion that her brother would be arriving in Liverpool the following week, to collect her in person. They weren't taking any chances this time. There was no question of Daisy being put on a boat alone, as Alison had argued.

'God alone knows where you would end up this time. We might

find ourselves answering a call from America. Only you, Daisy, could board the Liverpool to Dublin ferry and quite possibly end up in New York,' she had joked.

Despite that, they struggled to laugh. Everyone was keeping a very careful eye on Daisy, until she had been handed over to her brother.

The new commanding officer had explained the plan of action in detail to the gathered group – Daisy, Miss Devlin, Sister Evangelista, Harriet and Father Anthony – who had all listened intently over tea and hot toasted muffins, dripping with butter and strawberry jam. Harriet was never happier than when people left the Priory with a full stomach, whatever the time of day.

'We are on our way over to Ireland this afternoon,' Howard had said, 'to determine how the arrangements were made for Daisy to be delivered to the convent and why that particular convent was chosen. The police officer in custody is refusing to tell us anything, so, ladies, we are slightly stuck. However, it will take only a little good old-fashioned footwork to sort things out.'

They were all impressed with the competence of the commander who had taken over the reins of the investigation, immediately drafting Howard in as his number two. This made sense, given that Howard was completely up to date on all that had happened during the previous investigation and was already an invaluable member of the team. The commanding officer had even hinted at promotion, if the case reached a successful conclusion.

The fact that Howard and Alison had cancelled their honeymoon to the Isle of Man, losing their deposit on the bed and breakfast they had booked months ago, had not gone unnoticed by Howard's senior officers. The uniformed officers down at Whitechapel were hugely disappointed that one of their own was locked in a police cell, and stinking guilty as hell.

'Do you have to shout every single time you walk in through the front door, Harriet?' Father Anthony placed his finger to his lips, which were smiling at his little sister, always so full of life. 'Shh,' he said, 'I have a visitor in the office.'

'Oh, gosh, I'm sorry. Wayward housekeeper here, not doing her job properly.'

Harriett grimaced playfully.

'Not at all. Could you make tea? I have no idea what has happened to Annie O'Prey. Sheila knocked on the Priory door and Annie just disappeared without a by-your-leave. That woman is the end, Harriet. If you didn't like her so much, she would have to go. She makes delicious cakes but she is really a law unto herself. Anyway, fetch the tea, would you, and bring it to the study. I want you to join us as this is very much your project, not mine. Mr Manning is here to talk to us.'

Harriet felt a thrill run down her spine. Oh God, how should I act? Indifferent? Cold? Friendly?

'Mr Manning?' she hissed. 'Were you expecting him?'

'No, although I did tell him to call in if he had any news or if he wanted further information. But I didn't really expect him to just pop in without at least a phone call from his secretary first, unless, of course, he had an ulterior motive for visiting.' Anthony winked at Harriet who blushed from head to toe.

Harriet quickly checked her hair in the hall mirror. Licking her fingertips, she ran one along each eyebrow, pushing them into shape. Having fluffed up her hair and pinched her cheeks, she swept into the office where, without any warning whatsoever, her beauty knocked Benjamin Manning completely off his feet.

'Mr Manning,' Harriet trilled breezily.

Just in the nick of time, she erased from her face the instinctive look of sympathy that threatened to appear as Ben struggled to rise from his chair to greet her.

Harriet was beset by feelings she had never known before, despite her age, and she had no idea how to deal with them.

She blushed again, her palms sweated, her eyes shone and her heart fluttered like a trapped bird.

He noticed.

'Good morning,' he replied, but his mouth was so dry that his response was barely audible. He held out his hand, which trembled like a leaf in the breeze.

She noticed.

It had begun.

# Chapter Fifteen

Maggie and one of the orphan girls were in the process of removing fifteen loaves of hot bread from the oven when Sister Theresa arrived, unannounced.

As was her way, she issued no greeting.

'Are we managing to bottle enough gooseberries for the winter? Sister Perpetua thinks we have less in hand than last year, despite the good weather.'

'Oh, aye, we are that,' replied Maggie, barely hiding a hint of indignation. 'I have plenty bottled in the cellar and if there's any more late crop come through, Frank thinks we may be able to squeeze out another half-dozen jars or so from the plants in the glasshouse.'

Sister Theresa looked far from mollified.

'Good. Sister Perpetua also tells me some of the apples have been stolen.'

'Ah, well, I think one or two of the windfalls from the other side of the railings may have gone, but, sure, they would have been full of maggots and no good to us now,' Maggie replied.

'That's not the point, Maggie. Any child who steals from us should be up before the magistrate. Thou shalt not steal is an important lesson to be learnt.'

'But, sure, Sister Theresa, these children have walked a mile to steal a rotten apple, because they are hungry. Surely the good Lord wouldn't mind a bit of that in their bellies? It would give them the cramps as it is. Is that not a fair punishment?'

'There is no excuse for stealing, Maggie. It is wrong. If you see any child doing it, I want them caught and reported.'

'Yes, Sister,' said Maggie, with a heavy heart and no intention of doing any such thing.

The children hadn't stolen any apples. She and Frank had picked the windfalls and kept them in a basket behind the lodge. They knew every child from the village and their parents. Frank and Maggie dished out the apples when the children came along, to save them from the sin of stealing or, worse, being caught.

'We are using the salt fish today with tatties,' said Maggie, in a desperate attempt to change the subject.

As Sister Theresa looked round the kitchen, her gaze alighted on the orphan girl helping Maggie.

There was a note of alarm in her voice as she asked, 'Where's the girl?'

Maggie didn't need to ask, which girl? 'She has the vomiting bug and, sure, I don't want it, Sister, so I've confined her to her room. The last thing we need is vomiting to sweep through this place now and I don't want to be laid up or none of us will eat.'

Sister Theresa looked at the door of the storeroom where Daisy was expected to sleep and which opened straight onto the kitchen. It was closed and Maggie had locked it. The key felt as though it were burning a hole through her apron pocket and scalding her thigh.

Her heart beat wildly as the Reverend Mother stared at the door for what seemed like a lifetime. Suddenly she turned back to Maggie.

'Very well, but don't let her shirk, though. Back to work as soon as she is well. The bishop is in Liverpool for a meeting about the new cathedral, but he told me he wants to see her when he returns.'

'Yes, Sister,' said Maggie.

Maggie kept her head bent as she turned the loaves out onto the long wooden table. She daren't look up in case Sister Theresa detected the panic in her eyes.

Later that evening, when her work was done and she was back at the lodge, Maggie recounted the visit to Frank. They had settled in front of the fire, the way they did each night before bed. Rain was falling steadily, as it had done for most of the day. The fire struggled to catch and throw out a decent flame as smoke billowed back into the kitchen. In another of their familiar nightly rituals, each held an enamel mug of poteen, brewed by Frank himself in a still kept hidden, behind a false wall in the potting shed. He and Maggie often laughed at the thought of what the nuns would do, if they knew Frank brewed his own poteen in the convent grounds.

'Jesus, they would choke and die, wouldn't they just,' said Maggie as she took her first sip.

Tonight, they talked about the Reverend Mother's visit to the kitchen and Daisy's whereabouts.

'That's three days she has been gone now. I reckon we have another week. Reverend Mother, she never visits the kitchen more than once a week. What will we say, Frank, when they discover she has disappeared?'

'You will wail and cry, Maggie, about how that girl took advantage of you, letting her rest whilst she was sick, that's what. No finger of suspicion must ever point at us. Let's hope the police are listening to Daisy and her story.'

'Aye, if she is following the instructions I gave her and there is a God, all should be well.'

Maggie looked again at the letter they had received from the foreman, Jack.

'Carry on reading now, before the poteen knocks ye out for the night,' said Frank.

Frank had worked in the fields since he was six years old and had never learnt to read. Maggie had attended the local school religiously and had excelled at English and maths, despite frequently receiving the cane across her palms whenever she made the slightest error.

The nuns had failed to beat an aptitude for learning out of Maggie, as they had with most children. Rather, they beat a resilience and determination into her, to get her own back one day.

Maggie resumed reading.

> Because she told me on the way over that one of the men she needed to report was a policeman from Liverpool, I decided to take her to the police station in Holyhead.
>
> They were very good and kept her in overnight. I agreed to keep an eye on her, as promised, and booked into the pub next door to

the police station for the night. When I called back the next morning, they told me they had got a mighty statement from her and they were taking her to Liverpool where they were hopefully going to make an arrest before the day was out. I have no idea who he was, but a very senior man from the Welsh police came to the station. They let me go and told me that what Daisy had told them amounted to a kidnapping, which is a very serious offence.

I have to say, your comments in the letter about her brother being the state solicitor of Dublin made them jump and I know they telephoned him. I didn't mention your names as promised.

It was a pleasure to get to know you both and, Frank, I look forward to welcoming you to the Shamrock pub in Liverpool, for a return Guinness one day soon, mate.

Your pal from Liverpool,
JACK

'That makes me feel good, so it does, that such a bad man will get his due deserts because we have played our part.'

'Aye, it does. Me too, Frank,' said Maggie thoughtfully. 'Watch out for Sister Perpetua. She wants to see kids from the village locked up for stealing apples. Telling tales to the Reverend Mother so she is. She's a wicked one, that one. Watch yer back.'

'Aye, I've noticed her snooping around the vegetable gardens a few times. I will, Maggie, don't worry about me. I keep my wits about me at all times. No one can catch me out.'

Frank had no idea. Someone already had.

Sister Perpetua sat in her room, making yet another entry in the journal she had been keeping over the last month. She knew that when she approached the Reverend Mother, she would need to present a cast-iron case. Not of a single event that could be explained away, but a whole list, which would demonstrate a pattern of deceit, theft and bad behaviour.

Only a few weeks earlier, Sister Perpetua had caught one of the girls returning to the orphanage from the kitchen with her pockets stuffed full of biscuits. When they were removed from her and she was beaten, she confessed to Sister Perpetua that the cook, Maggie, had given them to her.

This had not been an isolated incident. Only the previous week, Sister Perpetua had seen Frank passing vegetables through the railings to the village children. Last night, she had seen him taking a bottle of clear liquid from the potting shed and slipping it into his jacket pocket. Her suspicions now thoroughly aroused, she kept an eye on Frank from the orphanage, which overlooked the vegetable gardens, and with her own eyes she had seen him sneakily carry a basket of apples round the back of the orchard to the lodge.

Sister Perpetua was sure in her own mind that the Reverend Mother had employed a pair of thieves and it was her duty to point this out. When she did so, maybe then she would be relieved of the job that she hated so much. Dealing day after day with ungrateful children and digging graves.

The Reverend Mother knew she could trust Sister Perpetua. Only two nuns were allowed to dig graves and Sister Perpetua was one of them. She was also the only nun entrusted with the paperwork, when children died. It was she who decided whether or not to obtain a death certificate and at what point to report the death to the authorities.

'We have no idea who will come asking questions or when,' Sister Theresa had said. 'We must keep everything as obscure as possible and, sure, if no one wanted these children in life, I am quite sure there will be no interest when they are dead, but you never know. Better to be safe than sorry. We must protect ourselves from any charge that could be brought to our door. There are people who indulge children and fail to discipline them. Sentimental, they are, and just the type to think they could do a better job than we have. No traces, Sister Perpetua. Always be vigilant. Nothing recorded that anyone at any time in the future could behold.'

Sister Perpetua had done her work well. There was at least one death a week at the orphanage. She knew this was high.

'We could blame a disease, Reverend Mother,' Sister Perpetua had commented. Sister Theresa was always anxious about the children sent to the orphanage by the authorities.

'Really, Sister Perpetua?' the Reverend Mother snapped. 'Then they would all have died in the same week, not at the rate of four or five a month. Just do as I say.

'There must be nothing that can be traced. No mass at the graveside. Most of those children were born out of wedlock. They are steeped in a sin that no mass could erase. No headstones. We don't ever want to encourage mourners.'

Sister Perpetua had created an environment of obedience and orderliness in which penitents could seek forgiveness, exactly as she had been asked. However, after four years of disciplining children and burying them, she was heartily sick of the orphanage. She knew it was difficult to ask for a transfer to the retreat. That was solely in the gift of the Reverend Mother. A reward for loyalty and discretion.

She bent over the journal in the orphanage office and continued with her record-keeping.

The cook and the gardener deserved to be in prison, and Sister Perpetua knew that she was the only nun in the convent sharp enough to make sure it happened. Her reward would be guaranteed and soon, God willing, she might have thrown the last lice-ridden, sin-soaked child into the pit.

# Chapter Sixteen

'That Harriet has ants in her pants, she cannot keep flamin' still,' said Kathleen as she dried her hands on her apron and took the leaflet out of Nellie's hands to read it for herself.

'But, Nana, it sounds so exciting, a Rose Queen of the docks and eight people in her retinue, and we can all enter the competition. There is going to be a big fair with a street party on the green and afternoon tea. I've never known the like. It is too exciting for words. I'm off to tell Angela.'

Nellie jumped up from the kitchen table and already had her hand on the back doorknob when Kathleen stopped her.

'Nellie, stop. Come here a minute while I tell ye something.'

Nellie knew what that meant. It was a summons to sit down and wait for a lecture. She knew from experience that she wouldn't be going anywhere until it was over. With a sigh, she walked back to the table and sat down.

'Now, child, listen to me. The Rose Queen, that's a fantastic idea and I'm not surprised that Harriet has dreamt it up, an' all. She has transformed these streets in the months she has been here. Jesus, she's even trying to make me run the Mothers' Union and the committee for the new nursery because she reckons that, if I do, it will be easier to get Maura to help. And she's right, it will be good for Maura. I won't have to do nothing, so I won't, I will just act stupid. We have to pray to God that Maura's famous spirit for organizing and bossing everyone will return, but that's not what's worrying me.'

Nellie could tell this was going to be a long one so she helped herself to a biscuit from the tin on the press. Nana Kathleen had made syrup oaties that morning, using a nice deposit from a load en route from the docks to the Lyons factory.

'I'm listening, Nana Kathleen,' she said, munching. 'Go on, don't stop, keep talking.'

'Cheeky madam,' said Kathleen, whacking Nellie's bottom with the tea towel. 'Look, Nellie, I'm just saying, have ye seen the date on that leaflet, the date of the Rose Queen competition?'

Nellie looked down at the leaflet. She hadn't noticed the date at all, so caught up had she been with the long list of events Harriet planned: a fancy-dress competition, a tombola, a beat-the-rat stall, a best-cake competition, a cake stall and a jumble sale too. There was so much, how did Harriet think they could fit it all in on one day?

Nellie picked up the leaflet and read it again.

'Oh God,' she said, placing her hand over her mouth. 'I feel terrible. Oh God, I am so stupid and she was like my sister too.'

Nellie began to cry. The shock of Kitty's death had numbed her, crushing her free spirit for what had seemed like a very long time. Not until recently had she started to seem like her old self. Kathleen and Jerry were only just beginning to notice the true signs of their old Nellie returning.

'Hush now, ye were so caught up with the news, I'm sure ye didn't even notice that the date was Kitty's birthday. I just wanted to point it out because when ye go over to Maura and Tommy's, they will notice it straight away, and Angela too, I've no doubt, so just be a little bit careful, eh?'

'Shall I not go over then?' said Nellie.

'Tell ye what, give me five minutes to finish these dishes and we will go together, shall we?'

Nellie dried her eyes and took the tea towel from Nana Kathleen. As she did so, Kathleen drew Nellie to her, burying the child's head in her chest for a brief moment, and then kissed the top of it, noting that in no time at all she would have to reach up, not bend down, to give their Nellie a kiss.

Meanwhile, Declan Doherty had taken the leaflet into the kitchen and read out the list of events with a similar degree of enthusiasm. Harry lay on the mat in front of the fire, reading his book.

He looked up on hearing the events that interested him the most: races for the children on the green, a street party and a kestrel-flying display.

'Well,' said Maura, in the subdued voice that had become the norm of late, 'that all sounds fantastic now. Angela, I think we should enter the cake competition and start practising with some recipes. What do you think?'

'When is it?' asked Harry after Declan finished.

As Declan read out the date, only Harry and Maura exchanged glances. Harry had realized immediately what day it was. None of the others had. Harry knew he couldn't say anything. Kitty's name had barely been mentioned since the day of the funeral. It was as if by pretending she had never existed, it would become easier for everyone to bear her absence.

It didn't work like that for Harry. Right now he wanted to yell out loud, 'That's our Kitty's birthday!' But he knew that if he did, his mother would cry and the others would cast their eyes downwards and behave as if he had never spoken.

Through the kitchen window Maura spotted Nellie and Kathleen, walking up the back path towards her door.

'Well now, there's a bit of news we have,' said Kathleen as she let herself into the kitchen.

'Cuppa tea, Kathleen?' said Maura.

Kathleen didn't stop to draw breath or to answer, saying, 'Would ye credit that Harriet and Miss Alison?' So Maura poured her one anyway, on the basis that never once had she known her to refuse. Kathleen even had her own cup and saucer in the Doherty kitchen.

'She's Mrs Davies now,' said Maura. 'Seems funny calling her Alison, as if it's disrespectful for someone in her position, her being a teacher.'

'Well, I'll never get used to that in a month of Sundays,' said Kathleen. 'It's not even an Irish name, so it's not. Maura, those women are on a mission to exhaust us, what with the nursery an' all. I hope Mrs Davies gets caught quick now that she's married and has her hands too full with a baby to be finding things for the rest of us to do.'

Kathleen sat herself down on the chair beside the fire and ruffled Harry's hair by way of a greeting. He looked up at Kathleen and smiled.

'You all right, lad?' she asked him with a wink. Her words went unnoticed by anyone else, below the noise of Nellie and Angela re-reading aloud to Maura from Harriet's proposed list of events.

'Yeah, ta, Nana Kathleen,' said Harry. He turned to look at Nellie and Angela and then back to Kathleen. 'It's on our Kitty's birthday,' he whispered earnestly, so that no one would hear him mention Kitty's name.

'I know, lad,' said Kathleen quietly, smoothing down errant wisps on the crown of his head. 'No one will forget such an important day, Harry. We will all go to the church and put our mass cards in and light a penny candle for her. She won't be forgotten, Harry. Kitty was like you, lad, very special. No one will ever forget her.' Whilst she spoke she continued to stroke Harry's hair, licking her fingertips and then pushing his fringe to the side, over and over. Harry pulled his head away.

'Get away with ye,' she laughed. 'Ye love it when I mess yer hair up now. Where's yer mate then? Little Paddy?'

'He's coming over now. His mammy has sent him with the pram to fetch a bag of coke. He will be back in a minute.'

Sometimes Kathleen wondered if Maura and Tommy were handling things the best way. Since Kitty's death, Harry always seemed to be hiding in a book.

When the girls had finished babbling, Maura sat next to Kathleen with her own cup of tea.

'Well, sure, that's got them two going and our Angela laughing and, God knows, that isn't easy. She works miracles, that Harriet.'

'Tell ye what, Maura.' Kathleen's face lit up as she carefully placed her cup back on the saucer. 'Why don't ye take the mop out and let's get the others in. This Rose Queen is big news. We had better start planning. Where are we going to find the frocks for this lot for a start? It's time for a pow wow.'

For a moment, Maura didn't respond. Over the past six months she hadn't banged on the wall once for her neighbours to meet in her kitchen for a natter. She wasn't sure if she was ready for rapid chatter and street gossip.

What did any of it matter? Their Kitty was dead, drowned. Who cared a fig about gossip? She looked sideways at Kathleen.

'Go on, love,' Kathleen urged her gently. 'Knock on for Peggy. They have all been patiently waiting and, sure, aren't the best days any of us have ever had been spent in this kitchen? We have solved more problems and had more laughs than most people do in their whole lives, sitting round your table. Everyone has been worried sick about you, Maura. Knocking on would be a sign to them and I think they deserve that.'

'Go on, Maura.' Kathleen put her hand on Maura's arm. 'Time to take the next step and this Rose Queen, 'tis a God-sent opportunity now.'

Maura sighed, knowing Kathleen was right. She walked over to the back door, picked up the mop and, as had always been the tradition, banged the handle against the wall that adjoined Peggy's kitchen, with three loud thumps.

The children fell silent. After a moment that seemed to last forever, they all heard it, Peggy knocking on her wall three times for Sheila. Moments later, Maura's neighbours began trotting down her path, chatting to each other, their heads full of bobbing curlers, balancing babies on hips, with cigarettes half smoked in one hand and their babies' bottles in the other. Each one walked over to Maura and hugged her.

They had been waiting patiently for Maura to let them know when she was ready. Now, they couldn't keep the smiles off their faces. Maura had turned a corner and they were turning it with her. Every single one of them breathed a sigh of relief when the Nelson Street mops once more began knocking.

'Enough of that,' shouted Nana Kathleen from the sink where she was in the process of filling the kettle. 'There's tea to be drunk and who has brought the biscuits?'

'I have, Kathleen,' said Deirdre above the chatter. 'I have a bag of broken which I got from the tin, in Keenan's.'

'And I've brought a brack, I made one extra today,' said Sheila, taking her plate to the press. 'Shall I run and fetch Annie?'

'Do you know, that's not a bad idea, Sheila. Aye, 'tis is a grand idea. The more the merrier.'

And with that, Sheila was back out of the door and across the entry to fetch Annie, back to where the beating heart of the four streets traditionally rested. In Maura's kitchen.

As they settled round the table, the chatter was so loud, Kathleen would have to shout to be heard. She breathed a deep sigh of relief. It felt as though she had been holding her breath for months and, for the first time, she could relax.

Suddenly there was an unfamiliar, tinkling sound. Little Harry looked up from his book and, catching Nana Kathleen's eye, he smiled. It was the sound of Maura laughing. A sound they had all forgotten.

# Chapter Seventeen

After her meeting with Sister Evangelista, Daisy walked down the convent steps with a confidence and self-assurance that had been wholly absent during the time she had worked as the dead priest's housekeeper. Sister Evangelista had insisted that Daisy stay with them in the convent guest room, until her brother arrived to collect her. As she reached the bottom step, Daisy spotted Harriet rushing down the Priory driveway.

'Morning, Daisy, love, isn't it a glorious day?' Harriet shouted across to her as she turned and almost ran down Nelson Street in the direction of Maura Doherty's house.

Daisy waved across the road and smiled. Although it was early, the river already shimmered in the bright sunlight. From years of observing how the river responded to the weather, Daisy could tell that today would be a scorcher. She liked Harriet. It was a very strange feeling seeing her run out of the house that had been Daisy's prison. She had arrived at the Priory as a young girl not knowing that it was the place where her childhood would be stolen.

Daisy had been nervous about her meeting with Sister Evangelista. Once she had finished her breakfast with Alison and the nuns, she had taken out Maggie's note and read it again. It told her exactly what she had to say and to whom she had to say it. This morning, it had been Sister Evangelista's turn.

Although the school was empty, with the children at home for the holidays, Sister Evangelista had been working in the school office.

'Morning, Daisy, come on in,' she said as she pulled out a chair next to her desk. 'I'm just preparing the lessons for next term as I want to visit Ireland myself. It is time I had a little break.'

Sister Evangelista had been alarmed to discover that whilst they had thought she was lost, Daisy had been held like a prisoner at the new convent near Galway. Sister Evangelista knew the Reverend Mother well, as Sister Theresa was related by blood to the bishop. Like the police, Sister Evangelista had plans to pay a visit to the convent personally and discover just what had been occurring.

She wanted to find out for herself who had told the police officer to take Daisy to St Vincent's and why. There were many hidden secrets still to be uncovered and she should know; she was probably hiding the very worst.

'Sister, I have something to say.' Daisy sounded very serious.

Sister Evangelista looked at Daisy, slightly amazed. This was the girl who would never say boo to a goose. Who would ever have thought it? Such a transformation.

Daisy continued, 'Sister, you and I, we found photographs in the priest's desk that were very bad.'

'Aye, we did, Daisy, but they are burnt now and that is all over.'

'Well, they weren't all burnt, Sister. There are some in the safe in the cellar and I don't think it is all over. If it was, I wouldn't have been taken to the convent, would I? There was a reason I was taken there—'

'What safe?' Sister Evangelista interrupted Daisy.

Sister Evangelista felt the return of a familiar feeling of panic that she was sure she would never shake off. Every night before she went to sleep, she often wondered: was this the effect of shock? Would she spend her remaining years looking over her shoulder, jumping each time a telephone rang or a door slammed? Her life until recently had been one of serenity and devotion. The most serious problem she ever had to tackle was a severe outbreak of nits at the school.

Since she had opened the desk drawer of the dead Father James and found it stuffed full of those disgusting photographs, nothing had been the same. As she closed her eyes at night, the images of schoolchildren once entrusted to her care swam before her eyes. It took prayers and tears to wash them away.

'The safe in the wall in the cellar,' Daisy said. 'Father James asked me to put a cardboard box of photographs in it. He kept them in there for a man called Arthur. He didn't like the dark, did Father James. At night he always liked the landing light to be left on. Down in the cellar, it is very dark, so he always sent me instead. I had the notion he was scared.

'There were some big flat round tins as well, with films in. Sometimes Arthur used to come to the Priory to collect them and sometimes he brought them to the father. Quite often, the two men who worked at the hospital came. You remember them, Sister, they came to the convent one night when the bishop sent them to collect me. 'But you know, Sister, it wasn't only Father James who was a bad man, it was the bishop too. I have to tell the police about that now. But I also have to tell them about the photographs in the desk drawer, the ones which you burnt.'

Sister Evangelista felt as though she were falling.

'No, Daisy,' she whispered. 'Do you realize what that would do? I am not fond of the bishop any more than you are, now, but he would be arrested and I might be as well. God only knows what would happen to the church and the school. Haven't I always taken care of you, Daisy? I think the best thing is if we keep all this to ourselves and make sure those two hospital porters get their come-uppance. But, please, keep it just between us about the bishop and Father James. Let us keep as our secret the photographs we found in the desk.'

'I can't, Sister.' Daisy's voice sounded stronger than she felt. 'I can't, because although you have been good to me since the father died and you are a good and kind Reverend Mother, you haven't always done the right thing. For years I was stuck in that Priory with Father James doing to me the same things you saw in the photographs, and the bishop too. And you want me to keep that just between us? I can't do that, Sister. I can't. I have to tell the police everything. That's what Maggie told me I had to do.'

Shocked, Sister Evangelista was unable to speak. Her life had been sent out of control with her future spinning away from her.

'I will also give the police the key to the cellar safe. I took it with me, because Father James told me to never let anyone have it and to always keep it hidden when he wasn't around. Maggie told me, that now that he is dead, I don't have to do that any more.'

'Who is this Maggie?' Sister Evangelista almost screamed the words.

'She is the person who looked after me and smuggled me out of the St Vincent's convent and got me back home. She told me I was no more simple than she was, Sister. Maggie said I only couldn't speak very well because no one ever spoke to me and I thought I was simple because everyone told me I was. Maggie said, if people didn't use their brains and keep their wits about them, everyone would be simple. Maggie told me, no one should keep secrets with the devil himself. If we don't tell the police, Reverend Mother, that is what we would be doing. That's not the right thing, is it? You should meet Maggie. You would really, really like her.'

With that, Daisy stood up and, with her head held high, she walked out of Sister Evangelista's office.

## Chapter Eighteen

'Is he still sleeping?' Mrs McGuire leant across and whispered to Mary.

She was sitting next to her daughter in the back seat of a taxi, travelling from the airport to Galway. The bags piled between them were now full of wet terry-towelling nappies and everything a baby could possibly need on a journey from Chicago to Galway.

Alice travelled in a cab following on with the remainder of the bags.

A large carrycot was wedged into the front seat and was also full of baby accessories. As she spoke, Mrs McGuire craned over the pile of bags to take a peep at the baby lying on her daughter's lap. He had slept for almost the entire journey.

Having had a blood transfusion before they left for Ireland, the sickly boy had transformed into a jolly pink bundle of joy.

'Aye, he is, but not for long, I reckon. He will have me awake all night now,' an exhausted Mary replied.

With a sigh, she gently ran her thumb across the latest dark bruise to appear on his leg. The gesture alone spoke volumes.

'*Look, Mammy, he's dying in my lap. This bruise, it tells me so.*'

Mrs McGuire pushed a bag aside and slipped her arm round her daughter's shoulders, her own gesture of concern encompassing both her daughter and her baby.

Mrs Mcguire was delighted they were returning home, even though, given the circumstances, that feeling had to be wrong. This made her feel guilty, which was the default position for every self-respecting Roman Catholic.

If the child had not been as sick they would never have attempted the journey whilst he was so young and it would have been a very long time before she set foot once again in her village on the outskirts of Galway.

However, Mary had insisted Mrs McGuire came too. She would find it hard to travel to Ireland alone with Dillon. If she had to travel to find his birth mother, they would do it together.

Mrs McGuire still knew her way around every back kitchen in every house in her village and, despite the many years she had spent in Liverpool and Chicago, Galway was the only place that truly felt like home.

'That's the thing about home,' Mary had explained to her. 'No one is anonymous. The chances are, someone we know will know someone who knows the people we are looking for and that's why I need you, Mammy, because, sure, don't you know half of the people in Ireland anyway.'

Every sensible person they knew in Chicago had tried to persuade Mary to leave the baby behind. She had refused to budge.

'He has been ours for only a few months and I have waited my whole life for him. I will not be parted from him for a day. God in heaven, he will have forgotten who his mother is if I leave him.'

Henry gave up trying to stop Mary from doing what she wanted to do. 'Jesus, she's like a woman possessed,' he had said to Sean as they stood in the garden, watching the new gardeners prune Henry's conifers. Henry didn't trust anyone to do anything he couldn't do himself. He might be a rich man now, but if he had had the time to do his own garden, he would have done.

'Ever since the baby has been sick, there has been no talking to her. She's driven, so she is. She will do whatever it takes to make him better and I for one am not standing in her way.'

'I wouldn't try, Henry,' Sean had replied. 'She is her mother's daughter. Nothing you can say will make a ha'p'orth of difference. Da would vouch for that if the poor man were still alive.'

Henry nodded in agreement as he lit two cigarettes and handed one to Sean.

'I'm glad Alice is travelling with Mary and Mammy to Ireland. I think it will take the three of them to manage the baby and all the luggage. I would feel better if she were with them.'

Sean agreed. Maybe Alice herself needed a break. They had been arguing a great deal of late. Sean was finding it impossible to say or do anything to please Alice. It felt as if everything had become an effort. Every single day at some point they would have the same argument and the last time had been just hours ago.

'Get your hands away from me,' Alice had said as she stormed out of bed. 'I am not falling for that. I know what your plan is. I have an appointment at the doctor's office today and I'm asking him for the new birth control pill. It takes a month to work and then I am safe. Until then you can keep your hands to yourself.'

As the bathroom door banged shut, Sean lay on his back and remembered Brigid, who had done everything in her power to make him happy. The images of his daughters' faces swam before his eyes as tears prickled. He wished it was he who could have travelled home and kept Mary company because, if it had been possible, wild horses wouldn't have kept him from visiting his children. For the first time, Sean realized he was a wealthy man. He had all he had ever dreamt about and yearned for, but without a loving wife and children to share it with, what did any of it mean?

He turned his head towards the bathroom door.

An en suite bathroom. Who had ever heard the like? He imagined the expressions on his children's faces if he could show them around Mary's house, how beyond excited they would be. He could see Emelda and Patricia bouncing up and down on his king-sized bed, jostling each other as usual to be picked up first. Then he saw the deep blue eyes of his baby, looking up at him trustingly from the pram as he had bent down to place a kiss on her cheek the morning he had left her, for the last time.

He allowed his tears to flow, because he knew that to see them all again was a dream that would never materialize.

As the taxi bumped along the uneven road, Mrs McGuire looked out of the window at the familiar countryside. She had already sent a letter on ahead to her daughter-in-law, Brigid, and her grandchildren, to let them know she would be visiting as soon as she arrived in Ireland. Neither her son, Sean, nor his mistress, Alice, were aware of this but, as far as Mrs McGuire was concerned, no one would keep her away from her own granddaughters, certainly not her son's fancy bit on the side.

'Are you sure you don't want to come with Alice and me to the convent tomorrow, Mammy?' asked Mary in a whisper, careful not to wake the sleeping baby.

'No, Mary, ye and Alice go. I have friends I want to catch up with and I have the taxi booked to take me. No point me coming all this way back home now and not saying hello to my friends, is there? That would just be a waste of a visit now. Ye and Alice, sure, that's enough to be dropping in on the nuns unannounced.'

'Well, if you are sure, Mammy. I don't want ye to think I don't want ye with me.'

'Sure, child, why would I think that? Just because my blockhead of a son thought I shouldn't visit my grandchildren? I know what's going on in his head all right. He doesn't want me carrying tales to Brigid and the girls about him and Alice. He should have stopped the boxing years ago. I swear to God it sent him mad.'

Mary looked out of the back window of the taxi. Alice was now following closely behind them in the second taxi.

'Are you off to see Brigid, Mammy?' Mary had seen right through her mother's story of visiting her friends and knew exactly what she was up to.

'I am, Mary, and nothing ye or anyone else can say is going to stop me. I almost brought those girls up. Your brother broke my heart, leaving them all like he did and landing us with that harlot back there.' This with a backwards nod towards Alice.

Seeing the taxi driver's eyes light up in the rear-view mirror as he heard the word 'harlot', Mary gently pressed her mother's arm and nodded towards the driver.

'Sure, I'm not bothered by Porick,' her mother replied. 'I knew his daddy when he was just a child and I've changed his nappies often enough. D'ye not remember him? Ye was at the convent together with his big sister. They live on the Knock Road. Porick, repeat a word ye hear in this car and I'll slap yer legs raw. D'ye understand?'

Porick, who was at least twenty years of age, winked at Mary in the rear-view mirror and replied with a grin, 'Aye, Mrs McGuire. Yer secrets are all safe with me, so they are. I'll not say a word to the harlot, so I won't.'

Mary smiled. She thought that there was possibly not a single person in all of Ireland that her mother didn't know. She also knew that by tonight every detail of their conversation would be the main topic of discussion in the pub.

'Can ye put me out at the main street, Porick,' Mrs McGuire said.

'What for? We are staying at the hotel, Mammy. You don't need to go to your house and we don't need anything until tomorrow.' Mary looked at her mother and frowned, knowing exactly what Mrs McGuire was doing. 'You can't wait, can you?' she whispered to her. 'You want to show off to your mates, don't you?'

Mary smiled indulgently, holding the baby tight to her chest so as not to wake him. If Mrs McGuire had a fault, it was that she could never resist the chance to brag.

'I don't know what you mean,' her mother replied, her voice loaded with indignation. 'Ye have Alice to help with the baby and Porick here will carry the bags into the hotel. Sure, Mary, ye have come a long way in the world. Ye don't need me to show ye how it works any more. I just want to have a bit of a wander round the shops now. To see what's changed an' all.'

Mrs McGuire had made sure that she was known by her friends and neighbours in Ireland as a bit of a jet-setter. It wasn't difficult, given that she was the only woman in the village to have ever set foot on a jet. Now she tried to change the subject.

'Let's go to the chippy for our tea tonight, Mary. God knows, I can't remember the last time I went to one.'

Mrs McGuire loved to regale her friends back home in Ireland with stories of the exotic delicacies to be found in Mr Chan's chippy on Liverpool's Dock Road.

Saveloys. Oh my, how she loved the way that word rolled off the tongue.

Was there ever a more exotic word?

'In Liverpool, I often pop to the chippy for saveloys,' she would say to her friends. Slowly.

'God in heaven, s-a-v-e-l-o-y-s? What would they be?' her friends would demand to know.

She loved the way their mouths fell open when she described sodas, burgers, corn dogs, barbecues, air-conditioning and ice-making machines.

And, as everyone knew, the person she most liked to impress with her stories was the butcher, Mr O'Hara, who also owned the village shop. Mr O'Hara was a man of business. He wore a brown overall and carried himself with the air of a man of the world.

Mr O'Hara often travelled as far as Dublin, which gave him some standing in the local community, Dublin being such a dangerous place by all accounts.

There was a time when Mrs McGuire could easily have become Mrs O'Hara, that's if Maisie O'Toole hadn't pushed herself in first.

Maisie had died ten years back and, a month later, so had Mr McGuire, leaving behind a pair of once-upon-a-time, almost-young lovers with stars uncrossed.

Mrs McGuire liked to pop into Mr O'Hara's shop and brag about her international travels, to which he would listen patiently before he responded with his own prepared tales of daring and bravery, as he sliced rashers and laid out pig's trotters.

It was a ritual they both engaged in, each and every time she returned home.

Tales at dawn.

And even though it was she who had travelled oceans and had shared experiences, she had yet to win their battle of words.

Mrs McGuire leant against the car window and peered at the low, white-stone cottages they passed. Closing her eyes for a moment, she remembered the last time she had come home and their parting conversation.

'Sure, now, I have to travel to Dublin most weeks. If ye were contemplating such a visit these days, Mrs McGuire, ye would need to carry a gun around in your handbag before ye set foot out of the bus.'

'Surely, Liverpool and Chicago are far safer places altogether, I think,' she had replied, never missing a chance to casually drop her jet-setting credentials into the conversation.

Mr O'Hara nodded sagely as he wrapped up her two pounds of bacon rashers in waxed paper, handing them over with a very solemn expression.

'I would think that would be so, Mrs McGuire, safer altogether I would be saying now,' he replied, in a tone as serious as if he were telling her the Pope had visited his shop and dropped dead, then and there, on the sawdust-covered floor, right on the spot where she was standing.

She had left that day feeling strangely empty. She had failed to impress.

It was a task unfinished, awaiting her return.

On a jet plane.

Porick pulled over in the main street for Mrs McGuire to alight.

The taxi with Alice pulled up behind. Mrs McGuire noticed that Alice's head was on the seat. She was fast asleep, so she had no need to explain herself. Mrs McGuire walked round to the front of the taxi and spoke through the driver's window. 'Porick, will ye meet me back here now in an hour to take me to the hotel?'

'Aye, Mrs McGuire. Should I meet ye here, or go straight to the butcher's?' Porick grinned from ear to ear, feeling very smug and pleased with himself.

Sure, apparently everyone knew there had been a thing between Mrs McGuire and Mr O'Hara.

His daddy had told him only that morning.

'If there have ever been two mismatches in marriage, it was them two not seeing the obvious right under their noses. But then, Maisie O'Toole, she was far from stupid, that one. She knew what she was up to and Mr O'Hara, he was just an eejit of a man who was knocked off his feet with a roll in the hay and a story of a babby on the way. God knows, that was the longest pregnancy in history. Two years until after the wedding, it lasted.'

'Ye cheeky beggar, Porick, I will meet ye here, as I said.'

She turned to Mary. 'I will be an hour now. I'll just say a few hellos.'

'Aye, take as long as ye want, Mammy,' Mary said. 'I'm going to have a nap and take the little fella with me.'

Mary was true to her word. The twenty-four hours she had spent in the company of Alice and her mother had been enough. She was in need of some peace and quiet of her own. Exhausted by the journey, she took herself off to bed within half an hour of checking into the hotel.

*

Mrs McGuire had walked for only a few minutes before regretting her hasty decision to leave the taxi, wishing she had popped into the hotel for a quick bath and a change of clothes before venturing out. She felt nervous, probably because this was her longest absence from home ever. Now she felt uncomfortable, like a stranger in her own village.

As she was continually halted on her way down the main street by people she had known all of her life, she made slow progress.

'Howarye?'

She answered this greeting a dozen times before finding herself at the kerbside, facing the butcher's shop belonging to the man who had passed her over all those years ago.

A young boy ran out of the school gates towards the tobacconist's shop, splattering her legs with dirt from the gutter. She recognized him from her own childhood. She knew his look. He was a Power, all right, and if she had to ask him, she would put money on him belonging to the eldest lad, who was the son of Colm, who was the son of PJ.

She knew them all. Grandfather, father and son.

The familiarity of his face, in his run, in his shouts to his friends, made her realize just how many of the years she had spent away.

From the opposite side of the road, she saw Mr O'Hara, standing in the same place, in the same brown coat, as he had done for almost forty years. Man and boy.

'Hello, howarye?' he shouted across to her, moving swiftly to fill the shop doorway with his bulky frame.

Mrs McGuire stepped off the kerb, ready to cross the mud-and-dirt road, towards the shop and the life that might once have been hers, if Maisie O'Toole hadn't slipped in first.

As she checked for traffic and looked towards the school gates, there they all were, their ghosts of the past: Maisie O'Toole and herself, running home, pigtails flying in the air. Maisie, her once best friend. Maisie, in whom she had confided her heart's deepest secrets and desires. Maisie. The thief. Dead but not forgiven.

'Howaryerself? I'm grand and glad to be back home,' she called back as she reached the front of the shop.

Now that she stood in front of him, feeling more like sixteen than sixty, she had forgotten all the boastful anecdotes she had dreamt up on the plane.

'Well, ye are a sight for sore eyes and that's for sure. I was wondering only the other day how long it would be before we saw ye back here. Mrs Kennedy, she said now, no, ye won't be seeing her back in these parts. Gone for good she is, to Chicago, and I thought, well now, isn't that a great shame.'

He had thought about her?

She was speechless. He had thought of her and spoken to others in the shop about her.

'Well now, I will always come back. 'Tis my home after all.'

'Aye, but many don't. Time passes and they forget. We have houses now standing empty for years and no one to sell them on or to claim them. Families in America, long gone. Old Catherine, over a hundred she was, now, when she died. Her house has stood empty these two years or so. Solicitors, they have tried but, sure, they cannot find the son. He emigrated to America sixty years back, and could be long dead himself now. It will stand empty forever, I would say.'

He smiled. 'I'm about to lock up. How d'ye fancy a glass in the pub and a catch-up over old times?'

Mrs McGuire nodded, but said nothing. She couldn't have spoken even if she had wanted to. He had asked her to the pub as though he were commenting on the weather. And yet her heart was beating as fast as it had when they had been teenagers, and he had kissed her, one burning hot day, when they had both helped out at the Finnegan's harvest for a penny each.

On that day, just as they were about to leave together, Maisie had interrupted and spirited Mrs McGuire away on a spurious excuse, saying she was needed urgently by her mother. Mrs McGuire found her an hour later, sitting in a bar drinking Guinness with no notion at all as to why anyone should be looking for her.

Leaving her mother, she had gone in search of Maisie and Mr O'Hara. It was Colm Power who had given her the news that had shattered her world.

'Would ye be looking for Maisie? Ah, well, ask yer man. They was sneaking off looking very sweet with one another, I would say now. Kissing the two prettiest colleens in the village in one day. Isn't he just the lucky bastard?'

Mr O'Hara turned the closed sign to face the window and put the key in the door ready to lock up.

She hesitated, thinking about Mary and Alice, back at the hotel.

Mary could manage. Alice could manage. They could all manage. Bugger them.

She was about to do something she had wanted to do for a very long time and a thrill shot down her spine. She would spend time alone with the man she had first fallen in love with, over forty-four years ago.

No one could ever say Mrs McGuire wasn't a patient woman.

The following morning, Porick drove Mary and Alice to the convent. Long before he reached its gravel drive he began to slow down.

'Shall I wait at the bottom of the drive for ye, Mary?' he said without turning round.

Porick didn't like the nuns and the closer he got to the convent steps, the more anxious he became. Given a choice, he would have preferred to have dropped both women and the baby at the bottom of the drive and agree to pick them up there later, or even at the gates of hell, anywhere they wanted. He just did not want to hang around outside the convent, waiting.

'I would prefer it if you waited outside the main building,' Mary replied. 'But, if you don't want to, park up outside the gates and we will walk down the drive to you when we have finished. Just keep an eye out for us now.'

'Why didn't Mrs McGuire want to come with us?' Alice asked Mary.

Alice was holding the baby while Mary used her compact mirror to reapply her lipstick and check her hair before they stepped out of the taxi. Mary had her own stories of being educated by the nuns. Lipstick was her warpaint. Her armour of defence.

Mary carefully outlined her lips. Her intense focus on keeping a straight line provided her with an excuse to act distracted, delaying the moment she might have to lie. She did not want to be the one to inform Alice that Mrs McGuire had taken herself off to see Brigid. Mary had wanted to join her herself to visit the woman who was legally married to her brother and see her lovely nieces. She had packed presents for them all in her suitcase. Alice didn't know that either. Unperturbed by Mary's silence, she continued, 'Do you think they will be able to tell I'm not a Catholic, Mary? Am I actually allowed to step inside?'

'Oh, for goodness' sake, Alice, we don't look any different.'

Mary sounded impatient, which was unusual for her. Alice didn't take offence; she understood that Mary was nervous about meeting the nuns.

'Mammy didn't come because she had a hangover, I reckon,' Mary now said to Alice. 'When I popped into her room this morning she said she felt as if a rocket had landed on her head and, my God, she did look ghastly. I thought it was best to leave her. I think she ended up in the pub with one of her friends last night.'

Mary was quite sure that, as soon as they had left the hotel, Mrs McGuire would recover and be on her way to visit Brigid.

Mary felt a moment of panic as she looked at Porick. She hoped he would keep his mouth shut and not mention Mrs McGuire this morning. It was his father who would be driving her mammy, she imagined, as soon as she and Alice were down the road and out of sight.

It was Sister Celia herself who answered the door of the Abbey.

She recognized Mary instantly. It was not often a parent offered three thousand dollars for a baby. Sister Celia's face instantly transformed from its normal grumpy setting to a smiling mask of compassion and care. A carefully crafted pretence, masking abject indifference.

'Ah, come on in now,' she said as she gently took hold of Mary's arm. 'Come in.'

Mary gratefully stepped into the hallway. 'This is Alice, my sister-in-law, Sister. We are so sorry to call in on you unannounced, but I did write ahead to Sister Assumpta. It's just that we didn't know what flights we would be able to catch and everything was so rushed as we left. I am so sorry.'

'Stop, would ye, stop, not at all, not at all,' said Sister Celia as she ushered Mary down the corridor. 'Reverend Mother has a visitor with her, Sister Theresa from St Vincent's, but, sure, she was on her way when the bell rang, which is why I was in the hall. Come along now, I will make sure ye go straight in.'

Alice hung back a little. Surrounded by statues of the sacred heart and paintings depicting scenes from the bible, she was uneasy, and felt as though the initials C of E burnt brightly on her forehead.

Alice and Mary stepped into the Reverend Mother's huge office with its vast expanse of Persian rug.

'Beautiful carpets,' Alice whispered to Mary. 'Just like the make we had in the foyer of the Grand in Liverpool. That was called Axminster, the best.' The opulence of the carpet made Alice feel at home. This was more like it.

'Come along in, ladies,' Sister Assumpta called out from behind the desk.

Alice felt she had better do something to make herself useful, as well as to divert the nuns' attention away from her, just in case they could spot a soul in limbo. While Sister Celia prattled on and pulled out chairs, Alice whispered to Mary, 'Give me the baby to hold so that you can concentrate.' As she held out her arms to take the sick baby, she noticed Sister Assumpta looking at her with more than a hint of curiosity. Alice smiled back, tentatively, as she rewrapped the shawl around Dillon. The smile was unreturned. God, she can tell, Alice thought. She began to tremble and all thought of defiance in the face of intimidation fled.

Nervously, but calmly, Mary began to explain her situation. She had practised her words over and over the evening before, but now, sitting in front of the Reverend Mother, she was unable to prevent the tears from filling her eyes and thickening her throat, making it difficult to speak without almost breaking down.

'I'm so sorry,' she sniffled as she opened the clasp on her handbag and took out a hankie.

Mary felt overwhelmed. Neither nun spoke or offered a gesture of comfort.

On the plane over, she had rehearsed this scene in her mind. In her imagined scenario, the nuns had been kindly. In reality, they were unyielding, devoid of compassion.

'We are in a desperate situation, Sister. We have no choice other than to come here and ask for your help. The baby is very poorly and we need to find his mother urgently, or he will die. There is almost no chance of finding a stranger with a good enough match. We must find the woman or the girl who gave birth to him.'

As Mary spoke, Sister Assumpta occasionally altered the position of something or other on her desk.

She moved her pen slightly further up. Straightened the blotter. Stroked the silver and ivory letter opener. Raised her eyebrows. Tipped her head to one side.

Mary felt she wasn't really listening and, worse, that the Reverend Mother had known what her answer would be and was waiting impatiently to deliver it.

'We desperately need a member of his family to donate a sample of bone marrow. 'Tis a simple operation and we would pay for the family member to be flown to America. Everything would be covered. There would be no problem with that. We would make sure the family were very comfortable.'

When Mary had finished talking, Sister Assumpta ceased the constant rearrangement of her desk. She remained quiet for an unnaturally long time, as though in prayer, and then, slowly looking up, she gazed first at the baby and then at Mary. For a moment, far too long for comfort as far as Alice was concerned, she fixed her eyes upon Alice. The clock chimed, the fire hissed and an air of expectation built in the room.

Mary felt as though something was wrong. Things were not quite as they should be. She had expected much greater concern. Sister Assumpta and Sister Celia appeared very different from how they had been when the baby was first offered for adoption.

At the time, they had been kindness itself. Had they really altered so much in those few short months? Had her recollection been warped by her own emotional state when she had collected her son? Mary felt sick to her stomach as every nerve in her body told her, this is not right, and yet what could she say? There could be few circumstances in life more serious than the one she was trying to explain and this was the one place she had expected to find help and compassion. She had even expected Sister Celia to be overfussy, just as she had on the day they had collected her baby boy.

The atmosphere in the room now was tainted and surreal. She wondered to herself, do they not understand? This is life and death.

Mary was about to speak again, fearing that maybe she had not explained the gravity of the situation clearly enough, when Sister Assumpta broke the silence.

'Well now, 'tis a dreadful problem you have there.' Sister Assumpta broke her silence at last.

She emphasized the word 'you'. This was not her problem, nor that of the convent. There would be no return of a faulty baby.

'We do, however, have the greatest sympathy for your situation, don't we, Sister Celia.'

Sister Celia had not taken a seat, but hovered near the door, waiting for the tea to arrive. 'Oh yes, Reverend Mother, sure, 'tis a shocking state of affairs.' She was saved from having to say anything more by a novice arriving with a tray of tea, which she gratefully took and placed on the table between the chairs occupied by Alice and Mary. Saved by the tray.

'Tea, ladies?'

Two words, which gave everyone a moment to think and Sister Assumpta, time to nuance her message.

She knew very well what her answer had to be. There must be no room for ambiguity when she delivered her response. This was the last time she would ever want this mother and baby in her office.

The ceremony of tea and cake commenced. Alice began to relax. No one had asked her a question and it didn't look as if anyone was about to. She breathed a sigh of relief, as she adjusted the baby in her arms and reached for her teacup. She really wanted to look occupied, too busy to speak.

Two doves had landed on a branch on the tree outside the window behind Sister Assumpta's chair. Alice tried not to look but became fixated by them. She wanted to be anywhere other than in this room. Mentally joining the two noisy birds on the branch in their mating ritual, she thought it as good a distraction as any.

'You see, the thing is, Mrs Moynihan, would ye believe, we have no idea at all who the mother is, do we, Sister Celia.'

Sister Celia, not expecting to be involved in the conversation until she was required to show Mary and Alice out of the office, looked up and, with her mouth full of cake, answered, 'Well now, no, Reverend Mother, I don't believe we do.'

Crumbs flew out and landed on her lap as she spoke. Sister Celia hurriedly stood and, waddling to the fireplace, held out the skirt of her habit to shake the contents into the hearth.

Mary began to feel angry. This was a farce. She sensed acutely that the nuns were not telling the truth and that, in the midst of this roomful of women, the only person fighting for her baby's life was herself.

The pitch of her voice rose. 'I'm sorry, Sister, but I cannot believe that to be the case and I'm afraid I cannot leave here, without some information. My son will die without help and I have to make contact with his mother and his family. I simply have to. This is not what I want to do. I do not want to meet his mother. I did not want to make the journey from America. But if this baby is to live, I have no choice.'

Tears ran silently down her cheeks.

'Please, please, I'm begging you, check your records for any information you may have. Anything will help.'

'Mrs Moynihan, we would love to do that, now, wouldn't we, Sister Celia, but I'm afraid it just isn't possible. You see, a few weeks ago we had the most desperate fire and all our records were destroyed, weren't they, Sister Celia. We have nothing, can ye imagine, nothing left. But let me check now as some of the paperwork survived. We may have the contract the girl signed when she handed the baby over for adoption.'

Sister Assumpta walked over to the long, tall press at the end of her study and opened one of the lower drawers. A few moments later, she returned to her desk.

Alice was confused. The words 'fire' and 'where?' ran through her brain as she looked round the spotless room.

The convent smelt of incense, not smoke, and there was no sign of the desperate fire Sister Assumpta had spoken of.

'Ah, here we have it now,' the Reverend Mother said with a flourish. Then her voice altered dramatically and took on a tone of disbelief. 'Sure, now, I think the girl may have signed the contract with a false name. Don't they often do that, Sister Celia?'

Sister Celia had just taken a bite of cake the size of a baby's head whilst Sister Assumpta had been distracted, searching through the drawer. She was not about to be caught out again and nodded furiously in agreement.

'Now, I know for a fact that the girl's name was Cissy. She was brought here by her family, but she was sent here by the matron midwife from the hospital, Rosie O'Grady and she wouldn't get a name wrong. But see here, on the contract the girl has signed her name Kitty Doherty, and yet her name was very definitely Cissy. The girl must have been deluded when she signed this. All we know is that she was from Liverpool. My best suggestion to you would be to travel to Dublin and visit the midwife because the girl obviously lied when she signed this.'

Sister Assumpta felt foolish. This was the first time she had bothered to check the signature.

The room grew dark as storm clouds gathered in the sky, resulting from the heat of the previous week.

As the light faded, the first drops of rain spattered the glass. The doves huddled together on the branch and Alice looked down at the baby on her lap.

Had she heard right?

The baby spat his dummy out onto the floor. He looked up and smiled seraphically at Alice. She stared back at him, dumbfounded.

She leant down to retrieve his brown rubber dummy from the rug and placed it in her hot tea to clean it, a trick she had learnt on the four streets. Her movements were studied and unhurried, concealing the pace of her thoughts, which were racing.

She spoke for the first time, slowly and deliberately.

'I'm sorry, what did you say the name was on the contract?'

Sister Assumpta held the document out towards Mary as though ignoring Alice.

'Here, see for yourself. Kitty Doherty.'

Maura had taken Kitty to Ireland to have the baby. Alice had read the letter that Kathleen had sent Maura.

Alice felt dizzy as her two worlds collided and became one.

Just at that second, the door to the office swung open and closed again. A novice re-entered with a jug of hot water for the teapot.

Bang. Bang. The door slammed shut.

Alice flinched. This could not be possible. She held out her hand to take the contract Sister Assumpta waved in front of Mary.

'Please, please, let me see,' she whispered.

A thousand reasons flew through her mind as to why it could not be Maura and Tommy's Kitty, but only one thought made any sense, drowning out all else and pounding in her brain.

The sickly baby sitting on her lap was Kitty's child and Maura's grandson. Alice struggled to breathe. This could not be. The reason for the night that no one would ever speak of was right here, on her knee. That awful night, when Alice had become an accomplice to murder. She looked back at the doves taking shelter from the rain, which now battered the windows, and felt the floor shift beneath her chair.

She looked round at the faces in the room, which were fixed upon her and the baby.

Oh good Lord, can the nuns see what I have done? Alice thought. Surely, this was a nightmare. This could not be really happening. The ghosts of her past life filled the room, laughing and taunting her.

Somewhere outside, in the rain, she heard Maura and Tommy crying. Alice rose slowly from her chair. She looked down at the baby in her arms and, as she did so, the eyes of a dead priest stared back at her.

# Chapter Nineteen

'Are you sure you witnessed this with your own eyes? 'Tis a grave accusation. God knows how we will manage without them if this is true. The kitchens run like clockwork and the garden is one of the most productive I have ever known.'

Sister Theresa peered over her glasses at Sister Perpetua who sat in front of her desk, still and calm, with her hands clasped loosely in her lap. A statue of poise, marbled with malice. Sister Theresa had read through the journal of evidence Sister Perpetua had placed before her and the facts were there, in black and white. The trouble was, she would so much rather they weren't.

'Yes, Reverend Mother. I have been keeping a watch for a month now and I have seen everything.' Sister Perpetua didn't even blink.

From the opposite side of the desk, she glanced across at her own handiwork, perched lightly in Sister Theresa's hands.

The list of accusations against Maggie and Frank was damning.

Feeding village children through the railings. Taking garden vegetables to their own kitchen. Giving food to the orphans and slipping bread up to the orphanage in the pockets of the kitchen helpers. The poteen still behind the secret wall in the potting shed.

'I will have to phone the Gardai, you realize that, don't you? This amounts to theft. We prefer to be private here, Sister Perpetua, and I have no notion of calling the Gardai every five minutes. Are you absolutely sure you have seen all this with your own eyes and there is no mistake?'

'Aye, Sister, I saw it all from the orphanage windows.'

'Holy Mother, I have two bishops arriving in an hour. We will leave this until our visitors have left. I cannot have visitors here and nothing to feed them and, besides, only Maggie knows how the kitchen runs, apart from, possibly, Maggie's kitchen helper.

'She was with us in the Dublin orphanage. We heard good reports about her from the bishop in Liverpool. When he arrives today, I shall ask him if he thinks she would be up to taking over the kitchen. She worked as a housekeeper for a priest in Liverpool and she will have had enough experience downstairs by now, I should think, wouldn't you?'

Sister Perpetua looked puzzled and frowned.

'What is it, Sister Perpetua? For goodness' sake, what is the problem now?'

Sister Theresa had never really liked Sister Perpetua. Putting her to work in the orphanage had been the ideal way to keep her out of sight. Or so she had thought. Sister Perpetua was methodical, pedantic and downright humourless. Not that Sister Theresa was in need of a laughing nun, but she did like to see them smiling every now and then. God knew, with the nature of the work they had to undertake and the amount of death they had to deal with, the odd smile was like a tonic to them all. But not Sister Perpetua. It was three years since she had taken her vows and, with each year, she had soured a little bit more than the last. Sister Theresa had never witnessed Sister Perpetua smile. She had also never known her to be wrong, which was why all of this was so depressing.

'Nothing, Sister, it just occurred to me that I haven't seen the new kitchen girl at mass for a little while now.'

Sister Theresa frowned. 'She has been sick, but she surely must be improved. I'm about to check on the meal for tonight, so I shall see her for myself. I have known her since she was a baby. We reared her. She was never a shirker, just a bit simple.'

Changing the subject quickly, she asked, 'Did you burn all the papers from the orphanage as I ordered?'

Sister Theresa closed the pages of the journal as she spoke and handed it across the desk to Sister Perpetua, who took it with her outstretched hand. Sister Theresa rose from her chair.

This was Sister Perpetua's cue to follow likewise.

'I did. Sister Clare helped me. We kept only the contracts the girls have signed at the mother and baby home, agreeing to never make contact with their babies, and we burnt all the death certificates from the orphanage. We lit a bonfire by the compost heap at the end of the potato patch and the furthest away from the house.'

Sister Theresa was now feeling better disposed towards Sister Perpetua. Her manner was tedious but her efficiency very useful.

'Very good. Sister Assumpta has done likewise at the Abbey. There is a midwife in Dublin who will not stop giving out to the authorities, which is making life very difficult indeed for us all. If we have nothing for them to see, if we don't keep any records, they can't look for anything, can they? If we are asked, it will be no sin if we do not have to lie. A simple explanation that the papers were lost in a fire will be all that is needed. That will be no word of a lie. Well done, Sister Perpetua. We should have a little talk when the bishops have left tomorrow about whether it is time you moved back down into the convent. But not yet. Now we have to prepare for our visitors.'

Maggie well knew the determined footsteps of Sister Theresa as they thumped down the stairs into the kitchen. Her inbuilt antennae were programmed to pick up the first step as soon as the top door was opened. By the sound of their tread alone, Maggie could tell even before she had reached the second step which sister was paying the kitchen a visit.

'As dainty as a bleeding elephant,' she muttered under her breath as the familiar black shoes and skirt came into view. She quickly slipped her smouldering pipe back into her apron pocket.

'Maggie.' Sister Theresa was already speaking while still on the stairs. 'Is all in order for our visitors tonight? Did we have a good side of beef delivered from the village? The bishop's teeth aren't that good, so we don't want tough meat now.'

'Have I ever served ye tough meat, Reverend Mother, visitors or not?' Maggie asked her question without impertinence, but her meaning was implicit.

She could feel the heat of her pipe burning in her pocket. It was rare for Sister Theresa to visit the kitchen in the middle of the morning, which was when Maggie always had a cuppa and a 'pull of me pipe'. It was also when she gave the girls from the orphanage or the mother and baby home a cuppa and a slice of bread and butter, telling them to rest their legs for a minute or two.

Maggie had learnt how to make the flour stretch by making slightly smaller loaves for the nuns, so that she could keep an extra one back for the helpers.

The girls had shoved their mugs and bread under the bench and were scrubbing the pots, just as they had been moments before.

Sister Theresa studied them. Maggie sweated.

'Where's the girl? Is she still sick?'

Daisy had supposedly been sick for the best part of a week. Maggie had known this moment would arrive.

Maggie was many things – kind, hurt, wise and damaged – but she was not stupid.

'She is off to the village to collect me baccy, Reverend Mother. She is the only one I can trust. Frank is busy digging up cabbage and I have run out. Did ye want me to send her to ye when she gets back?'

'Maggie, you don't send the girls to the village on your errands. For goodness' sake, not today of all days, and not on any day.'

'No, Sister, well, I can only say that with me baccy, you will likely have a better-tasting dinner and more tender beef, as it is a fact that if I am in a bad mood when I cook, the food never tastes as good and the milk often curdles.'

Sister Theresa stared at Maggie. She played an important role in the convent. Supplying three meals a day to the sisters and any visitors. This left the nuns free to run the mother and baby home, the nursery, the laundry, the orphanage and the retreat. Making money was the order of the day.

Using nuns to run the gardens and the kitchen would have been a waste of resources. The sisters had to be self-sufficient and, in the last few years, they had been successful in that. They were almost as successful as the Abbey, Sister Theresa guessed.

The bishops were visiting tonight and had asked to look over the bank books.

'They can do that gladly,' Sister Theresa had said to Sister Celia. 'We can hand them the books with pleasure. What we do not do is tell them about the biscuit tins with the money in the press. We have upwards of nineteen thousand pounds in there now, so we have, and it will be gone in a flash if the bishop knew we had it. If we ran into trouble, sure, we would have to beg on our knees for a handout. The money in the tins is ours and it stays that way.'

Her nuns were working long hours, for the benefit of the community, and she dreaded the disruption that losing Maggie and Frank would bring. As she stood in the kitchen, she knew she would have to be reconciled to that loss if Sister Perpetua's record-keeping was correct.

Right now, she was too busy to tackle the problem of Maggie or, for that matter, the errand-running kitchen girl. She needed to visit the orphanage to let them know the bishops were arriving and to ensure the sick children were in the isolation rooms. Every one of them would need a bath today and that would be a massive effort in itself.

Frank returned to the lodge, knowing that Maggie would be late back.

The nuns had been all of a flutter all day, preparing for the simultaneous visit of two bishops. Nothing but wailing and crying had been heard through the orphanage windows and, as Frank well knew, the rumpus was being caused by much more than the mere fact that all the children were being bathed in cold water. Tempers were flying.

It made his heart crunch when he saw a nun dragging a child by her hair from the washroom back to the orphanage and it was all he could manage not to say or do something.

'Heavenly Father, my blood boils, so it does, I have to calm me temper. Jaysus, I want to grab the nun by her fecking habit and drag *her* into a cold bath and then across the yard.'

It broke his heart to see the cruelty inflicted upon the children and every day he brought Maggie a different story.

Frank was often quiet when he arrived back at the lodge after work, and Maggie knew it was because he had seen things that upset him. Frank wasn't a great talker. Maggie would have to leave him be to eat his food, smoke his pipe and drink his poteen. Only then would he occasionally make a comment and, when he did, it was frequently shocking.

'Ye know the little one, the lad I told ye about who was only just walking, and so thin I could see the bones of his arse through his fecking trousers? Well, today I saw them putting him in the ground, so I did. They didn't even lay him down with a prayer or a blessing. They just rolled him off the edge, into that pit. Not a coffin in sight.'

Frank would finish speaking with a long drink from his mug of poteen and Maggie would not comment, merely sit in silence, knowing that Frank and she were both doing exactly the same thing: thinking of their own little lad. Frank threw a stick onto the range and then blew on the peat to make it glow red. The oven was still hot from earlier in the afternoon, when Maggie had run back to the lodge from the kitchen to set his dinner over a pan of hot water, with a lid on top to keep it warm.

Today he sat on the rocking chair by the fire with his dinner on his lap, his pot and pipe lying by his side, and he began to eat.

The food was delicious but the sights of the day made it stick in his gullet. He scraped most of it into the grate so that she wouldn't see. It was not to be. Maggie opened the door to the smell of burning beef.

'For feck's sake, ye eat as good as a nun and then throw it on the fire. Are ye crazy, Frank?'

Frank noticed that she looked exhausted.

Throwing her shawl over the back of one of the pair of chairs at the kitchen table, she made her tea, chatting away to Frank who remained sitting by the fire, still, staring into the flames.

'I suppose ye let the bishops and the band of followers in through the gates, did ye? Holy Mary, what a commotion today has been, but I tell ye what, Frank, Sister Theresa came into the kitchen, looking for Daisy, she did. She made a pretence at first, but I know that is what she was after. I know that woman like the back of my hand, I can see right though her, I can. Wanting to know if the beef was tough, my fecking arse. She was checking up. If I didn't know better, I would say someone was on to us.

'Daisy has been gone nearly a week now and do you know what else, Frank? I was shocked to see that bishop tonight. He's the same one, ye know, the one Daisy was on about, the dirty fecking bastard.

That has worried me because if Daisy did what we told her, surely to God he would not be a free man by now.'

'Don't believe it, Maggie, the bishops are as powerful as the Lord God himself. No man would dare arrest a bishop. They look after one another and poor girls like Daisy, they are just left to suffer.'

Maggie looked at Frank with disbelieving eyes. 'I cannot believe that. Not everyone in Liverpool is a Catholic. She would have no luck here in Ireland and, God knows, she would be put in the asylum for the rest of her days if she ever claimed such a thing. But in Liverpool, surely to God, they are more civilized altogether? Surely someone there will believe her?'

'What do you think about this then?' said Frank, as he removed what appeared to be bits of charred paper from his pocket. Smoothing the larger pieces out carefully, he said, 'Well, go on then, you are the reader, what do they say?'

'What are they?' asked Maggie, peering at the blackened, burnt papers.

'I don't know, but Sister Perpetua and Sister Clare spent three hours burning them at the back of the tatties. 'Tis something they was desperate to be rid of. They ran up and down from the orphanage and the mother and baby home with boxes flying everywhere, so they was, and Sister Perpetua, she was shouting to Sister Clare to get a move on before the rain came and, sure, I have never seen Sister Perpetua so much as speak above a whisper, never mind shout. 'Twas all very odd indeed.'

Maggie sat down in the chair, pulling towards her the largest and most complete document.

'It's a letter signed by a priest,' she said. 'Her family can no longer manage to contain the girl's nature for flirtation. No man is safe from her advances. She must seek penance and be punished for forcing her neighbour to commit a shameful sin. She is pregnant. Her father never wants to see her face again and they have committed her to your care.

'Here ye go, some of the letters have gone, but there's enough to make it out.'

'Jesus, who would that be?' asked Frank.

'It says here,' Maggie replied, 'her name was Julie, Julie Dempsey.'

Frank rubbed his bearded chin thoughtfully. 'Aye, Julie, that one died in childbirth, as did the child. She is one of the few to have a wooden cross with her name on. She was one of the first. The nun who asked me for a mallet to put the cross in told me. Not one of them has a cross now.'

As Maggie studied the remaining burnt pieces of document, the dog began barking; someone was ringing at the gate. They both moved to the window to see a Gardai car, waiting to be admitted.

'Well, what do you know?' said Frank, when he was back indoors. 'They asked, was the bishop here and I told him we have two tonight, and which one did he want? He has told me to leave the gate open as he won't be staying long.'

A smile leapt across Maggie's face. 'Do you think it could be to do with Daisy?'

'I have no idea, but ye may be right.'

Minutes later, as they stood at the door with their pipes, Frank waiting to lock the gate, the Gardai car drove past with a very white-faced bishop sitting in the back.

'Right,' said Maggie. 'We have two things to do. I want a drink with me pipe and I want to read through all those bits of paper and then keep them somewhere safe. They could be our insurance for the future, Frank. Things are happening but I tell ye what: those nuns, they need to run a little faster to keep up.'

## Chapter Twenty

Harriet tapped politely on Maura's back door. She had yet to become comfortable with the habit of walking uninvited into the houses on the four streets.

She spotted Maura's face at her back kitchen window, in the midst of a steam cloud, and waved as Maura beckoned her inside.

Harriet put her head round the back door, still feeling the need to ask. 'Hello, do you mind me popping in?'

'Not at all. Ye don't have to stand on ceremony with us, Harriet,' said Maura, who stood at the sink, drying her hands on her apron.

Harriet noticed an enamel bucket on the floor next to Maura. The smell of hot Napisan and ammonia filled the kitchen, stinging her nostrils and making her eyes water.

'Come on away in. I've just finished now, that was the last nappy. Come on, come on. Have ye time just to sit down and have some tea? God alone knows, I've washed out ten dirty nappies this morning and I need a cuppa. Or are ye here to give me a message or a list of instructions maybe?'

Harriet grimaced. She was aware that she moved at a pace slightly faster than that of the four streets.

It seemed to everyone as though Harriet never sat still and that she spent her every day organizing something or someone.

Tommy had formed a very firm opinion about Harriet.

'Miss Bossy Knickers, that Harriet one. I had to walk round the back of the Anchor last night, when I spotted her turning the corner at the top of Nelson Street. I daren't bump into her without she asks me to do something or help her with a committee. I'm not a committee man, Maura, tell her, will ye? It's not safe any more to walk down me own street, so it's not. She has Jerry on a mission to clean the untended graves in St Mary's. That was a wicked play on his conscience.' Then he whispered with a guilty glance at the back door, 'The last place we want to be is in the fecking graveyard, for feck's sake.'

Maura soothed his worried brow with a kiss and, sitting on the arm of his chair in front of the fire, she let him talk without interruption. That was a novelty in itself in their passionate and noisy marriage. She let Tommy speak for as long as it took. I can't remember when we were last like this, Maura thought. We used to do this all the time.

The thin wooden arm of the chair dug painfully into her backside, numbing it, but she didn't stir or break the spell. She shuffled slightly and re-crossed her legs, worried that even her slightest fidget would stem his flow, but he carried on, jumping from Harriet to Kathleen and Jerry without pausing for breath.

'Kathleen and Jer, they have been good to us. Better than our own family even. As God is true, no one ever had better neighbours than we do, thank God. What can we ever do to repay them? It is beyond me. I have nothing to repay a man who has burdened himself with the debt Jerry has on my behalf. He could be in prison, Maura, and, surely to God, without Kathleen these kids would have starved. I have no notion or recollection of the first few weeks. Do ye, Maura?'

Maura shook her head.

'Has the cat got yer tongue? Are ye fecking dumb all of a sudden?' said Tommy with a hint of surprise. It wasn't often that he was allowed to talk for so long without being interrupted. He looked up at Maura with suspicion.

'I'd rather he had my tongue than your langer,' Maura replied.

Tommy put his arm round Maura's waist and pulled her down onto his lap. The springs underneath the thin cushion groaned with their dual weight and they both rocked with laughter. They could now laugh about the dead priest and without guilt too. It felt strange and, at the same time, right. They hadn't laughed together for months. In the midst of their merriment the thought came to Maura: we are healing.

Tommy had complained about Harriet, but with affection. No one could do anything other than agree to whatever it was she asked.

It was impossible to refuse. Her manner was always so charming, and she implored in a way that made grown men melt and women feel sorry for her.

'Oh, I would love a cup of tea, thank you, Maura,' Harriet now replied.

''Tis a cuppa round here, Harriet, and ye don't have to thank me or stand on ceremony in my kitchen. Take the weight off your feet and sit down. The kettle is always on and we can spare a bit of tea. I'll even put fresh leaves in the pot as we have a guest.' Maura lifted the lid on the large tin teapot and peered inside. 'These leaves have been used three times today already, weak as a maiden's piss they will be by now.'

Maura set the kettle back on the range, where it simmered away all day and took only seconds to boil. Harriet, a maiden, was already blushing.

'Mary and Joseph, would ye look who is coming down the path,' said Maura. 'I swear to God she hears the clatter of the kettle on the range, that one, and pops in here to save the job of making herself a cuppa. Or, more like, she heard the back gate when ye arrived and has come for a nose to see who it is.'

Maura stopped talking just as Peggy opened the back door. As soon as Peggy saw Harriet by the fire, a look of disappointment crossed her face and she cried out, 'Oh, Jesus, no. I only came in for a cuppa tea and now I'm going to walk out with work to do. Fecking hell, how did that happen?'

'No, no,' Harriet said, as both her hands flew to her mouth in horror. 'I must have a terrible reputation for bothering people. I am here for something entirely different altogether, although I will admit there is a reason.'

Peggy didn't have time to respond, before Nana Kathleen joined them.

'Well now, a pow wow and no one invited me?' she said as she bustled in and placed a bulky white paper bag on Maura's press.

'Goodness me, it's like Lime Street station in here, it's so busy,' said Harriet.

'Aye, this kitchen was very rarely empty at one time,' said Maura. 'Some of the kids on the four streets used to be confused about where they lived, because their mothers spent so much time nattering round my kitchen table. My house has always been full of kids and friends and I don't have a problem with that now. My neighbours have been good to me, so they have.'

Harriet felt mildly embarrassed. She hadn't met or known Kitty, although she wished she had, as Maura might then have felt a closer connection to her. Harriet was always on the lookout for a lost soul to heal. She was as close as she could be to Kathleen's granddaughter, Nellie, and she knew they were aware of the role she had played in helping Nellie recover. It was that which made it possible for her to pluck up the courage to knock on Maura's door, seeking an answer to a question that was burning away in her mind.

'It wasn't a pow wow five minutes ago, Kathleen,' said Maura, 'but sure, 'tis about to become one. Peggy, go and knock on for Sheila and Deirdre with the mop, and tell them we have a guest. I feel guilty, them not being here.'

Peggy looked grumpy, but she stood up from the kitchen chair where she had made herself comfortable, preparing to waddle back into her own kitchen to bang the mop on her wall and send out the call.

'How do ye reckon I let them know there's a guest? D'ye think I bang on the wall in fecking Morse code now?' Unused to such raw language, Harriet blushed again.

They sat and listened to her footsteps shuffle down the yard, until they heard the back gate latch snap. Then Kathleen and Maura both began to laugh.

'Gosh, she was cross,' said Harriet.

'Not at all, no, she wasn't. Don't you be taking no notice of Peggy now,' said Maura. 'Peggy never stops grumbling. She's all right. Right as rain she will be in five minutes when she comes back in. There are a few things ye need to know about Peggy. She hates to move her backside and she loves her tea and cake. Apart from that, there's not a lot to her.'

'Apart from the smell,' Kathleen whispered and winked at Harriet.

'That's the reason I'm here, to be honest,' said Harriet.

'What, because of the way Peggy smells?' exclaimed Nana Kathleen.

'No, no. I wanted your advice, Maura. I'd like to get to know a bit more about the neighbours. Alison and I are good friends, but I want to know everyone else too.'

'Well, ye have come to the right place to be sure,' said Maura. 'We can do that. We can provide all the advice ye need and tell ye everything you need to know about everyone around here. There's nothing we don't know about on these four streets, isn't that a fact, Kathleen?'

Kathleen smiled. ''Tis true. Now, tell me, Harriet, ye haven't taken the veil and yet there's no husband in yer life. Why is that now?'

Harriet gasped. She had known people in Liverpool were direct and to the point, but she had at least expected them to be onto their second cuppa before being asked such deeply personal questions.

'Well, I have never taken to anyone, I suppose, and no one has ever taken to me. I had to look after Mammy and Daddy until they died. I don't know really. I was so busy and time just flew and then there I was, on my way to Liverpool with Anthony and no husband to speak of. I would love to be married and have children, but I expect it is too late now, though.'

Kathleen or Maura were saved from having to answer by the sound of the back gate opening and familiar chatter flooding the yard. The kitchen was crowded within minutes. Neighbours, old and new, sat round the yellow Formica table that had once belonged to Bernadette. The precious Formica table with which Maura refused to part, no matter how large her family grew.

Sheila had spotted Daisy, leaving the school office, and had called her over to join them.

Kathleen helped Maura pour the tea at the range.

'I bought the kids some custard slices in Sayers, your Harry loves them. They are in that bag on the press for when they get home from school.'

'Kathleen, ye spoil them kids but they do love it,' said Maura, smiling.

'Aye, well, they deserve a bit of spoiling with what they have been through,' replied Kathleen, pouring from the sterilized-milk bottle into the cups.

Kathleen nodded her head in the direction of the table.

'I will have ye a penny, that Harriet is here with troubles of the heart. I can hear it in her voice. Hope these is fresh tea leaves as we might have to give her a little reading.'

Maura wanted to say, 'Harriet, no,' but she knew better. Nana Kathleen was never wrong.

Life on the four streets was mundane. It was about survival and making ends meet. Harriet had lived in a large house in Dublin and had been brought up in a professional household. Her brother was a priest. She was a cut above. She wore stockings every day, never ever went outside her front door with curlers in her hair, and she carried a handbag with a fresh handkerchief in it at all times.

Harriet was a source of fascination to the women of the four streets, especially to Peggy.

'So, is there anyone takes ye fancy now?' she asked.

Harriet spluttered, 'Well, that was why I came to see Maura, er, there is and I have no idea what to do. And Alison, she told me Maura and Kathleen know the answer to everything, including things that haven't even happened yet. She was very mysterious, though, and wouldn't say why.'

Kathleen now spoke.

'Put three spoons of sugar in your tea, queen, drink it up as quick as yer can and then, with the last dregs, rinse them round your teacup three times, making a wish. Tip the cup up on the saucer, quick now, and then pass it to me. I will read your fortune and then we can decide what you should do.'

Harriet looked horrified. 'Read my tea leaves? Isn't that a sin?'

'Well, if it is, Harriet, we are all going to hell together. Tell me now, how do ye think your friend Alison got her man down the aisle? Do ye think she has never sat round this table and passed me her teacup?'

Harriet's hand shook as she spooned the sugar into her tea. If Alison had done it, she would too.

'No one must tell Anthony, though,' she added quickly before drinking her scalding tea as fast as she could. Then she told them all about Mr Manning. His caliper, his war wounds and his sad eyes.

'I'm sorry to burden you all but I don't know what to do. It is the first time I've been stuck. I usually know how to solve a problem and now it is just about me and I have no idea.'

Maura reached out and placed her hand over Harriet's. 'Don't worry, Harriet. If there is a way, we will find it here round this table, as we have done so many times with so many problems. I'm sure Alison won't mind me saying, but she was heartbroken when she called here to see me and Nana Kathleen. And do you know what?'

There was a sharp intake of breath as everyone leant forward and gasped, 'What?' at exactly the same time.

'Alison met Howard two weeks after she walked out of this back door, having had her reading. You don't know about Bernadette, Harriet, but she was my best friend, Nellie's mother and Jerry's wife. This is her table we are sitting at.'

'We know it's our Bernadette, and she works through Nana Kathleen. She will get ye sorted, have no worry about that,' said Maura.

Harriet felt scared and exhilarated at the same time. It was true, Alison had urged her to visit Maura, but hadn't said why. If she had, Harriet would probably never have come.

Nana Kathleen picked up Harriet's cup. 'Now then,' she said. 'I see him here, right in the middle of your cup.'

Harriet gasped and put her hand to her throat.

'He's not really in there,' said Peggy, looking sideways at Harriet, slightly alarmed at how frightened she looked. 'It's just the shape Bernadette makes in the tea leaves for Nana Kathleen that makes it look like him.'

'He works in a tall government building,' Nana Kathleen continued. 'He can't work today, as his mind is distracted and he keeps thinking about a woman he met recently who has turned his head. He hasn't eaten his lunch either. It is there on his desk in front of him, still wrapped in greaseproof paper, unopened. He feels sick and doesn't know what to do. He is daydreaming about her, about the things they could do together if he was brave enough to ask if he could court her, but he is too afraid in case she should say no. He thinks his caliper and walking stick would turn a woman off.'

A tear ran down Harriet's cheek. Maura jumped up to comfort her. 'Shush, don't cry,' she said. 'I know, it really gets to you, doesn't it? Alison was just the same.'

Everyone watched as Harriet undid the clasp of her handbag and took out her white linen handkerchief edged in lace. No one had ever seen such a pretty hankie.

'Well, 'tis as clear as the nose on yer face if ye ask me,' said Nana Kathleen. 'Ye organize everyone else, Harriet, and ye boss us all about with yer fêtes and committees and the Rose Queen. There's a man out there waiting to be organized by ye, I would say, and so ye had better get cracking. Ask him to join ye for a cuppa down by the docks. There's a nice café where Jerry proposed to Bernadette, not fancy, mind, but if Bernadette is helping us, I reckon she will make sure there's a bit of magic around on the day.'

'Well,' said Peggy, leaning back on her chair and folding her arms across her ample bosom. 'I'll say this, Kathleen, that is good advice, an' all. The only advice anyone ever gave me, before I met my Paddy, was to never trust a man who doesn't like potatoes, and, surely to God, what a ridiculous piece of advice that was. There was never a man in all of Ireland who didn't like his tatties now, was there?'

'Aye, and yer still chose Paddy,' said Kathleen.

The clock chimes could barely be heard over their laughter. Maura stood to refill the teacups as Deirdre asked Kathleen, 'Will ye do mine? Will I need to put more money in the club for Christmas or will I have enough?'

'Oh, my goodness me,' Harriet squealed. 'I have a meeting in town about an organizing committee for the cathedral they are planning to build.'

And with that, her chair was scraped back, her hat scooped up from the chair where she had placed it earlier, and she was heading for the back door, but not before running back to give Maura and Kathleen a hug.

They sat and waited silently until they heard the back gate slam.

Deirdre lit up a cigarette and narrowed her eyes against the haze of blue smoke. 'Reckon she'll be having her leg over within six months, that one.' Then she frowned, crossing her eyes to look down her nose. Picking a stray shred of tobacco from the tip of her extended tongue with her fingertip and thumb and flicking it into the ashtray, she added, 'Not before he takes his caliper off first, mind.'

And with that, the laughter continued, just as it always had, year after year.

Nana Kathleen joined in. She had no intention of telling anyone she'd had a nice little chat with Mr Manning after the meeting about the nursery. As for the rest of it, she had no idea where her words had come from. She didn't have a clue whether or not he took his sandwiches to work in greaseproof paper and normally she shied away from providing such detail.

But she felt in her heart what had really happened. There was no other explanation. Bernadette was back.

Nana Kathleen had been wondering where she had gone to. She seemed to have left them all for some time now. The catastrophic sequence of events that had hit them with the force of a tank had broken the spell.

First Alice had left, then Kitty had died and finally Brigid had moved away. All within days. It felt as though Bernadette had vanished too. No ghostly sightings, no feeling that she had joined them. Nothing.

Maura began collecting up the dirty cups for a quick rinse.

'No doubt we shall all have another round now,' she said as she carried them over to the sink.

And for the second time in twenty-four hours, Maura thought once again, I am healing.

Daisy had sat silent throughout the chatter but had joined in the laughter. She wondered what her life would have been if her parents had never placed her in the convent, believing her to be simple, for no other reason than following a difficult birth, she struggled as a baby. Maggie had told her it was a common practice, but Daisy still asked herself, why?

'I won't have any tea, thank you, Maura,' she said when asked. 'I have to go and meet the police at the Priory at half past.'

'The police, why?' asked Nana Kathleen, more than a little interested.

Maura had returned to the table, carrying the dripping cups by their handles, three in each hand. 'Harriet didn't mention that. Does she know?'

'I don't know,' Daisy replied. 'The police said they would telephone the Priory to let them know. I have to take them down into the cellar and give them the key to the safe.'

'What key?' said Nana Kathleen. 'If ye have the key, doesn't Father Anthony have one too?'

'I don't think so. I'm sure I have the only one and, besides, I don't think he would find the safe. Only me and Molly Barrett knew where it was and Molly only knew because I showed her. It's behind the bricks in the cellar. The police say 'tis very important they have everything that is in it.'

It was a full minute after Daisy had left the kitchen before Peggy said, 'Fecking hell, she's a dark horse, that one.'

Maura sipped her tea and, taking out the cigarette packet from her apron pocket, she removed the last one.

Maura held her hand out to Peggy and, without the need for words, Peggy gave Maura the lit cigarette from her lips for Maura to light her own.

'She's that, all right,' Maura said as she exhaled. 'Daisy and her Maggie.'

Astonished, everyone looked at Maura, awaiting an explanation.

Maura milked the moment. She liked this feeling, being first with the news. Walking to the hearth, she screwed up the empty cigarette packet and threw it onto the fire. Her face took on a warm glow from the sudden rush of flame.

Resting her forehead on the mantelshelf, with one hand in her front apron pocket and the other still holding her cigarette, she stared intently at the blaze. A small piece of foil from inside the packet had curled up on itself, refusing to catch alight, and now it dropped down into the ashes, where Maura would brush it away in the morning.

'Who the hell is Maggie?' six women asked in unison.

Maura walked back to the table and, as she sat, she smiled. 'Well, then.'

It was going to be a long pow wow today.

# Chapter Twenty-one

Father Anthony was far from happy at having to leave the new cathedral community meeting. Archbishops and bishops were attending from all over Europe and he was excited about meeting his friend from Rome.

As he left the Grand hotel to retrieve his car, he saw Harriet, running up the street for a meeting of the Mothers' Union. All this activity had one purpose: to ensure that the new cathedral, known by everyone as Paddy's wigwam, became a vibrant Christian community.

'I hope 'tis the last time the police want to spend time at the Priory,' Anthony grumbled at Harriet as he passed her in the street. 'I'm beginning to feel as though my office is a police cell.'

'Well, who's the grumpy one today then?' said Harriet, rushing past him, through the hotel's revolving doors.

She had deliberately not dallied. She did not want to lie to Anthony about where she had been and what she had been doing. She was on fire with excitement after having had her tea leaves read by Kathleen.

Harriet felt a thrill as she replayed Nana Kathleen's words in her mind. She had been told, with the help of a ghost, that she had to be bold and ask Mr Manning to meet her for a cup of tea in the café at the docks.

During the journey to Lime Street, her mind had raced ahead. It didn't matter what she, or anyone else, thought of Kathleen's fortune-telling. The fact was that her feelings, which were swamping her, were beyond explanation. How could she account for them?

It was as if someone had wrapped an invisible shawl of love around her shoulders. She knew, she just knew, it had come straight from Bernadette, the woman they all loved and spoke of with such fondness. She was sure that it was she who had sat down next to her, but no one else had appeared to notice. Did it happen all the time?

What was Bernadette like? Why on earth would Bernadette possibly want to help Harriet? All Harriet knew was that Bernadette was Nellie's mammy. As she ran up the wide carpeted staircase to the meeting room, Harriet resolved to visit the churchyard to place some flowers on Bernadette's grave. She would thank Bernadette and tell her, I love your little girl. I will always do whatever I can for Nellie.

If Bernadette had already talked to her through three sugars and a cup full of tea leaves, she might work a miracle, if Harriet took her some flowers, sat next to her plot of earth and said a prayer.

The police commander was waiting in the hallway of the priory when Daisy stepped through the open front door. Having spent years using a key, she now felt at a loss as to the correct etiquette. Should she knock?

Hearing the sound of tyres on gravel, she saw Father Anthony's car turn into the drive. Father James had never owned a car.

'My, how quickly times are changing,' said Daisy out loud.

'Hello, Daisy,' Father Anthony called as he joined them. 'Go along into my office. You know the way. I will be just one minute. Oh, for goodness' sake, what are the boys doing now?'

Father Anthony looked over the wall into the churchyard and saw Harry and Little Paddy, charging between the headstones, shouting.

'Scamp, Scamp, come here!'

But Scamp was faster than they were.

'Sorry, Father,' the boys shrieked as they flew past.

'Harriet wasn't in, so we were playing truth or dare in the graveyard,' Harry explained breathlessly, as he struggled to keep up with the errant Scamp.

'Priests in cars and little boys tearing through the graveyard, chasing a dog. I have never known the like.' Daisy laughed.

'Don't let them see me laughing, Daisy,' Father Anthony whispered. ''Twould be the end of me for sure.'

Daisy realized that, after all the years she had spent in the Priory as housekeeper, this was the first time she had laughed out loud.

*

The commander had been pacing up and down the Priory hallway, pondering aloud his dilemma to the officer who had accompanied him. It was the tall and tubby PC Shaw, who had successfully nicked Stanley.

'It is all becoming very complicated and we need to ensure we keep each crime isolated. We have a priest's murder, Mrs Barrett's murder, a kidnapping and what appears to be an organized paedophile ring. It is unlikely the kidnapping and the child abuse had anything to do with the poor priest. I am very sure that whoever killed Molly Barrett killed him too, eh, boyo? But it's unlikely we are ever going to find out who that was. Apart from the butt of a Pall Mall ciggie found on the outhouse floor next to the dead woman, Molly Barrett, we have not a single clue and that's the truth.'

'What about the fact that they all happened at around the same time?' said PC Shaw. 'Surely that links them all in some way.'

'I'm not sure it does, boyo. That may just be a coincidence. On the other hand the case is turning out to be something far bigger and deeper than we thought, with new developments unfolding by the day. In the cells we have the two hospital porters and a policeman. None of them is saying a word. You would think they were all bloody nuns who had taken a vow of silence and they all look as guilty as hell. What with a kidnapping, child abuse and a double murder. We should have clues coming out of our ears, and yet hardly a sausage. You wouldn't believe it, would you?

'Let's hope Daisy comes up trumps again, eh? God knows why she thought she needed to keep the safe a secret all this time. The priest must have been worried about robbers stealing the collection money and who could blame him? The O'Prey boys came from around here somewhere, didn't they? Bad lads, they were. The most notorious thieves on the docks. Let's hope they throw away the key on the oldest. They say Callum, the youngest, has turned over a new leaf, but I'll believe it when I see it.'

Annie O'Prey, standing at the bottom of the kitchen stairs, heard every word.

Her elderly eyes pricked with tears. She bent her weary back to rest the tea tray she was carrying for the officers on the stair in front of her and, taking her grey and tattered hankie from the sleeve of her cardigan, she wiped her eyes.

So alone, she missed her boys desperately. She was very proud of her Callum, who had been taken on by Fred Kennedy down at the docks, and she suspected and hoped that he had his eye on lovely young Fionnuala down the street. She was the first to admit that they were naughty lads, but they never nicked anything without sharing it with everyone else. She knew that many a house had gone without, now that her eldest lad was in the nick and Callum was doing his best to behave.

Everyone missed the antics of the O'Prey boys.

Annie took out her rosaries from her cardigan pocket, said her Hail Mary and asked for forgiveness for having wallowed in her own despair. Drying her eyes, she picked up the tray and carried on up the stairs as though she hadn't heard a thing.

PC Shaw was about to offer up an idea of his own regarding the murders. Anger boiled in his belly when he thought of the men involved and he knew what he would want to do to anyone who went near his own daughter.

He thought the commander was wrong to think the murders had nothing to do with the kidnapping, nor with the way Daisy had been abused, and she had described others being abused too.

When Daisy walked into the hall, his moment for speaking out was gone.

'Ah, Daisy, I don't know if you remember my name? I'm Commander Lloyd. I'm from Wales, across the border.'

Daisy nodded. 'I remember,' she replied. 'I'm not simple, you know.'

There, she had said exactly what Maggie told her she must say.

'No, quite, Daisy. I apologize if I caused any offence. Mrs Davies is also on her way. She thought you might need a bit of female company. Do you have the key to the safe? Where is this safe, anyway?'

Daisy reached into her blouse and pulled out a chain from around her neck. Her gold crucifix hung from it – the only possession to have accompanied her to the orphanage when she was a baby.

'It's down in the cellar,' said Daisy, 'and so we need to go through the kitchen first.'

'Well, that explains why the safe wasn't in the office,' said the commander.

Annie O'Prey heard them coming down the stairs. 'Daisy, are ye after your job back, queen? 'Cause I'm done in, I am. I'm too old for this malarkey now.'

Daisy gave Annie a hug. 'I have to go down to the cellar, Annie,' she said. 'I have the key for the safe.'

'The cellar?' said Annie, amazed. 'Well now, I haven't put one foot in that place since the new father arrived and, do you know, I don't think anyone else has. A creepy hole altogether, that is.'

Ten minutes later, the commander was on his way back up the stairs, loaded with round tin cans the size of dinner plates, a projector, a screen and a pile of envelopes. He laid them all out on the hall floor and sent his officer down to collect the rest.

Alison was turning into the drive to the Priory when she saw her page-boys, Little Paddy and Harry, walking through the gate from the graveyard. Paddy was carrying Scamp and Harry, something large and wooden.

'Paddy, Harry,' she shouted. 'Is Scamp misbehaving himself?'

Alison could see that something was up. 'Is something wrong, boys?'

'I don't know,' Harry replied. 'Scamp found this on the other side of the wall, on one of the graves. It was covered with ferns but it looks a bit weird.'

Harry struggled to hold what looked like a lump of wood while Scamp wriggled in Little Paddy's arms.

'Here, let me take Scamp,' Alison said, extracting the rather sheepish-looking dog from under Little Paddy's arm. But she gasped with shock as Harry held up the wooden mallet he was carrying.

The end was soaked in what was obviously old, stale blood.

*

Commander Lloyd sat in the temporary office he had been allocated in Whitechapel where he and his officer had set up the screen and projector. It was eight in the evening. They had been waiting for days for clearance to view the films, as well as for a lab-test result on the mallet. It was being examined for fingerprints, and, more importantly, to check whether the blood on it belonged to the murdered priest.

'Have you eaten, boyo?' he asked Howard.

'Yes, sir, but I'm half wishing I hadn't now, if these films are too bad.'

The commander looked at the brown paper bag on his desk.

'Now then, before we begin, nip down to the canteen and bring up a few empty cups.'

Howard looked confused. 'Empty?'

'Because, boyo, we need something inside us, to line our stomachs and give us a bit of Dutch courage.' He slipped a large bottle of whiskey out of the bag on his desk.

'Now then, let's see how this thing works,' said the commander, as he wound one of the films around the wheel and PC Shaw switched on the projector.

He took a large swig from the bottle and then turned out the lights.

Images appeared on the screen in black and white. Although the filming was obviously amateur, they were clear enough.

'Oh God, fucking hell,' he said. He took another swig of whiskey, just as Howard walked back into the room with three mugs.

'Come here, boyo,' said the commander. 'Do you recognize him?'

Howard joined PC Shaw, who was staring at the screen, transfixed. Howard wanted what he was watching not to be true. But it was. It was there in front of him in black and white.

'I do, sir, he's that politician fella, he's always on the news. Drives round here in a big black Rolls with a chauffeur, and eats a lot of pies by the look of him.'

Peter, from the main desk, had come into the room unnoticed. 'Eh, that's that politician, isn't it?' he said.

'Aye, boyo, it is that,' said the commander. 'But keep it under your hat, mate, we have a bigger problem here. Did you want something?'

'Yes, sir, your lab and fingerprint tests are through. One of our lads has just run back from the labs with them. If you thought you had a problem before, wait until you hear this. They managed to get a fingerprint from the mallet. It belongs to Simon, the copper. Thank God he's already in the cells, eh? And the blood, well, that isn't the priest's blood group, but we know whose it is, all right – it belongs to the old lady who was murdered, Molly Barrett. I reckon it will be only half an hour before the *Echo* are on to it.'

'Jesus, fucking Christ! So if he murdered the old woman, he murdered the priest too. Unless we have two crazed murderers running around the docks, who both happened to strike within weeks of each other.'

Howard slowly lowered himself onto a chair. Simon – the man he had worked with for years, who had driven him to his wedding and bought him and Alison a silver rose bowl as a wedding gift – was a murderer.

All of them stared at the screen for a second longer. Then the commander leant forward and flicked up the off button. The room became dark. He turned to Howard and PC Shaw.

'You guys look through the photographs, quickly, before we have the press breathing down our necks. Let's try to keep this to ourselves and make sure the *Echo* only get to hear about that dirty, stinking creep Simon being charged with the double murder. I need to speak to my boss, as this will go way above my pay grade. Number Ten will be involved in this.'

And with that, he left the room.

'I don't know what he's worried about,' said PC Shaw. 'No one is going to let anything like this concerning a politician get out to the public. It will definitely all be covered up. It will all be pinned on the policeman now. He's a goner with those lab results, and that's for sure.'

But when PC Shaw opened an envelope of photographs, he blanched in horror.

'And here we have it,' he said. 'Yet another link. Jesus, someone is shaking that tree pretty hard. They are falling like leaves.'

'Let me see,' said Howard. 'Well, what do you know? Here they are, both together, very cosy, the priest and Simon. So now we have it, the link that binds them together, that and a bloody mallet.' Howard sounded sorrowful when he added, 'Simon can only be hanged once, but hanged he will be, for both.'

There was something painfully sad and disappointing about the fact that Simon was one of their own. PC Shaw drained the last of the whiskey bottle into two mugs and handed one to Howard.

'Here, drink this,' he said. 'Makes it all much easier to stomach.'

## Chapter Twenty-two

Mrs McGuire sat in the window seat of the hotel foyer, looking out onto the main road, drinking her tea and pondering. What a strange situation it was indeed that, because of Mary's new affluence, she could now afford to do this.

Some of the local children were walking past, on their way home. They stared in at the three-tiered plate, piled high with fancies and millionaire's shortbread, just as she and Maisie had done when they were girls.

A scruffy-looking young boy, who looked as though he hadn't seen soap and water for a month and wearing a jumper with more holes than stitches, his face full of envy and resentment, put out his tongue at Mrs McGuire.

She was far from shocked. Sure, didn't me and Maisie do the same, she thought, as she leant forward and put out her own tongue back at him. The other boys laughed and pushed the cheeky boy to move him along.

'Sorry, Mrs McGuire,' shouted a boy she recognized, but for the life of her, could not name.

She smiled back, to let him know, she took no offence.

I've been away for too long and missed too much, she thought, as she sipped her tea and waited for Mary and Alice to return.

Mary had been delighted that Sister Assumpta was happy to hand over the contract signed by Kitty.

'All we have to do now is get ourselves to Dublin. We will talk to this Rosie O'Grady and then we can find the girl who gave birth to my baby. I know that, no matter what, she will want to help. Who wouldn't, Alice? No one would deny a child the gift of life, now, would they? I will make it worth her while. I bet she is just a poor girl from the country.'

'Of course she will help. Anyone would,' Alice replied. 'When do you think we should leave for Dublin?'

'Tonight, if Mammy agrees. We don't have hours to waste, never mind days.'

Alice was distracted. She wished she could speak to Sean. She knew who the mother of the baby was and, what's more, she knew where she lived. There was no need for any visit to Rosie O'Grady.

The baby was dying and only his parents could save him. Alice knew for sure that one was already dead. Alice was part of the conspiracy, an accomplice in that parent's murder, a murder that would never be spoken about.

And the other parent was Kitty. She could get them to Kitty Doherty within a couple of days.

'Oh God, this is awful,' Alice groaned.

'What is?' asked Mary, unwrapping the shawl from around the baby and laying him on his back on her knee. Holding his little feet in her hands, she smiled at him and blew him kisses. Her heart felt lighter than it had since the day she had first received his diagnosis.

'Oh, it's nothing, I'm just tired,' said Alice, pressing her forehead on the cold glass and looking out of the window.

How could Alice explain that Kitty lived on the four streets, doors away from Alice's own son, Joseph?

'No woman who leaves her son has the right to call herself a mother,' Mrs McGuire had said to Alice when she had first arrived in America. She was right. Alice had no business thinking of herself as a mother, but that didn't stop her heart from breaking every day for the baby boy she had never wanted, had finally learnt to love and then had left behind in running away with Sean. And now Sean wanted her to have another child, as though Joseph had never existed. Alice had never wanted children but she knew in her heart that Joseph had taught her to love. She might have left him, but she would not desert him. He would remain her only child.

If she told Mary where Kitty lived, she would have to return to Liverpool and face her demons. If she didn't tell Mary, this Rosie O'Grady would lead them straight there anyway.

A baby was dying. Alice would be obliged to tell Mary that she knew who Kitty Doherty was. It was going to happen. Alice would have to return to the four streets. The thought made her stomach clench and her heart scream, for a sight of Joseph. Sean no longer occupied all her thoughts. She was smart enough to realize that things were not as she had expected them to be. She loved America, the freedom and the way of life, but she was also beginning to acknowledge, if only to herself, that she no longer loved Sean.

Mrs McGuire watched the taxi pull up outside the window and asked the waiter to bring another tray of tea for Mary and Alice.

'Well, hello there, and how is the little man?'

Mrs McGuire stood up, to take the baby from Mary.

'He is grand, so he is, and so are we,' said Mary, grinning.

'Well, that's the first time I have seen a smile on your face for some weeks. So the visit must have been worthwhile then?'

'It was, Mammy. We have the name of the girl and the name of a midwife in Dublin who sent her with her family to the Abbey. All we need to do is travel to Dublin, find the midwife and then we will have the address of where the girl lives. It has all been much easier than I thought. I'm famished. Are those cakes for us?'

Mrs McGuire smiled. Tea and cake. Always her daughter's favourite. There wasn't a problem in the world that she and her Mary couldn't solve, over a cuppa and an almond tart.

'They are delicious fancies, so they are. Tuck in, Mary. And you, Alice. Sit down now while ye tell me, what was the Abbey like? Was it nice to see the Reverend Mother again? I bet she and Sister Celia made a great fuss of this little fella, didn't they just?'

Mary and Alice exchanged a glance that Mrs McGuire missed as she lifted the baby into the air and bounced him up and down in her arms, making cooing and gurgling baby noises at him.

'I will speak to Porick. He and his da will take us to Dublin to see the midwife. What hospital's she at, then? What is her name?'

Two waiters began to offload the contents of a trolley onto the low table, placing teacups and saucers in front of them. Alice felt as though they were taking forever, deliberately hovering, to eavesdrop on their conversation. The clinking of the china and the babbling of Mrs McGuire's chatter grated. She willed the waiters to hurry and felt her heart beating faster in panic. Her mouth became dry. The sooner she did it, the better.

'Mrs McGuire,' said Alice.

She hadn't realized that it would come out as a dry croak. Mrs McGuire didn't hear.

Alice tried again. 'Mrs McGuire, Mary.' She reached out and touched Mary's arm, to attract her attention. 'I know who the girl is. I know the name on the contract and, Mrs McGuire, so do you.'

Mary and Mrs McGuire stared at Alice, waiting for her to continue.

'Is this why you have been acting strange since we left the convent?' asked Mary. 'Who is she then?'

Alice stared Mrs McGuire straight in the face.

'It's Kitty Doherty, Mrs McGuire, Maura and Tommy's daughter.'

'My God, no,' Mrs McGuire replied.

'Well, Mammy, is that not good? It saves us the visit to the midwife. We can go straight to wherever the girl lives,' said Mary, sounding encouraged. But now, for reasons beyond her understanding, the atmosphere tightened as hope took flight.

Mrs McGuire looked pale. 'Kitty's mammy, Maura, was one of Brigid's best friends. They live on the four streets. But I am afraid I have bad news for you both. Kitty Doherty is dead.'

'What do you mean, dead? She can't be.'

Alice felt as though she had been hit. Tears sprang to her eyes and, for no apparent reason, an image of Bernadette, Maura's closest friend, leapt into her mind. Bernadette, whom Alice had usurped before her body was even cold in her grave, was here, in her mind's eye.

Alice spoke again. 'How do you know she is dead, anyway? I'm sure you must be wrong. Kitty is only, what, fifteen at the most? She can't be dead.'

'She is. She drowned in the river near Kathleen's farm on the Ballymara Road, about six months ago. By my reckoning, if she is his mother, it must have happened only days after she gave birth to this little fella, although no one knows about him and that's for sure.'

Mrs McGuire blessed herself as she laid the baby over her shoulder, hugging him tight.

Quietly, her voice loaded with sorrow, Alice asked, 'How do you know all this, Mrs McGuire?'

'Because today I visited the woman who is truly married to my son, the woman who carries my family name and who is the mother of my Sean's children. I didn't visit my friends. I travelled to see my daughter-in-law, Brigid, and she told me. She was at the wake in Liverpool. She rushed to the side of her friend as soon as she heard the news.'

Mary picked up the teapot and stared at her mother. The consequences of what she had just said sank in. The baby's mother was dead and no one knew who the father was.

Mrs McGuire took control.

'We will set off for Liverpool in the morning, Mary. The doctor said we needed a family member for a match, did he not? Well, Maura is this little fella's grandmother and Tommy is his grandad, and their children, Kitty's brothers and sisters, are his family too, and nicer people you could not meet. Maura is from Killhooney Bay and Tommy, well now, he is from Cork. And you, Alice, can come with us. Maybe ye would like to see your own little lad, while we are there.'

Now it was Alice's turn to cry.

Mrs McGuire slid the cup of tea that Mary had poured across the low table towards Alice, and handed the baby to Mary.

'Here, drink this,' she said, passing a cup to Mary and lighting herself a cigarette.

She felt compelled, always, to make Alice suffer for what she had done to her family, but, being a kind woman at heart, she felt bad afterwards.

Leaning back in the chair and taking a deep pull on her cigarette, she thought through what tomorrow would now hold. We will have to leave early, she thought. I have tonight. I have this one night finally to get even with Maisie.

While she pondered, she looked across the road and watched Mr O'Hara as he locked up the butcher's shop. It was why she had chosen this table. She and Maisie used to stare at this very table and imagine which cakes they would order, when they were ladies, taking afternoon tea in the hotel.

She was meeting him again, tonight, at O'Connolly's pub.

The lives, and the demands, of the younger generation were exhausting her. She was too involved. They were far too dependent upon her. Most of the time, she didn't mind at all. But the arrival of Sean, with Alice, in America had altered things. He had let her down, broken her heart. Mary's willingness to be complicit in their deceit had surprised her. The disappointment she felt in her son, for leaving his wife and daughters, never faded.

She had spent too long being a hands-on grandmother and, in the process, had lost much of her own life. Tonight, she would take some of that back. She would be daring, do something that no respectable woman, at sixty years of age, would even consider. If her friends in the village knew what she was planning, they would disown her.

To hell with them, she thought. Just one night, that's all I want. Just one. I want to remember the last time I ever slept with a man.

I want to grow old, thinking: that was it. It was him. It was there and it was then and I loved it.

She looked at her daughter and at her fake daughter-in-law. Mary was tucking the blanket around the baby in the carrycot.

'Right, Mammy. I'm off to pack. Alice, are you OK?'

Alice looked anything but OK.

Mrs McGuire answered for her.

'She has to face her own healthy little boy, Mary, and the women she deserted and the families she destroyed and the stepdaughter she left distraught and stunned into silence by her own grief when Kitty died. Where was Alice then? Why shouldn't she be all right? I hear Alice has always been good at getting her own way, so she shouldn't worry. Liverpool will be a breeze, won't it, Alice?'

'Mammy, enough, stop. You are only acting like this because Sean isn't here.'

Mary was shocked at the way her mother was behaving. Mary didn't like what Sean and Alice had done any more than her mother did. Every time she attended mass she prayed for their forgiveness, and she saw her job as acting as referee, to keep the peace as far as that was possible. It had been Mary's idea to bring Alice along. It was an act designed to involve her and make her feel part of the family.

'I for one am very glad you are here with us, Alice.' Mary threw a look to Mrs McGuire that said, stop, now.

Alice didn't bother to say anything. She thought of the fifty thousand dollars she had drawn from her bank account and had used to line her suitcase. Sean had entrusted her with the money that Henry had paid them for the house. She didn't have to return to America at all, nor put up with the likes of Mrs McGuire, nor Sean's demands for another baby. Fifty thousand dollars was a huge sum of money. With that amount she could be set for life in England. Even as she had placed the bundles in her suitcase, she had failed to acknowledge to herself that this was her intention all along.

As the lift door closed on Mrs McGuire, Alice whispered, 'Go to hell, you witch.'

That night, as Alice lay in bed, she hatched her plan. There was no court that would refuse a mother custody of her child. She would return to England with Mary and then claim back her son. Mrs McGuire might be no Kathleen and Sean no Jerry, but Alice had burnt her boats. She knew that neither Kathleen nor Jerry would ever want to know her again. She was alone now. She would take Joseph away and the two of them would find a little house, over the water in Birkenhead, or one of those nice suburbs, and they would live a quiet, gentle life, just Alice and her boy.

He already had her drink waiting when she arrived at O'Connolly's.

He was sitting at the corner table, as far away as possible from the toilets and the jukebox. For the first time since they were kids, she thought he looked nervous.

'I got ye a gin and orange squash, the same as before. Is that all right, now?'

He had stood up to greet her and removed his cap as she approached the table. Waiting for her reply, he stubbed his cigarette out in the ashtray, rolled up his cap and stuffed it deep down into his pocket. His black waistcoat strained against buttons that threatened to pop. The thought crossed her mind that it had been many a year since he had last worn it.

'Aye, that's grand, thanks. If you don't mind me saying, I need that right now and another to follow, after the day I have had.'

He picked up his Guinness. 'Aye, well, for a long time now mine has been much the same as every other day. There are never any surprises for me. It does always come as a great shock, I suppose, when a customer dies and hasn't paid their bill, but that is as bad as it gets.'

They both burst out laughing. She realized it wasn't something she did very often any more. Laugh. She was often concerned, busy, useful, needed, but not for herself, always for someone else. As their laughter abated, she looked into his eyes. She didn't see a sixty-year-old face, laughing back at her. She saw the face of over forty years ago, just the same. Unaltered. Hidden by extra weight and some wrinkles, it might have been, but she looked through that to the boy she had known before.

Be bold. Be bold. The words raced through her mind as they weighed each other up.

He still has nice eyes, she thought.

She has the figure of a woman half her age, he thought.

She knew he would be shy. He would have no idea of her wild thoughts or crazy intentions. If she weren't bold, she would lose her nerve and change her mind.

Be bold.

She leant across the table to say the most daringly outrageous words she had ever uttered, but, even as she began to speak, she had no idea what those words would be.

He surprised her and spoke first.

'Ye are a sight for sore eyes and one that hasn't left my mind for these forty years gone, now, do ye know that?'

'But you married Maisie,' she replied, very matter-of-fact.

'Aye, 'tis true and, sure, I was the father of a child that grew in the womb for two years. I was a stupid fool, easily led, and what lad isn't? But I will tell ye this: there was only one woman I wanted to marry and, God knows, I paid the price for my mistake every day for years. God rest her soul. She couldn't help it but, sure, nothing good comes from trickery, now does it, and so I feel no guilt.'

Mrs McGuire's heart was beating like the wings of a captive bird. 'No, I suppose not. I couldn't forgive ye for years.'

'Sure, didn't I know that. Ye bought yer meat in Castlefeale. Now that's a woman with a grudge, I'd say.'

Mrs McGuire turned round to look towards the bar and saw that, as she had guessed, they were under close scrutiny from Mrs O'Connolly, who repeatedly wiped the same section of the counter.

She turned back to face him. Be bold. She took a deep breath. This would be it. Her chance.

'Do ye have any gin at home? Because if ye do, why don't we pop back there for a drink, without Mrs O'Connolly watching? We can catch up on some of the fun we missed out on, forty years ago.'

It took him what felt like forever to respond. 'Jesus Christ, I missed out altogether all these years, didn't I just?'

Less than five minutes later, they sneaked in through his back door, giggling like a pair of errant teenagers. Thirty minutes later, they were in his bed.

At four in the morning as he lay next to her, gently snoring, she thought to herself, so this was it. It was here.

She gazed out of the window and listened to the rain gently fall, as it so often did. The window was open wide. She grinned to herself and thought, Holy Mother, I hope next door didn't hear me. But instead of feeling washed in shame, she felt exhilarated and half hoped that the neighbours, the miserable, God-fearing, mass-four-times-a-day O'Byrnes, had heard her after all.

She looked at the outline of his body, older and heavier but still fit and healthy, and thought to herself, I want a life of no surprises. I'm not going back to America. From now on, I'm going to squeeze two days into each one, to make up for lost time.

He opened his eyes and saw her leaning over him.

'Bloody hell,' he said. 'It was real, then. I thought maybe I had been dreaming.'

She smiled. Be bold.

'How about I don't go back to America, but stay here in the village? Would ye like that? Would ye like more nights like this?'

He reached up and pulled her down to him. 'No, I'm not dreaming, that's for sure I'm in fecking heaven.'

She laughed, as she hadn't done in a very long time. She felt like a girl. It was as though her wrinkles and her age were nothing to him. As she spoke she stroked the base of his neck and traced around the outline of his lips.

'It'll be a shock for them all, but, God, who helped me when I had my kids? No one. 'Tis time they learnt to manage without me. God knows, for sure, I'll be dead in ten years or so. I haven't much time left.'

And they made love again. Not as they would have done as teenagers, but gently and slowly, with a passion so intense that she knew she could never handle the sadness of knowing when it was to be the last time.

# Chapter Twenty-three

Harriet knelt at the foot of the headstone with a bunch of floppy-headed, deep-burgundy roses, which she had cut from the Priory garden just that morning. Annie O'Prey had wrapped wet newspaper round the base of the stems to keep them fresh but now that Harriet was at the graveside, she felt silly. Despite that, she was glad of the five minutes to sit down. The following day was the Rose Queen competition and parade, the first of what Harriet hoped would become a regular grand day of festivities, for everyone who lived on the four streets.

'Do you know, Anthony, no one who lives here has ever had a holiday. The Rose Queen fête is something for everyone to look forward to and to plan for. And it is great fun for the kids.'

'You are right, Harriet, and you always are.' Anthony had smiled. 'Just don't overwhelm yourself. It is a massive undertaking, if you don't have enough help.'

Even Harriet had been amazed at how many women had stepped forward to volunteer their services. Lots had their own ideas and Harriet had relished every minute of taking on the role of event co-ordinator.

This was the last quiet moment she would have until it was all over, so it seemed as good a time as any to pay her visit to Bernadette.

Annie had told her, 'There's an old pickling jar on Bernadette's grave. Brigid put it there. She was always leaving flowers. She thought none of us knew it was her but we knew, all right. I don't think it has cracked. You can put some water in from the fountain.'

'Do Jerry and Nellie visit the grave, Annie?'

'Oh Jesus, now, Jerry is there all the time. He always was, even when he was married to Alice. I shouldn't think she knew but, God only knows, I cannot even tell you the number of times I have seen that man standing there.'

'He must have loved her very much,' said Harriet.

'Loved her? Well now, listen while I tell ye. If I lived to be a hundred, never in all my life will I have known two people who loved each other as much as they did. It was as if the sky had fallen down, the day she died. Oh God, now you've set me off.'

And here Harriet was, at the grave of a woman people still spoke of as if she had died just yesterday and who appeared to have been one of the nicest women ever to have lived.

'These are for you, Bernadette,' Harriet whispered, as she placed the roses in the jar and looked carefully around to see if anyone was listening.

Kneeling back on her heels, she sat still for a moment and gradually became aware of the noise around her. Traffic passed by on the road, the cranes were lifting their loads down on the docks, tugs were tooting angry horns, and yet she felt as though she were in an oasis of peace and tranquillity.

Tentatively, she began. 'I just wanted you to know that I think the world of Nellie and I know she is hurting. Nana Kathleen is just the greatest woman, Bernadette, and everyone does their best, but I think you know that Nellie and I have a special bond. We are a similar age, you and I, Bernadette, and I think Nellie knows that. Anyway, I just wanted you to know that I will do my utmost for your little girl. My eye will always be on your Nellie and my heart will always be full of care for her.'

Harriet felt guilty for what she was about to say, but she knew, in her heart, that there was another reason she had visited the grave.

'Bernadette, Nana Kathleen and the women, they say you are like a guardian angel to everyone on the four streets. I think that's true, because I felt it. I know you and Jerry were very much in love too. I would so love to have someone special of my own. I always have. Just someone I can love and who would love me back. My mammy told me to find myself a nice Irish boy, but I don't care about things like that. I would just love someone kind. Bernadette, I think I have found someone I would like to get closer to, if you can be my guardian angel too.'

As Harriet spoke, it was as though a feeling of utter serenity and optimism swept over her. Without understanding why, she knew, without any doubt whatsoever, that the wish she had made to Bernadette would come true.

He will be mine and I will be happy, she thought.

Over at number forty-two, Maura Doherty felt that if she never saw another scone or jam tart again, it would not be too soon.

'Where did the flour and sugar come from, Tommy?' she asked as her husband brought a sack of each into the kitchen.

'Don't ask, queen,' Tommy replied. 'But if the captain of the *Cotopaxi* comes knocking on the door, you've never heard of me.'

'Thank the Lord for the *Cotopaxi* and all who sail in her,' said Maura. 'What in God's name would we have done without her all these years? I bet Harriet doesn't know where they have come from, does she?'

'Good God, no, are ye mad? That woman has me run ragged. I have to go now, to set out the road with marking chalk for the kids' races tomorrow, and then I have to help Jerry carry the weight for the strongest-man machine she has borrowed from God knows where.'

'Oh, stop complaining,' Maura laughed. 'The kids are beside themselves with excitement. The girls are trying on their retinue dresses upstairs and then they will be both off down to Mrs Green, who made the headdresses. I have enough to do, getting the cake stall ready without your moaning mouth. Nana Kathleen and Nellie are making coffee cake with Camp coffee and coconut golf balls, but they have run out of Camp, so Harry has run a message to buy another bottle. Deirdre is making giggle cake and fudge squares, and I am making the bannock cake.'

'Can I have one of those?' said Tommy, putting his arms round her. 'Ye are doing grand, queen, but don't let all the extra work or this Rose Queen fair get to you, d'ye hear me?'

Maura lifted her head. 'Tommy, I am loving all this activity, so I am. It's grand for the kids, to have something to be excited about. I just can't help thinking that our Kitty would have been in the Rose Queen competition and might well have won it. Can ye imagine the picture she would have made in that frock? Beside herself she would have been. Oh, and how big that head of hers would have quietly swollen. She never needed to brag, our Kitty, Angela would have given out forever more and without meaning to, done it all for her. There would have been no telling her now, no, there wouldn't. She would never have shut up and our Kitty, not a word would she have said back. But God, I'd put up with all that, if we could just have her back. She would have been the Rose Queen, Tommy. She was so beautiful.'

Tommy hugged Maura closer into him. He didn't want her to see the tears that sprang to his eyes as he imagined Kitty in the white Rose Queen dress. He didn't want to tell Maura that, on the day Alison Devlin got married, it was all he could do to hide the pain in his heart as he realized he would never walk his Kitty down the aisle, nor see her in her wedding gown.

He had never revealed to Maura that, when he closed his eyes, he could still see Kitty's face. It was the last time he ever saw her. She was looking out of the window of the wooden hut on the Pier Head, on the night when he had taken her to meet Nana Kathleen and Nellie. The night she left for Ireland and exile.

Maura felt his tears soaking through her hair and she held him tight, as they both stood there, in the same place, on that well-trodden, rocky road together.

Annie O'Prey was also baking, in her own kitchen. She had inherited Molly's handwritten cookbook and was in the middle of one of Molly's most famous recipes. Examining Molly's precise writing, she rested for a moment and took her rosary out of her cardigan pocket.

'Ah, Molly, I wish I knew what happened to you and why I didn't hear a thing that night. I have yer cat and I'm looking after him for yer. He's a good cat. Brings me a mouse every morning. Never a langer now, he saved that for ye, Molly, and I know in my heart that was why ye was killed. It was summat to do with the priest's murder, wasn't it, Molly?'

Annie peered out of the window to see the flatbed coal lorry easing its way down the entry, piled high with chairs and beds. She wiped her hands on her apron and, Molly and cakes forgotten, ran out of the back gate.

'What's going on?' she asked the coalman.

'New family moving in next door, into Molly's old house, Annie, to keep ye company.'

'Well, what a day to be moving. 'Tis the fair tomorrow – do they know?'

'I have no idea. Why don't ye tell them yourself? They will be along in a minute.

'Have ye heard the news? They have arrested the policeman for the murder of the priest and Molly. 'Twas the policeman himself that did it.'

'God, no, I didn't. How did ye know that?'

'The paper boy is shouting it outside Lime Street station. They found a mallet with his fingerprints and Molly's blood on it.'

'Does anyone else know yet? God, does anyone else on the four streets know?' Annie almost screamed the question.

'I shouldn't imagine so, not until the *Echo* is delivered here and that's not until six o'clock.'

He had barely finished speaking before Annie was away and over the road to be the first to break the biggest news to hit the street in months. The first kitchen she ran into was Tommy and Maura's.

'All right, you young lovers, break it up. Come here while I tell ye. Ye will never have a notion of what I'm about to say.'

The baby woke and began to scream at the sound of Annie's voice.

Maura shouted, 'Oh God, no, not again.'

The commotion brought the girls thundering down the stairs, as fast as they could, in their long dresses.

'What's going on?' said Angela. 'What is all the noise about?'

'I'm sure I have no idea,' Maura replied, picking the baby up. 'She's teething real bad,' she said to Annie, by way of an apology for having snapped.

Annie grinned at the girls. She was going to relish every minute of this.

'Would ye like some tea, Annie?' Even Tommy was intrigued by the high colour on Annie's cheeks and the twinkle in her eye. He wanted to stay and hear the latest news.

'Aye, I will, thanks, but, Maura, I reckon ye need to knock on because I have big news, so I do.'

Just as Annie finished speaking, Angela ran to the corner of the kitchen, picked up the mop and said, 'I'll do it, I have to learn soon enough.'

Tommy smiled at Angela as he put the kettle on the range. Suddenly the back door burst open and in ran Little Paddy, with Scamp hot on his heels. Little Paddy yelled at the top of his voice, 'Maura, Maura, the policeman is going to hang for murdering Molly and the priest, so he is.'

Behind him, Peggy puffed and panted up the path, shouting, 'Paddy, ye fecking little bastard, get out, 'tis my news.'

'No, it isn't!' yelled Little Paddy. 'I was the one who told you. The paper boy is shouting it on the Dock Road.'

Ducking the slap from his mother, which was meant for his head, he and Scamp legged it up Maura's stairs to find the boys.

The kitchen fell silent. Even the baby stopped grizzling. Maura wasn't even sure whether she had spoken the words, or whether someone else had, when she said, 'How do they know?'

'Because,' said Annie forcefully, peeved at Little Paddy's interruption and determined to deliver the last shred of the news, 'they found a mallet in the graveyard with the policeman's fingerprints on it and Molly's blood all over. He must have carried it from the outhouse and dropped it when he ran.'

'Will he hang?' said Maura, her face ashen.

'Aye, he will, but he can only be hanged once for one murder. They can't hang you twice, can they?'

Maura spoke quickly. 'How do they know 'twas him who murdered the priest as well, then, Annie?'

Annie was not happy. She had been expecting stardom, at the very least, not an inquisition.

'How would I know?'

'I do.' Tommy spoke. 'They think there can't be two murders so close together by two different people so it must be the same man who committed both.'

'Aye, that makes sense,' said Maura slowly, as she wondered why in God's name Molly would have been killed.

'I'm popping down to the shops, to buy the *Echo*.'

With that, Tommy slipped out of the front door, unnoticed by the women who began to arrive through the back gate as a result of Angela banging on the kitchen wall with the mop like a madwoman.

Running down the street, he met Jerry.

They fell into step, each not having to ask where the other was heading.

'Have ye heard then?' asked Jerry.

'Aye, I have and I have only one question: what the fecking hell is going on? Why would the policeman have murdered Molly? Why didn't we know? 'Twas us what did for the priest, so how can he be taking the rap for us?'

'That was more than one question, Tommy. Shall we call in to the Anchor on the way to the shop? Someone will have an *Echo* in there.'

'Grand idea, but only for a quick one. Then ye have to help me mark out the streets with this block of chalk Harriet has given me for the races tomorrow, 'cause I couldn't stand the thought of that one breathing down my neck, now, if it wasn't done.'

With that, both men turned up the Anchor steps and into their place of refuge, where even someone as determined as Harriet wouldn't dare try to reach them.

# Chapter Twenty-four

As soon as it was light Harriet woke and reached for the list on her bedside table. She read down the long line of additions that she had written, either before she went to sleep or when she had twice woken during the night.

'You couldn't function without that list, could you?' said Anthony, as they ate breakfast in his study.

'Do you know, Anthony, if I lost this list, I would surely die. I could not think of anything worse, so please stop hiding it, even as a joke. It is no longer funny.'

'Will your Mr Manning be coming to the Rose Queen competition today?' Anthony teased.

'I have no idea,' she replied.

'I only ask,' he said, 'because I know Alison is in charge of judging the Rose Queen and I saw his name, on her list of judges.'

Harriet looked at him, aghast.

'Stop,' she said. 'For goodness' sake, she hasn't done that, without telling me, has she? The judges are due here for tea and sandwiches, at one o'clock, before they begin judging, at two. Why would she do that? Not that it makes any difference. He's a judge, like any other.'

'Really?' said Anthony. 'I think your friend may be trying to play Cupid.'

Now that it was finally the morning of the Rose Queen fair, Harriet realized she had yet to sort out an outfit for herself. And if Mr Manning was to be a judge, she wanted to make an effort to look special. Alone in her room, her stomach filled with butterflies, she became giddy as she tore through her wardrobe, looking for a suitable dress, while downstairs Anthony was reaching for his bible and a reason to believe. Not just for Harriet, the doubt of true faith.

Outside, the women were already marching their young boys down the four streets, to carry kitchen tables outdoors and cover them with cloths for the afternoon street party. The dockers, who were taking a day off, were building a platform and erecting side poles, just as Harriet had asked them, for the judging of the Rose Queen.

The coalman had scrubbed his float almost clean and covered it with sacking, a skirt of hessian sackcloth hiding the wheels.

Mothers who had stood at St John's market at closing time the previous day, to buy leftover flowers and greenery, were laying them on the ground next to the float.

Two chairs, covered with white sheets and tied with pink-and-white ribbons, were being carried out of Mrs Green's front door, ready to be lifted onto the lorry, as thrones for the Rose Queen and her maid of honour. The attendants would sit in a circle on the floor around their feet.

Harriet pulled up the sash window in her bedroom and shouted out to Maura, who was walking past with a cardboard box full of cakes. She thought that Maura looked sadder than usual and on a morning like this, too.

'Morning, Maura. Are the girls excited?'

Maura looked up. 'Everyone is excited, Harriet. Ye have done a grand job. It is going to be a special day today. Look, the sun is out, too.'

Harriet laughed as she ducked back inside. Now all she had to do, on top of everything else on her list, was try to make herself look halfway decent. At the thought of Mr Manning, her stomach turned a somersault. Little did she know that, at that very moment, his was doing the same.

'Nellie, would ye get out of that bed. Everyone else is already out on the streets, doing their jobs. Come down and let me get those curlers out.'

Nellie stared at her Nana Kathleen. How could she tell her that she felt almost too sad to leave her bed? Her heart felt heavy and her legs even more so. Today was Kitty's birthday, but she wasn't here for the best party the four streets had ever known. It hurt too much. She didn't want to move an inch, unless it was to slip further under the bedclothes.

Nana Kathleen sat down on the edge of the bed.

'I know what's up, queen,' she said, 'but do you know who is outside already, setting up the cake stall and being as bright as she can for everyone else? 'Tis Maura, Kitty's own mother, and how do ye imagine she is feeling inside?'

Nellie felt embarrassed.

'And Angela and Niamh, well, a pair of troupers they are, already downstairs in the kitchen, with their hair done, waiting for ye to go with them, to have their headdresses clipped in. Kitty was their sister. How do ye think they feel?'

Nellie's eyes were full of tears as she threw her arms round Nana Kathleen and buried her head in her hair, breathing in the distinctive musty smell that was her nana: of tobacco and chips, mingling with her new, sticky, Get Set hairspray.

'I know, queen, I know. We all feel it,' said Nana Kathleen, as she stroked Nellie's back. 'Today is a first. A first birthday without her and for that we should be thankful for the Rose Queen. It will help it pass more quickly.'

By mid-afternoon the noise from the docks had been drowned out by the sound of music and laughter ricocheting around the four streets.

When Malachi and Little Paddy won the three-legged race, the cheers could be heard for miles.

To no one's surprise, Angela was crowned Rose Queen. Her twelve attendants were dressed in peach-coloured dresses, all handmade in the Priory by Harriet's sewing circle. They behaved regally, as though used to such grandeur and with no notion of the tattered clothes they would be dressed in the following morning. Maura and Kathleen did a roaring trade on the cake and jumble stalls, and with the bric-a-brac.

Little Harry had sidled up to Maura, holding out the purchase he had made with the sixpenny piece Tommy had given him for the morning.

'Look, Mammy, I got this for you.'

Harry held out a square glass ashtray, washed and sparkling. It was one Maura had used herself when visiting another house on the four streets and it had been donated as a contribution to the bric-a-brac stall.

'There's a glass sugar bowl, on three legs, as well. Shall I get that, with another penny? We don't have a sugar bowl.'

Maura looked at her son, whose pain was, she knew, as great as her own, yet his only thought was of how he could ease hers. She pulled him into her side.

'The money is for you to buy sweets and things with, Harry. It's for you to have a nice day with, not to buy things for me.'

As she ruffled his hair, Harry squeezed his mother's waist and said, 'I'm going to buy the sugar bowl.'

'I don't know what I did to deserve a lad as good as that,' said Maura to Nana Kathleen who was serving next to her.

But Kathleen was preoccupied with something else. She had noticed a woman with a baby, who had been looking hard at Maura and was now walking up to the stall. There wasn't a woman at the Rose Queen fair not known to either Maura or Kathleen. This woman wasn't from the four streets, Kathleen could tell that much straightaway. But she did look familiar.

Kathleen nudged Maura, who was wrapping a slice of giggle cake in greaseproof paper for the youngest McGinty girl.

'That'll be a ha'penny, queen,' she said.

The crestfallen look told Maura in a flash that the child had no money.

It was a look Maura knew well. She could smell shame a mile away.

Maura thrust the cake into the little girl's hand. 'Well, there you go, then, you have it anyway. I need to be rid of it now.'

The child's look of despair instantly vanished, to be replaced by one of gratitude. As she walked away, Maura watched her break the cake and hand half to her little brother, whom she was holding tightly by the hand.

'That bastard McGinty. He doesn't deserve to have kids as good as that,' said Maura.

'Are you Maura Doherty?'

It was a voice Maura did not recognize. She looked up to see the best-dressed woman she had ever laid eyes on, with an accent she could not identify, but which had a trace of Irish in it somewhere.

Maura looked instantly suspicious. 'Yes, I am. Why?' she replied. 'Do I know you?'

'No, you don't, but you do know my sister-in-law, Brigid.'

'Brigid?' Maura looked incredulous. 'Brigid doesn't live here any more. She moved back to Ireland months back.'

'Yes, I know,' the woman replied. 'My mammy visited her yesterday.'

'Your mammy?' said Kathleen, joining in the conversation. 'Mrs McGuire, would that be now?'

'Yes, that's right. I am Mary, her daughter. I live in America.'

'Jesus, by all the saints, would that be ye, so? That means ye are the sister of Sean, who ran off with my son's wife, Alice.'

'I am that, yes,' she replied wearily. 'And it is their sin, not mine. I am not here to talk about them, Maura.' The woman's voice began to tremble as she looked down at the baby in her arms.

The thought flashed through Maura's mind that it was the sickliest baby she had ever seen.

'This baby, Maura, is your grandson. I adopted him from the Abbey. He is the baby your daughter Kitty gave birth to. He is very ill and needs your help.'

Maura could not speak, but as she looked towards the Green, her eyes searching for Tommy, she saw her once again, on the very spot where Maura had first laid eyes on her on the day of Bernadette's funeral. Alice, standing on the corner of the street, tucking her hair back into her hat.

Jerry had lifted Joseph out of his pushchair. The excitement of the children running around was all too much for him and he wanted to be on his feet, not pushed by his da.

'Come here, little fella,' said Jerry as he bent down to unclip his reins.

Once on his feet, Joseph grasped the handle of the pushchair, which Jerry slowly propelled along, and toddled down the street.

'Let's visit Nana Kathleen on the cake stall, shall we, and see what treats she has for ye?'

'Shall I look after Joseph, Jer?' Little Paddy appeared out of nowhere.

'Aye, go on then, Paddy,' said Jerry, failing to hide the relief in his voice.

He put his hand into his pocket. 'And here's a threepenny bit, Paddy. I'll go and help Tommy now. You keep in my sight so I know where ye go. And buy yerself and Joseph a cake and play one of the games. '

'Aye, I will, Jerry, thanks, Jerry.'

Little Paddy tied to the pushchair handle the piece of string he used as a dog lead for Scamp and lifted Joseph into his arms. He half staggered as he wheeled the pushchair towards the cake stall. Scamp had become a local canine hero. It hadn't taken many minutes before everyone on the four streets knew that Paddy's little friend had found a murder weapon.

'I was thinking of charging people to stroke Scamp,' Little Paddy had confided to Harry, 'but I changed me mind. I don't want Scamp to get above himself. 'Tis magic, Harry, that the *Echo* took our photo with Scamp. Who would have known that us playing in the graveyard would lead Scamp to the mallet, to be sure it was a miracle, it was.'

Little Paddy was delighted to have money in his hand. He had felt slightly detached from the fun, not having had a penny with which to join in, but that was Little Paddy's life, always on the outside. Nothing in his life was quite enough.

He wasn't loved enough, fed enough or respected enough. The kids on the four streets sensed who was the weakest in the pack and it was always Little Paddy everyone made fun of. His only true friend had been Harry, until now. Little Paddy and Scamp were enjoying hero status for having found the murder weapon, which had elevated Little Paddy to a level of contentment he had never known existed before today.

Harriet was aware that some of the children would have been excluded from the fun because they had no money, so she made sure much of the entertainment was free. However, she was also mindful of the fact that the aim of the fair was to raise funds for the new library.

Jerry waved across at Tommy, who was red in the face from

blowing his brass whistle, trying to impose some sort of order on the eighty children running around, demanding to know which race was next.

Jerry ran over to help his mate and, as he did so, he noticed Harriet walking into the tea tent with one of the Rose Queen judges.

'Well, if she wasn't the priest's sister, I would say that they was flirting outrageously now, wouldn't you?' he said to Tommy.

'Jesus, I haven't a fecking clue. Would ye stop that fight at the finishing line, Jerry? It was definitely Brian what won, will ye tell them for me.'

Little Paddy, having struggled with Scamp and an objecting toddler, put his foot down and, with it, Joseph back into his pushchair. He was already salivating at the thought of buying one of the huge cheese scones that he had watched Maura pile high on a plate. Little Paddy had had only a slice of bread and dripping for breakfast and his stomach had begun to rumble the second Jerry had placed the money in his hand.

'Let's go and get some grub, eh?' Little Paddy said to Joseph who had voiced no objection to being put back in his pushchair, now that he was being pulled along by Scamp. Little Paddy spun the pushchair round to head towards the cake stall, but his progression was halted suddenly in midflight.

'Oh, Holy Jesus, Joseph, is that yer mammy?'

It took Little Paddy only seconds to recognize the woman walking towards them. Her eyes were fixed on Joseph, and she appeared sadder than Little Paddy had ever seen her when she lived on the four streets.

'Hello, Alice,' said Little Paddy nervously. 'Have ye come back?'

Alice glanced around. She was safe; everyone was busy. With her plain headscarf pulled low over her forehead and tied under her chin, she looked very unlike the Alice who had left the four streets only months before.

'I have, Paddy. I've come to collect Joseph. I'm taking him with me now.'

At the sound of his mother's voice, Joseph sat up in his pushchair and his bottom lip began to tremble. His mother had been absent for a large part of his very short life, but he knew her. He knew her features and her voice, and he put out his arms. He wanted to be close to her and feel her.

But Little Paddy swung the pushchair round, away from Alice. Joseph strained against the reins, beginning to turn red in the face and working himself up into a scream as he attempted to scramble his way out.

'Right, well, ye see, Alice, Jerry has paid me, like, threepence to look after Joseph, so I can't let him go until I take him back to Jerry first.'

'Don't be silly, Paddy.'

Alice spoke firmly but no louder than was necessary so as not to attract attention. The last thing she wanted was to alarm Little Paddy or her beloved son. The sight of him made her heart crunch in pain. She had been thousands of miles away, and here she now was, only six feet from him, yet the barrier between her and the child was just as if an ocean lay between them.

'Don't be silly, Paddy,' Alice said again, her tone laced with tension. 'I am his mammy and, look, he needs his mammy. He wants me to pick him up.

'Shh, Joseph, Mummy's here,' she whispered, moving forward and bending down to unclip the reins.

Little Paddy broke out in a sweat. He knew this wasn't right; he couldn't run off and leave Joseph but he had no idea how to stop Alice either.

'Oh God, no, please don't get me into trouble, Alice. Shall I shout for Jer to help ye?'

Little Paddy looked around frantically. Jerry was down at the bottom of the green, organizing children to collect their prizes. Tommy had lined up a group of children for the next race. There were adults everywhere, but each was busy and distracted, and not one was looking his way. Music drifted over from the accordion, competing with the sound of children squealing and laughing.

'Oh God, please, please help,' Little Paddy whispered to himself, jumping up and down frantically. He shouted to Harry, standing on the side of the green, watching the games with Declan.

Little Paddy knew Harry couldn't join in the races and so he shouted louder, 'Harry, Harry, over here!'

But the noise drowned him out and Harry didn't so much as turn round.

Little Paddy looked at Alice.

'Please, Alice,' he begged, 'I think Jer will be mad with me and ye know what my da's like. Please, Alice, don't take him until I fetch Jer.'

Alice was struggling with the reins. When Little Paddy had fastened them and put Joseph back in his harness, he had accidentally crossed the leather straps. Alice paid no attention to Little Paddy. It was as if he weren't there and she was in a world of her own, where only Joseph existed.

'Oh, for goodness' sake.' Her voice was heavy with frustration. 'I will just take the pushchair with me. Sit down, Joseph, Mummy is here now.'

Joseph held out his hands. Alice leant forward and wrapped her arms round the son who had so obviously missed her. It tore her heart apart that he remembered her, that he loved her and wanted to be in her arms, that he did not pull away or condemn her for leaving him. Love was forgiveness and her baby son had needed no words. He had only his open arms. Alice knew she was forgiven. Leaning against the pushchair, she held him tightly, but he didn't object. His crying subsided as hers began and her hot, salty tears ran onto his scalp, darkening his blond curls. Alice was not a woman known to cry, until today.

Joseph, comforted, allowed Alice to stand as she held onto his hand. He grasped her fingers tightly. He was not about to let her go or leave his sight. As she stood, she pressed the pushchair handle down and spun it round, ready to head towards the Dock Road.

Little Paddy had broken out into a sweat. He felt faint with fear and knew that, at any second, he would have to do something.

'Alice.' Little Paddy sounded stronger than he felt. 'Please don't take Joseph. I might have to do something drastic. The dog is tied to the pushchair. I might have to set him on to ye or sumthin'.'

Alice seemed not to hear as she strode quickly away. Suddenly Little Paddy saw Jerry wave towards him and then break into a sprint. He heaved a huge sigh of relief.

'Paddy, hold onto the baby,' Jerry shouted as he ran, but Alice was already on her way down the road.

Scamp now took exception to being separated from Little Paddy and, with one bound, he leapt up, bit Alice on the arm and lodged his teeth in her coat sleeve. Alice screamed. Joseph screamed. Little Paddy screamed. The air was filled with growling, snarling and screaming, and then as Joseph began to cry, Alice found her voice.

'Get this dog off, Paddy, get him away,' she yelled, as the dog's yellow teeth refused to dislodge from the woollen cuff of her Macey's coat.

In a split second, Jerry had reached the pushchair and detached the dog, while Little Paddy untied his well-knotted string dog lead from the handles.

'Thanks, Paddy, ye did a good job there. Take Joseph to Kathleen, please, will yer,' said Jerry.

Little Paddy felt sick with relief. 'Aye, Jerry. D'ye want the threepence back?'

Little Paddy held out the coin and was thankful that Jerry didn't notice. He quickly popped it back into his trouser pocket and ran with the pushchair over to Kathleen, bumping into Harry on the way.

'Jesus, Harry, Alice came back from nowhere. She just appeared like a ghost and scared the feckin' shite outta me she did. She stared at me with her weird eyes and I swear to all that is holy, she was trying to turn me into stone and then when it didn't work, she tried to kidnap Joseph and run away with himself sat in the pushchair. Scamp wasn't having that and attacked her, hung from her arm with his teeth he did and bit her, and then Jerry came and paid me for looking after Joseph and saving him. I'm away to Nana Kathleen with Joseph now, so we can be safe in case she comes after us and tries it again.'

Harry looked at Little Paddy gravely.

'Paddy,' he said, placing both hands on his hips, 'you have to stop telling lies and making stuff up, or, I swear to God, you will get locked up one day.'

*

Jerry held Alice by her arm and inspected the small puncture wound on her wrist. They could both hear Joseph crying for his mother as Little Paddy wheeled him away, and Jerry could see the pain in her eyes.

'The dog hasn't drawn blood, Alice, so ye will be fine. Have ye come back to steal my son?'

Alice hesitated. Her answer should be yes. But she knew that if she said that out loud, it would be a lie. She had returned for so much more.

She looked first at the man who had loved her without ever being loved back, then turning to the green and Joseph, saw the woman who had been a mother to her and who was now lifting Alice's baby into her own arms to comfort him.

Alice had discovered that it was nowhere near as difficult to leave behind a person as it was to leave behind an entire life. She hadn't just left Jerry; she had unfastened herself from her own existence. It felt now as though each day in America had passed in a haze of unreality.

Alice met Jerry's eyes. She stalled. 'How can you ask me that?'

'Because I can't believe, Alice, that even you would try to steal my own son away from under my very nose without so much as a by-your-leave. You did that when you walked away as my wife, but ye surely cannot think you can do it with my son?'

She could see Maura standing by Kathleen's side. Alice wanted to run over and tell her that she had loved Kitty and cared for her, and that her heart had broken for the first time ever when she had heard the news that Kitty was dead. That was why she had visited the abortionist on Kitty's account. Because she had wanted to help, to find a solution. She had wanted to find a way out for Kitty, because she had cared.

All around her, everything and everyone was familiar and safe and known to her. She was surrounded by the people who had helped her through her transition from that wretched woman she had once been, to a mother. And someone they regarded as one of their own. Although she had traded this life for a new one of opulence and opportunity, even Alice knew that no amount of money could buy the security she had here, with these people. She and they were bound forever by a secret, a deadly secret, one she would find hard to carry alone for the rest of her life, without them.

Jerry knew Alice well enough to read her thoughts and know exactly what was flashing though her mind.

'If you've not come to steal Joseph away, have ye come back to us then?'

'I can't. I've caused too much damage,' she whispered.

'If ye mean Sean and Brigid, he was always going to live in America and she never was. His leaving would have happened anyway.'

'Would ye have me back?' Alice looked at Jerry, but she dared not hope.

The money and the big house, they were as nothing compared to the homely comfort of the two-up, two-downs on the four streets. And what she and Sean McGuire, the man she hadn't really known and never would, had for each other was a sham compared with the love she had for her son, Joseph. It had taken another woman's desperate fight to save the life of a child who wasn't even her own flesh and blood to make her realize that.

She held her breath as she waited for his reply, knowing that, if he said no, the torrent of tears now building up inside her, for the second time in her life, would overwhelm her.

Jerry didn't answer straightaway, despite the words being on the tip of his tongue. He could deal only with how he felt. The imaginary arguments and discussions with Alice that he had had in his head in the minutes before he fell asleep each night appeared to have temporarily deserted him. Even so, the fact that she had left with his own friend, one of his workmates, was surely beyond healing or repair. Would his other workmates and friends understand? Would the four streets forgive her? Amongst them again, would she become a living scandal? Would they all shun her?

He made no reply as he let go of her arm.

'Alice.'

Jerry turned as he heard Maura's voice. She was coming towards them with a smart woman whom Jerry had never seen before, carrying a baby.

Alice looked at Maura. With tears rolling down her cheeks, she whispered, 'I'm so sorry, Maura.'

Jerry stared, amazed. It was the first time he had seen Alice cry.

'Are ye home to stay, Alice?' asked Maura.

Alice turned to look at Jerry.

In those few words, Maura had answered all of his doubts.

'Aye, she is,' he replied. 'She is.'

# Epilogue

*Six months later*
*The Ballymara Road*

Liam had collected Nana Kathleen and Nellie, as he always did, in the old van. He and Kathleen chattered away as they travelled cross-country. They talked about the farm and each and all of the people who now lived, or had ever lived, in Bangornevin and Ballymara, going back as far as Nana Kathleen could remember.

'Do ye remember the Reagans?' Kathleen asked. 'They farmed up on Craighorn, back in my grandmother's day. The youngest son did three jobs to save up to emigrate to America and he kept his money hidden in the cowshed. The oldest, who never lifted a stick, watched him hide the money away for years. Never touched it he didn't and, when there was enough for a passage, he nicked it himself and took a ship from Cobh. Well, Jesus, I hear now that the youngest saved and saved again and when he got to America, he hunted his brother down and shot him. He is now spending his life in an American gaol, for all his troubles.'

Liam laughed. 'I do, 'twas the news here for at least a week, Mammy. His family moved to Galway a good while back now.'

'Things never turn out as you may plan, or think they will, do they, Liam? Holy Mother, we have had a year of it in Liverpool.'

Kathleen looked over her shoulder at Nellie who, exhausted from the night crossing, was fast asleep.

'This one struggled to get over Kitty, now, even more than Kitty's sisters, it would appear, although who knows what goes on inside a girl's head? Nothing cheered her up but, thank the Lord, the fact that she could face coming back here, the place where Kitty died, that is progress, so it is, and 'tis all thanks to the priest's sister, Harriet. She worked wonders with Nellie, so she did. Harriet got married all of a sudden, to a nice Mr Manning from the City Corporation. My tea leaves and prophesizing helped there, Liam. Now, the wedding was a surprise and she only had one bridesmaid and that was Nellie, for no other reason than to make her feel special. Oh, and Jesus, you should have seen the dress she was put in and the cut of her. She looked like a princess. Did you get the pictures I sent ye?'

Liam nodded.

'Did ye hear about the court case?'

'We did, we read about the court case as well, Mammy. That was shocking. Some people over here don't even know what a paedophile is. The kidnapping in the convent, it was all over the papers over here and on the television.'

'Aye, there were bad things going on, all right. Poor Sister Evangelista, she thought she was going to cop it, but the judge was very lenient with her and let her off for concealing information. Thank the Lord he was an Irish Catholic. There are five men in prison, you know, Liam, and one of them is a bishop. We will never see that happen again in my lifetime, as God is my judge. We sat in the public gallery every day we did. We had to take it in turns to keep each other's seat, there was so many nosey buggers trying to get in. You would not believe how awful curious some women can be. 'Tis an affliction, surely?'

Liam smiled to himself and, without drawing breath, she continued.

'Have you seen much of Maura and Tommy since they moved to Killhooney Bay?'

Kathleen galloped so fast from one subject to the next, it was difficult for Liam to keep up.

'Aye, we do. Maeve and Maura visit each other every week and I've kept it a surprise from Nellie,' Liam whispered. 'Angela and Niamh are waiting at the house for Nellie to arrive and they are staying with us for the week. Maura and Tommy are coming over tonight to eat with us. Tommy is driving his own van now, and doing a grand job, with a bit of land on Killhooney. About to open his own pub he is. Tommy reckons that things are so bad in England and America that everyone who ever left will be so homesick and desperate to return, there will be a roaring tourist trade soon enough on the West Coast. Everyone seems to be mad about the salmon from our waters and Tommy reckons he will have a good business there.

'He has a couple from Galway, Maggie and Frank, who have come across to work for him and Maura. Grand people, so they are. They were in the papers, over the convent being closed down. Seems they had a bad time of it locally they did. Because they spoke to the police and gave a statement, they had to leave before they were hounded out of the village. Made the locals very mad, so it did. Meself, I reckon 'twas the priest behind all the bad feeling. He was the maddest of them all. They will be running the pub and helping Maura with the paying guests.'

'Who would ever have thought it, eh?' Nana Kathleen shook her head. 'Little Harry spends a few days in Alder Hey Hospital, saves a baby's life, and Maura and Tommy are handed a fortune.

'Well, I want to meet this Maggie. Daisy has a lot to say about her. She was due to set off to Dublin, was Daisy, to live with her brother, but the Priory was too much for Annie and so, with Harriet getting married, Daisy has stayed put. Her poor brother was distraught, they said, but Daisy visits them for nice holidays. She is attached, like, to the four streets, and to Alison and Harriet, I would say. She won't leave ever, I don't think.

''Tis a strange world, Liam, and getting stranger by the day. There was a lot of money flying around. Alice brought a suitcase-load with her from America and she gave it back to Mary and then, lo and behold, Mary gave her it back and wished her luck. I think she was feeling mighty generous, because she arrived in Liverpool with a sick baby, and left with a healthy one. Fifty thousand pounds it was and, Liam, there is some of it in my case for you. Jerry has sent ten over for you and Maeve to compensate for your trouble and for you to build a milking shed. And with the rest, he is going to buy a little house for Nellie and Joseph. The talk about the four streets being knocked down, 'tis nonstop, and our Jerry, he has said he would rather die than move to Speke with the rest of them. And, as I was saying before, Little Harry has to fly to America soon, to help out a bit, give some more of the jelly from his bones. God, doesn't even flinch he doesn't, but I reckon ye are more ahead on that news than I am, Liam. Ah, here she is, she's waking now.'

Nellie rubbed her eyes and yawned. 'Are we there yet?' she asked.

'Passing through Bellgarett now,' said Liam. 'Not long until we are on the Ballymara Road and, God, Nellie, 'tis a road that has missed yer footsteps.'

Nellie smiled. She put one hand to her other wrist, to check that it was still there: the gold charm bracelet, given to Kitty by Maeve, the last time she saw her, when Kitty had promised to return. Nellie turned the bracelet round and round. She wanted Maeve to notice that she was wearing it. She had missed Maeve so much and she knew that Maeve had sent the bracelet across to Liverpool to let Nellie know, it was time. She was to return to the Ballymara Road.

As the van turned into Bangornevin, Nellie noticed that not a thing had altered. The school looked just the same. The river, the shops and the children playing in the street: all as if it had been only yesterday when she had last been driven through the village. As they turned left and crossed the roaring river on to the Ballymara Road, Nellie felt overcome with emotion and her eyes flooded with tears.

'Nana, Nana Kathleen,' she whispered.

'Oh, God in heaven, would ye look at ye. In just two minutes we will be with Maeve. Now dry your eyes. God, she will be upset, so she will, if ye arrive crying.'

Kathleen looked to Liam for help.

'Come on, Nellie, we aren't that bad. Ye only have two weeks to put up with us now and I promise to behave.' Liam tried his best to raise a smile.

Both he and Nana Kathleen knew what was wrong. In a minute or so, they would reach the place in the river where Kitty had drowned.

Returning Nellie to the farmhouse and taking her back down the Ballymara Road was the last step on the road to her recovery.

The chain of events that had begun with an evil priest had been far-reaching.

The four streets had settled down and life had returned to normal. New concrete towns were being erected to the south of the city, but the people on the four streets had dug in and refused to move. Neighbours had died, new families had moved in and old ones, such as the Dohertys, had moved out. The community had altered in appearance but remained firm in the bonds of poverty, love and the instinct to survive, which kept it strong.

'Look,' whispered Nana Kathleen to Nellie, 'look out of the window.'

Nellie looked and there, on the Ballymara Road, in the same spot where she had last seen her, stood Maeve, with her hand shielding her eyes, squinting into the sunlight. As the van approached, Nellie saw a smile light up Maeve's face, and she began to wave.

'There she is, our Maeve. I imagine she got notice now, when we passed through Castlefeale. Not much changes around here, Nellie,' said Liam.

'Praise the Lord for that,' said Nana Kathleen. 'That's exactly what we need a little of.'

As the van began to slow down, Nellie spotted the others running out of the front door of the house, laughing and waving. There was Rosie, and Auntie Julia, and Aengus, and Mrs and Mrs McMahon. She could hardly believe her eyes when Angela and Niamh appeared, with Maura and Tommy behind them.

'Well, ye couldn't ask for a better welcoming committee than that, now, could you?' said Nana Kathleen, squeezing Nellie's hand.

Nellie's eyes blurred. She could barely focus and yet, through the river of tears which flooded her eyes, she saw her. Her mother, Bernadette, holding Kitty by the hand. They smiled and waved to her. Immediately she knew of the love that they brought to her and it filled her heart, which had ached and felt so empty for so long.

The car door opened and she was aware of Maeve, helping her out and sweeping her into her ample bosom.

'Would ye look at her now, almost as tall as meself,' said Maeve as she pulled Nellie into her arms. Nellie's tears turned to laughter as she heard everyone asking her questions, all at once.

In the midst of excited chatter, people fighting with each other to carry the bags and Angela trying to drag her out of Maeve's arms, she looked back towards the river and she just caught them as, with a last smile, they turned away from her and, walking together, faded into the blinding sunlight, down the Ballymara Road.